As the Second World War started, two sides were lined up against each other – Axis versus Allies. Mortal enemies. But suddenly they were forced to unite against a terrible foe, one whose frighteningly advanced technology seemed invincible.

With alien beings even worse than the Nazis loose on the Earth, humanity began its struggle against overwhelming odds. In Britain and Germany, where the banshee wail of hostile jets screamed across the land, secret caches of terrifying once-forbidden weapons were unearthed. Brilliant military strategists faced challenges unprecedented in the history of warfare.

The Earth's first atom bombs were created and city after city joined the radioactive pyre as the planet flared into fiery ruins. The tactics of daredevil guerrillas everywhere grew increasingly ingenious against a technologically superior foe whose desperate retaliation would grow ever more fearsome.

About the author

Harry Turtledove has lived in Southern California all his life. He has a Ph.D. in history from the University of California at Los Angeles and has taught at UCLA, California State University, Fullerton, and California State University, Los Angeles. He has written many works of speculative fiction and fantasy, as well as several nonfiction articles in the field of medieval history. He is married to the novelist Laura Frankos and they have three daughters.

Worldwar:
Upsetting the
Balance

Harry Turtledove

NEW ENGLISH LIBRARY
Hodder and Stoughton

Copyright © 1996 by Harry Turtledove

First published in Great Britain in 1996 by
Hodder and Stoughton

First published in paperback in 1996
by Hodder and Stoughton
A division of Hodder Headline PLC

A New English Library paperback

This edition published by arrangement with Ballantine/Del Rey,
a division of Random House, Inc.

The right of Harry Turtledove to be identified as the Author of
the Work has been asserted by him in accordance with the
Copyright, Designs and Patents Act 1988.

10 9 8 7

British Library Cataloguing in Publication Data
A CIP catalogue record for this book is available from the British Library

ISBN 0 340 66698 6

Printed and bound in Great Britain by
Clays Ltd, St Ives plc

Hodder & Stoughton
A division of Hodder Headline PLC
338 Euston Road
London NW1 3BH

WORLDWAR: UPSETTING THE BALANCE

DRAMATIS PERSONAE

(Characters with names in CAPS are historical, others fictional)

HUMANS

ANIELEWICZ, MORDECHAI	*Jewish partisan, eastern Poland*
Archie	*Military hospital orderly, Chicago*
Auerbach, Rance	*Captain, US Cavalry, Syracuse Kansas*
BEAVERBROOK, LORD	*British Minister of Supply*
Berkowitz, Benjamin	*Captain, US Army; psychiatrist, Hot Springs, Arkansas*
Beulah	*Receptionist, Hanford, Wahsington*
BLAIR, ERIC	*BBC newsreader and author, London*
Calhoun, Jake	*Cavalry trooper, US Army*
CHILL, KURT	*Wehrmacht Lieutenant General, Pskov, USSR*
Chung, Horace	*Laundryman, Lewiston, Idaho*
Daniels, Pete ('Mutt')	*Lieutenant, US Army, Chicago*
DIEBNER, KURT	*Nuclear physicist, Tübingen, Germany*
Doc	*Physician, Chicago*
Donnelly	*Bomb disposal expert, US Army, Chicago*
Dölger	*Wehrmacht, Captain, Pskov, USSR*
Edie	*Whore, Lewiston, Idaho*
EINSTEIN, ALBERT	*Physicist, Couch, Missouri*
EISENHOWER, DWIGHT	*General, US Army, Couch, Missouri*
Embry, Ken	*RAF pilot, grounded in Pskov, USSR*
Eschenbach, Wolfgang	*Panzer loader, Rouffach, Alsace*
FERMI, ENRICO	*Nuclear Physicist, Denver, Colorado*
Fleishman, Bertha	*Jew in Lodz, Poland*
Fred	*RAF Flight Sergeant, Watnall, England*
Friedrich	*Partisan, eastern Poland*
George	*Local resident, Hanford, Washington*

GERMAN, ALEKSANDR	*Partisan brigadier, Pskov, USSR*
GODDARD, ROBERT	*Rocket expert, Couch, Missouri*
Goldfarb, David	*RAF radarman, Bruntingthorpe England*
Gorbunova, Ludmila	*Red Air Force Pilot*
Grillparzer Gunther	*Panzer gunner near Breslau, Germany*
GROVES, LESLIE	*Brigadier General, US Army, Denver, Colorado*
Gruver, Solomon	*Jewish Fireman in Lodz, Poland*
Gus	*Private, US Army, Chicago*
Hagerman, Max	*Cavalry trooper, US Army*
HALIFAX, LORD	*British ambassador to the United States*
Henry	*RAF man, Nottingham, England*
Henry, Marjorie	*Physician, Hanford, Washington*
Hexham	*Colonel, US Army, Denver, Colorado*
Hines, Rachel	*Escapee from Lakin, Kansas*
Hipple, Fred	*RAF Group Captain, Bruntingthorpe, England*
Ho Ma	*Midwife, refugee camp west of Shanghai*
Horton, Leo	*RAF radarman, Bruntingthorpe, England*
Hou Yi	*Dung-beetle show man, Peking*
Howard	*Cavalry trooper, eastern Colorado*
Hsia Shou-Tao	*People's Liberation Army Officer, China*
HULL, CORDELL	*US Secretary of State*
Jacobi, Nathan	*BBC newsreader, London*
Jacobs	*Private, US Army, Chicago*
'Jacques'	*French farmer near Ambialet*
Jäger, Heinrich	*Panzer colonel, Rouffach, Alsace*
Jerzy	*Partisan, eastern Poland*
Jimmy	*Stretcher-bearer, Chicago*
Johannes	*Panzer driver near Breslau, Germany*
Jones, Jerome	*RAF radarman in Pskov, USSR*
Karpov, Feofan	*Red Air Force colonel south of Moscow*
Kennan, Maurice	*RAF Flight Lieutenant, Bruntingthorpe, England*
Kipnis, Jakub	*Interpreter, Lizard POW camp in Poland*
Larssen, Jens	*Nuclear physicist with the Metallurgical Laboratory*

Lidov, Boris	*Colonel, NKVD*
Liu Han	*Peasant woman in refugee camp south of Shanghai*
Magruder, Bill	*Lieutenant, US Cavalry, Syracuse, Kansas*
Mather, Donald	*Flight Lieutenant, Special Air Service, London*
Mavrogordato, Panagiotis	*Captain of tramp freighter Naxos*
Maxwell	*Cavalry trooper, eastern Colorado*
Meinecke, Klaus	*Panzer gunner, Rouffach, Alsace*
MOLOTOV, VYACHESLAV	*Foreign Commissar of the USSR*
Muldoon, Herman	*First Sergeant, US Army, Chicago*
MUSSOLINI, BENITO	*Italian Fascist leader, Couch, Missouri*
NIEH HO-TING	*People's Liberation Army Officer, China*
Nigel	*RAF corporal, Watnall, England*
Nordenskold, Morton	*Colonel, US Army, Lamar, Colorado*
Norma	*BBC worker, London*
Nussboym, David	*Jew in Lodz, Poland*
O'Neill, Red	*Cavalry trooper, US Army*
Okamoto	*Major, Japanese Army*
Oscar	*Sergeant, US Army, Denver, Colorado*
Pete	*US Army sentry, Denver, Colorado*
Pirogova, Tatiana	*Red Army sniper, Pskov, USSR*
Porlock	*Supply officer, Minneapolis*
RIBBENTROP, JOACHIM VON	*German foreign minister*
Roundbush, Basil	*RAF Flight Officer, Bruntingthorpe, England*
Russie, Moishe	*Jewish refugee and broadcaster, London*
Russie, Reuven	*Son of Moishe and Rivka Russie*
Russie, Rivka	*Moishe Russie's wife*
Schultz, Georg	*German soldier working as Red Air Force mechanic*
Sholudenko, Nikifor	*NKVD officer*
Silberman, Pinchas	*Jew in Lodz, Poland*
SKORZENY, OTTO	*SS Standartenführer*
Smithers	*British Army major*
Smitty	*Cavalry trooper, eastern Colorado*
STALIN IOSEF	*General Secretary, Communist Party of the USSR*
Stanegate, Fred	*British soldier*

Stansfield, Roger	*Royal Naval Commander; captain, HMS* Seanymph
Stella	*Barmaid, Bruntingthorpe, England*
Summers, Penny	*Escapee from Lakin, Kansas*
Summers, Roger	*Escapee from Lakin, Kansas; Penny's father*
Szabo, Bela ('Dracula')	*Private, US Army, Chicago*
SZILARD, LEO	*Nuclear physicist, Denver, Colorado*
Szymanski, Stan	*Captain, US Army, Chicago*
Terence	*Storekeeper, Couch, Missouri*
Tompkins	*Major, US Army, Hot Springs, Arkansas*
VASILIEV, NIKOLAI	*Partisan brigadier, Pskov, USSR*
Wiggs, Ralph	*RAF meteorologist, Bruntingthorpe, England*
Yeager, Barbara	*Sam Yeager's wife*
Yeager, Jonathan	*Son of Sam and Barbara Yeager*
Yeager, Sam	*Sergeant, US Army, Denver, Colorado*
'Yetta'	*Telephone operator, Lodz, Poland*
York, Hank	*Radioman, US Army, Chicago*

THE RACE

Atvar	*Fleetlord, conquest fleet of the Race*
Diffal	*Security officer*
Ekretkan	*Casualty, St. Albans, England*
Elifrim	*Airbase commander, southern France*
Hisslef	*Base commandant, Siberia*
Hossad	*Killercraft pilot*
Innoss	*Airbase armorer, southern France*
Jisrin	*Killercraft pilot*
Kirel	*Shiplord, 127th Emperor Hetto*
Msseff	*Researcher in China*
Nejas	*Landcruiser commander, Alsace*
Nivvek	*Killercraft*
Pshing	*Adjutant to Atvar*
Ristin	*Prisoner of war, Denver, Colorado*
Rokois	*Assistant to Pshing*
Skoob	*Landcruiser gunner, Alsace*
Sserep	*Killercraft pilot*
Straha	*Shiplord, 206th Emperor Yower*

Teerts	*Flight leader, prisoner of war, Tokyo*
Tessrek	*Researcher in human psychology*
Ttomalss	*Researcher in human psychology*
Ullhass	*Prisoner of war, Denver, Colorado*
Ussmak	*Landcruiser driver, Alsace*
Vesstil	*Shuttlecraft pilot for Straha*
Wuppah	*Smallgroup commander, Chicago*

1

The fleetlord Atvar had convened a great many meetings of his shiplords since the Race's conquest fleet came to Tosev 3. Quite a few of those meetings had been imperfectly happy; the Tosevites were far more numerous and far more technically advanced than the Race had imagined when the conquest fleet set out from Home. But Atvar had never imagined calling a meeting like this.

He used one eye turret to watch his leading officers as they gathered in the great hall of his bannership, the *127th Emperor Hetto*. The other eye turret swiveled down to review the images and documents he would be presenting to those officers.

Kirel, shiplord of the *127th Emperor Hetto* and a staunch ally, stood beside him on the podium. To him, Atvar murmured, 'Giving a good odor to what happened in the SSSR won't be easy.'

One of Kirel's eye turrets swung toward a hologram of the tall cloud rising from the nuclear explosion that had halted – worse, had vaporized – the Race's drive on Moskva. 'Exalted fleetlord, the odor is anything but good,' he said. 'We knew the Big Uglies were engaged in nuclear research, yes, but we did not expect any of their little empires and not-empires – especially the SSSR – to develop and deploy a bomb so soon.'

'Especially the SSSR,' Atvar agreed heavily. The *Soyuz Sovietskikh Sotsialesticheskikh Respublik* set a frisson of horror through any right-thinking male of the Race. A short span of years before, its people had not only overthrown their emperor but killed him and all his family. Such a crime was literally unimaginable back on Home, where emperors had ruled the Race for a hundred thousand years. Among the Big Uglies, though, impericide seemed stunningly common.

The gas-tight doors to the great hall hissed closed. That meant all the shiplords were here. Atvar knew it, but was still less than eager to begin the meeting. At last, Kirel had to prompt him: 'Exalted Fleetlord—'

'Yes, yes,' Atvar said with a hissing sigh. He turned on the podium microphones, spoke to the males waiting impatiently in their seats: 'Assembled Shiplords, you are already aware, I am certain, of the reason for which I have summoned you here today.'

He touched a button. Two images sprang into being behind him, the first of a brilliant point of light northeast of the Soviet city of Kaluga captured by an observation satellite, then that ground-level shot of the cloud created by the SSSR's atomic bomb.

The shiplords, no doubt, had already seen the images tens of times. All the same, hisses of dismay and fury rose from every throat. The tailstumps of several males quivered so hard with rage that they could not stay in their seats, but had to stand until their tempers eased.

'Assembled shiplords, we have taken a heavy blow,' Atvar said. 'Not only did this explosion take with it many brave males and a large quantity of irreplaceable landcruisers and other combat equipment, it also moved our war against the Big Uglies into a new phase, one whose outcomes are not easily foreseen.'

To the Race, few words could have been more ominous. Careful planning, leaving nothing to chance, was not only inherent in the temperament of most males but inculcated in all from hatchlinghood. The Race had sent a probe to Tosev 3 sixteen hundred years before (only half so many of this planet's slow revolution around its star), decided it was worth having, and methodically began to prepare. But for those preparations, little in the Race's three-world empire had changed in that time.

The Big Uglies, meanwhile, had gone from riding animals and swinging swords to riding jet aircraft, launching short-range missiles, using radio... and now to atomic weapons. The Race's savants would be millennia investigating and explaining how a species could move forward so fast. Neither the Race itself nor its subjects, the Hallessi and the Rabotevs, had ever shown such a pattern. To them, change came in slow, tiny, meticulously considered steps.

Atvar, unfortunately, did not have millennia to investigate the way the Big Uglies worked. Circumstances forced him to act on their time scale, and with too large a measure of their do it now, worry later philosophy. He said, 'In this entire sorry episode, I take comfort in but one thing.'

'Permission to speak, Exalted Fleetlord?' a male called from near the front of the hall: Straha, shiplord of the *206th Emperor Yower*, next senior in the fleet after Kirel – and no ally of Atvar's. To Atvar's way of thinking, he was so rash and impetuous, he might as well have been a Big Ugly himself.

But at a meeting of this sort, all views needed hearing. 'Speak,' Atvar said resignedly.

'Exalted Fleetlord—' Straha used the proper deferential title, but sounded anything but properly deferential. 'Exalted Fleetlord, how can any part of this fiasco cause you comfort?'

Some of the shiplords muttered in alarm at the harsh language Straha used; males of the Race, even those of highest rank, were expected to show – and to feel – respect for their superiors at all times. But a disquieting number of officers – and not just those of his faction – seemed to agree with Straha.

Atvar said, 'Here is the comfort, Shiplord.' He used Straha's title, high but not supreme in the conquest fleet, to remind him of his place, then went on, 'Analysis shows the plutonium the SSSR used in its weapon to have come from stocks stolen from us in a raid during Tosev 3's past autumn. The Big Uglies may be able to make a bomb if they get nuclear material, but we have no evidence they can manufacture it on their own.'

'Cold comfort to the thousands of males dead because you didn't think the Tosevites could do even so much,' Straha jeered.

'Shiplord, you forget yourself,' Kirel said from beside Atvar; sometimes a near-equal could call attention to a breach of decorum a superior might feel he had to ignore.

'By the Emperor, Shiplord, I do not,' Straha shouted back. At the mention of his sovereign, he cast down both eye turrets so he looked at the floor for a moment. So did every other male in the chamber, Atvar included. The murmurs among the shiplords grew; as Kirel had said, Straha's conduct was most out of place in a staid officers' meeting.

But Straha himself was anything but staid. 'Who, Exalted Fleetlord, led the raid in which we lost this nuclear material?' he demanded.

Atvar's gut knotted. Now he knew the direction from which Straha would attack, but knowing brought no comfort. He tried to head off the shiplord: 'That is not relevant to the matter before us now.'

Many males, probably even most, would have yielded to his authority. Straha, though, refused to be headed off. 'It most certainly *is* relevant, Exalted Fleetlord,' he howled. 'Wasn't the chief Big Ugly male the one named Skorzeny?'

With its hisses, the name might almost have belonged to a male of the Race. That, however, was not why it drew a sharp reaction from the assembled shiplords. The male called Skorzeny had given the Race grief ever since the conquest fleet landed on Tosev 3. And—

Straha continued as Atvar had known he would: 'Exalted Fleetlord, along with promising us the capture of Moskva at our previous meeting, did you not also promise us the imminent destruction of Skorzeny? Have we achieved either of these goals?'

His sarcasm made the murmurs in the great hall rise to a din. Males shouted angrily at one another. Though the uproar, Atvar answered steadily, 'Shiplord, you know we have not. I assure you, I find that at least as unfortunate as you do.'

The sardonic reply did nothing to calm the shiplords. It certainly did not calm Straha, who said, 'Instead of Moskva captured, we have a major force ruined. Instead of Skorzeny dead, we have the city of Split lost, Croatia more firmly in the Deutsch camp than ever, and Skorzeny boasting of what he did over every frequency on which the Deutsche broadcast. Assembled shiplords, I submit to you that these plans were not adequately developed.'

He couldn't have been much more provocative if he'd suggested that Atvar as in the Big Uglies' pay. Accusing a male of the Race of bad planning was as harsh a condemnation as you could make. Atvar had trouble replying, too, for the plan on which he'd relied in Split had come from the mind of an operative named Drefsab, who, despite being perhaps the best intelligence officer the Race possessed, was – or rather, had been – addicted to the Tosevite herb ginger, which could easily have clouded his judgment.

The fleetlord did say, 'Experience on Tosev 3 has been that plans cannot always be as immutable as we conceived them to be back on Home. Any male who does not see this is a fool.'

'Your pardon, Exalted Fleetlord, but you are the one who has failed to adapt to the conditions pertaining to this world,' Straha said. 'I have come to this conclusion reluctantly, I assure you; subordination to properly constituted authority has served the Race well for tens of thousands of years. But the SSSR's atomic explosion and our ignominious failure at Split, each in its own way, have shown beyond any possible doubt that our conduct of the campaign to conquer Tosev 3 has been dreadfully mishandled.'

'What should you have us do?' Atvar said angrily. 'Throw our own atomic weapons about with reckless abandon? For one thing, we do not have that many to throw. For another, we do not know how many bombs the SSSR constructed from the nuclear material it got from us. For a third, we also do not know how close the SSSR – and several other Tosevite empires – are to producing nuclear materials and weapons on their own. And for a fourth, we cannot devastate large areas of this planet, not with the colonization fleet already on its way here from Home.'

That should have made Straha shut up. Similar arguments had, many times before. Now, though, the shiplord's eye turrets twisted to let him glance toward males throughout the great hall. *Gauging his strength*, Atvar thought. For the first time, alarm prickled through him. Could Straha . . .?

Straha could. 'Assembled shiplords,' he declared. 'I hereby submit to you that because our present exalted fleetlord, by his repeated misjudgments of the Big Uglies and their capabilities, put the success of our conquest of Tosev 3 not only at risk but in desperate peril, he no longer deserves to hold the supreme rank with which the Emperor entrusted him and should be replaced by another, more able, male.' He did not say who that male should be, but the way he preened suggested he had at least one candidate in mind.

'Mutiny!' Atvar exclaimed.

'Mutiny,' Kirel echoed, but not quite as promptly as Atvar would have liked. The fleetlord gave him a quick, suspicious glance. After himself,

Kirel was the highest-ranking male in the fleet. If he was to be deposed, the shiplords might well decide they could not stomach Straha as his replacement – in which case Kirel might get the job.

'It is not mutiny,' Straha insisted – and now he did not give Atvar his title of respect. 'We would be insane if we did not provide for removing a superior who has shown himself to be incompetent. I have the right to request that we consider such a removal at this time.'

He was technically correct; he did have that right. But to use it – Prominent males who were removed from their posts got into the Race's history, not only as object lessons for later generations but also because they were so rare. Atvar wanted fame from this mission, not notoriety.

He said, 'Assembled shiplords, the right of which Straha speaks pertains to males who have gone mad under the stress of their work or suffered some other mental debilitation. If we contemplated removing every male who ever met a reverse, we would soon have few males left to do anything.'

'That is the ordinary standard, I admit,' Straha shot back, 'but the ordinary assignment does not carry such a burden of responsibility. If a transport planner back on Home fails, goods may be delivered late, to the annoyance of those who receive them. If the fleetlord fails here, however, our conquest of this plant fails with him. Less ineptitude is tolerable from him than from a male of lower rank.'

Shiplords commanded their inferiors and obeyed the fleetlord. They seldom found themselves in a gathering of equals, and even more seldom in a gathering of equals where they were called upon to decide something both vital and highly irregular. The Race shied away from irregularity wherever it could, one more thing that left it ill-prepared for a world as regularly irregular as Tosev 3.

Because the males had little practice at debate, they weren't very good at it. Straha's supporters shouted and hissed at those who backed Atvar, and the fleetlord's followers returned the compliment. They displayed their rows of pointed teeth, shoved one another, and generally behaved more like new hatchlings than staid males of respectable years.

Quietly, Kirel said, 'Exalted Fleetlord, the rule in such cases is that three-fourths of the males in the rank immediately inferior to that in question must concur that its present holder is incompetent to remain at his post.'

'By the Emperor, I am not incompetent!' Atvar raged.

'I did not for a moment assert that you were, Exalted Fleetlord,' Kirel said, 'but the question has been put in proper form and now must be decided.'

Atvar's suspicions doubled, then doubled again. But formality trapped him. He knew the rules for deciding the matter, though he's never really expected to have to use them. 'Very well, Shiplord,' he said, hating every word. 'Since you are next senior to me but were not personally involved in raising the question, I yield control of the meeting to you until it is settled. Be assured I shall appeal to the Emperor any action taken against me.'

'Of course, Exalted Fleetlord,' Kirel said politely, although he, Atvar, and all the assembled shiplords knew the warning was meaningless. Back on Home, an appeal to the Emperor would be heard promptly. On Rabotev 2 and Halless 1, the Emperor's viceroys performed that duty. But from here, a radio signal would take more than ten even of Tosev 3's long years to reach Home, while another ten of them would pass awaiting a reply. Effectively, Atvar was the Emperor's viceroy on Tosev 3, or would be if he retained his post.

Making no effort to hide his anger, he stepped away from the podium. Rather nervously, Kirel said, 'Assembled shiplords, we are gathered now in the most solemn proceeding known to the Race. We may answer the question of the exalted fleetlord's fitness to continue in office in one of two ways: either each male may enter an anonymous yes or no at his seat, the result to be displayed electronically here, or we may publicly record each shiplord's name and choice. How say you?'

He knows the rule very well, to bring it out so pat, Atvar thought. Had Kirel been loyal to him, or simply more cautious than Straha? Atvar would have to contemplate that ... if he remained in any position to act on the results of his contemplation. Straha said, 'Let it be done anonymously, Superior Shiplord. That way, should the question fail' – he did not sound as if he expected it to – 'the exalted fleetlord will not be in a position to take vengeance on those who questioned his competence.'

You'll get more support that way, too, from males who would be ashamed to condemn me openly, Atvar thought. In a way, though, that reassured him: had Straha been certain of his backing, he would have asked for a public record of names. *And no matter that the choice is anonymous, Straha: I'll remember what* you've *done.*

Kirel waited for any males who so desired to insist on a public record. When none did, he said, 'Very well, assembled shiplords, register your choices. When the tally is complete, I shall announce the result.'

Atvar did his best to look impassive, no matter how he writhed inside. Being subjected to this tribunal of his inferiors was humiliating. It was worse than humiliating, in fact: it reminded him of the way some of the Big Ugly not-empires tried to run their affairs. The Race had expected, had intended, to bring civilization to Tosev 3. Instead, the Tosevites seemed to be barbarizing not only the shiplords but all the males of the conquest fleet.

Time stretched. After what seemed like forever, Kirel said, 'Assembled shiplords, I shall now announce your decision.' Atvar stayed outwardly unconcerned, or tried to. Straha leaned forward in eager anticipation. The great hall grew as still as Atvar had ever known it; not a male wished to miss the result.

'Assembled shiplords,' Kirel said, 'those favouring the removal of fleetlord Atvar from his post constitute sixty-nine percent of your number; those favoring his retention constitute thirty-one percent. This fails to be a three-fourths majority.' He turned to Atvar. 'Command us, Exalted Fleetlord.'

Atvar walked back to the podium. He looked out at the assembled shiplords, and they back at him. *Command us*, Kirel had said. Even with the Race's traditions of obedience, could he command these males when two out of three of them had declared he was not fit to do so? He would have to find out.

And how was he supposed to treat with the Big Uglies, now that they could do serious damage not only to the Race but also to their precious planet. Before, negotiations had either been about small-scale procedural matters like treatment and exchange of prisoners or over terms of surrender to the Race. Now ... he'd have to find that out, too.

Vyacheslav Molotov hated flying. He reckoned going in a drafty biplane to Germany and then on a later air trip to England among the worst experiences of his life. But flying in a human-made airplane, however appalling that was, paled to insignificance beside taking off in a Lizard rocket ship to zoom up into outer space to talk with the commander of the imperialist aggressors from the stars.

He'd done that once before, so this time he'd known what to expect: the acceleration that pushed him back against the too-small padded seat and squeezed the air from his lungs; the sudden moment of transition, after which he seemed to weigh nothing at all and had to control his stomach as rigidly as he always controlled his face; the Saharalike temperatures the Lizards found comfortable. He'd prepared for that, at least, wearing a light cotton suit instead of his usual thick wool.

Even so, he was still sweating as he faced the fleetlord Atvar. A couple of small drops had escaped from his forehead and floated around the chamber in which he, the leader of the Lizards, and a Lizard interpreter hung at various improbable angles. The Lizards took their weightlessness utterly for granted, so he tried his best to do the same.

Atvar spoke several sentences in the Lizards' language of hisses, pops, and clicks. The interpreter turned them into Russian: 'The exalted fleetlord says you were most rash to use an atomic bomb against the Race, when we could turn so many of these weapons against you.'

Molotov had told Stalin the same thing – had, in fact, argued harder against using the atomic bomb than he'd dared argue with Stalin about anything else for years. But Stalin had overruled him, and no rain of destruction had fallen on the Soviet Union – yet. Instead, the Lizards had summoned him here to confer. Maybe that meant Stalin was right all along.

Such thoughts ran through the Foreign Commissar's mind as he asked the interpreter to repeat a couple of things he hadn't quite understood.

His face remained expressionless. He nodded to the interpreter to show he'd caught the gist this time. The Lizard was much more fluent than he had been on Molotov's previous trip to this immense spacecraft not quite a year before.

'Tell the exalted fleetlord the Race was rash to attack the peace-loving peasants and workers of the Soviet Union,' Molotov answered. 'Perhaps the means we used to repel you will show you how true this is.'

'Perhaps,' Atvar said through the interpreter. 'And then again, Vyacheslav Mikhailovich, perhaps not. We know you made this bomb with the quantity of element 94 you stole from us. Do not try to deny it; our analysis leaves no room for doubt. When will you be able to produce bombs altogether on your own?'

'If you renew your treacherous attacks on us, I assure you that you will find out, and that the answer will not please you,' Molotov said without hesitation. Again, his features showed nothing of the fear he felt. The true answer to that question was *On the order of three years*. If the Lizards learned the true answer, the Soviet Union was hideously vulnerable to them.

His prompt reply seemed to give Atvar pause. He was relieved to see that, and even more relieved when the fleetlord partially changed the subject: 'Do you not realize you destroy your own planet when you use atomic weapons?'

'That did not stop you when you bombed Berlin and Washington,' Molotov retorted. 'Why did you think it would concern us? And if you win this imperialist war against mankind, Earth will no longer be *our* planet in any case. Of course we shall use all our weapons to resist you.'

'This course can lead only to your own destruction,' Atvar said.

I think you may be right. But Molotov's demeanor would not have shown his wife what he was thinking, let alone a Lizard. He said, 'We know you have enslaved two races already, and want us to become the third. We know you have kept those other races under subjection for thousands of years, and that you plot the same fate for us. Since all this is true, and since you have not even tried to deny it is true, how can destroying ourselves be worse?'

'You would keep your lives, some of your private property—' Atvar began.

Even stone-faced as he normally was, even in the Lizards' power, even floating in hideously unfamiliar weightlessness, Molotov burst out laughing. It took him by surprise; it also seemed to take the Lizard fleetlord and his interpreter by surprise. Molotov said, 'There is no private property in the Soviet Union; private property is the result of theft. The state owns the means of production.'

Atvar and the interpreter went back and forth in their own language for a little while. When they were done, the interpreter swiveled his eyes back toward Molotov and said, 'The full meaning of the concept you describe escapes us.'

'I understand that,' Molotov answered. 'It is because the class struggle in your society has not progressed to the point where the dialectic of the transition from capitalism to socialism is above your mental horizon.'

As best he could, the translator rendered that into the Lizards' language. The fleetlord Atvar made a noise that might well have come from the safety valve of a powerful steam engine. Through the interpreter, he said, 'You dare, you presume, Tosevite, to call the *Race* primitive?' His mouth fell open in a Lizard laugh.

'In your system of social organization? Certainly,' Molotov said.

Despite the confidence with which he imbued his voice, he felt the paradox, for the Lizards' technical achievements were anything but primitive. The Soviets called them imperialists, but he did not think they were out to conquer the Earth for the sake of developing new markets, as highly advanced capitalist states had done in the past few generations to delay the inevitable proletarian revolution. The Lizards' society seemed more like that of the ancient empires, with masters ruling slaves and exploiting their labor. But the economic system of the ancient empires had been assumed to be incompatible with developing advanced technology. Marxist-Leninist theoreticians were still hammering out where the Lizards fit into the historical dialectic.

Atvar was laughing at him again, perhaps for his presumption. The fleetlord said, 'Well, we care nothing for what you Tosevites think of our arrangements, and I did not summon you here to discuss them. You have made this war more dangerous for us; I do not deny that. But you have also made it more dangerous for yourselves. If you think we will hold back from responding in kind, you are badly mistaken.'

'That was not our concern,' Molotov answered. *That was not Stalin's concern, anyhow.* 'We shall do what we think best, depending on the circumstances in which we find ourselves. Withdraw your forces from the Soviet Union and you will be in no more danger from us.'

Atvar laughed again, not, Molotov thought, pleasantly. 'This cannot be. I show my mercy by not treating you as a criminal, since your rulers came to power through murdering your emperor.'

The fleetlord and the translator both showed what looked like genuine revulsion. The version Atvar gave of what had happened in the Soviet Union wasn't strictly accurate, but Molotov didn't argue the niceties with him. The Bolsheviks had done what they had to do to stay in power; to do anything less would have been to betray the workers and common soldiers and sailors who had helped them overthrow their class enemies in the Kerensky regime.

Aloud, Molotov said, 'One day, when you have advanced sufficiently, you will do the same.'

If the two Lizards had been revolted before, now they were furious.

Again, they made noises that reminded Molotov of a samovar boiling with the fire too high. Atvar spat words. The interpreter proved his fluency had improved by turning them into precise, insulting Russian: 'You Big Uglies are the most uncultured, odious creatures anyone could ever have imagined, and you Soviets the most uncultured and odious of the Big Uglies. To suggest such a thing—' Atvar started bubbling and sputtering again.

Molotov took no notice of the insults, but in weightlessness his glasses kept trying to escape from his nose. When he had secured them, he said, 'We do not love one another. This much I already knew. Did you summon me here merely to remind me of it, or did you have serious diplomatic proposals to put to me?'

He granted Atvar a moment of professional respect when the fleetlord did return to business: 'I summoned you here to warn you that under no circumstances will we tolerate any further use of nuclear weapons by any Tosevite empire, and that we reserve the right to retaliate as we see fit.'

'I can speak only for the Soviet Union, whose peace-loving workers and peasants must of course reject demands made at gunpoint,' Molotov answered. 'We also reserve the right to retaliate as we see fit, especially since your forces invaded our land without reason or declaration of war. I can predict, though, that other nations will respond similarly.'

'Other empires—' Atvar let that hang in the air for a few seconds before resuming: 'Other Tosevite empires are also working on nuclear weapons; of this we are certain. How can you be assured that they will use these weapons against us rather than you? The Deutsche, for instance, are already developing rockets which could carry them.'

Molotov almost betrayed himself by bursting into laughter again. The Lizard was trying to sow rivalry among his human enemies, which would have been far from the worst of ploys if he hadn't been so obvious – and so bad – at the game. Even Ribbentrop would have seen through it.

'Before you came, Germany and the Soviet Union were enemies, true,' Molotov said. 'Germany and the United States were enemies, Germany and Great Britain were enemies, Japan and Great Britain were enemies, Japan and the United States were enemies. We are enemies among ourselves no more – you are more dangerous to all of us than we were to one another.'

For once, diplomacy and truth came together. Men fought each other on more or less even terms. The Lizards were far ahead of all human nations. Go under to them and you would never come up again. Even Hitler, wretched madman that he was, recognized the truth there.

Atvar said, 'Surely you realize this struggle is futile for you.'

'Class struggle is the engine of the historical dialectic,' Molotov answered. 'It is never futile.'

'I understand these words one by one, Vyacheslav Mikhailovich, but not their full meaning together,' the interpreter said. 'How shall I render them for the exalted fleetlord?'

'Tell him we shall go on fighting, come what may, and that we shall use whatever weapons we have to destroy his forces within the Soviet Union,' Molotov said. 'No threats he can make will keep us from defending ourselves.'

The translator hissed and popped and squeaked, and Atvar hissed and popped and squeaked back. The translator said, 'You will regret this decision.'

'I would regret any other decision more,' Molotov replied. That was true in an immediate, personal sense: if he dared step so much as a centimeter outside the limits Stalin had set for him, the General Secretary of the Communist Party of the Soviet Union would have him shot and worry afterwards no more than if he'd trimmed a fingernail. But it was also true in the wider way in which he'd intended it. Surrender to the Lizards meant long-term slavery not just for the Soviet Union but for the human race.

Like any true believer, Molotov was certain the historical dialectic would produce a proletarian revolution among the Lizards. Given what scraps he knew of their history, though, he was not prepared for mankind to wait the thousands of years the dialectic was liable to take.

Brigadier General Leslie Groves had a sign over his desk in the Science Hall at the University of Denver: DO IT ANYHOW. He scrawled his signature on a report and got up from the desk: a big, ginger-haired man with a big belly and enough driving energy for any three ordinary mortals. That energy, and a gift for organization that went with it, had made him a first-rate military engineer and led to his being put in charge of America's effort to build an atomic bomb.

As Groves put on his cap, he glanced back at the sign. He'd used all his impressive energy to make sure the United States built the first human-made atomic bomb, only to be beaten by the Russians, of all people.

That wounded his pride. Losing the race to the Germans would have been a catastrophe had the Lizards not come. Under the present circumstances, though, it wouldn't have surprised him – the Germans were the ones who'd discovered nuclear fission, after all. But the Russians—

'The Russians,' he muttered to himself as he tramped down the hall. 'Unfair advantages.' The Russians and Germans had split a load of plutonium they'd captured from the Lizards not far from Kiev. Thanks to Polish Jews who'd intercepted their courier, the Germans had had to split their half again; the American Metallurgical Laboratory physicists had the half the Germans had been forced to disgorge. Neither that half nor what the Germans had left was enough by itself to make a bomb. If the Russians had kept as much as the Germans had started out with, though, they'd have plenty.

'All right, so they didn't do it all by themselves,' Groves said. That they'd done it ahead of the United States in any way, shape, form, color, or size still rankled, no matter how much the bomb they'd used had helped the war effort against the Lizards.

It rankled more people than Groves, too. Ever since the Russian bomb went off, the Denver papers had been screaming that the USA should have been the first country to blow the Lizards to hell and gone. None of the reporters and editorial writers had shown that he knew his atoms from third base, and none of them (thank God!) seemed to have a clue that the Met Lab was operating out of the University of Denver these days.

On his way from Science Hall to the football stadium that housed the atomic pile the physicists had built, Groves passed a sergeant leading a couple of Lizard POWs. The man and the aliens were almost friends by now; they chatted in a mixture of English and Lizards' language.

'Morning, General,' the sergeant said, saluting.

'Superior sir,' the two Lizards added in their hissing English.

'Morning, Yeager.' Groves returned the salute. He even grudged the Lizards a nod. 'Ullhass, Ristin.' As individuals, they looked strange, but not particularly dangerous. They were about the size and build of skinny ten-year-olds, with scaly, green-brown skins. Their bodies leaned forward slightly at the hips, and had stubby little tails to balance. Their fingers and toes bore claws rather than nails. They had forward-thrusting muzzles filled with lots of small, sharp teeth, and long tongues they'd stick out like snakes. Their eyes were like a chameleon's, on independently rotating turrets so they could look in two directions at the same time. No mere humans had ever put the United States in such deadly danger, though.

Groves tramped on. Science Hall was near the north end of the campus, a long way from the stadium. The walk helped keep his weight down. So did the short rations everybody was on these days. He was a long way from skinny even so. Had things been a little different, he would have looked like one of the blimps the Navy flew (or, more likely, had flown) out of Lakehurst, New Jersey.

Outside the football stadium, a guard saluted Groves, who noted approvingly that the fellow was under cover so he couldn't be spotted from the air. One of the keys to the American atomic bomb project was not letting the Lizards know it existed.

It was shadowy under the stadium, but not cool. During the day, Denver was like a bake oven in summer, even though the mile-high air shed heat fast at night. The physicists and technicians in charge of the pile nodded as Groves approached. They didn't necessarily love him, but they took him seriously, which sufficed.

'How much closer are we?' he asked Enrico Fermi.

'We have gained another day,' the physicist answered. 'The output of plutonium from this pile does continue to increase.'

'Not fast enough,' Groves growled. The pile produced grams of plutonium per day. The United States needed several kilograms of the stuff to add to what they had received from inside the Soviet Union by way of a reluctant German courier, the Jewish irregulars in Poland, and a British submarine. Groves had shepherded that plutonium all the way from Boston to Denver, only to be told when he got it here that he hadn't brought enough. The memory still rankled.

Fermi shrugged a large Latin shrug. 'General, I cannot charge the laws of nature. I can learn to apply them more efficiently, and this I try to do: this is how we gain time on the date I first predicted. But to increase production to any really great degree, we need to build more piles. That is all there is to it.'

'That's not going fast enough, either,' Groves said. Another pile was going up under the stands at the opposite end of the football field. They had plenty of uranium oxide for it. Getting the super-pure graphite they needed was another matter. Groves was an expediter supreme, but the transportation snarl into which the Lizards had thrown the United States was more than enough to drive even expediters mad.

'What we really need is to build piles of more efficient design,' Fermi said. 'The Hanford site on the Columbia would be ideal – far more water for cooling than we can take from the South Platte, an area far removed from the Lizards—'

'I'm not so sure of that,' Groves broke in. 'They're supposed to have a base in Idaho, only a couple of hundred miles off to the east.'

'A small one.' Fermi pinched his thumb and forefinger together to show how small. 'As soon as Professor Larssen returns to confirm that the site is as good as it appears to be, we will begin centering more and more of our activities there.'

'As soon as Larssen gets back, yeah,' Groves said with a marked lack of enthusiasm. As far as he was concerned, Jens Larssen could stay away indefinitely. Yeah, sure, the guy had a beef: he'd been away from the Met Lab crew for a long time on a dangerous mission (any cross-country travel counted as a dangerous mission these days), and his wife, figuring he had to be dead, had fallen for Sergeant Sam Yeager – he'd been a corporal then – married him, and got pregnant. When Larssen turned out to be alive after all, she'd decided to stay with Yeager. None of that was calculated to improve a man's attitude.

But goddamn it, you couldn't let how you felt drag down your work the way Larssen had. It wasn't just his own work that had been hurting, either. He'd been taking his colleagues' minds off what they were supposed to be doing, too. Groves hadn't been sorry to see him volunteer to scout out Hanford, Washington, and would hold in his delight at seeing him come back.

'Professor Larssen has had a difficult time,' Fermi said, reacting to the dislike in Groves' voice.

'Professor Fermi, the whole country – hell, the whole world – has had a difficult time,' Groves retorted. 'It's not like he's the only one. He'd better stop whimpering and pull himself together.'

He leaned toward Fermi, using his physical presence to make his point for him. He wasn't that much taller than the Italian, but he was wider, and harder and tougher to boot. Fermi said, 'If you will excuse me, General, I have some calculations I must attend to,' and hurried away.

Groves grunted. Scoring a victory against a mild-mannered physics prof was like shooting fish in a barrel – yeah, you'd done it, but so what? When you'd cut your teeth on hard cases, you barely even noticed biting down on a Fermi.

And besides, you couldn't bite down too hard on Fermi. Without false modesty, Groves knew he was very good at what he did. There weren't a whole lot of people who were both the engineer and administrator he was. But if he dropped dead tomorrow, George Marshall would pick somebody just about as good to replace him. Who was just about as good as a Nobel Prize-winning physicist? In a word, nobody.

The bombs would be built. He had no doubt of that: first the one that incorporated the plutonium stolen from the Lizards, then others made entirely with human-produced nuclear material. The know-how and resources were in place; the United States merely had to await results.

Only trouble was, the United States couldn't wait. As things stood, that first bomb was a year away, maybe more. How much of the States would be left in American hands by the time it was ready to blow? *Not enough*, Groves thought gloomily; the guys with the guns and the tanks and the airplanes were doing all they could, but all they could was liable not to be enough.

That meant every day he could shave off getting the first bomb ready was a day that might save the country. Nobody in the United States had faced that weight of responsibility since the Civil War. He shrugged his broad shoulders. He had to hope they were strong enough to bear the burden.

Ristin threw a baseball to Sam Yeager. The Lizard POW handled the ball as if it were a grenade, but he threw pretty straight. The ball slapped leather in Yeager's beat-up glove. 'Good toss,' he said, and threw the baseball on to Ullhass.

Ullhass's mitt was even more battered than Yeager's but that wasn't his problem. He lunged at the ball with the glove, as if he were trying to push it away rather than catch it. Not surprisingly, he didn't catch it. 'Stupid egg-addled thing,' he said in his own language as he stooped to pick the ball up off the grass, and added the emphatic cough to show he really meant it.

Yeager felt a surge of pride at how automatically he understood what the Lizard was saying. He wasn't any big brain; he'd had his third stripe only a few days. He hadn't been a prof before the Lizards came, either.

He'd been an outfielder for the Decatur Commodores of the Class B Three-I League; the only reason the draft hadn't grabbed him was that he wore full dentures, uppers and lowers, a souvenir of the 1918 influenza epidemic that had almost killed him, and had left him so weak and debilitated that his teeth rotted in his head.

But prof or no, he'd been an avid reader of *Astounding* and the other science-fiction pulps. After the Lizards came, the Army didn't care any more whether you had teeth; all they worried about was a pulse – if you had one, you were in. So, when his unit captured some Lizards back in Illinois, he'd volunteered to try to communicate with the things ... and here he was in Denver, working hand in hand not only with the aliens but also with the high foreheads who were taking what Ullhass and Ristin knew and using it to help build an atomic bomb for the USA. *Not bad for an overage ball-player.*

Ullhass threw the baseball to Ristin. Ristin was a better natural athlete than the other Lizard, or maybe just smarter. He'd figured out how to catch with a glove, anyhow: let the ball come to him, then close his meat hand over it to make sure it didn't get out.

He still threw funny, though; Sam had to jump high to catch his next fling. 'Sorry, superior sir,' Ristin said.

'Don't worry about it. Nobody's keeping score.' Yeager brushed back into place a lock of dark blond hair that had escaped from under the fore-and-aft Army cap he wore. He threw Ullhass the ball. But for the nature of his friends, it was an all-American scene: three guys playing catch on a college campus on a bright summer's day. You didn't get any more Norman Rockwell than that – except Norman Rockwell had never painted a Lizard with a baseball glove.

Just to add to the *Saturday Evening Post* quality of the scene, here came Barbara. Sam waved and grinned enormously, partly because he was always glad to see her and partly because she was wearing the calico blouse and blue jeans in which she'd married him up in the great metropolis of Chugwater, by God, Wyoming. Even for Yeager, who in seventeen years of pro ball thought he'd seen every small town in the US of A, that had been a new one.

He wondered how long she'd be able to keep wearing those jeans. Not that they didn't look good on her – she was a little on the lean side, but she definitely had hips and a pert posterior – but her pregnancy was just beginning to show with her clothes off. As best he could tell, they'd started Junior on their wedding night.

'Hi, honey,' he said as she drew near. 'What's up?' The question came out more seriously than he'd expected; she wasn't smiling as she usually did.

'General Groves sent me out to find you himself,' she answered. 'You've got new orders, he said.'

'New orders?' Sam pulled a face. 'I was just thinking how much I liked what I was doing here. Did he say what they were?'

Barbara shook her head. Her hair, a couple of shades darker than his, flew around her head. 'I asked him, but he wouldn't tell me. He said he wanted to give them to you in person.'

'I don't like the sound of that,' Yeager said. Any time a general gave a sergeant orders in person, something out of the ordinary was going on, maybe something liable to get the sergeant killed. But if General Groves wanted to see him, he couldn't very well say no. He turned to Ullhass and Ristin, spoke in the mix of English and Lizard he usually used with them: 'Come on, boys, let's go see what the exalted projectlord wants with me.'

Ristin's mouth fell open in a Lizardy chuckle. 'You're a funny Big Ugly, superior sir.' He used the Lizard's slang name for people as unselfconsciously as Sam said *Lizard* instead of *male of the Race* around him.

The two humans and two Lizards strolled across the University of Denver campus toward Science Hall. A couple of times, people they knew waved to them. Ullhass and Ristin waved back as casually as Barbara and Sam did; they were an accepted part of the Met Lab staff by now. Technically, they remained prisoners, but nobody worried much about their trying to escape.

Groves was a big enough wheel to rate a guard outside his office: the same guard who'd been assigned to Jens Larssen for a while. Yeager didn't hold that against him. 'Morning, Oscar,' he said. 'You want to keep an eye on these two tough guys while the general tells me whatever he tells me? Try to keep 'em from stealing all our secrets here.'

'Sure, Sam,' Oscar answered. Even without his rifle, Yeager would have bet on him against Ristin and Ullhass both; dark and quiet he might be, but he'd seen nasty action somewhere – he had the look. Now he nodded to Barbara. 'Morning, ma'am.'

'Good morning, Oscar,' she answered. She spoke more precisely than Sam did. Hell, she spoke more precisely than most people did. She'd been a graduate student in medieval English out at Berkeley before the war; that was where she'd met Jens.

Oscar turned back to Sam. 'Go on in. General Groves, he's expecting you.'

'Okay, thanks.' Yeager turned the doorknob, feeling the same willies he'd had whenever a manager called to him in a certain tone of voice after a game. *Oh, God,* he thought. *Where have they gone and traded me to now?*

He went through the door, closed it after him. General Groves looked up from the notes he was scribbling on a typed report. Sam came to attention and saluted. 'Sergeant Samuel Yeager reporting as ordered, sir,' he said formally.

'At ease, Yeager. You're not in trouble,' Groves said, returning the salute. He waved to the chair in front of his desk. 'Sit down if you care to.' When

Sam had, Groves went on, 'Is it your opinion that we've wrung just about everything your two scaly accomplices know about nuclear physics out of them?'

'Yes, sir, I'd say that's probably true,' Yeager answered after a moment's thought.

'Good. I'd have thrown you out of here on your ear if you'd tried to tell me anything else,' Groves said. By the way the muscles shifted in his big shoulders, he'd meant it literally. 'The United States can still learn a lot about the Lizards from Ullhass and Ristin, though, even if what we learn has nothing directly to do with the Metallurgical Laboratory. Wouldn't you agree with that?'

'No doubt about it, sir,' Yeager said. 'The more we know about the Lizards, the better. They'll still be around from now on even if we manage to beat them, and that's not counting this colonization fleet of theirs. It's due in – what? – twenty years?'

'That's about right, yes.' General Groves looked intently across the desk at Sam. 'The way you answered that last question convinced me these are absolutely the right orders for you: you casually came to the same conclusion a staff of government experts has needed months to reach.'

Probably comes from reading science fiction, Yeager thought. He didn't say out loud; he had no idea how Groves felt about the Buck Rogers stuff. He did say, 'You haven't told me what the orders are, sir.'

'So I haven't.' Groves glanced down at some papers behind his IN basket that Yeager couldn't see. 'We've established a center for interrogation and research on Lizard POWs down in Arkansas. I'm going to send Ristin and Ullhass there, and I'm ordering you to accompany them. I think you can best serve your country by using your rapport with the Lizards, and that's the place for you to do it.'

'Yes, sir,' Sam said. He'd been traded, all right, but to a place he didn't mind going ... assuming he could get there. 'Uh, Sir, what sort of transportation will we have? There's a lot of Lizards between here and Arkansas that aren't prisoners, if you know what I mean.'

'I know exactly what you mean. Nevertheless, you'll fly,' Groves answered.

'Sir?' Yeager did his best to keep the surprise – to say nothing of the dismay – he felt from showing. His best, he feared, was none too good. He figured he'd better explain: 'They shoot down an awful lot of our planes, sir.' That would do for an understatement until a better one came along. The Lizards' aircraft had the same sort of advantage against the planes the Americans flew as a Lightning or a Warhawk would have against a World War I-vintage Sopwith Camel.

But Groves nodded his big head and said, 'You'll fly anyhow – what's more the Lizards will know you're coming.' Yeager must have looked as if he'd just been smacked in the kisser with a large carp, for the general chuckled a little before continuing, 'We always inform them before we move prisoners by air, and we paint the planes we fly them in bright yellow. It's worked pretty well; they don't like shooting at their own people any more than we would.'

'Oh,' Yeager said. 'I guess that's okay, then.' And if there were no such arrangement between Lizards and men and Groves had told him to fly anyway, he'd have damn well flown: that's what the Army was about. As it was, though, he asked, 'Do you think it's safe enough for my wife to come along, sir? Really, I'm not just asking for the sake of having her with me; she knows just about as much about the Lizards as I do. She'd be useful at this Arkansas place, at least until she has her baby.'

'Under normal circumstances, Sergeant, I'd say no,' Groves answered. He grimaced. 'I don't think there's any such thing as normal circumstances any more. As you say, your Barbara may be useful in Arkansas, but that's not why I'm going to tell you yes. Frankly, Sergeant, getting you and her out of here will simplify matters when Professor Larssen gets back from Washington State.'

'Yes, sir,' Sam said woodenly. Groves had to think like that, though; Jens Larssen was a talented nuclear physicist, and the general was running a project to build an atomic bomb. If he could help the Lizard prisoner research project at the same time ... *two birds with one stone* ran through Yeager's mind. 'When do we leave, sir?' he asked.

'Not for a few days,' Groves answered. 'We need to make the arrangements and be sure they're understood. Written orders will go out to you as soon as one of the secretaries gets around to typing them. Dismissed.'

Yeager stood, saluted, and left. He wasn't sure Groves even saw the salute; he'd already gotten back to work on the report he'd been scribbling on when Sam came in.

Barbara, Ullhass, and Ristin all took a couple of steps toward him when he came out into the hallway. 'You look green, Sam,' she said. 'What happened in there?'

'Pack your bags, hon,' he answered. 'We're moving to Arkansas.' She stared and stared. He had to remind himself that she'd never been traded before.

Heinrich Jäger stuck his head and torso up through the open cupola of his Panzer V for a look around, then ducked back down into the turret of the panzer. 'Lord, it feels good to have some centimeters of steel all the way around me again,' he said.

His gunner, a veteran sergeant named Klaus Meinecke, grunted at that. 'Colonel, you don't seem to have done too bad while you were out on your own, either.' He pointed to the Knight's Cross of the Iron Cross that Jäger wore at his collar.

Jäger's hand went to the medal. He'd earned it for helping Otto Skorzeny take the town of Split on the Adriatic back from the Lizards. He said,

'Sergeant, I was in the infantry during the last war. I thought one round of that had cured me forever. Just goes to show, you may get older, but you don't get smarter.'

Meinecke laughed as if he'd told a joke. But Jäger meant every word of it. Fighting from building to building inside the great stone walls of Diocletian's palace had been every bit as appalling as trench warfare in France a quarter of a century before.

The Alsation town of Rouffach, through which the Panther had rumbled a few minutes before, had been part of the German *Reich* during World War I, taken from France after the Franco-Prussian War. France had taken it back after the First World War; now it was German again ... for as long as the *Reich* could maintain itself against the Lizards.

Jäger stood up in the cupola again, looked back over his shoulder. The spires of Rouffach's church of Notre Dame still loomed against the sky; so did what the locals called the Witches' Tower, crowned by a huge, disorderly storks' next. 'Pretty country,' he said, lowering himself once more.

Klaus Meinecke grunted. 'I wouldn't know. All I get to see of it is a gunsight's worth, except when we stop for the night.' He smacked his lips. 'They make good wine around here, though; I'll give them that much.'

'That they do,' Jäger said. 'They didn't do badly farther south, either.'

He wouldn't let himself venture any more in the way of reproach than that. When he'd left the panzer forces in the west to head for Croatia, they'd had the Lizards stopped in their tracks between Besançon and Belfort. Since then, Belfort had fallen, and Mulhouse, too; the Lizards had pushed all the way up to the Rhine. *If I'd been here ...* Jäger thought, and then shook his head. Almost certainly, the same thing would have happened. He knew he was a damn fine panzer officer. He also knew he wasn't a panzer genius – and even a panzer genius might not have held the Lizards once they got rolling.

'Maybe we can push them out of Mulhouse again,' he said hopefully.

'That's what they said we'd do back in Colmar, anyhow,' Meinecke answered. He was a veteran, all right; he understood that what they said and what actually happened could be two very different animals. He pursed his lips, then added quietly, as if afraid of being overheard by malignant fate, 'Engine's been behaving pretty well, knock on wood.' He made a fist and tapped it against the side of his own head.

'Let's hope it keeps up,' Jäger agreed. Rushed into production, the Panther could be balky; among other things, fuel pump problems plagued it. But it was a great step forward from earlier German panzers, boasting a high-velocity 75mm gun and thick, well-sloped armor borrowed in concept from that of the Soviet T-34.

All of which meant you only had to be foolhardy to go up against the Lizards in a Panther, as opposed to clinically insane, which was about what opposing them in a Panzer III had required.

'Wish we had one of those bombs the Russians used to blow the Lizards to hell and gone,' Meinecke said. 'When do you suppose we'll get one of our own?'

'Damned if I know,' Jäger said. 'I wish to God I did.'

'If you don't, who does?' the gunner asked.

Now Jäger just grunted by way of reply. He wasn't supposed to say anything about that to anybody. He'd been part of the band of raiders that had stolen explosive metal from the Lizards in Russia – *like Prometheus, stealing fire from the gods*, said the part of him that, back before World War I, had planned on becoming a classical archaeologist. He'd taken Germany's share of the material across Poland on horseback, only to have half of it hijacked by Jewish fighters there.

Only luck they didn't kill me and take it all, he thought. In Russia and then in Poland, he'd learned what the *Reich* had done to the Jews who'd fallen into their hands; it made him sick, so he understood why the Polish Jews had risen in favor of the Lizards and against their German overlords.

He'd also been involved in the German physicists' efforts to build an atomic pile at Hechingen, although, again luckily, he'd been in combat in eastern France when the pile went out of control somehow and killed off a good many physicists, including Werner Heisenberg. How long the program would take to recover was anyone's guess.

Meanwhile, the unglamorous infantry and panzer troops would have to keep the Lizards from overrunning the *Vaterland*. If they didn't, the high foreheads would never get the chance to finish their research and make something that would go *boom!* In Hechingen, Jäger had felt useless; he'd been too ignorant to contribute properly. Now he was back to doing what he did best.

Off to one side of the road, an artillery piece barked, then another and another. 'Eighty-eights,' Jäger said, identifying them by the report. 'That's good.'

Meinecke understood him without any more discussion than that: 'So they can fire their salvo and then get the hell out of there, you mean?'

'Right the first time, Sergeant. They're easy to shift to a new firing position – a lot easier than the bigger guns.' Jäger paused meditatively. 'And Lizard counterbattery fire is better than anything we ever dreamt of.'

'Isn't that the sad and sorry truth, sir?' Meinecke agreed with a mournful sigh. 'They can drive nails into your coffin from halfway round the world, seems like, sometimes. If there were more of them, and if they had the doctrine to go with all their fancy equipment—'

'—The likes of us would have been dead for quite a while now,' Jäger finished for him. Meinecke laughed, though again the colonel had spoken nothing but the truth. Down lower in the turret, Wolfgang Eschenbach, the loader, laughed too. He was a big blond farm boy; getting more than half a dozen words out of him in the course of a day was just this side of miraculous.

For all their good points, 88s had drawbacks, too. They couldn't fire shells as heavy as the larger guns, and they couldn't throw the shells they did fire as far. That meant—

'We'll probably see action in the next few kilometers,' Jäger said. 'Bumping up against whatever the artillery boys are shooting at, you mean, sir?' Meinecke said. At Jäger's nod, he went on, 'Makes sense to me. Besides, south of Rouffach is where they told us we'd start running into the enemy, isn't it? They have to be right once in a while.'

'Your confidence in the High Command does you credit, Sergeant,' Jäger said dryly, which set the gunner and the loader to laughing again. 'I just hope the Lizards use the same kind of flank guards we did when we got stretched thin fighting the Russians.'

'How's that, *Herr Oberst*?' Meinecke asked. 'Me, I was playing games with the Tommies in the desert before they stuck me in the Flying Circus here.' When Panther and Tiger panzers started rolling off the assembly lines, the *Wehrmacht* put only the best crewmen into them.

'You, you didn't miss a thing,' Jäger said, mimicking his gunner's diction. 'But sometimes we'd have to concentrate our German troops at the *Schwerpunkt*, the decisive place, and cover our flanks with Romanians or Hungarians or Italians.'

'God save us.' Wolfgang Eschenbach used up half his daily quota of speech.

'They weren't the worst soldiers I've ever seen,' Jäger said. 'They might not have been bad at all if they were decently equipped. But sometimes the Russians managed to hit them instead of us, and it got pretty ugly. I'm hoping the Lizards are concentrating all their best troops up where they're trying to advance. I'd just as soon not have to fight the first team all the time.'

'Amen to that,' Eschenbach said; Jäger confidently expected him to fall silent till the morning.

The colonel stood up in the cupola again. That was a good way to get shot, but it was also far and away the best way to see what was going on, and if you didn't know what was going on, you had no business commanding a panzer, let alone a (rather battered) regiment of them. Slamming the lid down and peering through the periscopes made you feel safer, but it also made you miss things that were liable to get you killed.

Northbound shells whistled overhead, undoubtedly the Lizard's response to the Germans' 88s. Jäger hoped the artillerymen had moved their pieces elsewhere before the shells came down on them.

The countryside began to have a look of a land at war: wrecked and burned farm buildings, smashed trees, bloated dead animals, shell craters pocking fields. Jäger clucked sadly at the charred wreck of a German half-track. The Panther rolled past trenches and foxholes that showed the earlier limits of the German push to the south.

Stooping to get down into the turret for a moment, Jäger said, 'We're moving forward, anyhow.' Against the Lizards, that was no small novelty and boosted his hopes that they had only second-line troops on their flanks. Like a jack-in-the-box, he popped up out of the cupola again.

Through the rasping roar of the Panther's big Maybach engine came the rattle of small-arms fire ahead. A couple of German MG-42s were in action, their rapid rate of fire unmistakable – they sounded as if a giant were ripping enormous bolts of thick, tough cloth between his hands. Jäger was glad the German infantry had the machine guns; since all Lizard foot soldiers carried automatic weapons, the poor *Landsers* needed all the help they could get.

The German panzers deployed for action, moving into their blunt wedge formation: two companies forward, Jäger's command panzer and another company in the middle to support them, and a fourth company in the rear as a reserve. They chewed brown, muddy lines through the green of growing crops.

Without warning, a streak of fire lanced through the air toward a Panzer IV in one of the lead companies. New Panzer IVs had long-barreled 75mm guns almost as good as the ones Panthers carried, but their armor, though thicker than in the earlier models, wasn't excellent protection even against terrestrial foes. Against a Lizard antipanzer rocket, the armor might as well not have been there at all. The Panzer IV brewed up, orange flame billowing and a column of thick black smoke mounting swiftly into the air.

Confused, angry shouts filled the radio. Jäger grabbed the headset, shoved the earphones into place, and shouted orders into the microphone. The nearest surviving panzer poured machine-gun fire into the thick clump of bushes from which the antipanzer rocket had come, hoping to flush out or knock down the Lizards who had fired it.

Nothing without armor could have survived that hail of bullets. From more than four hundred meters farther to the rear, Jäger watched the bushes writhe under it, as if under torture. But a moment later, another rocket incinerated a German panzer.

'They've got one of their troop carriers in there?' Jäger shouted into the microphone. 'Give 'em your main armament.' Unlike German half-tracks, the Lizards' armored troop carriers bore light cannon that could chew up anything this side of a panzer, and carried those rockets on turret rails to either side of the cannon. With them, the troop carriers became deadly dangerous panzer killers.

But, while they were formidably armed, they were only lightly armored. They could withstand small-arms fire, but when a panzer shell came knocking, they opened up. The German panzer hit the brakes to fire into that stand of bushes. Moments later, the bushes went up in flames as part of the troop carrier's funeral pyre.

Jäger whooped like a Red Indian. He remembered all too well the bad days of the summer before, when killing any Lizard armored vehicle seemed to require divine intervention. He'd done it himself once, with the

50mm cannon of a Panzer III, but he didn't pretend he'd been anything but lucky.

Yet another rocket streaked out from cover and smote a Panzer IV. The rocket exploded in a ball of flame, but the panzer did not brew up. Jäger whooped again. 'The *Schürzen* work!' he shouted to the world at large. The hollow-charge warheads of the Lizard's antipanzer rockets sent a jet of white-hot flame through armor and into a panzer. Some bright engineer had figured out that 5mm plates – 'skirts,' he called them – welded into a panzer's turret and sides would make the rocket warhead go off prematurely and dissipate that jet. Now Jäger saw that the bright idea actually worked in combat.

The advancing German panzers kept on spraying the Lizard infantry positions with machine-gun bullets. Covered by that, German infantrymen ran forward, too. The only opposing fire came from small arms. Jäger's hopes rose. If the Lizards didn't have any panzers in this sector, the *Wehrmacht* really could make some gains. He hadn't taken the brass seriously when they talked about getting Mulhouse back and cutting the Lizards off from the Rhine, but he was starting to think that just might happen.

Then three Lizard helicopters popped up from behind cover, two from out of clearings in the woods and the third from behind a barn. Jäger's mouth went dry; helicopters were deadlier foes than panzers. They launched two rockets each. One blew a hole in the ground. The other five hit German panzers. Two of the machines survived, but the other three went up in flames. A couple of crewmen managed to bail out of escape hatches; most perished.

Then 20mm rapid-fire antiaircraft guns started hammering at the helicopters. On the raid that captured the plutonium from the Lizards, the Germans who'd joined with the Russian partisans had carried a mountain version of one of those guns, which broke down into man-portable loads. Now the *Wehrmacht* made a habit of posting the light guns as far forward as possible, to hold helicopters at bay.

The tactic worked. The helicopters sheered away from the antiaircraft guns. One of them was trailing smoke, though it kept flying. Jäger prayed for it to fall from the sky, but it refused.

The two lead panzer companies were already through what had been the Lizard front line. They hadn't cleared up all the holdouts; a bullet cracked past Jäger's head and several more ricocheted off the Panther. Like any sensible soldiers, the Lizards were trying to pick off the panzer commanders. For the time being, Jäger ducked down into the Panther turret.

'We're driving them,' he said, fixing his eyes to the periscopes that gave him vision even when buttoned up. 'With luck, maybe we can push far enough to get in among their artillery and do them some real harm.'

Just then a Lizard troop carrier that had lain low opened up with a rocket and took out a panzer less than a hundred meters from Jäger's. By luck, he was looking through the periscope that showed where the rocket had come from. 'Panzer halt!' he shouted, and then, 'Armor-piercing!'

'Armor-piercing.' Wolfgang Eschenbach had a dispensation to exceed his daily word quota if in the line of duty. Grunting a little, he lifted a black-tipped shell, set it in the breech of the Panther's cannon.

'Bearing 300 degrees, range 700 metres, maybe a little less,' Jäger said. The turret slewed anticlockwise. 'I see him, sir,' Klaus Meinecke said. 'Behind those bushes, *ja*?'

'That's the one,' Jäger said. 'Fire at—'

Before he could say 'will,' Meinecke fired. With the turret closed, the noise was bearable, but recoil rocked the Panther. The shell casing leaped out of the breech; Eschenbach had to move smartly to keep it from smashing his toes. The acrid reek of burnt cordite filled the air.

'Hit!' Jäger yelled. 'Hit! Got him in one, Klaus. Forward!' That to the driver; stopped, the Panther was hideously vulnerable to enemy fire. The Maybach bellowed. The panzer leaped ahead. The advance went on.

2

Captain Rance Auerbach led his cavalry company out of Syracuse, Kansas, heading east along the north bank of the Arkansas River toward Garden City. Somewhere before he got there, he expected to run into the Lizards.

People in Syracuse waved to him and his command. Like him, they were up with the sun. Most of them were heading out to their farms. 'God bless you, boys,' a man in overalls called. 'Give 'em hell,' somebody else said. Two people said, 'Be careful.'

'We'll do our best,' Auerbach said, brushing the brim of his hat with the forefinger of his right hand. He was a big, rawboned man; years out in the open in all weather had tanned and lined his long face till he looked a good deal older than his actual thirty-two. That was true of most of the farmers, too, but amid their flat Kansas accents his Texas drawl stood out like a bobcat in a pack of coyotes.

His second-in-command, Lieutenant Bill Magruder, came out of Virginia and had a softer version of a Southern accent. 'So't of hate to leave a nice little town like this,' he remarked.

'It is pretty, isn't it?' Auerbach said. Syracuse boasted a cool, green profusion of poplars, willows, and other trees. On this stretch of the Great Plains, there wasn't much like it. Folks drove from miles around to relax under those trees. Or rather, folks *had* driven, in the days before the Lizards came.

'Your grandfather ride this way during the States War?' Magruder asked.

'Two of my great-grandfathers were Texas cavalrymen, sure enough,' Auerbach answered. 'One of 'em did some fighting in the Indian Territory – what's Oklahoma now – and up in Missouri, so I reckon he went through Kansas a time or two, but probably not this far west. Wasn't anything here to speak of back then.'

'Mm, you're likely right,' Magruder said.

They rode on a while in silence punctuated only by the occasional jingle of harness and the steady clopping of their horses' hooves. A little to the north, US 50 paralleled the Arkansas, but bare ground was easier on the horses' feet and legs than the asphalt would have been.

Every few hundred yards, a dead car or a clump of them sat on or alongside the highway. Some had just run out of gas with no hope for getting more. The Lizards had strafed others in the early days of their invasion, back when their fighter planes roamed everywhere and shot up everything. Farther east along the road, there would be dead tanks, too. The Great Plains were wonderful country for armor; too bad the Lizards had the wonderful armor to take advantage of the terrain.

'Or maybe it's not too bad,' Auerbach murmured, leaning forward to pat the side of his gelding's neck. 'Otherwise you'd be out of a job and I'd be just another grease monkey.'

The horse snorted softly. Auerbach patted it again. If you sent cavalry charging tanks, the way the Poles had against the Nazis in 1939, you'd get yourself killed, but you wouldn't accomplish anything else. But if you used your horses to take you to places farther and faster than infantry could go, and if you made sure the garrisons you raided weren't big ones, you could still do some useful things.

'You know, we aren't really cavalry, not the way Jeb Stuart would have used the word,' Auerbach said.

'I know. We're dragoons,' Magruder answered calmly. If anything ever rattled him, he didn't let it show on the outside. 'We use the horses to get from here to there, then get down and fight on foot. Jeb Stuart might not have done things that way, but Bedford Forrest sure as hell did.'

'He'd have done better if he had our firepower too,' Auerbach said. 'Every trooper with an M-1 except for the boys with BARs, a couple of nice, light Browning 1919A2 machine guns and a mortar on our packhorses ... give 'em to Forrest and we'd all be singin' "Dixie" instead of "The Star-Spangled Banner".'

'If Forrest had 'em, the damnyankees would've had 'em, too,' Magruder said. 'It'd just ratchet the slaughter up a notch without doin' anything else much, seems to me. Right now, I'm not much worried about what we sing for the national anthem, as long as it's not the song the Lizards use.'

To that, Auerbach could only nod. The company rode past the ruins of Fort Aubrey, about four miles east of Syracuse. After the Civil War, the Army had used it as a base from which to fight Indians. There hadn't been any fighting in these parts since. There was now.

High overhead, a westbound Lizard airplane scribed a white contrail, straight as if drawn by a draftsman, across the blue sky – *a blueprint for somebody catching hell*, Auerbach thought. The deadly roar of the plane's jet engines came down to the ground as a thin, attenuated whisper.

Bill Magruder shook his fist at the flying silver speck. Auerbach understood that only too well. He said, 'I'm just glad it's not after us.'

'Yes, sir,' Magruder said. They'd both been through assaults by ground-attack aircraft. Those chewed up horse cavalry as bad as tanks did. Helicopters were even worse. They didn't just make strafing runs and leave; they stayed around and hunted you no matter which way you ran. If cavalry flew instead of riding, it would be mounted on helicopters.

Auerbach turned his head to follow the Lizard plane as it disappeared into the west. 'These days, I can't help wondering what those sons of bitches carry,' he said. 'I keep worrying it's another one of those bombs like the one they used on Washington or the Russians used on them south of Moscow. Once the gloves for that kind of fight come off, how do you put 'em back on again?'

'Damned if I know,' Magruder answered. 'I just wish to Jesus we had some of those bombs ourselves. You think we can make 'em?'

'I sure hope so,' Auerbach answered. He thought back to the knapsack that colonel – what was his name? Groves, that was it – had toted from Boston all the way to Denver, complete with a detour into Canada. He'd commanded the company that had escorted Groves on the cross-country jaunt. He didn't know for sure what was in that knapsack; Groves had been mighty tight-lipped about the whole business, like any good officer. But if it wasn't something to do with one of those fancy bombs, Auerbach figured his guesser needed repairing.

He didn't say anything about that to Magruder, who hadn't been with the company then. If Groves couldn't talk to him about it, he didn't figure he could talk to anybody else.

The company rode into Kendall, twelve miles east of Syracuse, a couple of hours before noon. If Syracuse had been a small town, Kendall was a dusty hamlet dozing by the Arkansas River. Auerbach let the horses rest, crop some grass, and drink from the river. He walked into the general store to see if it had anything worth getting, but the 150 Kendallians had pretty much picked it clean over the past year. They were living on whatever they got from their farms, the way their grandparents and great-grandparents had just after the War Between the States.

When the company left Kendall, Auerbach ordered a couple of scouts with radios well forward. He knew the Lizards were in Garden City, forty miles east. He didn't think they were in Lakin, fifteen miles east. He didn't want to find out he was wrong the hard way.

He also ordered the men to spread out wide. Even if the worst happened – the worst being attack from the air – some of them should escape.

One minute, one hour, melted into another. Sweat dripped from the end of Auerbach's pointed nose, soaked the armpits of his khaki jacket. He took off his hat and fanned himself with it. It didn't help much.

Just as if the world remained at peace, windmills spun, pumping water up from underground to nourish wheat and corn and sugar beets. Almost every farm had a big brooder house; every so often, Auerbach would hear chickens clucking. Cows and sheep cropped grass, while pigs wandered around eating anything that wasn't nailed down. Even though shipping had gone to the devil here no less than anywhere else, people still ate pretty well.

The company approached Lakin in the late afternoon. Auerbach didn't mind that at all: if the town did hold Lizards, they'd have the sun in their eyes when fighting started. 'Sir!' The radioman brought his horse up next to Auerbach's 'Henry and Red, they say they've spotted razor wire like the Lizards use. They're dismounting and they'll wait for us.'

'Right.' Auerbach reined in, got out a pair of binoculars. He didn't see any razor wire, but the scouts were a lot closer than he was. Far and away the biggest set of buildings ahead looked at first distant glance like military barracks. Auerbach turned the binoculars on them, whereupon he laughed at himself – they let him read the words painted in big letters on the side of one building, which said KEARNY COUNTY CONSOLIDATED HIGH SCHOOL. He turned back to the radioman. 'Tell 'em we're on our way.'

'Yes, sir.' The radioman spoke into the microphone.

'Horse holders!' Auerbach called, hoping the sun *would* keep the Lizards in Lakin from noticing him and his men. If it didn't that could prove embarrassing – maybe fatally embarrassing. In the States War, one man in four had held horses while the others went up to fight on foot. Auerbach's company was already about ten men under strength; he couldn't afford to lose any more effectives than he could help. Letting one man hold five horses also let the company bring four or five extra weapons to the front.

Some of the horse holders resented the duty; he had to rotate it through all the troopers to make it seem fair. Some, though, looked just as well pleased not to be going up against the firepower the Lizards could throw at them. He pretended not to notice that. Nobody had to be a hero all the time.

He wondered how big a garrison the Lizards had thrown into Lakin. They hadn't been there long; how well could they have fortified the place? He was bringing about seventy men with him; if they were going up against a battalion, they'd get slaughtered. But why in God's name would the Lizards stick a battalion into a godforsaken place like Lakin, Kansas? He hoped he didn't find out.

The company advanced at the best pace the crews for the machine guns and mortar could manage: they were the ones weighed down by their guns and ammunition. Auerbach would have liked to approach Lakin closer on horseback, but that was asking to get chewed up. Here on the plains, they could see you coming from a long way off.

About a mile outside of town, the mortar crew set up shop. A little bit closer, Red and Henry had tied their horses to fence posts. Red – his last name was O'Neill – pointed ahead. 'See that, Sir? They've got a perimeter out around the school.'

'Mmhmmm.' Auerbach studied it. 'Wire, yeah, and firing pits, too. I don't see anybody in 'em, though.'

'No, sir,' O'Neill agreed. 'They're there, all right, but they don't look like they're expecting company.

'Which may mean they aren't, and which may mean they're laying for us.' Auerbach rubbed his chin. Bristles rasped under his fingers. He was getting scruffy enough to make a good States War trooper, that was for sure. He sighed. 'I think we better find out.'

Nobody argued, but then nobody would; he was the captain, the fellow who got paid to make the choices. He wished someone would have tried to talk him out of this one. Instead, the men fanned out and started moving in on the consolidated high school. At his murmured orders, one of the machine-gun crews went straight toward it while the other circled around to the left, away from the Arkansas River.

Auerbach went straight in, too. With every step he took, he wished Kansas wasn't so blinking flat. He felt like a bug on a plate, walking toward a man with a fly swatter the size of Dallas. Before long, he wasn't walking any more; he was crawling on his belly through the grass.

Something moved inside the perimeter ahead. Auerbach froze. Somebody fired. As if that were a signal, the whole company opened up. Some of the high school's windows had been broken before. Abruptly, just about all of them were. The Lizards wasted no time shooting back. They had machine guns on the roofs of several high school buildings. Auerbach blew air out through his lips, making a snuffling noise amazingly like one a horse might produce. This wasn't going to be anything like a walkover.

A mortar bomb whistled through the air, landing about fifty yards short of the school buildings. Another round flew over the high school. *Bracketed*, Auerbach thought. Then bombs started falling on the buildings. One of the rooftop machine guns suddenly fell silent. Auerbach yelled himself hoarse.

After about fifteen rounds, the mortar stopped shooting. That was painfully developed doctrine. If you kept banging away from the same place too long, the Lizards would get you. Besides, they were going to be calling in air support any minute now. You didn't want to lose artillery, even a little old mortar. If they couldn't find you, they couldn't shoot.

One of the high school buildings had caught fire. Lizards skittered out of it. Auerbach drew a bead on one, fired. The Lizard sprawled on the ragged grass and lay there kicking. Auerbach shot at another one, to no visible effect. He swore.

Some of his men had got into Lakin itself, so fire came at the consolidated high school from three sides of a ring. Auerbach pricked up his ears – some of the weapons firing from that direction weren't regulation Army issue. That meant the locals had joined in the fight. Auerbach wanted to pound his head against the dirt of the shallow foxhole he'd scraped out for himself. The cavalry was going to have to get the hell out in a couple of minutes. Did the Lakinites or whatever they called themselves think the Lizards would give them a big kiss on the cheek for trying to make like soldiers?

He turned to the radioman. 'Call our boys in town and tell 'em to get

out. Tell 'em to bring out as many of the townies with guns as they can.'
He laughed. 'Those folks don't know it yet, but they just joined the Army.'
Several of his troopers had joined in the same highly informal way. If you
were willing to put your neck on the line to fight the Lizards, Uncle Sam
was more than willing to give you a chance to do it by the numbers.

When firing in Lakin began to die down, Auerbach also ordered his
troops on the left to pull back. Now he used his machine guns to cover the
retreat and keep the Lizards from getting too enthusiastic about pursuit.
The troopers had made a lot of raids on Lizard-held small towns. They
knew the drill. You wanted to get back to your horses and scatter before
the Lizards brought in their planes and helicopters and splattered you all
over the landscape.

You could tell at a glance the new fish the troopers were bringing out
of Lakin, and uniforms or their absence had next to nothing to do with it.
The civilians who'd taken up arms against the Lizards didn't know how
to take cover, they didn't know how to move, they hesitated before doing
what somebody told them. About what you'd expect from three or four
farmers in bib overalls and . . . two girls?

Auerbach did a double take. Sure as hell, a couple of young women toting
.22s were trotting back with his soldiers. One of them wore overalls, too; the
other was in a dress. He played back in his head the orders he'd given the
radioman. He'd said *townies*; he hadn't said *men*. If the troopers claimed
they were just following orders, they'd have a point.

'Oh, for God's sake,' he muttered. That sort of thing had happened
before, but, like anybody, he hadn't expected it to happen to him. He
hoped the girls could ride. He'd have horses for them; he'd seen a couple
of his men go down. Companions were helping others along.

There were the horses, in a little hollow that shielded them from being
spotted from the high school. The mortar was already broken down and
packed away. Here came the machine gun crews. The 1919A2 had been
developed especially for cavalry; with the weapons came light metal fittings
that attached to the standard pack saddle and carried gun, tripod, a spare
parts chest, a spare barrel, and three small ammunition chests. Getting
everything ready for travel took bare moments.

Auerbach turned to the civilians who'd taken up arms against the
Lizards. 'Can you ride, people?' Even in farm country like this, it wasn't
a given, the way it would have been a generation before.

But nobody said no, for which he was duly grateful. The newcomers
gave their names as they mounted – or, in a couple of cases, clambered
onto – the horses of cavalrymen who wouldn't need them any more. What
anybody called Lorenzo Farquhar was doing in Lakin, Kansas, was beyond
Auerbach, but it wasn't his business, either.

The woman in overalls was named Penny Summers; her father Wendell
was there, too. The other one was Rachel Hines. She said, 'I've wanted to
shoot those things ever since they came here. Thanks for giving me the

chance.' Though she showed a lot of leg mounting, she swung into the saddle as smoothly as any of the men.

When everyone was horsed, Auerbach said, 'Now we scatter. You new people, pick a trooper and stick close to him. Rendezvous point is Lamar, Colorado. See you there in a couple of days. Let's ride.'

Scattering was the best way to make sure attack from the air didn't wipe out your whole command. Some of the troops galloped off to the north, some to the south toward the Arkansas, some straight off to the west. Auerbach headed northwest himself, to be in the middle of things when the air attacks came. Not that he could do anything about them, but his job was to try . . .

Penny Summers and her dad rode with him. They weren't horsefolk like his troopers, but they kept up – and everyone was going flat out, too. Hearing a swelling roar in the air behind him, he roweled his gelding with his spurs, wringing out of it every ounce of speed it had. A hammering noise rang through the roar, as if God's jalopy had developed a knock.

The damage was done in the few seconds before the fighter plane screamed overhead, close enough for Auerbach to see the seams and rivets on the underside of its fuselage. Cannon shells chewed up the ground around the fleeing cavalrymen. A fragment tore his trouser leg and drew a bleeding line on the side of his calf.

He looked around as the plane streaked off after other targets. One of his troopers was down, dead. So was Wendell Summers. It looked as if one shell had got him and another his horse. Auerbach gulped. Even for war, it was ugly.

Penny Summers had reined in, staring in numb astonishment at the red smears and badly butchered meat that had been her father. 'Get moving!' Auerbach shouted at her. 'You want to end up just like him? We've got to get out of here.'

'But – he's dead,' she said disbelievingly, as if such things couldn't happen, as if this were peaceful 1938 rather than 1943.

'It's a chance you take, shooting back at the Lizards,' Auerbach answered. He wanted to be gentle, but he didn't have time. 'Look, miss, we can't hang around. That plane may be back for another pass, you know.'

Her eyes were green but white showed all around their irises. She was, he guessed, somewhere in her middle twenties, but shock left her face so blank, she looked years younger. But if she didn't pull herself together at least well enough to ride that horse in the next ten seconds, he was damn well going to leave her here.

She did. She was still stunned, but she booted the horse in the ribs and got rolling. Auerbach rode alongside her. When he had the time, he'd grieve for his lost men, too. Not now. Now getting away was all that mattered. If that stinking jet hadn't chewed up the rest of the company too badly, he might even have won himself a minor victory.

Ussmak said, 'If they keep pulling us out of the line, how do they expect us to maintain the advance against the Deutsche?'

Nejas let out a hissing sigh. 'I am but a landcruiser commander, Ussmak, just as you are but a driver and Skoob here but a gunner. I do not make these decisions, but I am a male of the Race. I obey.'

'Yes, superior sir.' Ussmak sighed, too, but quietly. High-ranking males made decisions, lower-ranking ones obeyed him . . . and paid the price. Two landcruiser commanders and one gunner with whom he'd fought were dead now, and another commander and gunner arrested for being ginger addicts – all that in what everyone had assumed would be a walkover campaign, back when males went into the cold-sleep tanks while the conquest fleet still orbited Home.

Nejas and Skoob were good crewmales, the best he'd had since his first commander and gunner. They didn't know he had his own little stash of ginger stowed away under one of the flameproof mats in the driver's compartment of the landcruiser. He wished he'd never got the habit, but when good males died around you, when half your orders made no sense, when you were hurt and bored and didn't look forward to more combat but knew you had no choice, what were you going to do?

He was no fleetlord or shiplord or grand strategist of any sort, but pulling the landcruisers back from the thrust they'd made struck him as stupid. They'd reached an important river (the locals called it the Rhine) and were poised to strike deep into Deutschland if they could force a crossing – and now this.

'You have to give the Deutsche credit,' he said reluctantly. 'No matter how hard we hit them, they hit back. And the Swiss – is that what the other tribe's name is? – are like that, too. They don't have weapons as good as the Deutsche, but—'

'I know what I want to give the Deutsche,' Skoob the gunner said. He pointed to the main armament of the landcruiser, a thin black line against the dark blue of the night sky. 'Better that than credit, if you ask me.'

Ussmak didn't argue. The landcruiser was pulled off the road north of Mulhouse (and hadn't going back through the wrecked Tosevite town been a delight?), parked in a meadow. Tosev 3's big moon spilled pale light on the mountains to the west, but only made the closer woods seem blacker and more forbidding.

Even by day, Tosev 3 was an alien world to Ussmak. It was too cold to suit him, while the light from the star Tosev paradoxically seemed whiter and brighter than he was used to. At night, though, the planet turned into the sort of haunted place a female might have used to frighten hatchlings.

Everything felt unfamiliar. The odors the chilly breeze brought to the scent receptors on Ussmak's tongue, some spicy, some bland, others redolent of decay, were all strange to him. The air itself felt heavy and wet to breathe. And the sounds – the chirps and tweets and occasional snarls – were none of them like those night creatures made back on Home. That was one reason Ussmak found them frightening. Another was that he could never be certain which of those night noises came from a Big Ugly sneaking up with the intent of doing him permanent bodily harm.

He said, 'I'm going to get my rest while I can. We'll probably be fighting tomorrow.' Somewhere altogether too close for comfort, the Deutsche were camped with their landcruisers, too, waiting for Tosev to rise. The landcruisers themselves weren't much, though the new models could sting. But by the way the Deutsche handled them, they could have served as instructors at any training center in the Empire.

New models. The thought ran through his head as he slid down into the landcruiser through the driver's hatch. The weapons with which the Race fought on Tosev 3 were not much different from the ones they'd used to conquer the Rabotevs and Hallessi, thousands of years before. They'd been on Tosev 3 a bit more than two years (only a little more than one of this planet's slow turns around its sun), and already the landcruisers and aircraft with which the Big Uglies fought them were vastly more dangerous than those they'd first met.

That was frightening in and of itself. Worse than frightening was the atomic bomb the Russkis had used. If the Big Uglies got nuclear weapons, the Race was liable to lose the war. Ussmak hadn't imagined that, not when he rampaged across the plains of the SSSR just after the Race landed. He closed the hatch after him, dogged it tight. Nejas and Skoob would sleep under the treads of the landcruisers; they didn't have enough room for comfort in the turret. But his seat reclined to make a fair bed. He lay there for a while, but sleep eluded him.

Ever so cautiously, he reached under the mat and took out a little plastic vial. It was full of brownish powder. He pulled off the top, poured a small mound of powder into the palm of his hand, and brought the hand up to his mouth. His scent receptors caught the ginger's spicy tang even before his tongue flicked out to lap up the powder.

As it made its way to his brain, well-being flowed through him: he felt wise and quick and powerful all at the same time, as if he were the fleetlord and part of the fleetlord's computer scrambled together. But he also felt *good*, almost as good as he would during mating season. With no females within light-years, mating hardly ever crossed his mind; to the Race, the habits of the Big Uglies seemed a planetwide dirty joke.

When ginger coursed through him, the Big Uglies were laughable, contemptible. Better yet, in his mind they were *small*. With ginger, the war looked not only winnable but easy, the way everyone had thought it would be before the conquest fleet left Home.

But Ussmak had learned better than to taste just before he went into combat. Ginger made you think you were smart and strong, but it didn't really make you smart and strong. If you soared into action convinced the Tosevites couldn't possibly hurt you, you were all too likely to end up dead before you realized you'd made a mistake.

Tasting ginger had two other problems attached to it. One was that the first thing a taste made you want was another taste. Ussmak knew he was an addict; he fought against it as best he could, but an addict he remained. The other problem was what happened when you didn't take that second taste. Ginger didn't just lift you. When it was through with you, it dropped you – hard. And the drop seemed all the worse because of how high you'd been before.

Ussmak made himself not reach for the vial again when exhilaration faded. 'I've done this a lot of times by now,' he said aloud, willing himself to stillness. Depression and fear crashed down on him just the same. He knew they weren't real, but they felt as real as the pleasure that had gone before them.

Infantrymales screened the landcruisers. In Ussmak's worried imagination, they fell asleep at their posts or simply failed to spy Deutsche males creeping through what were to the Race alien woods. The first the crewmales would know of their blunders was satchel charges chucked at their landcruisers. Ussmak dozed off shivering in terror.

He woke with a fresh spasm of alarm when the turret hatches clanged shut, but it was only Nejas and Skoob getting into the landcruiser. 'I thought you were a couple of Tosevites,' he said resentfully.

'If we were, you'd be dead meat,' Skoob retorted. A short pause showed he was letting his mouth fall open in laughter.

'Let's get moving,' Nejas said. 'Driver, start the engine.'

'It shall be done, superior sir.' The return to routine heartened Ussmak; however battered by fate he'd been, he was still a male of the Race. The hydrogen-burning turbine caught on the first try. He would have been astonished at anything else. The Race's engineering was solid.

'We'll clean up the Deutsche here and then resume our advance,' Nejas said as the landcruiser began to move. 'A little delay won't matter.' Ussmak wondered if he'd had his tongue in the ginger jar, too. But no. Nejas and Skoob had never developed the habit. They were everything males of the Race should be, and so unselfconscious about it that he couldn't even resent them.

Landcruisers and troop carriers rumbled up the road together. The farmland to either side had probably been fertile once, but armies going back and forth across it hadn't done much to help that. Ruins, craters, and the tumbled corpses of Tosevite animals were appalling. Ussmak didn't see any Big Uglies. They weren't too stupid to get out of the way of the war.

Not far ahead, a male in the gray sacks the Deutsche wore to protect themselves from their world's beastly climate popped up out of a concealed hole in the ground and pointed something at a troop carrier. Flame shot from the rear of the device; a projectile rocketed toward the carrier. Without looking to see whether he'd scored a hit, the Big Ugly ducked back into his hole.

Troop carriers were armored against small-arms fire but, unlike landcruisers, not against heavy weapons. The projectile struck just below the turret. The carrier burst into flames at once. Escape hatches popped open as its crew and the fighting males it bore tried to escape. Some did; fire from Deutsch gunners cut down others.

'Smash that Tosevite!' Nejas screamed from the intercom speaker taped to Ussmak's hearing diaphragm. Normally a calm, collected commander, he sounded as furiously excitable as any ginger-licker after three tastes.

By contrast, Ussmak was coldly furious. 'It shall be done, superior sir,' he said grimly, and steered straight for the foxhole from which the Big Ugly had emerged. He made sure he put a tread right on it, then locked that tread and turned the landcruiser in its own length, crushing the Deutsche male as if he were grinding an insect underfoot. Then he drove on.

'It's not revenge enough,' Skoob complained.

'It certainly isn't, by the Emperor,' Nejas agreed. 'The Deutsche came out ahead in that exchange.'

As he'd been trained since hatchlinghood to do, Ussmak cast down his eyes at the mention of his sovereign. Before he could raise them – WHAM! The impact against the front of the landcruiser was like a kick in the muzzle. He'd been in a landcruiser that had taken shell hits back in the SSSR, but never one like this. But the armor held – if it hadn't, he wouldn't have been sitting there thinking about how hard he'd just been hit.

Commander and gunner normally went through a series of orders identifying a target and designating it for destruction. This time, Skoob just said, 'With your permission, superior sir,' and fired after a tiny pause. That hesitation was enough to let the Deutsche fire again, too. WHAM! Again an impact that jolted Ussmak, again the shell failed to penetrate.

The landcruiser rocked with the round Skoob fired. 'Hit!' Ussmak shouted as flame and smoke spurted from behind bushes. Not even the best Big Ugly landcruiser gun could pierce the frontal armor of one of the Race's landcruisers, but the reverse did not hold true.

'Forward,' Nejas ordered. Ussmak gave the engine more throttle. The landcruiser leaped ahead.

More Deutsche, Ussmak discovered, were armed with those alarming rocket projectors. They killed two troop carriers that he saw, and managed to set one landcruiser afire. Few of the males who used the projectors escaped. The blast from the launchers showed just where they were, and gunners sent heavy fire their way – nor was Ussmak the only male to take more direct measures of extermination.

He'd almost reached a town marked on the map as Rouffach when Nejas ordered, 'Driver halt.'

'Halting, superior sir,' Ussmak said obediently, though the command puzzled him: despite the antivehicle rockets, they'd been driving the Big Uglies before them.

'Orders from the unit commander,' Nejas said. 'We're to pull back from this position and resume our previous offensive.'

'It shall be done,' Ussmak said, as he had to say. Then, not only because he'd been through a lot of combat with a lot of crews but also because the deaths of his previous crewmates made him much more an outsider than males of the Race usually became, he went on, 'That doesn't make a lot of sense, superior sir. Even if we were beating them, we haven't smashed the Big Uglies here, and by going off we've just given the Deutsche by the big river a couple of days' rest to strengthen their defenses. They were tough enough before, and they'd stay that way, even if we had forced our way through some of them.'

For a considerable time, Nejas did not answer him. At last, the landcruiser commander said, 'Driver, I fear you demonstrate imperfect subordination.' Ussmak knew he was imperfect in any number of ways. That was a long way from saying he was wrong.

'Take off your clothes,' Ttomalss said. The little scaly devil's Chinese held a thick, hissing accent, but Liu Han was used to it and followed it without trouble.

She used the little devils' speech in return. 'It shall be done, superior sir.' She wondered if Ttomalss could detect the weary resignation in her voice. She didn't think so. The little scaly devils were interested in learning everything they could about people, but only as people might be interested in learning everything they could about some new kind of pig. That people might have feelings didn't seem to have occurred to them.

Sighing, Liu Han pulled off her black cotton tunic, let her baggy trousers and linen drawers fall to the dirt floor of the hut in the refugee camp west of Shanghai. Outside, people chattered and argued and scolded children and chased chickens and ducks. The marketplace lay not far away; the racket that came from there was never-ending, like the splashing of a stream. She had to make a deliberate effort to hear it.

Ttomalss's weird eyes swiveled independently as they examined her. She stood still and let him look all he cared to; one thing more than a year's association with the little scaly devils had taught her was that they had no prurient interest in mankind ... not that she would have aroused prurient interest in many men, not with a belly that looked as if she'd swallowed a great melon whole. Her best guess was that the baby would come in less than a month.

Ttomalss walked up to her and set the palm of his hand on her belly. His skin was dry and scaly, like a snake's, but warm, almost feverish, against hers. The little devils were hotter than people. The few Christians in the camp said that proved they came from the Christian hell. Wherever they came from, Liu Han wished they'd go back there and leave here – leave everyone – alone.

The baby kicked inside her. Ttomalss jerked his hand away, skittered back a couple of paces with a startled hiss. 'That is disgusting,' he exclaimed in Chinese, and added the emphatic cough.

Liu Han bowed her head. 'Yes, superior sir,' she said. What point to arguing with the scaly devil? His kind came from eggs, like poultry or songbirds.

Cautiously, Ttomalss returned. He reached out again, touched her in a very private place. 'We have seen, in your kind, that the hatchlings come forth from this small opening. We must examine and study the process most carefully when the event occurs. It seems all but impossible.'

'It is true, superior sir.' Liu Han still stood quiet, enduring his hand, hating him. Hate filled her, but she had no way to let it out. After the Japanese overran her village and killed her husband and little son, the little scaly devils had overrun the Japanese – and kidnapped her.

The little devils had mating seasons like farm animals. Finding out that people didn't had repelled and fascinated them at the same time. She was one of the unlucky people they'd picked to learn more about such matters -- again, as people might explore the mating habits of pigs. In essence, though they didn't seem to think of it in those terms, they'd turned her into a whore.

In a way, she'd been lucky. One of the men they'd forced on her, an American named Bobby Fiore, had been decent enough, and she'd partnered with him and not had to endure any more strangers. The baby kicked again. He'd put it in her belly.

But Bobby Fiore was dead now, too. He'd escaped from the camp with Chinese Communist guerrillas. Somehow, he'd got to Shanghai. The scaly devils had killed him there – and brought back color photos of his corpse for her to identify.

Ttomalss opened a folder, took out one of the astonishing photographs the little scaly devils made. Liu Han had seen photographs in magazines before the little devils came from wherever they came from. She'd seen moving pictures at the cinema a few times. But never had she seen photographs with such perfect colors, and never had she seen photographs that showed depth.

This one was in color, too, but not in colors that seemed connected to anything in the world Liu Han knew: bright blues, reds, and yellows were splashed, seemingly at random, over an image of a curled-up infant. She could not see whether it was a boy or a girl. 'This is a picture developed by the machine-that-thinks from scans of the hatchling growing inside you,' Ttomalss said.

'The machine-that-thinks is stupid, superior sir,' Liu Han said scornfully. 'The baby will be born with skin the color of mine, except pinker, and it will have a purplish patch above its buttocks that will fade in time. It will not look like it rolled through a painter's shop.'

Ttomalss's mouth dropped open. Liu Han couldn't tell if he was laughing at her or if he thought the joke was funny. He said, 'These are not real colors. The machine-that-thinks uses them to show which parts of the hatchling are warmer and which cooler.'

'The machine-that-thinks is stupid,' Liu Han repeated. She didn't understand everything Ttomalss meant by the phrase; she knew that The scaly devils were pretty stupid themselves, even if they were strong – maybe they needed machines to do their thinking for them. 'Thank you for showing me all is well,' she said, and bowed to Ttomalss. 'How could the machine-that-thinks see inside me to know?'

'With a kind of light you cannot see and a kind of sound you cannot hear,' the little devil said, which left Liu Han no wiser than before. He held out other pictures to her. 'Here are earlier pictures of the hatchling. You see it looks more like you now.'

He was right about that. Foolish colors aside, some of the pictures hardly looked like anything human. But Liu Han had talked with women who'd miscarried, and remembered them speaking of the oddly shaped lumps of flesh they'd expelled. She was willing to believe Ttomalss wasn't lying to her.

'Will you take more pictures now, superior sir, or may I dress?' she asked.

'Not of the hatchling, but of you, that we may study how your body changes as the hatchling grows inside.' Ttomalss took out what had to be a camera, although Liu Han had never seen one so small in a human's hands. He walked all round her, photographing from front, back, and sides. Then he said, 'Now you dress. I see you again soon.' He skittered out the door. He did remember to close it after himself, for which Liu Han was duly grateful.

Sighing, she got back into her clothes. Other cameras hidden in the hut probably recorded that. She'd given up worrying about it. The little scaly devils had had her under close surveillance ever since she fell into their clutches, and that had grown closer yet after Bobby Fiore somehow managed to get out of the camp. Yet no matter how tight it was, there were ways around it. Ttomalss had told her something worth knowing. She took a couple of silver Mex dollars from a hiding place among her pots and pans, then left the hut herself.

A lot of people gave her a wide berth as she walked slowly down the dirt road that ran in front of the house – anyone who was so obviously involved with the little devils was not to be trusted. But children didn't skip alongside her chanting 'Running dog!' as they once had.

The market square brawled with life, merchants selling pork and chicken and ducks and puppies and vegetables of every sort, jade and silk and cotton, baskets and pots and braziers – anything they could raise or find or trade for (or steal) in the refugee camp. Women in clinging dresses with slits pasted alluring smiles on their faces and offered to show men their bodies, a euphemism for prostituting themselves. They didn't lack for customers. Liu Han pitied them; she knew what they had to endure.

She dodged a mountebank juggling knives and bowls as he strolled through the market. Her sidestep almost made her upset the ivory tiles of a mahjong player who made his living by matching wits against all comers (and maybe by unduly clever fingers as well). 'Watch where you're going, stupid woman!' he shouted at her.

Bobby Fiore had used a one-fingered gesture to answer shouts like that; he knew what it meant and the Chinese didn't, so he could vent his feelings without getting them angry. Liu Han just kept walking. She paused in front of a cart full of straw hats. As she tried one on, she said to the man behind the cart, 'Did you know the little scaly devils have a camera that can see how hot things are? Isn't that amazing?'

'If I cared, it would be,' the hat seller answered in a dialect she could hardly follow; the camp held people from all over China. 'Do you want to buy that hat or not?'

After haggling for a while, she walked on. She talked about the camera at several other stalls and carts, and bought some *bok choi* and a small brass pot. She'd wandered through half the market before she came to a poultry seller whose stand was next to that of a pig butcher. She told him about the camera, too, while she bought some chicken feet and some necks. 'Isn't that amazing?' she finished.

'A camera that can see how hot things are? That *is* amazing,' he said. 'You think I give you that much for thirty cents Mex? Woman, you are crazy!'

She ended up paying forty-five cents Mex for the chicken parts, which was too much, but she kept her temper about it. With the poultry seller, 'Isn't it amazing?' was a code phrase that meant she had information to pass, and his 'That *is* amazing' said he'd understood. Somehow – she had no idea, and didn't want to know – he'd get word to the Chinese Communists outside the camp.

She knew the little scaly devils watched her closely, not only because they were interested in her pregnancy but also because of what Bobby Fiore had done. But if she spread gossip all through the marketplace, how could they figure out which person who heard it was the one who mattered? She just seemed like a foolish woman chattering at random.

What she seemed and what she was were not one and the same. As best she could, she was getting her revenge.

Having a rifle in his hands again made Mordechai Anielewicz feel he was doing something wrong once more. The months he'd sent in the little Polish town of Leczna had been the most pleasant he'd passed since the Germans invaded in 1939 – especially the romance he'd had with Zofia Klopotowski, who lived next door to the people who had taken him in – but that memory made him feel guilty, not glad. With a war raging all around, what right did he have to take pleasure in anything?

Back in the Warsaw ghetto, he'd been readying an uprising against the Germans when the Lizards came. The Jews of the ghetto had risen, all right, against the Nazis and for the Lizards – and he'd become head of all the Jewish fighters in Lizard-held Poland, one of the most powerful humans in all the land.

But the Lizards, while they weren't interested in exterminating the Jews the way the Nazis had been, were intent on enslaving them – and the Poles and the Germans and the Russians and everybody else. Joining them for the short term had helped save his people. Joining them for the long term would have been ruinous for all peoples.

So, quietly, he'd begun working against them. He'd let the Germans smuggle explosive metal west, though he had diverted some for the British and Americans. He'd smuggled his friend Moishe Russie out of the country after Moishe couldn't stomach telling any more lies for the Lizards on the wireless. But the Lizards had grown suspicious of Mordechai, and so . . .

Here he was in the forest at dead of night with a rifle in his hands. Some of the partisans with him where Jews, some were Poles, a few were Germans. The Germans still alive and fighting in Poland a year after the Lizards came were some very tough customers indeed.

Somewhere up ahead, an owl hooted. He didn't mind that. A few nights before, he'd heard wolves howling. That had sent the hair on his arms and at the back of his neck prickling up in atavistic terror.

Also up ahead, but closer, the point man for the partisan band let out a hiss. Everybody froze. A whisper came back down the line: 'Jerzy's found the highway.'

The road from Lublin up to Biala Podlaska was paved, which by the standards of Polish country roads made it worthy of that handle. One of the Germans in the band, a hulking blond named Friedrich, thumped Anielewicz on the shoulder and said, 'All right, Shmuel, let's see how this works.'

'It worked once, or something like it,' Mordechai answered in German cleaner than the *Wehrmacht* man's. First names were customary in the partisan band. His was false – anybody who figured out who he really was might be tempted to betray him to the Lizards – but had to be Jewish in spite of his unaccented German and Polish. Languages were all very well, but some things they couldn't disguise.

'All right,' Friedrich said. 'We see if it works again.' His voice carried an implied threat, but Anielewicz didn't think that had anything to do with his own Judaism. Freidrich just didn't want things to go wrong. That much he still kept from his army days. Otherwise he didn't look much like the spit-and-polish soldiers who'd made life hell for the Jews in Warsaw and Lodz and everywhere in Poland. A floppy hat had replaced his coalscuttle helmet, he wore a fuzzy yellow beard, and the bandoliers crossed over the chest of his peasant blouse gave him a fine piratical air.

With a grunt of relief, Anielewicz unstrapped the crate he'd been carrying along with his knapsack. Some enterprising soul had stolen it from the Lizard's base at Lublin. It wasn't anything special, just an ordinary Lizard supply container. As he carried it toward the road, other partisans put in cans and jars of food, some from purloined Lizard stock, others of human make.

Up by the highway, Jerzy had the *pièce de résistance*: a jar full of ground ginger. 'Stick it in my pocket,' Mordechai whispered to him. 'I'm not going to put it in there yet.'

'This is your play,' the point man whispered back as he obeyed. He grinned, his teeth for a moment startling visible. 'You sneaky Jew bastard.'

'Fuck you, Jerzy,' Anielewicz said, but he grinned, too. He stepped out onto the asphalt, tipped the supply crate over sideways. Cans and jars rolled out of it along the surface of the road. He decided that wasn't good enough. He stomped on a couple of cans, smashed two or three jars.

He stepped back, considered the artistic effect, and found it good. The crate looked as if it had fallen off a supply lorry. He took the jar of ginger from his pocket, unscrewed the lid, and spilled half the contents over the cans and jars still inside. Then he set the jar and the lid by the crate and retreated back into the woods.

'Now we set up the ambush and we wait,' he told Jerzy.

The point man nodded. 'They're fools for not cutting the brush farther back from the sides of the road,' he remarked.

'Fools?' Anielewicz said. 'Well, maybe. You ask me, though, they just don't have the manpower to do everything they need. Good thing, too. If they did, they'd beat us. But trying to take on the whole world spreads them thin.'

He found a good hidey-hole behind a shrub – as a city boy, he couldn't identify it any more closely than that. He detached the bayonet from his Mauser and used it to dig himself a little deeper into the soft, rich-smelling dirt. He was too aware of how much better he could have done with a proper entrenching tool.

Then it was lie and wait. A mosquito bit him in the hand. He swatted at it. It or one just like it bit him on the ear. Somebody warned he was making too much noise. Another mosquito bit him. He lay still. Lizard vehicles weren't as nosy as the grunting, flatulent machines the Nazis used. Sometimes the racket from the German tanks and troop carriers was intimidating, but it always told you right where they were. The Lizards could sneak up on you if you weren't careful.

Mordechai was careful. So were the rest of the partisans; the ones who hadn't been careful – and some of the ones who had – were dead now. When the faint rumble of northbound vehicles came to his ears, he flattened himself against the earth, to be as nearly invisible as he could. The Lizards had gadgets that could see in the dark like cats.

A personnel carrier whizzed by the artistically arranged crate without stopping. So did three lorries in quick succession. Anielewicz's heart sank. If his ambush went for nothing, he'd lose prestige in the band. He might have been the leader of Poland's Jewish fighters, but the partisans here didn't know that. As far as they were concerned, he was just a new fish showing what he could do.

The last lorry in the convoy pulled to a stop. So did the troop carrier riding shotgun for it. Mordechai didn't raise his head. He strained to catch the noises from the highway. A door on the lorry slammed. His heart thumped. One of the Lizards was going over to investigate the crate.

His biggest worry was that the Lizards wouldn't touch it because they were afraid it was rigged to a land mine or a grenade. Actually, that wasn't a bad idea, but Mordechai was ambitious. He wanted to bag more Lizards than he could with such a ploy.

He knew the exact instant when the Lizard realized the ginger was there: the excited, disbelieving hiss needed no translation. He wanted to hiss himself, with relief. Not all Lizards were ginger tasters, by any means, but a lot of them were. He'd counted on there being at least one taster among those who investigated the spilled crate.

That hiss brought another male out of the lorry. Maybe the Lizard who'd made it had a radio with him, for a moment later hatches on the troop carrier came down, too. Anielewicz's lips skinned back from his teeth in a savage grin. Just what he'd hoped for!

Easy, easy ... patient. He willed his comrades to hold their fire until they could do the most damage. With a whole lot of luck, the fighting vehicle's crew would get down along with the infantry they transported. If they were smart, they wouldn't, but ginger tasters were more apt to be greedy than smart. Would they be foolish enough to forget about the heavy weapons the troop carrier bore?

One of the partisans couldn't stand to wait any more. As soon as one man opened up, everybody started shooting, intent on doing the most damage to the Lizards in the shortest time possible.

Anielewicz threw his rifle to his shoulder and, still prone, started squeezing off shots in the direction of the crate. You couldn't use aimed fire at night, not unless you had gadgets like those of the Lizards, but if you put enough bullets in the air, that didn't matter too much.

Hisses turned to screeches on the roadway. A couple of Lizards started firing back at the partisans. Their muzzle flashes gave the humans hidden in the woods better targets at which to aim. But then the turret-mounted machine gun and light cannon in the troop carrier opened up. Anielewicz swore, first in Polish, then in Yiddish. The Lizards hadn't been altogether asleep at the switch after all.

With that kind of fire raking the trees and bushes, there was only one thing to do. 'Let's get out of here,' Mordechai yelled, and he rolled away from the road. The Lizards weren't the only ones screeching now; screams from the darkness and Polish cries for the Virgin said some of those sprayed bullets and shells had found targets.

The advantage of opening fire from close to the highway was that you were right on top of the enemy. The disadvantage was that you took a long time to get away from his guns. Not until Anielewicz scrambled behind an oak tree whose trunk was thicker than his own did he begin to feel safe.

Firing from the road died away. Anielewicz didn't think the partisans had hurt the Lizards so badly they'd call in air strikes. This sort of warfare walked a fine line. If you did too little, you didn't harm the enemy. If you did too much, you were liable to provoke him into squashing you like a bug. The Lizards could do that almost anywhere in the world, if they wanted to badly enough. Keeping them too busy in a lot of places to concentrate on any one worked fairly well.

Mordechai was walking a line himself, but not a fine one. It involved fetching up against a tree with his nose, stepping into a hole and twisting his ankle (by luck alone, not too badly), and splashing through a tiny rill he discovered by the simple expedient of getting his feet wet. Some people moved through the woods at night silent as a lynx. He sounded more like a drunken wisent. He thanked God the Lizards were even less woodswise.

'That you, Shmuel?' somebody hissed – Jerzy.

'Yes, it's me,' Anielewicz answered in Polish. He had no idea the other partisan was within a kilometer till he spoke. Well, that was why Jerzy walked point while he shlepped along well back in the line.

But the Pole didn't sound angry at him. 'That was a good scheme you had there. The Lizards really like sticking their snouts into that stuff, don't they?'

'That they do,' Mordechai said. 'The ones who get hooked good, they'll do just about anything for a taste of ginger, and a lot of them are hooked – quite a lot of them, if what happened back there is any clue.'

'Might as well be pussy, eh?' Friedrich stepped out from behind a tree. He was twice Jerzy's size, but just about as light on his feet – and it didn't do to think him stupid, either. He'd understood Polish and answered in the same language.

None of which made Mordechai feel easy around him. 'I don't think they keep their brains in their pricks, unlike some people I could name,' he said. He tried to keep his tone light, but wasn't sure how well he succeeded; having to deal with *Wehrmacht* men made his hackles rise.

'If men keep brains in their pricks, why do you Jewish make yourselves stupider by cutting some off?' Friedrich retorted. Was that just raillery, or did the German mean something more by it? Who could tell what a German had been up to in Poland before the Lizards came? Anielewicz gave it up. They were – supposed to be – on the same side now.

Jerzy said, 'Come on – we go this way now.' Mordechai was damned if he knew how Jerzy could tell which way to go, or, for that matter, which way *this* way was. But the Pole was rarely wrong – and Mordechai had no idea which way he was supposed to be going. He followed. So did Friedrich.

The point man's skill or instinct or whatever it was led them back to the partisans' camp deep in the forest. No one risked a fire even with thick tree cover overhead; the Lizards had too many eyes in the air. They just found blankets, rolled themselves in them, and tried to go to sleep.

For Anielewicz, that proved impossible. For one thing, adrenaline still sang through him from the fight. For another, he wasn't used to sleeping in a blanket on the hard ground. And for a third, men – and a few women – not lucky enough to have been guided by Jerzy kept stumbling into camp all night long. Some of them moaned with wounds.

Some of them couldn't sleep, either. He joined one of the little knots of fighters sitting in the darkness and trying to figure out how well they'd done. One fellow claimed four Lizards downed, another twice that many. It was hard to figure out the partisans' losses, but at least two men were known dead, and four or five wounded. What morning would prove remained to be seen.

Mordechai said, 'If we hit them this hard every time, we'll make them know we're there. We can afford to trade one for one longer than they can.' That produced thoughtful silence, then grunts he took as agreement.

Sirens screaming, airplanes roaring overhead, bombs crashing down, antiaircraft guns pounding maniacally – Moishe Russie had been through that in Warsaw in 1939, when the *Luftwaffe* methodically pounded the Polish capital to pieces. But this was London almost four years later, with the Lizards trying to finish the job the Germans had started here, too.

'Make it stop!' his son Reuven cried, one more wail lost in the many that filled the Soho shelter.

'We can't make it stop, darling,' Rivka Russie answered. 'It will be all right.' She turned to Moishe. She didn't speak again, but her face held two words: *I hope.*

He nodded back, sure he bore an identical expression. Having to admit your powerlessness to your child was awful, and being afraid you were lying when you reassured him even worse. But what else could you do when you had no power and were dreadfully afraid things wouldn't be all right?

More bombs hit, somewhere close by. The mattresses strewn across the floor of the shelter jumped with the impact. The outcry inside the shelter rose to a new pitch of polylingual panic. Along with English and the Russies' Yiddish, Moishe heard Catalan, Hindustani, Greek, and several languages he couldn't identify. Soho held immigrants and refugees from all over the world.

Reuven squealed. At first, Moishe was afraid he'd hurt himself. Then he realized the flickering candlelight had been enough to let his son spot the Stephanopoulos twins, who lived in the flat across the hall from his own. Reuven had no more than a handful of words in common with Demetrios and Constantine, but that didn't keep them from being friends. They started wrestling with one another. When the next flight of Lizard planes dropped another load of death, they paid hardly any attention.

Moishe glanced over at Rivka. 'I wish I could be so easily distracted.'

'So do I,' she said wearily. 'You at least don't look like you're worried.'

'No?' he said, surprised. 'The beard must hide it, because I am.' His hand went to his whiskery chin. A lot of men were sporting whiskers in London these days, what with shaving soap, razor blades, and hot water all in short supply. He'd worn a beard in Warsaw, though, and felt naked when he shaved it off to escape to Lodz one step ahead of the Lizards after he refused to be their radio mouthpiece any more.

They'd captured him anyhow, a few months later. Growing the beard again had been the one good thing about the prison into which they'd clapped him. He shook his head. No, there had been one other good thing about that prison – the commando raid that got him out of it. The trip to England by submarine had followed immediately.

He peered around the shelter. Amazingly, some people managed to sleep despite the chaos. The stink of fear and stale piss was the same as he'd known back in Warsaw.

Rivka said, 'Maybe that was the last wave of them.'

'*Alevai omayn*,' Moishe answered fervently: 'May it be so – amen!' The vigor of his reply made Rivka smile. Wishing didn't make things so, worse luck, but he didn't hear any more explosions, either nearby or off in the distance. Maybe Rivka was right.

The all-clear sounded half an hour later. Friends and neighbors woke the men and women who'd slept in spite of everything. People slowly went back above ground to head back to their homes – and to discover whether they had homes to head back to. It was about as dark on the street as it had been inside the shelter. The sky was overcast; the only light came from fires flickering here and there. Moishe had seen that in Warsaw, too.

Fire engines screamed through the streets toward the worst of the blazes. 'I hope the Lizards didn't wreck too many mains,' Moishe said. 'They'll need all the water pressure they can get.'

'I just hope our block of flats is still standing,' Rivka said. They turned the corner. 'Oh, thank God, it is.' Her voice changed timbre: 'Get away from there, Reuven! That's broken glass – you could cut yourself.'

A woman lay groaning in front of the apartment building. Moishe hurried over to her. He'd been a medical student when the war started, and used what he'd learned in the Warsaw ghetto – not that all the medical training in the world did any good when people were starving to death.

'My leg, my leg,' the woman moaned. Russie was just starting to learn English, so that didn't mean much to him. But the way she clutched at the injured part, and the way the shin bent where it had no business bending, told him everything he needed to know.

'Doctor,' he said; he'd made sure he learned that word. He pointed to himself. It wasn't quite true, but he was the closest thing to a doctor the poor woman would see for a while, and thinking he was the genuine article might give her more confidence in him. He wanted that; he knew how to set a broken leg, but he also knew how much the process hurt.

The woman sighed, he hoped with relief. A small crowd had gathered around her and Moishe. He looked up to the people and said, 'Fetch me a couple of flat boards and some rags to tie them to her leg.'

Nobody moved. Russie wondered what was wrong until Russie said gently, 'Dear, they don't understand Yiddish.'

He thumped his forehead with the heel of his hand, feeling seventeen different kinds of idiot. He tried again, this time in the clear German he'd learned in school. Every time he had to use it, irony rose up to choke him. Here, in the heart of Germany's most important enemy, the irony was doubled.

But no one in the crowd followed German any better than Yiddish. In desperation, Moishe tried Polish. 'Here, I'll get what you need,' somebody said in the same language. Better yet, he translated Russie's request into English. Several people hurried away. In the rubble from years of bombings, boards and rags were easy to come by.

Moishe said to the fellow who spoke Polish, 'Tell her I'm going to set her leg and splint it. Tell her it will hurt.' The man spoke in English. The injured woman nodded. 'Maybe you and a couple of other men should hold her while I work,' Moishe went on. 'If she thrashes around, she's liable to make things worse.'

The woman tried to thrash. Moishe didn't blame her; he admired the way she did her best to keep gasps from turning into shrieks. He got the broken bones aligned and tied the splint tight to keep them from shifting again. When he was through, the woman whispered, 'Thank you, Doctor.'

He understood that. It warmed him. When he stood up, his own knees clicked. The sky was growing light. He sighed. No point in going to bed. He had an early broadcast scheduled at the BBC Overseas Service. Yawning, he said to Rivka, 'I may as well just get my script and go on in.'

'Oh, dear,' she said sympathetically, but nodded. He and his family went upstairs together. He found the manila folder with the papers inside, then realized he was wearing only a greatcoat over pyjamas. He threw on a white shirt and a pair of trousers and headed out to face the world. A stretcher party had taken away the woman with the broken leg. Moishe hoped she'd do well. He wouldn't sleep, but he thought his wife and son might.

The building that housed the BBC Overseas Services was at 200 Oxford Street, not far west of his Soho flat and a few blocks east of Hyde Park. As he walked to work, London came to life around him. Pigeons cooed and sparrows chirped – lucky creatures, they knew nothing of war, save that it made the air sharp with smoke. Bicycles, men and women afoot, and horsedrawn wagons and even buggies taken out of sheds where they'd moldered for a generation clogged the streets. Petrol was in as desperately short supply here as in Warsaw or Lodz; only fire engines had all they needed.

Nathan Jacobi approached the building that housed the studios from the other direction at the same time as Moishe reached it. The two men waved to each other. Moishe broadcast in Yiddish and German; Jacobi translated his words into English. His Yiddish was polished and elegant. If his English came close to it – Russie wasn't qualified to judge, but doubted the BBC would have hired him if it didn't – he made a very effective newsreader indeed.

Now he surveyed Moishe with a sympathetic eye. 'Bad for you last night? You look done in.'

'I *am* done in,' Russie said. 'I hope the tea in there has a jolt to it this morning. If it doesn't, I'm apt to fall asleep in front of the microphone.'

'It'll be hot, anyhow,' Jacobi said, which was true. 'As for the jolt, you never can tell from day to day, not with these messes of leaves and roots and rose hips we get instead of the proper stuff.' He sighed. 'What I wouldn't give for a cup of vintage Darjeeling – Bloody war.'

The last two words were in English. Moishe knew what they meant, but took the adjective literally. 'Bloody war is right. And the worst of it is, we can't make the Lizards out to be as black as we would otherwise, because they haven't done much worse to us than we were already doing to ourselves.'

'You would know best about that. Anyone who was in Poland—' Jacobi shook his head. 'But still, if we hadn't been geared up to a fever pitch to fight each other, could we have put up such a battle against the Lizards?'

'I suppose not, but it's no credit to us that we were,' Russie answered. 'It's not as if we knew they were coming. We'd have gone right on slaughtering ourselves if they hadn't come, too. Still, I admit that's neither here nor there at the moment. They are here, and we have to make life miserable for them.' He waved the pages of his script, then fished out his pass and showed it to the guard at the door. The guard nodded. Russie and Jacobi went in to get ready to broadcast.

3

'Forgive me, Exalted Fleetlord, but I have an emergency call for you from the *206th Emperor Yower*,' Atvar's adjutant said. In the vision screen, the younger male looked as worried as he sounded.

'Very well, Pshing, patch it through,' Atvar said, setting aside for a moment the war against the Big Uglies for his private conflict with the shiplord Straha. After Straha failed to topple him from command of the conquest fleet, the shiplord should have known revenge was on its way. Atvar wondered what sort of lying nonsense Straha would come up with to justify himself.

Pshing's face disappeared from the vision screen. It was not, however, replaced by that of Straha. Instead, Atvar's chief security officer, a male named Diffal, turned his eye turrets toward the fleetlord. Diffal was earnest and capable. All the same, Atvar yearned for the cunning deviousness Drefsab had brought to the job. Even as a ginger taster, he'd been the best in the fleet. But now he was dead, and Atvar had to make do. 'Do you have the shiplord Straha in your custody?' he demanded.

'Exalted Fleetlord, I do not.' Diffal also sounded worried. 'I am informed that, shortly before the arrival of any team aboard the *206th Emperor Yower*, the shiplord Straha left this vessel and traveled down from orbit to confer with Horrep, shiplord of the *29th Emperor Jevon*, whose ship has landed in the central region of the northern portion of the lesser continental mass, near the city called St Louis.'

Atvar hissed. Horrep was a member of Straha's faction. Pshing, who must have been monitoring the conversation from his outer office, came onto the screen for a moment. 'Exalted Fleetlord, the *206th Emperor Yower* did not report this departure to us.'

Diffal said, 'I have been in communication with the *29th Emperor Jevon*. Straha is not aboard that ship, nor has his shuttlecraft landed nearby. I examined the radar records of the trajectory of the shuttlecraft. Computer analysis of the course they indicate gives a landing point relatively close to the *29th Emperor Jevon*, but not as close as would be expected if Straha truly intended to confer with Horrep. The shiplord Horrep, I should inform you, vehemently denies that Straha sent messages announcing a visit, as custom and courtesy would have required.'

'Ever since we came to Tosev 3, custom and courtesy have been corroding,' Atvar said. Diffal stared back at him, not replying. One couldn't expect a male in security to be concerned with philosophy as well. Atvar dragged himself back to the matter in hand: 'Well, where is the shiplord Straha, then?'

'Exalted Fleetlord,' Diffal said, 'I don't know.'

Jens Larssen was sick and tired of bicycles. He was sick and tired of pedaling all over creation on missions he shouldn't have had to take on and knew he wouldn't get thanked for, and, of all the things he never would have expected before he set out from Denver, he was sick to death of pine trees.

'First the Arapaho goddamn National Forest, now the Payette goddamn National Forest – or is it the Nez Perce goddamn National Forest yet?' he asked as he worked his way up US 95 toward Lewiston, Idaho. He was used to talking to himself on the road; days often went by when he didn't talk to anybody else. The longer he spent on his bike, the better he liked being alone.

He wiped sweat off his forehead with a sleeve. The day was hot, but he wore long sleeves and a long-brimmed cap anyway – he was so fair that he worried more about burning in the sun than baking in his clothes. His ears, which the cap didn't protect, were a permanently raw red peeling mess.

'Not that anybody gives a damn what I look like these days,' he said. Self-pity notwithstanding, he wasn't a bad-looking fellow: a skinny blond Viking, just past thirty, with bright blue eyes. A sour twist to his mouth marred his features, but since he couldn't see it, he didn't know it was there.

A Lizard jet screamed by, high overhead, flying west. The Lizards held the Snake River valley from Idaho Falls to Twin Falls, and used it as an air base against the Pacific Northwest. Outside of their airfields, though, they didn't seem to give a damn about the area – a sentiment in which Jens heartily concurred. He'd gone through several towns – even what passed for cities hereabouts – without seeing a one of the little scaly bastards.

'Maybe I should have stopped and gone looking for them,' he said to the trees. He knew enough to make the Lizards have kittens. What better way to pay back Barbara for dumping him, to pay back Colonel Hexham for helping him lose his wife, to pay back Oscar the guard for slugging him when he grabbed her to try to get her back, to pay back the Metallurgical Laboratory and the whole stinking human race on general principles? Denver might not earn an atomic bomb all on its own, but it would sure as hell get leveled.

A mountain stream chuckled by, close to the road. Jens ran his sleeve over his forehead again, then decided he'd earned a break. He pulled the bike over to the shoulder, let down the kickstand, and climbed off. He pulled a tin cup out of the pack tied behind the bike saddle and headed for the stream. He had to think about walking the first few steps; his legs kept wanting to go round and round.

The water, undoubtedly snowmelt, was very sweet, but so cold it gave him a savage headache for a few seconds after his first long swig. He swore as he waited for the pain to subside. A gray and blue jay scolded him from the branches of one of those pines.

'Oh, shut up,' he told it. 'You'd say the same thing if it happened to you.'

He unslung the Springfield he carried on his back and looked around. He wasn't much of a hunter, but if a deer came down for a drink, he wouldn't say no to trying for some venison. The jay screeched again. He swung the rifle its way, then laughed at himself. He'd probably miss, and even if he didn't, nailing a jay with a .30 caliber slug was about like smashing a roach by dropping an anvil on it. You might have a few feathers left, floating on the breeze, but that was it.

Since he was siting by the stream, he drank another cup of water. If Bambi didn't show up, he'd be gnawing on beef jerky for lunch. He'd traded a few rounds of rifle ammo for it just outside of a tiny town incongruously called Cambridge; the more he thought about the deal he'd made, the more he figured he'd been snookered.

The water had its usual effect. He got up and walked over to a tree – not the one in which the jay still perched. He undid his fly and, setting his teeth, took a leak against the tree trunk. It didn't hurt as much as it had just after he came down with the clap; for a while there, he'd been wishing his joint would drop off every time he used it. But it still wasn't what anybody in his right mind would call fun.

'Goddamn bitch,' he ground out between his teeth as he fastened himself up again. The first time he'd got laid after Barbara left, and that was the present the stinking waitress had given him. Better he should have stayed a monk.

No sign of any deer. No sign of any bears, either, but Larssen, at the moment, was not inclined to look on the bright side of things. Cursing that slut of a waitress all over again (and conveniently forgetting how much he'd enjoyed having her while she lay in his arms), he got up, went back over to the bicycle, and used his belt knife to carve off a lunch-sized slab of jerky.

Chewing on the stuff was about like gnawing well-salted shoe leather. 'Good thing I've got a decent set of choppers,' Jens said, and the jay, as if carrying on a bad-tempered conversation with him, peevishly screeched back. 'I told you once to shut up,' Larssen reminded it. It took no more notice of him than anybody else had lately.

He gulped down a mouthful of the jerky. Even after he'd been chewing on it, little sharp edges scraped his throat. His laugh wasn't a friendly sound. 'I'd like to see Mr Sam fucking Yeager eat this stuff with his store-bought teeth,' he said. The more he thought about it, the more he figured that if Barbara could go for a guy like that, she wasn't such a bargain after all.

But even figuring he was well rid of her didn't make the burn of being thrown over go away. She shouldn't have decided he was dead, not anywhere near so soon. Even if she had, even if she'd ended up in bed with that Yeager son of a bitch a time or two, she shouldn't have married him, and she sure as hell shouldn't have let him knock her up. That had put the kibosh on any hope she'd come to her senses, all right.

'Security,' Larssen snarled, making it into a curse word fouler than any of the others he'd been throwing around. If that stinking Colonel Hexham had just let him write to her as the Met Lab wagon train made its slow way across the northern Great Plains, everything would have been fine. But he'd literally had to go on strike in Denver to get Hexham to let him send a letter. By the time it got to her, it was too late. She was already married and already pregnant.

In peacetime, some lawyer probably would have been able to buy himself a new Packard from the fees he'd have made trying to sort out the whole mess. With the Lizards giving the whole world hell, nobody bothered with much in the way of legal niceties any more. Barbara decided she wanted to stay with Mr Dentures, so she damn well did.

'And I'm the one who gets screwed – or rather, who doesn't get screwed any more,' Larssen said. 'Isn't that a hell of a note?'

It was, in more ways than one. Not only did his wife up and leave him but, just because he was too burned up about it to let her go quietly, he'd been all but booted off the Met Lab team. And so, instead of the nuclear physics he loved and for which he'd spent a lifetime training, he got to play Natty Bumppo in the wilderness instead.

If he hadn't refused to admit he was beaten, he never would have managed to make it back from White Sulphur Springs, West Virginia, to Chicago. He never would have found out where the Met Lab crew had gone, nor managed to beat them there on his own (of course, if he hadn't been quite so efficient there, he might have had a better chance of hanging on to Barbara).

Well, he owed the Lizards a good deal, for fouling up his life beyond all recognition. So he'd go on to Hanford and see if it made a good place for building an atomic pile to blow them to hell and gone. So much seemed only fair.

'But after I do that, I'll get even with all the people who fouled me up, too,' he said softly. 'You just bet I will.' He got up from the streamside rock he'd been sitting on, walked over to the bicycle, climbed aboard, and started rolling north again.

Ludmila Gorbunova had seen more bomb craters, from closer range, than she'd ever imagined before the war began. But she'd never seen, never dreamt of, a crater like the one over which her little U-2 biplane skimmed now.

The burned area was most of a kilometer across, maybe more than a kilometer. The ground near the center had been baked into something that looked like glass, and gave back dazzling reflections of the sun. Well beyond that, trees, houses – essentially everything – had been knocked flat. It was as if God had decided to step on the land a few kilometers northeast of Kaluga.

Ludmila did not believe in God, not in the top part of her mind. She was a child of the Revolution, born in Kiev in the midst of civil war. But sometimes, in moments of stress, reactionary patterns of speech and thought emerged.

'We've not yet built true socialism,' she reminded herself. 'Even with the German invasion, the generation born after the war might have lived to see it. Now—'

The air blowing in over the windscreen flung her words away. Having confessed her imperfection, if only to herself, she was willing to admit that stopping the Lizards' drive on Moscow had taken something that looked very much like divine intervention.

She'd been flying back from a harassment mission against the Lizards when the bomb went off. Then she'd thought at first that the Lizards were visiting on the Soviet Union the same kind of destruction they'd meeted out to Berlin and Washington. Only gradually had she realized her own country had matched the invaders at their murderous game.

The *Kukuruznik* – Wheatcutter – buzzed over the hulks of three Lizard tanks. Their guns slumped limply, as if they'd been made not of steel but of wax and left too close to the fire. Measuring the revenge the Soviet Union had finally taken on its tormentors filled her with fierce joy. She fired a burst from her machine guns at the dead tanks, just to mark her own hatred. The recoil made her aircraft shudder for a moment. The U-2 had been a trainer before the war, but proved an excellent raider against the Germans and then against the Lizards. It was quiet – the Germans had dubbed it the Flying Sewing Machine – and flew at treetop height and below. Speed wasn't everything.

'I'm still alive,' she remarked. Again, the slipstream blew her words away, but not the truth in them. The Lizards hacked higher-performance Red Air Force planes out of the sky as if they knew they were coming – no, not *as if*, for Intelligence was sure they *did* know, with help from electronics of the kind that the Soviet Union was just beginning to acquire. The U-2, though, was small enough – maybe slow enough, too – to escape their notice.

Ludmila patted the fabric skin of the plane's fuselage. She'd been in the *Osoaviakhim*, the Soviet pilot training organization, before the war. When she joined the Red Air Force after getting out of Kiev just before the Germans took it, she'd wanted to fly bombers or real fighters. Getting assigned to a *Kukuruznik* squadron had seemed a letdown: she'd flown in U-2s to learn to handle other, more deadly, aircraft.

Time changed her perspective, as time has a way of doing. She patted the U-2's fabric skin again. It kept flying, kept fighting, no matter what. 'Good old mule,' she said.

As she neared Kaluga, she grew alert once more. The Lizards still held the town, though they hadn't tried to push north from it since the bomb went off. She knew only too well that she hadn't been invulnerable till now, just lucky – and careful. If you stopped being careful, you wouldn't stay lucky.

Far off in the distance, she spotted a couple of Lizard trucks stopped right out in the open by a haystack. Maybe one of them had broken down, and the other paused to help. Any which way, they made a tempting target. Her thumb slid to the firing button for the U-2's machine guns.

A moment later, she used stick and pedals to twist the little biplane away from the trucks in as tight a turn as she could manage. That haystack didn't have quite the right shape to be sitting in a Russian field – but it was just the right shape to serve as *maskirovka* for one of the Lizard's antiaircraft tanks.

She headed back toward the airstrip from which she'd taken off. If anything, dignifying the place with that description was flattery: it was just a stretch of field with underground shelters for the pilots and groundcrew, and with barley-draped camouflage nets to cover up the planes. A few hundred meters away, a false strip with dummy aircraft, tents, and occasional radio signals was much more prominent. The Lizards had bombed it several times. Soviet *maskirovka* really worked.

As Ludmila approached the airstrip, a fellow who looked like any other peasant took off his hat and waved at her with it in his left hand. She accepted the course correction and shifted slightly more to the north.

The *Kukuruznik* bounced to a stop. It was light enough to have no trouble on plowed-up dirt, and to stop very quickly once the wheels touched down. Like moles emerging from their burrows, groundcrew men dashed toward the biplane, and reached it before the prop had stopped spinning.

'Out, out, out!' they yelled, not that Ludmila wasn't already descending from the U-2. No sooner had her boots touched ground than the groundcrew manhandled the biplane toward what looked like just another piece of field. But two of them had run ahead to pull aside the camouflage netting that covered a broad trench. In went the aircraft. Back went the netting. Within two minutes of landing, not a trace of the *Kukuruznik* remained visible.

Ludmila ducked under the netting, too, to help ready the biplane for its next mission. She'd made herself into a good mechanic. Red Air Force pilots needed to be good mechanics, because very often the groundcrew weren't. That wasn't the case here; one of the fellows at the base was as good a technician and repairman as she'd ever known.

Even so, she helped him as much as she could. It was, after all, her own neck.

'*Zdrast'ye*, Comrade Pilot,' the mechanic said in accented Russian. He was a tall, lean, ginger-bearded fellow with a grin that said he refused to take her or anything else too seriously.

'*Zdrast'ye*,' she answered shortly. Georg Schultz was a genius with a spanner in his hands, but he was also a dedicated Nazi, a panzer gunner who'd attached himself to the airbase staff when they were still operating out of the Ukraine. She'd helped him get his place there; she'd known him and his commander, Heinrich Jäger, before. Every so often, she wondered how wise she'd been.

'How did it go?' he asked, this time in German, of which she had a smattering: more than that now, thanks to practice with Jäger and with Schultz.

'Well enough,' she answered in the same language. She turned away from him toward the *Kukuruznik* so she wouldn't have to notice the way his eyes roamed up and down her body as if she were naked rather than covered by a heavy leather flight suit. His hands had tried roaming up and down her body a couple of times, too. She'd said no as emphatically as she knew how, but *nyet* wasn't a Russian word he seemed to have grasped. For that matter, he wasn't what you'd call solid on *nein*, either.

Maybe her indifference was finally getting through to him, though; the next question he asked seemed strictly business: 'Did you fly over the crater from the big bomb you people set off a little while ago?'

'*Aber natürlich*,' she answered. 'It's a good direction from which to approach: I can be sure no Lizard guns will be waiting for me from that position, and it lets me penetrate deep into their lines.'

Schultz puffed out his chest. 'Me and Major Jäger – Colonel Jäger now – we were part of the raiding crew that got you Russkis the metal I expect you used to build that bomb.'

'Were you?' She wanted the words to come out cold as ice, but they didn't, quite. One thing she reluctantly granted Schultz was his habit of telling the truth as he saw it. She found that sort of bluntness alarming in a way: how had he managed to keep it without getting raked over the coals by the *Gestapo*? Any Russian so outspoken would have ended up in a *gulag*, if he wasn't simply executed as an enemy of the state. But Ludmila was willing to believe Schultz wasn't lying just to impress her.

He preened some more. 'Yes, we certainly were. Hadn't been for us Germans, you Reds never would have been able to build your bomb at all.'

Ludmila felt like slapping his smug face. 'I don't suppose you Germans' – she deliberately used the Russian word, *nemtsi*, with its overtones of barbarism and unintelligible babbling – 'would do anything like that if you didn't get your own share of the metal, too. As you say, we built a bomb with ours. Where is the German bomb?'

Georg Schultz went a dull red. Ludmila chuckled under her breath. The Nazis thought of themselves as the lords of creation and of their Slavic neighbors as subhuman, certainly incapable of a scientific feat like the explosive-metal bomb. Reminding them that wasn't so always gave a Russian pleasure.

'Let's look over the aircraft,' Schultz mumbled. Ludmila didn't argue with him – that was what they were supposed to be doing. With tools in his hands, Schultz became useful enough for her to overlook, if not to forgive, his appalling politics. His piggish approaches to her she already discounted. Plenty of Russian men were just as uncultured – Nikifor Sholudenko, for instance. The NKVD man would be debriefing her as soon as she was done inspecting the U-2.

Schultz grunted as he pried through the five-cylinder Shvetsov radial engine. Ludmila had come to know that grunt. 'What's wrong?' she asked.

'One of the springs in your oil pump is starting to go,' he said. 'Here, come see for yourself.'

She inspected the part. Sure enough, it wasn't as strong as it should have been. She nodded with professional respect. The German got into everything, with monomaniacal thoroughness. She couldn't imagine a Russian technician stripping down a part that wasn't giving trouble. 'Do we have spares for it?' she asked.

'I think so, yes, or if not I can steal one from a plane that's down for some other reason,' Schultz said. Ludmila nodded; cannibalizing machines for parts happened all the time.

'Good. Do that at once,' she said.

He gave her an odd look. 'But I have not yet seen what else may need fixing,' he said. 'What do you think I am, some slapdash Russian? Finding one thing wrong does not mean there will be no more.' After a moment, he grunted again, and pointed up into the greasy bowels of the engine. 'Here. Look.'

Ludmila, who was close to twenty centimeters shorter, had to stand on tiptoe to see what he was talking about. As she did so, he turned his head and planted a quick kiss on her cheek. then he stepped back, grinning. As his advances went, that one was downright gentlemanly. She shook her head, exhaling through her nose in exasperation. 'You ought to now better than that by now.'

'Why? Maybe I'll get lucky one of these days,' he said, altogether unabashed. He grinned at her. 'After all, Major Jäger did.'

She hoped the light under the camouflage netting was too dim and gray for him to notice her flush, but if she'd seen him go red, he could probably see her. And she was sure she was red as fire now. She'd had a brief liaison with Jäger when she'd flown Foreign Commissar Molotov to Berchtesgaden while Jäger happened to be there to get a medal from Hitler for bringing explosive metal back to Germany.

'The major is a gentleman,' she said. 'You—' She stopped in confusion. In the classless society the Soviet Union was building, you weren't supposed to think or talk about gentlemen, let alone prefer them.

'Maybe,' Schultz said. 'But I'm here and he's not.'

Ludmila made a wordless sound of fury. She made it again when Schultz laughed at her, which only made him laugh harder. What she wanted to do was stalk indignantly out of the underground shelter. Wriggling out from under the camouflage net was a poor substitute, but it had to do.

A groundcrew man came hurrying over to smooth the netting and preserve the *maskirovka*. He said, 'Comrade Pilot, they are ready to debrief you on your mission now.'

'Thank you,' she said, and hurried over to the underground bunkers that housed the air base's personnel. More camouflage netting concealed the entrance. She pushed it aside to go in.

There had always been the hope that Colonel Karpov, the base commandant, would take her report, but no such luck. Behind a folding table in a chamber lit by four stinking candles sat Nikifor Sholudenko. She signed internally; she and the NKVD man had come to the base together out of the Ukraine, so his presence here, like Schultz's, was her own fault. That didn't make him any easier to take.

'Sit, Comrade Pilot,' he urged, waving her to a battered armchair. Like hers, his Russian had a bit of a Ukrainian flavor in it. He handed her a glass. 'Here, drink, this. It will make you feel better after your dangerous flight.'

The glass held a reddish liquid. Weak tea? She sipped cautiously. No – pepper vodka, smoother than anything she'd had in quite a while. All the same, she sipped cautiously.

'Drink, drink,' Sholudenko urged her. His eyes glittered avidly in the candlelight. 'It will relax you.'

He wanted her relaxed, all right. She sighed again. Sometimes facing the Lizards was easier than coming back and trying to deal with her own side.

A few kilometers south of Pskov, Lizard artillery hammered at the line the Russians and Germans had built together to try to hold the aliens away from the northwestern Russian city. George Bagnall watched the explosions from Pskov's *Krom*, the old stone fortress that sat on the high ground where the Velikaya and Pskova rivers came together. The *Krom* wasn't quite in range of the Lizards' guns – he hoped.

Beside him, Ken Embry sighed. 'They're catching it pretty hard out there.'

'I know,' Bagnall answered. 'There but for mistrust go we.'

Embry snorted, though it wasn't really funny. He'd piloted the Lancaster bomber on which Bagnall had served as flight engineer when they brought an airborne radar to Pskov to help the Soviets in their struggle against the Lizards. The mission had been hurried, and imperfectly conceived. Nobody'd bothered to tell the RAF men, for instance, that Pskov wasn't altogether in Soviet hands. The Russians shared it uneasily with the Germans, each side hating the Lizards just a little – sometimes a very little – more than it did the other.

Nikolai Vasilev and Aleksandr German came into the makeshift office, the one black-bearded and stocky, the other red-whiskered and foxy-faced. Before the Lizards came, they'd commanded the First and Second Partisan Brigades in what they called the Forest Republic, harassing the Nazis who'd held Pskov. Now they made up an uneasy triumvirate with *Generalleutnant* Kurt Chill, who had led a German infantry division and commanded all German forces in the Pskov area.

'Gentlemen,' Bagnall said in German, and then amended that in Russian: '*Tovarishchi* – comrades.'

'These are not the same thing,' Aleksandr German said reprovingly. 'Russia had gentlemen. The Soviet Union has comrades – we got rid of the gentlemen.' His smile showed yellow, pointed teeth, as if he'd had some of those gentlemen for supper. He was a Jew; he spoke Yiddish, not German, and Bagnall had to struggle to understand him. But Bagnall's Russian, picked up word by word since he'd come to Pskov, was much worse.

The partisan leader translated what he'd said for his companion. '*Da!*' Nikolai Vasiliev boomed. He drew his thumbnail across his throat, under his beard, as if to show what had happened to the gentlemen of old Russia. Then he came out with one of the handful of German words he knew: '*Kaputt!*'

Bagnall and Embry, both comfortably middle class by upbringing, shared a look. Even in the middle of a war, such wholehearted enthusiasm about the virtues of liquidation was hard to stomach. Cautiously Bagnall said, 'I hope this command arrangement is working to your satisfaction.'

This time, Aleksandr German spoke to Vasiliev before he replied. Vasiliev's answer was voluble but unintelligible, at least to Bagnall. Aleksandr German said, 'It works better than we had expected, maybe because you Englishmen seem more honest than we had expected.'

When Bagnall translated that for Embry, the pilot said, 'General Chill told us the same thing.'

'That's the idea, old man,' Bagnall told him, and then turned the remark into German for the benefit of the partisan brigadiers. The Reds didn't want Chill giving orders to their men, and he would sooner have swallowed his monocle than let them command his – but if Pskov didn't have some sort of unified command, it would damn well fall. Both sides, then, appealed orders they reckoned unsatisfactory to the RAF men, and both sides had agreed to abide by their decisions. So far, both sides had.

'If you can keep the Nazis and us equally dissatisfied, you are doing well,' Aleksandr German said.

'Bloody wonderful,' Ken Embry muttered. Without a moment's hesitation, Bagnall translated that as '*Ochen khorosho* – very good.' Here he was willing to sacrifice the spirit to preserve the letter – and good feeling all around.

Vasiliev and Aleksandr German walked over to study the situation map tacked up on the wall. The Lizards were still about twenty miles south of town. They hadn't tried a big push in a while – *busy elsewhere*, Bagnall supposed – but the work of building new defensive lines against them went on day and night, not that Pskov had much night during high summer.

Bagnall waited for the Russians to ask something, complain about something, demand something. They didn't. Vasiliev pointed to one of the defensive positions under construction and grunted a mouthful of consonants at Aleksandr German. The other partisan brigadier grunted back. Then they both left the room, maybe to go have a look at that position.

'That was too easy,' Embry said when they were gone.

'Can't have disasters every day,' Bagnall said, though he wondered why not as soon as the words were out of his mouth. Given his own experience, disasters seemed almost as common as sparrows. He went on, 'Can you tend the shop by yourself for half a moment? I'd like to get outside for a bit and stretch my legs.'

'Go ahead,' Embry answered. 'I owe you one or two there, I think, and this is a bloody gloomy room.'

'Too right, and not just because it's poorly lit, either,' Bagnall said. Embry laughed, but they both knew Bagnall hadn't been joking.

When he escaped the massive medieval stone pile of the Pskov *Krom*, he let out a long sigh of relief. Now that summer truly was here, Pskov seemed a very pleasant place, or could have seemed such if you ignored war damage. Everything smelled fresh and green and growing, the weather was warm and pleasant, the sun smiled down from a bright blue sky ornamented with puffy little white clouds, linnets chirped, ducks quacked. The only trouble was, you had to go through eight months of frozen hell to get to the four nice ones.

The Lizards had bombed the Sovietsky Bridge (older Russians in Pskov, Bagnall had noted, sometimes still called it the Trinity Bridge) over the Pskova. Their accuracy was fantastically good, as the flight engineer noted with professional jealousy; they'd put one right in the middle of the span. Men could cross over the timbers laid across the gap, but machines couldn't.

A German on a bicycle rode by and nodded to Bagnall. '*Heil Hitler?*' the fellow said, probably taking the Englishman for one of his own. Bagnall contented himself with a nod. Having Stalin for an ally had felt strange back in 1941. Having Stalin and Hitler both for allies felt surreal, as if the world had turned upside down.

'Well, it bloody well has,' Bagnall muttered.

Boards climbed under his feet as he crossed the bridge into the Zapsokvye district on the west side of the river. Behind a stone fence that looked old enough to have been there before the city itself stood the church of Sts. Cosmas and Damian on Primostye, its tall onion dome surmounted by an Orthodox cross with a diagonal below the horizontal arm.

Unlike a lot of the bigger buildings in the area, the church hadn't been bombed. It looked run-down anyway, with paint peeling and pigeon droppings resembling snow on the green copper sheathing of the dome. Bagnall wondered if the Communists had let anybody worship in there since the Revolution.

A soldier in Red Army khaki was sitting on the fence that surrounded the church. He – no, she – waved to Bagnall. '*Zdrast'ye*, Tatiani Fyodorovna,' he said, waving back.

Tatiana Fyodorovna Pirogova swung down from the fence and strode toward him. Her blonde curls gleamed in the bright sunshine. She was pretty – hell, she was more than pretty – in the broad-faced, flat-featured Russian way, and not even baggy Red Army tunic and trousers could altogether disguise her shape. As she came up to Bagnall, she ran her tongue over her full lower lip, as if she were contemplating what sort of *hors d'oeuvre* he'd make.

She probably was. She'd been after him ever since he'd co-ordinated the defense that beat back the last Lizard push against Pskov. Up till then, she'd been with Jerome Jones, the radarman Bagnall and Embry and Alf Whyte (poor Alf – he'd caught a bullet south of the city) had flown into Russia with an airborne set.

Not poaching on his countryman's turf wasn't what made Bagnall shy about taking advantage of Tatiana's abundant charms. The Moisin-Nagant rifle with telescopic sight she wore slung over her right shoulder had a lot more to do with it. She was a sniper by trade, and a damn good one. Bagnall wasn't in the least ashamed to admit she scared the whey out of him.

He pointed to the church and said, '*Schön.*' Tatiana understood a little German, though she didn't speak it.

That luscious lip curled. She let loose with a spate of Russian he had no hope of following in detail. She repeated herself often enough, though, that after a while he got the gist: the church and everything it stood for were primitive, uncultured (an insult to conjure with, in Russian), superstitious rubbish, and too bad neither the Nazis nor the *Yashcheritsi* – Lizards – had managed to blow it to kingdom come.

Then she pointed to the church itself, mimed opening the door, and asked him a question so bluntly coarse that the bad language he'd picked up from Red Army officers and men let him understand it perfectly: did he want to go in there for a quick poke?

He coughed and choked and felt himself turn red. Not even English tarts were so bold, and Tatiana, maneater though she might have been, was no tart. He wished to God she'd been content with Jones instead of setting her sights on him. Stuttering a little, he said, '*Nyet. Spasebo, aber nyet.* No – thanks, but no.' He knew he was mixing his languages, but he was too rattled to care.

'Bourgeois,' Tatiana said scornfully. She turned on her heel and strode off, rolling her hips to show him what he was missing.

He was perfectly willing to believe there'd be never a dull moment in the kip with her. All the same, he'd sooner have bedded down with a lioness; a lioness couldn't put one between your eyes at fifteen hundred yards. He hurried back over the Sovietsky Bridge toward the *Krom*. After an encounter with Tatiana, trying to figure out what the Lizards would do next struck him as a walk in the park.

Mutt Daniels hunkered down in the Swift and Company meat-processing plant behind an overturned machine whose gleaming blades suggested a purpose he'd sooner not have thought about. Was that something moving toward him in the gloom? In case it was, he fired a burst at it from his tommy gun. If it had been moving before, it didn't afterwards, which was what he'd had in mind.

'Meat-processing plant, my ass,' he muttered. 'This here's a slaughter-house, nothin' else but.'

His thick Mississippi drawl didn't sound too out of place, not when summer heat and humidity turned Chicago's South Side Southern indeed. He wished he had a gas mask like the one he'd worn in France in 1918; the heat and humidity were also bringing out the stink of the slaughterhouse and the adjacent Union Stockyards, even though no animals had gone through the yards or the plant in the past few months. That smell would hang around near enough forever as to make no difference.

The huge bulks of the Swift meat factory, the Armour plant beside it on Racine Avenue, and the Wilson packing plant not far away formed the keystone to the American position in the south side of Chicago. The Lizards had bombed them from the air and shelled them to a fare-thee-well, but GIs still clung to the ruins. The ruins were too ruinous for tanks, too; if the Lizards wanted the Americans out, they'd have to get them out the hard way.

'Lieutenant Daniels?' That was Hank York, the radioman, who habitually talked in an excited squeak.

'What's up, Hank?' Mutt asked without taking his eyes off the place where he thought he'd seen movement. He wasn't used to being called 'Lieutenant'; he'd joined up as soon as the Lizards invaded, and went in with two stripes because he was a First World War vet. He'd added the third one pretty damn quick, but he'd only gotten a platoon when the company commander, Captain Maczek, went down with a bad wound.

He didn't much blame the Army for being slow to promote him. When the Lizards came, he'd been managing the Decatur Commodores, but in normal times who'd want a platoon leader nearer sixty than fifty? Hell, he'd been a backup catcher for the Cardinals before most of the guys he led were born.

But times weren't normal, no way. He'd stayed alive in spite of everything the Lizards had thrown at him, and so he was a lieutenant.

Hank York said, 'Sir, word from HQ is that the Lizards have asked to send somebody forward under a white flat to set up a truce to get the wounded out. He'll be coming from that direction' – York pointed past a ruined conveyor belt – 'in about ten minutes. They say you can agree to up to three hours.'

'Hold fire!' Mutt yelled, loud as he would have shouted for a runner to slide going into third. 'Spread the word – hold fire. We may get ourselves a truce.'

Gunfire slowly died away. In the relative quiet, Bela Szabo, one of the fellows in the platoon who toted a Browning Automatic Rifle, let out a yip of glee and said, 'Hot damn, a chance to smoke a butt without worryin' about whether those scaly bastards can spot the coal.'

'You got that one right, Dracula,' Daniels answered the BAR man. Szabo's nickname was as universally as his own; nobody ever called him Pete, the handle he'd been born with. The cigarettes were also courtesy of Dracula, the most inspired scrounger Mutt had ever known.

The limit of vision in the ruined packing plant was about fifty feet; past that, girders, walls, and rubble obscured sight as effectively as leaves, branches, and vines in a jungle. Daniels jumped when a white rag on a stick poked out of a bullet-pocked doorway. He swore at himself, realizing he should have made a flag of truce, too. He jammed a hand in a pants pocket, pulled out a handkerchief he hadn't been sure he still owned, and waved it over his head. It wasn't very white, but it would have to do.

When nobody shot at him, he cautiously stood. Just as cautiously, a Lizard came out of the doorway. They walked toward each other, both of them picking their way around and over chunks of concrete, pieces of pipe, and, in Mutt's case, an overturned, half-burned file cabinet. The Lizard's eyes swiveled this way and that, watching not only the floor but also for any sign of danger. That looked weird, but Mutt wished he could pull the same stunt.

He saluted and said, 'Lieutenant Daniels, US army. I hear tell you want a truce.' He hoped the Lizards were smart enough to send out somebody who spoke English, because he sure as hell didn't know their lingo. *Sam Yeager might understand it by now, if he's still alive*, Mutt thought. He hadn't seen Yeager since his ex-outfielder took some Lizards prisoners in Chicago a year before.

However strange the Lizards were, they weren't stupid. The one in front of Mutt drew himself up to his full diminutive height and said, 'I am Wuppah' – he pronounced each *p* separately – 'smallgroup commander of the Race.' His English was strange to the ear, but Mutt had no trouble following it. 'It is as you say. We would like to arrange to be able to gather up our wounded in this building without your males shooting at us. We will let you do the same and not shoot at your males.'

'No spying out the other side's positions, now,' Daniels said, 'and no moving up your troops to new ones under cover of the truce.' He'd never arranged a truce before, but he'd gathered up wounded in France under terms like those.

'It is agreed,' Wuppah said at once. 'Your males also will not take new positions while we are not shooting at each other.'

Mutt started to answer that that went without saying, but shut his mouth with a snap. Nothing went without saying when the fellow on the other side had claws and scales and eyes like a chameleon's (just for a moment, Mutt wondered how funny he looked to Wuppah). If the Lizards wanted everything spelled out, that was probably a good idea. 'We agree,' Daniels said.

'I am to propose that this time of not shooting will last for one tenth of a day of Tosev 3,' Wuppah said.

'I'm authorized to agree anything up to three hours,' Daniels answered.

They looked at each other in some confusion. 'How many of these "hours" have you in your day?' Wuppah asked. 'Twenty-six?'

'Twenty-four,' Mutt answered. Everybody knew that – everybody human, anyhow, which left Wuppah out.

The Lizard made hissing and popping noises. 'This three hours is an eighth part of the day,' he said. 'It is acceptable to us that this be so: my superiors have given me so much discretion. For an eighth part of a day we and you will do no shooting in this big and ruined building, but will recover our hurt males and take them back inside our lines. By the Emperor I swear the Race will keep these terms.' He looked down at the ground with both eyes when he said that.

Truces with the *Boches* hadn't required anybody to do any swearing, but the Germans and Americans had had a lot more in common than the Lizards and Americans did. 'We'll keep 'em, too, so help me God,' he said formally.

'It is agreed, then,' Wuppah said. He drew himself up straight again, though the rounded crown of his head didn't even come up to Mutt's Adam's apple. 'I have dealt with you as I would with a male of the Race.'

That sounded as if it was meant to be a compliment. Mutt decided to take as one. 'I've treated you like a human being, too, Wuppah,' he said, and impulsively stuck out his right hand.

Wuppah took it. His grip was warm, almost hot, and, though his hand was small and bony, surprisingly strong. As they broke the clasp, the Lizard asked, 'You have been injured in your hand?'

Mutt looked down at the member in question. He'd forgotten how battered and gnarled it was: a catcher's meat hand took a lot of abuse from foul tips and other mischances of the game. How many split fingers, dislocated fingers, broken fingers had he had? More than he could remember. Wuppah was still waiting for an answer. Daniels said, 'A long time ago, before you folks got here.'

'Ah,' the Lizard said, 'I go to tell my superiors the truce is made.'

'Okay.' Mutt turned and shouted, 'Three-hour ceasefire! No shootin' till' – he glanced at his watch – 'quarter of five.'

Warily, men and Lizards emerged from cover and went through the ruins, sometimes guided by the cries of their wounded, sometimes just searching through wreckage to see if soldiers lay unconscious behind or beneath it. Searchers from both sides still carried their weapons; one gunshot would have turned the Swift plant back into a slaughterhouse. But the shot did not come.

The terms of the truce forbade either side from moving troops forward. Mutt had every intention of abiding by that: if you broke the terms of an agreement, you'd have – and you'd deserve to have – a devil of a time getting another one. All the same, he carefully noted the hiding places from which the Lizards came. If Wuppah wasn't doing the same with the Americans, he was dumber than Mutt figured.

Here and there, Lizards and Americans who came across one another in their searches cautiously fraternized. Some officers would have stopped it. Mutt had grown up listening to his grandfathers' stories of swapping tobacco for coffee during the War Between the States. He kept an eye on things, but didn't speak up.

He was anything but surprised to see Dracula Szabo head-to-head with a couple of Lizards. Dracula was grinning as he came back to the American lines. 'What you got?' Mutt asked.

'Don't quite know, Lieutenant,' Szabo answered, 'but the brass is always after us to bring in Lizard gadgets, and the scaly boys, they traded me some.'

He showed them to Mutt, who didn't know what they were good for, either. But maybe some of the boys with the thick glasses would, or could find out. 'What did you give for 'em?'

Dracula's smile was somewhere between mysterious and predatory. 'Ginger snaps.'

A blast of chatter greeted David Goldfarb when he walked into the Friend In Need. The air in the pub was thick with smoke. The only trouble was, it all came from the fireplace, not from cigarettes and pipes. Goldfarb couldn't remember the last time he'd had a smoke.

He worked his way toward the bar. The Friend In Need was full of dark blue RAF uniforms, most of them with officers' braid on the cuffs of their jacket sleeves. Just a radarman himself, Goldfarb had to be circumspect in his quest for bitter.

If it hadn't been for the RAF uniforms, the Friend In Need couldn't have stayed in business. Bruntingthorpe was a tiny village a few miles south of Leicester: a greengrocer's shop, a chemist's, a few houses, the pub, and damn little else. But the RAF experimental station just outside the place brought hundreds of thirsty men almost to the door of the Friend In Need. The place not only survived, it flourished.

'Goldfarb!' somebody bawled in a loud, beery voice.

The radarman's head whipped around. There at a table, waving enthusiastically, sat Flight Lieutenant Basil Roundbush, who, along with Goldfarb, was part of Group Captain Fred Hipple's team that labored to incorporate Lizard knowledge into British jet engines and radars. Goldfarb often thought that was the equivalent of trying to incorporate the technology of smokeless powder into the Duke of Wellington's infantry squares, but carried on regardless.

Roundbush, by some miracle, had an empty chair next to him. Goldfarb made for it with mixed feelings. On the one hand, sitting down would be nice. On the other, if he sat next to the flight lieutenant, not a barmaid in the world, let alone the ones in Bruntingthorpe, would look at him. Besides being an officer, Roundbush was tall and blond and ruddy and handsome, with a soup-strainer moustache, a winning attitude, and a chestful of medals.

Goldfarb had a Military Medal himself, but it didn't match up. Nor did he: other rank, medium-sized, lean, with the features and dark, curly hair of an Eastern European Jew. Sitting down next to Roundbush reminded him of how un-English he looked. His parents had got out of Poland a little before the First World War. A lot of people hadn't been so lucky. He knew that very well.

'Stella, darling!' Roundbush called, waving. Because it was he, the barmaid came right away, with a broad smile on her face. 'Pint of best bitter for my friend here, and another for me as well.'

'Right y'are, dearie,' Stella said, and swayed away.

Roundbush stared after her. 'By God, I'd like to take a bite out of that arse,' he declared. His upper-class accent made the sentiment sound a trifle odd, but no less sincere for that.

'As a matter of fact, so would I,' Goldfarb said. He sighed. He didn't have very much chance of that, not just with Roundbush next to him but with the pub – with the whole experimental station – full of officers.

Stella came back with the tall glasses of beer. Roundbush banged his teeth together. If Goldfarb had done that, he'd have got his face slapped. For the mustachioed fighter pilot, Stella giggled. *Where is justice?* Goldfarb wondered, a thought that would have been more Talmudic had it been directed to something other than trying to end up in bed with a barmaid.

Basil Roundbush raised his glass on high. Goldfarb dutifully followed suit. Instead of proposing a toast to Stella's hindquarters, as the radarman had expected, Roundbush said, 'To the Meteor!' and drank.

'To the Meteor!' Goldfarb drank, too. When you get right down to it, a jet fighter was more toastworthy than a barmaid's backside, and less likely to cause fights, too.

'On account of the Meteor, we're going to be good chaps and pedal on back to barracks at closing time,' Roundbush said. 'We're going up tomorrow afternoon, and the powers that be take a dim view of improving one's outlook, even with such camel piss as this allegedly best bitter, within twelve hours of a flight.'

The thin, sour beer did leave a good deal to be desired, even by wartime standards. Goldfarb was about to agree to that, with the usual profane embellishments, when he really heard what the flight officer had said. '*We're* going up?' he said. 'They've installed a radar in a Meteor at last, then?'

'That they have,' Roundbush said. 'It will give us rather better odds against the Lizards, wouldn't you say?'

He spoke lightly. He'd flown a Spitfire in the Battle of Britain, when a fighter pilot's life expectancy was commonly measured in days. But a Spitfire had had an even chance against a Messerschmitt Bf-109. Against Lizard aircraft, you had to be lucky just to come back from a combat mission. Actually shooting the enemy down was about as likely as winning the Irish Sweepstakes.

'D'you think we'll actually be able to accomplish something against them now?' Goldfarb asked.

'We add the radar, which is your wicket, and we add a good deal of speed, which is always an asset,' Roundbush said. 'Put them together and I'd say they improve our chances all the way up to bloody poor.'

As a joke, that wouldn't have been bad. The trouble was, Roundbush wasn't joking. Goldfarb had tracked Lizard aircraft on ground-based radar down at Dover before the aliens openly revealed their presence. They'd gone so high and fast, he and everybody else had wondered if they were real or defects in the mechanism. He and everybody else knew the answer to that now.

Roundbush said, 'You've flown airborne radar before, haven't you? Yes, of course you have; that's why Group Captain Hipple wanted you as part of the group. Don't mind me. I'm a silly ass tonight.'

'That's right.' Goldfarb hoped the pilot would realize he was agreeing about his experience, not the later parenthetical comment. He'd been in charge of a set flown in a Lancaster to see if the thing could be done. 'Rather more room to fit the set in a bomber fuselage than in the Meteor.'

'Rather,' Roundbush said, and drained his glass.

Goldfarb finished his bitter too, then held up a hand to buy a round in turn. That was inviolable pub custom: two men together, two rounds; four men together, four rounds; eight men together and they'd all go home half blind.

Stella took her time about noticing a mere radarman, but Goldfarb's half-a-crown spent as well as anyone else's. When she went off to get change, though, she didn't put as much into her walk for him as she had for Roundbush.

The pilot said, 'We'd be better off still if we had guided rockets like the Lizards'. Then we'd knock their planes out of the sky at twenty miles, as they can with us. Once we're inside gun range, we have an almost decent chance, but getting there, as the saying goes, is half the fun.'

'Yes, I know about that,' Goldfarb said. The Lizards had fired radar-homing rockets in his Lanc. Turning off the radar made them miss, but a turned-off radar was of even less use than no radar at all, because it added weight and made the aircraft that carried it slower and less maneuverable.

'Good. One less thing to have to brief you about.' Roundbush poured down his pint, apparently in one long swallow, then waved to get Stella's attention. 'We'll just have ourselves another one before we toddle on back to base.'

Another one turned into two: Goldfarb insisted on buying a matching round. Part of that was pub custom. Another part was a conscious effort on his part to give the lie to the Jews' reputation for stinginess. His parents, products of a harsher world than England, had drilled into him that he should never let himself become a spectacle for the Gentiles.

Pedaling back to the airbase with four pints of best bitter in him gave a whole new meaning to Roundbush's mock-aristocratic 'toddling'. He was glad he wasn't trying to drive a car. He expected to have a thick head come morning, but nothing that would keep him from doing his work, and certainly nothing that would keep him from flying the next afternoon.

The headache with which he did wake up wasn't what left him abstracted when he headed for the Nissen hut Hipple's team shared with the meterological staff. He had his mind too focused on the flight ahead to be as efficient as he might have been in trying to decipher the secrets of a captured Lizard radar, though.

Basil Roundbush had had more than four pints the night before – how many more, Goldfarb didn't know – but seemed fresh as a daisy. He was whistling a tune the radarman hadn't heard. Flight Lieutenant Maurice Kennan looked up from a sheaf of three-view drawings and said, 'That's as off-key as it is off-color, which is saying something.'

'Thank you, sir,' Roundbush said cheerfully, which made Kennan return to his drawings in a hurry. If Roundbush hadn't been a flier, he would have made a masterful psychological warfare officer.

Goldfarb's pretense of its being a normal day broke down about ten o'clock, when Leo Horton, a fellow radarman, nudged him in the ribs and whispered, 'You lucky sod.' After that, he was only pretending to work.

An hour or so later, Roundbush walked over and tapped him on the shoulder. 'What say we go don our shining armor and make sure our steed is ready to ride?' From another man, the Arthurian language would have sounded asinine. He was not only a spirit blithe enough to carry it off without self-consciousness, he'd fought a great many aerial jousts already. Goldfarb nodded and got up from his desk.

The flight suit of leather and fur was swelteringly hot in the bright sunshine of an English summer's day, but Goldfarb zipped zippers and fastened catches without complaint. Three or four miles straight up and it wouldn't be summery any more. For that matter, the Meteor surely had a higher ceiling than the trudging Lanc in which he'd flown before.

In the Lancaster, he'd tended the radar in the cavernous space of the bomb bay. In the new two-seater version of the Meteor, he sat behind the pilot in a stretched cockpit. The radar set itself was mounted behind and below him in the fuselage; only the controls and the screens were where he could get at them. If something went wrong with the unit, he'd have to wait till he was back on the ground to fiddle with it.

Groundcrew men pulled the plane out of its sandbagged, camouflaged revetment and onto the runway. Goldfarb had heard jet engines a great number of times, but being in an aircraft whose engines were being started was a new experience, and one he could have done without: it reminded him of nothing so much as taking up residence inside a dentist's drill. 'Bit noisy, what?' Roundbush bawled through the interphone.

The moment the Meteor began to taxi, Goldfarb realized he'd traded a brewery horse for a thoroughbred. The engine noise grew even more appalling, but the fighter sprang into the air and climbed as if it were shot from a boy's catapult.

So Goldfarb thought, at any rate, till Basil Roundbush said, 'This Mark is on the underpowered side, but they're working on new engines that should really pep up the performance.'

'Overwhelming enough for me already, thanks,' the radarman said. 'What's our ceiling in this aircraft?'

'Just over forty thousand feet,' Roundbush replied. 'We'll be there in less than half an hour, and we'll be able to see quite a long way, I expect.'

'I expect you're right,' Goldfarb said, breathing rubbery air through his oxygen mask. The Lancaster in which he'd flown before had taken almost twice as long to climb a little more than half as high, and Roundbush was complaining about this machine's anemia! In a way, that struck Goldfarb as absurd. In another way, given what the pilot would have to face, it seemed only reasonable.

The Meteor banked gently. Through puffs of fluffy white cloud, Goldfarb peered out through the Perspex of the cockpit at the green patchwork quilt of the English countryside. 'Good show this isn't a few months ago,' Roundbush remarked casually. 'Time was when the ack-ack crews would start shooting at the mere sound of a jet engine, thinking it had to belong to the Lizards. Some of our Pioneers and Meteors took shrapnel damage on that account, though none of them was shot down.'

'Urk,' Goldfarb said; perhaps luckily, that hadn't occurred to him. Down in Dover, the antiaircraft crew had opened up at the roar of jets without a second thought.

'How's the radar performing?' Roundbush asked, reminding him of why they were flying the mission.

He checked the cathode-ray tubes. Strange to think he could see farther and in greater detail with them than with his eyes, especially when, from this airy eyrie, he seemed to be the king of infinite space, with the whole world set out below for his inspection. 'Everything seems to be performing as it should,' he said cautiously. 'I have a couple of blips that, by their height and speed, are our own aircraft. Could you fly a southerly course, to let me search for Lizard machines?' 'Changing course to one-eight-zero,' Roundbush said, obliging as a Victorian carriage driver acknowledging his toff of a master's request to convey him to Boodle's. Like a proper fighter pilot, he peered ahead and in all directions as the Meteor swung through its turn. 'I don't see anything.'

Goldfarb didn't see anything, either: his screens remained serenely blank. In a way, that was disappointing. In another way, it was a relief: if he could see the Lizards, they assuredly could also see him – and Roundbush had made no bones about their planes' remaining far superior to the Meteor.

Then, off in the electronic distance, he thought he detected something – and then, an instant later, the radar screens went crazy with noise, as if the aurora borealis had decided to dance on them. 'I'm getting interference,' Goldfarb said urgently. 'I spied what seemed to be a Lizard plane, right at the edge of where the set could reach, and then everything turned to hash – which means he likely detected me, too.'

'Which also means we're apt to have a rocket or two pay us a visit in the not too distant future,' Roundbush said. 'I don't propose to wait around for them, all things considered.'

He threw the Meteor into a dive that left Goldfarb's stomach some miles behind and thousands of feet above the aircraft. He gulped and did his best to keep his breakfast down; vomiting while you were wearing oxygen gear was not a good idea. Roundbush didn't make it easy, twisting the plane from side to side in evasive maneuvers violent enough to make the wings groan in protest. Goldfarb suspected he was stretching the Meteor's performance envelope, and hoped it had enough stretch in it.

The radarman had shut down his set to keep any rockets from homing on its signal. Now he was just a passenger, useless weight, as Roundbush shed altitude. The ground rushed up as if thrown at him. Not knowing whether the Lizards had fired and missed or contented themselves with simply scrambling his signal made the descent all the more harrowing.

The first thing he said when the nose wheel touched down at Bruntingthorpe was, 'Thank you.' The next thing was, 'We have a bit more work ahead of us, haven't we?'

*　　*　　*

Teerts was getting quite handy with the eating sticks the Nipponese used. He shoveled rice with bits of raw fish into his mouth, hardly spilling a grain or a morsel. The Big Uglies were feeding him better than they had when they first took him prisoner. He shuddered. They could hardly feed him worse.

His *hashi* discovered a thin, reddish piece of pickled ginger. He picked it up, turned both eye turrets toward it. Not so long ago, he'd been a killercraft pilot, a proud male of the conquest fleet of the Race. Now, thanks to bad luck, he was a prisoner in an empire of Big Uglies convinced that no worthy warrior ever let himself be taken prisoner. To help squeeze all they could out of him, they'd addicted him to this perfidious Tosevite herb.

With a convulsive jerk of his hand, he popped the piece of ginger into his mouth. He went rooting through the bowl with the eating sticks, looking for others. He found them and gobbled them up. The Nipponese cook had been unusually generous. He wondered what that meant; the Nipponese were not given to generosity unless they expected to realize something from it.

Then, as the ginger took effect, he stopped worrying about why the Nipponese had given it to him. That they had was enough. He felt smart enough to outwit every Big Ugly interrogator and nuclear physicist, strong enough to bend the bars of his Tokyo prison cell and escape the life of torment that he led.

Those were only feelings. He knew it all too well. The interrogators and physicists had drained him dry; everything he'd known about splitting atoms, they now knew. They'd known much of it already. The Russkis had already built a bomb. How the Nipponese gloated over that! How they strained every fiber to get one of their own!

Could Teerts have torn out the bars of his cell, he would have. Thinking he could wasn't enough to make it real. He'd tried, the first few times ginger had made him feel like a machine. In somber fact, he was just a male of the Race, and steel bars defeated him.

Usually when they fed him so much ginger, an interrogation was in the offing. The Nipponese liked to question him when the herb made his tongue loose and lively. He waited for Major Okamoto, his interpreter, interrogator, and occasional tormentor, to come down the hall. But Okamoto did not come.

From the top of the lift ginger gave him, Teerts slid into the trough of despair that followed. Just as he started to curl up in the farthest corner of his cell with the blanket drawn up over him both for warmth and to cut himself off from the unpleasant outside world, heavy Tosevite footsteps came echoing down the corridor.

The jailer unlocked his cell, 'Come along,' Major Okamoto said in Teerts's language. By now, Teerts paid little attention to his accent.

'It shall be done, superior sir,' Teerts said, but Okamoto had to shout at him before he would get up. The silent guard who always accompanied the major gestured with his bayoneted rifle for Teerts to precede him.

Before they left the prison, Okamoto decked Teerts in a conical straw hat like the ones some Nipponese wore, and also gave him trousers and tunic. He looked ridiculous, but that was not the point: the point was to keep him from being spotted from the air or by the Race's reconnaissance satellites.

The beast-drawn wagon that waited outside did not head off toward the nuclear physics laboratory, as it usually did. Instead, it took an unfamiliar path through the narrow, crowded streets of Tokyo. Teerts asked, 'Where are we going, superior sir?'

'To the train station, and then on to Kobe,' Okamoto answered. 'Dr Nishina does not think you can tell him any more of use in his plutonium bomb project, so the naval aviators will resume their questioning of you.'

'I see,' Teerts said dully. Now something more than the absence of ginger weighed down his spirits. The scientists, on the whole, had been restrained when he didn't know something. The military males – he shuddered.

The train station was packed with Nipponese, some in gowns, some in shirts and trousers, many in the uniforms of army and navy. Using a separate service for the water struck Teerts as absurd, but Tosev 3 had oceans where Home had small seas, so perhaps there was some justification for the idea.

Most of the train was even more crowded than the station as a whole, but Teerts, Major Okamoto, and the stolid guard had a car all to themselves, with tea and food already laid on. Okamoto did not object to Teerts's feeding himself. His rice had ginger in it, which buoyed his spirits.

A jerk said the train was in motion. Puffs of smoky steam flew from the engine. Teerts reckoned the coal-burner an unbelievably filthy machine, but on such matters the Big Uglies did not solicit his opinion.

Above the racket of the engine, above the clicking of the cars it pulled over the rails, came another sound, one Teerts knew intimately: the high, screaming wail of a turbofan engine. Major Okamoto looked up in alarm. 'Air raid!' he shouted, just as bombs and cannon fire began chewing up the train.

Shells punched through the roof of the car as if it were made of tissue. A bomb exploded right next to it. Teerts felt as if he were caught in the egg from which all earthquakes hatched. Glass sprayed around him. The car derailed and overturned.

When the crashing and the spinning stopped, he found himself sitting on what had been the roof. 'I'm alive,' he exclaimed, and then, even more surprised, 'I'm not hurt.' Major Okamoto and the silent, stolid guard lay on the roof, too, both of them bleeding and unconscious.

Teerts snatched up the guard's rifle and scrambled out through a shattered window. Ahead, the engine was a shattered wreck. Behind, some of the other passenger cars were in flames. The Big Uglies who had managed to escape from them were more interested in rescuing their trapped and endangered comrades than in a male of the Race, especially since he still wore Tosevite-style clothes and from a distance might have looked like one of them.

He knew the rifle would fire once if he squeezed the trigger. He wasn't sure how to work the bolt. But one shot was more than he'd had since he fell into Nipponese captivity. If all else failed, he could use it on himself. He put more distance between himself and the train wreck as fast as he could. He didn't know what he'd do for food or ginger, but he didn't much care. As soon as he found a place that was out of sight of the railway cars, he took off the hideous clothes the Big Uglies had given him and stretched his arms up to the planes and satellites he devoutly hoped were watching.

'Come and get me!' he cried. 'Oh, please, come and get me!'

4

Sam Yeager had been staring out the window of the bright yellow DC-3 ever since it took off from Lowry Field outside Denver. He'd never been in an airplane before, and found looking down at the ground from two miles in the air endlessly fascinating.

Ullhass and Ristin kept looking out the window, too, but anxiously. Every time turbulence shook the aircraft, they hissed in alarm. 'You are certain this machine is safe to fly?' Ullhass demanded for the dozenth time.

'Hasn't crashed yet,' Yeager answered, which for some reason did not fully reassure the Lizard POWs. He added, 'The pilot wouldn't take it up if he didn't think he could bring it down again. Biggest thing we have to worry about is having one of your friends shoot us out of the sky, and everything's supposed to be taken care of to make sure that doesn't happen.'

Ullhass jerked a clawed thumb at Barbara Yeager, who had the single seat in front of Sam's on the right side of the aisle. She'd closed the curtain over her window and was snoring gently. 'How can she sleep in this trap of death?' the Lizard said indignantly.

'Well, for one thing, being in a family way tires you out so you want to sleep all the time,' Yeager said, 'and for another, she doesn't think this is one – a death trap, I mean. Relax, boys. We'll be down on the ground pretty soon now.'

He looked out the window again. The endless flat expanse of the Great Plains had given way to rather rougher ground, much of it covered with pine woods. The airliner's two engines changed their note as it descended, and it bounced a little when the flaps came down.

'What's that?' Ristin and Ullhass exclaimed together.

Sam didn't answer; the flaps had caught him by surprise, too. Off to the north, the Arkansas River was a silvery ribbon of water. Here and there, buildings poked out of the forest. More rumblings and thumpings came from under the DC-3. The Lizards started having conniptions again.

The noise and the bumping were enough to wake Barbara. 'Oh, the landing gear is down,' she cried, stretching, which told Ullhass and Ristin and, incidentally, her husband what was going on.

After one bounce, landing was as smooth as takeoff had been. As soon as the plane rolled to a stop in front of a building made of corrugated sheet metal, a fellow in khaki brought up a wheeled ladder up to the door behind the left wing. 'Everybody out!' he shouted. He had a rifle on his back, just in case Ullhass and Ristin proved friskier than they looked. The only friskiness they showed was grumbling over how far apart the rungs were on a human-built ladder.

The hot, muggy air hit Sam like a blow when he got down onto the tarmac. He hadn't played in the Southeast for a good many years; he'd forgotten how sticky and unpleasant it could be.

He stood at the base of the ladder to help Barbara down in case she needed it. She didn't, but her eyes widened just the same. 'Thank goodness the baby's not due till winter. If I were going to have it in August in this weather, I think I'd sooner die.'

'Come on, let's get you folks under cover, too,' the guard said, pointing to the door in the airport building through which the Lizards had already gone. As they moved away from the ladder, a couple of colored men in overalls climbed up into the DC-3 to get out their luggage.

It was even hotter inside the building than it had been on the runway. Yeager felt as if he were stuck inside an upside-down-frying pan. Ullhass and Ristin strutted around, obviously enjoying the heat. 'If it didn't seem like too much work, I'd strangle them,' Sam said. Barbara nodded. Even the tiny motion made sweat leap out on her forehead.

A two-horse team pulling a covered wagon a lot like the one in which they'd traveled from Chicago to Denver left from the other side of the building. A moment later, so did another one, and a moment after that another one still. 'What are those all about?' Barbara asked, pointing.

'Come on – you people and the POWs go in the next one,' the guard answered. 'We send 'em out in all different directions to keep the Lizards from swooping down and tryin' a rescue while we move the prisoners to their camp.'

'Where is this camp, anyway?' Yeager asked.

'Hot Springs, maybe sixty miles west and a little south of here,' the fellow answered.

'Haven't ever been there,' Yeager said.

A gleam of mischief in her eye, Barbara said. 'What with your baseball and all, I thought you'd been everywhere, Sam.'

Yeager shook his head. 'I played in El Dorado in the Cotton States League back maybe ten years ago, the year after I broke my ankle. The league went under partway through the season. Hot Springs wasn't in it then, though I hear it joined up after the league started up again a few years later.'

The negroes had already stowed their suitcases in the back of the wagon and had made themselves invisible again. Yeager had forgotten what things were like in the South, how many colored people there were and how they mostly got the short end of the stick. He wondered if they wouldn't have been just as well pleased to see the Lizards win the war The Lizards would treat everybody, white and black, like niggers.

After flying more than nine hundred miles from Denver to Little Rock in a little over five hours, Sam and Barbara and the Lizards took two days to go the sixty miles from Little Rock to Hot Springs. All the same, Yeager didn't complain. Till they got there, he was essentially on leave. It was pretty country, too: pine woods more than halfway to Hot Springs, after which black gum and sweet gum began to predominate in the bottomlands by the creeks. Everything smelled green and alive and growing.

Arkansas didn't seem to have seen a lot of war. When he asked the wagon driver about that, the fellow said, 'The Lizards bombed the aluminium plants over the bauxite pretty good when they first got here, but those are going again now. Otherwise it ain't been too bad.'

'Just looking at the highway tells me that,' Barbara said, and Sam nodded. They'd passed only a few wrecked, rusted cars dragged off to the side of US 70. Most of them had their hoods gaping open, as if visiting an automotive dentist – whatever was useful in their engine compartments had been salvaged.

By the time the wagon got into Hot Springs, Sam envied Ristin and Ullhass their scaly hides. Mosquitoes had made him and Barbara miserable, but didn't seem to bother the Lizards. 'Maybe we do not taste good to them,' Ristin said.

'I wish I didn't,' Yeager answered darkly.

Hot Springs was a medium-sized town, tucked in among the deep green slopes of the Ouachita Mountains. US 70 entered it from the northeast, and swung south past what the driver called Bathhouse Row, where in happier times people had come from all over the world to bathe in the springs that gave the town its name and its fame. The wagon rolled past the greensward of Arlington Park, the limestone-and-brick Fordyce Bathhouse, the plastered Quapaw Bathhouse with its red tile roof and mosaic dome, and the Hot Springs National Park administrative building before turning left on Reserve and stopping at the magnificent five-storey towers of the Army and Navy General Hospital.

The wagon pulled past the one-storey white stone front and up under an awning that led into one of the towers. 'We're here, folks,' he announced. He looked back over his shoulder at the Lizard POWs. 'You'll want to stay under the awning when you go inside.'

'It shall be done, superior sir,' Ristin answered, though whether he actually wanted to obey remained an open question. But Lizard aerial intelligence was uncannily good, so if you were smart you revealed as little as you could to the sky. Yeager wondered where the decoy wagons were unloading their feigned prisoners.

He left his bags in the wagon, helped Barbara down, and hurried after his charges into the hospital building. Barbara followed him. Inside there,

Ullhass and Ristin were talking in a mixture of English and their own language with a bright-looking man some years younger than Sam who wore captain's bars. Sam waited for the officer to notice him, then saluted and said, 'Sergeant Samuel Yeager reporting from Denver as ordered, sir, with my wife Barbara and the Lizard prisoners Ristin and Ullhass.'

The captain returned the salute. 'Pleased to meet you, Sergeant, Mrs Yeager.' He had a New York accent. 'I'm Benjamin Berkowitz.' He glanced down at some papers stuck in a clipboard. 'General Groves speaks highly of your abilities with the Lizards, Yeager. From what I've heard, any praise from him is high praise. How did you get so good with them? Were you a translator or something like that before the war?'

'No, sir, I was a baseball player.' Sam's face heated as he admitted, 'All I knew about creatures from outer space before the war, sir, I got from reading science fiction.'

Berkowitz grinned. It made him look like a kid. 'You know what, Sergeant? I'm just the same way. You know what else? That starts us out two jumps ahead of everybody else, because our minds are flexible.' He looked down at the papers in the clipboard again. 'We've got you and your wife and the POWs assigned to rooms 427 and 429 upstairs. Why don't you get settled in tonight – supper's at 1800, about half an hour from now – and report with the Lizards at 0800 tomorrow.'

'That sounds fine, sir,' Sam said. 'Uh – our bags are still in the wagon, sir.'

'Somebody will carry them up for you,' Berkowitz said. 'Your job is to ride herd on your friends here.'

A room in a hospital wasn't going to be as nice as an apartment across the street from the University of Denver, but Yeager was in no position to argue. He hoped Barbara wouldn't mind the change too much. She wasn't in the Army, but it still jerked her around.

When he and his companions trudged up to the fourth floor, the rooms proved bigger than he'd expected. The window to 429 had iron bars fitted – on the inside, so they wouldn't show from the air – which meant that one was intended for the Lizards.

A Negro in khaki brought up the luggage. Sam pulled a half-dollar out of his pocket. The black man shook his head. 'Sergeant, I'm in the Army, jus' like you. This here's my job.'

'I don't care if you're a congressman, buddy. You do that kind of work in this kind of weather, you ought to get something special for it.' Yeager tossed the man the half-dollar. He picked it out of the air with an infielder's smoothness, sketched a salute, and went down the hall whistling something Dixieland.

Drawn by the noise in the hallway, a Lizard came out of room 431 to see what was going on. He had the fanciest body paint Sam had ever seen. Ristin and Ullhass hadn't kept themselves painted for months, which made the contrast all the more striking: this male's body gleamed with spirals and swirls of silver and gold and red.

Ullhass and Ristin turned and stared, their eye turrets swiveling toward the fancily painted Lizard as if drawn to him by magnets. Then they started spluttering honorifics Yeager had never heard before: 'Supreme sir!' 'Splendid Shiplord!' 'How did you come here, splendid sir?'

Barbara didn't follow the Lizards' language as well as Sam, but tone and gesture spoke volumes by themselves. 'That's an *important* Lizard,' she said quietly.

'No kidding,' Yeager murmured back. His two scaly buddies were reacting to the fellow with the bright paint job the way a couple of bobby-soxers would have reacted to Frank Sinatra. He walked over to the Lizard, gave forth with his best interrogative cough, and said, 'May I ask your name and rank?' He didn't use any of the formal titles of respect Ullhass and Ristin had employed; the Lizard was, after all, a prisoner.

The male turned from his two fellow aliens to Yeager. 'You speak our language as well as any Tosevite I have heard,' he said, and added the emphatic cough. Sam grinned a wide, foolish grin, as if he'd just knocked in the game-winning run in the bottom of the ninth. The Lizard went on, 'I am Straha, shiplord of the *206th Emperor Yower*. Former shiplord, I should say – no more, thanks to the exalted incompetence of Atvar the fleetlord.'

Yeager stared. How the devil had the Americans bagged a shiplord? From what he knew, a lot of them stayed up in outer space where nothing human could touch them, let alone capture them. Ristin said, 'This is our third-highest male, superior sir, in all the fleet. Above him are only the shiplord of the bannership and the exalted fleetlord himself.'

Most of that was in English, so Barbara caught it, too. It was her turn to gape. 'What's he doing here?' she asked, a split second ahead of her husband.

'What *are* you doing here, Shiplord?' Sam asked in the Lizard's language. He granted Straha his title, but not the flowery language that went with it.

The Lizard didn't take offense. He said, 'When the Russkis set off their plutonium bomb – you know about this?' He waited for Yeager to say he did, then went on, 'And when other parts of our campaign were botched and mishandled, I alone had the courage to stand up and propose that we replace the inept exalted fleetlord. My motion had large majority, but not the three parts in four our law requires. It was defeated.'

'Oh, lord,' Yeager said softly. The scene sounded like something out of South America or the Balkans. Somehow he hadn't imagined the Lizards with political squabbles of their own. It made them seem much more – human. He switched back to their language: 'What happened then?'

'I knew the exalted incompetent would have his revenge,' Straha said. 'Nowhere in the conquest fleet would I be safe from his injustice. And so, with my pilot, I brought my shuttle down and gave myself into the hands of you Tosevites here.'

'God, it's almost like Rudolf Hess flying to England,' Barbara said when Sam translated that.

'Yeah, it sure is,' he said, and, sticking to English, went on, 'I wonder if we have the spaceship he flew down in. If we do, I wonder if we can make one like it. If we can do that—'

'If you can, you will be a greater danger to the Race,' Ristin said in the same language. Sam wondered why he didn't translate that for Straha. Maybe he wasn't happy with him for giving the USA that kind of chance.

Letting that go, Yeager gave his attention back to Straha. 'Shiplord, now that you are here with us, what will you do?'

'I have already begun,' the alien answered. 'I have made one radio broadcast telling the males of the Race that this war will be lost because of the stupidity of the males who lead them – either that, or this plant will be wrecked in the fighting. I tell them the best thing for them to do would be to give up to the males of the empires in whose lands they are situated.'

'Do you?' Yeager said with something like delight. Lizard POWs had broadcast to their comrades before, but they were the alien equivalent of dogfaces: nobody to take seriously on account of who they were. But Straha was a big wheel. If he was turning collaborator – the world might become a very interesting place.

The recording of the broadcast was scratchy, full of hisses and pops and bursts of static. Tosevite radio equipment left a great deal to be desired, and the Big Uglies' broadcasts were vulnerable to interference from their star and from atmospheric electrical phenomena. Nonetheless, the message being sent was perfectly comprehensible, and made Atvar perfectly furious.

Straha was saying, '—because our campaign has been misadministered at the highest level, we have no hope of the victory for which the Emperor sent us forth. We have been betrayed by the arrogance and over-confidence of the exalted fleetlord, who consistently refuses to listen to advice from those who know better than he. And if we cannot win this war, what must we do?'

'Getting rid of traitors would be a good first step,' Kirel said savagely.

'Who could have imagined this?' Atvar agreed. 'To be captured in battle is one thing, and no disgrace. To flee to the enemy, especially when the enemy is not of the Race ... such has never been done in all our history, not since the Empire first covered all of Home.' In his mind, breaking a precedent a hundred thousand years old was a crime as appalling as betraying the Race.

Straha's ranting had gone on while Atvar and Kirel vented their fury. The fleetlord ran the recording back and let it play once more: 'We must make the best terms with the Tosevites we can. I am treated well here by the Americans, though I was a shiplord in the force that vainly tried to overcome them. Males of lower rank enjoy treatment equally good here, as is true in many of the other empires on this world. Take yourselves out of danger you should never have been in.'

Atvar stabbed out a clawed forefinger and turned off the recording. 'How many of our males will hear this poisonous nonsense?' he demanded.

Kirel looked unhappy. 'Some of these broadcasts are on our entertainment frequencies: no doubt the Big Uglies learned those from prisoners. Others – translations – use the frequencies the Tosevites more commonly employ, and are no doubt intended to boost their morale. Exalted Fleetlord, my opinion is that both uses are extremely damaging to us.'

'I should say so!' Atvar snarled. 'The Race is hierarchical by nature and training. Foolish males who hear the third-highest officer in the conquest fleet tell them all is lost are all too likely to believe him. What can we do to suppress his treacherous twaddle?'

Kirel looked unhappier still. 'Exalted Fleetlord, of course we attack transmitters, but that does only so much good. The Americans quickly rebuild and relocate them. And Straha, I am certain, is not present at the transmission sites. Our engineers say these broadcasts are made from recordings.'

'Where is he, then?' Atvar demanded. 'His shuttle landed not far from one of the sites to which the Big Uglies fly prisoners. Surely they must have a facility somewhere in this area.'

'No doubt they do, but they have gone to great pains to keep us confused as to where it might be,' Kirel said. 'So far, they have succeeded, too. Besides, they may well have shifted Straha away from that region to prevent us from reacquiring him through a raid on the prisoner-holding facility. In short, we do not know where he is and have no immediate hope of learning.'

'Most unsatisfactory,' Atvar said. 'We can jam the frequencies where Straha's babbling is directed at other Big Uglies, but if we jam those on which he seeks to speak to our males, we jam our own entertainment channels, which is also unsatisfactory. Straha—' He let out a long hiss. 'I was angry at him for trying to overthrow me, but even then I never expected *this*.'

'Nor I, Exalted Fleetlord,' Kirel said. 'He must have greatly feared the might of your vengeance.'

Atvar wondered if that was polite, oblique criticism. Should he have tried to come to terms with Straha after the shiplord failed to oust him? How could he, without relinquishing some of the power the Emperor had granted him? In any case, no point worrying about that now: far too late.

'Did we at least succeed in destroying the shuttle Straha used to escape?' he asked.

'I – believe so, Exalted Fleetlord,' Kirel answered cautiously. 'The Big Uglies show an amazing capacity for deception, though, so I cannot be quite certain.'

'We'd better have destroyed it,' Atvar said. 'The Deutsche are already throwing their own missiles at us, but those are just short-range weapons with bad guidance, small playloads, and no chance of achieving orbital velocity, much less velocity to escape this planet. If the Big Uglies get proper rocket motors, though, and a couple of them with atomic weapons—'

He and Kirel stared at each other in horror. Kirel said, 'If that happens, Exalted Fleetlord, the entire conquest fleet is at risk. We may have to think about wrecking this world for the sake of our own survival.'

'This fleet's survival, yes, but the colonization fleet will be thrown away if it arrives to discover a world unsuitable for colonization.'

'It will also be thrown away if it arrives to discover a world that is the base for space-traveling Big Uglies with atomic weapons,' Kirel replied.

Atvar would have given him a hot answer, if only he could have come up with one. At last, he said, 'Let us hope we did destroy the shuttle. That will buy us the time we need to complete the conquest before the Tosevites become spacefarers.' But when you bought time against the Big Uglies, somehow you always ended up buying less than you thought you were paying for.

Marching. Nieh Ho-T'ing sometimes thought he'd been born marching. He would have bet a goodly sum that he would die marching. If his death advanced the cause of the proletarian revolution, he would have accepted it without a qualm, although he had no more interest in immediately dying than any other healthy man of thirty-five.

He'd been on the Long March with Mao, commanding a ragged division of the Communist Army as it fled Chiang Kai-Shek's counter-revolutionary forces. That had been a march worthy of the name. Now he personally commanded only a squadron of men on the road northwest from Shanghai to Peking. It looked like a demotion. It wasn't. Responsibility for guerrilla resistance to the scaly devils – and, when necessary, to other foes of the revolution as well – through that whole stretch of territory rested in his hands.

He turned to his second-in-command, Hsia Shou-Tao, and said, 'This is surely the most complicated piece of warfare the world has ever known.'

Hsia grunted. He was a big, burly man with a wide, tough-looking face, the archetype of a stupid, brutal peasant. He had a deep, rasping voice, too, and had used it and his appearance to escape trouble any number of times. He was, however, anything but stupid. Laughing a little, he said,

'Why on earth would you say that? Just because we, the little scaly devil imperialists, the Kuomintang and Chiang's counter-revolutionary clique, and the remnants of the eastern devil imperialists from Japan are *all* struggling over the same territory?'

'No, not just because of that.' Nieh paused a moment to fan himself with his straw hat. Peasant dress – the hat, loose-fitting black cotton shirt and trousers, sandals – was as good as anything at withstanding the muggy heat of a Chinese summer. 'If we faced merely a four-cornered struggle, everything would be simple.'

'For you, maybe,' Hsia Shou-Tao said. Sometimes he played the role of foolish boor so well that he even seemed to convince himself with it.

'I mean what I say,' Nieh Ho-T'ing insisted. 'This is not a war with corners, this is a war in a spider's web, with threads running from each force to all the others, and sometimes sticking when they cross. Consider: sometimes the men of the Kuomintang co-operate with us against the scaly devils, sometimes they betray us to them. Knowing when they will do the one and when the other is a matter of life and death, of success or failure for the progressive forces.'

'We've sold them out a few times, too,' Hsia said with a reminiscent chuckle.

'Exactly so, and they are as wary of us as we are of them. But sometimes we do work with them, as we do sometimes with the Japanese, and sometimes with even stranger allies,' Nieh said.

'That foreign devil, the American, you mean?' Hsia asked. 'Yes, he was useful. I've never seen a man who could throw like – what was his name?'

'Bobby Fiore,' Nieh answered, pronouncing the foreign sounds with care. 'Yes, without him we probably would not have escaped after we assassinated that scaly devil back in Shanghai. Pity he was killed; he could have taught our men his skill.'

'He was a reactionary, of course,' Hsia said. 'Of course,' Nieh Ho-T'ing agreed. 'Also a lecher.' Bobby Fiore had made full use of the services of the Shanghai brothel in which Nieh had based himself while preparing the assault on the scaly devil official. Like a lot of his Communist comrades, Nieh looked on such looseness with disdain. But he was a pragmatic man. 'As you say, though, he was useful, not only for his throwing but also because he understood the little devils' language.'

'We would have had to liquidate him sooner or later,' Hsia said. 'He was ideologically most unsound.'

'Of course,' Nieh said again. 'I think he may even have known that. But he had a true hatred for the little scaly devils, even if it was just personal and not ideological.'

'Personal hatred for the little devils is too easy to come by to be much of a virtue,' Hsia Shou-Tao said. There Nieh could not disagree with him.

Pick up a foot, put it down, pick it up, put it down ... If you let your feet work and didn't think about it, you covered more ground than you dreamt you could. The Long March had drilled that into Nieh. He looked back over his shoulder. The men he led were strung out along a *li* – a third of a mile – of the dirt road. That was all right. The less they looked like part of an armed force, the less likely the little devils were to give them trouble.

Peasants labored in the fields and paddies to either side of the road. They looked up warily from their labor as Nieh and his followers went by. They were wiser than the scaly devils; they knew soldiers when they saw them. A couple of men waved to Nieh: they knew what kind of soldiers he led, too. That pleased him. If at need his men could become but a single minnow in the vast school of the peasantry, they would be impossible for any enemy to root out.

One of the peasants called, 'Are you people going by the camp the little devils built up ahead? You want to be careful if you are; they don't like anyone snooping around there.'

'Thank you for the warning, friend. We'll steer clear,' Nieh Ho-T'ing said. He waved to the peasant, who nodded and went back to work. Nieh and Hsia nodded, too, to each other. As long as the people supported your efforts, you could not be beaten.

As a matter of fact, Nieh wanted as close a look at the prison camp as he could get without making himself appear an obvious spy to the scaly devils. The camps they'd set up to oppress the people had become fertile sources of intelligence against them. From this one, for instance, had come word that the scaly devils had cameras that could somehow see heat. The news had tactical implications: no campfires at night when in close contact with the enemy – except as diversions, travel through cool water whenever possible, and more.

The camp, set in the middle of the fields that might otherwise have raised a good crop of beans, was as big as a fair-sized city. The stink of its night soil came sharp on the breeze. 'A lot of shit there that's not going into the fields for fertilizer as it should,' Hsia Shou-Tao said. He thought like a peasant, too.

'True,' Nieh said, his voice abstracted. As casually as he could, he peered across the fields toward the perimeter of the camp: razor wire, with sentry posts and little forts all around. Liberating it would be suicidally expensive, however grand to contemplate.

Down the road, swiftly drawing nearer, came a rising cloud of dust. Its speed meant motor vehicles were kicking it up, and motor vehicles, in these days, meant little scaly devils. Nieh did not break his stride. his submachine gun was hidden in the blanket roll he carried slung over one shoulder. He could get at it in a hurry if he had to, but hoped the occasion would not arise. Motor vehicles were usually armored against weapons like his.

Hsia walked along as nonchalantly as he did. They stepped off the road into the field beside it when the vehicle – a troop carrier – sped past. Had they not moved, Nieh thought, the driver would have run them down: what were peasants to an imperialist aggressor, especially one of alien race?

'What we ought to have,' Hsia said thoughtfully, 'is more land mines. The little devils would lose some of their arrogance if they had to worry about blowing up as they barreled down the road.'

'We have people manufacturing some of them,' Nieh answered. 'If we want to get them fast and in quantity, though, we'd do best to dicker with the Japanese. They don't have many vehicles of their own left in this part of China, so they shouldn't mind trading us some mines. I wonder what we'd have to give in exchange. Food, probably. They're always hungry.'

'As if we aren't.' But Hsia nodded. After a few seconds, he nodded again, for a different reason: 'You're right, Comrade – this *is* a complicated war.'

Heinrich Jäger felt like a soccer ball, with the continent of Europe his pitch. Since the war started in 1939, he'd been to just about every corner of it: Poland, France, the Soviet Union, France again, back to Germany, Croatia, France one more time ... and now Germany again.

He turned to Kurt Diebner, who stood beside him on the walls of Schloss Hohentübingen. 'Professor, I tell you again that I am not needed for this recovery operation. I would be of far more use to the *Vaterland* leading panzer troops against the Lizards.'

Diebner shook his head. 'It has to be you, Colonel,' the physicist said, running a hand through his greasy, dark brown hair. 'We need someone with a military background to supervise those engaged in recovering the material from the failed pile down in Hechingen, and you also have the required security clearances. We prefer you to anyone from the *Schutzstaffel*, and the SS itself has no objection to your employment. So you see—' He beamed at Jäger through thick, black-rimmed spectacles and spread his hands, as if he'd just proved some abstruse piece of math relating to quantum mechanics.

The explanation made sense to Jäger, which did not mean he liked it. He wondered how he'd got a good character from the SS: Otto Skorzeny's doing, most likely. Skorzeny no doubt thought he was doing him a favor. Jäger supposed it *was* a favor, but having Himmler's approval, however useful it might be, was also slightly chilling.

Jäger also noted the bloodless language Diebner used: the 'failed pile' twenty kilometers south in Hechingen had poisoned a good stretch of the local landscape, and would have poisoned Tübingen, too, had the wind been blowing out of the south rather than from the north and west after the accident. Soldiers talked the same way; they spoke of 'maintaining fire discipline' when they meant not shooting until the enemy was right on top of you.

A Geiger counter sat on the wall between Jäger and Diebner. It rattled away, a good deal more quickly than it would have had everything gone right in Hechingen. Diebner insisted the level of radiation they were getting wasn't dangerous. Jäger hoped he knew what he was talking about. Of course, nobody had thought the pile would go berserk before it did, either.

Diebner glanced down at the Geiger counter. 'It's good enough,' he said. Maybe he needed to reassure himself every so often, too.

'Good enough for us, yes,' Jäger said. 'What about the poor devils who're getting that stuff out of there?' Getting pulled away from the front line was one reason he hated the assignment here. Having to deal with the men who went into Hechingen to recover uranium from the pile was another.

Kurt Diebner shrugged. 'They are condemned by the state,' he said, as if he were Pilate washing his hands. 'If this did not happen to them, something else would.'

Nothing like this, Jäger started to say, but the words did not cross his lips. Some of the men who went into the background chamber with shovels and lead boxes wore pink triangles on their striped uniforms; others wore six-pointed yellow stars. In the *Reich*, anything was liable to happen to Jews and homosexuals.

'You have of course told them the sickness from which they are suffering is only temporary, and that they will make a full recovery,' Diebner said.

'Yes, I've told them – the first group, and then the ones who replaced them when they got too sick to work.' No one had argued with Jäger when he spoke what he knew to be a lie. The thin, weary men just stared back at him. They didn't believe a word he said. He didn't blame them.

Diebner shifted uncomfortably. Like Jäger, he was a fairly decent man in a nation whose regime did horrible things as a matter of course. If you weren't directly involved in them, you could pretend they weren't there. Even if you were directly involved, pretending not to see was one way of preserving in your own mind your sense of personal decency. Very few *Wehrmacht* officers admitted to knowing what the SS had done to Jews in Poland and Russia; Jäger hadn't admitted it to himself until a Russian Jew rubbed his nose in it.

Diebner said, 'If we do not recover the nuclear material, Colonel Jäger, we are all the more likely to lose the war against the Lizards, at which point all ethical arguments become irrelevant. Whatever we must do to get it back, we have to have it.'

Jäger turned his back and walked several paces along the parapet. Arguments from military necessity were hard to refute, and losing the war against the Lizards would be disastrous not just for Germany but for mankind as a whole. And yet – Jäger took the physicist by the arm. 'When you say these things, Professor, you should know firsthand whereof you speak. Come along with me.'

Diebner was not a small man, nor a weak one. He hung back, protesting,

'This is not my concern; it is why we had you brought here. My business is with the nuclear pile itself.'

Though a couple of centimeters shorter than the nuclear physicist, Jäger was wider through the shoulders and better trained at wrestling. Not only that, his will burned hotter. He frog-marched the reluctant Diebner off the wall and down into the bowels of Schloss Hohentübingen.

The castle's cellar was a different world from the light and fresh air of the wall. It was dank and gloomy; somewhere out of sight, water dripped continuously. A startled bat dropped from the roof and flew chittering between Jäger and Diebner. The physicist jumped back with a startled oath. Jäger wasn't dragging him along any more, but he followed nonetheless; officers learned ways to get themselves obeyed.

In happier times, the cellar had contained a monster wine cask that held 300,000 liters of Burgundy. The cask was gone now, probably chopped into firewood. In its place were the miserable cots of the prisoners who got the uranium out of the pile at Hechingen.

'Faugh!' Diebner said, a noise of disgust.

Jäger wrinkled his nose, too; the cellar stank, not least because the only sanitary arrangements were some buckets off in a corner. Not everything went into the buckets, either. Jäger said, 'One of the symptoms these people seem to have is diarrhea.'

'Yes, I knew of this in principle,' Diebner said in a small voice that suggested he was much more used to dealing with abstract principles than this reeking reality.

'Ah.' Jäger clicked his heels in exquisite irony. 'Are you also aware – in principle, of course – of the other symptoms this work brings with it?'

'Which ones do you mean?' the physicist asked. 'The burns from actually handling the metal, the loss of hair, the bleeding gums and nausea? I am familiar with these, yes, and also with the cancer that is likely to result some years from now as a result of this exposure. I know these things, Colonel.'

'You know of them,' Jäger said coldly. 'Here – see what they do to real people who are not just abstracted principles.'

A man with a pink triangle on the front of his striped shirt was spooning cabbage soup into the mouth of a Jew who lay on a straw pallet, too sick to get up. When the Jew retched and coughed up the soup, the homosexual held his head so he would not foul himself too badly, then got a rag and put it on the patch of vomit. Then he started trying to feed the Jew again.

'It doesn't have to be like this,' Jaeger insisted. 'Maybe we do have to use condemned people, as you call them, for this work, but we don't have to make their lot worse by treating them like beasts of burden.'

Diebner nodded to the several wooden platforms that had been built around the edges of the cellar – incongruously, they reminded Jäger of the lifeguards' stands by a lakeshore or along a popular stretch of riverbank. Each held, not a lifeguard in white tank top and colorful trunks, but a uniformed, helmeted guard who cradled a submachine gun. Quietly, the physicist said, 'Without coercion, this work would not be done – and it *must* be done. For that matter, neither the guards nor we are entirely safe.'

Jäger looked at him sharply. 'How do you mean?'

'How do you think, Colonel?' Diebner answered. 'We, too – and the guards – are exposed to these radioactive materials, at lower levels than the prisoners, yes, but certainly exposed. What the long-term consequences of this may be, I cannot say with certainty, but I doubt they will be good. We have lined the roof of this cellar with lead to keep the Lizards from detecting the radioactivity gathered here; that we are close to Hechingen will help account for a higher level than might otherwise be expected, and gives us some added security.'

'I – see,' Jäger said. He rubbed his chin, remembering the raid in which he, along with Russians and other Germans, had stolen explosive metal from the Lizards, and remembering riding across Poland with the German share of the explosive metal showed in lead-lined saddle bags. He wondered what he'd done to himself in the service of the *Reich*.

The classically trained part of him thought of Prometheus, who'd stolen fire from the gods and brought it down to mankind. Zeus had chained Prometheus to a rock, with a vulture gnawing at his liver. The gods weren't much in the habit of manifesting themselves these days, but Jäger wondered what might be gnawing at his own entrails.

Despairingly, Teerts turned his eye turrets toward the heavens. Those heavens remained empty, silent. If they remained so much longer, he would either starve or be recaptured – or use the one shot he was sure he could fire from his Nipponese rifle.

He counted himself lucky not to have been recaptured already. So much of the train on which he'd been riding had gone up in flames. However savage and backward they were, though, the Big Uglies were not stupid enough to take his demise for granted. A search would be mounted. Teerts was gloomily certain of that.

A little stream trickled by the stand of brush where he was holed up; at night he could come out to drink. He'd caught a couple of crawling and scurrying things and eaten them raw, but hunger gained on him regardless. He did his best to remember how used to hunger he'd got while the Nipponese were mistreating him, but it wasn't easy. He hungered for ginger, too, all the way down to the depths of his spirit.

Every once in a while, when he saw no Tosevites around, he emerged from the shrubbery during daylight, to show himself for aircraft or satellites that might be passing overhead. If they'd spotted him, they'd certainly given no sign of it.

Now he lay curled up in a nest he'd made of branches and twigs and dry leaves. It was the sort of thing in which an animal might live, not a male of the Race. The Nipponese had done their best

to make him into an animal, and failed. Now he was doing it
himself.

A noise in the sky – Teerts' head came up, but only for a moment.
Some of the flying creatures of Tostev 3 were noisy as they made their
way through the air. His hearing diaphragms stretched tight with hope
he'd mistaken their wingbeats for the thutter of a rescue helicopter again
and again. He couldn't fool himself any more.

But this sound swelled and swelled. Teerts jumped to his feet, crying
the Emperor's name. From above, in a voice like thunder, came a call
in his own language: 'Male of the Race, show yourself! This is hostile
airspace; we cannot stay long!' The accent was pure and clean – that of
Home. Teerts had been listening to the mushy, barking way the Nipponese
mangled his speech for so long, he needed a moment to recognize this was
how it should be spoken.

He sprang from cover, waved his arms frantically, and did everything
but turn backflips in the wild effort to make himself as visible as he could.
His swiveling eyes caught sight of the helicopter – and one of the crewmales
saw him, too, and the big, ungainly, ever so beautiful machine swung in his
direction. Its rotor kicked up gravel and dust; nicitating membranes slid
across his eyes to protect them from flying grit.

The helicopter hovered, its landing wheels not quite touching the ground.
Its side door came open; a male inside let down a chain-link ladder. Teerts
was already running toward the copter. He scrambled aboard. 'We've got
him!' the male shouted to the pilot and weapons officer in their cockpit
forward.

The fellow hauled in the ladder, slammed and dogged the door. The
helicopter was already gaining altitude and scurrying out toward the sea.
'Thank you!' Teerts gasped. 'The Emperor grant you bounty. You don't
know—'

'Don't thank me yet,' the crewmale answered. He hurried to a machine
gun that stuck out one of the windows. 'We're a long way from safe. We've
got a killercraft overhead, but if the Big Uglies send enough aircraft after
us, they're liable to catch up with us and shoot us down. They're a lot
faster than we are.' He turned one eye back toward Teerts. 'Who are you
anyway?'

'Teerts, killercraft pilot and fight leader,' Teerts answered. Stating his
specialization and rank made him consciously aware for the first time in
a very long while that he was without his body paint.

That didn't seem to bother his rescuer, who said, 'Good. You know how
to handle one of these things, then.' He patted the machine gun. 'In case I
get hit, keep shooting till we go into the water.'

'It shall be done, superior sir,' Teerts said. Actually, he outranked the
male at the gun, but he was not part of the helicopter crew – and, after so
long in Nipponese captivity, he was used to attaching honorifics to anyone
with whom he spoke. As the land of Nippon receded behind them, his wits

began to work again. 'You couldn't have flown straight here from any land the Race controls: you must have used in-flight refueling.'

'That's right,' the crewmale said. 'We're on our way out for more hydrogen now, too. That should be enough to take us back to base.' He paused, listening to the microphone fastened to one hearing diaphragm. 'Pilot says our killercraft cover just shot down three of the Big Uglies' aircraft and the rest have broken off pursuit. Now I really start to think we're going to be all right.'

'Emperor be praised,' Teerts said, dropping his eye turrets to the grimy mats on the floor of the helicopter. When he raised them again, he asked, 'How is the conquest faring? I've been away from our kind for what has to be more than a year.'

'Between you, me, and this gun here, not so well,' the crewmale answered. 'We were driving the Russkis hard, and then they somehow exploded an atomic bomb and made us stop there. These Big Uglies are a thousand times worse than we expected when we got to this stinking planet.'

'You don't know the half of it,' Teerts said feelingly. 'The Nipponese told me about – gloated about – the Russkis' atomic bomb. I was afraid they were telling the truth, but I wasn't sure.' He suddenly sat bolt upright on the hard, uncomfortable seat. 'They're working on their own nuclear project, too. They spent endless time interrogating me about atomic energy. They got everything out of me, too. That's how I managed to escape: they were taking me somewhere else so they could ask me about different things.'

'We'll send *that* news upstairs, by the Emperor,' the crewmale exclaimed, lowering his eyes as Teerts had. 'And after that, unless I miss my guess, we'll have a present for these Big Uglies. You can show us where this work was being done?'

'The city was Tokyo,' Teerts answered. 'Where in the city—'

'—Likely won't matter,' the crewmale finished for him.

Teerts shivered. The male was probably right: the Nipponese would discover firsthand what nuclear weapons were like. They were only Big Uglies, and vicious ones to boot, but did they deserve that? Whether they did or not, he would have bet they were going to get it.

No point in arguing about that; the decision would come from levels far higher in the hierarchy than himself or the crewmale. He said, 'Do you have any food here? The Nipponese didn't give me a lot to eat.'

The crewmale unsnapped a pouch on the side of the helicopter wall, pulled out a couple of ration packs, and tossed them to Teerts. They were unheated and inherently unexciting: just fuel for the body to keep a male going until he had a chance to stop and rest and eat something better. Teerts thought he'd never eaten anything so wonderful in his life.

'After so long without the tastes of home, this may be the best meal I ever had,' he said ecstatically. His tongue cleansed the hard outer surfaces of his mouth. Every crumb it encountered brought him fresh delight.

'I've heard others we rescued say the same thing,' the crewmale

answered. 'That may be true for them, but I just can't see it.' He let
his mouth fall open to show he didn't expect to be taken altogether
seriously.

Teerts laughed, too; he remembered the rude jokes he and the rest
of his flight had made about ration packs in the days before he'd been
captured. He also remembered something else, remembered it with a
physical longing more intense than anything he'd ever known outside
of mating season. Hesitantly, he said, 'The Nipponese fed me a Tosevite
herb. They made me depend on it; my body craves it still. I don't know
what I'll do without it.'

To his surprise, the crewmale laughed again. He rummaged in a pouch
he wore on one of his belts, pulled out a tiny plastic vial, and offered
it to Teerts. 'Who says you have to do without it, friend? Here, have a
taste on me.'

Liu Han grunted as the labor pain washed over her. 'Oh, that is a good
one!' Ho Ma, the midwife, said enthusiastically. She'd been saying that for
a long time now. She went on, 'Soon the baby will come, and then you will
be happy.' She'd been saying that for a long time, too, which only proved
she didn't know Liu Han very well.

Several midwives had set up shop in the prison camp. Liu Han recognized
the red-tasseled signs they set up outside their huts, and knew what the
characters on those signs said even if she could not read them: 'light cart
and speedy horse' on one side and 'auspicious grandmother-in-law' on the
other. The midwife who'd worked in her now-wrecked village had had just
the same sign.

Ttomalss said, 'Move aside, please, female Ho Ma, so the camera can
see as it should.'

The midwife grumbled under her breath but moved aside. The little
scaly devils were paying her extravagantly in silver and food and even,
she'd boasted to Liu Han, in tobacco they'd got from who could say where.
They had to pay her extravagantly to ignore the bright lights they'd put
into Liu Han's hut, to ignore their presence and that of their cameras,
and to ignore the way that, contrary to all custom and decency, they'd
insisted on Liu Han's being naked through the entire delivery so those
cameras could do their work as the little scaly devils thought proper.

To the scaly devils' payment, Liu Han had added several dollars
Mex from her own pocket to persuade Ho Ma not to gossip about the
humiliations she would witness. The midwife had agreed at once – for
money, a midwife would agree to almost anything. Whether she would
keep her promise afterward was a different question.

Another contraction shook Liu Han. Ho Ma peered between her legs. 'I
can see the top of the baby's head,' she said. 'Lots of nice black hair . . .
but then, the father had proper black hair even if he was a foreign devil,
didn't he?'

'Yes,' Liu Han said wearily. Bobby Fiore's being the baby's father would just add to the scandal of this already extremely irregular delivery. Liu Han feared she could never bribe Ho Ma enough to be sure of keeping her quiet.

Then her body made its own demands, and she stopped worrying about what Ho Ma would say. The urge to push the baby out of her became overwhelming. She held her breath and bore down with all her might. A squealing grunt told of her effort.

'Again!' Ho Ma exclaimed when Liu Han had to stop because, like a punctured pig's bladder, she had no more air left in her. Liu Han needed no urging. She panted for a moment, gathering her strength, took a deep breath and held it, and pushed once more. The urgency seemed unbearable, as if she were passing night soil at last after months of complete constipation.

'Once more!' Ho Ma said, reaching down to help guide the baby out. A couple of the little scaly devils with their accussed cameras shifted so they could still see what they wanted to see. Caught up in her body's travail, Liu Han barely noticed them.

'Here, I have the head,' the midwife said. 'A pretty baby, considering who its father was – not big-nosed at all. One more push, now, and I'll bring the baby out of you.' Liu Han pushed. Now that the head had emerged, the rest was easy. A moment later, Ho Ma said, 'A girl baby.' Liu Han knew she should have been disappointed, but she was too worn to care.

A couple more pushes brought out the afterbirth, looking like a great bloody chunk of raw liver. One of the little scaly devils set down his camera and ran out of the hut, slamming the door behind him.

Ho Ma tied off the umbilical cord with two pieces of silk thread. Then she cut the cord with a pair of shears. She pinched the baby's feet. After a moment, it began to squall like an angry kitten. The midwife thrust an iron poker into the flames of the fireplace, then touched the hot tip of it to the end of the umbilical stump.

'Do you do that to kill the little invisible demons – not the word I want, but as close as your language has – that cause sickness?' Ttomalss asked.

'I do that because it is the custom to do that,' Ho Ma answered, rolling her eyes at the foolish questions the scaly devils asked. She wrapped the afterbirth in a cloth to take it away and bury it in some out-of-the-way place.

Liu Han had long since resigned herself to the little devils' ignorant and presumptuous questions. 'Give me the baby, please,' she said. Just talking was an enormous effort. She remembered that crushing weariness from the son she'd borne to her husband not long before a Japanese attack killed him and the boy.

Ho Ma handed her the child: as she'd said, a girl, her private parts swollen as newborns' often were. Liu Han set the baby to her breast. The tiny mouth rooted, found the nipple, and began to suck. Liu Han turned to Ttomalss and said, 'Have you seen everything you need? May I put my clothes on again?' She wanted to put some rags between her legs; she knew she would pass blood and other discharge there for weeks to come.

The little scaly devil did not answer, not directly. Instead, he asked another question: 'Why do you not clean off the hatchling, which is still covered with these disgusting substances from inside your body?'

Liu Han and Ho Ma exchanged glances. How stupid scaly devils were! The midwife answered, 'The baby is still too new to the world to bathe. On the third day after it is born, it will be more solid. We will wash it then.'

Ttomalss spoke to one of his machines in his own language. The machine answered back. Liu Han had seen that too often to be amazed by it any more. The scaly devil switched to Chinese and said, 'My information is that other groups of Big Uglies do not do this.'

'Who cares what foreign devils do?' Ho Ma said scornfully. Liu Han nodded. Surely Chinese ways were best. Cradling the baby in one arm, she sat up, ever so slowly and carefully – she felt as if she'd aged about fifty years this past half-day – and reached for her tunic and trousers. When Ttomalss did not object, she set the baby down for a moment and got dressed, then picked up the child again, set it to her shoulder, and patted it on the back till it belched out the air it had sucked in with her milk.

Ho Ma gave her some tea, a single hard-boiled egg (had she had a son she would have got five), round sugar cakes of fermented dough, and little sponge cakes shaped like fans, pomegranates, and ingots of silver. She devoured the traditional food, for she'd eaten nothing and drunk only a glass of hot sugar water with a dried shrimp in it – she hadn't eaten the shrimp – since her labor began. She was stuffed when she was through, but felt she could have eaten twice as much.

One of the little scaly devils holding a camera spoke to Ttomalss in their language: 'Superior sir, that was one of the most revolting processes I have ever had the misfortune to observe.'

'I thank you for maintaining your position,' Ttomalss answered. 'We may have lost valuable information when Dvench fled this hut; he failed in his duty to the Race.'

'You are generous in your praise, superior sir,' the other scaly devil said. 'Shall we now proceed with the experiment?'

Liu Han had listened to their hisses and squeaks with half an ear; not only was she exhausted from childbirth and distracted by her newborn daughter, but she also had only a halting command of the scaly devils' tongue. But the word 'experiment' made her start paying close attention, though she tried not to show it; she'd been part of the little devils' experiments ever since they first appeared. They had their purposes, which emphatically were *not* hers.

Ttomalss said, 'No, the matter is not yet urgent. Let the Chinese carry on with their ceremonies. These may conceivably produce an increased survival rate for infants: more Tosevites appear to be of this Chinese variety than any other.'

'It shall be as you say, superior sir,' the other little devil said. 'My opinion is that it's surprising the Big Uglies retain their numbers, let alone increase them, with this system of reproduction. Passing an egg is far simpler and less dangerous and harrowing to the female involved than this gorefilled procedure.'

'There we agree, Msseff,' Ttomalss said. 'That is why we must learn to understand how and why the Tosevites do in fact increase. Perhaps the risks inherent in their reproductive processes help explain their year-round sexual activity. This is another connection we are still exploring.'

Liu Han stopped listening. Whatever their latest experiment was, they weren't going to tell her any more about it now. Ho Ma took up the cloth with the afterbirth and carried it away. Even Ttomalss and the other scaly devils got out of the hut, leaving Liu Han alone with the baby.

She set the sleeping little girl in the scrapwood cradle she'd readied. As Ho Ma had said, it did look like a proper Chinese baby, for which she was glad. If she ever escaped the camp, she could raise it properly, too, with no awkward questions to answer.

If she ever escaped the camp – her laugh rang bitter. What chance of that, with or without the baby? Then all thought, no matter how bitter, dissolved in an enormous yawn. Liu Han lay down on top of the *k'ang* – the raised, heated platform in the middle of the hut – and fell deeply asleep. The baby woke her a few minutes later. She had groggy memories of her first child doing that, too.

The next two days passed in a blur of fatigue. Ho Ma came back with food, and the little scaly devils with their cameras. Then on the third day the midwife brought incense, paper images of the gods and paper goods to sacrifice to them, and a basin to be filled with water and a spicy mixture of ground locust branch and catnip leaves.

Ho Ma prayed to the family kitchen god, the goddess of smallpox, the goddess of playmates, the goddess of breast milk, the six minor household gods, the god of heaven and the god of earth, and the god and goddess of the bed, and burned offerings to each. She set out round cakes in a row before their images.

Msseff said to Ttomalss, 'Superior sir, if all this is necessary for survival, then I am addled egg.' Ttomalss' mouth fell open.

The midwife bathed the baby, dried her, and sprinkled alum on her here and there. Then she laid the child on her back and set slices of ginger by the blackened stump of the umbilical cord. She put a little smoldering ball of catnip leaves on the ginger, and another at the baby's head. A couple of the scaly devils let out hisses of longing for the ginger. Ttomalss took no notice of those, perhaps not recognizing what they signified.

Other ritual objects made their appearance: the small weight that portended a big future, the padlock to ward off impropriety, the tap of the onion punningly used to impart wisdom (both were pronounced *ts'ung*), and the comb for the child's hair. The onion would be tossed on the roof of the hut, to predict the sex of Liu Han's next child by the way it landed.

Ho Ma extinguished the burning balls of catnip and lit the paper images of the gods, who, having done their duty, were thus urged to depart the scene. The hut filled with smoke. Coughing a little, the midwife took her leave. The onion thumped up onto the roof. 'The root points to the eaves,' Ho Ma called. 'Your next baby will be a boy.'

Liu Han couldn't remember what the onion had foretold after the birth of her first child. She wondered how many fortune-tellers made a good living by counting on their bad predictions being forgotten. A lot of them, she suspected, but how could you tell which ones till after the fact?

As if Ho Ma's leaving the hut had been a signal, several little scaly devils came in. They were not carrying cameras; they were carrying guns. Alarm flared in Liu Han. She snatched up the baby and held it tight.

Ttomalss said, 'That will do you no good. We now go to the next step of the experiment – we of the Race will raise this hatchling apart from you Tosevites, to learn how well it can acquire duty and obedience.' He turned to the males and spoke in his own language: 'Take the hatchling.'

Liu Han screamed and fought with all she had in her. It did no good. Individually, the scaly devils were little, but several of them together were much stronger than she. The threat of their guns drove back the people who came out to see why she was screaming. Even the sight of a wailing infant in their arms was not enough to make men brave those terrible guns.

Liu Han lay on the ground in the hut and moaned. Then, slowly, she rose and made her painful way through the staring, chattering people and into the marketplace. Eventually, she came to the stall of the poultry seller. The little scaly devils might think they were through with her, but she was not through with them.

Half past two in the morning. Vyacheslav Molotov wished he were home and asleep in bed. Stalin, however, had not asked his opinion, merely summoned him. Stalin was not in the habit of asking anyone's opinion. He expected to be obeyed. If he kept late hours, everyone else would, too.

The doorman nodded politely to Molotov, who nodded back. Normally he would have ignored such a flunky, but the doorman, a longtime crony of Stalin's, knew as many secrets as half the members of the Politburo – and he had his master's ear. Slighting him was dangerous.

Stalin was writing at his desk when Molotov came in. Molotov wondered if he'd become dominant simply because he needed less sleep than most men. No doubt that wasn't the whole answer, but it must have played its part.

'Take some tea, Vyacheslav Mikhailovich,' Stalin said, pointing to a samovar in a corner of the cramped room. 'Thank you, Iosef Vissarionovich,' Molotov answered. When Stalin told you to take tea, you took tea, even if it was the vile mix that passed for the genuine article these days – much worse than the coarse *makhorka* everyone, even Stalin, had to smoke. Molotov poured a glassful, sugared it – as long as the Soviet Union had beets, it would have sugar – and drank. He had to work to keep from betraying surprise. 'This is – excellent.'

'The real leaf,' Stalin said smugly. 'Brought in from India, thanks to the lull in the fighting with the Lizards after we showed we could match them bomb for bomb.' *So there*, his eyes added. He'd gone against Molotov's advice and not only got away with it but prospered. Not only was that bad in itself, it meant he would pay less attention to Molotov the next time.

The Foreign Commissar sipped his tea, savoring its warmth and its rich flavor. When he was through, he set the glass down with real regret. 'What do you need, Iosef Vissarionovich?' he asked.

'The lull is slowly dying away,' Stalin answered. 'The Lizards begin to suspect we have no more bombs than that first one.' He sounded as if that were Molotov's fault.

'As I have noted, Comrade General Secretary, they are aware we used their metal to produce that bomb,' Molotov said cautiously; telling Stalin *I told you so* was as dangerous as defusing any other pyrotechnic device. Molotov tried to put the best face on it he could: 'They cannot know, however, whether we have enough of that metal to use it for more bombs.'

'We should,' Stalin said. 'Sharing with the Germans was a mistake.' His mouth twisted in annoyance at the irrevocability of the past. '*Nichevo*.' Try as he might, Stalin could not utter *It can't be helped* with the fatalism a native Russian put in the word. His throaty Georgian accent gave it a flavor of *But someone ought to be able to do something about it*.

Molotov said, 'Creating the impression that we *do* have more bombs available will be a cornerstone of our policy against the Lizards for some time to come. They suspect our weakness now. If they become certain of it, the strategic situation reverts to what it was before we used the bomb, and that was not altogether to our advantage.'

He stood up and got himself another glass of tea, both because he hadn't any real tea in a long time and because he was all too aware of how large an understatement he'd just loosed. If the Soviet Union hadn't set off that bomb, the Lizards surely would have been in Moscow by now. If Stalin and he had escaped the fall of the city, they'd be trying to run the country from Kuibyshev, in the heart of the Urals. Would the workers and peasants – more to the point, would the soldiers – of the Soviet Union have continued to obey orders from a defeated government that had had to abandon the national capital?

Maybe. Neither Molotov nor Stalin had been anxious to attempt the experiment.

Stalin said, 'Kurchatov and his team must accelerate their efforts.'

'Yes, Comrade General Secretary,' Molotov said dutifully. Igor Kurchatov, Georgi Flerov, and the rest of the Soviet nuclear physicists were doing everything they could to isolate uranium 235 and to produce the equally explosive element 94. Unfortunately, before the war nuclear physics in the Soviet Union had lagged several years behind its course in the capitalist and fascist nations. The mere search for abstract knowledge had not seemed vitally urgent then. Now it did, but with their limited expertise and limited cadre, the physicists were still years away from producing homegrown nuclear material.

'The fascists in Germany are not idle,' Stalin said. 'In spite of their setback, espionage confirms that their explosive metal project goes forward. I believe the same is true in the United States and Britain, though communications with them both are not everything we might wish.' He slammed a fist down on the top of the desk. 'And the Japanese – who knows what the Japanese are doing? I don't trust them. I never trust them.'

The only man Stalin had ever trusted was Hitler, and that trust almost destroyed the Soviet Union. But here Molotov agreed with him. He said, 'If Zhukov hadn't treated them roughly in Mongolia in '39, they would have joined with the Nazis two years later, and that might have been very difficult for us.'

It would have been altogether disastrous, but Molotov didn't have the nerve to tell that to Stalin. No one had the nerve to tell Stalin such things. The Moskva Hotel had two wings that spectacularly didn't match. The architects had chosen to show Stalin their plans, expecting him to pick one design or the other. He'd just nodded and said, 'Yes, do it that way,' and no one dared do anything else.

The doorman tapped on the door. Stalin and Molotov looked at each other in surprise; they weren't supposed to be interrupted. Then the doorman did something even more surprising: he stuck his head in and said, 'Iosef Vissarionovich, the officer here bears an urgent message. May he deliver it?'

After a moment, Stalin said, '*Da*,' with clear overtones of *It had better be*.

The officer wore the three red squares of a senior lieutenant and the green backing on his collar tabs that meant he was from the NKVD. Saluting, he said, 'Comrade General Secretary, Lizard propaganda broadcasts report – and Japanese radio confirms – that the Lizards have detonated an explosive-metal bomb over Tokyo. They say this was because the Japanese were engaged in nuclear research there. Casualties are said to be very heavy.'

Molotov waited to see how Stalin would react, intending to match his own response to his leader's. Stalin said, 'The Germans were inept, and blew themselves up. The Japanese were careless, and let the Lizards get wind of what they were about. We can afford neither mistake. We already knew that, but now we are, mm, strongly reminded once more.'

'Truth, Comrade General Secretary,' Molotov said. Stalin did have an eye for the essential. Not for nothing had he dominated the Soviet Union these past twenty years. Molotov wondered where – or if – the USSR would be in another twenty.

5

The engineer in the room next to the broadcast studio gave the *you're on* signal through the large window the two rooms shared. Nodding, Moishe Russie began reading from his Yiddish script: 'Good day. This is Moishe Russie, coming to you by way of the BBC's Overseas Service. Another great world capital has fallen to the malice of the Lizards.'

He sighed. The sigh was part of the script, but also heartfelt. 'When the Lizards destroyed Berlin last year, I confess that I was not altogether broken-hearted. The Germans had done dreadful things to the Jews under their control. I thought the Lizards, who helped the Jews of Poland escape the Nazi yoke, were our benefactors.

'I was wrong. The Lizards used us, too. They were willing to let us live, yes, but only as their slaves. And that holds not just for us but also for all mankind. When the Lizards destroyed Washington, they made that plain for anyone with eyes to see. When they destroyed Washington, they showed they were fighting freedom.

'And now Tokyo. The Lizards no longer even try to pretend. They come straight out and tell us they dropped one of their hellish bombs on it because the Japanese were seeking to build weapons there that could meet them on even terms. That some hundreds of thousands of human beings, most of them civilians, died in the bombing is to the Lizards of no consequence.

'Mankind has employed one of these bombs, against a purely military target. The Lizards have now incinerated three historic cities, seeking to terrify humanity into surrender. London, from which I am broadcasting, has already been bombarded by both Hitler and the Lizards, yet still endures. Even if, in their madness, the Lizards treat it as they did Tokyo, the British Isles and the British Empire will continue not only to endure but also to *resist*. We hope and expect that all of you who are unfortunate enough to live in territory overrun by the aliens, yet can hear my voice, will continue to resist, too. In the end, we shall prevail.'

He came to the end of the script just as the engineer drew a finger across his throat. Beaming at the good timing, Nathan Jacobi took over, in English rather than Yiddish: 'I shall translate Moishe Russie's remarks in a moment. First, though, I should like to note that no one is better qualified to judge the perfidy in the Lizards' promises than Mr Russie, for he watched them turn what he'd thought to be liberation into the enslavement and wholesale murder they bring to the entire world. As he said ...'

Moishe listened to the introduction with half an ear. He was picking up more English day by day, but remained far from fluent: by the time he'd figured out what most of one sentence meant, two others would have gone by.

Jacobi went through an English version of Russie's speech for Eastern European listeners who had no Yiddish. Since Moishe already knew what he'd said, he did better at following that than he had with the introduction. When the engineer signaled that they were off the air, he leaned back in his chair and let out a long sigh.

Switching from English to Yiddish for Moishe's benefit, the newsreader said, 'I do wonder at times whether any of this does the least bit of good.'

'It does,' Moishe assured him. 'When the Lizards had me locked up in Lodz, it wasn't just my English cousin who helped me get out, but plenty of Jewish fighters from Poland. They need encouragement, and to be reminded they're not the only people left in the whole world who want to stand up to the Lizards.'

'No doubt you're right,' Jacobi said. 'You would know better than I, having been on the spot. I just seem to have spent almost all of the last four years broadcasting messages of hope into occupied Europe – first Nazi-occupied Europe, now Lizard-occupied Europe – with what looks like very little return for the effort. I do want to feel I'm actually contributing to the war effort.'

'The Lizards don't like truth any better than the Germans did,' Russie answered. 'Next to what the Nazis were doing in Poland, they looked good for a moment, but that was all. They may not be out to exterminate anyone, but they are aiming to enslave everyone all over the world, and the more people realize that, the harder they'll fight back.'

'All over the world,' Jacobi repeated. 'That takes thinking about. We called it a world war before the Lizards came, but the Americans, Africa, India, much of the Near East – they were hardly touched. Now the whole world really is in play. Rather hard to imagine.'

Moishe nodded. It was harder for him than for the British Jew. Jacobi had grown up in London, the center of the greatest empire the world had ever known and also closely linked to the United States. Thinking of the world as a whole had to come easy for him. Moishe's mental horizons hadn't really reached beyond Poland – indeed, seldom beyond Warsaw – until the day von Ribbentrop and Molotov signed the Nazi-Soviet friendship pact and guaranteed that war would not only come but would be disastrous when it came.

Through the glass, the engineer motioned Russie and Jacobi out of the studio. They got up quickly; another broadcaster or team would soon be taking over the facility.

Sure enough, out in the hall stood a tall, skinny, craggy-faced man with a thick shock of dark hair just beginning to go gray. He was looking at his wristwatch and holding a sheaf of typewritten pages like the ones Jacobi carried. 'Good morning, Mr Blair,' Russie said, trotting out his halting English.

'Good morning, Russie,' Eric Blair answered. He slid off his dark herringbone jacket. 'Warm work closed up in the coffin there. I'd sooner be in my shirtsleeves.'

'Yes, warm,' Moishe said, responding to the part he'd understood. Blair broadcast for the Indian Section of the BBC. He'd lived in Burma for a time, and had also fought and been badly wounded fighting on the Republican side in the Spanish Civil War. Somewhere there, or perhaps back in England, he'd picked up a wet cough that was probably tubercular.

He pulled out a handkerchief to stifle it, then said, 'Excuse me, gentlemen, I'm going to take some tea to get the scaling out of the pipes.'

'He's astonishing,' Jacobi murmured in Yiddish as Blair walked away. 'I've known him to bring up bloody phlegm after a broadcast, but you'd never imagine anything was the matter if you listened to him over the air.'

Blair returned in a moment with a thick, white china cup. He gulped down the not-quite-tea, made a wry face, and hurried into the studio. No sooner had he gone inside than the air-raid sirens began to wail. Russie blinked in surprise; he heard no Lizard jets screaming overhead. 'Shall we go down to the shelter in the cellar?' he asked.

To his surprise, Jacobi said, 'No. Wait – listen.'

Moishe obediently listened. Along with the howling sirens came another sound – a brazen clangor he needed a moment to identify. 'Why are the church bells ringing?' he asked. 'They've never done that before.'

'In 1940, that was going to be a signal,' Jacobi answered. 'Thank God, it was one we never had to use.'

'What do you mean?' Russie asked. 'What was it for?'

'After the *Luftwaffe* began to bomb us, they silenced all the bells,' Jacobi said. 'If they ever started ringing again, it meant – invasion.'

The church bells rang and rang and rang, a wild carillon that raised the hair of Moishe's arms and at the back of his neck. 'The Germans aren't going to invade now,' he said. However much it grated on him, relations between England and German-occupied northern France and the Low Countries had been correct, even sometimes approaching cordial, since the Lizards landed. The Lizards – '*Oy!*'

'*Oy!* is right,' Jacobi agreed. He cocked his head to one side, listening to the bells and the sirens. 'I don't hear any Lizard airplanes, and I don't hear any antiaircraft guns, either. If they are invading, they aren't coming down on London.'

'Where are they, then?' Moishe asked, as if the newsreader had some way of learning that to which he himself was not allowed access.

'How should I know?' Jacobi answered testily. Then he answered his own question: 'We're in a BBC studio. If we can't find out here, where can we?'

Russie thumped his forehead with the heel of his hand, feeling very foolish. 'Next thing I'll do, I'll ask a librarian where to find books.' He hesitated again; he still didn't know the overall layout of the BBC Overseas Section all that well, being primarily concerned with his own broadcasting duties.

Jacobi saw his confusion. 'Come on; we'll go to the news monitoring service. They'll know as much as anyone does.'

A row of wireless sets sat on several tables placed side by side. The resultant dinning mix of languages and occasional squeals and bursts of static would swiftly have driven any unprepared person mad. The mostly female monitors, though, wore earphones, so each one of them gave heed only to her assigned transmission.

One phrase came through the Babel again and again: 'They're here.' A woman took off her earphones and got up from her set for a moment, probably for a trip to the loo. She nodded to Jacobi, whom she obviously knew. 'I can guess why you're hanging about here, dearie,' she said. 'The buggers have gone and done it. Parachutists and I don't know what all else in the south, and up in the Midlands, too. That's about all anyone knows right now.'

'Thank you, Norma,' the newsreader said. 'That's more than we knew before.' He translated it for Moishe Russie, who had understood some of it but not all.

'The south and the Midlands?' Russie said, visualizing a map. 'That doesn't sound good. It sounds as if—'

'—They're heading for London from north and south both,' Jacobi interrupted. He looked seriously at Moishe. 'I don't know how much longer we'll be broadcasting here. For one thing, God may know how they'll supply a city of seven million with invaders on both sides of it, but I don't.'

'I've been hungry before,' Moishe said. The Germans had had no logistic problem in keeping the Jews of the Warsaw ghetto fed; they simply hadn't bothered.

'I know that,' Jacobi answered. 'But there's something else, too. We would have fought the Germans with every man we had. I don't expect Churchill will do anything less against the Lizards. Before long, they'll come for us, put rifles in our hands, give us as many bullets as they happen to have for them, and send us up to the front line.'

That had the ring of truth to it. It was what Russie would have done had he been running the country. All the same, he shook his head. 'To you, they'll give a rifle. To me, they'll give a medical bag, probably with rags for bandages and not much else.' He surprised himself by laughing.

'What's funny?' Jacobi asked.

'I don't know if it's funny or just *meshuggeh*,' Moishe said, 'but here I'll be a Jew going to war with a red cross on my arm.'

'I don't know which, either,' Jacobi said, 'but you haven't gone to war. The war's come to you.'

Ussmak was afraid. The lumbering transport in which his landcruiser rode was big and powerful enough to haul two of the heavy machines at a time, but it wasn't much faster than the killercraft the Big Uglies flew. Killercraft of the Race were supposed to be flying cover missions and making sure no Tosevite aircraft got through, but Ussmak had seen enough war on Tosev 3 to know that the Race's neat, carefully developed plans often turned to chaos and disaster when they ran up against real, live perfidious Big Uglies.

He wondered if this plan had turned to chaos and disaster even before it ran up against the Big Uglies. Into the intercom microphone, he said, 'I don't see why we were ordered away from fighting the Deutsche just when we'd finally starting making good progress against them.'

'We are males of the Race,' Nejas replied. 'The duty of our superiors is to prepare the plans. Our duty is to carry them out, and that shall be done.'

Ussmak liked Nejas. More to the point, he knew Nejas was a good landcruiser commander. Somehow, though, Nejas had managed to come through all the hard fighting he'd seen with his confidence in the wisdom of his superiors unimpaired. Not even when Ussmak was happy almost to the point of imbecility with three quick tastes of ginger could he sound so certain everything would be all right. And Nejas didn't even taste.

Neither did Skoob, the gunner. He and Nejas had been together ever since the conquest fleet touched down on Tosev 3, and he was every bit as enamored of the straight and narrow as his commander. Now, though, he said, 'Superior sir, I believe the driver has a point. Dividing and shifting effort in combat creates risks, some of which may be serious. While we and our equipment are transferred to attack the British, we grant the Deutsche time to recover, even to counterattack.'

'The Deutsche are staggering, ready to fall on the tailstumps they don't have,' Nejas insisted. 'The British have seen little of the war till now. Their miserable little island has been a base for endless mischief against us. Because it is an island, we can conquer it completely, remove this threat, and then resume our campaign against the Deutsche secure in the knowledge that Britain can no longer threaten our rear.'

He sounded like the dapper officers who had briefed the landcruiser units as they pulled them out of line against the Deutsche. Those officers had exuded wholesome confidence, too, so much confidence that Ussmak was certain they'd never led males in combat against the Big Uglies.

He said, 'I don't think military needs have all that much to do with it, or not in the usual way. I think more of it comes down to politics.'

'How do you mean, driver?' Nejas asked. The interrogative cough with which he punctuated his question was so loud and explosive, Ussmak knew he didn't follow that all: a good commander, yes, but a natural-hatched innocent.

'Superior sir, when Straha fled to the Big Uglies, the Emperor only knows how many of our plans he took with him. They probably know just what we intend to try for the next two years. To keep them confused, we have to do different things now.'

'Curse Straha. May the Emperor turn his eye turrets away from him forever, now and in the world to come,' Nejas answered fiercely. After a moment, though, he said, 'Yes, some truth may hatch from that eggshell. We—'

Before he could finish what he was saying, the transport, without warning, dropped like a stone. The chains that held the landcruiser secure in the fuselage groaned and creaked, but held. Ussmak's seat belt held, too, to his relief, so he didn't bounce all over the driver's compartment as the aircraft dived.

As landcruiser commander, Nejas had a communications link with the pilot of the transport. He said, 'We had to take evasive action against a Tosevite killercraft there. The machine guns stitched us up a bit, but no serious damage. We should land without trouble.'

'A good place not to have trouble, superior sir,' Ussmak agreed, and tacked on an emphatic cough to show he really meant it.

'What happened to the Big Ugly aircraft?' Skoob demanded. He had the proper attitude for a gunner: he wanted to be sure the foe was gone.

Unfortunately, this time the foe wasn't gone. Nejas said, 'I am told that the Tosevite male escaped. The British apparently had more aircraft available than we anticipated, and are throwing them all into the battle against our forces. Here and there, sheer numbers let some of them get through.'

'We've seen that before, superior sir,' Ussmak said. Individually, a landcruiser or killercraft of the Race was worth some large number of the machines the Big Uglies manufactured. But the Tosevites, after they'd lost that large number, proceeded to manufacture several more. When the Race lost a machine, it and the male or males who crewed it were gone for good.

Nejas might have picked the thought from his head. 'With luck, our conquest of this island of British or whatever its name is will make it harder for the Big Uglies, at least in this part of Tosev 3, to continue building the weapons with which they oppose us.'

'Yes, superior sir, with luck,' Ussmak said. He'd given up on the idea that the Race would get much luck in its struggle with the Big Uglies. Maybe, along with their aircraft and landcruisers, the Tosevites manufactured luck in some hidden underground factory ...

Nejas broke into his reverie, saying, 'We are on the point of landing. Prepare yourselves.'

Sealed up in the landcruiser, Ussmak hadn't noticed maneuvres less violent than the ones the transport had used to escape the Big Ugly raider. Now he braced himself for a jolt as the aircraft touched down. It came, hard enough to make his teeth click together. The airstrip, made by combat engineers in country for which 'hostile' was a polite understatement, would be short and rough and probably pocked with shell holes, too. He wondered if any transports – and the males they were transporting – had been caught on the ground.

Things started happening very fast once the transport landed. The scream of its engines reversing thrust to help slow it made Ussmak's head ache even through the aircraft fuselage and the steel and ceramic armor of the landcruiser. Deceleration shoved him forward against his seat belt.

The instant the transport stopped, Nejas ordered, 'Driver, start your engine!'

'It shall be done, superior sir,' Ussmak replied, and obeyed. The hydrogen-burning turbine purred smoothly. Ussmak stuck his head out through the driver's hatch to get a better view. At the moment he did so, the nose door of the transport opened, swinging up and back over the cockpit while the aircraft's integral ramp rolled down to the ground. Air from outside flowed into the fuselage, bringing with it the smells of powder and dirt and alien growing things. It was also cold, cold enough to make Ussmak shiver. The idea of being on an island, entirely surrounded by water, was less than appealing, too; back on Home, land dominated water, and islands on the lakes were small and few and far between.

A male with a lighted red wand ran up to guide the landcruiser out of the transport. 'Forward – dead slow,' Nejas ordered. Ussmak engaged the lowest gear and eased forward. The landcruiser rattled over the metal floor of the fuselage, then nosed down onto the ramp. The male with the wand hadn't done anything but urge Ussmak straight ahead – he might as well not have been there. The Race, though, took *Better safe* as a general working rule.

By the way they fought, the Big Uglies had never heard of that rule.

A buzzing in the air, like the wingdrone of a flying biter immensely magnified ... Ussmak hadn't heard that sound often, but knew what it meant. He ducked back into the landcruiser, slammed the hatch shut. The Big Uglies' killercraft shot by at a height not much greater than the top of the transport's tail. Machine-gun bullets rattled from the glacis plate of Ussmak's landcruiser. A couple hit the just-closed hatch. Had his head been sticking out through it, they would have hit him.

The male who'd been directing him out of the transport reeled away, blood pouring from two or three wounds. 'Forward – top speed!' Nejas screamed into the microphone taped to Ussmak's hearing diaphragm. Ussmak's foot was already mashing the accelerator. If the Tosevite killercraft had poured bullets into the front end of the transport, what had it done to the rest of the machines?

'Superior sir, is the other landcruiser following us out?' he asked. With the prisms in the cupola, Nejas could see all around, while Ussmak's vision was limited to ahead and a bit to the sides.

'Not quickly enough,' the commander answered. 'And oh, he'd better hurry – there's flame from one wing of the transport, and now from the fuselage, and—' The blast behind him drowned his words. The rear of the heavy landcruiser lifted off the ground. For a terrifying instant, Ussmak thought it was going to flip end over end. But it thudded back down, harder than any of the jolts it had given the crew while the transport took evasive action in the air.

More explosions followed, one after another, as the ammunition of the landcruiser trapped in the inferno of the fuselage began cooking off. 'Emperors past, take the spirits of the crewmales into your hands,' Skoob said.

'May they take *our* spirits into their hands, too,' Nejas said. 'Until that wreck is cleared, no traffic will be using the runway – and we need all the traffic we can get. More landcruisers, more soldiers, more ammunition, more hydrogen to keep our machines running—'

Ussmak hadn't thought of that. When he'd rolled across the plains of the SSSR, he'd thought the conquest of Tosev 3 would be as easy as everyone back on Home had expected before the fleet left. Even though the Big Uglies had opposed him with landcruisers of their own rather than the animal-riding, sword-swinging soldiers he'd been led to expect, he and his fellow males disposed of them easily enough.

Even then, though, things had gone wrong: the sniper who'd killed his first commander, the raider who'd wrecked his landcruiser – he'd been lucky to get out of that alive, even if he'd had to jump into radioactive mud to do it. He'd picked up his ginger habit recovering in the hospital ship.

Things had got tougher in France. The terrain was worse, the Deutsche had better landcruisers, and they knew what to do with them. The Français were hostile, too. He hadn't thought that would matter, but it did. Sabotage, bombings, endless nuisances, all of which caused damage and forced the males of the Race to divert efforts and guard against them.

And now this – trapped on an island, partially cut off from resupply, with the Big Uglies, even the ones who weren't soldiers, more certain to be dangerous than the ones in France. 'Superior sir,' Ussmak said, 'the deeper we get into this war, the more it looks as if we might lose it.'

'Nonsense,' Nejas declared. 'The Emperor has ordained that we bring this world into the light of civilization, and it shall be done.' Ussmak thought him optimistic to the point of idealism, but even protesting to a superior as unusual; arguing with his commander would have got him punished.

A male with fancy body paint ran up to the landcruiser, waving his arms. 'Driver halt,' Nejas said, and Ussmak did. The male clambered up onto the landcruiser. Ussmak heard Nejas open the cupola lid. The male shouted, his voice deep with excitement. 'Yes, we can do that, superior sir,' Nejas answered him, 'provided you have a clearing blade to fit to the front of the vehicle.'

Even really hearing only one side of the conversation, Ussmak had no trouble figuring out what the male wanted: help pushing the wrecked transport off the runway. The officer ran off. Not much later, a truck with a winch came rumbling up to the landcruiser. Combat engineers began attaching the blade.

Not far off, dirt suddenly rose into the air in a graceful fountain. One of the engineers screamed loud for Ussmak to hear him through Nejas's microphone: 'Emperor protect us, they've snuck a mortar inside the perimeter again!'

Another bomb landed, this one even closer. Fragments of the casing rattled off the sides of the landcruiser. A combat engineer went down, kicking; blood spurted from a wound in his side. A medical technician gave him first aid, then summoned a couple of other males to take him away for further treatment. The rest of the engineers kept on bolting the clearing blade to the landcruiser.

Ussmak admired their courage. He wouldn't have done their job for all the money – maybe not even for all the ginger – on Tosev 3. For that matter, his own job didn't look like such a good risk at the moment.

Mordechai Anielewicz huddled in a deep foxhole in the middle of a thick clump of bushes. He hoped it would give him good enough cover. The forest partisans must have miscalculated how much their raids were annoying the Lizards, for the aliens were doing their best to sweep them into oblivion.

Firing came from ahead of him and from both sides. He knew that meant he ought to get up and move, but getting up and moving struck him as the quickest and easiest way to get himself killed. Sometimes sitting tight was the best thing you could do.

The Lizards were worse in the woods than even an urban Jew like him. He heard them skittering past his hole in the ground. He clutched his Mauser. If the Lizards started poking through the bushes that shielded him, he'd sell his life as dear as he could. If they didn't, he had no intention of advertising his existence. The essence of partisan warfare was getting away to fight another day.

Time crawled by on leaden feet. He took a *Wehrmacht*-issue canteen from his belt, sipped cautiously – he had less water than he wanted, and didn't know how long it would have to last. Going out to find more didn't strike him as a good idea, not right now.

The bushes rustled. *Sh'ma yisroayl, adonai elohaynu, adonai ekhod* ran through his head: the first prayer a Jew learned, the last one that was supposed to cross his lips before he died. He didn't say it now; he might have been wrong. But, as silently as he could, he turned toward the direction of the rustling. He was afraid he'd have to pop up and start shooting; otherwise the Lizards could finish him off with grenades.

'Shmuel?' A bare thread of whisper, but an unmistakably human voice.

'Yes. Who's that?' The voice was too attenuated for him to recognize it, but he could make a good guess. 'Jerzy?'

By way of reply, he got a laugh as discreet as the whisper had been. 'You damn Jews are too damn smart, you know that?' the partisans' point man answered. 'Come on, though. You can't hang around here. Sooner or later, they'll spot you. I did.'

If Jerzy said staying around wasn't safe, it probably wasn't. Anielewicz scrambled up and out of his hidey-hole. 'How'd you notice me, anyway?' he asked. 'I didn't think anybody could.'

'That's just how,' the point man answered. 'I looked around and I saw an excellent hiding place that didn't look like it had anyone in it. I asked myself, who would be clever enough to take advantage of that kind of place? Your name popped into my head, and so—'

'I suppose I should be flattered,' Mordechai said. 'You damn Poles are too damn smart, you know that?'

Jerzy stared at him, then laughed loud enough to alarm them both. 'Let's get out of here,' he said then, quietly once more. 'We'll head east, in the direction they're coming from. Now that the main line of them is past, we shouldn't have any trouble slipping away. They're probably aiming to drive us against some other force they have waiting. That's how the Nazis hunted partisans, anyhow.'

'We caught plenty of you Pole bastards, too,' someone behind them said in German. They both whirled. Friedrich sneered at them. 'Poles and Jews talk too fucking much.'

'That's because we have Germans to talk about,' Anielewicz retorted. He hated the arrogant way Friedrich stood there, feet planted on the ground as if he'd sprung from it, every line of his body proclaiming that he thought himself a lord of creation, just as if it had been the winter of 1941, with the Lizards nowhere to be seen and the Nazis bestriding Europe like a colossus and driving hard on Moscow.

The German glared at him. 'You've got smart answers for everything, haven't you?' he said. Anielewicz tensed. A couple more words to Friedrich and somebody was liable to die right there; he resolved he wouldn't be the one. But then the Nazi went on, 'Well, that's just like a Jew. You're right about one thing – we'd better get out of here. Come on.'

They headed east down a game track Mordechai never would have noticed for himself. Just as if they were raiding rather than running, Jerzy took the point and Friedrich the rear, leaving Anielewicz to move along in the middle, making enough noise to impersonate a large band of men.

Friedrich said, 'This partisan business stinks.' Then he laughed softly. 'Course, I don't remember hunting you bastards was a whole lot of fun, either.'

'Hunting us bastards,' Mordechai corrected him. 'Remember which side you're on now.' Having someone along who'd been on both sides could be useful. Anielewicz had theoretical knowledge of how partisan hunters had operated. Friedrich had done it. If only he weren't Friedrich ...

Up ahead a few meters, Jerzy let out a hiss. 'Hold up,' he said. 'We're coming to a road.'

Mordechai stopped. He didn't hear Friedrich behind him, so he assumed Friedrich stopped, too. He wouldn't have sworn to it, though; he hadn't heard Friedrich when they were moving, either.

Jerzy said, 'Come on up. I don't see anything. We'll cross one at a time.'

Anielewicz moved up to him as quietly as he could. Sure enough, Friedrich was right behind him. Jerzy peered cautiously from behind a birch, then sprinted across the rutted, muddy dirt road and dived into the brush there. Mordechai waited a few seconds to make sure nothing untoward happened, then made the same dash and dived himself. Somehow Jerzy had done it silently, but the plants he dived into rustled and crackled in the most alarming way. His pique at himself only got worse when Friedrich, who would have made two of him, also crossed without producing any noise.

Jerzy cast about for the game trail, found it, and headed east once more. He said, 'We want to get as far away from the fighting as we can. I don't know, but—'

'You feel it too, eh?' Friedrich said. 'Like somebody just walked over your grave? I don't know what it is, but I don't like it. What about you, Shmuel?'

'No, not this time,' Anielewicz admitted. He didn't trust his own instincts, though, not here. In the ghetto, he'd had a fine-tuned sense of when trouble was coming. He didn't have a feel for the forest, and he knew it.

'Something—' Jerzy muttered, just before the shooting started. The Lizards were ahead of them and off to one flank. At the first gunshot, Mordechai threw himself flat. He heard a grunt and a groan from in front of him. He groaned, too – Jerzy was hit.

In Lizard-accented Polish, a tremendously amplified voice roared, 'You have been tracked since you crossed the road. Surrender or be killed. You cannot escape. We shall cease fire to allow you to surrender. If you do not, you will die.'

As promised, the hail of bullets stopped. By the noises in the trees, more Lizards were moving up on the side opposite the one from which the shooting had come. A helicopter thrummed overhead, sometimes visible through the leafy forest canopy, sometimes not.

Anielewicz weighed the odds. The Lizards didn't know who he was. That counted for a great deal – what they didn't know he knew, they couldn't squeeze out of him. Wearily, he set down his Mauser and got to his feet, arms high over his head.

Five or ten meters behind him, Friedrich was doing the same thing. The German managed a wry grin. 'Maybe we'll get away, eh?'

'That would be good,' Anielewicz agreed. He'd managed to arrange it for other people (he wondered how Moishe Russie was getting along these days), and he'd managed to slip out of Warsaw right under the Lizards' snouts. Whether he could get out of a prison camp once he was inside it was another question, though.

And it was going to be one he'd have to answer. Several Lizards, all of them with automatic rifles at the ready, approached him and Friedrich. He stood very still, not wanting to spook them and get himself shot. One of the Lizards gestured sharply with the barrel of his gun – *This way.* 'Go!' he said in barely understandable Polish. Anielewicz and Friedrich shambled into captivity.

Rance Auerbach and his troopers rode into Lamar, Colorado, after another hit-and-run raid into Lizard-held Kansas. A couple of horses had bodies tied across their backs; nothing came easy when you fought the Lizards. But the company had done what it set out to do.

Auerbach turned to Bill Magruder. 'Old Joe Selig won't play footsie with the Lizards any more.'

'Sir, that's a fact, and a good thing, too,' Magruder answered. His face was soot-grimy; he'd been one of the band that had torched Selig's barn. The rest of the company had burned Selig's farmhouse, and Selig inside it. Magruder leaned down and spat right in the middle of Main Street. 'God-damn collaborator. I never thought we'd see bastards like that, not in the United States.'

'Me, neither,' Auerbach said glumly. 'Just goes to show there's some bastards everywhere, I guess. Hate to say it – hate to see it, by God – but I reckon it's true.'

Near the railroad station, right where Main Street crossed the Santa Fe tracks, stood the Madonna of the Trail monument, dedicated to all the pioneer mothers. Too bad some of those pioneer mothers had snakes in the grass for grandchildren.

A pigeon flew overhead, making a beeline for the county courthouse. Auerbach spotted the little aluminium tube fastened to its left leg. Spying it took some of the bitter taste out of his mouth. 'I'd like to see the Lizards figure out a way to jam that,' he said.

Magruder hadn't noticed the bird, but he figured out what the captain had to be talking about. 'Homing pigeon, was it?' he said. At Auerbach's nod, he went on, 'Yeah, as long as we stick to the nineteenth century, the Lizards don't have a clue about what we're doing. Only trouble is, when we get up to the here and now, we get licked.'

'Isn't it the truth?' Auerbach said ruefully. 'And if we have the nineteenth-century stuff and they have the twentieth and the Buck Rogers gadgets, too, we're going to keep right on getting licked unless we're a damn sight smarter than we've been so far.' The beginning of an idea flickered across his mind but was gone before he could capture it.

Before the war, Lamar had been a medium-sized town: four thousand people, maybe a few more. Unlike a lot of places, it was bigger now. A lot of the original inhabitants were dead or fled, but soldiers made up for a good many of them because it was an important forward base against the Lizards. And, because it remained firmly in American hands, it was a magnet for refugees from farther east.

Army headquarters was in the First National Bank building, not far from the courthouse (not that Lamar was a big enough town for anything to be real far from anything else). Auerbach dismissed his troopers to see to their horses, then went in to report.

Colonel Morton Nordenskold, the local commander, heard him out and made encouraging noises. 'Well done,' he said. 'Traitors need to know they'll pay for treason.' Nordenskold had to be from somewhere in the upper Midwest; his voice held a trace of singsong Scandinavian intonation.

'Yes, sir.' Auerbach felt his own Texas drawl coming out more strongly in reaction to that very northern accent. 'What are your orders fro the company now, sir?'

'As usual,' Nordenskold answered: 'Observe, patrol, raid. Given what we have, what else can we do?'

'Nothing much I can see, sir,' Auerbach said. 'Uh, sir, what do we do if the Lizards push west with armor, the way they did last summer to get into Kansas? I'm proud to be a cavalryman – don't get me wrong – but you go horses against tanks once and you won't do it again with the same horses. Probably not with the same men, either.'

'I know.' Nordenskold wore a small, precise gray mustache – too small and precise to fluff out when he sighed. 'Captain, we'll do the best we can under the circumstances: we'll harass, we'll counterattack when we can ...' He sighed again. 'Take away the Army guff, and a lot of us are going to get killed trying to hold them back. Any further questions, Auerbach?'

'Uh, no, sir,' Rance answered. Nordenskold had been more forthright than he'd expected. Things weren't good, and they weren't likely to get better any time soon. He'd known that, but having his superior come right out and say it made it feel as real and immediate as a kick in the teeth.

'Dismissed, then,' the colonel said. His desk was piled high with papers, some of them reports and notes handwritten on the backs of old bank forms. He bent to them once more before Auerbach was out of the office.

Without electric lights, the room where First National Bank customers would have stood was dark and gloomy. Rance blinked several times when he went out into the bright sunshine of the street. Then he blinked again, and touched the brim of his cap with a forefinger in what was more a polite gesture than a salute. 'Hello, Miss Penny. How are you today?'

'I'm all right, I suppose,' Penny Summers answered indifferently. She'd been like that ever since Auerbach had brought her back to Lamar from Lakin, Kansas. Nothing seemed to matter much to her. He understood that; watching your father smashed to cat meat right before your eyes was plenty to leave you stunned for a while.

'You look mighty nice,' he offered gallantly. She was a nice-looking girl, true, but that wasn't the same thing. Her face still had a wounded look to it and, like a lot of faces in Lamar, was none too clean. She still wore the overalls she'd had on when she and her father decided to pitch in and help the cavalry against the Lizards in Lakin. Under them she had on a man's shirt that had seen better years – maybe better decades – and was also several sizes too big for her.

She shrugged, not because she didn't believe him, he judged, but because she didn't care one way or the other.

He tried again: 'The folks you're staying with here, are they treating you okay?'

'I guess so,' she said, still so flat that he started to give up hope of bringing her back into full contact with the world. But then her voice picked up a little as she went on, 'Mr Purdy, he tried peekin' at me when I got undressed one night, but I told him I was your girlfriend and you'd whale the stuffing out of him if he ever did it again.'

'I ought to whale the stuffing out of him for doing it once,' Auerbach growled; he had definite, even vehement, notions about what you should and shouldn't do. Taking advantage of somebody you were supposed to be helping fell with a thud into the second category.

'I told him I'd tell his wife on him, too,' Penny said. Was that amusement in her voice? Auerbach wasn't sure, but it was something, and he hadn't heard anything there since the Lizard plane swooped low over her father.

He decided to risk laughing. 'That was a good idea,' he said. Then he asked, 'Why did you say you were my girlfriend? Not that I wouldn't like it if it were so, mind you, but—'

'On account of Mr Purdy knows you brought me here, and he knows you're half his age and twice his size,' Penny Summers answered. If she had noticed the last sentence he'd politely tacked on, she didn't show it.

He signed. He wished he could do something for her, but had no idea what that something might be. When he said goodbye, Penny only nodded and went on down the street. He didn't think she was going anywhere in particular, just wandering around – maybe she and the Purdys got on one another's nerves in ways other than the one she'd mentioned, too.

He turned a corner and headed for the stables (funny to think of towns having stables again; they'd been going out of business since about the time he was born) to see to his horse: if you didn't worry about your animal before you worried about yourself, you didn't belong in the cavalry.

Somebody sang out, 'Hello, Captain Rance, sir!'

Auerbach whirled. Only one person called him Captain Rance. To his men, he was Captain Auerbach. To his friends, he was just Rance – or rather, he'd been just Rance; the people he'd called friends were a lot of duty stations away from Lamar, Colorado. Sure enough, there stood Rachel Hines, grinning at him. He grinned back. 'Hello yourself.'

Where Penny, weighed down by her father's death, had withdrawn into herself since she came to Lamar, Rachel had blossomed. She was still wearing the dress in which she'd come to town, and it wasn't any too clean, but she wore it with a flair Penny had forgotten – if she'd ever known it. From God knows where, Rachel had managed to come by makeup which highlighted her blonde good looks. And, perhaps for no better reason than to keep life interesting, she still had her .22 slung over a shoulder.

Or perhaps she did have a reason: perhaps she was trying to make a point. She walked up to Auerbach and said, 'When am I going to get to ride out with your men against the Lizards?'

He didn't dismiss the idea out of hand, as he would have before the Lizards came. The position of the United States was, in a word, desperate. In a situation like that, whether you could take a leak standing up suddenly looked a lot less important than whether you could ride hard, shoot straight, and follow orders.

He studied Rachel Hines. She stared saucily back at him. He wasn't sure about that last one, not where she was concerned. Some women wouldn't be any trouble on campaign, but Rachel enjoyed flaunting what she had. That could make trouble. So Auerbach temporized, saying, 'I can't tell you yes or no yet. Colonel Nordenskold is still thinking that one over.' That had the additional virtue of being more or less true.

She took another step toward him; now she was so close, she made him want to take a step back. She ran her tongue over her lips, which made him notice again that she'd painted them red. 'I'd do just about anything to get the chance to go along,' she murmured a breathy little voice he wasn't used to hearing anywhere outside the bedroom.

The sweat that sprang out on his forehead had nothing to do with the heat of Colorado summer. Women had been few and far between for him this past crazy summer, and, like a lot of guys, he always came back from action horny, probably because he was so relieved to be coming back alive.

But if Rachel would go to bed with him to get what she wanted, she'd do the same thing with somebody else. Politely, in case he'd somehow misunderstood her (though he knew damn well he hadn't), he said, 'I'm sorry, but it isn't in my hands. Like I said, it's up to the colonel.'

'Well, I'll just have to talk with *him*, then, won't I?' She sashayed off toward the First National Bank. Auerbach wondered if Colonel Nordenskold would be able to resist her blandishments, and if he'd even try.

The cavalry captain went on to tend to his horse, also wondering how much he'd regret turning her down. 'Damn, if she'd only wanted something easy from me,' he muttered under his breath. 'Robbing the bank here, say ...'

Leslie Groves did not pretend to be a combat general, even to himself. Engineers fought nature and they fought the efforts of ill-intentioned people in the wrong kinds of uniforms who wanted to knock down the things they ran up. They weren't supposed to worry about fighting the bad guys, not directly.

On the other hand, engineers had to be able to fight in a pinch. You never could tell what might happen to the officers who made battle their proper business. If enough of them went down, you were liable to be the man on the spot for a while.

So Groves had plenty of experience reading situation maps. Just to keep himself in practice, he often tried to figure out strategy for each side. With pardonable pride, he thought he was pretty good at it.

When he looked at the situation map on the wall of his office, he grimaced. You didn't have to be Napoleon to realize that, if the Lizards wanted to, they could stroll across Colorado and seize Denver without breathing hard, let alone slowing down.

'What's going to stop them?' Groves snorted. 'Cavalry, for God's sake?' He hadn't seen cavalry symbols on a map for a long time; he'd felt mild pride for remembering what they meant.

Cavalry, against the Lizards? Cavalry had had trouble with the Sioux Indians, and he didn't see that the state of art had improved enough in the past three generations to give the horse soldiers much of a chance of holding off creatures from another planet. If the Lizards took it into their toothy heads to go after Denver, cavalry wouldn't be enough to hold them back.

More armored divisions than the U.S. Army owned might not be enough to hold them back, either, but Groves didn't worry about might-have-beens. What *was* posed quite enough difficulties.

'They can't find out we're working on the atomic bomb here,' he announced, as if he expected someone to materialize in an empty chair across the desk from him and nod at his wisdom.

Of course, if the Lizards did find out the Metallurgical Laboratory had settled down here, they probably wouldn't bother mounting an armored drive across Colorado. They'd just do unto Denver what they'd done unto Tokyo: they'd blow it off the face of the earth. If they did that, and especially if they did that before the United States had made any bombs, the war would be as good as lost, at least on this side of the Atlantic.

'Japan's smashed, England's invaded,' he said. Astonishing how much the destruction of Tokyo worried him. Not much more than a year before, Jimmy Doolittle had won himself a Congressional Medal of Honor for bombing the Japanese capital, and the whole USA had stood up and cheered. Now – 'If we go under now, everything rides on the Reds and the Nazis,' Groves said, scowling. That was a hell of a thought, depending on a couple of the nastiest regimes ever invented to save the day for everybody else. Living under the Lizards might almost be better ...

Groves shook his head. Nothing was worse than living under the Lizards. He held one finger in the air, as if to show he'd had a good idea. 'The thing to do is not to let them know,' he declared. So far, they hadn't tumbled. With luck and care, they wouldn't.

What really worried him, though, was that they wouldn't have to figure out that the Americans were doing nuclear research to want to conquer Denver. If they decided to head west from where they already were, it was the biggest city in sight. Maybe the Met Lab team would escape, the way they had from Chicago, but where would they go next? He hadn't the faintest idea. How much precious time would they lose? He didn't know that, either, but a lot. Could the United States – could the world – afford to have them lose all that time? There, for once, he knew the answer. No.

He got up from his desk, stretched, and headed out the door. Instead of his officer's cap, he grabbed a civilian-style fedora. He was finally wearing a brigadier general's stars on his shoulders, but he'd daubed gray paint on them so they wouldn't sparkle and perhaps draw the notice of Lizard aerial reconnaissance. The last thing he wanted the Lizards wondering was what a general was doing on a university campus. If they were smart enough to figure out that that meant military research, they might also be smart enough to figure out what kind of research it meant ... in which case, goodbye, Denver.

The walk to the pile under the football stadium was, aside from eating and sleeping, almost the only break Groves allowed himself in his days of relentless toil. Off to the east, civilians, men and women alike, were out digging tank traps and trenches. Those might not come to anything without the soldiers and guns they'd need to make them effective, but the civilians were giving their all. He could hardly do anything less – and it wasn't in his nature to do anything less, anyhow.

A chart was thumbtacked to a hallway wall of the stadium by the atomic pile. It kept track of two things: the amount of plutonium produced each day, and how much had been produced overall. That second number was the one Groves watched like a hawk.

Leo Szilard came round the corner. 'Good morning, General,' he said in the thick Hungarian accent that always made Groves – and a lot of other people – think of Bela Lugosi. Something else beside the accent lurked in his voice. Groves suspected it was scorn for anybody who put on his country's uniform. Groves's reaction to that was returned scorn, but he did his best to hide it. He was, after all, fighting to keep the United States a free country.

And besides, he might have been reading altogether too much into a three-word greeting, although other encounters with the physicist made him doubt that. 'Good morning, Dr Szilard,' he answered as cordially as he could – and the chart gave him some reason for cordiality. 'We've been up over ten grams a day this past week. That's excellent.'

'It is certainly an improvement. Having the second pile operational has helped a good deal. More than half the production now comes from it. We were able to improve its design with what we learned from this one.'

'That's always the way things go,' Groves said, nodding. 'You build the first one to see if it will work and how it will work, whatever "it" happens to be. Your second one's a better job, and by the third or fourth you're about ready to enter regular production.'

'Adequate theory would enable the first attempt to be of proper quality,' Szilard said, now with a touch of frost. Groves smiled. That was just the difference between a scientist, who thought theory could adequately explain the world, and an engineer, who was sure you had to get in there and tinker with things before they'd go the right way.

Groves said, 'We're bringing down the time until we have enough plutonium for a bomb every time I look at the chart, but next year still isn't good enough.'

'We are now doing everything we can here at Denver, given the materials and facilities available,' Szilard answered. 'If the Hanford site is as promising as it appears to be, we can begin producing more there soon, assuming we can set up the plant without the Lizards' noticing.'

'Yes, assuming,' Groves said heavily. 'I wish I'd sent Larssen out as part of a team. If something goes wrong with him . . . we'll just have to judge going ahead at Hanford on the basis of theory rather than experience.'

Szilard gave him a surprised look. The physicist owned a sense of humor, a rather dry, puckish one, but seemed surprised to find anything similar lurking in the soul of a military man. After a moment's hesitation, he said, 'The atomic piles we have in mind for that facility are truly elegant, and will make these seem like clumsy makeshifts. The Columbia has enough cooling flow to let them be enormously more efficient.'

'Getting equipment and people to Hanford is going to be complicated,' Groves said. 'Getting anything anywhere is complicated these days. That's what having aliens occupying half the country will do to you.' 'If we do not establish additional facilities, our production rate for plutonium here will remain cruelly slow,' Szilard said.

'I know,' Groves answered. So many things the United States had to do if it was going to win the war. So many things, also, the United States couldn't do. And if the United States couldn't do the things it had to do … Groves was an excellent logician. He wished he weren't, because he hated the conclusion to which logic led him.

David Goldfarb drew himself to attention as Fred Hipple walked by, which meant he looked down on the crown of the diminutive group captain's service cap. 'Permission to speak to you a moment, sir?'

Hipple stopped, nodded. 'What is it, Goldfarb?'

The rumble of artillery was plainly audible in the moment Goldfarb used to gather his thoughts. The Lizards' northern perimeter was only a few miles away. Up till now, it had been a defensive perimeter; their main effort went into the southward push toward London. That didn't mean the British were attacking it with any less ferocity, though.

Goldfarb said, 'Sir, I'd like your endorsement on a request to transfer from this unit to one where I can get into combat.'

'I thought that might be what you would say.' Hipple rubbed at the thin line of his mustache. 'Your spirit does you credit. However, I shall not endorse any such request. On the contrary. As long as this research team exists, I shall bend every effort toward maintaining it at full strength.' He scratched at his mustache again. 'You are not the first man to ask this of me.'

'I didn't think I would be, sir, but this is the first chance I've had to speak to you in any sort of privacy,' Goldfarb said. Being one of the other ranks, he didn't share quarters with Hipple, as did the officers on the jet propulsion and radar research team. Stealing this moment outside the Nissen hut where they all worked wasn't the same thing – although the roar of cannon and the cloud of dust and smoke that obscured the southern horizon lent his words urgency.

'Yes, yes, I understand all that. Quite.' Hipple looked uncomfortable. 'I might add that my own request to return to combat duty was also rejected, and I must admit I found the reasons for its rejection compelling enough to apply them myself.' He shifted from foot to foot, a startling gesture from such a usually dapper little man.

'What are those reasons, sir?' Goldfarb gestured violently. 'With the country invaded, seems to me we need every man who can carry a rifle to do just that.'

Hipple's smile was rueful. 'Exactly what I said, though I believe I used the phrase "climb into a cockpit" instead. I was told, quite pointedly, that this was penny wise and pound foolish, that we have a sufficiency of fighting men who are only that and nothing more, but that technical progress had to continue lest in winning this fight we sow the seeds of losing the next one, and that – you will forgive me, I trust, for quoting the words of the Air Vice Marshal – I was to bloody well stay here till we were either evacuated or bloody well overrun.'

'Yes, sir,' Goldfarb said. Then, greatly daring, he added, 'But sir, if we lose this fight, can we make another?'

'A cogent point,' Hipple admitted. 'If by "we" you mean the British Isles, I daresay the answer is no. But if you mean by it mankind as a whole, I believe the answer to be yes. And if we are evacuated, I believe we shan't go into the Welsh mountains or up into Scotland or across the Irish Sea to Belfast. My guess is that they may send us across to Norway, and from there to join forces with the Germans – no, I don't care for that, and I see from your face that you don't, either, but neither of our opinions has anything to do with anything. More likely, though, we'd sail across the Atlantic and set up shop in Canada or the United States. Meanwhile, we soldier on here. Is that clear?'

'Yes, sir,' Goldfarb repeated. Hipple nodded as if everything were settled and went on his way. Sighing, Goldfarb walked into the Nissen hut.

Basil Roundbush was in there, poring over a blueprint with a singular lack of enthusiasm. He looked up, saw Goldfarb's hangdog expression, and recognized it for what it was. 'The Old Man wouldn't let you go and fight either, eh?'

'Too bloody right.' Goldfarb waved to the Sten guns and spare magazines that had gone up on hooks and in bins on the walls of the hut, ready to be grabbed. 'I suppose those are there to make us feel like soldiers, even if we're not.'

Roundbush laughed, but without much humor. 'That's well put. I never should have learned so blinking much. If I were just a pilot, I'd be in there battling, not chained to a draughtsman's table away from it all.'

One of the meterologists said, 'If you were just a pilot, you'd have been in there battling all along, and odds are you'd've long since bought your plot.'

'Oh, bugger off, Ralph,' Basil Roundbush said. For a crack like that, he would have beaten most men to a jelly, but Ralph Wiggs had had an artificial leg since the day when, a generation before, he'd gone over the top at the Somme. Having seen that and been lucky enough to survive it, he knew everything worth knowing about senseless slaughter.

Now he said, 'Oh, don't get me wrong, lad. I tried to get back into it, too – if they'd take Tin-Legs Bader to fly a Spit with both legs gone, why wouldn't they take me to fight with just one? Blighters said I'd best serve His Majesty by keeping an eye on air pressure and wind direction.'

'It's a filthy job, Ralph, but someone's got to do it,' Roundbush said. 'I just wish I'd never heard of turbines. Teach me to be an engineer—'

Goldfarb couldn't make complaints like that. If he hadn't been mad for wireless sets and the like before the war, he wouldn't have become a radarman in the first place; he'd have gone straight into the infantry. He might have come back from Dunkirk, but then again he might not have. So many good chaps hadn't.

He stuck a lead onto one of the sub-units he and Leo Horton had salvaged from the radar of a crashed Lizard fighter. Little by little, they were figuring out what the unit did, if not always how it did it.

Just as he was about to take his first reading, the air-raid alarm began to wail. Swearing in English and Yiddish, he dashed for the trench right outside the Nissen hut and jumped down into it.

Basil Roundbush landed almost on top of him. The flight officer clattered as he dived into the trench; on the way out, he'd grabbed several Sten guns and enough ammunition to fight a small war. When the first Lizard plane screamed overhead, he fired off a long burst. 'Just on the off chance, don't you know,' he shouted to Goldfarb through the hellish din.

Bombs slammed down all around, jerking them and the other men in the trench around like so many rag dolls. 'Odd pattern,' Goldfarb remarked; he'd become something of a connoisseur of bombing runs. 'Usually they go after the runways, but it sounds more as though they were hitting the buildings today.' He stuck up his head. 'That's what they were doing all right.'

Most of the huts and barracks and other buildings of the Bruntingthorpe Experimental Air Station had just taken a dreadful pounding. The Nissen hut from which he'd fled was still intact, but all its windows had blown in.

Roundbush also peered this way and that. 'You're right – not a scratch on the runways,' he said. 'That isn't like the Lizards, not even a little bit. It's almost as if they wanted them—' His voice faded before the last word '—intact.'

No sooner had that passed his lips than Goldfarb's battered ears caught a thuttering roar from out of the south. It seemed to be coming from the air but he'd never heard anything like it. Then he caught sight of something that reminded him of a tadpole slung beneath an electric fan. 'Helicopter!' he yelled.

'Helicopters,' Roundbush corrected grimly. 'And they're coming this way – probably want to seize the airstrip.'

Goldfarb kept his head up another moment. Then one of the helicopters let loose with a salvo of rockets. He threw himself flat again. Several of them tore into the Nissen hut; a piece of hot corrugated iron landed on him like an overaggressive player in a rugby scrum. 'Oof!' he said. A couple of precious Meteors blew up in their revetments.

The radarman started to shake the slab of metal off and get up, but Roundbush sat on him. 'Stay low, you bloody fool!' the flight officer shouted. As if to underscore his words, machine-gun bullets kicked up dirt all around. When a fighter plane strafed you, it made its pass and flew on. The helicopters hung in the air and kept shooting and shooting.

Over the racket of the guns, Goldfarb said, 'I think Group Captain Hipple's research team has just broken up.'

'Too bloody right it has,' Roundbush answered.

'Here, give me one of those Sten guns,' Ralph Wiggs said. 'If they're going to shoot us, we may as well shoot back as long as we can.' The middle-aged, one-legged meteorologist sounded a great deal calmer than Goldfarb felt. After the Somme, Wiggs might not have found a mere airborne invasion worth showing excitement.

Roundbush passed him a submachine gun. He chambered the first round, stuck his head up, and started shooting regardless of the bullets still raking the trench. The Somme had been machine-gun hell, hundreds of them firing at the overburdened British troops slogging toward their positions. Next to that, what the Lizards were throwing at Bruntingthorpe had to seem negligible.

If Wiggs could get up and fight, Goldfarb supposed he could also manage it. He peered over the lip of the trench. The helicopters still hovered above the runway, covering the Lizards who skittered along the tarmac, shooting as they ran. Goldfarb blazed away at them. Several of them went down, but whether he'd hit them or they were just taking cover he could not say.

All at once, one of the helicopters turned into a blue-white fireball. Goldfarb whooped like a Red Indian. Antiaircraft guns ringed Bruntingthorpe. Nice to know that, aside from almost shooting down British jet fighters, they could also do some damage to the enemy.

The remaining helicopter whirled in the air and fired more rockets at the ack-ack gun that had brought down its companion. Goldfarb couldn't imagine anyone living through such a barrage, but the gun kept pounding away. Then the helicopter lurched in the air. Goldfarb screamed louder than he had before. The helicopter did not explode, but did flee, trailing smoke.

Basil Roundbush bounded out of the trench and fired at the Lizards on the ground, who had halted in dismay. 'We have to wipe them out now,' he shouted, 'before they get their air cover back.'

Goldfarb got up into the greensward, too, though he felt horribly naked outside the trench. He fired a burst, went down on his belly, wriggled forward, fired again.

Other men came up and started shooting, too, from their slit trenches, from others, and from the wreckage of the buildings the Lizards had bombed. Ralph Wiggs limped straight toward the Lizards, as if this were 1916 all over again. A bullet caught him. He went down but kept on shooting.

'You hurt badly?' Goldfarb asked.

Wiggs shook his head. 'I took one through the knee there, so I can't walk, but otherwise I'm right as rain.' He fired again.

He didn't sound like a man who'd just been shot. Goldfarb stared for a moment, then realized the Lizard bullet must have wrecked the knee of Wiggs's artificial leg. Even out in the open, with precious little cove and bullets whistling all around, he burst out laughing.

'They can't have more than two squads on the ground,' Roundbus said. 'We can take them, I really think we can.'

As if to underline his words, the antiaircraft gun the helicopters hadn' been able to silence opened up on the Lizard infantry. Using ack-ack a regular artillery was unconventional, although the Germans were suppose to have started doing it as far back as their blitzkrieg through France i 1940. It was also deucedly effective.

Goldfarb scurried forward toward some wreckage strewn over th runway. He got in behind it with a grateful belly flop; any bit of cove was welcome. He poked the barrel of his Sten gun up over the edge o the torn wood and metal and blazed away.

'Hold fire!' somebody yelled from across the runway. 'They're tryin to give up.'

One weapon at a time, the insane rattle of small-arms fire died away Goldfarb ever so cautiously raised his head and peered toward the Lizards He'd seen them as blips on a radar screen, and briefly in the raid on th prison in Lodz that had freed his cousin, Moishe Russie. Now, as th survivors of the force threw down weapons and raised hands high, h got his first good look at them.

They were only the size of kids. He'd known that intellectually; he' even seen it for himself. But it hadn't really registered on an emotional leve The Lizards' technology was so good that they seemed nine feet tall. Excep for size, they didn't remind him of children. With their forward-slanting posture and scaly skins, they looked something like dinosaurs, but thei helmets and armored jackets gave them a martial air – probably a bette martial air than he had himself right now, he thought, glancing down a his grimy RAF uniform.

Basil Roundbush tramped up beside him. 'By Jove, we did it,' he said

'So we did.' Goldfarb knew he sounded surprised, but couldn't help it He was surprised to be alive, much less victorious. Musingly, he went on 'I wonder if one of those bulletproof waistcoats would fit me.'

'Now there's a thought?' Roundbush exclaimed. He appraised Goldfarl with his eyes. 'You're smaller and leaner than I am, so you stand a chance I hope for your sake one does, because the time for research in merry old England, I fear, is past.' He kicked at a broken slide rule lying on the tarmac. 'Till we throw those scaly buggers out, there's nothing but fighting left.'

6

O God! I could be bounded in a nutshell and count myself a king of infinite space, were it not that I have bad dreams.

What the devil was that from? *Macbeth? Hamlet? King Lear?* Jens Larssen was damned if he could remember, but it was something out of Shakespeare, sure as hell. The lines came floating up into his conscious mind the moment he reached the top of Lewiston Hill.

Looking west from the hilltop, he could certainly count himself a king of infinite space. Even in a land full of spectacular scenic vistas, this one stood out. There was the endless rolling sagebrush prairie of Washington State – desert might have been a more accurate name for it, if less kind.

Nearer, though, were the towns of Clarkston, Washington, and, on this side of the Snake River, Lewiston, Idaho, itself nestled between the Snake and the Clearwater, with mountains pinching it off north and south so that at first glance it seemed to consist of nothing but one long street.

Rafts of logs floated on the Snake, to head downstream to be made into who could say what to help fight the Lizards. As if the clock had turned back a generation, more and more aircraft parts were wood these days.

But did Jens really care these days how the war against the aliens went? Having the Lizards conquer the world was a nightmare of a bad dream. But when the people who had the best chance of stopping them were also the people who'd done him the most dirt, how was he supposed to feel?

'Like hell,' he announced to the air, and kicked his bicycle into motion to roll down into Lewiston.

Roll down into were the operative words; in the ten miles between Lewiston Hill and Lewiston itself, US 95 dropped two thousand feet, about a four percent average grade. Averages were tricky – it was a lot steeper than that in some places. And going down was the easy way; if he came back by this route, he'd have the long slog up to the summit of the hill. Just thinking about it made his thighs ache.

Lewiston bustled in a way he hadn't seen since he left Denver, or maybe since he left Chicago. Loggers swaggered down the street. So did sawmill workers; not all the timber cut around here headed into Washington, not by a long shot. The bulk of what had to be one of the world's biggest lumber plants was just a mile down the Clearwater. By the smoke that poured from its chimneys, it was going flat out, too. The world was a big place, too big for the Lizards to knock out every factory in it, no matter how thoroughly destructive they were.

The sawmill was interesting in the abstract, but it didn't make Jens want to stop for a closer look. When he came up to a YMCA building, though, he stopped so hard, he almost pitched himself over the handlebars of his bicycle. Several bikes were parked out front, with a pistol-toting guard to keep an eye on them. Larssen had seen that in Denver and elsewhere, too. Bicycles now were what horses had been in the old days – come to that, there were also a good many horses on Lewiston's streets.

Jens nodded to the guard as he let down the kickstand to his bike. When he went inside, he asked the clerk at the front desk, 'You have hot water?'

'Yes, sir,' the man answered, unfazed by the sudden appearance of a grimy stranger with a knapsack and a rifle on hi back. He'd probably seen a lot of such strangers, for he went on, 'A hot shower is two dollars. If you want a shave, you can use a straight razor and – hmm – probably a scissors for you, too, for another fifty cents. If you'll give me your goods there, you can have them back when you pay.'

Larssen passed him the Springfield and the knapsack. 'Thanks, pal. I'll take a miss on the razor; I'm used to the beard by now.'

'A lot of men say the same thing,' the clerk answered, nodding. 'If you want your clothes washed, too, Chung's laundry down the street does a first-class job.'

'I'm just passing through, so I don't think I can stay for that, but thanks again,' Jens said. 'But a hot shower! Hot dog!' He followed the signs back to the shower room.

As promised, the water was hot, almost hot enough to scald. The soap took off not only the dirt but part of his top layer of hide, too. It was obviously homemade, mushy and full of lye and strong-smelling. But when he turned off the water and toweled himself dry, he was pink again, not assorted grimy shades of brown.

Putting stale clothes over his clean body made him wrinkle his nose. He'd been rank for so long, he'd stopped noticing it. Maybe he'd stop at Chung's after all. He combed back his hair and walked out to the front desk, whistling.

When he gave the clerk a couple of dollar bills, he got his chattels back. He checked the knapsack to make sure nothing was missing. The clerk looked pained, but said nothing. He'd probably seen that a hundred times, too.

Jens tossed the bike guard a dime, climbed onto his machine, and headed toward the bridge, over the Snake that would lead into Washington State. A couple of blocks west of the YMCA, as the clerk had said, was Chung's laundry, with Chinese characters below the English name of the shop. Jens was about to roll past it, however regretfully, when he saw the place simply called Mama's next door.

He stopped. If this Chung worked fast, maybe he could get his clothes washed while he had a leisurely lunch. 'Why the hell not?' he muttered. An hour this way or that wasn't enough to worry about.

The laundryman – his first name, you learned inside, was Horace – spoke perfect English. He giggled when Larssen said he was going into Mama's for lunch, but promised to have his clothes ready in an hour.

When Jens opened the door to Mama's place, he didn't smell the friendly odors of home-cooked food he'd expected. Perfume hit him in the nose instead. The joint reeked like a cathouse. After a moment, he realized the joint *was* a cathouse. It made sense. All those lumberjacks would want something to do besides chopping down trees all day. But no wonder Horace Chung had broken up when he said he was coming over here to eat.

A big, blowsy woman, maybe Mama herself, came out of a back room. Jens's rifle didn't seem to bother her, either. 'Ain't you squeaky clean?' she said, eyeing his just-washed face and camp hair. 'Bet you been over to the Y. That's right thoughtful of you, it sure is. Now come on back with me and pick yourself out a pretty girl.'

Jens opened his mouth to tell her he'd thought the place was a restaurant, but then he shut it again and followed her. He wasn't going anywhere till the laundryman got done with his clothes, and this would be more fun than lunch.

The girls weren't particularly pretty, no matter what Mama said, and most of them looked mean. The lingerie they were wearing had seen better years. He wondered again if he really wanted to do this. But then he found himself nodding to a girl with curly, dark blonde hair. She looked a little like Barbara had back when they were married, but he didn't notice that; he just thought she was the best-looking woman there.

She got up and stretched. As she headed for the stairs, she said, 'A straight screw is forty. Ten bucks more than that for half and half, another ten for French. You want anything else, find yourself a different gal.'

That bald announcement almost made Jens turn on his heel and walk out. If Horace Chung hadn't had his clothes, he might have done it. As it was, he went after the hooker. The linen on the bed in the little upstairs room was frayed but clean. Larssen wondered if Horace did the laundry for Mama's place and, if so, how he got paid.

The girl kicked off her shoes, pulled her nightgown up over her head, and stood impassively naked. 'What'll it be, buddy?'

'Tell me your name, at least,' Jens said, unnerved by such straightforward capitalism.

'Edie,' she answered, and didn't bother asking his. Instead, she repeated, 'What'll it be?'

'Half-and-half, I guess,' he said with dull embarrassment.

'Show me the money first. You don't pay, you don't play.' She nodde when he tossed the bills onto the bed, then warned, 'You come while I' sucking you, you gotta pay the extra ten for full French, okay?'

'Okay, okay.' He shook his head, horny and disgusted with himself at th same time. This wasn't what he'd been used to getting in his happier day It bore about as much resemblance to love as the painting on an orang crate did to the Mona Lisa. But it was all he could find right now.

He shrugged out of his knapsack, set it and the Springfield in a corne by the bed. Then he undressed. Edie looked him over like somebod inspecting a slab of meat. As Mama had, she said, 'You're clean, anyhov That's something. Haven't seen you round these parts before. You stop a the Y before you came here?'

'Yeah, I did,' he answered, cherishing any human contact between them it was the first thing she'd said to him that wasn't strictly business.

It was also the last. 'Sit on the edge of the bed, will you?' she asked. Whe he did, she got down on her knees in front of him and went to work.

She knew what she was doing, no doubt about that. Presently he patte the mattress with one hand. She lay down on the bed, her legs open. Sh didn't respond when he caressed her, but gave him a good professiona ride after he got on top. Afterwards, the first thing she did was scoop u the money.

He was dressing again when he realized he hadn't put on a rubber. *To bad for her*, he thought coldly. If you were in her line of work, you too your chances with things like the clap.

She said, 'You want another round, half price?'

'No, that's all right,' he answered; what he was thinking about wa going back to the YMCA for another shower. He probably had time, bu he didn't feel like explaining himself to the desk clerk – or not explaining himself, but bearing up under the guy's fishy stare.

'You want a drink downstairs, then?' Edie asked. 'We got home-brew beer, moonshine, even a little real whiskey if you feel like payin' for it.'

She should have been peddling used cars instead of her ass and related amenities. 'That's all right,' Jens said again; all he wanted to do was ge the hell out of there. Edie's look said, *Cheapskate*. He ignored it.

When he went back into Chung's laundry, the proprietor asked, 'You have a nice lunch, sir?' and giggled louder than he had the first time. Then he called something in Chinese into the back room. A woman's laugh floated out. Jens's ears felt on fire. He thought seriously about abandoning his clothes and riding west as fast as he could go.

In the end, he decided to say. But as soon as Horace Chung handed him the hot laundry, he shoved it into his knapsack and fled without changing and getting the clothes he had on clean, as he'd intended to do.

The steel suspension bridge over the Snake River was history – the Lizards hadn't missed it, as they had the sawmill. the only way across the river was by rowboat. The oarsmen all wanted fifteen bucks for the trip, too. Jens flashed his letter that said he was on important government business. One of the boatmen said, 'I'm as patriotic as the next guy, Mac, but I gotta feed my face.' Jens paid.

Eastern Washington, as seen from US 410, reminded him of Utah: very fertile when next to a river or irrigated, otherwise pale alkali flats with not much more than sagebrush growing on them. He'd always thought of Washington as full of pines and moss and ferns, with water dripping everywhere all the time. This part of the state didn't live up to the description.

The roads hereabout hadn't been badly bombed. Most of the bridges over rivers smaller than the Snake remained intact. Timber makeshifts let light traffic cross some of the spans that had been destroyed from the air. A couple of times, he had to pay his way across.

He got his ashes hauled again in Walla Walla, on the third day after he'd crossed into Washington. Again he picked a dark blonde girl; again he didn't think anything of it. This time, he didn't have any laundry to reclaim when he left the bordello. He knew nothing but relief that that was so.

About thirty miles west of Walla Walla, US 140 swung north along the eastern bank of the Columbia toward its junction with the Snake. The country had been irrigated farmland once upon a time. Some of it looked to have been abandoned for quite a while; maybe the farmers hadn't been able to pay their water bills.

Other stretches, though, especially where the two big rivers joined, were just now fading. Irrigation ditches were nothing but muddy, weed-choked grooves in the ground. Here and there, farmers still cultivated small orchards and berry patches, but big stretches of land between them baked brown under the summer sun. Jens wondered what had gone wrong till he pedaled past the ruins of a pumping station, and then of another. If the water couldn't reach land, the land wouldn't bear.

The town nearest the Snake River bridge (not that Jens expected to find it standing) was called Burbank. Just before he got into it, he pulled off the highway to contribute his own bit of irrigation to the roadside plants. No sooner had he started to piss than he stopped again with a snarl of pain. Now he knew without having to think about it what that burning meant.

'*Another* dose of clap?' he howled to the sky, though that was not where he'd got it. The next week or two, till things calmed down in there, were going to be anything but fun.

Then, half to his own surprise, he started to laugh. From everything he'd heard, the clap didn't usually make a woman as sore as it did a man, but that didn't mean she didn't have it. And this time, there was every chance he'd given as good – or as bad – as he'd got.

*   *   *

When Nikifor Sholudenko poked his head unannounced into the underground chamber where Ludmila Gorbunova slept and rested between missions, her first thought was that the NKVD man had hoped to catch her half dressed. But Sholudenko said, 'Comrade Pilot, you are ordered to report to Colonel Karpov's office at once.'

That was different. That was business. Ludmila jumped to her feet. 'Thank you, Comrade. Take me to him at once, please.'

Colonel Feofan Karpov was not a big man, but in his square solidity reminded Ludmila of a bear nonetheless. The stubble on his chin and the decrepit state of his uniform only added to the impression. So did the candles flickering in the underground office; they gave the place the look of a lair.

'Good day, Comrade Pilot,' Karpov said after returning Ludmila's salute. His voice, which was on the reedy side, did not sound particularly ursine, not even when he growled, 'That will be all, Comrade,' at Sholudenko. But the NKVD man disappeared even so.

'Good day, Comrade Colonel,' Ludmila said. 'I report to you as ordered.'

'At ease, Ludmila Vadimovna – you're not in trouble, certainly not from me,' Karpov said. Ludmila did not ease; the colonel was a stickler for military formality, and not in the habit of addressing her by name and patronymic. The first reason she came up with for his changing his tune was that he was doing to make advances at her. If he did, she decided, she'd scream.

But instead of coming around the desk to lay a 'comradely' hand on her shoulder or any such thing, he said, 'I have orders for you to report to Moscow immediately. Well, not quite immediately.' He made a wry face. 'A wagon is waiting above ground to transport you. It brought a replacement pilot and a replacement mechanic.'

'A replacement mechanic, Comrade Colonel?' Ludmila asked, puzzled.

'*Da.*' Karpov scowled an angry bear's scowl. 'They are robbing me not only of one of my best pilots in you, but also of that German – Schultz – you roped into this unit. Whatever bungler they've sent me, he won't measure up to the German; engines don't care if you're a fascist.'

The prospect of riding in to Moscow with Georg Schultz was less than appealing; the prospect of being paired with him on whatever mission followed the trip to Moscow was downright appalling. Hoping she might find out why the two of them had been ordered to the capital, she asked, 'Where and to whom are we to report, Comrade Colonel?'

'To the Kremlin, or whatever may be left of the Kremlin after the Lizards have done their worst.' Karpov looked down at a scrap of paper on his desk. 'The order is signed by a certain Colonel Boris Lidov of the People's Commissariat for the Interior.' He saw Ludmila stiffen. 'You know this man?'

'Yes, I know him, Comrade Colonel,' Ludmila said in a small voice. She glanced around out through the doorway to see if anyone was loitering in the hall.

Karpov's gaze followed hers. 'An NKVD bastard, eh' he said roughly – but he didn't raise his voice, either. 'I thought as much, just from the way the order was framed. No help for it that I can see. Go gather your belongings and get into the wagon – you'll see it when you come out of the tunnels here. Wear something civilian, if you can; it will make you less likely to be shot at from the air. And good luck to you, Ludmila Vadimovna.'

'Thank you, Comrade Colonel,' Ludmila saluted again, then walked back down the hall to her chamber. Mechanically, she packed up her flight suit, coveralls, and pistol. She had no civilian blouses, but at the bottom of her duffel bag she did find a flowered skirt. She couldn't remember the last time she'd worn it.

When she came out of the tunnels, she blinked like a mole suddenly in daylight as she replaced the grass-covered netting that concealed the entrance. As Colonel Karpov had said, a high-wheeled *panje* wagon waited there, the driver in the baggy blouse, trousers, and boots of the *muzhik*, the horse making the most of the moment by pulling up weeds.

The wagon carried a load of straw. When Georg Schultz sat up in it, he looked like a scarecrow, although Ludmila had never seen a scarecrow with a coppery beard. He was dressed in his old *Wehrmacht* tunic and Red Army trousers; he didn't have any civilian clothes this side of wherever in Germany he came from.

He grinned at her. 'Come on back here with me, *liebchen*,' he said in his mixture of Russian and German.

'One minute.' She rummaged in her pack until she found the Tokarev automatic pistol. She belted it on, then climbed into the wagon. 'You never listen to me when I tell you to keep your hands where they belong. Maybe you will listen to this.'

'Maybe.' He was still grinning. He'd faced worse things than pistols. 'And maybe not.'

The driver twitched the reins. The horse let out a resentful snort, raised its head, and ambled off toward Moscow. The driver whistled something from Mussorgsky – after a moment, Ludmila recognized it as 'The Great Gate of Kiev.' She smiled at the reference, no matter how oblique, to her hometown. But the smile quickly faded. Kiev had passed from the Nazis' hands straight into those of the Lizards.

Although they moved ever farther from the front line, the countryside showed the scars of war. Bombs had cratered the dirt road that ran northeast toward Moscow; every couple of hundred meters, it seemed, the *panje* wagon had to rattle off onto the verge.

George Schultz sat up again, spilling straw in all directions. 'These stinking dirt roads played hell with us, all through Russia. The map would say we were coming up to a highway, and it'd either be dust and dirt like this or mud when it rained. Didn't seem fair. You damn Russians were so backwards, it ended up helping you.'

The driver didn't move a muscle; he just kept driving. In spite of that, Ludmila would have bet he knew German. If he was from the NKVD, he'd have more talents than his rough-hewn exterior revealed.

Every so often, they'd pass the dead carcasses of tanks rocketed form the air by the Lizards before they ever reached the front. Some had been there long enough to start rusting. Most had their engine compartments and turret hatches open: the Soviets had salvaged whatever they could from the wreckage.

Even as scrap metal, the T-34s looked formidable. Pointing to one, Ludmila asked with no small pride, 'And what did you think of those when you were up against them, Comrade Panzer Gunner?'

'Nasty buggers,' Schultz answered promptly, ignoring the ironic form of address. 'Good armor, good gun, good engine, good tracks – all better than anything we had, probably. The gunsight, not so good. Not the two-man turret, either – the commander's too busy helping the gunner to command the panzer, and that's his proper job. He should have a cupola, too. And you need more panzers with wireless sets. Not having them hurt your tactics, and they weren't that great to begin with.'

Now Ludmila hoped the driver was listening. She'd been aiming to twit the German tankman; she hadn't expected such a serious, thoughtful answer. Being a Nazi didn't automatically make a man a fool, no matter what propaganda claimed.

The journey in to Moscow took two days. They spent the first night in a stand of trees well off the road. The Lizards still flew by at night, smashing up whatever they could find.

Moscow, when they finally reached it, made Ludmila gasp in dismay. She'd last been there the winter before, after she'd flown Molotov to Germany. The Soviet capital had taken a beating then. Now …

Now it seemed that every building possibly large enough to contain a factory had been pounded flat. A couple of the onion domes of the Kremlin and St Basil's had crumpled. Walls everywhere were streaked with soot; the faint odor of wet, stale smoke hung in the air.

But people hadn't given up. *Babushkas* sold apples and cabbages and beets on the street corners. Soldiers carrying submachine guns tramped purposefully along. Horse-drawn wagons, some small like the one in which Ludmila rode, others pulled by straining teams, rattled and clattered along. No guessing what they held, not with tarpaulins lashed down tight over their beds. If the Lizards couldn't see what was in them, they wouldn't know what to bomb. Flies droned around lumps of horse dung.

The driver knew which bridge over the Moscow River was in good enough repair to get them up to the Kremlin, and which parts of the battered heart of Moscow – of the Soviet Union – were still beating. He pulled the *panje* wagon up in front of one of those parts, stuck a feed bag on the horse's head, and said, 'I am to escort you to Colonel Lidov.' But for the snatches of whistling he'd let out from time to time, that was almost the first sound he'd made since he set out from the air base.

Some of the walls in the corridor were cracked, but the electric lights worked. Off in the distance, a petrol-fired generator chugged away to keep the lightbulbs shining. 'Wish *we* had electricity,' Schultz muttered under his breath.

The corridor was not the one down which Ludmila had gone on her earlier meeting with Boris Lidov; she wondered if that part of the Kremlin still stood. The wagon driver opened a door, peered inside, beckoned to her and to Georg Schultz. 'He will see you.'

Ludmila's heart pounded in her chest, as if she were about to fly a combat mission. She knew she had reason to be nervous; the NKVD could kill you as readily, and with as little remorse, as the Germans or the Lizards. And Lidov had made plain what he thought of her after she got back from Germany. She might have gone to a *gulag* then, rather than back to her unit.

The NKVD colonel (Ludmila wondered if his promotion sprang from ability or simply survival) looked up from a paper-strewn desk. She started to report to him in proper military form, but Schultz beat her to the punch, saying breezily, 'How goes it with you, Boris, you scrawny old prune-faced bastard?'

Staring, Ludmila waited for the sky to fall. It wasn't that the description didn't fit; it did, like a glove. But to say what you thought of an NKVD colonel, right to his prune face ... Maybe he didn't follow German.

He did. Fixing Schultz with a fishy stare, he answered in German much better than Ludmila's: 'Just because Otto Skorenzy could get away with speaking to me so, Sergeant, does not mean you can. He was more valuable than you are, and he was not under Soviet discipline. You, on the other hand—' He let that hang, perhaps to give Schultz the chance to paint horrid pictures in his own mind.

It didn't work. Schultz said, 'Listen, I was one of the men you sent on the raid that gave you people the metal for your bomb. If that doesn't buy me the right to speak my mind, what does?'

'Nothing,' Lidov said coldly.

Ludmila spoke up before Schultz got himself shot or sent to a camp, and her along with him: 'Comrade Colonel, for what mission have you summoned the two of us away from the front line?'

Lidov's look suggested he'd forgotten she was there, and utterly forgotten he'd ordered the two of them to Moscow for any specific reason. After a moment, he collected himself and even laughed a little. That amazed Ludmila, who hadn't suspected he could. Then he explained, 'Curiously enough, it has to do with Soviet-German friendship and co-operation.' He'd answered Ludmila in Russian; he translated the reply into German for Scultz's benefit.

The panzer gunner laughed, too. 'Till the Lizards came, I was giving you co-operation, all right, fifty millimeters at a time.'

'What are we to do, Comrade Colonel?' Ludmila asked hastily. Lidov had warned Georg Schultz twice. Even once would have been surprising. Thinking he'd forbear three times running was asking for a miracle, and Ludmila, a good product of the Soviet educational system, did not believe in miracles.

Lidov's chair squeaked as he turned in it to point to a map pinned to the rough plaster on the side of the wall. 'Here by the lake – do you see it? – is the city of Pskov. It is still in the hands of mankind, although threatened by the Lizards. Some of the defenders are *Wehrmacht* troops, others partisan members of the Red Army.' He paused and pursed his lips. 'Some friction in the defense has resulted from this.'

'You mean they're shooting at each other, don't you?' Schultz asked. Ludmila had wondered if he was too naive to see what lay beneath propaganda, but he proved he wasn't. Goebbels probably used the same techniques as his Soviet counterparts, which would have sensitized Schultz to them.

'Not at present,' Lidov said primly. 'Nonetheless, examples of co-operation might prove to have a valuable effect there. The two of you have done an admirable job of working together, by all the reports that have reached me.'

'We haven't worked together all that close,' Schultz said with a sidelong glance at Ludmila. 'Not as close as I'd like.'

She wanted to kick him right where it would do the most good. 'By which you mean I don't care to be your whore,' she snarled. Before she said something worse to him, something irremediable, she turned to Boris Lidov. 'Comrade Colonel, how are we to get to Pskov?'

'I could have you sent by train,' Lidov answered. 'North of Moscow, rail service works fairly well. But instead, I have a U-2 waiting at a field not far from here. The aircraft itself will prove useful in defending Pskov, as will the addition of a pilot and a skilled mechanic who can also serve a gun. Now go – you spent too much time getting here, but I was not willing to detach a plane from front-line service.'

Ludmila was unsurprised to find the driver waiting for them when they left Colonel Lidov's office. The driver said, 'I will take you to the airport now.'

George Schultz scrambled up into the *panje* wagon. He reached out a hand to help Ludmila join him and laughed when she ignored it, as if she'd dome something funny. Once more she felt like kicking him. Being sent to Pskov was one thing. Being sent there in the company of this smirking, lecherous lout was something else again.

She brightened for a moment: at least she would be escaping Nikifor Sholudenko. And – exquisite irony! – maybe his reports on her had helped make that possible. But her glee quickly faded. For every Sholudenko she escaped, she was only too likely to find another one. His kind was a hardy breed – *like any other cockroaches*, she thought.

Atvar nervously pondered the map that showed the progress of the Race's invasion of Britain. In one respect, all was well: the British could not stop the thrusts of his armored columns. In another respect, though, the picture was not as bright: the Race's armor controlled only the ground on which it sat at the moment. Territory where it had been but was no longer seethed with rebellion the moment the landcruisers were out of sight.

'The trouble with this cursed island,' he said, jabbing a fingerclaw at the computer display as if it were actually the territory in question, 'is that it's too small and too tightly packed with Tosevites. Fighting there is like trying to hold a longball game in an airlock.'

'Well put, Exalted Fleetlord.' Kirel let his mouth fall open in an appreciative chuckle. Atvar studied the map with one eye and the shiplord with the other. He still mistrusted Kirel. A properly loyal subordinate would have played no role in the effort to oust him. Yes, next to Straha, Kirel was a paragon of virtue, but that was not saying enough to leave the fleetlord comfortable.

Atvar said, 'The cost in equipment and males for territory gained is running far higher than the computer projections. We've lost several heavy transports, and we cannot afford that at all. Without the transport fleet, we'll have to use starships to move landcruisers about – and that would leave them vulnerable to the maniacal Tosevites.'

'Truth, Exalted Fleetlord.' Kirel hesitated, then went on, 'At best, computer projections gave us less than a fifty percent chance of succeeding in the conquest of Britain if the campaign in the SSSR was not satisfactorily concluded first.'

Kirel remained unfailingly polite, but Atvar was not in the mood for criticism. 'The computer's reasoning was based on our ability to shift resources from the SSSR after we conquered it,' he snapped. 'True, we did not conquer it, but we have shifted resources – after the Soviets exploded that atomic bomb, we've scaled back operations in their territory. This produces something of the effect the computer envisioned, even if by a different route.'

'Yes, Exalted Fleetlord.' If Kirel was convinced, he did a good job of hiding it. He changed the subject, but not to one more reassuring: 'We are down to our last hundred antimissiles, Exalted Fleetlord.'

'That is not good,' Atvar said, an understatement that would do until a bigger one came along, which wouldn't be any time soon. As was his way, he did his best to look on the bright side of things: 'At least we can concentrate those missiles against Deutschland, the only Tosevite empire exploring that technology at the moment.'

'You are of course correct,' Kirel said. Then he and the fleetlord stopped and looked at each other in mutual consternation – and understanding.

With the Race, saying something was not happening at the moment meant it would not happen, certainly not in a future near enough to require worry. With the Big Uglies, it meant what it said and nothing more: it was no guarantee that the Americans or the Russkis or the Nipponese or even the British wouldn't start lobbing guided missiles at the Race tomorrow or the day after. Even more unnerving, both males had come to take that possibility for granted. With the Tosevites, you couldn't tell.

Kirel tried again: 'We continue to expend the antimissile missiles at a rate of several per day. We also seek to destroy the launchers from which the Deutsch missiles come, but we have had only limited success there, as they are both mobile and easy to conceal.'

'Any success on Tosev 3 seems limited,' Atvar said with a sigh. 'We might do better to blast the factories in which the missiles are manufactured. If the Deutsche cannot produce them, they cannot fire them. And missiles require great precision; if we destroy the tools needed to make them, the Big Uglies will be a long while coming up with more.' He realized he was once more reduced to buying time against the Tosevites, but that was better than losing to them.

'This course is also being attempted,' Kirel said, 'but, while it pains me to contradict the exalted fleetlord, the Tosevite missiles are astonishingly crude. Their guidance is so bad as to make them no more than area weapons, extremely long-range artillery, but the prospect of large weights of high explosive landing behind our lines remains unpleasant; some have evaded our countermeasures and done considerable damage, and that situation will grow far worse as we run out of countermissiles. The corresponding point is that they are far easier to build than the missiles that shoot them down. We attack factories we've identified as producing missile components, but the Deutsche continue to produce and launch the pestilential things.'

Atvar sighed again. There in an eggshell was the story of the war against the Big Uglies. The Race took all the proper steps to contain them – and got hurt, anyhow.

A screen on his desk lit up, showing the features of his adjutant, Pshing. Atvar immediately started to worry. Pshing wouldn't interrupt his conference with Kirel for anything that wasn't important, which meant, in practice, for anything that hadn't gone wrong. 'What is it?' Atvar demanded, putting a fierce snarl into the interrogative cough.

'Forgive me for troubling you, Exalted Fleetlord,' Pshing said nervously, 'but Fzzek, commander of invasion forces in Britain, has received under sign of truce a disturbing message from Churchill, the chief minister to the petty emperor of Britain. He requests your orders on how to proceed.'

'Give me the message,' Atvar said.

'It shall be done.' Pshing swung an eye turret to one side, evidently reading the words from another screen. 'This Churchill demands that we begin evacuating our forces from Britain in no more than two days or face an unspecified type of warfare the Tosevites have not yet employed against us, but one which is asserted to be highly effective and dangerous.'

'If this Churchill uses nuclear arms against us, we shall not spare his capital,' Atvar said. 'The island of Britain is so small, a few nuclear weapons would utterly ruin it.'

'Exalted Fleetlord, Churchill specifically denies the weapons he describes are nuclear in nature,' Pshing replied. 'They are new, they are deadly. Past that, the British spokesmale declined detailed comment.'

'Having begun the conquest of Britain, we are not going to abandon it on the say-so of a Tosevite,' Atvar said. 'You may tell Fzzek to relay that to Churchill. For all we know, the Big Ugly is but running an enormous bluff. We shall not allow ourselves to be deceived. Relay that to Fzzek as well.'

'It shall be done,' Pshing said. The screen holding his image went blank.

Atvar turned back to Kirel. 'Sometimes the presumption Tosevites show astonishes me. They treat us as if we were fools. If they have a new weapon, which I doubt, advertising it will produce nothing from us, especially since we've seen for ourselves that liars they are.'

'Exactly so, Exalted Fleetlord,' Kirel said.

Mutt Daniels crouched in ruins, hoping the Lizard bombardment would end soon. 'If it don't end soon, there ain't gonna be nothin' left of Chicago,' he muttered under his breath.

'What's that, Lieutenant?' Dracula Szabo asked from the shelter of a shell hole not far away.

Before Mutt could answer, several Lizard shells came in, close enough to slam him down as if he'd been blocking the plate when a runner bowled him over trying to score. He thanked his lucky stars he'd been breathing out rather than in; blast could rip your lungs to bits and kill you without leaving a mark on your body.

'Come on,' he said, and charged west across the ruined campus of Poro College toward the rubble that had been shops and apartments on the other side of South Park Way. Szabo followed at his heels.

Somewhere close by, a Lizard opened up with an automatic rifle. Daniels didn't know whether the bullets were intended for him, and didn't wait to find out. He threw himself flat, ignoring the bricks and stones on which he landed. Bricks and stones could hurt his bones, but bullets ... he shuddered, not caring for the parody on the old rhyme.

Bela Szabo returned five with his BAR. 'Ain't this a hell of a mess?' he called to Mutt.

'You might say that, yeah – you just might,' Mutt answered. Off to the west, some Americans still fought in the Swift and Armour plants; every so often, little spatters of gunfire rang out from that direction. The plants themselves were worse rubble than the Bronzeville wreckage amidst which he crouched. The Lizards had finally pushed around them and driven halfway toward Lake Michigan. That put them and Chicago's American defenders smack in the middle of Bronzeville, Chicago's Black Belt. Nobody had any real solid claim to the land between the packing plants and where Mutt now lay.

Dracula jerked a thumb back at what had been, in happier times, Poro College. 'What the hell kind of place was that, anyways?' he asked. 'I seen pictures of colored women all gussied up scattered along with all the other junk.'

'That there was what they call a beauty college,' said Mutt, who'd seen a sign on the ground. 'I guess that's where you went to learn how to gussy up colored folk, like you said.'

'Not me, Lieutenant,' Dracula said.

'Not me, neither, but somebody,' Mutt answered. Like most white men from Mississippi, he automatically thought of Negroes as ignorant share-croppers who were fine as long as they kept to their place. Barnstorming against black ballplayers in the winter and endless travels through the north and west, where things worked a little differently, had softened his attitude without destroying it.

That complicated life at the moment, because Bronzeville held, along with Lizard assault troops and American defenders and counterattackers, a fair number of Negro civilians living in cellars and makeshift shelters cobbled together from the wreckage of what had once been fine houses. They were nonpareil scavengers; that they'd stayed alive in the hell Chicago had become proved as much. They found all sorts of goodies – canned food, medicine, sometimes even smokes and booze – for the Army units fighting hereabouts. But not for Mutt: as soon as they heard his drawl, they dummied up. One, more forthright than the rest, had said, 'Mistuh, we came no'th to git away from that kind o' talk.'

As if picking the worry from Mutt's mind, Dracula Szabo said, 'Lieutenant, we gotta get some more help from the spooks around here. I mean, I ain't the worst scrounger ever born—'

'You're a sandbaggin' son of a bitch, is what you are, Dracula,' Daniels answered. Szabo was the best scrounger he'd ever seen, and he'd seen some real pros, Americans and British and especially Frenchmen, in France during the First World War. Hadn't been for Dracula, the platoon would have been hungrier and grouchier. Mutt still had a couple of precious cigarettes stashed against a day when he'd have to smoke one or die.

Dracula grinned, unabashed. As if Mutt hadn't spoken, he took up where he'd left off: '—but the thing of it is, the spooks know where most of the stuff is, account of they're the ones who stashed it in the first place. I'm just goin' around, maybe finding things by luck, know what I mean? Luck's a handy thing, no doubt about it, but having an angle's a damn sight better.' He spoke with the calm assurance of a man who tucked an ace up his sleeve every now and again.

'I'm not saying you're wrong, kid. Tell you what – next time we're tryin' to get somethin' from 'em, you handle it. Tell 'em the lieutenant made you the official US Army special duty supply bloodhound for the platoon. We'll see how that goes for a while – if we don't get pushed outta here and don't walk into a shell.'

'Okay, Lieutenant, if that's how you want it.' Szabo kept his voice so carefully neutral that Mutt had to put his sleeve up against his mouth to keep from laughing out loud. He knew he'd just given the fox the keys to the henhouse. Dracula would be scrounging for himself, not just for the platoon, and he'd turn a handsome profit on some of the things he came up with. But he was smart enough to do that after the things that really needed doing. Or he'd better be smart enough, because if he wasn't, Mutt would land on him like a ton of bricks.

From somewhere not far back from the shore of Lake Michigan, a mortar started lobbing bombs onto the Lizards over on Calumet Avenue. 'Come on!' Mutt shouted, and ran forward toward a house that was more or less intact. The men he led came with him, rifles and submachine guns banging away as they sprinted from one piece of cover to the next.

More bombs fell, these just ahead of the advancing Americans, so close that a couple of fragments flew past Daniels with an ugly whistling noise. The mortars chewed up the landscape even worse than it was already. Mutt peered out from behind a corner of the house, fired a burst at what might have been a Lizard even if it probably wasn't, and ran forward again to flop down behind a pile of bricks that once upon a time had been somebody's chimney.

He rested there for a couple of minutes, breathing hard – hell, panting. War was a young man's business, and he wasn't a young man any more. As he tried to catch his breath, he wondered whether pushing the Lizards back across a couple of miles of landscape-turned-trash-dump was worth the blood it would cost.

He'd wondered the same thing Over There. Once you were in 'em, the stretches of shell-pocked German trench you'd taken didn't seem as if they could possibly make up for the guys who got shot while you were taking them. But you kept doing it, over and over and over, and eventually the *Boches* couldn't stand the hammering any more and gave up.

Mutt had figured it was what Mr Wilson called it: the war to end war. But then up popped Hitler and up popped the Japs, and you had to go off and do it all over again. And then along came the Lizards, and all of a sudden you weren't fighting in some godforsaken place nobody'd ever heard of, you were fighting in Chicago, for God's sake. Hell, Comiskey Park, or whatever was left of it, couldn't have been more than a mile away.

Freight-train noises overhead said the Lizards were going after the mortar crews. Mutt didn't wish those crews any harm, but he was just as glad to have the aliens' artillery pounding at something in back of the line.

On his belly, he scrambled toward the bulk of a dead Model-A Ford th. sat on four flat tires. Small-arms fire was picking up; the Lizards didr feel like leaving the neighbourhood. He was almost to the car when I got shot.

He'd gone through months in France and more than a year in Illino without a scratch. He hadn't thought he was invulnerable; he knew bett than that. But he hadn't thought his number was up, either.

At first he felt just the impact, as if somebody had kicked him in tl rear, hard. 'Ahh, shit,' he said, as if an umpire had blown a close call third base and wouldn't change it back no matter how obviously wrong l was. He twisted around, trying to see the wound. Given where he'd bee hit, it wasn't easy, but the seat of his pants was filling up with blood.

'Jesus God,' he muttered. 'Everybody goes and talks about gettin' the ass shot off, but I went and did it.'

Then the wound started to hurt, as if he had a red-hot skewer stuck in his hindquarters. 'Medic!' he bawled. He knew he sounded like a brande calf, but he couldn't help it.

Dracula Szabo slithered over to him. When he saw where Mutt was hi he started laughing. 'Sorry, Lieutenant,' he said after a moment, and eve halfway sounded as if he meant it. 'I was just thinkin', I'll be damned I'm gonna kiss it and make it better.'

'I ask for a medic an' I go an' get W. C. Fields,' Mutt said. 'You ge a field dressing on you?' At Szabo's nod, he went on, 'Stick it on ther will you?'

'Sure thing. Lift up a little, so I can get your pants down and ge at where you're hit.' When Mutt obeyed, Dracula bandaged him wit cool competence that spoke of the practice he'd had at such things. Hi appraisal also told of that experience: 'Doesn't look too bad, sir. Not quit a crease, but it's a through-and-through, and it's just in the ham, not in th bone. You sit tight an' wait for the medics to take you outta here. You'r gonna be okay, I think.'

'Sit tight?' Mutt rolled his eyes. 'I ain't goin' anyplace real fast, ne with that, but I don't wanna sit on it, neither.'

'Yeah, well, I can see that,' Dracula answered. He swatted Mutt lightl on the shoulder. 'You take care. Good luck to you.' Then he was gone, bac to the fight. In the space of a moment, Daniels had gone from platoon leade – essentially, God's right-hand man – to part of the detritus of war.

He sang out again: 'Medic!' That ran the risk of drawing Lizards t him, but he was willing to take the chance. The Lizards were prett decent about not butchering wounded men, probably better than eithe the Germans or the Americans had been in the last war.

'Where you hit, soldier?' The man with the Red Cross armband wa black; at that moment, Mutt wouldn't have cared if he'd been green.

'Right in the butt,' he answered.

'Okay.' The black man had a partner who was white. Mutt noticed that but didn't say anything about it, even when the Negro kept on being the spokesman: 'We'll get the stretcher over by you, and you slide onto it on your belly, right?'

'Right.' Mutt did as he was told. 'Got me what the limeys used to call a Blighty wound: too bad to go on fightin', but not bad enough to wreck me for good. They'd get shipped back to England and they were done with the war. Me—' He shook his head.

The Negro chuckled sympathetically. 'Afraid you're right about that, Lieutenant. They'll fix you up and send you out again.' He turned to the white stretcher bearer. 'Come on, Jimmy. Let's get him back to the aid station.'

'Right, Doc.' Jimmy picked up his end of the stretcher.

'Doc?' Mutt said. He'd wondered why the colored guy had done all the talking. 'You a doctor?' he asked. He'd learned not to tack 'boy' onto that.

'That's right.' The Negro didn't look back at Daniels. For the first time, his voice got tight. 'Does it bother you, Alabama? If I'm not lily-white enough to take care of you, I can leave you right here.' He sounded deadly serious.

'I'm from Mississippi,' Mutt said automatically. Then he thought about the rest of the question. 'I been out of Mississippi a while, too. If you're American enough to want to patch my ass, I reckon I'm American enough to say thank-you when you're done.' He waited. He'd run into a few educated black men who were just as good at hating as any Ku-Kluxer.

Doc didn't say anything for a couple of steps. Then he nodded. 'Okay, Mississippi. That sounds fair.'

It damn well better, Daniels thought. *You're not gonna get anything more out of me.* But he didn't say so out loud. The colored doctor was doing his job, and seemed willing to meet him halfway. Given Mutt's own present circumstances, that was about as much as he had any right to expect.

The aid station had a big Red Cross flag flying in front of it, and several more on the roof. It was a big, foursquare brick building not far from Lake Michigan. Doc said, 'Hey, Mississippi, you know what this place was before the war?' 'No, but that don't matter, on account of I got the feeling you're just about to tell me,' Daniels said.

'You're right,' the Negro said. 'You don't let much bother you, do you? This was – still is, I guess – the Abraham Lincoln Center.'

'Just another damnyankee,' Daniels said, so deadpan that the colored doctor gave him a sharp look over his shoulder before chuckling ruefully. Mutt went on, 'Doc, I've done two turns of soldiering now, and in between 'em I was a bush-league manager for about a hundred years. So a smartmouth, even a smartmouth doc, that don't bother me much, no. Gettin' shot in the ass, now, *that* bothers me.'

'I can see how that would mess up a man's day,' Jimmy, the other stretcher bearer, put in.

Some dogfaces trudged past Mutt on their way up to the front. About half of them were grimy veterans like him, the rest fresh-faced kids. Some of the kids looked at the blood stained bandage on his backside and gulped. That didn't bother Mutt. He'd done the same thing the first time he saw wounded in France. War wasn't pretty, and you couldn't make it pretty.

What did bother him was that about one rifle-toting trooper in four was black. The Army was segregated, like any decent and proper outfit. Seeing white and colored soldiers together in the same outfit bothered Mutt as much as having white and colored ballplayers on the same team would have.

Doc didn't look back, but he didn't have to be a mind-reader to figure out what Daniels was thinking, either. He said, 'When you're fightin' to stay free, sometimes you get freer.' Mutt just grunted.

Doc and Jimmy lugged him into the aid station. His nose wrinkled at the stink of wounds gone bad. 'How messed up is this one?' somebody called from farther in.

'Not too,' Doc answered. 'Needs a tetanus shot, if we have any antitoxin, and some stitching. Should be okay, though.'

'Yeah, there's antitoxin,' the somebody – a worn, harassed somebody by his voice – said. 'It's slow right now, so why don't you sew him up quick before they bring in half a dozen bad ones all at the same time?'

'Right.' Doc and Jimmy set Mutt down where he wouldn't be in the way of other stretcher parties carrying in the wounded. Doc came back with a syringe, a glass jar partly filled with a clear, oily liquid, and a clean rag. He jabbed Mutt in the backside with the needle.

'Ow!' Mutt said. 'Why didn't you give me the ether first?'

'Mississippi, if you can grouse about a needle after you took a bullet in the cheek, I think you're probably going to live,' the colored doctor told him. He opened the jar, soaked the rag, and held it to Daniels' face. The stink of the ether made Mutt cough and choke. He tried to pull away, but the doctor's hand at the back of his head wouldn't let him. His vision got frayed and fuzzy and faded out like a movie.

When he woke up, his mouth was dry as a salt mine and tasted like a latrine. He hardly noticed; he had a headache worse than any he'd ever got from moonshine, and that was saying something. His backside felt as if an alligator had taken a good bite out of it, too.

'Doc?' Mutt's voice was a hoarse croak.

'The doctors are busy,' an orderly said. 'Can I get you some water?'

'Oh, Lord, I wish you would,' Mutt answered. The orderly sounded like some kind of pansy, but if he'd bring some water, Mutt didn't care what he did in his spare time. He shook his head, which made it hurt worse. A nigger doctor and a pansy orderly, colored troops fighting side by side with white men ... what the hell was the world coming to?

The orderly brought not only water but a couple of little white pills with BAYER on them. 'I found some aspirin,' he said. 'It may do your head a little good. You probably don't feel real well right now.'

'Buddy, you ain't kidding,' Mutt answered. His hand trembled when he held it out for the aspirin tablets. He grimaced in self-reproach. 'You'd think I had the DTs or somethin'.'

'You're still woozy from the anesthetic,' the orderly said. 'That happens to everybody, not—' He shut up and held out the water to Daniels.

Not just to old geezers like you: Mutt could fill in the blanks for himself. He didn't care; what with his head and his ventilated backside, he felt as elderly as he probably looked. He popped the aspirins into his mouth, washed them down with some water. It probably came straight out of Lake Michigan; Chicago didn't have running water, or ever guaranteed clean water, any more. But you had to go on drinking, even if you did get the runs now and again.

'Thank you, friend,' he said with a sigh. 'That was mighty kind of you, even if I do wish it was a bottle of beer instead.'

'Oh, so do I!' the orderly exclaimed, which made Mutt blink; when he thought about queers – which he didn't spend a lot of time doing – he pictured them sipping wine, not knocking back a beer. The fellow studied Mutt's bandages, which made him shift nervously from side to side. Just because he had to lie on his stomach didn't mean ... Then the orderly said, 'You're probably one of the few people who's glad – for a while, anyhow – the toilets don't work. With that wound, squatting over a bucket will hurt you a lot less than sitting down would.'

'That's true,' Daniels said. 'Hadn't much thought about it yet, but you're right.' He was beginning to feel a little more like himself. Maybe the aspirin was starting to work, or maybe the ether cobwebs were going away.

'You have trouble or need help, you just sing out for me,' the orderly said. 'My name is Archie. Don't be shy, I don't mind – it's why I'm here.'

I bet you don't mind. But Mutt kept his mouth shut again. Like the colored doctor, this guy was doing his job. He was entitled to enjoy it – if he did – so long as he didn't make a nuisance of himself. Mutt sighed. The world got crazier day by day, though he wished it hadn't got crazy enough to shoot him in the ass. 'Thanks, Archie. If I have to take you up on that, I will.'

Sweat ran down George Bagnall's face. When summer finally got to Pskov, it didn't fool about. The grass on the hills outside of town was turning yellow as the sun. The forests of pine and fir to the east and south, though, remained as dark and gloomy in summer as at any other time of year.

A lot of German troops in Pskov went around bare-chested to get a suntan. The Russians didn't go in for that. The ones who weren't in uniform and were lucky enough to have a change of clothes switched to lighter, baggier tunics and trousers. Bagnall's RAF uniform wasn't much more than tatters these days. He mostly wore Russian civilian clothes, with a Red army officer's cap to give him a semblance of authority.

As happened on account of that, somebody came up to him and asked him something in Russian. He got the gist – which way to the new stables? – and answered in his own halting Russian. 'Ah!' the fellow said. '*Nyemets?*'

'*Nyet,*' Bagnall answered firmly. '*Anglichani.*' You never could be sure how a Russian would react if he thought you were a Jerry – better to set him right straightaway.

Ah, *Anglichani, khorosho,*" the Russian said: Englishman – good. He rattled off something Bagnall thought was thanks for the directions and hurried off toward the street to which Bagnall had pointed.

Bagnall headed on toward the market square. As a fighting man, he got plenty of black bread, the cabbage soup called *shchi*, and borscht, along with the occasional bit of hen or mutton or pork. The Russians ate and thrived, the Germans ate and didn't complain – the winter before the Lizards came, they'd been eating horses that froze to death in the snow. Bagnall wanted something better, or at least different; he wanted to see if any of the *babushkas* would part with some eggs.

The old and middle-aged women sat in rows behind rickety tables or blankets on which they'd laid out what they had for sale. With their solid, blocky figures and the outlines of their heads smoothed and rounded by the scarves they all wore, they reminded Bagnall of nothing so much as figures from those cleverly carved, multilayered sets of Russian wooden dolls. The immobile stolidity with which they sat only enhanced the illusion.

No one was displaying any eggs, but that didn't necessarily signify. He'd found out good stuff often got held back, either for some special customer or just to keep it from being pilfered. He walked up to one of the *babushkas* and said, '*Dobry dyen.*' The woman stared at him, expressionless. '*Yaichnitsa?*'

She didn't bother returning his good-day. She didn't even bother scowling at him; she just looked through him as if he didn't exist. It was one of the most effortlessly annihilating glances he'd ever received. He felt himself wilting as she let him know she didn't have any eggs, and that even if she had had some eggs, she wouldn't have had any for a German.

Before the Lizards came, before the partisans emerged from the forest to reclaim a share of Pskov, she never would have dared to act so to a German, either. If she'd had eggs, she would either have turned them over or hidden them so well the Nazis would never had suspected they were there. As it was, he got the notion she was just taunting him.

'*Nyet nyemets,*' he said, as he had before. '*Anglichani.*'

'*Anglichani?*' She gave forth with a spate of Russian, much too quick for him to follow in detail. What he did get, though, suggested that that made a difference. She plucked a few sorry-looking potatoes out of a bowl – you'd have to have been starving to want them. Underneath lay more equally unprepossessing spuds – and, nestled among them, several eggs.

'*Skolko?*' he asked. 'How much?'

She wanted five hundred rubles apiece, or 750 marks. German money had been falling against its Soviet equivalent ever since Bagnall arrived in Pskov. The Soviet Union and Germany were still going concerns, but the Lizards in Poland and to the south of Pskov screened the city away from much contact with other German forces. The Soviet presence, on the other hand, was growing. That might lead to trouble one day, as if the Reds and the Nazis didn't already have enough trouble getting along.

'*Bozhe moi?*' Bagnall shouted, loud enough to draw glances from *babushkas* several places away. He'd learned you'd best forget all you'd ever known of British reserve if you wanted to get anywhere dickering with Russians. If you stayed polite, they thought you were weak and they rode roughshod over you.

He knew he mixed his cases and numbers in a way that would have got him a caning in sixth-form Latin, but he didn't care. This wasn't school; this was the real world. However inelegant his Russian might have been, it worked, and he didn't think the *babushka* was any budding Pushkin, either. He ended up buying three eggs for seven hundred rubles, which wasn't half bad.

'*Nyet anglichani,*' the *babushka* said, pointing at him. '*Zhid.*'

Bagnall remembered an old, beautifully dressed Jewish man he'd seen walking slowly along a Paris street with a six-pointed yellow star with the word *Juif* on it sewn to his jacket pocket. The expression of dignified misery that man had worn would go with him to his grave. But the sneer in the *babushka's* voice told him something of how others had thought it a good idea to make the old Jew wear a yellow star.

'*Zhid?*' Bagnall said quietly. '*Spasebo.* Thank you.' The *babushka's* gray eyes went blank and empty as a couple of stones. Bagnall took the eggs and headed for the house he shared with Ken Embry and Jerome Jones. He hoped he wouldn't run into Tatiana the sniper.

A buzz in the sky made him turn as he walked past a grassy park on whose greensward sheep grazed under the watchful eyes of Red Army and *Wehrmacht* guards. After a moment, he spotted an approaching plane: not a Lizard fighter, lean and graceful as a shark and a millionfold more deadly, but a human-built machine that hardly looked as if it belonged in the same sky as Lizard aircraft or even those of the RAF.

It was, nonetheless, the first human-built airplane – and, not coincidentally, the first plane not loaded with ordnance intended to punch his ticket – he'd seen in a long time. That alone sent his spirits soaring. The Red Army guards raised a cheer when they spied the red stars painted on the wings and fuselage and tailplane.

The Russian aircraft was coming into Pskov at treetop height. At first Bagnall thought that was just because it skimmed the ground to give the

Lizards a harder time spotting it. Then, as it lowered its flaps, he realized the pilot intended to bring it down right in the park.

'He's out of his bloody mind,' Bagnall muttered. But the pilot wasn't. The biplane wasn't going very fast and wasn't very heavy; it rolled to a stop with better than a hundred yards of meadow to spare. It even managed to avoid running over a sheep or butchering one with its prop as it taxied. Bagnall trotted toward it with the vague notion of congratulating whoever had done the flying.

First out of the aircraft was a tall, skinny fellow with a thick red beard. He wore a field-gray tunic, but Bagnall would have guessed him for a German even without it – his face was too long and beaky to belong to most Russians.

Sure enough, he started yelling in German: 'Come on, you dumbheads, let's get this stinking airplane under cover before the Lizards spot it and blow it to hell and gone.'

The pilot stood up and shouted support for the Nazi. Bagnall didn't follow all of it, but he knew *maskirovka* meant camouflage. That wasn't what made him stop and stare, though. He'd heard the Reds used female pilots, but he hadn't more than half believed it till now.

Yet there she was. She took off her leather flying helmet, and hair the color of ripe wheat spilled down almost to her shoulders. Her face was wide and rather flat, her skin fair but tanned except around the eyes, where her goggles shielded it from the sun. The eyes themselves were intensely blue.

She saw him and the officer's cap he was wearing, climbed down out of the biplane, and walked up to him. Saluting, she said, 'Comrade, I am Senior Lieutenant Ludmila Gorbunova, reporting to Pskov as ordered with the German sergeant Georg Schultz, a tank gunner and highly capable mechanic.'

Fumblingly, Bagnall explained he wasn't really a Red Army officer, and who he really was. Without much hope, he added, *'Gavoritye li vuy pa-angliski?'*

'No, I don't speak English,' she replied in Russian, but then she did switch languages: *'Sprechen Sie Deutsch? Ich kann Deutsch ein wenig sprechen.'*

'I speak a little German also. Perhaps more than a little now,' he answered in the same tongue.

Hearing German, Georg Schultz came up and greeted Bagnall with a stiff-arm salute and a loud, *'Heil Hitler.'*

Bugger Hitler, was the first thought that came to Bagnall's mind. If it hadn't been for the Lizards, he and Schultz – and, for that matter, Schultz and Ludmila Gorbunova – would have been at each other's throats. The Germans made even more uncomfortable allies than the Russians.

Senior Lieutenant Gorbunova looked pained. 'He is a dedicated fascist, as you hear. But he has also done very good work for the Red Air Force. With tools in his hand, he is a genius.'

Bagnall studied Schultz. 'He must be,' he said slowly. If the Nazi hadn't been bloody good, the Communists would have got rid of him on general principles. That they hadn't was probably a measure of their own desperate situation.

Men came running up to drag the biplane as far in among the trees over to one side of the park as its wings would permit. Others draped it with camouflage netting. Before long, it had all but disappeared.

'That *may* do,' Ludmila said, casting a critical eye its way. She turned back to George Bagnall. 'I think I am glad to meet you. You English here in Pskov, you are—' She ran out of German, then tried a couple of Russian words Bagnall didn't understand. Finally he got the idea she meant something like *arbitrators*.

'Yes, that is right,' Bagnall answered in German. 'When the *Wehrmacht* commander and the partisan brigadiers cannot agree, they bring their arguments for us to decide.'

'What if they don't like what you decide?' Georg Schultz asked. 'Why should they listen to a pack of damned Englishmen?' He stared at Bagnall with calculated insolence.

'Because they were killing each other here before they started listening to us,' Bagnall answered. Schultz looked like one very rugged customer, but Bagnall took a step toward him anyhow. If he wanted a scrap, he could have one. The flight engineer went on, 'We do need to stick together against the Lizards, you know.'

'That is part of why the two of us were sent here,' Ludmila Gorbunova said. 'We are German and Russian, but we have worked well with each other.'

Schultz leered at her. Bagnall wondered if she meant they were sleeping together. He hoped not. She wasn't as pretty as Tatiana, but on three minutes' acquaintance she seemed much nicer. Then she noticed Schultz's slobbering stare, and answered it with one that would have made any long-suffering English barmaid proud.

It also made the world seem a much more cheerful place to George Bagnall. 'Come with me,' he said. 'I'll take you to the *Krom*, where both sides have their headquarters.' Ludmila Gorbunova smiled at him as she nodded. He felt like bursting into song.

7

"Do you know what one of the troubles with Big Uglies is?" Atvar said to his English-speaking interpreter as they waited for the emissary from the United States to be shown into the conference chamber.

'They have so many, Exalted Fleetlord,' the interpreter answered. 'Which in particular are you thinking of today?'

'They are *untidy* creatures,' Atvar said with distaste. 'Their clothes flap about them like loose skins, the tufts they grow on their heads either flap about, too, or else are held down with enough oil to lubricate a landcruiser engine, and they spew water from their hides instead of panting, as proper people should. They are disgusting.'

'Truth, Exalted Fleetlord,' the interpreter said gravely.

Pshing, Atvar's adjutant, came on one of the communications screens. 'Exalted Fleetlord, the Tosevite from the United States is here. I remind you, his name is Cordell Hull; his title is Secretary of State. Before we came, he was the chief aide in dealing with other Big Ugly empires for his not-empire's leader.'

'Send him in,' Atvar said.

Cordell Hull looked uncomfortable in weightlessness, but made a good show of pretending he wasn't. Even for a Big Ugly, he was long, though not especially wide. The tuft of fuzz on top of his head was almost white. Atvar knew that meant he was aging. So did the wrinkles and sags in his integument. He was not attractive, but then, to Atvar's eyes, no Big Ugly was.

After the polite greetings customary even between enemies, Atvar plunged straight in: 'I demand from you the immediate return of the traitorous shiplord Straha, who fled to you in violation of all law.'

Cordell Hull spoke a single sharp word: 'No.' The translator indicated that that was a negative; Atvar had suspected as much. Hull went on at some length afterwards: 'The United States does not give back people who come to us seeking shelter. My land is made up of people who came seeking freedom. We welcomed them; we did not turn them away.'

'You welcomed criminals?' Atvar said, and then, in an aside to the interpreter. 'It does not surprise me a bit, though you needn't tell him that.'

'We did,' Hull answered defiantly. 'Many things that were called crimes were really nothing more than disagreeing with the leaders of the lands they left.' His eyes, though sunk deep in his head like any Tosevite's, bored into Atvar's with disconcerting keenness.

The fleetlord said, 'Do you not call stealing a shuttlecraft a crime? Straha is a robber as well as a traitor. Is your not-empire also in the habit of keeping stolen goods? We demand the shuttlecraft's return, too.'

'Go ahead and demand,' Hull replied. 'In war, if one side is generous enough to help the other, it doesn't get its toy back.'

'In war, the side that is losing is usually wise enough to deal politely with the side that is winning,' Atvar said. 'So the ancient records of the Race tell us, at any rate; the Race has never lost a war against another species.'

'If you think we're losing, look at Chicago,' Hull said. In his own way, he was as exasperating an opponent as the SSSR's Molotov. The latter Big Ugly was as inflexible as a poorly programmed machine, mechanically rejecting everything Atvar said. Hull instead tried to twist things.

Atvar said, 'Look at Chicago yourself. Our forces continue to advance through the city. The large factories you defended for so long are now practically cleared of Tosevites, and soon our victorious males will reach the shore of the lake by which the city lies.'

'Bully for them,' Hull answered, which caused the interpreter considerable confusion. After the misunderstanding was straightened out, the US Secretary of State said, 'Some of your victorious males may make it to Lake Michigan, but how many of 'em won't? How many of 'em are dead and stinking in the streets of Chicago?'

'Far fewer than the males you throw away like wastepaper in a futile effort to halt us,' Atvar snapped. He didn't like being reminded of the casualties the conquest of Chicago was costing the Race.

Cordell Hull's face twisted into one of the leers the Big Uglies used to show emotion. ('This is an expression of amusement and irony,' the interpreter told Atvar in a brief aside.) He said, 'We have more men to spend than you do, and more of everything else, too. Before long, you're going to have to start robbing Peter to pay Paul if you want reinforcements.'

The interpreter needed to go back and forth with Hull a few times, but when he finally made sense of that, it made sense to Atvar, too. Worst of it was that the Tosevite was right. Every time fresh males went into Chicago, an offensive somewhere else on Tosev 3 necessarily suffered, either that or a garrison in a 'safely conquered' region was reduced, whereupon, more often than not, the region was found not to be so safely conquered after all.

Trying to match Hull's irony, the fleetlord said, 'What would you have us do, then, Exalted Tosevite?'

'Who, me? I'm just a jumped-up Tennessee lawyer,' Hull replied, which occasioned still more translation difficulties. Once they were resolved, Hull went on, 'We don't hold with fancy titles in the United States – never have, never will. We figure part of being free is getting away from all that nonsense.'

Atvar stared at him in honest bewilderment. Every society built by every intelligent race was hierarchical – how could it be otherwise? Why pretend such a manifest and obvious truth did not exist?

He had no time to ponder that; Hull was still talking: 'If you really want to know what I want you to do, what the people of the United States want you to do, what the people of the world want you to do, it's not what anybody would call complicated: quit killing people and go back to your own planet.'

The fleetlord tried to imagine his reception if he returned to Home with a beaten army in cold sleep, bearing word that the species that had defeated him was now seeking to develop space travel on its own and would in a short time (as the Race reckoned such things) be heading out toward the Empire. 'It cannot be,' he answered quickly.

'Well, I allow I reckoned you'd say as much,' Cordell Hull told him. 'Next best would be for you to stay here – we'd set aside land somewhere for you, maybe – and make peace with us.'

'You Tosevites are not in any position to grant us terms,' Atvar said angrily. 'We are in the process of conquering you, of bringing you into the Empire, and we shall continue until victory is won, in Chicago and everywhere else.'

'If you're going to take that attitude, why did you bring me up here to this spaceship in the first place?' Hull asked. 'Flying up here was a big jolt for an old man like me.'

'You were summoned to hear our demand for the return of the traitor Straha, which you have insolently refused, and to take a warning back to your emperor,' Atvar said.

'We don't have an emperor, or want one, either,' Hull said.

'Your leader, then – whatever you call him.' Atvar hissed in exasperation. 'The warning is simple: if you seek to produce nuclear weapons, you will be utterly destroyed.'

Hull studied him for a while before answering. Every so often, despite their weird features, the Tosevites could look disconcertingly keen. This was one of those times. Being divided up into tens or hundreds of ephemeral little squabbling empires, each always trying to outdo or outcheat its neighbors, had given them a political sophistication – or perhaps just a talent for chicanery – the Race, despite its long history, had trouble matching.

Slowly, Hull said, 'You intend to conquer us whether we make these weapons or not. Why should we give up the best chance not just to hurt you but to beat you? What's the percentage in it for us?'

'We shall conquer you with or without your nuclear weapons,' Atvar answered. 'More of your not-empire, more of your people, will survive if you do not force us to extremes.'

Cordell Hull made a strange noise, half gasping, half barking. 'This is what the Big Uglies use for laughter,' the interpreter said.

'Yes, I know that,' Atvar answered impatiently. 'What did I say that was so amusing?'

When the US Secretary of State spoke again, he made a grim kind of sense: 'Why should we care? In your scheme of things, we're all going to be your slaves forever anyhow. To keep that from happening, we'll do anything – *anything*, I tell you. Men are meant to live free. When you came here, we were fighting among ourselves to make that happen. We'll fight you, too.'

Now Atvar was the one who hesitated. The Big Uglies constantly prated of freedom. The best analysts of the Race kept trying to understand, and kept having trouble. Atvar didn't find the concept attractive; what the Tosevites meant by it seemed to him nothing more than anarchy.

'Do you not care what happens to the males and females under your rule?' he asked. To any civilized male, the Race came first. Any individual's fate paled in importance beside the welfare of the group.

If the Tosevites thought like that, they did a good job of hiding it. Cordell Hull said, 'If the United States isn't free, if her people aren't free, there's no point to the whole business. Time you figured that out. You get your soldiers and your bases out of our country, maybe we have something to talk about. Until then, forget it.'

Molotov had made the same demand, although he'd couched it in terms of – what had he called it? – the ineluctable historical dialectic, a notion that gave analysts even more trouble than did the mysterious and quite possibly unreal thing called freedom. The Big Uglies had a gift for dreaming up concepts unsupported by evidence.

Atvar said, 'If you cannot make us do something, you are in a poor position to tell us we must do it as a price for beginning talks.'

'The same applies to you,' Hull retorted. 'You can't make us quit trying to beat you by any way that comes to hand, so you'd just as well give up on that. Maybe after we've battered you some more, you'll be more wiling to talk sense.'

The fleetlord's breath hissed out in a long sigh. 'You will regret your obstinacy.' He turned to one of the males who had brought Hull to the conference chamber. 'We are finished here. Take him back to the shuttle; let him convey to his emperor – his not-emperor, I should say – the substance of our discussion.' When the Tosevite was gone, Atvar sighed again. 'They refuse to see reason. The more readily they yield and accept the Emperor's supremacy, the higher their place within the Empire will be. If we cannot trust them, if they are always rising in futile revolt—'

Before he could finish the thought, Pshing's face appeared on the screen once more. 'Exalted Fleetlord, urgent new reports from Britain.'

By his adjutant's tone, the new reports weren't good ones. Urgent news from the surface of Tosev 3 was seldom good. 'Give them to me,' Atvar said.

'It shall be done. As threatened, the British have turned loose their new weapon or weapons against us. Chemicals – of what sort we are still investigating – are being delivered by artillery and aerosol to poison our males. Casualties have occurred as a result of this. These poisonous gases have also adversely affected morale; when the Big Uglies employed them, they are sometimes able to achieve local successes in their wake. Commanders in Britain urgently request countermeasures.'

Atvar stared at Pshing, who looked back at him as if expecting him to produce countermeasures from a pouch on his belt. 'Refer all this to our scientific teams, with a highest priority tag,' the fleetlord answered. Then he asked, 'Are the Tosevites indiscriminately poisoning their own fighting males in an effort to harm us?'

One of Pshing's eye turrets swiveled down toward his desktop to study to report there. 'Exalted Fleetlord, this does not appear to be the case. They wear masks which give them at least some protection against their own chemical agents. Some of these have been captured. We are endeavouring to modify them to serve our own needs, and doing the same with our antiradiation masks. Unfortunately, we have very limited quantities of the latter.'

'Good that you thought of it, though,' Atvar said. For a moment there, he'd wondered if he was the only male in the entire Race left with a working brain. Then he realized that now, instead of worrying about whether the Big Uglies were able to match the technical developments of the Race, he was worrying about whether the Race could duplicate something the Big Uglies had invented.

It was a very unpleasant way to come full circle.

When the Lizards first came to Earth, Moishe Russie had been starving in the Warsaw ghetto, praying for a sign from God that He would not abandon His people. Russie had taken the nuclear bomb they'd exploded high above Central Europe as a sign his prayer was being answered, though he'd learned later that the Lizards had hoped to use the blast to scramble communications and disrupt electronics generally. For reasons he didn't altogether understand, it hadn't worked out as they'd expected.

That wasn't the point, though. When the light in the sky answered his prayer, people in the ghetto had started calling him *Reb* Moishe, and some of them had even looked on him as a prophet. He hadn't believed that himself, not really, but sometimes you wondered.

Now, crouched down in the rubble-strewn St Albans street between a theater left over from the days of ancient Rome and even more battered ruins of what had been some wealthy noble's mansion a couple of hundred years before, he wondered again. As he'd predicted to Nathan Jacobi, here he was in British service, wearing a Red Cross armband.

'I didn't think about the gas mask, though,' he said. The mask distorted his voice and made him sound like something from another planet, although not, thank God, a Lizard. With its long snout and the tube running down to the chemical canister that purified the air, the mask made him look inhuman, too: rather like a kangaroo with an elephant's trunk.

Not only did it change the way he looked, it changed the way he saw. Peering out at the world through a pair of portholes that got dirty whenever they felt like it and stayed more or less permanently steamed up made him appreciate what a marvel normal vision was.

Somewhere north of St Albans, the Lizards were licking their wounds. They'd been in the city itself till a barrage of mustard gas and phosgene, followed by a desperate infantry attack, drove them out again. Now St Albans was in British hands once more. Moishe wondered when the Lizards would start using poison gas of their own. It probably wouldn't be long. He also wondered if anyone on either side would be alive when the war was over.

Down in the Roman theater, someone called out 'Help!' in a drowned, choking voice. The cry wasn't Yiddish or Polish; Moishe had to translate it into a language he habitually used. Then he realized it wasn't English, either. That was a hurt Lizard down there.

He hesitated no more than a heartbeat before he scrambled down into the remains of the theater. He wondered for a moment what sort of plays the ancient inhabitants of St Albans (which surely hadn't been the Roman name for the place) had watched there. The theatre was shaped like a capital C, with a colonade – one column still miraculously standing – behind the rectangular stage that occupied what would have been the open space keeping the C from becoming an O. Curved banks of earth formed the letter itself, and showed where the seats had been.

The Lizard lay in the flat, open area in the center of the theater. Would that have been called the orchestra? Moishe knew only slightly more of the classical theater than he did of the fine points of Chinese calligraphy.

That also held true, he realized, for what he knew about how to treat injured Lizards – not that any human being was likely to be expert in that field. 'I'll do what I can,' he muttered inside the mask. He'd dealt with the Lizards long enough in Warsaw to come to see them as people, too. And Lizard prisoners were valuable. He hadn't had much in the way of a briefing before they sent him out to do his best for King and Country (not his king nor his country, but that was irrelevant now), but they'd made that crystal clear.

Then he got a clearer look through his dirty, steamy windows on the world and realized this Lizard wasn't going to live long enough to be worth anything as a captive. Its body was covered with blisters, some of them bigger than Moishe's fist. The blisters destroyed the patterns of its body paint. They seemed to cluster under its arms and at the join of its legs, although it also had one that swallowed up an eye turret. From the bubbling way it breathed, Russie was sure the mustard gas was wrecking its lungs as well.

The Lizard could still see out of the eye the gas had not destroyed. 'Help me,' it gasped, not caring in the least that he was a despised Tosevite. 'Hurts.' It added the emphatic cough, then kept on coughing and couldn't stop. Bloody bubbles came out of its mouth and nostrils.

'Help how?' Russie asked with an interrogative cough. 'Not know.' Seeing what the gas had done left him sick to his stomach, although being sick inside a gas mask was anything but a good idea.

'I don't know how,' the Lizard answered, more fluent now that Russie had spoken to it in its own language. 'You Big Uglies made this horrible stuff. You must have the antidote for it.'

'No antidote,' Moishe answered. There was an ointment that was supposed to do some good on mustard gas burns and blisters, but he had none and, in any case, word was the stuff didn't really help.

'Then kill me,' the Lizard said. 'Kill me, I beg.' Another emphatic cough turned into another paroxysm that tore the Lizard to pieces from the inside out.

Moishe stared at it in dismay. Everything he'd learned in medical school, everything trained into him as a Jew, made him want to cry 'No!' and to flee from the abominable act he'd been asked to perform. One of the things they had warned him about in medical school was that you didn't learn everything you needed to become a doctor there. He'd seen that in Warsaw from 1939 on; now he saw it again, even more starkly.

'I beg,' the Lizard said.

He looked around. The Lizard must not have been gassed here, for he didn't see its rifle. He had no weapons himself; medical personnel were supposed to be noncombatants. What was he supposed to do, bash in its head with a rock? He didn't think he could, no matter how much the Lizard wanted him – *needed* him – to do just that.

While he stood there in his own mental torment, yet another coughing fit wracked the Lizard. The coughs subsided to gasps; the gasps stopped. 'Oh, thank God!' Moishe exclaimed. Sometimes even death could be a blessing – and he hadn't had to inflict it.

Since Lizards didn't wear clothes, they carried what they needed in a pack on their back and in belt pouches. Russie peeled off the pack and undid the pouches. Then, because sitting out in the middle of the orchestra made him feel naked and exposed to artillery and whatever live Lizards might still be in the neighbourhood, he took the chattels first up onto the stage, where he could shelter behind the one intact column and the stubs of the others, and then down into a shell hole behind it. He didn't think he could find better cover than that.

He opened the pack first. In it were several full magazines for the automatic rifle the Lizards used. Those would be useful; a few Englishmen carried captured Lizard weapons, and they were always crying for ammunition.

He also found half a dozen little bricks of what the Lizards reckoned field rations, each one wrapped in stuff that reminded him of cellophane but was thicker, more pliable, and less shiny. Lizard prisoners were welcome to the rations, which struck him as distinctly unappetizing. He wondered more about their wrapping: what it was and how they made it. It wasn't really like anything mankind turned out.

Something else spilled out of the pack, a case about the size of a ration brick. 'Better and better,' Moishe said to no one in particular. The case was a wireless set, though how the Lizards managed to build such a tiny wireless was beyond him – and beyond the best human scientists and engineers in the world, too.

In the same way that the ration wrappers reminded him of cellophane, the material from which the case was made put him in mind of Bakelite. But it wasn't Bakelite; it was another one of the types of stuff the Lizards could manufacture and people couldn't.

Along with such practical things as food, ammunition, and communications gear, the Lizard also carried in its pack a whole sheaf of papers, more than Russie would have expected to find on any ten human casualties. One of the papers was a map; Moishe recognized the street grid of St Albans down in one corner.

The map and notations in the squiggly Lizard script. Moishe did his best to puzzle them out. Back in Warsaw, he learned the characters the Lizards used for their written language. It hadn't taken him long: he already dealt with two versions of one alphabet for Yiddish and Hebrew and two versions of another for Polish and German. The trouble was that, while he could read the words, he mostly didn't know what they meant. He hadn't had time to build up anything but the most basic vocabulary.

'Too bad,' he said, and tucked the papers into his medical bag. Somebody would understand what they meant. One thing that had impressed him about the English was the amount of scholarly talent they could bring to bear on almost anything.

He fumbled at one of the belt pouches before he finally got it open: the closure would have been much easier to work if he'd had claws on his fingertips rather than nails. A card a little bigger than a standard business card spilled out onto the ground.

When he picked it up and turned it over, he found himself staring into one of the Lizards' three-dimensional pictures. It showed the male who had just died in the Roman theater. Letter by letter, he sounded out the Lizard's name: 'Ekretkan.'

He wondered what sort of person Ekretkan had been, how he'd lived before he came to Earth, what he'd thought of the Race's war before he became one of its victims. The card offered no clue to that. Next to

Ekretkan's photo was a complicated network of golds and greens that reminded Russie of the body paint pattern the Lizard had worn. He supposed it showed the dead male's rank, seniority, and specialization, but had no idea how to read it.

The card went into his bag with the papers. Moishe went through the rest of the pouches, looking for more clues to Ekretkan the individual, as opposed to Ekretkan the soldier. Even Nazis had parents, wives, children, dogs, and often carried pictures of them. Not Ekretkan. He had a couple of pictures Moishe thought were of himself, one with him astride a contraption that looked like a four-wheeled motorcycle, another with him wearing a somewhat simpler version of the body paint in which he'd died.

Ekretkan also had a couple of photos of a flat, empty of other Lizards but filled with gadgets that did things incomprehensible to Russie. *Home sweet home*, he thought. And the Lizard carried a photo of a street scene that looked like the New York Moishe had seen in the cinema, only more so: tall, thrusting buildings of steel and glass, streets crowded with vehicles, sidewalks full of Lizards who looked as if they were in a hurry. *His hometown?* Russie wondered.

He set the meager handful of photographs on the ground in a row and stared at them, trying to draw meaning from them. If Ekretkan was a typical male, what did that say about how the Race lived? Could a male's life be as barren as the pictures made it look? Most of the males Moishe had known in Warsaw had seemed happy enough, and no crazier than human beings filling similar social roles.

'And so?' he muttered. The Race had mating seasons, not families; he'd learned that back in Warsaw, too. The Lizards thought human mating customs just as strange and revolting as most humans found theirs. Russie examined the pictures again, searching for clues like a Talmudic scholar contemplating a difficult text.

The most important difference he saw between Lizards and people was that Lizards didn't have families. That meant – what? That they were alone a lot, especially when they weren't working. They probably liked it that way, too. Ekretkan's pictures showed either himself or his empty flat, which argued in favor of Moishe's line of reasoning.

What about the street scene, then? Moishe picked that one up, set it aside from the others, and thought about families some more. No Lizard families. That didn't mean lonely Lizards, even if the Lizards were often alone. But it did mean the family wouldn't get in the way of whatever loyalty the Lizards gave to any entity bigger than the individual.

He nodded, pleased with himself. That fit. He didn't know whether it was true, but it fit. All the loyalty each Lizard didn't reserve for himself went straight to the Race. Moishe had seen that; the Race and the Emperor were as important to each male, if in a less vicious way, as the *Volk* and the *Führer* were to a Nazi.

Moishe gathered up the pictures and put them in his black bag along with the rest of the luckless Ekretkan's effects. He got out of the shell hole and headed back toward regimental headquarters. Other people needed to evaluate what he'd found.

He wondered how his conclusions would stack up against those of a real Lizard expert.

'You know, Sergeant,' Ben Berkowitz said, clasping his hand behind his head and leaning back in his chair, 'the Lizards are plenty to drive a psychiatrist *meshuggeh*. I ought to know, I am one.' He paused. 'You know what *meshuggeh* means? No offense, but you don't sound like you're from New York.'

Sam Yeager chuckled. 'I better not – I'm from Nebraska. But yeah – uh, yes, sir – I know what it means. Something like crazy, right? I've played ball with a few Jewish guys; it's one of the things they'd say. But why do the Lizards drive you nuts? Except because they're Lizards, I mean.'

'How much do you know about psychiatry?' Berkowitz asked.

'Not much,' Yeager admitted. *Astounding* had run some great articles about the physical sciences, and even about weird things like linguistics for time travelers, but zilch about psychiatry.

'Okay,' Berkowitz said equably. 'One of the basic principles of Freudian analysis is that a big part of why people do what they do comes from their sex drive and the conflicts that revolve around it.'

'No offense, sir, but it doesn't seem to me like you have to be a psychiatrist to figure that one out.' Yeager chuckled in fond reminiscence. 'I think about some of the crazy things I used to do to get myself laid—'

'Yeah, me, too, except I'm still doing 'em.' Berkowitz's hand was bare of wedding ring. That didn't have to signify, not with a man, but evidently it did. 'But like you say, if it was that simple, anybody could see it. It's not. Freud relates sex to all sorts of things that don't look like they have anything to do with it at first glance: the competitive drive, the urge to create, the way you relate to people the same sex as you.' He hastily held up that ringless hand. 'Don't get me wrong – I don't mean you in particular and I'm not calling you queer.'

'It's okay, Captain. I worked that out,' Sam said. Even if he was a shrink, Ben Berkowitz was a regular guy, too. Yeager hadn't got to the point of realizing it might be important for a psychiatrist to be able to make like a regular guy to help him do the rest of his job better.

'You with me so far?' Berkowitz asked.

'I guess so,' Yeager said cautiously. 'I never really thought about sex tying in to all that other stuff, but maybe it does.'

'You'll go with it for the sake of argument, you mean.'

'I guess so,' Sam repeated.

Berkowitz laughed at him. He was engagingly ugly; when he grinned he looked about eighteen, like one of the bright – or sometimes smartass – kids who filled the letter column in *Astounding*. He said, 'Careful son of a gun, aren't you? Remind me not to play poker with you. Well, for the sake of argument, let's say we can get all sorts of useful insights into the way the human mind works when we use Freudian analysis. It would be nice if we could do the same thing with the Lizards.'

'So why can't you?' Yeager asked. Then a lightbulb went on in his head. 'Oh. They've got a waddayacallit – a mating season.'

'Right the first time.' Ben Berkowitz grinned again. 'You may look like a farm boy, Yeager, but you're pretty damn sharp, you know that?'

'Thank you, sir.' Sam didn't think of himself as pretty damn sharp. Barbara, for instance, could run rings around him. But she didn't seem bored with him, either, so maybe he wasn't quite the near-hick he'd often felt hanging around with fast-talking big-city ballplayers.

'"Thank you, sir."' Just like some of those fast-talking city guys, Berkowitz had a flare for mimicry. Unlike a lot of them, he didn't spike it with malice. He said, 'Believe me, Sergeant, if you were a dimbulb, you wouldn't be in Hot Springs. This and the project you came from are probably the two most important places in the United States – and you've had your hand in both of them. Damn few people can say as much.'

'I never thought of it like that,' Yeager said. When he did, he saw he had something to be proud of.

'Well, you should have,' Berkowitz told him. 'But back to business, okay? Like you said, the Lizards have a mating season. When their females smell right, they screw themselves silly. When they don't—' He snapped his fingers. 'Everything shuts off, just like that. It's like they're sexually neutral beings ninety percent of the time – all the time, if no lady Lizards are around.'

'They think what we do is funny as hell,' Yeager said.

'Don't they just,' Berkowitz agreed. 'Straha tells me they have a whole big research program going, just trying to figure out what makes us tick, and they haven't come close yet. We're in the same boat with them, except we're just starting out, and they've been doing it ever since they got here.'

'That's 'cause they're winning the war,' Sam said. 'When you're ahead, you can afford to monkey around with stuff that isn't really connected to the fighting. When you're losing like we are, you have enough other problems closer to home, so you can't worry about stuff out on the edge.'

'Ain't it the truth,' Berkowitz said. The colloquialism dropped from his lips without sounding put-on, though Sam was sure he knew his whos and whoms as well as Barbara did. Not sounding put-on was also part of his job. He went on, 'So how do we figure out what makes a Lizard tick, way down deep inside? It isn't sex, and that makes them different from us at a level we have trouble even thinking about.'

'Ristin and Ullhass say the other two kinds of bug-eyed monsters the Lizards have conquered work the same way they do,' Yeager said.

'The Hallessi and the Rabotevs. Yes, I've heard that, too.' Berkowitz leaned back in his chair. Sweat darkened the khaki of his uniform shirt under the arms. Sam felt his own shirt sticking to him all down the back, and he wasn't doing anything but sitting still. If, say, you wanted to go out and play ball ... He recalled wringing out his flannels after games down here. You thought you remembered what this kind of weather was like, but when you fond yourself stuck in it week in and week out, you learned your memory – maybe mercifully – had blocked the worst of it.

He ran the back of his hand across his forehead. Since one was about as wet as the other, that didn't help much. 'Hot,' he said inadequately.

'Sure is,' Berkowitz said. 'I wonder about the Rabotevs and the Hallessi, I really do. I wish we could do something for them; the Lizards have held them down for thousands of years.'

'From what I've heard, they're supposed to be as loyal to the Emperor as the Lizards are themselves,' Yeager answered. 'They're honorary Lizards, pretty much. I guess that's what the Lizards had in mind for us, too.'

'I think you're right,' Berkowitz said, nodding. 'You want to hear something funny, something I got out of Straha?' He waited for Sam to nod back, then went on, 'About eight hundred years ago, the Lizards sent some kind of people to probe Earth. It beamed a whole bunch of pictures and I don't know what else back to the planet the Lizards call Home ... and they figured we'd be a piece of cake, because we couldn't possibly have changed much in that short a time.' Sam thought that one over for a few seconds. Then his eye caught Berkowitz's. They both started to laugh. Yeager said, 'You mean they thought they'd be fighting King Arthur and Richard the Lion-Hearted and, and ...?' He gave up; those were the only two medieval names he could come up with.

'That's just what they thought,' Berkowitz agreed. 'They expected to run tanks and fighter planes up against knights on horseback. The conquest would have taken maybe twenty minutes, and the only way a Lizard would have gotten hurt was if he fell down and stubbed his toe.'

'We gave 'em a little surprise, didn't we?' Sam said. 'A lot's happened since' – he paused to subtract in his head – '1142 or so.'

'Uh-huh. Good thing for us it has, too. But you know, here's the strange part: if they'd sent the probe in 342 and come in 1142, things wouldn't have changed that much – they'd still have had a walkover. Or if they'd sent it in' – now Berkowitz paused for subtraction—' 458 B.C. and come in 342 A.D., it would have been the same story. So they might have been right when they figured things wouldn't change much, and they could take their own sweet time getting ready to squash us flat.'

'I hadn't thought about it like that,' Yeager admitted. He didn't care to think about it like that, either. Something else occurred to him. 'They sure came loaded for bear if they expected to be taking on knights in shining armor.'

'Didn't they just?' Berkowitz ruefully shook his head. 'I asked Straha about that. He kind of reared back, the way they do when they think you're being stupid, you know what I mean? Then he said, "You do not go to war without enough tools to win it. This is what we thought we had." '

'He may still be right,' Sam said.

'So he may.' Berkowitz looked at his watch. 'And I've got to run and interview a Lizard tank officer about armor-piercing shells. I enjoy chewing the fat with you, Sergeant – you've got the right kind of mind to deal with the Lizards. People who start out too sure of themselves end up, you should pardon the expression, nuts.'

Laughing, Yeager went up to the fourth floor. He found Ullhass and Ristin in a state of high excitement. 'Look, Exalted Sergeant Sam,' Ristin said, holding up a set of what looked like bottles of nail polish. 'The grand and magnificent shiplord Straha brought with him a great store of body paints. He will share them with us. Now we no longer need be naked.'

'That's nice,' Sam agreed equably. 'Does each of you paint himself, or do you paint each other?'

'We paint each other.' Ullhass let out a mournful, hissing sigh. 'But we really should not paint our old rank patterns on our bodies. We hold those ranks no longer. We are only prisoners.'

'Then paint yourselves to show that,' Yeager said.

'There are markings to show one is a prisoner,' Ristin said, 'but a prisoner who has done something wrong and is being punished. We did nothing wrong; you Big Uglies captured us and made us prisoners. We have no markings for that.'

Probably didn't think it would ever happen when you set out from Home, Yeager thought. He said, 'If you don't have those markings, why not invent some?'

Ristin and Ullhass looked at each other. Obviously, that idea hadn't occurred to them, and wouldn't have, either. 'Such markings would not be official,' Ullhass said, as if that doomed the notion in and of itself.

But Sam said, 'Sure they would. They'd be official US Lizard POW at Hot Springs marks. If you're our prisoners, you should use our marks, right?'

The two Lizards looked at each other again. They took suggestions from superior authority very seriously indeed. 'What are these US Lizard POW at Hot Springs marks?' Ristin asked.

Yeager was about to tell him to make up his own when he had a better idea – much more than most people, Lizards liked doing as they were told. He said, 'You should paint yourselves with red and white stripes and blue stars. That way you'll look like you're wearing American flags.'

Ristin and Ulhass talked back and forth in their own language. Sam was getting fluent enough now to follow them pretty well. He hid a smile as he listened to their enthusiasm grow. Before long, Ristin said, 'It shall be done.'

When they were through, Yeager thought they looked gaudy as all get out, but nobody'd hired him for base art critic, so he kept his big mouth shut.

Ullhass and Ristin were delighted, which was the point of the exercise. In the next few days, several other formerly paintless Lizards started sporting stars and stripes. Sam's highly unofficial suggestion looked as if it might turn official after all.

Then one day, as Sam was coming out of the room he shared with Barbara, a peremptory hiss stopped him in his tracks. 'You are the Tosevite who devised these – these unpleasant prisoner color combinations?' Straha demanded.

'That's right, Shiplord,' Sam answered. 'Is something wrong with them?'

'Yes, something is wrong.' Straha used an emphatic cough to show how wrong the something was. Past that, he looked angry enough to be twitching; he reminded Yeager of nothing so much as a tent-show revival preacher testifying against the evils of demon rum and loose women. 'This you have done with the paint, this is wrong. This is a mark the Race does not use. It must be cleansed at once from the scales of the males. It is an—' Yeager hadn't heard the next word before, but if it didn't mean something like *abomination*, he'd eat his hat.

'Why is that, Shiplord?' he asked, as innocently as he could.

'Because it destroys all order and discipline,' Straha replied, as if to an idiot child. 'Body paint shows rank and assignment and seniority; it is not to be used for frivolous purposes of decoration.'

'Shiplord, it does show assignment: it shows that the males who wear it are prisoners of the United States,' Sam said. 'If you want it to show seniority, too, the males who have been prisoners longer can wear more stars than the others. Would that be all right?'

He tried to sound quiet and reasonable. All the same, he expected Straha to blow up like a pressure cooker with its safety valve stuck. But the shiplord surprised him: 'The trouble with dealing with Tosevites is that one forgets how perspective shifts. Do you understand this?'

'I don't think I do, Shiplord,' Sam answered. 'I'm sorry.'

Straha made an exasperated noise, rather like a water heater with a slow leak. 'I explain further, then. With the Race, all is as it has been. We do not casually invent body paint designs. They all fit into a system we have been refining for more than a hundred thousand years.' Yeager knew enough to divide that by two to convert it into Earthly years, but it was still a hell of a long time. Straha went on, 'You Big Uglies, though, you just casually invent. You care nothing for large-scale system; all that matters to you is short-term results.'

'We're at war, Shiplord. We were at war before the Race got here,' Yeager said. 'Whatever it takes to win, we'll do. We change all the time.'

'This we have noticed, to our sorrow,' Straha said. 'The weapons with which you fight us now are better than the ones you used when we first came. Ours are still the same. This is what I meant about looking at you from a different perspective. If something suits you for the moment, you will seize upon it, not caring a bit how it accords with what you formerly did. You invent a body paint pattern on the spur of the moment.' The shiplord hissed again. 'I suppose I should be used to that sort of thing, but every now and again it still shocks me. This was one of those times.'

Yeager thought of all the pulp science fiction stories he'd read where an inventor had an idea one day, built it the next, and mass-produced it the day after that, generally just in time to save the world from the Martians. He'd always taken those with a grain of salt about the size of the Great Salt Flats outside Salt Lake City. Real life didn't work that way.

To the Lizards, though, Earth must have seemed the embodiment of pulp science fiction run amok. In not a whole lot more than a year, human beings had rolled out long-range rockets, bazookas, and jet planes, to say nothing of the atomic bomb. That didn't count improvements to already existing items like tanks, either. And by all accounts, poison gas, which dated back to World War I, was new and nasty to the Lizards.

'So you'll forgive the other prisoners here for using American-style body paint, then?' Sam asked.

'I am not a prisoner; I am a refugee,' Straha said with dignity. 'But yes, I forgive it. I was hasty when I condemned it out of hand, but haste, for the Race, is to be actively discouraged. The captive males may wear any sort of marking Tosevite authorities suggest.'

'Thank you, Shiplord,' Yeager said. As Lizards went, Straha seemed like a pretty adaptable guy. If you actively discouraged haste, though, you didn't make life any easier for yourself, not on Earth, you didn't.

Teerts sometimes felt guilty about what had happened to Tokyo. Millions of intelligent beings dead, and all because he'd warned of what the Nipponese Tosevites were attempting.

The guilt never lasted long, though. For one thing, the Big Uglies would have blown up a similar number of males of the Race without a qualm. For another, the way the Nipponese had treated him deserved revenge.

He wasn't flying in the eastern region of the main continental mass any more. His commanders realized his life would end quickly – or perhaps slowly – if the Nipponese captured him again. Now he undertook missions for the Race from an airfield almost halfway round Tosev 3 from Nippon. France, the local Big Uglies called the place.

'These are the toughest Big Uglies you'll face in the air,' Elifrim, the base commander, told him. 'Our friends across the ocean who fight the Americans might argue, but take no notice of them. The Deutsche fly jets more dangerous than any others the Tosevites use, and the British had airborne radar before we invaded their island.'

'I don't mind facing them in the air, superior sir,' Teerts answered. 'I can shoot back at them now.' He remembered too well lying in Tosevite hands, unable to strike his Nipponese captors. He'd never know or imagined such loneliness, such helplessness.

'Shoot first,' Elifrim urged. 'That's what I mean: you could take your time with the Big Uglies before, but not so much now. The other thing is, you'll want to use your cannon more and your missiles less.'

'Why, superior sir?' Teerts asked. 'I can kill with my missiles from much greater range. If the Big Uglies' weapon systems are better than they were before the Nipponese captured me, I ought to be more cautious about closing with them, not *more* eager to do it.'

'Under normal circumstances, you would be right,' the base commander answered. 'When it comes to Tosev 3, though, precious little is normal, as you'll have discovered for yourself. The problem, Flight Leader, is that stocks of air-to-air missiles are dwindling planetwide, and we haven't found a way to manufacture more. We have plenty of shells for the cannons, though, from our own factory ships and from Tosevite plants here in France and in Italia and the USA. That's why we prefer you to use the guns.'

'I – see,' Teerts said slowly. 'How good is this Tosevite ammunition we're using? I hate trusting my life to something the Big Uglies turn out.'

'We had some quality control problems at first,' Elifrim said; Teerts wondered how many males had ended up dead as a result of such an innocuous-sounding thing. The commandant went on, 'Those are for the most part corrected now. Several Tosevite aircraft have been brought down using shells of Tosevite manufacture.'

'That's something, anyhow,' Teerts said, somewhat reassured. Elifrim reached into a desk drawer and drew out two shell casings. Teerts had no trouble figuring out which chunk of machined brass had traveled from Home and which was made locally: one was gleaming, mirror-finished, while the other had a matte coating, with several scratches marring its metal.

'It looks primitive, but it works,' Elifrim said, pointing to the duller casing. 'Dimensionally, it matches ours, and that's what really counts.'

'As you say, superior sir,' Teerts was less than enthusiastic about using those shell casings in his killercraft, but if the Race had plenty of them and a dwindling supply of both proper shells and missiles, he didn't see that he had much choice. 'Are the armorers satisfied with them?' Armorers were even fussier about guns than pilots.

'On the whole, yes,' Elifrim answered, though for a moment his eyes looked to the side walls of the office, a sign he wasn't telling everything he knew. When he spoke again, he attempted briskness: 'Any further questions, Flight Leader? No? Very well, dismissed.'

Teerts was glad to leave the office, lit only by a weak electric bulb left over from the days when the Tosevites had controlled the air base, and to go out into the sunlight that bathed the place. He found the weather a trifle cool, but pleasant enough. He walked over to his killercraft to see how the technicians were coming along in readying it for the next mission.

He found a senior armorer loading shells into the aircraft's magazine.

'Good day, Flight Leader,' the male said respectfully – Teerts outranked him. But he was an important male, too, and everything in his demeanor said he knew it.

'Good day, Innoss,' Teerts answered. He saw that some of the shells the armorer was using were shiny ones of the Race's manufacture, others with the duller finish that marked Big Ugly products. 'What do you think of the munitions the Tosevites are making for us?'

'Since you ask, superior sir, the answer is "not much,"' Innoss said. He lifted a Tosevite shell out of the crate in which it had come. 'All the specifications are the same as they are for our own ammunition, but some of these don't feel quite right.' He hefted the shell. 'The weight is fine, but the balance is off somehow.'

'Are all the ones the Tosevites produce like that?' Teerts asked.

'No,' the armorer answered. 'Only a few. With their primitive manufacturing techniques, I suppose I should not be surprised. The miracle is that we get any usable shells at all.'

Suspicion flared in Teerts. 'If it is not a universal trait, these shells with the odd balance will be somehow flawed,' he predicted. 'Believe me when I say this, Innoss. I know the Big Uglies and their tricks better than I ever dreamt I would. Sure as I had an eggtooth to help me break out of my shell, some ingenious Tosevite has found a way to diddle us.'

'I don't see how,' Innoss said doubtfully. 'The weight is proper, after all. More likely some flaw in the process. I have seen video of what they call factories.' Derision filled his hiss.

'Their weapons may be outdated next to ours, but they are well made of their kind,' Teerts said. 'I'll bet you a day's pay, Innoss, that close enough examination of that misbalanced shell will turn up something wrong with it.'

The armorer sent him a thoughtful look. 'Very well, Flight Leader, I accept that wager. Let us see what this shell has to say to us.' He carried it away toward his own shack by the ammunition storage area.

Teerts thought about how he would spend his winnings. Reaching a conclusion didn't take long.: *I'll buy more ginger.* Amazing how easy the stuff was to get. Every other Big Ugly who swept up or brought food onto the air base seemed to have his own supply. Every so often, Elifrim caught a user and made an example of him, but he missed tens for every one he found.

Teerts was still busy inspecting his aircraft when Innoss returned. The armorer drew himself up in stiff formality. 'Superior sir, I owe you a day's pay,' he said. 'I have already requested a file transfer between our accounts.' He spoke more respectfully than he ever had before; till now, Teerts had been just another officer as far as he was concerned.

'What did the Big Uglies do?' Teerts asked, doing his best not to show the relief he felt. He'd gained prestige by being right; only now did he think about how much he'd have lost had he been wrong.

'I X-rayed three shells: one of ours, one of theirs with proper balance, and one of theirs with improper balance,' Innoss said. 'The first two were virtually identical; as you said, superior sir, they can do good enough work when they care to. But the third—' He paused, as if still not believing it.

'What did the Big Uglies do?' Teerts repeated. By Innoss's tone, he guessed it was something perfidious even for them.

'They left out the bursting charge that goes behind the penetrating head,' the armorer answered indignantly. 'If they'd just done that, the shells would have been light, and quality control would have found them easily. But to make up for the empty space within the shells, they thickened the metal of the head just enough to match the missing weight of powder. I wonder how many shells have done far less damage to the enemy than they should have because of that.'

'Have you any way to trace down which Tosevite plane turned out the sabotaged shells?' Teerts asked.

'Oh, yes,' Innoss opened his mouth not in a laugh but to show off all his teeth in a threat display that made it clear the distant ancestors of the Race had been fierce carnivores. 'Vengeance shall fall on them.'

'Good,' Teerts said. This wasn't like vengeance on the Nipponese, where many thousands who had done nothing to him had died simply because they lived near where the Big Uglies had chosen to undertake nuclear research. The Tosevites who suffered now would have earned what they got, each and every one of them. 'The Race is in your debt,' Innoss said. 'I telephoned the base commandant and told him what you had led me to discover. You shall be recognized as you deserve; your body paint will get fancier.'

'That was generous of you,' Teerts said. A promotion, or even a commendation, would mean more pay, which would mean more ginger. After so many horrors, life was good.

Like Shanghai, Peking had seen better days. The former capital's fall to the Japanese had been relatively gentle – *Chiang's corrupt clique simply cut and ran*, Nieh Ho-T'ing thought disparagingly. But the Japanese had fought like madmen before the little scaly devils drove them out of Peking. Whole districts lay in ruins, and many of the palaces formerly enjoyed by the emperors of China and their consorts and courtiers were only rubble through which scavengers picked for bits of wood.

'So what?' Hsia Shou-Tao growled when Nieh spoke of that aloud. 'They were nothing but symbols of oppression of the masses. The city – the world – is better off without them.'

'It could be so,' Nieh said. 'Were it up to me, though, they would have been preserved as symbols of that oppression.' He laughed. 'Here we are, arguing over what should be done with them when, first, they are already destroyed and, second, we have not yet the power to say what any building's fate will be.'

'A journey of a thousand *li* begins with but a single step,' Hsia answered. The proverb made him grimace. 'More than a thousand *li* from Shanghai to here, and my poor feet feel every stinking step I took.'

'Ah, but here we are in the hibiscus-flower garden,' Nieh Ho-T'ing said with an expansive wave. 'Surely you can take your ease.'

'Hibiscus-flower night soil,' Hsia said coarsely; he reveled in a peasant's crudity. 'It's just another dive.'

The Jung Yüan (which meant hibiscus-flower garden) had been a fine restaurant once. It looked to have been looted a couple of times; soot running up one wall said someone had tried to torch the place. Those efforts were all too likely to succeed; Nieh wondered why this one had failed.

He sipped tea from a severely plain earthenware cup. 'The food is still good,' he said.

Hsia grunted, unwilling to admit anything. But, like Nieh, he'd demolished the *lu-wei-p'in-p'an* – ham, minced pork, pigs' tripes and tongue, and bamboo shoots – all in thick gravy – that was one of Jung Yüan's specialities. Pork and poultry were the only meat you saw these days; pigs and chickens ate anything, and so were eaten themselves.

A serving girl came up and asked, 'More rice?' When Nieh nodded, she hurried away and returned with a large bowlful. Hisia used the lacquerware spoon to fill his own eating bowl, then held it up to his mouth and shoveled in rice with his chopsticks. He slurped from a bowl of *kao liang*, a potent wine brewed from millet, and belched enormously to show his approval.

'You are a true proletarian,' Nieh Ho-T'ing said, not at all ironically. Hsia Shou-Tao beamed at the compliment.

A couple of tables over, a group of men in Western-style suits was having a dinner party, complete with singsong girls and a raucous orchestra. Despite all Peking had been through, the men looked plump and prosperous. Some had their arms around singsong girls, while others were trying to slide their hands up the slits in the girls' silk dresses. A couple of the girls pulled away; not all entertainers were courtesans. Most, though, accepted the attentions either as their due or with mercenary calculation in their eyes.

'Collaborators,' Nieh said in a voice that would have meant the firing squad in territory controlled by the People's Liberation Army. 'They could not be so rich without working hand in glove with the little scaly devils.'

'You're right,' Hsia grunted. He filled his bowls of rice again. With his mouth full, he added, 'That one there, in the dark shiny green, she's a lot of woman.'

'And her beauty is exploited,' Nieh answered. Like a lot of Communist officials, he had a wide puritanical streak in him. Sex for sport, sex for anything but procreation, made him uneasy. His stay in a Shanghai brothel had reinforced that opinion rather than changing it.

'So it is,' Hsia said; Nieh's doctrine was true. But the other man did not sound happy to concur.

'You are not an animal. You are a man of the revolution,' Nieh Ho-T'ing reminded him. 'If joy girls are what you wanted in life, you should have joined the Kuomintang instead.'

'I am a man of the revolution,' Hsia repeated dutifully. 'Coveting women who are forced to show their bodies' – a Chinese euphemism for prostitution – 'to get money to live proves I have not yet removed all the old corrupt ways from my heart. Humbly, I shall try to do better.'

Had he made the self-criticism at a meeting of Party members, he would have stood with head bowed in contrition. Here, that would have given him away for what he was – and the scaly devils and their running dogs were as eager as either Chiang's clique or the Japanese had been to be rid of Communists. Hsia stayed in his seat and slurped millet wine ... and, in spite of self-criticism, his eyes kept sliding toward the singsong girl in the green silk dress.

Nieh Ho-T'ing tried to bring his attention back to the matter at hand. Keeping his voice low, he said, 'We have to put fear into these collaborators. If a few of them die, the rest will serve the little devils with less attention to their duties, for they will always be looking over their shoulder to see if they will be next to pay for their treacheries. Some may even decide to co-operate with us in the struggle against imperialist aggression.'

Hsia Shou-Tao made a face. 'Yes, and then they'd sell us back to the scaly devils, along with their own mothers. That kind of friend does our cause no good; we need people truly committed to revolution and justice.'

'We would be fools to trust them very far,' Nieh agreed, 'but intelligence is always valuable.'

'And can always be compromised,' Hsia shot back. He was a stubborn man; once an opinion lodged in his mind, a team of water buffaloes would have had trouble dragging it out.

Nieh didn't try. All he said was, 'The sooner some are slain, the sooner we have the chance to see what the rest are made of.'

That appealed to Hsia, as Nieh had thought it might: his comrade was a man who favored direct action. But Hsia said, 'Not that the miserable turtles don't deserve to die, but it won't be as easy even as it was in Shanghai. The little scaly devils aren't stupid, and they learn more about security every day.'

'Security for themselves, yes,' Nieh said, 'but for their parasites? There they are not so good. Every set of foreign devils that has tried to rule China – the Mongols, the English, the Japanese – worked with and through native traitors. The little scaly devils are no different. How will they gather in food and collect taxes if no one keeps records for them?'

Hsia noisily blew his nose on his fingers. A couple of the scaly devils' running dogs looked at him with distaste; they'd learned Western manners to go with their Western clothes. He glared back at them. Nieh Ho-T'ing had seen him do such things before: he needed to hate his enemies on a personal level, not just an ideological one.

Nieh set down five Mex dollars to cover the cost of the meal; war and repeated conquest had left Peking, like Shanghai, an abominably expensive place to live. Both men blinked as they walked out into the bright sun of the western part of the Chinese City of Peking. Monuments of the past glories of imperial China were all around them. Nieh Ho-T'ing looked at the massive brickwork of the Ch'ien Mên Gate with as much scorn as he'd given to the scaly devils' puppets. Come the revolution, all the buildings war had spared deserved to be torn down. The people would erect their own monuments.

He and Hsia shared a room in a grimy little lodging house not far from the gate. The man who ran it was himself progressive, and asked no questions about his lodgers' political affiliations. In return, no one struck at the oppressors and their minions anywhere close to the lodging house, to keep suspicion from falling on it.

That evening, over tea and soup, Nieh and his comrades planned how best to harass the little devils. After considerable comradely discussion – an outsider would have called it raucous wrangling – they decided to attack the municipal office building, an ugly modern structure close to the western shore of the Chung Hai, the Southern Lake.

Hsia Shou-Tao wanted to do there what Nieh Ho-T'ing and his followers had done in Shanghai: smuggle guerrillas and weapons into the building under the cover of waiters and cooks bringing in food. Nieh vetoed that: 'The little scaly devils are not stupid, as you yourself said. They will know we have used this trick once, and will be on their guard against it.'

'We will not be using it against them, only against the men who lick their backsides,' Hsia said sulkily.

'We will not be using it at all,' Nieh Ho-T'ing repeated. 'The risk is too large.'

'What *shall* we do, then?' Hsia demanded. That brought on another round of comradely discussion, even more raucous than the one before. But when the discussion was done, they had a plan they could live with – and one which, with luck, not too many of them would die with.

The next morning, Nieh Ho-T'ing went with several of his comrades to the national library, which was just across Hsi An Mên – Western Peace Gate – Street, to the north of the municipal offices. They all wore Western clothes like those the running dogs in the Hibiscus-Flower Garden had had on; Nieh's shoes pinched his feet without mercy. The librarians bowed to them and were most helpful – who could have guessed they were not carrying papers in their briefcases?

The day was hot and sticky; the windows on the south side of the library were open, to help the air move. Nieh smiled. He had counted on that. All his companions could read. Not all of them had been able to when they first joined the People's Liberation Army, but ignorance was one means through which warlords and magnates held the people in bondage. The Communists fought it hard. That was useful generally, and a special advantage now: they fit right in until the time came for them to go into action.

Nieh Ho-T'ing knew just when that moment arrived. The noise on Hsi An Mên Street suddenly doubled, and then doubled again. Nieh looked out the window, as any curious person might have done. Clerks and officials were filing out of the municipal office building, gathering in knots on the sidewalk, blocking traffic on the street itself, and generally complaining up a storm.

He caught the word 'bomb' several times and smiled again, now more broadly. Hsia Shou-Tao had phoned in his threat, then. He had a deep, raspy voice, and could sound threatening quite without intending to. When he did intend to, the result was chilling indeed.

To make the joke complete, he'd said the Kuomintang had hidden the explosive. When the little scaly devils got around to laying blame for what was going to happen, they'd lay it in the wrong place.

Nieh nodded to his comrades. As one, they opened their briefcases. The grenades inside – some round ones, bought from the Japanese, and some German-style potato mashers, bought from the Kuomintang – had been wrapped in paper, to keep them from rattling about. The men pulled pins, yanked igniters, and hurled them down into the crowd below.

'Fast, fast, fast!' Nieh shouted, flinging grenade after grenade himself. The first blasts and the screams that followed them were music to him. Thus always to those who would oppress not just the peasants and proletarians but all of mankind!

When almost all the grenades were gone, Nieh and his comrades left the chamber. Already there were cries from inside the library. Nieh tossed the last two grenades back into the room he and his men had just abandoned. The grenades went off with twin roars. The diversion worked just as he'd hoped. Feet pounded toward that room. His band of raiders left by a small door on the north side of the library.

He had a pistol ready in case the guard gave trouble, but the fellow didn't. All he said was, 'What's that racket all about?'

'I don't know,' Nieh answered importantly. 'We were busy with research for the Race.' Running dogs often used the little scaly devils' name for themselves.

The guard waved him and his comrades by. Instead of fleeing the area, they walked down toward Hsi An Mên Street. A shouting policeman ordered them to help move some of the wounded. Nieh obeyed without a word of complaint. Not only did it let him evaluate how much damage he'd done, it was also the best possible cover against investigators.

'Thank you for your help, gentlemen,' the policeman said to Nieh and his group. 'Everyone needs to struggle together against these stinking murderers.' To Nieh in particular, he added, 'Sorry, you got blood on your clothes, sir. I hope it can be laundered.'

'I hope so, too. Cold water, they say, is good for such things,' Nieh answered. The policeman nodded. In times like these, knowing how to get bloodstains out of clothes was more than merely useful; it was necessary.

Nowhere did the policeman's uniform display a name or number that would identify him. That was clever, it helped prevent reprisals. Nieh Ho-T'ing carefully studied the man's face. He would start inquiries tomorrow. A policeman who spoke of 'stinking murderers' was too enthusiastic in his support for the little scaly devils. He struck Nieh as ripe for liquidation.

8

Ttomalss wondered more and more often these days why he had ever found the psychology of alien races an interesting study. If he'd taken up, say, landcruiser gunning, he would have dealt with the Big Uglies only through the barrel of a cannon. If he'd taken up something like publishing, he'd probably still be back Home, comfortably getting on with his career.

Instead, he found himself trying to raise a Tosevite hatchling without any direct help from the Big Uglies. If he could, that would teach the Race a lot about how the Tosevites would do as subjects when the Empire finally succeeded in establishing its control here. If ...

The more he worked on the project, the more he wondered how any Big Uglies ever survived to adulthood. When a male or female of the Race emerged from its egg, it was in large measure ready to face the world. It ate the same foods adults did, it could run around, and the biggest problem in civilizing it was teaching it the things it should not do. Since it was obedient by nature, that didn't usually present too big a challenge.

Whereas the hatchling Big Ugly female Ttomalss had taken from Liu Han ...

He glared resentfully at the lumpish little thing. Not only couldn't it run around, it couldn't even roll over. It thrashed its arms and legs as if it hadn't the slightest idea they were part of it. Ttomalss marveled that natural selection could have favored the development of such an utterly helpless hatchling.

The hatchling also couldn't eat just anything. It had evolved as a parasite on the female from whose body it emerged, and was able to consume only the fluids that female secreted. Not only did Ttomalss find that disgusting, it also presented him with an experimental dilemma. He wanted to raise the Tosevite hatchling in isolation from others of its kind, but required the stuff Big Ugly females produced.

The result, like so many things connected with Tosev 3, was a clumsy makeshift. One thing – almost the only thing – the hatchling could do was suck. Some of the Big Uglies had developed artificial feeding techniques which took advantage of that with elastomeric nipples. They also used artificial equivalents of the female's natural product.

Ttomalss didn't care to do that. Very little of what the Race had learned about the Big Uglies' medical technology impressed him. He made arrangements for females in the Race's camps who were already secreting for their own hatchlings to give some additional secretion for the one he was trying to raise. He'd feared that would make the Tosevites volatile, but, to his relief, it didn't, and his hatchling enthusiastically sucked from an elastomer copy of the bodily part evolution had given Big Ugly females.

The hatchling also voided enthusiastically; Tosevite excretory arrangements were much messier than those of the Race. The liquid wastes from Big Ugly adults strained the plumbing facilities of the Race's spacecraft. But adults, at least, had conscious control over their voiding.

As far as Ttomalss could tell, the hatchling didn't have conscious control over anything. It released liquid and solid waste whenever it felt the need, no matter where it was: it could be lying in its little containment cage, or he could be holding it. More than once – he'd had to wash off the evil-smelling liquid it passed, and to refurbish his body paint afterwards.

For that matter, its solid wastes barely deserved the adjective. They clung to the hatchling; they clung to everything. Keeping the little creature clean was nearly a full-time job. Ttomalss learned the Big Uglies lessened the problem by wrapping absorbent cloths around their hatchlings' excretory organs. That helped keep the hatchling's surroundings cleaner, but he still had to wash it every time it voided.

And the noises it made! Hatchlings of the Race were quiet little things; they had to be coaxed to talking. From an evolutionary point of view, that made sense: noisy hatchlings new drew predators, and didn't survive long enough to reproduce. But natural selection on Tosev 3 seemed to have taken a holiday. Whenever the hatchling was hungry or had fouled itself, it howled. Sometimes it howled for no reason Ttomalss could find. He'd tried ignoring it then, but that didn't work. The hatchling could squall longer than he could ignore it, and he also feared ignoring it might lead to damage of some kind.

Gradually he began picking it up when it raised a ruckus. Sometimes that made it belch up some air it had swallowed along with the secretions it ate (and sometimes it belched up those secretions, too, in a partially digested and thoroughly revolting state). When that happened, it sometimes brought the hatchling enough relief to make it shut up.

Sometimes, though, the hatchling had nothing whatever wrong with it and still made noise, as if it wanted to be held. And holding it would sometimes calm it. That bewildered Ttomalss, and made him wonder if the Tosevites didn't start the socialization process earlier in life than the Race did.

His colleagues' mouths dropped open when he suggested that. 'I know it sounds funny,' he said defensively. 'They've fragmented themselves into tens of tiny empires that fight all the time, while we've been comfortably united for a hundred millennia. On the other hand, they have that powerful year-round sexual drive to contend with, and we don't.'

'You're tired, Ttomalss,' his fellow psychologists said, almost in chorus.

Ttomalss *was* tired. Adult Tosevites had the decency to be respectably diurnal – one of the few decencies they did have. The hatchling was asleep whenever it felt like sleeping and awake whenever it felt like waking, and when it was awake, Ttomalss was perforce awake, too, feeding it or cleaning it (or feeding it *and* cleaning it) or simply holding it and trying to persuade it to calm down and go back to sleep and let him go back to sleep. No wonder his eye turrets felt as if someone had poured sand in them when they swiveled.

As days passed, the hatchling gradually began to develop a pattern to its sleeping and waking. That was not to say that it didn't wake up once or twice or sometimes three times in the night, but it seemed more willing to go back to sleep then and to be awake during the day. Little by little, Ttomalss began to reckon himself capable of coherent thought once more.

He also began to believe the hatchling might one day be capable of coherent thought – or thought as coherent as that of Big Uglies ever got. It began to make noises more complex than its first primordial yowls. It also began to look at him with more attention than it had formerly shown him or anything else.

One day, the corners of its mouth lifted in a facial twitch the Tosevites used to express good humor. Ttomalss wished he could return the twitch and reinforce it, but his own features were respectably immobile.

In spite of the hatchling's increasing responsiveness, in spite of everything he was learning from it, there were a great many times when he wished he'd left it with the Tosevite female from whose body it had come. Better it should drive her mad than him, he thought.

It was not the proper attitude for a scientist, but then again, a proper scientist got enough sleep.

Liu Han's breasts ached with milk. She'd earned money and food as a wet nurse on her way to Peking, but for the past day and a half she hadn't found anyone with a baby that needed to nurse. If she didn't come on one soon, she'd have to squeeze out some milk by hand. She hated to waste it that way, but being so painfully full was no delight, either.

Sometimes, when she was worn and hungry and her feet felt as if they couldn't take another step, she almost wished she was back in the camp. She'd had plenty to eat there, and not much to do. But she'd also had the little scaly devils spying on everything she did, and finally stealing her baby. Even if it was a girl, it was *hers*.

Getting away from camp hadn't been easy. Not only did the little devils have cameras mounted inside the hut, they also frequently followed her when she went out and about – and she could hardly walk through the gates in the razor wire. No human walked out through those gates.

If it hadn't been for the poultry seller who was a Communist, she never would have got out. One day when he was shutting up his stall, he said to her, 'Come with me. I'd like you to meet my sister.'

She didn't think the hut to which he'd taken her was his own; that would have been too dangerous. In it sat a woman who probably was not the poultry seller's sister. She wore her hair in a short bob, as Liu Han did, and was of about the same age and build.

The poultry seller turned his back on them. The woman said, 'Oh, Liu Han, I love your clothes so much. Will you trade them for mine, right down to your sandals and underwear?

Liu Han had stared down at herself for a moment, wondering if the woman was out of her mind. 'These rags?' she said. The 'sister' nodded emphatically. Then Liu Han understood. The scaly devils were very good at making small things. They might have put some of those small things in her clothes, even in her drawers, to keep track of where she was.

She undressed without bothering to see whether the poultry seller peeked at her. So many men had seen her body that her modesty had taken a severe beating. And anyhow, so soon after childbirth, her body, she was sure, hadn't been one to rouse a man's lust.

When the exchange was complete, the poultry seller had turned around and said to the other woman, 'I will take you back to your own home, Liu Han.' He turned to Liu Han. 'Sister, you wait here for me. I will be back soon.'

Wait Liu Han did, marveling at his gall. She knew the scaly devils had trouble telling one person from another. If the poultry seller's 'sister' dressed like her, they might think she was Liu Han, at least for a while. And while they were fooled . . .

As he'd promised, the poultry seller had soon returned. He took Liu Han through deepening twilight to another hut that was bare but for mats on the floor. 'Now we wait again,' he said. Twilight had given way to night. The camp fell as nearly silent as it ever did.

She'd expected him to demand her body, lumpy from childbirth though it was. She'd even made up her mind not to protest; he was, after all, risking his life to help her, and deserved such thanks as she could give. But he made no advances; he used the time to talk of the paradise China would become when Mao Tse-Tung and the Communists freed it from the scaly devils, the eastern devils from Japan, the foreign devils, and its native oppressors. If a quarter of what he said was true, no one would recognize the country after a generation of new rule.

At last, he'd unrolled a mat near one wall. It concealed a wooden trap-door that he'd slid aside. 'Go down this tunnel,' he said. 'Keep going ahead, no matter what. Someone will be waiting for you at the far end.'

She'd quaked like bamboo stalks when the wind blew through them. Bobby Fiore had gone down a tunnel like this, and he'd never come back; he'd ended up lying in a pool of his own blood on a Shanghai street. But down the wooden ladder she'd climbed, and then on hands and knees through damp and the smell of earth and blackness so perfect and intense, it seemed to close in on her until she wanted to huddle where she was and wait for it to swallow her.

But on and on she'd crawled, and at last she came to a rock barring the way. When she pushed it aside, it fell with a splash into an irrigation ditch and she could see again. 'Come on,' a voice hissed to her. 'This way.'

Liu Han had done her best to go 'this way,' but, like the stone, she fell into the ditch. She stood up, wet and dripping, and staggered in the direction from which the voice had come. A hand reached out to pull her onto dry land. 'That's not so bad,' her rescuer whispered. 'The cold water will make it harder for the scaly devils to see your heat.'

At first she'd just nodded. Then, though the night breeze on her dripping clothes left her shivering, she drew herself up very straight. This man knew the little scaly devils could see heat! That information had come from her, and people outside the prison camp were using it. In a life without much room for pride, Liu Han cherished the moments when she knew it.

'Come on,' the man hissed to her. 'We have to get farther away from the camp. You're not safe yet.'

Safe! She'd wanted to laugh. She hadn't known a minute's safety since the little scaly devils had attacked her village – not even before that, for the town had been full of Japanese when the little devils came in their dragonfly planes and turned her whole life – to say nothing of the world – upside down.

But as the days went by, as she tramped through the Chinese countryside, one of uncounted thousands of people going along the dirt tracks, she did begin to feel safe, or at least safe from the little scaly devils. She still saw them now and again: soldiers in their vehicles, or sometimes marching on foot and looking no more happy about it than human troops. Every so often, one would turn an eye turret her way, but only idly, or perhaps warily, to make sure she was not a danger to him. But to them, she was just another Big Ugly, not a subject for study. What a relief that was!

And now Peking. Peiping – Northern Peace – it had been renamed, but no one paid much attention to that. Peking it had been, Peking it was, and Peking it would remain.

Liu Han had never seen a walled city before; the closest to such a thing she'd known was the razor wire around the camp in which the little devils had confined her while waiting for her to give birth. But Peking's walls, in the shape of a square perched atop a broader rectangle, ran for almost forty-five *li* around the perimeter of the city; further internal walls separated the square – the Tartar City – from the rectangle – the Chinese City.

Broad streets ran north and south, east and west, paralleling the walls. The little scaly devils controlled those streets, at least to the point of being able to travel on them by day or night. Between the avenues, there twisted innumerable *hutungs* – lanes – where the bulk of the city lived its life. The little scaly devils took their lives in their little clawed hands when they went along the *hutungs*. They knew it, too, so they seldom went there.

Ironically, prison camp had been Liu Han's best preparation for life in bustling, crowded Peking. Had she come straight from her village, she would have been altogether at sea. But the camp had been a fair-sized city in its own right, and readied her to deal with a great one.

She quickly had to learn how to get around in the Chinese City, for the Communists kept shifting from one dingy lodging house to another, to throw off any possible pursuit from the little devils. One day they took her to a place not far from the Ch'ien Mên, the Western Gate. As she came in, one of the men sitting around and talking over rice spoke a few syllables that were not Chinese, Liu Han recognized them anyway.

She broke away from her escort and walked up to the man. He was a few years older than she, compact, clever-looking. 'Excuse me,' she said politely lowering her eyes, 'but did I hear you speak the name of a foreign devil called Bobby Fiore?'

'What if you did, woman!' the man answered. 'How do you know this foreign devil name?' 'I – knew him in the scaly devils' prison camp west of Shanghai,' Liu Han said hesitantly. She did not go on to explain that she had borne Bobby Fiore's child; now that she was fully among her own people once more, having lain with a foreign devil seemed shameful to her.

'You know him?' The man's eyes raked her. 'Are you then the woman he had at that camp? Your name would be—' He looked up to the ceiling for a moment, riffling through papers in his mind. 'Liu Han, that was it.'

'Yes, I am Liu Han,' she said. 'You must have known him well, if he spoke to you of me.' That Bobby Fiore had spoken of her left her touched. He'd treated her well, but she'd always wondered if she was anything more than an enjoyable convenience to him. With a foreign devil, who could say?

'I was there when he died – you know he is dead?' the man said. When Liu Han nodded, the man went on 'I am Nieh Ho-T'ing. I tell you this, and tell you truly: he died well, fighting against the little scaly devils. He was brave; by doing what he did, he helped me and several others escape them.'

Tears came into Liu Han's eyes. 'Thank you,' she whispered. 'They brought his picture – a picture of him dead – to me in the camp. I knew he died in Shanghai, but not how. He hated the little devils. I am glad he had revenge.' Her hands curled into fists. 'I wish I could.'

Nieh Ho-T'ing studied her. He was an alert, thoughtful-looking man, with the controlled movements and watchful eyes that said he was probably a soldier. He said, 'Do I remember right? You were going to have a child.'

'I had it – a girl,' she answered. If Nieh thought she was a slut for bedding Bobby Fiore, he didn't show it. That by itself was enough to earn her gratitude. She continued, 'You may know the little scaly devils do things to try to understand how real people work. They took my baby from me when it was just three days old, and they keep it for themselves.'

'This is a great wickedness,' Nieh said seriously. He looked up at the ceiling again. 'Liu Han, Liu Han …' When they swung back to her, his eyes had brightened. 'You are a woman who learned the scaly devils had machines that could see heat.'

'Yes – they used one of those machines on me, to help see inside my womb before the baby was born,' Liu Han said. 'I thought they would use it for other things as well.'

'And you were right,' Nieh Ho-T'ing told her, his voice full of enthusiasm. 'We have used this to give us a tactical advantage several times already.' He *was* a soldier, then. He went back from tactics to her: 'But if you want revenge against the little scaly devils for their heartless oppression and exploitation of you, you shall have your chance to get it.'

Not just a soldier, a Communist. She easily recognized the rhetoric now. It came as no surprise: the poultry seller, after all, had been a Communist, and passed on her information to his comrades. If the Communists were best at resisting the scaly devils, then she didn't see anything wrong with them. And she owed those little devils so much. If Nieh Ho-T'ing would help her get her own back … 'Tell me what you want me to do,' she said.

Nieh smiled.

Razor wire. Huts. Cots. Cabbage. Beets. Potatoes. Black bread. The Lizards no doubt intended it to be a prison camp to break a man's spirit. After the privations of the Warsaw ghetto, it felt more like a holiday resort to Mordechai Anielewicz. As gaolers, the Lizards were amateurs. The food, for instance, was plain and boring, but the Lizards didn't seem to have thought of cutting back the quantity.

Mordechai felt on holiday for another reason as well. He'd been a leader of fighting men for a long time: of Jews against Nazis, of Jews for the Lizards. Then he'd been a fugitive, and then a simple partisan. Now the other shoe had dropped: he was a prisoner, and didn't need to worry about getting captured.

In their own way, the Lizards were humane. When the Germans captured partisans, they shot them without further ado – or sometimes with further ado, if they felt like trying to squeeze out information before granting the grace of a bullet. But the Lizards had taken him and Jerzy and Friedrich across Poland to a POW camp outside Piotrków, south of Lodz.

No one here had the slightest idea who he was. He answered to Shmuel, not to his own name. As far as Friedrich and Jerzy knew, he was just a Jew who'd fought in their band. Nobody asked a would-be partisan probing questions about his past. Even in the camp, the freedom of anonymity was exhilarating.

One morning after roll call, a Lizard guard official read from a list: 'The following Tosevites will fall out for interrogation—' His Polish was bad, and what he did to the pronunciation of Anielewicz's alias a caution.

Nonetheless, Mordechai fell out without a qualm. They'd already interrogated him two or three times. To them, interrogation meant nothing worse than asking questions. They knew about torture, but the idea appalled them. There were times when Anielewicz savored the irony of that. They hadn't even questioned him particularly hard. To them, he was just another Big Ugly caught with a rifle in his hands.

He started to sweat as soon as he went into the wooden shed the Lizards used for their camp headquarters. That had nothing to do with fear; the Lizards heated their buildings to their own comfort level, which felt to him like the Sahara.

'You Shmuel, you go to room two on the left,' one of his guards said in execrable Yiddish.

Mordechai obediently went to room two. Inside, he found a Lizard with medium-fancy body paint and a human interpreter. He'd expected as much. Few Lizards were fluent enough in any human language to be efficient questioners. What he hadn't expected was that he'd recognize the interpreter.

The fellow's name was Jakub Kipnis. He had a gift for languages; he'd been translating for the Lizards in Warsaw, and he got on better with them than most people did.

He recognized Mordechai, too, in spite of the curly beard he'd grown and his general air of seediness. 'Hullo, Anielewicz,' he said. 'I never thought I'd see you here.' Mordechai didn't like the look on Kipnis's thin pale face. Some of the men the Germans had set up as puppet rulers of the Warsaw ghetto had fawned on their Nazi masters. Some of the Lizards' helpers were all too likely to fawn on them, too.

The Lizard sitting next to Kipnis spoke irritably in his own language. Anielewicz understood enough to know he'd asked the interpreter why he'd called the prisoner by the wrong name. 'This is the male Shmuel, is it not?'

Mordechai figured he could safely show he'd heard his own name. 'Yes, Shmuel, that's me,' he said, touching the brim of his cloth cap and doing his best to leave the impression that he was an idiot

'Superior, sir, this male is now calling himself Shmuel,' Jakub Kipnis said. Mordechai had less trouble following him than he'd had understanding the

Lizard; Kipnis spoke more slowly, thinking between words. 'In Warsaw, this male was known as Mordechai Anielewicz.'

Flee? Utterly futile. Even if the Lizard guard behind him didn't cut him down, how could he break out of the prison camp? The answer was simple: he couldn't. 'You are Anielewicz?' he asked, pointing to Kipnis. The most he could hope to do now was confuse the issue.

'No, you liar, you are,' the interpreter said angrily.

The Lizard made noises like a steam shovel with a bad engine. He and Jakub Kipnis went back and forth, now mostly too fast for Mordechai to keep up with them. The Lizard said, 'If this is Anielewicz, they will want him back in Warsaw. He has much to answer for.' Anielewicz shook his head. If he had to understand two sentences, why those two?

'Superior sir, it is Anielewicz,' Kipnis insisted, slowing down a little. 'Send him to Warsaw. The governor there will know him.' He stopped in consternation. 'No – Zolraag has been replaced. His aides will know this male, though.'

'It may be so,' the Lizard said. 'Some of us are learning to tell one Big Ugly from another.' By his tone, he didn't find that an accomplishment worth bragging about. He turned his eyes to the guard behind Anielewicz. 'Take this male to the prison cells for close confinement until he is transported to Warsaw.'

'It shall be done,' the Lizard said in his own language. Gesturing with his rifle barrel, he dropped into Yiddish: 'Come along, you.'

Mordechai sent Jakub Kipnis a venomous glance. Since he was still claiming to be Shmuel the partisan, that was all he could do. He wanted to give the *tukhus-lekher* of an interpreter something more than a glare by which to remember him, but consoled himself by thinking the traitor's turn would come some day. It wasn't as it had been under the Nazis. A lot of Jews had weapons now.

'Come along, you,' the Lizard guard repeated. Helplessly, Anielewicz stepped out into the corridor ahead of him. The Lizard interrogator said something to the guard, who paused in the doorway to listen.

The world blew up.

That was Anielewicz's first confused thought, anyhow. He'd been under aerial bombardment before, in Warsaw from the Nazis and then from the Lizards. One moment Mordechai was glumly heading toward prison – and probably toward much worse trouble than that. The next, he was hurled against the far wall of the hallway while ceiling timbers groaned and shifted and tore away from one another to let him see streaks of gray-blue sky.

He staggered to his feet. A meter or two behind him, the Lizard guard was down, hissing piteously. The window in the interrogator's office had blown in, skewering him with shards of shattered glass like shrapnel. His automatic rifle lay forgotten beside him.

Head still ringing, Anielewicz snatched it up. He fired a short burst into the Lizard's head, then looked into the office where he'd been grilled. The Lizard interrogator in there was down, too, and wouldn't get up again; flying glass had flensed him.

By the chance of war, Jacob Kipnis was not badly hurt. He saw Mordechai, saw the Lizard rifle, and made a ghastly attempt at a smile. 'The German flying bomb—' he began. Mordechai cut him down with another short burst, then made sure of him with a shot behind the ear.

That took care of the two Lizards and the man who'd known Anielewicz was Anielewicz. Behind him, an alarm began to ring. He thought it had to do with him till he smelled smoke – the building was afire. He set down the rifle, scrambled out of the now glassless window (actually, almost glassless; a sharp shard sliced his hand), and dropped to the ground. With any luck at all, no one would know he'd been in there, let alone that he'd been found out.

Not far away, smoke still rose from an enormous crater. 'Must have been a tonne, at least,' muttered Mordechai, who had more experience gauging bomb craters than he'd ever wanted to acquire. At the edge of the crater lay the wreckage of the flying bomb's rear fuselage.

He spared that barely a glance. The rocket or whatever it was had done more than wreck the prison camp's administrative building. It had blown up in the middle of the yard. Broken men, and pieces of men, lay all around. Groans and shrieks in several languages rose into the sky. Some men, those nearest the crater and those who'd been unlucky enough to stop a chunk of the fuselage, would never groan or shriek or cry again.

As he trotted over to do what he could for the wounded, Anielewicz wondered whether the Nazis' aim with their rocket had been that bad or that good. If they'd intended to drop it in the middle of the prison camp, they could't have done a better job. But why would they want to do that, when so many of the men held here were Germans? But if they intended to hit anyplace else – the town of Piotrków, say – then they might as well have been playing blind man's buff.

He bent over a man who wouldn't live long. The fellow stared up at him. 'Bless me, Father, for I have sinned,' he said in a choking voice. Blood poured from his nose and mouth.

Mordechai knew what last rites were, but not how to give them. It didn't matter; the Pole died before he could do anything. Anielewicz looked around for someone he actually had some hope of helping.

WHAM! Off to the north, toward Piotrków, another explosion came out of nowhere. Distance made it faint and attenuated. If the Germans had aimed the last rocket and this one at the same place, their aiming left a lot to be desired. Kilometers separated the two impacts.

WHAM! Yet another explosion, this one a lot closer. Anielewicz staggered, went to one knee. A chunk of sheet metal crashed to the ground a couple of meters from where he had stood. Had it landed on top of him ... He tried not to think about things like that.

Men started running toward the northern edge of the camp. Looking around, Anielewicz saw why: the flying bomb had landed almost directly on top of a Lizard guard tower and had blown a great hole in the razor wire that confined the prisoners. Moreover, fragments from it had played havoc with the towers to either side. One was on fire, the other knocked off its leg.

Anielewicz started running, too. He'd never had a better chance to escape. The Lizards opened fire from more distant guard towers, but they hadn't figured on losing three at once. Some men went down. More scrambled into the crater the rocket had made and out the other side to freedom.

As with the first flying bomb that had fallen in the camp, this one left part of its carcass behind by the crater. Some of the metal skin had peeled off, including the piece that had almost mashed him. He'd been an engineering student before the war, and peered curiously at tanks – fuel tanks? – wrapped in glass wool, and as much clockwork and piping as he'd ever seen all in one place. He wished he could take a longer, closer look, but getting away was more important.

Bullets rattled off the flying bomb, then went elsewhere in search of more prey. Mordechai ran. The bullets came back, kicking up dirt around his feet. He rolled on the ground and thrashed wildly, in the hope of convincing the Lizard gunner he'd been hit. When the bullets stopped playing around him again, he got up and ran some more.

'Sneaky bastard!' someone shouted from behind him in German. His head whipped around. He might have known Friedrich would get out while the getting was good.

The fleeing men fanned out broadly, some making for the brush a few hundred meters away, others pelting up the road toward Piotrków, still others heading east or west across the fields toward farmhouses where they might find shelter.

Friedrich slogged up even with him. 'Damned if I don't think we're going to get away with this,' he bawled.

'Kayn aynhoreh,' Mordechai exclaimed.

'What's that mean?' the big German asked.

'Something like, don't tempt fate by saying anything too good.' Friedrich grunted and nodded. Most of the bullets were behind them now. The Lizards seemed to have given up on the prisoners who'd escaped fastest, and were concentrating on keeping any more men from getting out through the hole the flying bomb had blown in the wire.

Friedrich swerved to put some of the brush between him and the prison camp. Panting, he slowed to a fast walk. So did Anielewicz. 'Well, Shmuel, you damned Jew, it's just the two of us now,' Friedrich said.

'So it is, you stinking Nazi,' Mordechai answered. They grinned at each other, but cautiously. Each of them sounded as if he were making a joke, but Anielewicz knew he'd meant what he said, and had a pretty good notion Friedrich had been kidding on the square too.

'What do we do now?' Friedrich asked. 'Besides keep moving I mean.'

'That comes first,' Anielewicz said. 'We ought to try to get far enough away so they can't track us with dogs, or whatever they use. Afterwards . . . maybe we can hook on with a local guerilla band and keep on making life interesting for the Lizards. Or maybe not. This part of Poland is pretty much *Judenfrei*, thanks to you Nazi bastards.'

Now Anielewicz didn't sound like a man who was joking. Friedrich said, 'Yeah, well, I can tell you stories about that, too.'

'I'll bet you can,' Mordechai said. 'Save 'em, or we'll be trying to kill each other, and that would just make the Lizards laugh. Besides, the Poles around here may not like Jews—'

'They don't,' Friedrich said with a grim certainty Anielewicz didn't want to explore.

Mordechai went on, '—but they don't like Germans, either.' Friedrich scowled, but didn't interrupt. Anielewicz finished, 'Best bet, as far as I can see, is heading up to Lodz. It's a good-sized city; strangers won't stick out the way they would in Piotrków. And it still has a good many Jews left.'

'As if I should care about that.' Friedrich snorted, then sobered. 'Or maybe I should – you Jew bastards have had practice with an underground, haven't you?'

'You Nazi bastards made us practice with one,' Anielewicz said. 'So – Lodz?'

'Lodz,' Friedrich agreed.

Cabbage, black bread, potatoes. For variety, turnips or beets. Heinrich Jäger wished he were back at the front, if for no other reason than the tinfoil tubes of meat and butter front-line soldiers got. You didn't starve to death on cabbage, black bread, and potatoes, but after a while you started to wish you would. No matter how important the work he was part of, life in Germany these days felt cold and gray and dull.

He speared the last piece of potato, chased the last bit of sauerkraut around his plate, soaked up the last juices from the sauerkraut with his bread – which, he had to admit, was better than the really horrid stuff the bakers had turned out in 1917. That still didn't make it good.

He got to his feet, handed the plate and silverware to a kitchen worker who took them with a word of thanks, and started out of the refectory. Opening the door, he almost ran into a tall man in a black SS dress uniform gaudy with silver trim.

The SS colonel folded him into a bearhug. 'Jäger, you miserable son of a bitch, how the hell are you?' he boomed. A couple of physicists who had been eating in the refectory with Jäger stared in misbelief and dismay at the raucous apparition invading their quiet little corner of the world.

Life might remain cold and gray, but it wouldn't be dull any more. 'Hullo, Skorzeny,' he said. 'How goes it with you?' Life might abruptly end around *Standartenführer* Otto Skorzeny, but it would never, ever be dull.

The scar that furrowed the SS man's left cheek pulled half his grin up into a fearsome grimace. 'Still going strong,' he said.

'As if you knew any other way to go,' Jäger replied.

Skorzeny laughed, as if that had been some sort of clever observation rather than simple truth. 'You know someplace where we can talk quietly?' he asked.

'You don't have any idea how to talk quietly,' Jäger said, and Skorzeny laughed again. 'Come on, I'll take you to my quarters.'

'I'd need a trail of bred crumbs just to find my way around this place,' Skorzeny grumbled as Jäger led him through the medieval maze of Schloss Hohentübingen. Once in Jäger's room, he threw himself into a chair with such abandon that Jäger marveled when it didn't collapse under him.

'All right, how do you want to try to get me killed now?' Jäger asked.

'I've come up with a way, never you fear,' the SS man said airily.

'Why does this not surprise me?'

'Because you're not a fool,' Skorzeny answered. 'Believe me, I have come to know fools in all their awesome variety these past few years. Some of them wear uniforms and think they're soldiers. Not you – so much I give you.'

'And for so much I thank you,' Jäger said. He remained unsure whether Skorzeny qualified as a fool in uniform, even after most of a year's acquaintance. The man took chances that looked insane, but he'd brought off most of them. Did that make him lucky or good? His string of successes was long enough for Jäger to give him some benefit of the doubt. 'How are you going to twist the Lizards' stumpy little tails this time?'

'Not their tails, Jäger – the other end.' Skorzeny gave that grin again. Perhaps he intended it as disarming; no matter how he intended it, the scar twisted it into something piratical. 'You've heard that the English have started using mustard gas against the Lizards?'

'Yes, I've heard that.' Jäger's stomach did a slow lurch. He'd spent hours sealed into a stifling gas mask during the First World War. He also remembered comrades who hadn't got their masks on and sealed in time. His mouth curled down. 'I don't blame them, not really, but it's an ugly business. And why did they have that gas ready, d'you think? – to use against us when we got over the Channel, unless I miss my guess.'

'Probably.' Skorzeny waved a dismissive hand. He didn't care about why; what and how were all that mattered to him. He added, 'Don't get up on your high horse, either. If the English had tried gassing us, we'd have shown them mustard gas is a long way from the nastiest thing around. We do things better these days than they did in the last war.'

'No doubt.' Skorzeny sounded very certain. Jäger wondered how he knew, how much he knew, and how the new gases, whatever they were, had been tested – and on whom. Asking such questions was dangerous. To Jäger's mind, so was *not* asking them, but few of his fellow officers agreed.

Skorzeny went on, 'We didn't use gas against the Lizards for the same reason we didn't use gas against the English: for fear of getting it back in turn. Even if we have better, being on the receiving end of mustard gas wouldn't have been any fun.'

'You're right about that,' Jäger said wholeheartedly.

'With the Lizards on their island, though, the English stopped worrying about things like that.' Skorzeny chuckled. 'What's the old saying? 'Nothing concentrates the mind like the prospect of being hanged tomorrow?' Something like that, anyhow. The English must have figured that if they were going down, they wouldn't go down with any bullets left in the gun. And do you know what, Jäger? The Lizards must not have used gas in their own wars, because they don't have any decent defenses against it.'

'Ah,' Jäger said. 'So someone has found an Achilles heel for them at last, eh?' He had a sudden vision of sweeping the Lizards off the Earth, though he had no idea how much gas it would take to do that, or how many – or how few – people would be left alive after it was done.

'A weak place, anyway,' Skorzeny said. 'But they aren't stupid, any more than the Russians are. Do something to them and they'll try to figure out how to stop you. They don't have many masks of their own – maybe they don't have any; nobody's sure about that – but they're sure to have captured English samples by now, and they do have collaborators. There's a factory in the south of France that's gearing up to turn out gas masks to fit snouty Lizard faces.'

'A light begins to dawn,' Jäger said. 'You want something dreadful to happen to this factory.'

'Give the man a cigar!' Skorzeny exclaimed, and from an inner pocket of his tunic he produced a veritable cigar, which he handed to Jäger with a flourish. Jäger seized it with no less alacrity than he would have accepted the Holy Grail. Now Skorzeny's grin, though lopsided, seemed genuinely amused. 'I know just what I want to happen to the building, too.'

'Do you?' Jäger said. 'How does it involve me?'

'Think of it as – poetic justice,' Skorzeny answered.

One of Rance Auerbach's troopers kept singing 'Lydia the Tattooed Lady' over and over again. Auerbach was damn sick of the song. He wanted to tell the cavalryman to shut up, but couldn't make himself do it. You dumped your worries however you could when you headed into a fight.

And Lydia, Kansas, was where the two companies of cavalry were supposed to be going: a tiny, nowhere town on Kansas State Highway 25, a two-lane stretch of nowhere blacktop that paralleled US 83's north-south path through Kansas a few miles to the west of the federal road, but that petered out well before it reached the Nebraska state line.

Lieutenant Bill Magruder said, 'The damned Lizards should have moved into Lydia by now.'

'They'd better have moved into Lydia by now,' Auerbach answered feelingly. 'If they haven't, a lot of us are going to end up dead.' He shook his head. 'A lot of us are going to end up dead any which way. Riding horses against the Lizards isn't your basic low-risk business.'

'Radio traces have been telling 'em right where we're at ever since we set out from Lamar,' Magruder said with a tight grin. 'They should know we're gettin' ready to hit Lydia with everything we've got.'

'They should, yeah.' Auerbach's smile was tight, too. The Lizards loved their gadgets, and believed in what those gadgets told them. If they intercepted radio signals that said two companies were heading toward Lydia to try to take it away from them, they'd take that seriously – and be waiting to greet the Americans when they arrived.

But it wasn't two companies heading toward Lydia: it was just Auerbach's radioman and half a dozen buddies, plus a lot of horses lashed together and carrying cloth dummies in the saddle. They never would have fooled anybody from the ground, but from the air they looked pretty good. The Lizards used aerial recon the same way they used radio intercepts. If you fed 'em what they already thought they were seeing or hearing, you could fool 'em. They went to Lydia – and you went to Lakin.

Thinking about carrier pigeons and nineteenth-versus twentieth-century warfare had given Auerbach the idea. He'd sold it to Colonel Nordenskold. Now it was his to execute ... and if he'd guessed wrong about how the Lizards' minds worked, they'd do some serious executing of their own.

He held up a leather-gauntleted hand to halt his command when they came to a tall stand of cottonwoods along the banks of the Arkansas River. We'll hold horses here,' he ordered, 'We're a little farther out than usual, I know, but we've got more horses along, too, since this is a two-company raid. We won't find better cover for concealing them any closer to town. Mortar crews, machine gunners, and you boys with the bazooka, you'll bring your animals forward. If we're lucky, you can use 'em to haul the weapons out when we pull back.'

'If we're real lucky, we'll hold the place a while,' Lieutenant Magruder said quietly. Auerbach nodded, grateful the Virginian didn't trumpet that thought. If everything went perfectly, they might push the Lizard-human frontier a few miles back toward the distant Mississippi and make the push stick. But how often did things go perfectly in war?

He swung himself down from his horse, tossed the reins to one of the troopers who was staying behind. Only about twenty or twenty-five men would hold horses today; the cottonwoods' trunks and low branches made convenient tethering points for the animals. He wanted to get as many soldiers into the fight as he could.

The troopers and the packhorses carrying what passed for their heavy firepower spread out into a broad skirmish line as they advanced on Lakin. Some of the sweat that darkened the armpits of Auerbach's olive-drab tunic had to do with the weather and the hike. Some came from worry – or rather, fear. If the Lizards hadn't taken the bait and reinforced Lydia at Lakin's expense, a lot of good young men weren't going to make it home to Lamar.

Lots of L's, he thought. If the similarity in names had confused the Lizards, they wouldn't have reacted as he'd hoped. And if they hadn't, his two companies were going to get massacred. Then, a few days or a few weeks or a few months from now, some hotshot captain back in Lamar would have some new brilliant idea about how to drive the Lizards out of Lakin. Maybe Colonel Nordenskold would let him try it out – assuming the Lizards weren't in Lamar by then, or in Denver.

From way off to the left of the advancing skirmish line came a loud, flat *bang*! and a shriek. 'Oh, hell,' Auerbach muttered under his breath. He raised his voice: 'They've laid some mines since we were here last, boys. Watch where you put your feet.' Not that that would do much good, as he knew only too well.

The Lizards inside Lakin hadn't been asleep at the switch, either. As soon as that mine went off, a siren in town began to wail. The Kearny County Consolidated High School looked like hell from the last time the cavalry had come to call, but the Lizards were still using it for their base. Off in the distance, Auerbach saw little skittering shapes heading for cover. He bit down hard on the inside of his lower lip. He'd counted on being able to get closer to town before his plan started going to pot.

But what you counted on in war and what you got weren't always the same critter. Sometimes they weren't even the same kind of critter. A machine gun started chattering in one of the battered high school buildings. Auerbach threw himself flat amid dark green beet tops. He pounded a fist into the dirt. Cries here and there said his command was taking casualties. If they spent the next hour crawling toward Lakin on their bellies, the Lizards would be able to bring back whatever forces they'd moved up to Lydia.

'Tell Schuyler's mortar crew to take out that machine gun!' he shouted. The man to his left passed on the message. No radios here – they were all part of the simulated attack on Lydia. Now for the first time Auerbach missed them desperately. He shrugged. His great-grandfathers' COs had managed to run battles under conditions like these, so he figured he could do it, too, if he had to.

And he had some pretty good people playing on his team, as had those officers in Confederate gray. Long before any order could have reached him, Schuyler – or maybe one of the other mortar men – opened up with his stovepipe. A bomb fell behind the place from which the machine gun was sending forth its firefly flashes, then another in front. The third bomb was long again, but by less than half as much as the first. The fourth was a hit. The machine gun fell silent.

Cheers rolled up and down the skirmish line. But when some of the troopers got up and started to run toward town, the machine gun began its hateful stutter once more. The mortar when *whump, whump, whump* – three rounds in quick succession. The machine gun stopped firing again. This time, it didn't start up when the Americans came to their feet.

Auerbach let out a Rebel yell as he advanced. Quite a few of his men echoed him; cavalry units drew a disproportionate number of Southerners. Some of the Lizards in the consolidated high school opened up with their automatic rifles. Those were bad, but didn't have the reach or sustained firepower of the machine gun.

Mortar bombs began stalking the rifle positions, one by one. Some were silenced, some weren't. At worst, though, not a whole lot of Lizards were shooting at the cavalrymen.

Auerbach's confidence rose. 'Boys, I think most of 'em have gone off to visit up in Lydia,' he yelled. That brought fresh cheers and more Rebel yells. Getting through the razor wire around the high school wasn't going to be any fun, but once they managed it—

Manage they did. The Lizards lacked the defenders to prevent it. They shot a couple of men attacking the wire with cutters, but others kept up such a heavy stream of fire on their positions that they probably lost as many fighters as they wounded.

Once through the barriers, the Americans fanned out and went Lizard hunting. 'Always wanted to do this to my old high school,' one trooper said, chucking a grenade into a likely-looking doorway. No Lizard came out. Ever so cautiously, Auerbach peered into the room. Desks and tables were randomly scattered over the dirty floor, some of them overturned. Dust and cobwebs covered the blackboard, but he could still read the social studies lesson some teacher had chalked there the day before the world changed forever. The corners of his mouth turned down. Whatever the kids had learned in that lesson, it wasn't helping them now.

The snarl of a Lizard automatic rifle said the fighting wasn't done yet. Auerbach hurried toward the sound of the shooting. The Lizard was holed up in what had been a girls' bathroom. 'Surrender!' he shouted to it. Then he made a noise that reminded him of bread popping out of an electric toaster. That was supposed to mean the same thing in Lizard talk.

He didn't think it would do any good. But then the door to the rest room opened. The Lizard slid out its rifle. 'Hold fire!' Auerbach called to his men. He made the popping-toast noise again. The door opened wider. The Lizard came out. He knew enough to stand there with his hands high. All he was wearing was body paint; he'd left his equipment behind in the john. He repeated the Lizard word

Auerbach had repeated, so it probably did mean *surrender* after all.

'Hagerman! Calhoun! Take charge of him,' Auerbach said. 'Théy really want Lizard POWs; we'll get a pat on the fanny for bringing him in, if we can do it.'

Max Hagerman gave the Lizard a dubious look. 'How we gonna keep him on a horse all the way back to Lamar, sir?'

'Damned if I know, but I expect you'll figure something out,' Auerbach said cheerfully, which meant Hagerman was stuck with it. Turning to Jack Calhoun, the captain went on, 'Go in there and gather up his gear. The intelligence staff'll want that, too.' The cavalryman assumed a dubious expression, too, his on account of the GIRLS sign on the battered door. 'Go, on,' Auerbach told him. 'They aren't in there now.'

'Yeah, that's right,' Calhoun said, as if reminding himself.

That seemed to be the last combat inside the school grounds. Auerbach hurried to the northern edge of the school. The mortar teams and the .50-caliber machine-gun crew were already digging themselves in. 'You boys don't need me,' Auerbach said. 'You could run this show by yourselves.'

The troopers just grinned and went on setting up. The mortar teams began logging bombs up Highway 25, getting the range and zeroing in on the highway itself. 'They'll have to work to get past us,' a sergeant said. 'We've each got a different stretch of road to cover, from long range to almost right down on top of us. And as they pass the longer-range weapons, those'll drop down to keep the pressure on.'

'That's how we set it up,' Auerbach agreed. 'Now we find out if we're as smart as we think we are.' If the Lizards sent a tank or two west from Garden City, instead of bringing the garrison back from Lydia to Lakin, his men were in big trouble. Sure, they'd packed the bazooka launcher and a dozen or so rounds for it, but you needed to be lucky to take out a Lizard tank with a bazooka, and you didn't need to be lucky to smash up some cavalrymen with a tank.

One of his troopers let out a yell and pointed north. Auerbach took his field glasses out of their case. The little specks on the road swelled into one of the Lizards' armored personnel carriers and a couple of trucks. They were southbound, coming fast.

'Get ready, boys,' he said, stowing the binoculars again. 'That APC is gonna be tough.' A Lizard APC could give a Lee tank a tough fight. A bazooka would make it say uncle, though.

He shouted for more troopers to come up and find cover in the buildings and ruins of the school. For once the Lizards were doing the dirty work, attacking Americans in a fortified position. Outside of Chicago, that didn't happen often enough.

The sergeant dropped a finned bomb down the tube of his mortar. *Bang!* Off it flew, quite visible against the sky. It was still airborne when he fired the second. He got off the third before either of the first two hit. Then dirt and asphalt fountained up from Highway 25, right behind the APC. The second bomb hit between two trucks, the third alongside one of them.

The trucks and the APC came on harder than ever, into the next mortar's zone. That crew was already firing. Screams of delight rose from the Americans when a bomb landed on top of a truck. The truck slewed sideways, flipped over, and started to burn. Lizards spilled out of it. Some lay on the roadway. Others skittered for cover. The .50- caliber machine gun opened up on them, and on the other truck.

The APC had a heavy machine gun, too, or a light cannon. Whatever it was, it put a lot of rounds in the air, and in a hurry. Auerbach threw himself flat behind what had been a wall and was now a substantial pile of rubble. With the Lizards' gun chewing at it, he hoped it was substantial enough.

He swore when the .50 fell silent. The mortar teams were shooting up and over cover, but the machine gunners had to be more exposed, and their weapon's muzzle flash gave the Lizards a dandy target. The Americans needed that gun. Auerbach crawled toward it on his belly. As he'd feared, he found both gunners down, one with the top of his head blown off, the other moaning with a shoulder wound. He quickly helped bandage the wounded man, then peered out over the long gun's sights.

Fire spurted from the second truck. It stopped but didn't roll onto its side. Lizards bailed out into the fields on either side of Highway 25. Auerbach fired at them. He came to the end of a belt, bent to fasten on another one from the ammunition box.

'I'll take care of that, sir,' a trooper said. 'I've done it with a .30- caliber weapon often enough. This here one's just bigger, looks like.'

'That's about right,' Auerbach agreed. He squeezed the triggers. The heavy machine gun felt like a jackhammer in his hands, and made a racket like a dozen jackhammers all going flat out. Even with the flash hider at the end of the muzzle, he blinked against the spearhead of flame that spat from the barrel. A stream of hot brass cartridge cases, each as big as his thumb, spewed from the breech and clattered down into the growing pile at his feet.

He swore again when the APC's weapon, which had gone on to other targets after wrecking the machine-gun crew, now swung back his way. 'Get down!' he yelled to the corporal feeding him with ammo. Bullets slammed into the wreckage all around him. Flying concrete chips bit into the back of his neck.

All at once, the shells stopped coming. Auerbach looked up, wondering if a sniper was waiting to put one through his head. But no – smoke poured from the APC. A mortar bomb had pierced the armor over the engine compartment. With the enemy machine dead in the water, all the mortar teams poured fire on it. In seconds, another bomb tore through the roof. The APC went up in a Fourth of July display of exploding ammunition.

A few Lizards out in the field kept up a rattle of small-arms fire. Next to what had been going on, it was Easy Street now. The Mortar teams and Auerbach on the .50- caliber shot back whenever they found decent targets. The Lizards couldn't hit back, not at long range.

'We beat 'em.' Lieutenant Magruder sounded as if he couldn't believe it.

Auerbach didn't blame him; he was having trouble believing it himself. 'Yeah, we did,' he said. 'We'll send a pigeon back to Lamar, let 'em know we did it. And we'll send back our prisoner with a guard. Otherwise, though, we'll bring the horses forward into town.'

'Yes, sir,' Magruder said. 'You aim to stay in Lakin, then?'

'Till I get orders otherwise or till the Lizards come up from Garden City and run me out, you bet I do,' Auerbach answered. 'Why the hell not? I won it, and by God I'm going to keep it.'

Leslie Groves stared at the telephone in disbelief, as if it were a snake that had just bitten him. 'I'm sorry, General,' the voice on the other end said, 'but I don't see how we're going to be able to get those tubes and explosives and detonator wiring to you.'

'Then you'd better look harder, Mister,' Groves growled. 'You're in Minneapolis, right? You still have a working railroad, for God's sake. Get 'em across the Dakotas or up through Canada; our track north by way of Fort Greeley is still open most of the time. You get moving, do you hear me?'

The fellow from Minneapolis – Porlock, that's what his name was – said, 'I don't know whether we'll be able to make that shipment. I'm aware your priority is extremely high, but the losses we've suffered on rail shipments made me hesitate to take the risk. Transporting the goods by wagon would be much more secure.' His voice trailed away in a sort of peevish whine.

'Fine. Send us a set by wagon,' Groves said.

'Oh, I'm so glad you see my difficulty,' Porlock said, now in tones full of bureaucratic relief.

Porlock, Groves reflected, should have been named Morlock, after one of the subterranean creatures in *The Time Machine*. Then he shook his head. Morlocks were machine tenders; they would have had a proper appreciation for the uses of technology, no matter how lamentable their taste in entrées had grown over the millennia.

Snarling, Groves said, 'I wasn't done yet, Porlock. God damn it to hell, sir, if I tell you I want your breakfast fried eggs and toast chucked into a fighter plane and flown out here, they'd better still be hot when I meet 'em at the airport. *That's* what the priority this project has is all about. You want to send me backups for my requisitions, you can send 'em any damn way you please. But you will send me a set my way, on my schedule, or the President of the United States will hear about it.

Do you have that down loud and clear, Mister? You'd better, that's all I have to say.'

Porlock had tried to interrupt him a couple of times, but Groves used his loud, gravelly voice the same way he used his wide, heavy body: to bulldoze his way ahead. Now, when he paused for breath, Porlock said, 'There are more projects than yours these days, General. Poison gas has had its priority increased to—'

'Three levels below ours,' Groves broke in. When he felt like interrupting, he damn well interrupted. 'Poison gas is a sideshow, Mister. The Lizards'll figure out proper masks sooner or later, and they'll figure out how to make gas of their own, too. If they don't manage it by themselves, you can bet your bottom dollar some helpful frog or wop'll give 'em a hand. The thing we're working on here, though' – he wouldn't call it a bomb, not over the telephone; you never could tell who might be listening – 'the only way to defend against that is to be somewhere else when it goes off.'

'Rail travel isn't safe or secure,' Porlock protested.

'Mister, in case you haven't noticed, there's a war on. Not one damned thing in the United States is safe or secure these days. Now I need what I need, and I need it when I need it. Are you going to send it to me my way, or not?' Groves made the question into a threat: *You are going to send it to me my way, or else.*

'Well, yes, but—'

'All right, then,' Groves said, and hung up. He glared at the phone after it was back on the hook. Sometimes the people on his own side were worse enemies than the Lizards. No matter that the united States had been at war for more than a year and a half. Some people still didn't get the idea that if you didn't take occasional risks – or not so occasional risks – now, you'd never get the chance to take them later. He snorted, a full-throated noise of contempt. For all the initiative some people showed, they might as well have been Lizards themselves.

He snorted again. Nobody would ever accuse him of failing through lack of initiative. Through rushing ahead too fast, maybe, but never through hanging back.

He had a picture of his wife on his desk. He didn't look at it as often as he should, because when he did, he remembered how much he missed her. That made him inefficient, and he couldn't afford inefficiency, not now.

Thinking of his own wife made him think of what had happened to Jens Larssen. The guy had caught a bunch of bad breaks, no doubt about that. Having your wife take up with another man was tough. But Larssen had let it drive him – oh, not round the bend, but to a nasty place, a place where people didn't want to work with him anymore. He'd had real talent, but he'd given up on the team and he wasn't quite brilliant enough to be an asset as a lone-wolf theorist. Sending him out had been a good notion. Groves hoped he'd come back better for it.

'Hanford,' Groves muttered discontentedly. It had seemed a great idea at the time. The Columbia was about as ideal a cooling source for an atomic pile as you could imagine, and eastern Washington a good long way away from any Lizards.

But things had changed since Larssen got on his trusty bicycle and pedaled out of Denver. The project was running smoothly here now, with plutonium coming off the piles gram after gram, and with a third pile just starting construction.

Not only that, Groves had his doubts about being able to start up a major industrial development in a sleepy hamlet like Hanford without having the Lizards notice and wonder what was going on. Those doubts had grown more urgent since Tokyo vanished in a flash of light and an immense pillar of dust, and since Cordell Hull brought back word that the Lizards would treat any American nuclear research facility the same way if they found it.

Just because Hanford was such a good site for a pile, Groves feared the Lizards would suspect any new work there was exactly what it really was. If they did, it would cease to exist moments later, and so would the hamlet of Hanford. Of course, if they got suspicious about Denver, the same thing would happen here – and Denver had a lot more people in it than Hanford did. Most of them – Groves devoutly hoped – knew nothing whatever about the atomic bombs being spawned here. They were hostages to the secret's being kept, just the same.

They were also camouflage. The Lizards flew over Denver a good deal, and bombed the plants that turned out tires and bricks and mining equipment and furniture (some of the latter plants were making wooden aircraft parts these days instead). The United States needed everything the factories produced. All the same, Groves didn't too much mind seeing them bombed. As long as Lizards hit them, they weren't hitting anything of greater importance. And here, unlike Hanford, new industrial facilities could go up without being reckoned anything out of the ordinary.

Even if Larssen did come back with the news that Hanford could be the earthly paradise for atomic research, Groves figured the Metallurgical Laboratory would stay here, east of Eden. Packing up and moving would be tough, doing it secretly would be tougher, and keeping things in Washington State secret would be toughest of all. Accepting Denver's drawbacks and exploiting its advantages seemed a better bet.

'That'll tick Larssen off, too,' Groves muttered under his breath. If Larssen came back from risking his neck for project and country with a recommendation to go yonder, he wouldn't be dancing with glee when he found out they'd decided to stay hither no matter what. 'Too damn bad,' Groves told the ceiling. 'If he doesn't like it, he can go back to Hanford by his lonesome.'

He turned to the report he'd been studying when that idiot Porlock called. Keeping the atomic piles cool as they cooked plutonium took a lot of water from Cherry Creek and the South Platte. Separating the plutonium from the uranium took chemical reactions that used more water. Every bit of that water, by the time it finished doing its job, ended up radioactive. A radioactive trail in the South Platte leading back to Denver might as well have been a sign to the Lizards, saying AIM HERE.

Heavy-duty filters sucked as much radioactive goop out of the water as they could. They did a good job; Geiger counters downstream from the University of Denver were pretty quiet. But that didn't end the problem. The glass wool and diatomaceous earth and other goodies in the filter (the report had a long list) grew radioactive themselves after a while. When they got cleaned out and replaced, they had to go somewhere. To keep the Lizards from detecting them, 'somwhere' meant lead-lined tubs and trash cans.

The major who'd written the report was complaining that he had trouble getting enough lead sheeting to line the tubs and cans. Groves scribbled a note in the margin: *This is silver-mining country, for heaven's sake. Wherever there's silver, there's going to be lead. If we aren't exploiting that as well as we should, we have to get better at it.*

If he had to requisition lead from outside of town, God only knew how long it would take to get here. If he stayed local, he could control the whole process of getting it from start to finish. All at once, he understood how old-time feudal barons, living off the produce and manufactures of their own estates, must have felt.

He smiled. 'Lucky bastards,' he said.

9

The mustard-gas burn on David Goldfarb's leg throbbed painfully. His trousers had pulled up over his socks just for a moment, while he was scrambling through grass near a shell hole that must have come from a gas round. That was all it took.

He pulled up his trousers now. In spite of the slimy stuff the medic had smeared on it, the burn remained red and inflamed. It looked infected. Mustard gas was nasty stuff. It could linger for days. He was just glad he'd been wearing his gas mask while he was near that hole. The idea of trying to breathe with a burn on his lungs made him shiver all over.

'Ow's it doin', flyboy?' Fred Stanegate asked in Yorkshire dialect so broad Goldfarb had trouble following it. Stanegate was a big blond chap with cheekbones that made him look more like a Viking than an Englishman. The Sten gun he carried seemed hardly more than a pistol in his massive, thick-fingered hands. It also seemed anachronistic; he should have been toting a battle-axe and wearing a hauberk, not filthy army battledress.

'I expect I'll live,' Goldfarb answered. Stanegate chuckled as if he'd said something funny. From the Yorkshireman's point of view, maybe he had; by all appearances, he bemused Fred at least as much as the other way round.

'Right peculiar they didn't want you back,' Stanegate said. 'Peculiar.' He repeated the word with relish, making four distinct syllables of it: pee-kyou-lee-yuhr.

'Wasn't much of a "they" left at Bruntingthrope by the time the Lizards got through it with,' Goldfarb said, shrugging. After the first Lizard attack on the air base, Basil Roundbush had been recalled to piloting at once, but no orders had come for Goldfarb to return to a proper radar station. Then the Lizards started pounding Bruntingthrope with pilotless aircraft, and after one of them hit the officer's barracks in the middle of the night, nobody much was left in RAF blue who could give him orders.

The local army commander had been happy enough to take him on. He'd said, 'You know how to handle a weapon and obey orders, and that gives you a leg up – two legs up – on a lot of the lads we're giving the king's shilling to these days.' Goldfarb pictured himself with two legs up, and crashing to earth immediately thereafter. He didn't argue with the major, though. He'd wanted to get into the scrap firsthand.

Now he waved about him and said, 'And so we find ourselves approaching the lovely metropolis of Market Harborough and all its amenities, which—'

'All its what?' Fred Stanegate broke in.

'All the good stuff it has in it,' Goldfarb said. Next to Bruntingthorpe, Market Harborough, a town of ten or fifteen thousand people, was indeed a metropolis, not that that in itself said much for Market Harborough. Goldfarb had pedaled into it a few times; it was no farther from Bruntingthorpe than Leicester was. 'The Three Swans served some very fine bitter, even in wartime.'

'Aye, that's so. Ah recall now.' Stanegate's face grew beatific at the memory. 'An' in the market – you know, the one by t'old school – you could get a bit o'butter for your bread, if you knew the right bloke t'ask.'

'Could you?' Goldfarb hadn't known the right bloke, or even that there was a right bloke. Too late to worry about it now, even if the margarine he'd been spreading on his bread had tasted like something that dripped from the crankcase of a decrepit lorry.

'Aye, y'could.' Fred Stanegate sighed. 'Wonder how much of the place is left.' He shook his head gloomily. 'Not much, I wager. Not much o' anything left these days.'

'Pretty country,' Goldfarb said, waving again. Occasional shell holes marred the green meadows and fields or shattered fence gates, but the Lizards hadn't quite moved up into Market Harborough itself, so it hadn't been fought over house by house. 'Can't you just see the hounds and riders chasing a fox into those woods there?'

'Ah, well, Ah always used t'pull for the fox, if tha knows what Ah mean, whenever the hunt went by my farm.'

'You're one up on me, then,' Goldfarb said. 'The only hunts I've ever seen were in the cinema.'

'Looked to me like it'd be a fair bit of a lark, if you had the brass to keep up the 'ounds and the 'orses and the kit an' all,' Stanegate said. 'Me, Ah was getting by on a couple o' quid a week, so Ah wasn't about t'go out ridin' t'the 'ounds.' He spoke quite without malice or resentment, just reporting on how things had been. After a moment, he grinned. 'So here Ah am in the army now, at a deal less than a couple o' quid a week. Life's a rum 'un, ain't it?'

'Won't quarrel with you there.' Goldfarb reached up to straighten the tin hat on his head. His right index finger slid toward the trigger of his Sten gun. Houses were growing thicker on the ground as they got into Market Harborough. Even though the Lizards had never been in the town, they'd bombed it and shelled it, and a lot of their bombs and shells sprayed submunitions that stayed around waiting for some unlucky or careless sod to tread on them. Goldfarb did not intend to be careless.

A lot of people who had lived in Market Harborough had fled. A good many others, no doubt, were casualties. That did not mean the place was empty. Far from it: it bulged with refugees from the fighting farther south in the Midlands. Their tents and blankets filled the grassy square around the old grammar school – the place where, before the Lizards invaded England, Fred Stanegate had bought his butter.

Goldfarb had seen his share of refugees the past few weeks. These seemed at first glance no different from the men and women who'd streamed north before them: tired, pale, thin, filthy, many with blank faces and haunted eyes. But some of them were different. Nurses in white (and some with no uniform but for a Red Cross armband on a sleeve) tended to patients with burns like Goldfarb's but worse, spreading over great stretches of their bodies. Others did what they could for people who wheezed and coughed and tried desperately to get air down into lungs too blistered and burned to receive it.

'Filthy stuff, gas,' Goldfarb said.

'Aye, that it is.' Stanegate nodded vigorously. 'My father, 'e was in France the last war, and 'e said it were the worst of anything there.'

'Looking at this, I'd say he was right.' That England had resorted to poison gas in the fight against the Lizards bothered Goldfarb, and not just because he'd had the bad luck to get hurt by it. His cousin Moishe Russie had talked about the camps the Nazis had built in Poland for gassing Jews. How anyone could reckon gas a legitimate weapon of war after that was beyond Goldfarb.

But Fred Stanegate said, 'If it shifts the bloody Lizards, Ah don't care how filthy it is. Manure's filthy, too, but you need it for yer garden.'

'That's so,' Goldfarb admitted. And it *was* so. If you were invaded, you did whatever you could to beat the invaders, and worried about consequences later. If you lost to the Lizards now, you lost forever and you never had the chance to worry about being moral again. Wouldn't that make gas legitimate? Churchill had thought so. Goldfarb sighed. 'Like you said, it's a rum world.'

Fred Stanegate pointed. 'Isn't that the Three Swans there?'

'That used to be the Three Swans, looks more like to me,' Goldfarb answered. The inn had boasted a splendid eighteenth-century wrought-iron sign. Now a couple of finger-length chunks of twisted iron lay in the gutter. A shell hit had enlarged the doorway and blown glass out of the windows. 'Bloody shame.'

'They're not dead yet, seems to me,' Stanegate said. Maybe he was right, too. The building hadn't been abandoned; somebody'd hung blankets over the doorway. And, as Goldfarb watched, a man in a publican's leather apron slipped out between two of those blankets and looked around in wonder at what Market Harborough had become.

Spying Goldfarb's and Stanegate's draggled uniforms, he waved to the two military men. 'Come in and have a pint on me, lads.'

They looked at each other. They were on duty, but a pint was a pint. 'Let me buy you one, then, for your kindness,' Goldfarb answered. The innkeeper did not say no, but beckoned them into the Three Swans.

The fire crackling in the hearth was welcome. The innkeeper drew three pints with professional artistry. 'Half a crown for mine,' he said. Given what England was enduring, it was a mild price. Goldfarb dug in his pockets, found two shillings. He was still rummaging for a sixpence when Fred slapped one on the bar.

Goldfarb leered at him. 'Pitching in on the cheap, are you?'

'That Ah am.' Stanegate sipped his beer. One blond eyebrow rose. So did his mug, in salute to the publican. 'Better nor I looked for. Your own brewing?'

'Has to be,' the fellow said with a nod. 'Couldn't get delivery even before the bloody Lizards crashed in on us, and now – Well, you'll know more about now than I do.'

A good number of tavern keepers were brewing their own beer these days, for just the reasons this one had named. Goldfarb had sampled several of their efforts. Some were ambrosial; some were horse piss. This one ... He thoughtfully smacked his lips. Fred Stanegate's 'Better nor I looked for' seemed fair.

Someone pushed his way between the blankets that curtained off the Three Swans. Goldfarb's gulp had nothing to do with beer: it was Major Smithers, the officer who'd let him embark on his infantry career.

Smithers was a short, chunky man who probably would have run to fat had he been better fed. He had a hand through thinning sandy hair. His forward-thrusting, beaky face was usually red. Goldfarb looked for it to get redder on his discovering two of his troopers in a public house.

But Smithers had adaptability. Without it, he would have taken Goldfarb's RAF uniform more seriously. Now he just said, 'One for me as well, my good man,' to the innkeeper. To Goldfarb and Stanegate, he added, 'Drink up quick, lads. We're moving forward.'

David Goldfarb downed his pint in three long swallows and set it on the cigarette-scarred wood of the bar, relieved not to be placed on report. Stanegate finished his at a more leisurely pace, but emptied it ahead of Major Smithers even so. He said, 'Moving forward. By gum, Ah like the sound o' that.'

'On to Northampton,' Smithers said in tones of satisfaction. He sucked foam from his mustache. 'That won't be an easy push; the Lizards are there in force, protecting their perimeter, and they have outposts north of town – their line runs through Spratton and Brixworth and Scaldwell.' He swallowed the last of his pint, did that foam-sucking trick again, and shook his head. 'Just a pack of bloody little villages nobody'd ever heard of except the people who lived in 'em. Well, they're on the map now, by God.'

He meant that literally; he drew from a pocket of his battledress an Ordnance Survey map of the area and spread it on the bar so Goldfarb and Stanegate could see. Goldfarb peered at the map with interest; Ordnance Survey cartography, so clear and detailed, always put him in mind of a radar portrait of the ground it pictured. The map seemed to show everything this side of cow tracks in the fields. Brixworth lay along the main road from Market Harborough down to Northampton; Spratton and Scaldwell flanked the road to either side.

Major Smithers said, 'We'll feint at Spratton. The main attack will go in between Brixworth and Scaldwell. If we can roll them out of Northampton, their whole position north of London unravels.' He glanced at the gas masks hanging from the soldiers' belts. 'Canisters in there fresh?'

'Yes, sir,' Goldfarb and Stanegate said together. Goldfarb clicked his tongue between his teeth. The question probably meant another mustard gas bombardment was laid on as part of the attack. After a moment, he asked, 'Sir, how do things stand south of London?' 'Not as well, by what I've heard.' Smithers made a sour face, as if the admission tasted bad to him. 'They put more men – er, more Lizards – into that one, and seized a broader stretch of territory. In spite of the gas, it's still very much touch and go in the southeast and the south. I've heard reports that they're trying to push round west of London, by way of Maidenhead and such, to link their two forces. Don't know whether it's so, but it would be bad for us if it is.'

'Just on account of you're goin' good one place, you think it's the same all around,' Fred Stanegate said. He sighed. 'Wish it were so, Ah do.'

Major Smithers folded the map and returned it to the pocket whence it had emerged. 'Let's be off,' he said. Reluctantly, Goldfarb followed him out of the Three Swans.

Not far outside Market Harborough, they passed a battery of 17-pounders bombarding the Lizards farther south. The men serving the three-inch field guns were bare-chested in the summer sun, but wore gas masks. 'Gas shells,' Goldfarb said, and took a couple of steps away from the guns. If one of those shells went off by accident, that wouldn't do much good, but he couldn't help it.

The 17-pounders barked and bucked, one after another. As soon as they'd fired three shells each, their crews hitched them to the backs of the lorries from which the shells had come and rattled off across the crater-pocked meadow to a new firing position.

They hadn't gone more than a couple of hundred yards when incoming shells tore fresh holes in the greensward where they'd been. Goldfarb dived for a hole. Fred Stanegate, half a step slower, chose the same hole and landed on top of him. 'Ow!' he said; Stanegate's knee dug into his left kidney.

'Sorry,' Stanegate grunted. 'Blighters are quick to shoot back, aren't they?'

'Too bloody accurate, too,' Goldfarb answered, wriggling toward greater comfort, or at least less discomfort. 'They always have been. I shouldn't wonder if they don't slave their guns to radar somehow.' He had no idea how to do such a thing, but it would account for both speed and accuracy in the Lizards' response.

Fred Stanegate shifted, too, and not in the right direction. 'What's radar?' he asked.

'Never mind. I talk too bloody much, that's all.' The shells stopped falling. Goldfarb scrambled out of the hole. So did Stanegate. He looked at the radarman curiously. Goldfarb felt himself flushing. He muttered, 'Trust me, Fred, you don't Need to Know.'

Stanegate heard the capital letters. 'It's like that, is it? All right, Ah'll say nowt further.'

Three clanking, smoking, rumbling monsters clattered south on iron tracks: two Cromwell tanks and a heavy Churchill. The Cromwells were a vast improvement over the Crusaders they supplanted, but not as good as the tanks the Nazis were turning out these days. The Churchill had thick armor, but a weak engine and a popgun 2-pounder for a cannon. Against Lizard armor, either model was woefully inadequate. They were, however, what Britain had, and into the fight they went.

Fred Stanegate waved to the commander of a Cromwell, who was standing up and peering out his hatch to get a better view. The tankman waved back. In his gas mask, he looked as alien as any Lizard. Stanegate said, 'Ah didn't know we had so many cards left in t'hand.'

'If we don't play them now, we'll never get to use them,' Goldfarb said. 'They'll do some good against Lizard infantry, I hope. From all I've heard, gas is the only thing that really does much against their tanks, unless somebody climbs on top and tosses a Molotov cocktail down a hatch.'

The farther south they went, the more chewed up the ground became. They passed the hulks of several burned-out British tanks, as well as tin hats hung on rifles stuck bayonet-first into the ground to mark hastily dug graves. Then, not much later, they came on a Lizard tank in the middle of a field.

Had it not been for the men in masks climbing in and out of the monster machine, Goldfarb would have expected to die in the next moments. The Lizard tank was not much bigger than its English foes, but looked more formidable. Its armor was smooth and beautifully sloped, so that it brought to mind the 'cars of the future' magazines sometimes hired artists to draw. As for its cannon – 'If that's not a four-inch gun, or maybe a five-, I'm a Lizard,' Goldfarb said. 'I wonder if the shell would even notice one of our tanks on the way through.'

'We knocked it out some kind of way,' Stanegate said. 'Don't look like it's burned – could be they got a mite too much mustard in their sandwiches.' He laughed at his own wit.

'I don't care why it's dead. I'm just glad it is.' Goldfarb set his gas mask on his head, made sure the seal was tight. 'Time to start using 'em, I'm afraid.' His voice sounded muffled and alien, even to himself.

Fred Stanegate understood him. 'Right y'are,' he said, and put on his own mask. 'Hate this bloody thing,' he remarked halfway through the process, although without much rancor. When the mask was in place, he added, 'Better nor breathing that stinkin' mustard, now, mind tha.' Goldfarb's burned leg twinged, perhaps in sympathy.

Off to the north, British field guns opened up again, pounding the Lizard defenses between Brixworth and Scaldwell. 'Not goin' to be much of a surprise, with them hammering away so,' Goldfarb said, after first glancing around to make sure Major Smithers was out of earshot.

'Aye, well, if they don't give 'em a nice dose o' gas first off, the buggers'll be waiting for us with all their nasty guns,' Stanegate said. Goldfarb smiled inside the mask where his companion couldn't see him: the Yorkshire accent made the last sound like *nahsty goons*. But however regional he sounded, that didn't mean he was wrong.

Smithers's Ordnance Survey map had shown a country road going northeast to southwest from Scaldwell down to Brixworth. The Lizards' line ran just behind it. Or rather, the line had run there. Some Lizards still held their posts and fired on the advancing Englishmen, but others had fled the rain of mustard gas and still others lay in the trenches, blistered and choking. Goldfarb hadn't been worse than moderately terrified by the time they forced their way through the foxholes and razor wire and pushed on.

'By gum, if it's this easy the rest o' the way, we'll roll right into Northampton, we will,' Fred Stanegate said.

Before Goldfarb could answer, a flight of Lizard warplanes roared low over the battlefield. Mustard gas didn't bother them; they had their own independent oxygen supplies. They flailed the English with cannons and rockets. Everywhere men were down, dead or screaming. Several tanks sent greasy black pillars of smoke up into the sky. the Lizards on the ground rallied and peppered survivors with small-arms fire.

Digging himself in with his entrenching tool, Goldfarb panted, 'I don't think it'll be this easy any more.' Digging just as hard beside him, Fred nodded mournfully.

Mutt Daniels huddled inside the Chicago Coliseum, waiting for the place to fall to pieces around him. The Coliseum had been built with the battlemented façade of Richmond's Libby Prison, which had housed Union prisoners during the War Between the States. Mutt didn't know how the hell the façade had got to Chicago, but here it was. He did know that, even if he thought of himself as a very mildly reconstructed Johnny Reb, he sure felt as if he were a prisoner in here, too.

Only bits and pieces of that battlemented façade were left; Lizard artillery and bombs had chewed holes in it and in the roof. The destruction didn't bother Mutt. The wreckage scattered in the interior of the building made it a better place in which to fight. With any luck at all, the Americans could give the Lizards as much grief here as they had in the meat-packing plants off to the southwest. Rumor said some holdouts were still holed up in the ruins of the Swift plant, sniping at any Lizard dumb enough to show his snout inside rifle range.

'How you doing, Lieutenant?' asked Captain Stan Szymanski, Daniels's new CO. He couldn't have been more than half Mutt's age (these days, nobody seemed more than half Mutt's age): blond as a Swede, but shorter, stockier, wider-faced, with gray eyes slanted almost like a Jap's.

'I'm okay, sir,' Mutt answered, which was more or less true. He still didn't get up and yell 'whoopee' at the prospect of sitting on his ass, but he didn't get up much chance to sit on his ass these days, anyhow. Or maybe Szymanski was trying to find out if his new platoon leader was going to be able to stand the strain generally. Mutt said, 'Captain, I been in this shit since the git-go. If I ain't fallen to pieces by now, don't reckon I'm gonna.'

'Okay, Mutt,' Szymanski said with a nod – yes, that was what he'd been worrying about. 'Why do they call you Mutt, anyway?'

Daniels laughed. 'Back when I first started playin' bush-league ball – this woulda been 1904, 1905, somethin' like that – I had me this ugly little puppy I'd take on the train with me. You take one look at it, only thing you want to say is, 'What a mutt.' That's what everybody said. Pretty soon they were sayin' it about me instead of the dog, so I been Mutt now goin' on forty years. If it wasn't that, I figure they'd've called me somethin' worse. Ballplayers, they're like that.'

'Oh.' Szymanski shrugged. 'Okay. I just wondered.' He'd probably figured there was a fancier story behind it.

'Sir, we ever gonna be able to hold the Lizards around these parts?' Mutt asked. 'Now that they done broke through to the lake—'

'Yeah, things are tough,' the captain said, as profound a statement of the obvious as Daniels had ever heard. 'But they don't have all of Chicago, not by a long shot. This is still the South Side. And if they want all of it, they're going to have to pay the price. By the time they're done here, they'll have paid more than it's worth.'

'Lord, I hope so,' Daniels said. 'We've sure paid a hell of a price fightin' 'em.'

'I know.' Szymanski's face clouded. 'My brother never came out of one of those meat-packing plants, not so far as I know, anyhow. But the idea is that the more they pour down the rathole here, the less they have to play with someplace else.'

'I understand that, sir. But when *you're* at the bottom of the rathole and they keep pourin' all that stuff down on top of you, it wears thin after a while, it really does.'

'You can sing that in church,' Szymanski said. 'Eventually, though, they're supposed to run out of stuff, and we're still making more. The more we make 'em use, the faster that'll happen.'

Mutt didn't answer. He'd heard that song a lot of times before. Sometimes he even believed it: the Lizards did have a way of playing it close to the vest now and again, as if they were short of soldiers and ammunition. But you'd end up dead if you counted on them doing that all the time, or even any one time.

Szymanski went on, 'Besides, if they're still stuck in downtown Shytown when winter comes around again, we'll give 'em a good kick in the ass, same way we did last year.'

'That'd be pretty fine,' Mutt said agreeably. 'They don't like cold weather, and that's a fact. 'Course, now that you get right down to it, I don't much like cold weather, neither. But what worries me is, the Lizards, they're peculiar, but they ain't stupid. You can fool 'em once, but you try foolin' the same bunch again the same way and they'll hand you your head.'

Captain Szymanski clicked his tongue between his teeth. 'You may have something there. I'll pass it on to Colonel Karl next time I talk with him, see if he wants to bump it up the line. Meanwhile, though—'

'We gotta stay alive. Yeah, I know.'

The Lizards weren't going to make that easy, not if they could help it. Their artillery opened up; shells landed just west of the Chicago Coliseum. Chunks of masonry crashed down. Mutt huddled in his rubble shelter. So did his comrades. When the shelling slowed, they came out and dragged newly fallen boards and pieces of sheet metal back to their positions, strengthening them.

Mutt liked that. It meant he had a good bunch of veterans in his new platoon. He wondered how his old gang of thugs was getting on without him. He'd miss Dracula Szabo; he'd never known anybody else with such a nose for plunder. Somebody here would have a talent for scrounging, though. Somebody always did.

A Lizard jet shrieked past, not far above the Coliseum's battered roof. A bomb hit just outside the building. The noise was like the end of the world. For anybody out there, it *was* the end of the world. More of the nineteenth-century façade crumbled and fell into the street.

Another bomb crashed through the roof and thudded down onto the bricks and boards and broken chairs strewn below. It landed maybe twenty feet from Mutt. He saw it fall. He buried his head against the rough wall of his shelter, knowing it would do no good.

But the explosion that would have thrown and torn and smashed him did not come. The Lizard plane dropped a couple more bombs a little north of the Chicago Coliseum, close enough to make it shake, but the one inside lay inert where it had fallen.

'Dud!' Mutt shouted in glad relief, and sucked in as wonderful a breath of air as he'd ever enjoyed, even if it did smell like a cross between an outhouse and a forest fire. Then he realized that wasn't the only possible explanation. 'Or else a time bomb,' he added, his voice more subdued.

Captain Szymanski spoke to the company communications man: 'Gus, call back to division headquarters. Tell 'em we need a bomb disposal unit fast as they can shag ass up here.'

'Yes, sir.' With a happy grunt, Gus slipped from his shoulders the heavy pack that contained a field telephone and batteries. He cranked the telephone and spoke into it. After a couple of minutes, he told Szmanski, 'They're on their way.' He closed up the phone back and, sighing, redonned it.

Mutt scrambled to his feet and walked over toward the bomb. It wasn't bravado: if the stupid thing went off, it would kill him just as dead in his shelter as out in the open. 'Don't touch it!' Captain Szymanski called sharply.

'Touch it? Captain, I may be a damn fool sometimes, but I ain't crazy. I just want to look at it – I thought it had my name on it.'

'You and me both,' Szymanski said. 'Okay, Mutt, go ahead.'

The bomb looked like a bomb: sheet metal casing painted olive drab, a boxy tail section for aerodynamics. If it hadn't been for the complicated gadget that replaced a normal twirl fuse, and for the wires that ran back from the gadget to flaps attached to the tail section, he would have taken it for an American weapon, not one the Lizards had made at all.

'Goddamn,' Mutt said quietly after he'd walked all the way around the bomb. 'That don't just look like one of ours, it *is* one of ours, wearin' a Lizard vest and spats.' He raised his voice: 'Captain, I think maybe you want to take a good close look at this thing your own self.'

Szymanski came; nothing was wrong with the size of his balls. As Mutt had, he walked around the bomb. By the time he'd got back to where he'd started from, he looked as bemused as Daniels did. 'That's a US Army Air Force 500-pounder, either that or I'm Queen of the May. What the hell have the Lizards gone and done to it?'

'Damfino,' Mutt answered. 'But you're right, sir, that's what it is, all right. Seems to me somebody ought to know about this.' He reached under his helmet to scratch above one ear. 'Reckon those bomb disposal people'll be able to say more about it than we can – if they make it here alive, that is.'

They did. There were four of them, all quiet and unhurried men who didn't look as if anything got on their nerves. If you were nervous when you started out disposing of bombs, odds were you wouldn't last long enough to get good at it.

Their leader, a first lieutenant in his middle thirties, nodded when he saw the bomb. 'Yeah, we've run into a fair number of these,' he said. He'd stuck a toothpick in one corner of his mouth, maybe in lieu of a cigarette. 'It's one of ours, but the fixtures there make it nastier than it used to be.' He pointed to the Lizards' additions at the nose and tail of the bomb. 'Some way or other – don't quite know how – they can guide these things right into a target. You fellas are lucky to be here.'

'We figured that out, thanks,' Szymanski said dryly. 'Can you pull its teeth for us?'

The toothpick waggled. 'Sir, if we can't, you won't be around to complain about it.' The first lieutenant turned around and studied the bomb. With his back to Mutt and Szymanski, he said, 'Now that I think about it, we've run into too damn many of these. I used to think the Lizards had raided an arsenal or something, but now my guess is that they're making bombs for themselves – or having us make 'em for them, I mean.'

'I don't even like to think about it,' Mutt said. 'How can you go to a weapons plant, work all day, know the Lizards are going to use whatever you make to blow up other Americans, and then go home at night and look at yourself in the mirror?'

'Beats me,' the bomb disposal man said. He and his companions stooped beside the bomb and got to work. Their talk reminded Mutt of what you heard in movie operating rooms, except they asked one another for wrenches and pliers and screwdrivers instead of scalpels and forceps and sutures. The real doctors and medics in the aid station he'd just escaped had been a gamier crew; they'd sounded more like ballplayers than anybody's conventional notion of medical men. On the other hand, if they made a mistake on one of their patients, they wouldn't blow them sky high. That might have a way of concentrating the mind on the job at hand.

One of the men grunted softly. 'Here we go, Sir,' he said to the first lieutenant. 'The fuse assembly in the nose is fouled up eight ways till Sunday. We could use this one for a football and it still wouldn't go off.'

The first lieutenant's sigh was long and heartfelt. 'Okay, Donnelly. We've seen a fair number of those, too.' He turned back to Mutt and Szymanski. Sweat was pouring down his face. He didn't seem to notice. 'I think maybe the guys who work the bomb factory do a little bit of sabotage when they can get away with it. When the Lizards were using all their own ordnance, they hardly ever had duds.'

'So are they all out of theirs?' Mutt asked.

'Don't know,' the bomb disposal man answered, with a shrug to dramatize it. 'If it blows up, who can say who made it?'

'Plenty of them blew up outside.' Captain Szymanski's voice was harsh. 'This probably wouldn't have been the only Made in the USA bomb in whatever load that airplane carried. They may be sabotaging some, but they sure as hell aren't sabotaging all of 'em.'

'Sir, that's the God's truth,' the first lieutenant said. He and his men set up what looked like a heavy-duty stretcher next to the bomb. With much careful shifting, they loaded it onto the stretcher and carried it away. Their chief said, 'Thanks for calling us on this one, sir. Every time we get one of these guiding mechanisms in one piece, it bumps up the odds we'll figure out how they do what they do, sooner or later.'

Staggering under the weight of weapon and stretcher, the bomb disposal crew hauled their burden out of the Chicago Coliseum. Mutt watched anxiously till they were gone. Yeah, Donnelly had said the bomb was harmless, but high explosive was touchy stuff. If one of them fell and the bomb went thud on the ground, the bad guys might still win.

Szymanski said, 'Sabotage one in ten, say, and you hurt the enemy with that one, yeah, but the other nine are still gonna hurt your friends.'

'Yes, sir,' Mutt agreed, 'but even if you're just sabotaging one in a hundred, you're making it so you can live with yourself afterwards. That counts, too.'

'I suppose so,' Szymanski said unwillingly.

Mutt didn't blame him for sounding doubtful. Being able to live with yourself counted, sure. But giving the Lizards a good swift kick in the balls counted for more in his book. Having them bomb American positions with American bombs ... it stuck in his craw.

But if they were running out of their own, maybe it wasn't so bad after all.

Crash! The shell smote Ussmak's landcruiser in the glacis plate. The driver's teeth clicked together. The shell did not penetrate. The landcruiser kept rolling forward, toward the village that topped the wooded hill. Crash! Another shell struck, with the same result, or rather lack of result.

'Front!' Nejas said, back in the turret.

'Identified,' Skoob answered. The turret hummed as it traversed, bringing the landcruiser's main armament to bear on the little gun that was hammering away at them. Through his vision slits, Ussmak saw Tosevites dash about in the deepening twilight as they served the gun. The landcruiser cannon spoke; the heavy machine rocked back on its tracks for an instant from the recoil. At the same time, Skoob called, 'On the way!'

He hadn't finished the sentence when the high-explosive round burst alongside the Tosevite gun. The cannon overturned; the Big Uglies of its crew were flung aside like crumpled papers. 'Hit!' Ussmak shouted. 'Well placed, Skoob!' Even now, he could still sometimes recapture the feeling of easy, inevitable triumph he'd known when the war on Tosev 3 was newly hatched. Most of the time, he needed ginger to do it, but not always.

Skoob said, 'The British here, they don't have such good antilandcruiser guns. When we were down there fighting the Deutsche, now, and they hit you, you knew you'd been hit.'

'Truth,' Ussmak said. Deutsch antilandcruiser guns could wreck you if they caught you from the side or rear. The British hand-launched antilandcruiser weapons weren't a match for the rockets the Deutsch infantry used. Unfortunately, that didn't make the campaign on this Emperor-forsaken island any easier. Ussmak shivered, though the inside of the landcruiser was heated to a temperature he found comfortable. 'The British may not have good antilandcruiser guns, but they have other things.'

'Truth,' Nejas and Skoob said in identical unhappy tones. Nejas went on, 'That accursed gas—'

He didn't say any more, or need to. The landcruiser crew was relatively lucky. Their machine shielded them from the risk of actually being splashed with the stuff, which, if it didn't kill you, would make you wish it had. They'd stuck makeshift filters over all the landcruiser's air inlets, too, to minimize the danger of getting it into their lungs. But the landcruiser wasn't sealed, and minimizing the danger didn't make it go away.

In a pensive voice, Skoob said, 'You couldn't pay me enough to make me want to be an infantrymale in Britain.'

Now Ussmak and Nejas chorused, 'Truth.' Gas casualties among the infantry had been appalling. They moved from place to place in their combat vehicles – a couple of those were advancing up the hill toward the village with Ussmak's landcruiser – but when they got to where they were going, they had to get out and fight. Getting out was dangerous at any time. Getting out with the gas in the air and clinging to the ground was worse than dangerous.

Machine-gun fire pattered off the landcruiser. At Nejas's orders, Skoob pumped high-explosive shells into the buildings that sheltered the gunners. The buildings, made largely of timber, began to burn.

'We'll seize that village,' Nejas declared. 'The native name is' – he paused to check his map – 'Wargrave, or something like that. The height will give us a position from which we can look down on and shell the river beyond. Tomorrow we advance on the ... the' – he checked again – 'the Thames.'

'Superior sir, should we consider a night advance?' Skoob asked. 'Our vision equipment gives us a great advantage in night fighting.'

'Orders are to stop at Wargrave,' Nejas answered. 'Too many casualties have been suffered and machines lost charging through territory still heavily infested with Big Uglies. The gas only makes that worse.'

The shelling had not taken out all the British gunners. Skoob poured more rounds into Wargrave. The mechanized combat vehicles also opened up on the village with their smaller guns. Smoke rose high into the evening sky. Down on the ground, though, muzzle flashes said the British were still resisting. Ussmak sighed. 'Looks as if we'll have to do it the hard way,' he said, wishing for a taste of ginger. The resigned comment might have applied to the Race's whole campaign on Tosev 3.

'Landcruiser halt,' Nejas said.

'Halting, superior sir.' Ussmak stamped down on the brake pedal. Nejas, he thought approvingly, knew what he was doing. He'd stopped the landcruiser outside the built-up area of Wargrave, but close enough so it could still effectively use not only its cannon but also its machine gun. Firepower counted. Being literally in the middle of action didn't.

Ussmak had had a couple of commanders who would have charged right into the middle of Wargrave, guns blazing. One of them had got his bravado from a vial of ginger; the other was just an idiot. Both males would have wondered where the satchel charge or bottle full of blazing hydrocarbons or spring-fired hollow-charge bomb had come from ... for as long as it left them alive to wonder. Nejas hung back and didn't have the worry.

The mechanical combat vehicles, unfortunately, did not enjoy such luxury. If they disembarked their infantrymales too far from the fighting, they might as well have stayed back at the base – enemy fire would chew those poor males to pieces. They pulled up right at the edge of the village. The infantrymales skittered out, automatic rifles at the ready. Ussmak wouldn't have wanted their job for all the ginger on Tosev 3.

One of those males went down. He wasn't dead; he kept firing. But he didn't advance with his fellows any more. Then a British male in the wreckage of Wargrave launched one of their antilandcruiser bombs at a combat vehicle. The thing was all but ludicrous against the landcruisers. It couldn't defeat their frontal armor, and usually wouldn't penetrate from side or rear, either.

But a mechanized combat vehicle was not a landcruiser, nor was it armored like one. Flames and smoke shot from the turret, and from the door by which the infantrymales had exited. Escape hatches popped open. The three-male crew bailed out. One of them managed to reach the second combat vehicle. The Big Uglies shot the other two on the ground. A moment later, the stricken combat vehicle brewed up.

'Advance, driver,' Nejas said. 'We're going to have to mix it up with them whether we want to or not, I fear. Move forward to the outermost buildings. As we clear the village of enemies, we may be able to go farther.'

'It shall be done.' The landcruiser rumbled forward. Shell casings clattered down from the machine gun to the floor of the fighting compartment.

'What's that?' Nejas said in alarm. With his limited vision, Ussmak had no idea what it was. Of itself, one eye turret swung up to the hatch above his head. If whatever it was hit the landcruiser, he hoped he could dive out in time. Then Nejas said, 'Rest easy, males. It's only a couple of combat vehicles bringing up fresh troops. These egg-impacted British are too stubborn to know they're beaten.'

Skoob said, 'If we have to send in more males here than we'd planned, so be it. We have to get across the river and link up our males in the northern pocket.'

And why did they have to do that? Ussmak wondered. The short answer was, because the males in the northern pocket not only weren't beating the British, they were having a dreadful time staying alive. Neither Nejas or Skoob seemed to notice the contradictions in what the two of them had just said. They were both solid males, gifted militarily, but they didn't examine ideas outside their specialties as closely as they did those within them.

Ussmak's lower jaw fell slightly open in an ironic laugh. Since when had he become a philosopher fit to judge such things? Only alienation from the rest of the Race had let part of his mind drift far enough from his duties to notice such discrepancies. Those who still reckoned themselves altogether part of the great and elaborate social and hierarchical web were undoubtedly better off than he was.

Night had fallen by the time the males either killed or drove out the last British defenders of Wargrave. Even then, small-arms fire kept rattling from the woods below the crest of the hill atop which the village sat.

An aggressive officer would have sent males into those woods to clear out the nuisance. The local commander did nothing of the sort. Ussmak didn't blame him. Even with infrared gear, Tosevite forests were frightening places at night for males of the Race. The Big Uglies belonged in amongst those trees and bushes, and could move quietly through them. The Race didn't and couldn't. A lot of males had ended up dead trying.

'Shall we get out and stretch our legs and wiggle our tailstumps?' Nejas asked. 'The Emperor only knows when we'll see another chance.'

As he'd been trained, Ussmak cast down his eyes at the mention of his sovereign. Skoob said, 'It'll be cold out there, but I'll come. Even a Big Ugly town is better than looking at my gunsight and autoloader all day.'

'What about you, driver?' Nejas asked.

'No, thank you, superior sir,' Ussmak said. 'With your permission, I'll sit tight. I've already seen more Big Ugly towns than I ever wanted.'

'You don't want to hatch out of your nice steel eggshell,' Nejas said, but jokingly, not in a way that would cause offense. 'As you will, of course. I can't say I disagree with you for not caring about Tosevite towns. They're generally ugly before we smash them up, and uglier afterwards.'

He scrambled out through the cupola. Skoob opened his escape hatch and joined him. Ussmak waited till they both jumped down from the landcruiser. Then he reached under the mat below the control pedals and pulled out his little jar of ginger. He'd been twitchy with need for it all through the fighting, but made himself refrain. Males who went snarling into combat with a head full of herb were braver than they would have been otherwise – and also stupider. It was a bad combination.

Now, though – He pulled off the stopper to the vial and hissed in dismay. The little bit of brownish powder that poured into the palm of his hand was all he had left. His forked tongue flicked out and lapped it up.

'Ah!' he said. Well-being flowed through him. Fear, loneliness, even cold fell away. He felt proud to be a male of the Race, bringing the benighted Tosevites into the domain of civilization. He thought he could singlehandedly force a crossing of the Thames ahead and effect a junction with the rest of the Race's males north of London.

With a distinct effort of will, he made himself keep his hands away from the wheel and his foot away from the accelerator. He'd been using ginger a long time now, and knew he wasn't as omnipotent as he thought he was.

He hadn't been all that smart before he tasted, though. Had he remembered how low on the herb he was, he could have got out of the landcruiser and found an infantrymale who had more than he could taste at the moment. Now, though, he'd look foolish if he emerged. Worse, he'd look suspicious. Nejas and Skoob both had untainted tongues. They thought he did, too. If they ever found out otherwise, he'd be sent off for punishment, with green stripes painted on his arms.

But if he didn't find some ginger somewhere, before long his condition would be apparent to them anyhow. He'd be a red-nostriled nervous wreck. Once you started tasting ginger, it got its claw in you and you had to keep doing it.

The exaltation of the herb faded. He sank as low as he had been high. Now the only thing he wanted to do was sit quietly and pretend the world outside the landcruiser didn't exist. Nejas had had the right of it: he was using the vehicle as an eggshell to separate himself from everything around him. The world wouldn't come in here.

But it did, in the persons of Nejas and Skoob. The landcruiser commander said, 'You were wiser than we, driver. Nothing here worth seeing, nothing worth taking. Better we should have stayed inside.'

'We'll sleep in here, no matter how cramped it is,' Skoob added. 'I don't want to be out in the open if the British start throwing gas at us.'

'No arguments there,' Nejas said, whereupon they did start arguing about who would try to sleep in the turret and who would have the dubious privilege of stretching halfway out next to Ussmak's reclining driver's seat. Being the landcruiser commander, Nejas won the argument. The victory proved of dubious value because, among other things, he tried lying down on the spent machine-gun cartridges that littered the floor.

He sat up suddenly, cracking his head on the low ceiling of the driver's compartment, and hissed in pain. 'Help me clean up these miserable things,' he snapped. 'You think my hide's armored in steel and ceramic?' There wasn't room for anyone to give him a lot of help, but Ussmak opened the hatch above his head. He and Nejas threw the spent cartridges out of the landcruiser. They jingled on the flagstones outside. A soon as most of them were gone, Ussmak dogged the hatch again. As his commander had said, poison gas made sleeping in the open even less attractive than it had been before.

Even for Ussmak, who had the best resting place in the landcruiser, sleeping in it was no bargain, either. He twisted and turned and once almost fell off his seat onto Nejas. Except for feeling elderly, he was glad to see light build up when he peered through his vision slit. Day came early at these latitudes.

Nejas started to sit up again, but thought better of it just in time. He called back to the turret: 'Are you awake, Skoob?'

'Superior sir, the question is, "Skoob, have you been asleep?"' the gunner replied in aggrieved tones. 'And the answer is, "Yes, but not nearly enough."'

'That holds for all of us,' Nejas said. 'Toss down a couple of ration bars, would you?'

'It shall be done.'

The ration bars almost landed on Nejas's toes. He twisted around so he could pick them up, then handed one to Ussmak. When they were done eating, the commander scrambled back up into the cupola with Skoob and said, 'Driver, advance us to the point where we have a good view of the river and that town by it ... Henley-on-Thames.' After a moment, he added, '"On" must mean something like "alongside of" in the local Big Uglies' language.'

Ussmak cared for the local Big Uglies' language about as much as he'd cared for his egg tooth after it fell off his snout in earliest hatchlinghood. He started the landcruiser engine. 'Super sir, we're a little low on hydrogen,' he said as he studied the gauges. 'We can operate today, I think, but a supply tanker should have come up last night.'

'I'll radio Logistics,' Nejas answered. 'Maybe they did try to send one, and Tosevite bandits ambushed it behind the line. The Big Uglies are pestilentially good at that kind of thing.'

The landcruiser rumbled forward. Ussmak listened with a certain malicious satisfaction to paving stones breaking under the pressure of the tracks. When Nejas ordered him to halt, he hit the brake.

He leaned forward and peered through the vision slit. It didn't give him anywhere near the view Nejas had from the turret, but what he saw, he didn't like. The Big Uglies had spent the night – and who could say how much time before that? – fortifying the slope that led down to the river. Belts of the spiky stuff they used in place of razor wire were everywhere. So were trenches, browns scars on green, plant-covered earth. Ussmak was willing to bet that greenery also concealed cleverly hidden mines.

'We shall begin shelling Henley-on-Thames,' Nejas said. 'Gunner, high explosive.'

'It shall be done,' Skoob said, 'but we are also low on high-explosive shells. We used a good many yesterday, and, as with the hydrogen, we got no resupply afterwards.'

Before Skoob began firing, the English down below opened up with their own artillery. Whitish puffs, different from the usual clouds of smoke and dust, rose from the Tosevite shells as they burst. Nejas slammed the lid of the cupola down with a clang. 'That's gas!' he exclaimed, with less than the equanimity a landcruiser commander should have displayed.

Nor was Ussmak delighted at having to drive the landcruiser through a thickening curtain of the horrid stuff. The filters that shielded the landcruiser's air intakes were makeshifts, and he distrusted them for no other reason than that. The Race did not think well of makeshifts. They went wrong too easily. Properly engineered solutions worked right every time. Trusting your life to anything less seemed a dreadful risk to take.

But at least Ussmak and his crewmales enjoyed, if that was the word, some protection against the poison the British spread with such enthusiasm. The poor males in the infantry had next to none. Some males wore masks, patterned either after those the Race used to fight radiation or based on Big Ugly models. But there weren't nearly enough masks to go around, and the gas also left hideous burns and blisters on bare skin. Ussmak wondered if that was one of the reasons the Tosevites wrapped themselves in cloth.

The landcruiser's main armament started hammering away, searching for the British guns. Not all the flying rubble came from that cannon's shells. Radar-guided counterbattery fire also rained down on the sites from which the gas shells had been launched. Low-flying killercraft poured rockets and their own cannon shells into Henley-on-Thames.

'Forward!' Nejas ordered, and Ussmak took his foot off the brake. A moment later, to his surprise, the commander said, 'Landcruiser halt.' Halt Ussmak did, as Nejas went on, 'We can't move forward, not against positions like those, without infantry support to keep the Tosevites from wrecking us as we slow down for their egg-addled obstacles.'

'Where are the infantrymales, superior sir?' Ussmak couldn't see them, but that didn't prove anything, not with the narrow field of view his visions slits gave. He wasn't about to unbutton and look around, either, not with gas shells still coming in. 'Have they got back into their mechanized combat vehicles?'

'Some of them have,' Nejas said. 'They don't do us much good in there, though, or themselves, either; the combat vehicles will have to slow down for the wire and trenches. But some of the males' – his voice sputtered in indignation – 'are running away.'

Ussmak heard that without fully taking it in at first. A few times, especially during the hideous northern-hemisphere winter, Tosevite assaults had forced the Race to fall back. But he slowly realized this was different. These infantrymales weren't falling back. They were refusing to go forward. He wondered if the like had ever happened in the history of the Race.

Skoob said, 'Shall I turn the machine gun on them, superior sir, to remind them of their duty?' His voice showed the same disbelief Ussmak felt.

Nejas hesitated before he answered. That in itself alarmed Ussmak; a commander was supposed to know what to do in any given situation. At last he said, 'No, hold fire. The disciplinarians will deal with them. This is their proper function. Hold in place and await orders.'

'It shall be done.' Skoob still sounded doubtful. Again, Ussmak was taken aback. Nejas and Skoob were a long-established unit; for the gunner to doubt the commander was a bad sign.

Orders were a long time coming. When they came, they were to hold in place until the field guns in Henley-on-Thames and the bigger British cannon farther north could be silenced. Aircraft and artillery rained destruction on the town. Ussmak watched that with great satisfaction. All the same, gas shells and conventional artillery kept falling on Wargrave.

Fresh hydrogen eventually reached the landcruiser, but the ammunition resupply vehicle never came. The males of the Race did not move forward, save for a probe by the infantry that the entrenched Big Uglies repulsed.

Ussmak wasn't very happy about where he was. He would have been even less happy, though, he decided, had he been in the northern pocket. That one wasn't just stalled. It was shrinking.

Atvar paced back and forth. That helped him to think, to some degree. It didn't mean he wasn't always staring at the situation map of Britain; one eye always swiveled toward it, not matter how his body was aligned. That kept the pain constant, as if it were festering in several tooth sockets at once.

He hissed in rage and frustration. 'Perhaps you were right, Shiplord,' he said to Kirel. 'Perhaps even Straha was right, though his egg should have addled before it hatched. We might have done better to deal with the British by means of a nuclear weapon.'

'Exalted Fleetlord, if that be your pleasure, we can still accomplish it,' Kirel said.

'Using nuclear weapons is never my pleasure,' Atvar answered. 'And what point to it?'

'Securing the conquest of Britain?' Kirel said.

'The accursed island is so small, it's scarcely worth having after a couple of these devices detonate on it,' Atvar answered gloomily. 'Besides, our losses there have been so dreadful that I fear even keeping pacification forces on it will be more expensive than it's worth. And besides—' He stopped, unwilling to go on.

Kirel, a reliable subordinate, did it for him: 'And besides, now that the British have introduced the use of these vile poisonous gases, every Tosevite empire still in the field against us has begun employing them in large quantities.'

'Yes.' Atvar made the word a hiss of hate. 'They were not using them against one another when we came to this miserable iceball of a world. Our analysis leaves no possible doubt as to that point. And yet all their leading empires and not-empires had enormous quantities of these munitions stored and ready for deployment. Now they know we are vulnerable to them, so bring them out. It seems most unjust.'

'Truth, Exalted Fleetlord,' Kirel agreed. 'Our historical analysis unit has perhaps uncovered the reason for the anomaly.'

'Seeking rational reasons for anything the Big Uglies do strikes me as an exercise in futility,' Atvar said. 'What did the analysis unit deduce?'

'The Big Uglies recently fought another major war, in which poisonous gases played an important part. Apparently, they were so appalled at what the gases did that, when this new war broke out among them, no empire dared to use them first, for fear of retaliation from its foes.'

'One of the few signs of rationality yet detected among the Tosevites,' Atvar said with heavy sarcasm. 'I gather this unwillingness to use the poisonous gases did not keep them from producing such gases in limitless quantities.'

'Indeed not,' Kirel said. 'No empire trusted its neighbors not to do so, and no empire cared to be without means of retaliation should its neighbors turn the gases against it. And so production and research continued.'

'Research.' Atvar made that into a curse. 'The blistering agent the British threw at us is quite bad enough, but this stuff the Deutsche use – Have you seen those reports?'

'I have, Exalted Fleetlord,' Kirel said. His tailstump curled downward in gloom. 'First a male finds the day going dim around him, then he has difficulty breathing, and then he quietly dies. I am given to understand, though, that there is an injectable antidote to that gas.'

'Yes, and if you inject it thinking you have breathed the gas but are mistaken, it makes you nearly as ill as the gas would without treatment.' Atvar hissed mournfully. 'A perfect metaphor for Tosev 3, would you not agree? When we do nothing, the Big Uglies wreck us, and when we take steps against them, that presents problems just as difficult in a different way.'

'Truth,' Kirel said. He pointed to the map. 'In aid of which, what are we to do about the northern pocket in Britain? We have not been able to suppress British artillery, and it can reach every spot within the pocket. The closer our males get to London, the more built-up areas they have to traverse, and fighting in built-up areas means heavy losses in males and matériel both.'

'That's not the worst of it, either,' Atvar said. 'Flying transports over Britain gets riskier by the day. Not only do the British seem to keep pulling aircraft out from under flat stones, but the Deutsche in northern France strike at our machines as they fly back and forth to Britain. We have lost several transports, and cannot afford to lose many more.' 'Truth,' Kirel repeated glumly.

'If we have to start using starships instead, and if we start losing starships in significant numbers—' Atvar didn't go on. He didn't need to go on. If the Race started losing starships in significant numbers, the war against the Big Uglies would be within shouting distance of being lost along with them.

'What then is our course in regard to the northern pocket in Britain, Exalted Fleetlord?' Kirel asked.

Atvar hissed again. He heartily wished the northern pocket did not exist. If the British kept pounding on it, it wouldn't exist much longer. That, however, was not what he'd had in mind as a means for disposing of it. Bitterly, he said, 'If only the sweep around London to the west from the southern force hadn't been halted at the river line, we could have withdrawn the males north of London without undue trouble.'

'Yes, Exalted Fleetlord,' Kirel said dutifully. Although he had every right to, he didn't remind Atvar that 'ifs' like this had no place in military planning.

'Bringing the males out from the north would be feasible,' Atvar said, 'but with the heavy transports having such difficulty there – with all manner of fixed-wing aircraft having such difficulty there – we would be compelled to leave behind a great deal of equipment.'

Not until the words had left his mouth did he realize he'd abandoned all hope of salvaging the northern pocket. The battle there was one the Race would lose, and he couldn't do anything about it except make the defeat less costly.

He hoped kirel would contradict him. He'd phrased his comment hypothetically; the shiplord might well find reason for optimism where he saw none. But Kirel said, 'Exalted Fleetlord, if we stay in the pocket we shall lose not only the equipment but the males as well. We should do our best to deny the matériel to the British, lest it be turned against us.'

Now Atvar said, 'Truth.' In a way, acknowledging defeat was liberating. In another way, it was terrifying. The fleetlord said, 'If we withdraw from the northern pocket, the political consequences will be unpredictable but surely unfortunate.'

'They shouldn't be as bad as that, Exalted Fleetlord,' Kirel said, his voice soothing. 'We will have kept the British from meddling on the main continental mass for some time to come, and other Tosevite empires opposing us can hardly be stimulated to more effort than they are already making.'

'Those were not the consequences to which I was referring,' Atvar answered. 'I was thinking of possible developments within the ranks of the shiplords themselves.'

'Ahh,' Kirel said. 'Now I see.' He paused thoughtfully. 'My view is that, with Straha gone, it will likely be too divisive an issue for any male to raise. His defecting to the Big Uglies has worked to your advantage, because it discredits in advance those who would rebel against your leadership.'

'Yes, I have made a similar calculation,' Atvar said. He carefully did not send Kirel a suspicious look. Straha had also been Kirel's chief rival for leadership among the shiplords. Now Kirel had no chief rival among them. After only himself, Kirel was supreme. If he took it into his head to claw aside the fleetlord ... Kirel hadn't played that role when he'd had the chance, but then Straha had been the one calling for his head.

Kirel said, 'As I mentioned before, we have met some of our goals for the invasion of Britain, if not all of them. We need not be ashamed of our efforts on the island.'

'No,' Atvar agreed. He let his mouth fall open and nodded slightly: a rueful laugh. 'Anywhere in the Empire but Tosev 3, partial fulfillment of goals is a matter for shame and reproach. Here, against the Big Uglies, we feel like celebrating whenever we can accomplish that much.'

'More is relative than the behavior of objects at speeds approaching that of light,' Kirel said. 'Among ourselves and when dealing with the Rabotevs and Hallessi, planning can take into account all known variables, and almost all variables are known. When we deal with the Big Uglies, almost all variables have indeterminate values.'

'Truth,' Atvar answered sadly. 'Sometimes we don't even know a variable exists until it rises up and bites off the tip of our tailstump. These poisonous gases, for instance: the Tosevites had them in unlimited quantity, but weren't using them against each other or against us. For all we know, we may have overrun considerable stores of them without noticing – and the Big Uglies would hardly have gone out of their way to point them out to us.'

'There's a notion, Exalted Fleetlord,' Kirel said. 'We should explore the weapons stocks in empires under our control. That may enable us to retaliate in kind against the Tosevites.'

'See to that,' Atvar said. 'We will still be at a disadvantage against them, as their protection technology is ahead of ours' – he opened and closed his hands in embarrassment at the admission – 'but having the tool in our kit will prove useful, as you say. Start the investigation today.'

'It shall be done,' Kirel said.

Atvar went on, 'Whether or not we come upon stores of these gases, though, the point is that we were unaware the Tosevites even had them until we made the British desperate enough to use them against us.'

'With all too much success,' Kirel said.

'With all too much success,' Atvar agreed. 'The Big Uglies care nothing for the long term. If something will help them for a moment, they seize on it. In the long run, their species may well have wrecked itself had we not come along at this particular time.' He hissed a sigh. 'But come we did, and now we must make the best of it.'

'The Soviets' use of the nuclear device was a similar phenomenon, I believe,' Kirel said. 'When we press the Tosevites – or some of them, at any rate – they are liable to do astonishing things.'

'Astonishing, yes,' Atvar replied dryly. 'To say nothing of appalling. And several of their other empires and not-empires are sure to be working on nuclear weapons for themselves. And if we press hard enough to make them desperate—' He paused.

'But if we don't, Exalted Fleetlord, how are we to win the war?' Kirel said.

'Planners back on Home never have to worry about dilemmas like that,' Atvar said. 'By the Emperor, how I envy them!'

10

Ludmila Gorbunova was used to flying over the endless plains of the Ukraine and central Russia. She'd seen little of the great forests of pine and fir and beech and birch that blanketed the more northerly reaches of her country.

Around Pskov, trees dominated, not steppe. The great dark green expanse to the east had been called the Forest Republic when Soviet partisans used it as their base and stronghold against the Nazis who held the city. Now Russians and Germans both used the woods in their struggle against the Lizards.

The Lizards used them, too. Ludmila was still discovering one major difference between forest and steppe: out on the steppe, despite vigorous Soviet *maskirovka*, concealing soldiers and weapons and machines was hard work. Here in the woods, it was second nature.

An aircraft that flew low and slow like her little U-2 biplane was the only sort of machine with much of a chance to look down and see what the enemy was doing. As she buzzed along, she wished the *Kukuruznik* could also fly low and fast. A Lizard helicopter could run her down and shoot her out of the air with no trouble at all, if it chanced to notice her.

She skimmed over a path in the forest. On the path she spied a pair of lorries, pushing north. They were of human manufacture – one a German model, the other an American one probably captured from the Soviets – but where they were and the direction in which they were going declared them to be under Lizard control. And where she'd seen two, there were likely to be two dozen more she hadn't seen, plus armored personnel carriers and tanks.

Ludmila had heard stories of Red Air Force pilots who'd flown below treetop height right down paths like that, shooting up everything in their paths. People who did things like that got the Hero of the Soviet Union award pinned on their tunics, sometimes by the Great Stalin himself. It was tempting, but ...

'I'd only get myself killed,' Ludmila said, as if someone were in the *Kukuruznik* arguing with her. It wasn't that she was afraid the Lizards would shoot her down; she'd signed up for the risk of getting shot down when she joined the Red Air Force. But she didn't think the lane was wide enough to let her get the U-2 down it. Tearing the wings off your aircraft by running into a tree was not what they taught you in flight school.

That left her with one choice. She spun the little – but not little enough – biplane through a tight turn and headed back toward Pskov. The Germans had artillery that could pound this position and the area north of it. It wouldn't be a guaranteed kill, not by any means, but it would make the Lizards unhappy.

Again she wished she could wring a better turn of speed from the Wheatcutter. The sooner she got back to Pskov, the shorter the distance the supply convoy would have traveled and the better the chance for a hit. The tall stone pile of the *Krom* and the onion domes of the churches marked the town. The old citadel wasn't badly damaged, but some of the domes had bites taken out of them and others leaned drunkenly away from the perpendicular. Some churches, along with a great many secular buildings, were in ruins.

Ludmila was a loyal child of the October Revolution, and had no great use for churches. Had the Soviet government knocked them down, she wouldn't have missed them a bit. But to have them destroyed by invading aliens was something else again. Even the Nazis, albeit for reasons of their own, had usually refrained from wrecking churches.

Instead of using the airstrip to the east of Pskov, as she usually did, Ludmila brought the *Kukuruznik* down in the park in the middle of town, the way she had when she first came to the city. Again, she managed to keep from running over people or livestock. Men came running to get the U-2 under the shelter of friendly trees.

She scrambled out of the aircraft and hurried toward the *Krom*, where *Generalleutnant* Kurt Chill had his headquarters. Having a Nazi in overall command of the defenses of a Soviet city galled her, but she couldn't do anything about it, not now. And if Chill didn't fight hard against the Lizards, it was assuredly his backside, too.

People shouted to her, asking what she'd seen that made her want to land in the middle of Pskov. 'I can't tell you that,' she answered. Some of the Pskovites seemed never to have heard of security. Well, if they hadn't, she certainly had.

She hurried over to the *Krom*. No sentries, Soviet or German, stood outside. Nobody wanted to give the Lizards a clue that anything important went on in there. Inside the entrance, a couple of tall Nazi soldiers leered at her. The Germans often found the idea of women in the fighting forces funny. '*Was wilst du, Liebchen?*' one of them asked. His companion, a very rough-looking customer indeed, broke out in giggles.

'*Ich will Generalleutant Chill sofort zu sehen,*' Ludmila answered in the iciest German she could muster. 'I want to see Lieutenant General Chill immediately.'

'Give me a kiss first,' the guard said, which made his comrade all but wet himself with mirth.

Ludmila drew her Tokarev automatic, pointed it not at the fellow's head or chest but at his crotch. 'Stop wasting my time, *dummkopf*,' she said sweetly. 'If the Lizards get away on account of you, it won't be my neck that goes into the noose.'

'Bitch,' muttered one of the Germans. 'Dyke,' the other said under his breath. But both of them moved aside. Ludmila didn't put the pistol back in its holster till she got round the corner.

Another German, a captain, sat at a desk in the antechamber outside Lieutenant General Chill's office. He treated Ludmila like a soldier, but was no more helpful on account of that. 'I am sorry, Senior Lieutenant, but he is away at the front, the German said. 'I do not expect him back for several days.'

'I need to have an artillery barrage laid on,' Ludmila said, and explained what she'd seen moving up the forest track from the south.

The German captain frowned. 'I have no authority to commit artillery to action except in immediate defense of the front,' he said doubtfully. 'Using it is dangerous, because Lizard counterbattery fire so often costs us guns and men, neither of which we can afford to lose.'

'I risked my life to get this information and bring it back here,' Ludmila said. 'Are you going to sit there and ignore it?' The captain looked too clean and much too well fed to have seen the front lines lately, no matter where Lieutenant General Chill was.

Instead of blowing up at her, he said, 'If the matter is as important as all that, Senior Lieutenant, I suggest you take it to the Englishmen down the hall.' He pointed out the direction. 'In the absence of the commander, they have the power to bind and to loose.' He sounded like a man quoting something. If he was, Ludmila didn't recognize it. He also sounded like a man unhappy about command arrangements. He didn't need to be happy, though – he just had to obey. Germans were supposed to be good at that.

'Yes, I'll try them, thank you,' Ludmila said, and hurried out.

All three of the Englishmen were in their map-bedecked office, along with a blonde woman in Red Army uniform, a rifle with telescopic sight slung on her back. She was so decorative, Ludmila doubted at first that she had any right to the uniform and sniper's weapon. A second glance at the woman's eyes changed her mind. She'd seen enough action herself to recognize others who had done likewise.

One of the Englishmen – Jones – had his hand on her shoulder. She stood close to him, but she was watching the one called Bagnall, the one Ludmila had met in the park when she first came to Pskov. She felt as if she'd walked into something out of *Anna Karenina*, not a place where battles got planned.

But Ken Embry, the third Englishmen, saw her and said, '*Chto* – What?'

His Russian remained on the rudimentary side. Even so, he attracted the others' attention to Ludmila. Jones jerked his hand away from the woman's shoulder as if she'd suddenly become red-hot.

Best, probably, for Ludmila to pretend she hadn't seen anything. What the Englishmen did in their private lives was their private business, although she wished they hadn't brought their private lives with them to the *Krom*. In German interspersed with Russian, Ludmila explained what she'd seen and what she'd wanted.

George Bagnall translated her words into English.

'Come to the map,' he said in German when he was done. He pointed to the forests south of Pskov. 'Where exactly did you see these lorries, and how long ago?'

She studied the map. It made her slightly nervous; in the Soviet Union, maps were secret things, not to be shown to the generality. She pointed. 'It was here, west of this pond. I am sure of it. And it was' – she glanced at the watch strapped to her left wrist – 'twenty-three minutes ago. I came in to report as soon as I saw them.'

George Bagnall smiled at her. By Russian standards, his face was long, thin, and bony. He was not, to Ludmila's way of thinking, a particularly handsome man, but that smile lit up his face. He said, 'You did well to note the exact time, and to get back to Pskov so fast.'

After that, he dropped back into English to talk with his comrades. Ludmila, who had no English, at first thought that rude. Then she realized the RAF men had business to do and needed their own language for it. Her irritation faded.

Bagnall returned to the same mixture of German and Russian as Ludmila used: 'By the time we can get the guns to open up, the lorries will be almost to the Lizards' front line – do you see?' He drew their probable track up to the line south of Pskov marked in red ink. Seeing Ludmila's disappointed expression, he went on, 'But the Lizards may not be done unloading them. A few shells might do us some good. Wait here.'

He left the map chamber, returning a few minutes later with a different sort of smile on his face. 'Captain Dölger does not approve of us, but he is a good soldier. If he is ordered to do something, it will get done.'

Sure enough, within a couple of minutes field guns off to the north and east of Pskov began hammering away in the short, intense bombardment that seemed best calculated to hit the Lizards. They shifted position before counterbattery fire could wreak full havoc.

And sure enough, Ludmila heard incoming rounds hard on the heels of the last outgoing ones. 'I hope they managed to move their cannon,' she said, and then shook her head. 'Hoping anything good for the Germans still feels wrong to me.' Saying that in German felt wrong to her, too. She repeated it in Russian.

The woman with the sniping rifle nodded emphatically. In fair Russian of his own, Jones, the youngest Englishman, said, 'For us also. Remember, we were at war with the Hitlerites for almost two years before the Soviet Union joined that fight.'

Ludmila did remember. For those almost two years, in the Soviet Union, Hitler's Germany could do no wrong. It was dealing blow after blow to the imperialist powers ... until it dealt a blow to the Soviet Union that almost wrecked it forever. Ludmila said, 'They are our allies against the Lizards. I try to forget everything but that. I try – but it is not easy.'

'No, it is not easy,' George Bagnall said. 'Things I've seen here, things I saw in France, make me glad we were dropping bombs on Jerry's head. And yet the Nazis give the Lizards a thin time of it. Very strange.'

Most of that had been in German, but the blonde Russian woman understood enough of it to say, 'Nobody says the Nazis cannot fight. Or if anyone does say it, it is a lie; we have all seen enough to know better. But they do not think why they fight. Someone tells them what to do, and they do it well. And for what? For Hitlerism!' Her cornflower-blue eyes blazed contempt.

No one argued with her. A couple of minutes later, Captain Dölger came running into the room. His fleshy, handsome face glowed. 'Field telephones from the front say our artillery touched off secondary explosions – some of those lorries were carrying shells,' Bagnall had told him what to do, and he'd done it well.

The blonde with the rifle threw her arms around Bagnall and kissed him on the mouth. Captain Dölger coughed; he left the Englishmen's office as fast as he'd come in. Jerome Jones flushed till he looked like a boiled crayfish. Ludmila turned away, embarrassed. Such behavior by a Soviet woman was uncultured in the extreme.

She expected Bagnall to take all he could get from the shameless sniper. For one thing, men were like that. For another, he was an Englishman, therefore a capitalist, therefore an exploiter. But he broke the kiss as soon as he decently could, and looked as embarrassed about it as Ludmila felt.

She scratched her head. Bagnall wasn't behaving the way school had taught her Englishmen were supposed to behave. What did that say about her lessons? She didn't really know, but the more you looked at things, the more complicated they got.

Jens Larssen pedaled wearily into Hanford, Washington. He stopped in the middle of the main street. 'God, what a dump,' he muttered. He could see why the physicists back at the Met Lab had been hot for the place. He could hear the murmur and splash of the Columbia as it flowed by next to the town. It was all the river anybody could ask for, and he knew what the Mississippi was like.

Not only that, the place already had a railroad line coming into it from the north: the train station was much the biggest building in town. No tracks came out of Hanford going south; it was the end of the line. *In more ways than one*, Jens thought. But the railroad line was a point in favor of the place. With it, you could conveniently move stuff in and out. Without it, that wouldn't have been so easy.

River and railroad: two big pluses. Everything else, as far as Jens could see, was a minus. Hanford couldn't have held more than a few hundred people. Any major industrial activity here would stand out like a sore thumb. Hanford didn't have any major industries. Just to make up for it, Hanford didn't have any minor industries, either. If it suddenly developed some, the Lizards couldn't help but notice.

Jens looked around. Both the pile and the plant to get the plutonium out of its fuel elements would have to go underground; there were no buildings big enough to conceal them. Could you do that much digging and keep it a secret? He had his doubts.

'It's too damn little,' he said, as if someone were arguing with him. The only reason Hanford existed was to act as a market town for the nearby farmers. Some of the fields to the north, south, and west were still green; more, thanks to the job the Lizards had done on pumping stations, lay brown and dry under the sun.

Besides the railhead, Hanford's amenities were of the basic sort: a couple of general stores (one of them now closed), a gas station (also closed), a school (it being summer vacation, Jens couldn't tell if that was closed or not), and a doctor's office. The doctor's office was open; Jens saw a pregnant woman walk into it.

He scratched absently at a flake of peeling skin on his wrist. Back in Ogden, Utah, that doctor – Sharp, that was his name – had said some smalltown doc might have some sulfa to give him to get rid of the clap. He'd tried once or twice on his way here, but no sawbones had had any, or been willing to use it on somebody just passing through. As long as he was here, he figured he might as well ask this one, too. If he heard no, he heard no. He'd heard it before.

He walked his bike over in front of the doctor's office, put down the kickstand with his foot. On second thought, he shook his head and carried the bike upstairs. If a local absconded with it, everyone else would pretend he hadn't seen a thing. Jens had grown up in a small town. He knew what they were like.

The waiting room was clean and pleasant. All the magazines were more than a year old, but that might have been true even if the Lizards hadn't come. Behind the desk sat a pleasant-faced middle-aged woman in a gingham dress. If the arrival of an unkempt, rifle-toting, bike-hauling stranger fazed her, she didn't show it.' 'Good morning, sir,' she said. 'Dr Henry will be able to see you soon.'

Okay, thanks,' Jens sat down. He hadn't paid any attention to the name on the sign outside. As long as it had MD after it, that would do. He leafed through a *Life* with pictures of Germans retreating through the snow of the fierce Russian winter. Worse things than Nazis were loose in the world these days, even if that hadn't seemed possible in the early days of 1942.

'Uh, sir,' the receptionist asked, 'what's your name?' Larssen gave it, then spelled it for good measure. People always fouled up either his first name or his last one, sometimes both of them.

The door by the receptionist opened. The pregnant woman came out. Except for being big as a blimp, she looked fine. She was smiling, too, so the doc had probably told her she was fine.

A woman a few years younger than the receptionist poked her head out the door. 'Come in, Mr uh, Larssen,' she said. She wore a frayed but clean white coat and had a stethoscope slung round her neck.

Jens went into the room to which she waved him. She weighed him, stuck a blood-pressure cuff on his arm, and asked him what his trouble was. He felt his ears get hot. 'I'd sooner talk about that with the doctor,' he mumbled.

She raised an eyebrow. She had a long, rather horsey face, and wore her dark hair pulled back from it and caught behind in a short ponytail. 'I *am* the doctor,' she said. 'I'm Marjorie Henry. Did you think I was the nurse?' By the way she asked the question, a lot of people over a lot of years had thought she was the nurse.

'Oh,' Jens said, embarrassed now for a different reason. 'I beg your pardon.' That new embarrassment was piled on top of the old one, which hadn't gone away. How was he supposed to tell a woman, even a woman doctor, he had the clap? He wished to Jesus he'd read the sign out front. Gonorrhea wouldn't kill you, and he could have looked for a different doctor to do something about it.

'What seems to be the trouble?' Dr Henry repeated. When Larssen didn't answer, that eyebrow went up again. 'I assure you, Mr Larssen: whatever it is, I've probably seen it and dealt with it before. And if I haven't seen it before, I'll just send you on your way, because with things as they are I won't be able to do anything about it anyhow.'

She had a no-nonsense attitude Jens liked. That made things easier, but not enough. 'I, uh, that is, well, I—' He gave up. No matter how he tried, he couldn't make himself say it.

Dr Henry got up and shut the door to her office. 'There. Now Beulah can't hear,' she said. 'Mr Larssen, am I to infer from his hemming and hawing that you are suffering from a venereal disease?' He gulped and nodded. She nodded, too, briskly. 'Very good. Do you know which disease you are suffering from?'

'Gonorrhea,' he whispered, looking down at his Army boots. Of all the words he'd never imagined saying to a woman, that one was high on the list. Gathering courage, he went on, 'I've, uh, heard that sulfa can cure it, but no doc I've talked to has had any to spare.'

'No one has anything to spare any more,' she said. 'But you're lucky here. Just before the Lizards came, I received a large shipment of sulfanilamide. I expect I can spare you a few grams. Believe me, actually being able to attack germs rather than just defending against them is quite an enjoyable sensation.'

'You really will give me some sulfa?' he said, happy and disbelieving at the same time. 'That's great!' His opinion of Hanford underwent a quick 180-degree shift. *Great town, friendly people,* he thought.

Dr Henry unlocked a drawer full of medications. As she'd said, she had several large jars of sulfanilamide tablets in there. The tablets were small and yellowish-white. She said, 'Take three of these five times a day your first day with them, four times a day the second day, three times a day the third day, and twice a day after that until you've taken them all. Do you have something to carry them in? I have plenty of pills, but I'm desperately short on jars and bottles and vials.'

'Here, I've got a spare sock,' he said, digging it out of his pack. Dr Henry started to laugh, but she filled the sock full of pills. There were an awful lot of them. Larssen didn't care. He would have swallowed a bowling ball if he could get rid of the clap that way. When the doctor was done counting pills, he asked her, 'What do I owe you?'

She pursued her lips. 'Mr Larssen, these days you can't really buy medicine for money. You can still buy other things, though, so money has some use ... A fair price, I'd say, would be about two hundred dollars. If you don't have that, and you probably don't—' Jens reached into a hip pocket and pulled out a roll of bills fat enough to choke a horse. Dr Henry's eyes widened as he started peeling off twenties. 'Here you go,' he said. 'You may just be surprised about medicine, too.'

'Really?' she said. 'Who are you, anyway?'

Who was that masked man? ran through his head. It was a fair question, though. People who looked like unshaven bums didn't often go around with enough loot to make them seem like apprentice John Dillingers. And people who did go around with that kind of loot probably weren't in the habit of dropping in on small-town doctors to get their social diseases treated.

Instead of answering in words, he took out the fancy letter with which General Groves had equipped him and handed it to her. She carefully read it through, gave it back to him. 'Where are you going, Mr no, Dr Larssen, on this important government mission of yours?' she asked. She didn't add, *And where did you pick up the clap along the way?* – just as well, too, since he'd picked it up twice.

He grinned at her. 'As a matter of fact, I was coming here. Now I have to get my bicycle out of your waiting room and head on back to make my report.'

'You were coming here? To Hanford?' Marjorie Henry burst out laughing. 'Excuse me, Dr Larssen, but what on earth does Hanford have that you couldn't get ten times as much of somewhere – anywhere – else?'

'Water. Space. Privacy,' he answered. Those were absolutely the only things Hanford had going for it, with the possible exception of Dr Henry, but Larssen had already changed his mind about the dreadful review he'd first thought he would give to the place.

'Yes, we have those things,' Dr Henry admitted. 'Why are they important enough for the government to send someone out looking for them?'

'I'm sorry; I really can't tell you that.' Jens started to regret pulling out the letter. He said, 'Please don't spread it around, either. In fact, I'd be grateful if you just told Beulah – did I get her name right? – I won the money in a poker game or something like that.'

'All right,' she said. 'I can do that. You can't afford to gossip as a small-town doctor, anyway. If you do, you lose all your patients after about the first week. I will ask one question, though: are you going to put a hospital in here? You may be Dr Larssen, but I don't think you're an MD.'

'I'm not, and no, that's not what's planned,' Jens said, and let it go at that. Telling her what kind of doctorate he had might have told her other things, too, things she didn't need to know. Now that he was here, security seemed to matter again. He hadn't worried much about it while he was on the road.

Dr Henry was visibly disappointed, but didn't ask any more questions. Maybe she'd really meant what she said about not gossiping. She stuck out her hand and shook his, man-fashion. 'Good luck to you,' she said. 'I hope the sulfanilamide tablets do as well for you as they commonly do. I also hope you won't need such medications again.' Before he could decide if that was patronizing, or get mad about it if it was, she went on, 'Will we see you again in Hanford, then?'

'You may very well,' he answered. That didn't seem to make her angry. In spite of her jab, she was a doctor, and didn't think of gonorrhea as the end of the world. He nodded to her, opened the door, and walked down the hall to the waiting room.

Dr Henry called after her, 'Mr Larssen has paid me for the visit, Beulah.' Jens nodded again, this time to himself. If she remembered to call him Mr Larssen in public, she would probably remember not to talk about his letter. He could hope so, anyhow.

In the waiting room sat another pregnant woman, this one less rotund than the one who'd preceded Larssen, and a farmer with a hand wrapped in a blood-soaked rag. They both gave Jens a curious look as he recovered his bicycle. Beulah said, 'Go on in, George. The doctor will clean that out and sew it up for you.'

'She got any o' that tetanus stuff left?' George asked as he rose from his chair.

Jens didn't find out whether or not Dr Henry had antitetanus serum. He walked out of her office, lugging the bicycle. Sure enough, the sign outside gave her name in good-sized letters; he just hadn't noticed. If he had, he wouldn't have gone in, and he wouldn't have got the sulfa tablets. Sometimes ignorance worked out pretty well.

He swung onto the bike and began to pedal, southbound now. Dr Henry was also the first woman he'd met in a long time who hadn't screwed him, one way or another. She knew what her job was and she went out and did it without any fuss or feathers.

'If she'd been waiting for me, she'd have *waited*, by Jesus,' Jens said as he rolled out of Hanford. 'She wouldn't have fallen into bed with some lousy ballplayer.' When he got back to Denver, he'd have some choice things to say to Barbara, and if Sam Yeager didn't like it, well, there were ways to deal with Sam Yeager, and with Barbara, too.

He reached around behind his back and patted the wooden stock of his Springfield. Then he bent low over the bicycle handlebars and started pumping hard. Colorado was still a long way away, but he could hardly wait to get back.

Lugging a heavy picnic basket uphill on a hiking trail in Arkansas summer wasn't Sam Yeager's idea of fun. But getting away from the Army and Navy General Hospital for a while – to say nothing of getting away from the Lizards – was worth some discomfort. And he wasn't about to let Barbara carry the picnic basket, not when her belly was starting to bulge.

She glanced over at him. 'You're red as a beet, Sam' she said. 'Really nothing will happen if I take that for a few minutes. Just because I'm expecting doesn't mean I'm made out of cut glass. I won't break.'

'No,' Yeager answered stubbornly. 'I'm all right.' The path rounded a corner. The pines to either side opened out onto a grassy meadow. 'Besides,' he went on with a grin not altogether free of relief, 'this looks like a perfect spot.'

'Why, so it does,' Barbara said. At first he thought that was hearty agreement. Then, when he listened to it again in his mind, he suspected she would have agreed had the meadow been a dismal swamp. She was ready to stop walking, and she was ready to have him stop toting that basket.

The meadow wasn't as closely trimmed as it might have been had the federal government not had more urgent things to worry about. Long grass didn't bother Yeager; he'd played in outfields where it wasn't a whole lot shorter. He saw down the basket, blipped open the lid, pulled out a blanket, and spread it on the ground. As soon as Barbara sat down on it, he did, too.

No that the hauling was done, the picnic basket became her responsibility. She reached in and got out ham sandwiches wrapped in cloth napkins from the hospital – waxed paper was a thing of the past. The bread was homemade and sliced by hand; the ham came from a Hot Springs razorback; the mustard had never seen the inside of a factory. It might have been the best sandwich Sam had ever eaten. After it came hard-boiled eggs and a peach pie that gave the ham sandwich a run for its money.

The only rough spot in the road was the beer. Several people in Hot Springs were brewing, but what they turned out didn't stack up too well against store-bought brands. It wasn't cold, either. But Sam could drink it, and he did.

When he was through, he lay back on the blanket with a sigh of contentment. 'I wish I had me a cigarette,' he said. 'Otherwise, the world looks like a pretty fine place right now.' Barbara didn't answer. He glanced over to her. She hadn't done justice to either that magnificent sandwich or the peach pie. 'Come on,' he told her. 'You're eating for two.'

'I know,' she said. 'Sometimes I still have trouble keeping down food for one, though.' She looked a trifle green. Defensively, she added, 'It's better than it was a couple of months ago. Then I thought having a baby meant starving to death – or rather, eating something and then tossing it up right away. Thank heaven I'm not doing that any more.'

'You said it,' he answered. 'Well, I'm not going to agitate you about it, not now. It's too nice a day – now that that picnic basket's sitting here on the blanket.' He consoled himself: 'It's downhill on the way back – and the basket'll be lighter, too.'

A lazy breeze drifted through the pines, filling the meadow with their spicy scent. High overhead, a hawk circled. Blue larkspur and violets, great blue sage and purple cone, splashed the rainbow here and there across the green grass. Bees buzzed from one flower to another. Flies snacked on the remains of the feast, and on the picnickers.

Barbara let out a squeak. Sam jumped; he'd been lulled by the peaceful surroundings – the most peace he'd known in quite a while. 'What's the matter?' he asked. He reached into the pocket of his chinos. If peace dissolved, as it had a way of doing, he was armed with nothing better than a pocketknife.

But Barbara pointed to the blanket and said, 'A little green lizard just ran across there. I didn't see it till it jumped out of the grass. Now it's gone again.'

'I know the ones you mean,' Sam said, relaxing. 'They can change colors – sometimes they're brown instead of green. People around here call 'em chameleons on account of that, but I don't think they are, not really. They don't have the funny eyes real chameleons do, the ones that go every which way like Lizards' eye turrets.'

Barbara sniffed. 'I was looking for sympathy, not herpetology,' she said, but she was laughing while she said it. Then everything but concentration drained from her face. Her face was turned toward Sam, but she was looking inward. 'The baby's moving,' she murmured. Her eyes got wide. 'Moving, heck – he's kicking like nobody's business. Come here, Sam. You should be able to feel this.'

He slid across the blanket toward her. She pulled the shirttail of her thin white cotton blouse out from the waistband of her pleated skirt. He set his hand on her belly, just below her navel. When she had clothes on, you couldn't see she was pregnant, not and be sure, but you could feel the mound that had begun to rise there. Her flesh was warm and beaded with sweat from the sticky day.

'He's stopped,' Barbara said, disappointed. 'No, wait – did you feel that?'

'I sure did,' Yeager said. Something had – fluttered – under his palm. He'd felt it a few times before, but it never failed to awe him. He closed his hand into a fist, tapped gently on her belly. 'Hello? Anybody home?'

Barbara made her voice high and squeaky: 'I'm sorry, I'm not ready to come out yet.'

They both laughed. Somewhere back in the forest, a wood thrush trilled. But for the droning of the bees, that was the only sound. The two of them might have had the national park to themselves. Lazily, Sam slid his hand up under the blouse to cup her left breast through the fabric of her brassiere – gently, because she was still often sensitive.

'What do you think you're doing?' Barbara said. She looked around to see who might be watching. No one was. No one, probably, was within a mile of them.

'I think – I hope – I'm getting ready to make love to my wife,' he answered. 'How about that?' He pulled the blouse all the way out of her skirt, bent down to kiss the spot where his hand had rested to feel the baby move.

'How about that?' she said softly. She reached around to the back of her neck. Through endless practice, women learn to work buttons behind them as smoothly as men do those they can see. She pulled the blouse up and over her head.

Sam unhooked her bra, tossed it on the blanket. Her breasts were fuller than they had been, her nipples larger and darker. He lowered his head to one of them. Barbara sighed. Her head lolled back; her breasts were sensitive to more than pain these days.

Presently he got out of his own clothes. In weather like this, bare skin felt best anyhow. Barbara was still wearing her skirt. He slid his hand under it, peeled down her panties, and tossed them on top of the bra. Then his hand returned. When he kissed her at the same time, she set one hand on the back of his head and pulled him to her. Her other hand toyed with him.

After a couple of minutes of that, he couldn't stand to wait any more. He started to hike up her skirt, but she said, 'No. Take it off me,' in such urgent tones that he quickly did as she asked. Sometimes being smart didn't amount to anything more than knowing when not to ask questions.

They both glistened with sweat when they were through; their skins slid greasily across each other. Barbara dressed in what seemed like no time flat. 'Hurry up!' she hissed to Sam when she saw he wasn't in quite such a rush.

He looked down at his still-bare self and shrugged. 'Okay,' he said, and sped up. As he buttoned his shirt and tucked it into his trousers, he went on, 'I guess I've spent so much time in the buff in locker rooms and things, I don't much worry about getting caught that way.'

'All well and good,' Barbara answered, 'but getting caught naked with me is different from getting caught naked with a bunch of baseball players – or at least I hope it is.'

'You better believe it,' he said, and got a chuckle out of her. He folded up the blanket and stowed it inside the picnic basket. The napkins that had wrapped the sandwiches went in there, too. So did the empty bottles of beer, and even their cork-sealed lids. You couldn't afford to waste anything, not with the war going the way it was. Even so, the picnic basket had been a good deal heavier on the way up the trail.

They were almost out of Hot Springs National Park when Barbara said in a small voice, 'I'm sorry I barked at you back there.' Sam raised a questioning eyebrow. Looking down at the ground, Barbara went on, 'I mean about hiking up my skirt. I remembered a time when—' She didn't go on.

Yeager kicked at the dirt. What she probably meant was that she remembered a time when Jens Larssen had hiked up her skirt. If she hadn't thought Jens was dead, she never would have ended up with him. He knew that damn well. After a few seconds – maybe a couple of seconds too long – he said, 'Don't worry about it. Nobody here but the two of us now. That's what counts.' With a laugh, he set his hand on her belly again. 'Nobody here but the three of us, I mean.'

Barbara nodded. They walked on. *That's what* really *counts*, Sam thought. If she hadn't been pregnant, dollars to doughnuts she would have gone back to Larssen when she found out he was alive. Yeager still marveled that she hadn't. You play half your life in the minor league – and most of that in the low minors, to boot – you get used to winding up on the short end of the stick. Winning a big one like having the woman you've fallen in love with pick you instead of the other guy – that was pretty special.

When they rounded the last corner and came into sight of the Army and Navy General Hospital, Barbara slipped her hand into his. He squeezed it gratefully. Every once in a while, he wondered whether she regretted the choice she'd made. That was another question he was smart enough never, ever to ask.

A horse-drawn wagon pulled up in front of the two towers of the hospital building just as he and Barbara got to the entrance. A GI – even if the fellow was in civvies, Yeager knew one when he saw one – took a gadget, a Lizardy-looking gadget, from the bed of the wagon and started to carry it in.

'What the devil you got there?' Yeager asked him. The thing, whatever it was, was cylindrical, maybe a foot long and three or four inches wide, with a glittering lens at one end and some wires trailing off the other.

'Bomb guider,' the man answered, which left Sam unenlightened. The fellow went on, 'We took it from a Lizard dud up in Chicago, figured we'd bring it down here to get the straight skinny on what it does and how it does it. We've got several up there, and we can't make 'em work worth a damn.' He pointed at Yeager. 'You talk Lizard talk?'

'Matter of fact, I do, not too bad,' Yeager answered.

'Okay. I figured a lot of guys down here would,' the GI said. 'You know what *skelkwank* means? That's what the Lizard POWs say when they talk about this stupid thing, and nobody up north can make it make sense.'

'*Skelkwank*?' Yeager echoed. 'Yeah, that's a word I've run into.' He was damn glad it was, too. Saying you were an expert and then showing you weren't got old fast. 'It's something to do with light – I'm not sure exactly what, and I'm not sure anybody else human is, either. I've heard LIzards say *skelkwank* when they're talking about rangefinders, things like that.'

'That helps some,' the fellow said, nodding. 'How's *skelkwank* light different than any other kind, though?'

'There you've got me,' Sam admitted. 'Tell you what – bring that thing inside and we'll round up a Lizard or two and ask 'em some questions. They're pretty good about giving straight answers. As soon as they get captured, they figure we're their superiors now, and they have to obey us. They're not as ornery as people, you know what I mean?'

'Once they're caught, they're not, maybe,' the man with the *skelkwank* device said. 'Long as they're still carrying guns, they're no fun at all.'

Sam gave an emphatic cough to show he agreed with that. The other fellow understood and nodded. Barbara said, 'Here, Sam, you're working again. Give me the picnic basket. I'll take care of it.'

'Okay, honey.' Sam held the door open for her and for the soldier with the Lizard gadget, then followed them into the lobby of the hospital building. He spotted Ristin there, talking with one of the human doctors. Ristin waved to him, a human gesture he'd picked up. Sam waved back, and then waved him over.

Ristin came up, gaudy in his American-flag style 'official' POW body paint. 'Hello, superior sir,' he said in his hissing English. 'You need me?'

'Sure do, pal.' Yeager pointed to the device the other man held. 'Tell me about that thing, will you?' Ristin turned one eye turret toward it. 'That? That is a *skelkwank* sight, I think maybe from a bomb. Artillery shells use a smaller model. *Skelkwank* in your language is ... is—' He paused and fluttered his fingers, a Lizardy way of showing frustration. 'I think your language has not this word. Yep, that is what I think.'

The fellow with the *skelkwank* sight snorted in amusement. 'First time I ever heard a Lizard go, "Yep".'

Yeager kicked at the carpet. 'He got that from me,' he said, mildly embarrassed. 'I'm the guy he learned English from, and I say it. Made me laugh, too, first time I heard it from him.' He turned back to Ristin. 'Okay, we don't have a word for it. *Skelkwank* has to do with light, right? What makes *skelkwank* light special?'

'Why, it comes from a *ftaskwelkwank*, of course,' Ristin said. Tacking *fta-* onto the front of a word in Lizard talk was about like taking *-er* onto the back of one in English. A *ftaskelkwank* was something that turned light *skelkwank*: a *skelkwanker*, in other words. The only trouble was, that didn't help much with *skelkwank* still undefined.

'Of course,' Yeager said with a sigh. 'What does the *ftaskelkwank* do with the light to change it from regular to *skelkwank*?'

'It makes the light—' Ristin used another Lizard word.

Sam turned to the fellow with the gadget. 'I've heard that term before, too. It means something like "coherent". I don't know what that means here, though.'

'Coherent, yep.' Ristin liked learning new English words. 'Most light, ordinary light, is of waves of all different lengths, photons – is right word? – of all different energies. Coherent light has only one length of wave, only one energy. Is all exact same color, you could say.'

'So if I put red cellophane on top of my flashlight lens, I'd have coherent light?' Sam asked, trying to figure out what the Lizard meant.

'Nep. I mean, nope.' Ristin's mouth fell open: he was laughing at himself. 'Not all photons of exact same energy, only close. Not all going in exact same direction. This is what coherent means.'

The GI with the Lizard *skelkwank* device said. 'Okay, how *do* you get this, uh, coherent light?'

'Take rod made of right kind of crystal,' Ristin answered. 'Grind ends very, very flat, put on coating like mirror. Pump energy into the crystal. Coherent light will come out. Is one way. Are others.'

For all the sense he made, he might as well have suddenly started speaking Tibetan. Yeager had seen that happen before when the Lizards talked about goodies they had and people didn't. He said, 'Never mind how. What can you do with a *ftaskelkwank* once you've got it?'

'Aim it at, say, one of your landcruisers – no, tanks, you say. *Skelkwank* sight here sees that coherent light reflected, guides rocket or bomb straight to it. This is why we do not miss much when we use these sights.'

The soldier stuck the device under Ristin's snout. 'How does it see the coherent light and not any other kind?'

'How?' Ristin turned one eye on the sight, the other on the soldier. He started to answer, spluttered, stopped, started over, stopped again. 'I do not know how it does this. I only know that it does this.'

'He's just a dogface like me,' Yeager said, 'or a dogface like I used to be – I've got three stripes when I'm not in civvies. You want more than that, friend, we've got a couple of Lizard technicians down here who'll talk as long as you'll listen.'

The fellow with the sight stared at Sam. 'You got this much out of an ordinary Lizard soldier? Holy Jesus, Sergeant, up north they've been beating around the bush with technicians who haven't said as much in weeks as I just got in ten minutes here. You're doing a hell of a job.'

'Thanks very much,' Sam said. 'Here, let me take you to Major Houlihan. He'll be able to fix you up with the Lizards who can tell you the most.' He patted Ristin on his scaly shoulder. 'Thanks for helping us out.'

'It is for me a pleasure, superior sir,' Ristin said.

Yeager was still grinning when he got upstairs. He told the story to Barbara, who listened while he burbled on. When he was done, she said, 'Why should you be so surprised when somebody tells you you're good at what you do?'

'Because it's not anything like something I imagined I could be good at, and because I don't have any education to speak of – you know that, honey – and because it's important to the country,' he answered. 'Suppose you got into riveting some kind of way, and after a little while on the job you riveted more wings onto B-17s than anybody else at the plant, even people who've been riveting for twenty years. Wouldn't you be surprised about that?'

'But Sam, nobody's been talking with the Lizards for twenty years,' Barbara reminded him. 'You have more experience at that than just about anyone else here. And you may not have thought you'd be good at it, but by now you should have seen that you are.' She gave him the kind of appraising look that always made him nervous, lest she sees less than she wanted. 'Isn't that what you'd call bush-league thinking, thinking you're not good enough for the big time?'

He stared at her. 'What are you doing using baseball talk on me?'

'I'm married to you, remember?' she answered, sticking her tongue out at him. 'Don't you think I'd look for some way to get ideas through your thick head?'

Sam walked over and gave her a big kiss. 'I'm a heck of a lucky guy, you know that? When I got you, I wasn't thinking bush league at all, not even a little bit.'

'That's good,' she said. 'We keep on like this for another thirty or forty years and we'll have something pretty fine.' He nodded. She pulled back a little as his beard rasped her cheek. That, unfortunately, reminded him how unlikely they were to live another thirty or forty years, or to be free if they did live so long.

The pitching deck of a ship in the Baltic did not strike Vyacheslav Molotov as the ideal locale on which to hold diplomatic negotiations. Stalin, however, had not asked his opinion, merely sent him forth.

Being aboard ship had one advantage: it meant he could avoid flying, an experience he heartily loathed. Molotov watched the fishing vessel approach. It flew a Danish flag, white cross on red. His own ship sported the red, gold, and green ensign of Lithuania, even though that unhappy land had first been incorporated into the USSR and then overrun by the Nazis. But the Lizards were more likely to shoot at vessels displaying German and Soviet flags than those of small, weak nations.

A signal light blinked across the water from the fishing boat. 'Comrade Foreign Minister, it is indeed the vessel of the German foreign minister,' the captain said. 'They ask permission to come alongside.'

'I am ready to meet with von Ribbentrop,' Molotov said – not eager, but ready. 'As for matters of shiphandling, that is why you are here, is it not?'

'Yes, Comrade Foreign Commissar.' The captain met icy sarcasm with wooden obedience. 'I shall have them convey the foreign minister to this vessel.'

'You had better,' Molotov answered. 'Anyone who thinks I am going to board that – scow – is sadly mistaken.' The Soviet ship in Lithuanian colors was a rust-bucket freighter. Next to the fishing boat now sidling up to it, it seemed a decadent capitalist luxury liner by comparison. A strong odor of stale herring made Molotov wrinkle his nose – or perhaps, he thought, it was only Ribbentrop and his Nazi policies he was smelling.

A couple of sailors let down a rope ladder to the deck of the fishing boat. The German foreign minister scrambled up to the Soviet ship like a monkey, closely followed by his interpreter, who rather resembled one. Molotov's own interpreter appeared at his elbow. Each side guarded itself against twisted meaning from the other.

Ribbentrop turned his complacent pop-eyed face, marbled with fat like expensive beef, toward the Lithuanian flag. Half sketching a salute to that banner of a country which no longer existed, he said, 'I honor the brave Lithuanian people.'

Molotov was more than a little surprised his opposite number remembered that flag represented Lithuania rather than Estonia or Latvia. He was also coldly furious, though he kept his face and voice expressionless as he replied, 'If you honor them so much, why did Germany include Lithuania in the territory designated as a Soviet sphere of influence in the Soviet-German nonaggression pact of 1939, which you helped negotiate? You do recall that clause, I trust?'

Ribbentrop coughed and spluttered and turned a mottled shade of red. Thanks to Hitler's favor, he could bluster his way through the Nazi hierarchy, but that meant nothing to Molotov. 'Well, let us speak of the present and not of the past,' Ribbentrop said with the air of a man making a great concession.

'You would have been well-advised to do that from the beginning,' Molotov said.

'Do not take that tone with me,' Ribbentrop snapped, the bluster returning to his voice. What was the old saying? – *The German was either at your throat or at your feet*. Much truth there – no middle ground.

The foreign minister went on, 'Just because you have managed to set off one explosive-metal bomb, you should not count yourselves little tin gods. We Germans are nearly to the point of being able to do that as well, and we are also deploying other new weapons in the fight against the Lizards.'

'Your nerve gases, you mean,' Molotov said. Reluctantly, Ribbentrop nodded. Molotov remarked, 'You Germans seem as reluctant to speak of your successes gassing Lizards as you were of your earlier successes gassing Jews.'

The eyes of Molotov's interpreter slid to him for a moment. Maybe he shaded the translation, for Ribbentrop's man murmured into his principal's ear afterwards. Ribbentrop said, 'I am given to understand that the chemical weapon bureau of the Red Army has made inquiries as to the formula for these gases – both kinds.'

Molotov changed the subject, the closest he would come to acknowledging the hit: 'Let us detail the ways in which our two governments can co-operate in our common struggle against the imperialist aggressors.' Stalin was nervous about the Germans' poison gas. Nuclear bombs, as yet, were too bulky to fit into any rocket mere humans could build. The same did not hold true for gas. Only the stretch of Lizard territory in what had been Poland kept the soil of the Soviet Union from being vulnerable to German rockets loaded with invisible death.

Ribbentrop said, 'This is why we were to meet here in this way. The rudeness that has gone on is distracting.' He seemed blithely unaware he had begun the rudeness himself. That probably was no affectation, either. The Nazis had a remarkable knack for ignoring their own flaws.

'Let us try to be polite to each other for the rest of this meeting, then.' Molotov was not sure that was possible, but he would make the effort. 'Since the *Führer* requested this meeting of General Secretary Stalin, I presume you will enlighten me as to what he intended to accomplish by it.'

Ribbentrop gave a fishy stare, as if suspecting sarcasm. Molotov doubted he would recognize it till – or perhaps even after – it chewed out the seat of his pants. The German foreign minister said, 'Indeed yes. The *Führer* wishes to discuss with you the possibilities of coordinating our future use of explosive-metal bombs against the Lizards.'

'Does he?' Molotov had a good reason to stall for time: having nearly exhausted its store of explosive metal with its first blast, the Soviet Union, despite frantic work, was nowhere near ready to loose another one. Hearing that the Nazis were close enough to having a weapon of their own to want to talk with the USSR about how best to use it was disquieting, to say the least.

But Ribbentrop nodded, his pop eyes bulging like a netted bream's. 'That is his purpose, yes. Between these explosive-metal bombs and our poison gas, we are in a position to make this world a very unpleasant place for the invaders.'

'And for ourselves,' Molotov said. 'The last time I discussed with Hitler the use of explosive-metal bombs, his principal aim was to level Poland with them, and to use the poisons that spread from them to wreck the Soviet Union as well. To this we could not possibly agree. I hope also that your engineers and scientists are more careful than they were earlier at producing explosive metal without wrecking themselves in the process.'

He wondered if Ribbentrop would resent any of that. It sounded sardonic, but every word of it was true. The German foreign minister said, 'Production problems seem well on their way to solution.'

'That is good news,' Molotov lied.

'Is it not?' Ribbentrop agreed, not noticing the lie at all. *Like a fat puppy*, Molotov thought scornfully. *And then he wonders why he gets kicked*. Ribbentrop went on, 'We were fortunate when the Lizards diverted forces from their offensive against us to assail England. That let us stop them at the Rhine. They had come uncomfortably close to our research facilities.'

'How fortunate for you that they were halted,' Molotov agreed tonelessly. If he'd been Himmler, he would have had Ribbentrop's interpreter reporting back to him. And, if he'd been Himmler, he'd have had some sharp things to say to Ribbentrop about talking too much. Molotov knew better than to reveal, even in the most general terms, where the Soviet nuclear weapons project was based.

'Yes, wasn't it?' Ribbentrop said without a shred of guile. 'The *Führer* still is of the opinion that punishing the Lizards and the Jews in Poland is the best strategic course to take. It would open up that blocked passage between Germany and the Soviet Union and permit direct communications between our two great countries once more. This could be vital in carrying on the war.'

'The war against whom?' Molotov asked. 'General Secretary Stalin views the Lizard presence in Poland, at least for the time being, as a useful buffer between us. If we do not touch, we cannot fight.' *And you cannot resupply your troops inside the Soviet Union. As they exhaust their stores, they become more and more dependent on us – and vulnerable to us.*

Ribbentrop looked so innocent, Molotov expected a halo to spring into being above his head at any moment. 'The *Reich* has no intention of continuing its former campaign against the Soviet Union. Circumstances have changed.'

'Circumstances changed, as you put it, in 1939, and then changed again in 1941. They could change yet again at a moment's notice,' Molotov said. 'Thus the value of the buffer.'

'If we do not co-operate against the Lizards, we shall never have the chance to pursue our private grievances,' Ribbentrop answered.

That was the first sensible thing he'd said since he boarded the Russian freighter. Molotov eyed him warily. 'True enough, but co-operation must run both ways. If you enjoy all the advantages, you must not expect us to be your dupes.'

'If we did not honestly co-operate with you, you would not have got the explosive metal from which to make your bomb,' Ribbentrop said. 'Do remember that half the team which took the metal was made up of German soldiers, who supplied all the heavy weapons for the raid.'

'True enough,' Molotov said, and then paused to think. Ribbentrop had now made sense twice running, which, as far as the foreign commissar knew, equaled his all-time record. Was the jumped-up champagne salesman actually developing competence in his old age? An alarming notion, if true. More cautiously than he'd spoken before, Molotov asked, 'When will your country have its own explosive-metal bombs? We cannot very well co-ordinate our strategy if we do not know when that strategy becomes effective.'

'Ja,' Ribbentrop said, not very happily. He paced up and down along the deck, his interpreter an obsequious half pace behind and to his left. At last he said, 'Gott mit uns, we shall have our first bomb next spring, with others following quickly on its heels. What of Soviet Russia? When will you be ready to give the Lizards another dose of their own medicine?'

'Our timetable is tightly similar to yours,' Molotov answered. For years, he had trained himself to reveal nothing with his face, with his voice, with his stance. That training served him in good stead now. The Soviet program would not produce a bomb of its own next spring, and probably not for a couple of years thereafter.

Molotov wished he could pace. What to do, what to do? If Ribbentrop was telling the truth, the Nazis had not only recovered from the disaster their nuclear program had suffered but were also ready to produce their own explosive metal in large amounts.

What to do? Ribbentrop had let slip that the heart of the German effort lay somewhere not far from the Rhine. Word ever so discreetly leaked to the Lizards would mean they – and the Soviet Union – might be freed of the threat of explosive-metal bombs in the hands of a madman like Hitler.

But the Nazis were also putting up a stubborn resistance against the Lizards. If they collapsed under a cloud of nuclear fire, the imperialist aggressors from the stars would be able to turn more force on the peace-loving people of the Soviet Union. They were already giving signs of realizing the USSR was not in a position to deploy more nuclear weapons against them. Keeping Germany in the fight might keep the Soviet Union alive, too.

It was a delicate calculation. Molotov knew the final decision would not be his. Only Stalin would make it. Stalin's cult of personality maintained that the General Secretary of the Communist Party of the Soviet Union was never wrong. Molotov knew better, but this time Stalin had to be right.

Nieh Ho-T'ing maneuvred his pedicab through the streets of Peking. He swerved to avoid a horse-drawn wagon, then again to keep from being run down by a lorry full of Lizards with guns. He wished he could fling a grenade into the back of the truck, but no, not now. If you couldn't be patient, you didn't deserve to win.

Men on foot got out of the way for Nieh. When they didn't move fast enough to suit him, he screamed at them: 'Move, you stupid wooden-headed son of a turtle mother!' The men he abused shouted insults back at him. They also grinned and waved, as did he. It was all good fun, and helped pass the time.

Nieh did not swear at men afoot who were dressed in Western-style clothes. Instead, he called out to them in beseeching tones: 'Ride, noble sir?' Sometimes he varied that by using the little scaly devil's phrasing: 'Ride, superior sir?' Other pedicab drivers also loudly solicited the little devils' running dogs. So did rickshaw men, who toiled between the shafts of their cars like bullocks. Anyone rich enough to dress like a foreign devil was also rich enough to pay for a ride.

Little scaly devils patrolled the streets on foot. No one asked them if they wanted a ride: people knew better. The scaly devils skittered along in squad-sized packs. They didn't go out in Peking by ones and twos: they knew better.

'Ride, superior sirs?' Nieh Ho-T'ing called to a couple of men in white shirts and ties who walked along with jackets slung over their shoulders. They looked tired, the poor running dogs.

They climbed into the back of the pedicab. 'Take us to the *Chi'i Nien Tien*,' one of them said. 'Go fast, too; we need to be there quickly.'

'Yes, sir.' Nieh Ho-T'ing started to pedal. 'The Hall of Annual Prayers it is. You pay me five dollars Mex, all right?'

'Stop the cab. We will get out,' the man answered. 'We do not need to ride with a thief. If you asked for two dollars Mex, that would still be too much.'

Nieh slowed down but did not stop. 'If I let you out, gentlemen, you will be late on your important journey. Suppose you give me four Mex fifty; I suppose, if I am stingy, my wife and children will not starve on that fare.'

'Do you hear the gall of this man?' one of the scaly devils' henchmen said to the other. 'He talks of his wife and children, but thinks nothing of ours, who will suffer if we meet his extortionate demands. Anyone who expects to get more than three dollars Mex for such a short journey would surely steal coppers from a blind beggar.'

'Rich men who refuse to share their bounty – something dreadful will surely happen to them in the next life if not in this one,' Nieh said. 'Even four Mex twenty-five would not be altogether without virtue.'

They finally settled on three Mex dollars seventy-five cents, by which time they'd nearly reached the Hall of Annual Prayer. Nieh scorned the running dogs as inept hagglers; anything over three dollars Mex was too much to pay for that ride. When he worked as a pedicab driver, he *became* a pedicab driver. Anything else, anything less, was dangerous.

The two lackeys of the scaly devils paid him, alighted, and headed off toward the tall circular building with its domed triple roof of blue tiles. Nieh slowly pedaled away, every now and then jingling a brass bell to try to lure in another fare. He soon did, a worn-looking woman with a straw basket filled to overflowing with chicken feet, rooster combs, giblets, and other bits of meat no one who could afford better would want. She told him to go to a little cookshop in one of Peking's innumerable *hutungs*, not to a fancy public building.

'Your load there will make many tasty soups,' Nieh said. The woman nodded. He hardly haggled with her at all; solidarity between proletarians came ahead of desire for profit. She noticed his generosity and smiled at him. He took note of where her eatery was. The Party needed all the friends it could find, and all the hiding places, too.

He pedaled back out onto the bigger streets, jangling his bell. He felt dispirited; those two men in Western clothes should have sent him where he wanted to go. If worse came to worst, he might have to head for the *P'an T'ao Kung* without anyone in his pedicab. Going to the Spiral Peach Palace with an empty pedicab was risky, though. He would be remarked upon. But how long could he wait for just the right fare?

'Patience,' he said out loud, reminding himself. The revolution was built one small step at a time. If anyone tried to rush it, it would fail. He picked up another meaningless fare, won the haggle without effort, and took the man where he wanted to go.

Back and forth across the city Nieh pedaled. Sweat soaked through his black cotton tunic and ran down his face from under the straw hat that shielded him from the merciless sun. That sun slid steadily across the sky. Soon it would be evening, and time for Nieh Ho-T'ing to go back to his lodging till morning came again. For a whole cadre of reasons, Nieh did not want to do that.

'You! Driver!' a fat man shouted imperiously. Anyone fat in Peking these days surely trafficked with the little scaly devils. Nieh zoomed toward him, cutting off another fellow with a pedicab whom he might also have been calling.

'Where to, superior sir?' he asked as the man climbed in.

'The *P'an T'ao Kung*,' the fat man answered. Springs creaked under him as his large, heavy fundament pressed down on the seat. 'Do you know where that is?'

'Yes – just south of the Eastern Wicket Gate,' Nieh answered. 'I can take you there for five dollars Mex.'

'Go.' The fat man waved, disdaining even to dicker. His pudgy face puffed out farther with pride. 'I am to meet with the little scaly devils in the Spiral Peach Palace, to show how my factory can work for them.'

'*Eee*, you must be a very powerful man,' Nieh said, pedaling harder. 'I will get you there, safe, never fear.' He raised his voice: 'Move, you sluggards! I have here a man who cannot waste the day.'

Behind him, his passenger shifted smugly on the padded seat, enjoying the face he gained by having his importance publicly proclaimed. Traffic did not vanish for Nieh's pedicab as he rolled east down *Hua Erh Shih* – Flower Market Street. He hadn't expected it would. Most of the people on the street would have sworn at Nieh's passenger had they dared, and desisted only for fear he might have been important enough to get them in trouble if he wanted. Some went out of their way to obstruct Nieh's progress. In their sandals, he would have done the same.

Along with the artificial flowers that gave it its name, Flower Market Street also boasted a number of shops that sold cheap costume jewelry. Hsia Shou-Tao probably would have loved the area, for a great many pretty women frequented it. Nieh Ho-T'ing frowned. Hsia was politically progressive, but he remained socially exploitive. The two should not have coexisted in the same man.

Nieh Ho-T'ing turned north off *Hua Erh Shih* toward the Spiral Peach Palace. It was not a prepossessing building, having only two small rooms, but it ws the headquarters of the little scaly devils in charge of turning the output of human factories to their own advantage.

Nieh steered the pedicab right up to the entranceway of the Spiral Peach Palace. A scaly devil stood guard outside it. Nieh's passenger dropped five silver Mex dollars into his hand, got down from the pedicab, and strutted over to the guard. He showed him a card and gained entrance to the palace.

After reaching down to the frame of the pedicab, as if to adjust the chain, Nieh also went over to the guard. 'You watch my cab, hey?' he said in slow Chinese. He pointed across the street to a couple of men selling noodles and pork and fish from two big pots. 'I go over, get some food, come back, all right?'

'All right, you go,' the guard said. 'You come back fast.'

'Oh yes, of course I will, superior sir,' Nieh answered, speaking faster now that he saw the guard understood him.

Several people crowded round the noodle-seller for late lunch, early supper, or afternoon snack. As soon as he got into the crowd, Nieh let his hat fall onto the back of his neck; the string under his chin held it in place there. Even that small change in his appearance should have been plenty to confuse the guard about exactly who he was. He asked the noodle-sellers their prices, exclaimed in horror at the answer he got, and departed.

He did not go back to reclaim the pedicab. Instead, he ducked into the first narrow little *hutung* he came upon. He took the first chance he got to doff the straw hat and throw it away. All the while, he rapidly walked south and east, turning corners every chance he got. The more distance he put between himself and the Spiral Peach Palace—

Blam! Even though he'd gone better than a half a *li*, the blast was plenty to stagger him. Men shouted. Women shrieked in alarm. Nieh looked back over his shoulder. A very satisfactorily thick cloud of smoke and dust was rising from the direction of the Spiral Peach Palace. He and his comrades had loaded more than fifty kilos of high explosive and a timer under the seat of the pedicab and in the steel tubing of the frame. The blast had surely killed the sentry. With luck, it had knocked down the palace and disposed of the little scaly devils who exploited mankind for their own advantage. The little devils needed to remember not every man could be made into a running dog or a traitor.

He came out on a street big enough to have pedicabs on it, and hailed one for the journey back to his lodging house in the western part of the city. He haggled with the driver for form's sake, but yielded sooner than he might have had his heart been in the dicker. He knew just how hard the gaunt fellow was working for his coins.

11

Teerts sat, worn and depressed, in the debriefing room at the Race's air base in southern France. He spoke into a recorder: 'On this mission, I shelled and bombed targets on the island known by the Big Ugly name of Britain. I returned to base with minimal damage to my aircraft, and inflicted substantial damage on Tosevite males and matériel.'

Elifrim, the base commander, asked, 'Did you encounter any Tosevite aircraft during your support mission over Britain?'

'Superior sir, we did,' Teerts answered. 'Our radar identified several Big Ugly killercraft circling at what is for them extreme high altitude. As they were limited to visual search, they spotted neither us nor our missiles, and were shot down without even having the opportunity to take evasive action. Later, at lower altitude, we met more skilled Tosevite raiders. Because we had exhausted our missiles, we had to engage them with cannon fire. Pilot Vemmen in my flight did have his killercraft badly damaged, while I am told two other males in different flights were shot down.'

Elifrim sighed heavily. 'These Tosevite aircraft at high altitudes ... They were merely circling? They did not seek to dive on you?'

'No, superior sir,' Teerts said. 'As I say, we knocked them down before they knew we were in the vicinity. I admit it did strike me as a little odd. Most British pilots are more alert. The ones who attacked us at low altitude certainly were. We had to fly slowly then, to enhance the accuracy of weapons delivery, and were only a little faster than their machines, and, frankly, not as maneuverable. That was a difficult encounter.'

'Your reports of losses in it are correct,' Elifrim said. 'It was made more difficult by the fact that you had expended your antiaircraft missiles, was it not?'

'Yes, certainly,' Teerts said. 'But—'

The commandant overruled him. 'But nothing, Flight Leader Teerts. Over the past several days, our forces on the ground in Britain have recovered wreckage from some of these high-altitude circles. It is their opinion that these aircraft were never piloted, that some sort of automatic device flew them to altitude and set them circling as diversionary targets, with the deliberate intent of inciting our males to expend missiles without bagging skilled Tosevite pilots in exchange.'

Teerts stared at him. 'That's – one of the most underhanded things I've ever heard,' he said slowly. 'Superior sir, we cannot afford to ignore aircraft circling above us. If they are not bluffs such as the one you describe, they dive on us and have the potential to hurt us badly.'

'I am painfully aware of this,' Elifrim said, 'and I have no good solution to offer. The British have concluded – and it is a conclusion that strikes me as reasonable – that one of their aircraft, if not piloted, is worth exchanging for one of our missiles. They can produce aircraft faster and more cheaply than we can manufacture missiles. And, by making us use missiles early and on the wrong targets, they improve their pilots' chances of survival in subsequent encounters.'

'Truth.' Teerts also sighed. 'After my experiences, no Tosevite perfidy should much surprise me.'

'No Tosevite perfidy should surprise any of us,' the commandant agreed. 'I am given to understand that no more missions will be flown in support of the northern pocket in Britain.'

'I see,' Teerts said slowly. He did, too, and didn't like what he saw. The Race had lost that battle. Before long, he feared, no flights would be going into the southern pocket of Britain, either. That one wasn't shrinking, but it wasn't getting any bigger, either. Resupply by air let it hold its own, but the cost there was high, not just in the males on the ground but in the irreplaceable males and aircraft without which the infantry and armor could not long function.

'Dismissed, Flight Leader Teerts,' the commandant said.

Teerts left the debriefing room. Another worn-looking pilot, his body paint smudged, went on to take his place. Teerts headed for the door that led outside. After his interrogations at the hands of the Nipponese, debriefing by an officer of his own kind was so mild as to be hardly worth noticing. Elifrim hadn't kicked him or slapped him or threatened him with hot things or sharp and pointed things or things that were hot and sharp and pointed or even screamed that he was a liar and would suffer for his lies. What kind of questioning was that supposed to be?

Tosev shone down brightly on this part of its third world. The weather struck Teerts as about halfway between crisp and mild – better than it was most of the time over most of the planet. Tosev 3 might not have been such a bad place ... if it weren't for the Tosevites.

Thanks to them, though, the Race was fighting not just for victory here but for survival. Thanks to them, most of the males who'd flown into Britain with such high hopes of knocking a foe out of the war would fly out wounded or wrapped in plastic for final disposal – or would never fly out at all.

With a deliberate effort of will, Teerts made himself not think about the fiasco Britain had become. But when his eye turrets swiveled in his head to let him look over the air base, he found nothing to cheer him here, either.

When the Race first came to Tosev 3, it had let its aircraft rest openly on their strips, confident the Big Uglies could not reach them. Now Teerts's killercraft, like those of his comrades – by the Emperor, like those of the Big Uglies! – huddled in earthen revetments. Antiaircraft-missile emplacements still ringed the base, but they were short of missiles. *A good thing the Big Uglies don't know how short we are*, Teerts thought. Sooner or later, though, they'd find out. They had a knack for that. They'd spent so much time and effort spying on each other that, low technology or not, they found ways to figure out what the Race was doing.

To try to make up for the missile shortage, technicians had slaved Français antiaircraft cannon to radars provided by the Race. That made the guns far more accurate than they'd been before, but still left them without either the range of the killing power the missiles had had. And the Big Uglies would eventually notice the cannons, and, worse, figure out why they were emplaced. When they did, the revetments would start paying for themselves.

The debriefing room lay not far from the edge of the air base. Teerts watched a couple of Tosevites shambling along the road that passed by the base. Even by the low standards the Big Uglies set for themselves, these were travel-worn specimens, their clothes (even they needed protection against their home planet's wretched weather) dirty and stained, their hides grimy. One of them, the bigger one, must have seen war or other misfortune somewhere, for a long scar furrowed one side of his face.

In Teerts's mind, that just made the Big Ugly uglier. Plastic surgery techniques on Tosev 3 were as backwards as the other arts on the planet, which struck Teerts as a shame, since Tosev 3 offered the unwary so many chances to maim and disfigure themselves. The Race was used to machines and systems that always worked and never hurt anybody. The Big Uglies just wanted results, and didn't much care how they got them.

Teerts understood that better than he would have before he came to Tosev 3, or, to be specific, before the Nipponese captured him. He felt the same restless craving for ginger as the Big Uglies did for everything in their lives. He wanted a taste, he wanted it now, and, as long as he got it, nothing else mattered to him.

Getting it wasn't hard, either. Many of the groundcrew males had been here since the Race seized the air base. They'd had plenty of time to make connections with Tosevites who could supply what they needed. Teerts had feared only the Nipponese knew about the herb to which they'd addicted him, but it seemed almost weed-common all over Tosev 3.

And to the Big Uglies, it was nothing more than a condiment. Teerts's mouth fell open. What irony! The Tosevites were biologically incapable of appreciating far and away the best thing their miserable planet produced.

He spied a fuel specialist and stepped out into the male's path. 'How may I help you, superior one?' the specialist asked. His words were all they should have been, but his tone was knowing, cynical.

'My engines could use a cleaning additive, I think,' Teerts answered. The code was clumsy, but worked well enough that, by all accounts, no one here had got in trouble for using ginger. There were horror stories of whole bases closed down and personnel set to punishment. When ginger-users got caught, those who caught them were disinclined to mercy.

'Think you've got some contaminants in your hydrogen line, do you, superior sir?' the specialist asked. 'Well, computer analysis should be able to tell whether you're right or wrong. Come with me; we'll check it out.'

The terminal to which the fuel specialist led Teerts was networked to all the others at the air base, and to a mainframe in one of the starships that had landed in southern France. The code the specialist punched into it had nothing to do with fuel analysis. It went somewhere into the accounting section of the mainframe.

'How far out of spec are your engines performing?' the male asked.

'At least thirty percent,' Teerts answered. He keyed the figure into the computer. It unobtrusively arranged for him to transfer thirty percent of his last pay period's income to the fuel specialist's account. No one had ever asked questions about such transactions, not at this air base. Teerts suspected that meant a real live male in the accounting department was suppressing fund transfer data to make sure no one asked questions. He wondered whether the male got paid off in money or in ginger. He knew which he would rather have had.

'There you are, superior sir. See? Analysis shows your problem's not too serious,' the fuel specialist said, continuing the charade. 'But here's your additive, just in case.' He shut down the terminal, reached into a pouch on his belt, and passed Teerts several small plastic vials filled with brownish powder.

'Ah. Thank you very much.' Teerts stowed them in one of his own pouches. As soon as he got some privacy, this cold, wet mudball of a planet would have the chance to redeem itself.

Walking with Friedrich through the streets of Lodz made Mordechai Anielewicz feel he was walking alongside a beast of prey that had developed a taste for human flesh and might turn on him at any moment. The comparison wasn't altogether accurate, but it wasn't altogether wrong, either. He didn't know what Friedrich had done in the war, or in the time between the German conquest of Poland and the invasion of the Lizards.

Whatever he'd done, Friedrich had sense enough to keep his mouth shut now, even with Jews swarming all about him. The Lodz ghetto wasn't as large as Warsaw's, but it was just as crowded and just as hungry. Next to what the ghettos had endured in Nazi times, what they had now was abundance; next to abundance, what they had now wasn't much.

Anielewicz scowled at the posters of Mordechai Chaim Rumkowski that stared down from every blank wall in the ghetto. Some of the posters were old and faded and peeling; others looked to have been put up yesterday. Rumkowski had run things here under the Nazis, and by all appearances was still running them under the Lizards. Mordechai wondered how exactly he'd managed that.

Friedrich noticed the posters, too. 'Give that old bastard hair and a little mustache and he could be Hitler,' he remarked, glancing slyly over at Anielewicz. 'How does that make you feel, Shmuel?'

Even now, surrounded by Jews, he didn't leave off his baiting. Neither did Anielewicz. It wasn't particularly vicious; it was the sort of teasing two workmen who favored rival football clubs might have exchanged. 'Sick,' Mordechai answered. That was true, for before the war he'd never imagined the Jews could produce their own vest-pocket Hitlers. But he wouldn't give Friedrich the pleasure of knowing he was irked, so he added, 'Hitler's a much uglier man.' As far as he was concerned, that was so both literally and metaphorically.

'Ah, rubbish,' Friedrich said, planting a playful elbow in his rigs. One of these days, the Nazi would do that once too often, and then something dramatic would happen. He hadn't done it quite often enough for that, not yet.

Something dramatic happened anyhow. A Jew in a cloth cap and a long black coat stopped in the middle of Lutomierska Street and stared at Friedrich. The Jew had a wide, ugly scar across the right side of his face, as if a bullet had creased him there.

He walked up to Anielewicz, waggled a forefinger in front of his nose. 'Are you a Jew?' he demanded in Yiddish.

'Yes, I'm a Jew,' Mordechai answered in the same language. He understood why the newcomer sounded a little uncertain. Even with the light brown beard on his cheeks, he looked more like a Pole than the swarthy, hook-nosed stereotype of a Jew.

'You *are* a Jew!' The newcomer clapped a hand to his forehead, almost knocking the cap from his head. He pointed at Friedrich. 'Do you know whom you're walking with? Do you know *what* you're walking with?' His hand quivered.

'I know that if there's a fire, the engine is going to come out of there and smash us flat as a couple of *latkes*,' Anielewicz answered, nodding over toward the fire station in front of which they stood. The ghetto fire engine still had petrol. As far as he knew, it was the only vehicle in the Jewish quarter of Lodz that did. He gently took the Jew by the elbow. 'Come on, let's go over on the sidewalk.' He gathered in Friedrich with his eyes. 'You come, too.'

'Where else would I go?' Friedrich said, his voice easy, amused. It was not an idle question. A lot of the young men on the street had rifles slung over their shoulders. If he ran, a shout of 'Nazi'! would surely get him caught, and likely get him shot.

The Jew with the scarred cheek seemed ready to give that shout, too. His features working, he repeated, 'Do you know what you're walking with, you who say you are a Jew?'

'Yes, I know he's a German, Mordechai answered. 'We were in a partisan band together. He may have been a Nazi soldier, but he's a good fighting man. He's given the Lizards many a kick in the arse.'

'With a German, you might be a friend. With a Nazi, even, you might be a friend,' the Jew answered. 'The world is a strange place, that I should say such a thing. But with a murderer of his kind—' He spat at Friedrich's feet.

'I said I was his comrade. I did not say I was his friend,' Anielewicz replied. The distinction sounded picayune even to him. He stared at Friedrich with a sudden, horrid suspicion. A lot of men in the partisan band had been reticent about just what they'd done before they joined it. He'd been reticent himself, when you got down to it. But a German could have some particularly good reasons for wanting to keep his mouth shut.

'His comrade.' Now the Jew spat between Mordechai's feet. 'Listen to me, *comrade*. He freighted the word with the hate and scorn a Biblical prophet might have used. 'My name is Pinchas Silberman. I am – I was – a greengrocer in Lipno. Unless you are from there, you would never have heard of it: it is a little town north of here. It had a few Jews – fifty, maybe, not a hundred. We got on well enough with our Polish neighbors.'

Silberman paused to glare at Friedrich. 'One day, after the Germans conquered Poland, in came a – platoon, is that what you call it? – of a police battalion. They gathered us up, men and women and children – me, my Yetta, Aaron, Yossel, and little Golda – and they marched us into the woods. He, your precious comrade, he was one of them. I shall take his face to the grave with me.'

'Were you ever in Lipno?' Anielewicz asked Friedrich.

'I don't know,' the German answered indifferently. 'I've been in a lot of little Polish towns.'

Silberman's voice went shrill: 'Hear the angel of death! I've been in a lot of little Polish towns,' he says. 'No doubt he was, and left not a Jew alive behind him, except by accident. Me, I was an accident. He shot my wife, he shot my daughter in her arms, he shot my boys, and then he shot me. I had a great bloody head wound' – he brought a hand up to his face—' so he and the rest of the murderers must have thought I was dead along with my family, along with all the others. They went away. I got up and I walked to Plock, which is a bigger town not far from Lipno. I was half healed before the Germans emptied out Plock. They didn't shoot everyone there. Some, the able-bodied, they shipped here to Lodz to work – to slave – for them. I was one of those. Now God is kind, and I can have my revenge.'

'*Police* battalion?' Anielewicz stared at Friedrich with undisguised loathing. The German had always acted like a soldier. He'd fought as well as any soldier, and Anielewicz had assumed he'd been a *Wehrmacht* man. That was bad enough, but he'd heard of an even known a few decent *Wehrmacht* men even before the Lizards came. A lot of them were soldiers like any other country's, just doing their jobs. But the men in the police battalions—

The most you could give them was that they didn't always kill all the Jews in the towns and villages they visited. As Silberman had said, some they drafted into slave labor instead. And he'd fought beside Friedrich, slept beside him, shared food with him, escaped from the prison camp with him. He felt sick.

'What can you say for yourself?' he demanded. Because he'd done all those things with Friedrich – because he was, in part, alive thanks to the German – he hesitated to shout for one of those armed Jews right away. He was willing, at least, to hear how the German defended himself.

Friedrich shrugged. 'Shall I tell you I'm sorry? Would it do me any good?' He shrugged again; he hadn't intended that second question to be taken seriously. After a moment, he went on, 'I'm not particularly sorry. I did what my officers told me to do. They said you Jews were enemies of the *Reich* and needed eliminating just like our other enemies. And so—' Yet another shrug.

Anielewicz had heard that same argument from Nazis the Jews had captured when they helped the Lizards drive the Germans out of Warsaw. Before he could say anything, Pinchas Silberman hissed, 'My Yetta, my boys, my baby – these were enemies? They were going to hurt you Nazi bastards?' He tried to spit in Friedrich's face, but missed. The spittle slid slowly down the brick wall of the fire station.

'Answer him!' Anielewicz barked when Friedrich kept silent for a moment.

'*Jawohl, Herr Generalfeldmarschall!*' Friedrich said, clicking his heels with exquisite irony. 'You have me. You will do as you like with me, just as I did as I liked before. When England dropped bombs on us and blew up our women and children, they thought those women and children were enemies. And, before you start shouting at me, when we dropped bombs on the English, we did the same thing, *ja*. How does that make me any different from a bomber, except I did it retail with a rifle instead of wholesale with a bombing plane?'

'But the Jews you murdered had never done anything to you, Mordechai said. He'd run into that peculiar German blind spot before, too. 'Parts of Poland used to be Germany, and some of the Jews here fought for the Kaiser in the last war. What kind of sense does it make to go slaughtering them now?'

'My officers said they were enemies. If I hadn't treated them as enemies, who knows what would have happened to me?' Friedrich said. 'And let me ask you another question, Shmuel – if you could make a giant omelet out of all the Lizards' eggs, would you do it so they'd never trouble us again?'

'A Nazi *tzaddik* we don't need,' Silberman said. 'Answer me this, Nazi *schmuck* – what would you do if you found the man who'd killed your wife and children? What would you do if you found him *and he didn't even remember doing it?*'

'I'd kill the motherfucker,' Friedrich answered. 'But I'm just a Nazi bastard, so what the devil do I know?'

Silberman looked at Mordechai. 'Out of his own mouth you heard it. He puts the noose around his neck – and if he didn't, I would.'

Friedrich looked at him, too, as if to say, *We fought together, and now you're going to kill me? You already knew part of what I was a long time ago. How much were you pretending so we didn't go for each other's throats?*

Anielwicz signed. 'Friedrich, I think we'd better go over to the Balut Market square.' The square didn't hold the market alone; the administration offices for the Lodz ghetto were there, too. Some of the Jewish fighting men there would know Mordechai was not Shmuel, a simple partisan. With some of those who knew who he really was, that would work to his advantage. Others, though, might be inclined to reveal his true name to Chaim Rumkowski – or to the Lizards.

'So you're going to tell them to hang me, too, eh?' Friedrich said.

'No,' Anielewicz said slowly. Pinchas Silberman let out an outraged howl. Ignoring it, Mordechai went on, 'Silberman here will tell what you did before the Lizards came. I'll tell what you've done since, or what I know of it. It should tilt the balance toward—'

Friedrich laughed in his face. 'You Jews took it when you were on the bottom. You think I believe you won't give it now that you're on top?'

'We believe in something you Nazis never heard of,' Anielewicz answered. 'It's called justice.'

'It's called *Scheisse*, is what it's,' Friedrich said. 'So in the name of justice, you're going to—' In the middle of the sentence, without shifting either his eyes or his feet to give warning, he hit Anielewicz in the belly and ran.

'Oof!' Mordechai said, and folded up like a concertina. *Shlemiel*, he thought as he gasped for air his lungs didn't want to give him. Friedrich might have started out in a police battalion, but he'd picked up a real soldier's skills from somewhere – and a partisan's, as well. Not letting your foe know what you were about to do until you did it ranked high on both lists.

But the German, who knew Anielewicz was dangerous, had not reckoned that Pinchas Silberman might be, too. The Jew from Lipno dashed after him, screaming 'Nazi murderer!' at the top of his lungs. Anielewicz made it up to his knees just in time to see Silberman spring on Friedrich's back. They went down in a thrashing heap. That was a fight in which Silberman was bound to get the worse of it, and quickly, but Friedrich hadn't beaten and kicked him into unconsciousness before a couple of Mauser-carrying Jewish fighting men put an end to the scrap with peremptory orders.

Silberman gasped out his story. One of the fighting men asked Friedrich a one-word question: '*Nu?*'

Friedrich gave a one-word answer: '*Ja.*'

Two rifles barked, almost in the same instant. The gunshots made men who didn't know what was going on cry out; a couple of women screamed. Pinchas Silberman burst into tears. Joy? Rage? Sadness that yet another death didn't bring back his slaughtered family? Anielewicz wondered if he knew himself. One of the Jewish fighters said to the other, 'Come on, Aaron, let's get rid of this garbage.' They dragged Friedrich away by the heels. His body left a trail of blood on Lutomierska Street.

Mordechai slowly got to his feet. He still bent at the midsection; Friedrich was strong as a mule, and had hit the way a mule kicked, too. He'd been a pretty good companion, but when you set what he'd done before against that – Anielewicz shook his head. The German had probably deserved to die, but if all the people who deserved to die on account of what they'd done in the war dropped dead at once, there'd be hardly more people left alive than after Noah's flood. The world would belong to the Lizards.

He shook his head again. The Lizards didn't have clean hands, either. He started slowly and painfully down the street. He was altogether on his own again. One way or another, though, he expected he'd manage to make a nuisance of himself.

'God, I pity the poor infantry,' Heinrich Jäger said, putting one foot in front of the other with dogged persistence. 'If I haven't lost ten kilos on this blasted hike, it's a miracle.'

'Oh, quit moaning,' Otto Skorzeny said. 'You're in the south of France, my friend, one of the prime holiday spots in all the world.'

'Yes, and now you can ask me if I give a damn, too,' Jäger said. 'When you're marching across it, it might as well be the Russian steppe. It's just about as hot as the steppe was in summer, that's certain.' He wiped the sleeve of his shirt over his face. He wore a workman's outfit, none too clean. It wouldn't fool a Frenchman into thinking he was French, but it had done well enough with the Lizards.

'It's not as cold as the steppe in winter, and that's a fact.' Skorzeny shivered melodramatically. 'It's not as ugly, either. Now shake a leg. We want to get to the next safe house before the sun goes down.' He lengthened his already long stride.

Sighing, Jäger kept up. 'Were you in such a tearing hurry that you had to march us straight past that Lizard air base the other day?' he grumbled.

'We got away with it, so quit your bellyaching,' Skorzeny said. 'The bold line is always the way to go when you mess with those scaly bastards. They're so cautious and calculating, they never look for anybody to try something risky and outrageous. They wouldn't be that stupid themselves, so they don't expect anyone else to be, either. We've taken advantage of it more than once, too.'

'All very well, but one of these days you're going to stick your *Schwantz* on the chopping block, and I don't fancy having mine there beside it,' Jäger said.

'Why not? How much use are you getting out of it now?' Skorzeny asked, laughing. He turned back toward the air base. 'And did you see the pop-eyed stare that one pilot gave us?' As best he could, he imitated a Lizard's swiveling eyes.

Jäger laughed, too, in spite of himself. Then he sobered. 'How could you tell the Lizard was a pilot?'

'Gold and blue bands on his chest and belly, yellow on the arms, and those red and purple squiggles on his head. He's medium-senior, I'd say – otherwise he'd have fewer of the purple ones. I've been studying their paint for a long time, my friend. If I say something along those lines is so, you can take it to the bank.'

'Oh, I will,' Jäger said, with some irony but not much.

They trudged on. To their right, the river Tarn chuckled between its banks. Sheep and cattle pulled up grass and shrubs in the fields. Every so often, a dog barked. A hammer rang on an anvil in a blacksmith's shop in a tiny village, just as it might have done a thousand years before.

'I'll tell you what I like about this countryside,' Jäger said suddenly. 'It's the first I've seen in the past four years that hasn't been fought over to a fare-thee-well.'

'*Aber natürlich,*' Skorzeny answered. 'And when we find a café, you can order yourself some vichyssoise, too.'

'Vichyssoise?' Jäger said, and then, a moment too late. 'Oh. *Ja.* The French gave up before we got down here, and this part of France wasn't occupied. Then the Lizards came, and they gave up to them, too. They're good at it.' He grunted. 'And a whole lot of them are alive now who would be dead if they'd fought more. Does that make them cowards, or just smarter than we are?'

'Both,' Skorzeny answered. 'Me, though, I'd rather stand up on my hind legs and not lie down till somebody knocks me over – and I'll try and kick the feet out from under him as I'm falling, too.'

Jäger thought that over, slowly nodded. A bell sounded behind him. He stepped aside to let a French policeman on a bicycle roll past. With his kepi and little dark mustache, the fellow looked like a cinema Frenchman. In the carrying basket under the handlebars, he had a couple of long, skinny loaves of bread and a bottle of red wine. Perhaps his mind was more on them than on anything else, for he rode by the Germans without a second glance.

They strode past the little hamlet of Ambialet. A long time ago, a lord had built a castle on a crag that stuck out into the Tarn. Later, a church and a monastery sprang up close by. They were all ruins now, but the hamlet remained.

Not far beyond it, they came to a farmhouse screened off from the road by a stand of willows. Ducks quacked in a pond close by. From off in a barn, a pig grunted. A stocky, stoop-shouldered Frenchman in a straw hat that almost made him look American put down the bucket he was carrying when the two Germans approached.

'*Bonjour, monsieur*,' Jäger said in his halting, heavily accented French. '*Avez-vous une cigarette? Peut-être deux?*'

'I regret, *monsieur*, that I have not even one, let alone two.' The farmer's shrug was so perfectly Gallic that Jäger forgot about the straw hat. The fellow went on, 'You will be from Uncle Henri?'

'*Oui*,' Jäger said, completing the recognition phrase. He didn't know who Uncle Henri was: perhaps a Frenchified version of Heinrich Himmler.

'Come in, both of you,' the farmer said, waving toward the building. 'My wife and daughter, they are staying with my brother-in-law down the road for a few days. They do not know why, but they are glad to visit René for a time.' He paused. 'You may call me Jacques, by the way.'

That didn't necessarily mean his name was Jacques, Jäger noted. Nonetheless, he said, '*Merci*, Jacques. I am Jean, and this is François.' Skorzeny snickered at the alias he'd been given. François was a name for a fussy head-waiter, not a scar-faced fighting man.

Jacques's eyes had heavy lids, and dark pouches under them. They were keen all the same. 'You would be Johann and Fritz, then?' he said in German a little better than Jäger's French.

'If you like,' Skorzeny answered in the same language. Jacques's smile did not quite reach those eyes. He, too, knew aliases when he heard them.

The interior of the farmhouse was gloomy, even after Jacques switched on the electric lamps. Again, Jäger reminded himself no one fought a war in this part of France for generations; the amenities that had been here before 1940 were still likely to work.

Jacques said, 'You will be hungry, yes? Marie left a stew I am to reheat for us.' He got a fire going in the hearth, hung a kettle above it. Before long, a delicious aroma filled the farmhouse. Jacques poured white wine from a large jug into three mismatched glasses. He raised his. 'For the Lizards – *merde*.'

They all drank. The wine was sharp and dry. Jäger wondered if it would tan his tongue to leather inside his mouth. Then Jacques ladled out the stew: carrots, onions, potatoes, and bits of meat in a gravy savory with spices. Jäger all but inhaled his plateful, yet Skorzeny finished ahead of him. When drunk alongside the stew, the wine was fine.

'Marvelous.' Jäger glanced over at Jacques. 'If you eat this well all the time, it's a wonder you don't weigh two hundred kilos.'

'Farming is never easy,' the Frenchman answered, 'and it has grown only harder these past few years, with no petrol at hand. A farmer can eat, yes, but he works off his food.'

'What kind of meat is it?' Skorzeny asked, looking wistfully back toward the kettle.

'Wild rabbit.' Jacques spread his hands. 'You must know how it is, *messieurs*. The livestock, it is too precious to slaughter except to keep from starving or *peut-être* for a great feast like a wedding. But I am a handy man with a snare, and so—' He spread his work-gnarled hands.

He made no more to offer Skorzeny more stew, and even the brash SS man did not get up to refill his plate uninvited. Like Jäger, he likely guessed Jacques would need what was left to feed himself after the two of them had moved on.

Jäger said, 'Thank you for putting us up here for the night.'

'*Pas de quoi,*' Jacques answered. His hand started to come up to his mouth, as if with a cigarette. Jäger had seen a lot of people make gestures like that, this past year. After a moment, the Frenchman resumed: 'Life is strange, *n'est-ce pas?* When I was a young man, I fought you *Boches*, you Germans, at Verdun, and never did I think we could be allies, your people and mine.'

'Marshal Pétain also fought at Verdun,' Skorzeny said, 'and he has worked closely with the German authorities.'

Jäger wondered how Jacques would take that. Some Frenchmen thought well of Pétain, while to others he was a symbol of surrender and collaboration. Jacques only shrugged and said, 'It is late. I will get your blankets.' He took for granted that soldiers would have no trouble sleeping on the floor. At the moment, Jäger would have no trouble sleeping on a bed of nails.

The blankets were rough, scratchy wool. The one Jäger wrapped around himself smelled of a woman's sweat and faintly of rose water. He wondered whether it belonged to Jacques's wife or his daughter, and knew he couldn't ask.

Skorzeny had already started snoring. Jäger lay awake a while, trying to remember how long it had been since he'd lain with a woman. Occasional visits to a brothel didn't really count, except to relieve pressure like the safety valve of a steam engine. The last one that mattered had been Ludmila Gorbunova. He sighed – most of a year now. Too long.

Breakfast the next morning was slabs of bread cut from a long, thin loaf like those the policeman had carried in his bicycle basket. Jäger and Skorzeny washed the bread down with more white wine. 'You might prefer coffee, I know,' Jacques said, 'but—' His Gallic shrug was eloquent.

'By me, wine is plenty good,' Skorzeny said. Jäger wasn't so sure he agreed. He didn't make a habit of drinking part of his breakfast, and suspected the wine would leave him logy and slow. Skorzeny picked up the loaf from which Jacques had taken slices. 'We'll finish this off at lunch, if you don't mind.'

His tone said Jacques had better not mind. The Frenchman shrugged again. Jäger would have taken the bread, too, but he would have been more circumspect about how he did it. Circumspection, however, did not seem to be part of Skorzeny's repertoire.

To smooth things over, Jäger asked, 'How far to Albi, Jacques?'

'Twenty kilometers, perhaps twenty-five,' the farmer answered indifferently. Jäger projected a mental map of the territory inside his head. The answer sounded about right. A good day's hike, especially for a man who was used to letting panzers haul him around.

The sun beat in his face and Skorzeny's when they set out. Sweat started running down his cheeks almost at once. *The wine*, he thought, annoyed. But it was not just the wine. The air hung thick and breathless; he had to push through it, as if through gauze, to move ahead. When the sun rose higher in the sky, the day would be savagely hot.

A stream of Lizard lorries came up the road toward Jäger and Skorzeny. They scrambled off onto the verge: what were a couple of human beings dead by the side of the road to the Lizards? He kicked at the tarmac. If a couple of Russian civilians hadn't gotten out of the way of a German motor convey, what would have happened to them? Probably the same thing.

Skorzeny hadn't been thinking about civilians of any sort. He said, 'You know what they're hauling in those lorries?'

'If it isn't gas masks, one of us will be the most surprised man in France, and the other will be runner-up,' Jäger answered.

'How right you are,' Skorzeny said, chuckling. 'Our job is to make sure they don't keep shipping them out of their in such great lots.'

He sounded as if that posed no more problems than hiking along this all but deserted road. Maybe he even believed it. After his coups – playing Prometheus by stealing explosive metal from the Lizards, absconding with Mussolini from right under their snouts, doing the same with a Lizard panzer, and driving the aliens out of Split and out of all of Croatia – he had a right to be confident. There was, however, a difference between confidence and arrogance. Jäger thought so, anyhow. Skorzeny might have had other ideas.

They rested for a while in the heat of midday, going down to the banks of the Tarn to drink some water and to splash some on their faces. Then, under the shade of a spreading oak, they shared the bread Skorzeny had appropriated from Jacques. A kingfisher dived into the river with a splash. Somewhere back in the brush, a bee-eater took off with a cry of '*Quilp, quilp!*'

'I should have lifted some of that wine, too,' Skorzeny said. 'God only knows how many Frenchmen have been pissing in this river, or what we're liable to catch from drinking out of it.'

'I used to worry about that, too,' Jäger answered. 'I still do, but not as much. Do it often enough and you stop thinking about it.' He shook his head. 'Like you stop thinking about killing people, but on a smaller scale, if you know what I mean.'

Skorzeny's big head bobbed up and down. 'I like that. It's true, too, no doubt about it.'

Cautiously, Jäger said, 'Like killing Jews, too, don't you think, Skorzeny? The more you do, the easier it gets.' There were just the two of them, here in the quiet of southern France. If you couldn't speak your mind, or at least part of it, here, where could you? And if you couldn't speak your mind anywhere, was life really worth living? Were you a man or just a mindless machine?

'Don't start in on me about that,' Skorzeny said. Now he tossed his head like a man shaking flies. 'I didn't have anything to do with it. I fought alongside those Jews in Russia, remember, same as you did, when we raided the Lizards for their explosive metal.'

'I remember,' Jäger said. 'I don't have anything to do with—' He stopped. How many of the prisoners extracting uranium from the failed nuclear pile outside Hechingen and bringing it to Schloss Hohentübingen had been Jews? A good many, without a doubt. He might not have condemned them himself, but he'd exploited them once they were condemned. He tried again: 'When the *Reich's* hands are dirty, how can anyone's hands be clean?'

'They can't,' Skorzeny said placidly. 'War is a filthy business, and it dirties everything it touches. The whole business with the Jews is just part of that. Christ on His cross, Jäger, are you going to feel clean after we give Albi our little dose of joy and good tidings?'

'That's different.' Jäger stuck out his chin and looked stubborn. 'The Lizards can shoot back – they shoot better than we do. But marching the Jews up to a pit and shooting them a row at a time – or the camps in Poland ... People will remember that sort of thing for a thousand years.'

'Who remembers the Armenians the Turks killed in the last war?' Skorzeny said. 'When they're gone, they're gone.' He rubbed his dry palms back and forth, as if washing his hands.

Jäger couldn't match that callousness. 'Even if you were right—'

'I *am* right,' Skorzeny broke in. 'Who worries about the Carthaginians these days? Or, for that matter, about the – what's the right name for them, *Herr Doktor Professor* of archaeology? – the Albigensians, that's it, from the town just ahead?'

'Even if you were right?' Jäger repeated, 'they aren't all gone and they won't be all gone, not with the Lizards holding Poland. And those ones who are left will see to it that our name stays black forever.'

'If we win the war, it doesn't matter. And if we lose the war, it doesn't matter, either.' Skorzeny climbed to his feet. 'Come on. We'll get into Albi by sundown, and then it's just a matter of waiting for our toys to arrive.'

That closed out the possibility of more talk. Jäger also got up. *I shouldn't have expected anything else*, he told himself. Most German officers wouldn't talk about Jews at all. In a way, Skorzeny's candor was an improvement. But only in a way. Sighing, Jäger tramped on toward Albi.

Liu Han felt invisible. With a wicker basket in her hand, she could wander from one of Peking's markets to the next without being noticed. She was just one more woman among thousands, maybe millions. No one paid the least attention to her, any more than you paid attention to one particular flea among the many on a dog's back.

'Think of yourself as a flea,' Nieh Ho-T'ing had told her. 'You may be tiny, but your bite can draw blood.'

Liu Hun was sick to death of being a flea. She was sick to death of being invisible. She'd been invisible all her life. She wanted to do something bold and prominent, something to make the scaly devils regret they'd ever interfered with her. Of course, the one time she'd not been invisible was when she'd been in the little devils' clutches. She prayed to the Amida Buddha and any other god or spirit who would listen that she never attain such visibility again.

'*Bok choi*, very fresh!' a merchant bawled in her ear. Others hawked barley, rice, millet, wheat, poultry, pork, spices – any sort of food or condiment you could imagine.

Back in another market, somebody had been selling canned goods: some Chinese, others made by foreign devils with their foods inside. Liu Han's gorge rose, thinking about those. The little scaly devils had kept her alive with them while they held her prisoner on the plane that never came down. If she tasted them again, she would remember that time, and she wanted to forget. The only good that had come from it was her baby, and it was stolen and Bobby Fiore, its father, dead.

She'd stayed close to the can salesman for some time, though. Canned goods were scarce in Peking these days, especially canned goods produced by foreign devils. To show a stock, the fellow who was selling them had to have connections with the little scaly devils. Maybe they would come around to his stall – and if they did, she would eavesdrop. Nieh Ho-T'ing had told her he'd used Bobby Fiore the same way in Shanghai; people who could make sense of the scaly devils' language were few and far between.

But the can seller, though he might have been what Nieh called a running dog, was no fool. 'You, woman!' he shouted at Liu Han. 'Do you want to buy something, or are you spying on me?'

'I am just resting here for a moment, sir,' Liu Han answered in a small voice. 'I cannot afford your excellent canned goods, I fear.' That was true; he asked exorbitant prices. For good measure, she added, 'I wish I could,' which was a crashing lie.

She did not mollify the can seller. 'Go rest somewhere else,' he said, shaking his fist. 'I think you are telling lies. If I see you again, I will set the police on you.' He was a running dog, then; the

Peking police, like police in any Chinese city, were the tools of those in power.

Liu Han retreated across the little market square to the edge of a *hutung*. She pointed back at the man who sold cans, screeched, 'See the fool with his nose up the little devils' back passage!' as loud as she could, and vanished down the alleyway. With a little luck, she'd have created ill will between the can seller and his neighbors in the market, maybe even cost him some customers.

She couldn't reckon it a victory, though, because he'd driven her away before any scaly devils showed up at his stall. She bought some *liang kao* from a man with a basket of them – rice cakes stuffed with mashed beans and peas and served with sweet syrup – ate them and then left the *hutungs* for Peking's more prominent avenues. The scaly devils did not usually venture into the lanes and alleys of the city. If she wanted to find out what they were doing, she would have to go where they were.

Sure enough, when she came out on the *Ta Cha La*, the Street of Large Gateposts, she found scaly devils aplenty. She was not surprised' the street was full of fancy silk shops and led to neighborhoods where fine eateries abounded.

But the scaly devils bought no silks and sought no restaurants. Instead, they gathered several deep around a mountebank whose show might have enlivened a child's birthday party. 'See how fat my mules are, and how warm my carriages!' the fellow cried.

Because the little devils were so short, Liu Han was able to see over them to the folding table the fellow had set up. His carriages were about six inches long, made of cast-off bits of cardboard, and used thin sticks for axles. The little scaly devils hissed with excitement as he pulled out a tin can from the box that held his paraphernalia. Out of the can he took one large, black dung beetle after another. He deftly fastened them to the carriages with reins of thread. They pulled those carriages – some of which resembled old-fashioned mule carts, others Peking water wagons – around and around the tabletop; every so often, he had to use a forefinger to keep his steeds from falling off the edge.

Even in the village where Liu Han had grown up, a beetle-cart show was nothing out of the ordinary. By the way the scaly devils reacted, though, they'd never seen anything like it in their lives. Some of them let their mouths hang open in mirth, while others nudged each other and exclaimed over the spectacle. 'They make even pests into beasts of burden,' one of the little devils said.

'See, that one has upset the cart. Look at its little legs wave as it lies on its back,' another replied. He tossed a dollar Mex, and then another, to the mountebank. His comrades also showered the fellow with silver.

The little devils paid Liu Han no attention. The only way they would have noticed her was if she'd got in their way while they were watching the antics of the beetles. But those antics had so fascinated them, they weren't talking about anything else. After a while, Liu Han decided she wouldn't hear anything worthwhile here. The *Ta Cha La* was full of scaly devils. She headed up it toward the next group she saw.

When she got to them, she discovered they were all staring at a monkey circus going through its paces. Like most of its kind, the circus also included a Pekinese dog and a trained sheep. Both men who ran it clanged brass gongs to draw a bigger crowd.

Growing impatient, one of the little scaly devils said, 'You show us these creatures, what they do, *now*.'

The two men bowed nervously and obeyed. The monkey, dressed in a red satin jacket, capered about. It put on masks, one after another, cued by more taps on the gong.

'See how it looks like a little Tosevite,' one of the scaly devils said in his own language, pointing to the monkey. His mouth opened in mirth.

The little devil beside him said, 'It's even uglier than the Big Uglies, I think. All that fuzz all over it—' He shuddered in fastidious disgust.

'I don't know,' yet another little scaly devil said. 'It has a tail, at least. I think the Big Uglies look funny without them.'

Liu Han pretended she was watching the show without listening to the little devils. She'd known they had no proper respect for mankind – were that not so, they never would have treated her as they had. But hearing their scorn grated. Liu Han rocked slowly back and forth. *You will pay*, she thought. *Oh, how you will pay for all you've done to me.* But how to make them pay? Vowing revenge was easy, getting it something else again.

The monkey went through the rest of its turns, imitating a wheelbarrow man and a rickshaw puller and then playing on a swing at the top of a bamboo pole. The little devils showered the men who ran the monkey circus with coins. After the monkey itself came the Pekinese. It jumped through hoops of different sizes that the men held at varying heights above the ground. Even in her village, Liu Han had seen dogs that could leap much higher. But the little scaly devils admired the Pekinese as much as they had the monkey.

For the finale, the sheep came out and the monkey sprang onto its back, riding it around in circles like a jockey on a racehorse. The little scaly devils had only to look about them to see men on horseback. They caught the analogy, too, and laughed harder than ever. When at last the show as over, they gave the two men who ran it still more silver – they seemed to have an unlimited supply – and went off in search of further entertainment.

'*Eee*,' one of the men said, letting Mex dollars jingle through his fingers, 'I used to hate the little scaly devils like everyone else, but they are making us rich.'

The other animal trainer did not answer. He picked up the gong and started pounding on it, trying to lure more scaly devils to the next show.

He had competition. A little way up the street, a fellow with a horn was playing old, familiar tunes. He didn't play very well, but skill on the trumpet was not how he made his living: it was just the traditional signal a fellow who exhibited trained mice used to draw a crowd.

And, sure enough, a crowd gathered. It had children in it, and old people with time on their hands, but also a good many little scaly devils. Because the little devils stood and watched, so did Liu Han.

'Hello, hello, hello!' the mouse show man boomed jovially. He was wearing a square wooden box, held on by a shoulder strap. From the box rose a wooden pole two feet high, on top of which were mounted a pagoda, a wooden fish, a little hanging bucket made of tin, and a hollow wooden peach. 'Do you want to see my little friends perform?'

'Yes!' the children shouted, loud and shrill as a flock of starlings. The little scaly devils who understood Chinese added their hissing voices to the cries.

'All right, then,' the man said. 'You don't have any cats, do you?' He looked sly. 'If you do, kindly keep them in your pockets till we're finished.'

He waited till the children's giggles and the silent laughter of the scaly devils subsided, then rapped three times on the side of the box. It had a latched hole in the front. He lifted the latch. Four white mice came out and climbed a little ladder of string and sticks of bamboo. They went through their paces on the apparatus, scrambling down into the bucket and swinging in it, pulling the fish up by the string that held it, running to the top of the pagoda and jumping inside, and scrambling into the peach and peering out, whiskers quivering, little red eyes aglow.

The mouse show man said, 'How'd you like to bite down and find *that* inside your peach?' The children giggled once more.

The little scaly devils, though, did not react to that with mirth. One of them said, 'The Big Uglies have filthy habits – always parasites in their food.'

'Truth,' another said. 'And they *joke* about it.'

'They are disgusting,' a third chimed in, 'but they also manage to be entertaining. We don't have beast-shows back on Home to match these. Who would have thought animals – especially Tosevite animals – could learn to do so many interesting things? I spend as much free time as I can watching them.'

'And I,' said the scaly devil who had spoken second. A couple of others sputtered agreement.

Liu Han watched the performing mice a minute or two more. Then she tossed the man who exhibited them a few coppers and walked down the *Ta Cha La*, thinking hard. More little devils congregated in a vacant lot from which the wreckage of a shop had been cleared away. A trained bear was going through its run of tricks there. The scaly devils exclaimed as it wielded a heavy wooden sword with a long handle. Liu Han walked by, hardly noticing.

Nieh Ho-T'ing was always looking for ways to get close to the little scaly devils, the better to make their lives miserable. If trained animals fascinated them so, a troupe of men with such performers might well gain access even to important males, or groups of important males. Anyone who showed Nieh a new way to do that would gain credit for it.

Liu Han scratched her head. She was sure she had a good idea, but how could she use it to best advantage? She was no longer the naive peasant woman she'd been when the little devils carried her away from her village. Too much had happened to her since. If she could, she would take her fate back into her own hands.

'Not to be a puppet,' she said. A man with a thin wisp of white beard turned and gave her a curious look. She didn't care. Nieh Ho-T'ing hadn't treated her badly; he'd probably treated her better than anyone except Bobby Fiore. But one of the reasons he did treat her so was that he found her a tool to fit his hand. If she was lucky, if she was careful, maybe she could make him treat her as someone to be reckoned with.

After the lamplit gloom of the *Krom*, George Bagnall had to blink and wait for his eyes to adjust to daylight. Even after the adjustment, he looked about curiously. Something about the quality of the light, the color of the sky, had changed, ever so slightly. The day was bright and warm, and yet—

When Bagnall remarked on that, Jerome Jones nodded and said, 'I noticed it, too, the other day. Somebody Up There' – the capitals were quite audible – 'is telling us summer shan't last forever.' He looked wistful. 'Now that it's beginning to go, it seems hardly to have been here at all.'

'Weren't you the blighter who swore to us Pskov had a mild climate by Russian standards!' Ken Embry demanded with mock fierceness. 'This, as I recall, while we were flying above endless snow and a frozen lake.'

'By Russian standards, Pskov *does* have a mild climate,' Jones protested. 'Set alongside Moscow, it's very pleasant. Set alongside Arkhangelsk, it's like Havana or New Delhi.'

'Set alongside Arkhangelsk, by all accounts, the bloody South Pole looks like a holiday resort,' Embry said. 'I knew Russian standards in matters of weather were elastic before we got here; I simply hadn't realized how much stretch the elastic had to it: rather like a fat man's underclothes, I'd say.'

'That may end up working to our advantage,' Bagnall said. 'The Lizards like Russian winter even less than we do. We should be able to push them farther south of the city.'

'A consummation devoutly to be wished,' Ken Embry leered at him. 'In aid of which, when will they be posting the banns for you and that little Russian flier?'

'Oh, give over such nonsense.' Bagnall kicked a clod of dirt down the street. 'Nothing is going on between us.'

The other two Englishmen snorted, either disbelieving or affecting disbelief. Then Jerome Jones sighed. 'I wish I thought you were lying. That might make Tatiana stop throwing her fair white body in your direction. We've had rows about it, once or twice.' He kicked moodily at the dirt.

'And?' Embry asked. 'Leaving us in suspense that way is bad form.'

'And nothing,' Jones answered. 'Tatiana does what she bloody well pleases. If one were mad enough to try stopping her, she'd blow off his head.'

Neither of the other Englishmen thought that was in any way figurative language. Bagnall said, 'Whoever came up with "The female of the species is more deadly than the male" must have had your fair Russian sniper in mind.'

'Too true.' Jones sighed again. He glanced sidelong at Bagnall. 'That's why she's keen on you, you know: she thinks you're better at killing than I am – I'm just a radarman, after all. The idea makes her motor go.'

Bagnall sent him a sympathetic look. 'Old chap, I don't mean to give offense, but have you never wondered if you'd be better off without her company?'

'Oh, many a time,' Jones said feelingly.

'Well, then?' Bagnall asked when the radarman failed to draw the obvious conclusion.

Now Jones looked shamefaced. 'For one thing, if I give her the boot, she's liable to give me something out of the barrel of that sniper's rifle of hers.' He touched a forefinger to a spot just above the bridge of his nose, as if to say the bullet would go in there.

'Something to that, I expect,' Ken Embry said. 'But a "for one thing" generally implies a "for another," what? Rather like a *mén* implying a *dé*, if you've read your Greek like a good fellow.'

'*Nai, malista,*' Jones said, which made all three Englishmen laugh. Bagnall had trouble imagining anything further removed from the classical world than Pskov during wartime. They walked on for another few steps. Slowly, reluctantly, Jerome Jones continued, 'Yes, there's a "for another." The other reason I don't send her packing is that – that – I seem to have fallen in love with her.' He waited for his companions to mock him.

Now it was Bagnall's turn to sigh. He set a sympathetic hand on Jones's shoulder. The radarman quivered under his touch like a restive horse. Bagnall said, 'Steady, there. If we're being classical, let's be downright Socratic and define our terms, shall we? Are you truly in love with her, or is it just that she pleases you in the kip?'

Jerome Jones turned a vermilion not commonly seen this side of a sunset. *How young he is,* Bagnall thought from his superior altitude of three or four years. 'How does one tell the difference?' the radarman asked plaintively.

'Always a good question,' Embry said with a cynical chuckle.

'Let's try answering it, then,' Bagnall said, for Jones looked not only very young but very lost: he'd meant the question with every fiber of his being. Bagnall went on, 'Socratics we are, having another go at the *Symposium*.'

That pleased Jones. Embry chuckled again and said, 'Fair young Alcibiades is right out.'

'Fair young Tatiana is quite enough trouble all on her own,' Jones said. 'She and Alcibiades, they'd deserve each other.'

'Here's one fast clue to your feelings, for starters,' Bagnall said: 'If you only want to have anything to do with your possibly beloved when the two of you are naked between the sheets, that should tell you something about your state of mind.'

'So it should.' The radarman looked thoughtful. 'Not as simple as that, I'm afraid; I wish to heaven it were. But I like being around her, whether we're' – he coughed – 'or not. It's rather like setting up a tent next to a tiger's lair: you never know what will happen next, but it's apt to be something exciting.'

'And you're liable to end up as the *hors d'oeuvres*,' Embry put in.

Bagnall waved the pilot to silence. 'How do you think she feels about you, Jones?' he asked.

Jerome Jones's face furrowed with thought. 'I am of the opinion her fidelity leaves something to be desired,' he said, to which Bagnall could but nod. Jones went on, 'She set her cap at me, not the other way round. This bloody country – I'd be afraid to chat up a girl, because next thing you know, you'd be talking to the NKVD instead.' He shivered. 'Some of my university chums, they weren't just pink, they were red. If any of them had actually seen Russia, that wouldn't have lasted long, and there's the God's truth.'

'You're certain to be right about that,' Bagnall said. 'The same thing has occurred to me, oh, once or twice during our delightful sojourn here. But it's not to the point now. That centers on the fair Tatiana.'

'I know.' Jones walked on for several paces without continuing.

Bagnall waited for him to say something, anything, that would clarify what he felt, what Tatiana felt, and might even help all of them get out of their present complications without falling into new ones that were worse. He realized that was asking a lot, but he'd never wanted Tatiana to set her sights on him.

After a bit, the radarman said, 'I chased a lot of skirt back in England; I don't think there was a barmaid in any pub I went into whom I didn't try to chat up. But we all know there's a deal of difference between chasing it and catching it, don't we?' He chuckled wryly. 'And so, when we got here and I had this gorgeous creature chasing me, it made me fell about ten feet high. And, of course—' He didn't go on, but his expression was eloquent.

Ken Embry put that expression into words: 'When you're sleeping with a pretty woman, there is a certain natural disinclination to do anything which will result in your not sleeping with her in future.'

'Well, yes,' Jones said, coloring a little. 'In her own bloodthirsty way, I think, Tatiana is fond enough of me, too. Speaking a bit of Russian does me no harm there. But she keeps complaining I'm too soft to quite suit her, that she'd like me better if I stuck a knife between my teeth and crawled about through the bushes slitting Lizards' throats.'

Bagnall nodded. His own rugged masculine charm (if any) hadn't been what drew Tatiana to him. He knew that perfectly well. Tatiana wanted him because she thought he was good at hurting the Lizards. She hadn't made any bones about it, either.

Embry said, 'With that cast of mind, it's a miracle she didn't throw in her lot with a Jerry.'

'If she hadn't been trying to pot them before the Lizards came, she would have done just that, my guess is,' Jones said. 'But she hates them worse than any other Russian I've ever seen, and she thinks her own menfolk are a pack of swine. Which left – me. Except nowadays I'm not good enough, either.'

'Maybe I should make a play for Senior Lieutenant Gorbunova,' Bagnall said meditatively. 'It's the easiest way I can think of to get Tatiana out of my hair for good.'

'Except that if she really is out to have you come hell or high water, losing you to Ludmila is liable to endanger that young lady,' Ken Embry said.

'There I have my doubts,' Bagnall said. 'Ludmila is not as outwardly ferocious as Tatiana, that I grant you, but she can take care of herself.'

'I should hope so,' Jerome Jones burst out. 'How many combat missions has she flown in that rickety little biplane of hers? More than I like to think about, that's certain. You wouldn't get me up in the air in one of those things, especially not where people are trying to shoot me down.'

'Amen to that,' Bagnall said. 'She doesn't go any too high in the air, either – leaves herself a target for any bloke on the ground with a rifle.' He knew she would have been a target for worse things than rifle fire had she strayed high enough for radar to pick her up, but the idea of being vulnerable to simple infantry weapons chilled him to the marrow.

'If she can take care of herself, you really should make a play for her,' Embry said. 'That would get you out of harm's way, and might even reconcile Tatiana to Jones here. See what a Leonora Eyles I'm getting to be?' he added, naming the advice columnist for *Women's Own* magazine.

'This ointment does have one fly in it,' Jerome Jones said, 'namely, the Jerry who flew into Pskov with our intrepid pilot: Schultz, that's what he's called. Have you never seen him casting sheep's eyes at her?'

'I've seen that, yes,' Bagnall said, 'but I've never seen Ludmila casting any back his way. He's a rugged specimen, but I'm not afraid of him.' He rubbed his chin. 'I'd not care to put us in a bad odor with the Germans, either, though. If we're not seen to be honest brokers between the Nazis and the Reds, everything we've accomplished goes up in smoke – and so, very likely does Pskov.'

'Bloody hell of a thing,' Ken Embry remarked, 'when you can't even make a play for a pretty girl for fear of causing an international incident.'

'International incidents be damned,' Bagnall said. 'I don't care about that aspect of it at all. But if making a play for a pretty girl will get me killed and this town blown up and around my ears, that does make me thoughtful, I admit.'

'Nice to know something can,' Embry said with a grin.

South of Pskov, antiaircraft guns began to hammer. A moment later, cannon inside the city started throwing shells into the air. With training instilled when the *Luftwaffe* had been pounding England, the three RAF men leaped into the nearest hole in the ground: a large bomb crater.

The crater was muddy at the bottom, but Bagnall didn't care about that, not when a couple of Lizard jets were screaming overhead, low enough that their banshee wail all but deafened him. As he buried his face in the cool, wet dirt, he tried to remember what sort of targets were nearby. In a mechanized war, such matters determined who lived and who died.

Bombs raining down made the ground shake. Bagnall had never experienced an earthquake, but was of the opinion that being bombed made a satisfactory substitute.

Still pursued by shells, the Lizard fighter-bombers streaked away to the north. Every so often, the antiaircraft gunners got lucky and brought down a Lizard plane. They expended a great whacking lot of shells between kills, though.

Shrapnel pattered down like hot, jagged hailstones. Bagnall wished for a tin hat. Shrapnel wouldn't tear you into gory rags the way bomb fragments did; it wasn't going fast enough. But a big chunk could fracture your skull or do other unpleasant things to the one and only wonderful and precious body you ever got.

When the AA guns fell silent and the rain of machined brass and steel stopped, Ken Embry got to his feet and began brushing dirt and muck from his clothes. The other two Englishmen followed rather more slowly.

'All in a day's work,' Embry said. 'Shall we brew up some of the Russians' alleged tea when we get back to our digs?'

'Why not?' Bagnall answered. His heart was still pounding in animal response to the bombing, but his mind remained untroubled and collected. As Embry had said, it was all in a day's work – and that struck Bagnall as the most damning indictment of all.

12

Rance Auerbach hated everything about Lamar, Colorado. It reminded him all too vividly of the medium-small west Texas town where he'd grown up, and which he'd left as soon as he could. That would have been bad enough all by itself. But just being in Lamar also reminded him the Lizards had thrown him and his men out of Lakin, Kansas.

That being so, he sneered at everything pertaining to Lamar. The town was dirtier than it had been when he and his force sallied against Lakin. It smelled of horse manure. Normally, that smell bothered him not in the least: he was a cavalryman, after all. There wasn't a town in the United States that didn't smell of horse manure nowadays, either. Auerbach was determined not to let facts get between him and his anger.

One thing Lamar did boast was a goodly number of watering holes. What they served these days was moonshine, liquor so raw it would have made better disinfectant than booze. No one who drank it complained, not with nothing better available.

Auerbach would not have imagined a small town like Lamar could hold surprises, but he was proved wrong about that. Coming out of one of the local watering holes was a cavalry trooper who filled a uniform in ways the Quartermaster General's Office never would have imagined before the Lizards landed.

Seeing him, the trooper snapped to attention. 'Captain Auerbach!' she said.

'At ease, Private,' Rance answered. 'We're both off duty right this minute.' He shook his head in bemusement. 'And since we are off duty, do you mind if I still call you Rachel?'

'No, sir, not at all,' Rachel Hines answered, smiling.

Auerbach shook his head again. He could have picked her up with one hand, but somehow she still looked like a cavalry trooper, even if she wasn't exactly a cavalryman. She lacked the devil-may-care relish for danger some of his men had, but she didn't look as if she'd flinch from it, and she did look as if she wouldn't lose her head while it was going on. But all of those things, in a way, were beside the point. He came to the point: 'How the devil did you talk Colonel Nordenskold into letting you enlist?'

She smiled again. 'You promise you won't tell anybody else?' When Auerbach nodded, she lowered her voice and went on, 'He tried putting his hand where it didn't belong, and I told him that if he did it again I'd kick him right in the nuts – if he had any, that is.'

Auerbach knew he was gaping, but couldn't help it. That wasn't the way he'd imagined Rachel Hines persuading the colonel to sign her up: just the opposite, in fact. If she'd been smart enough to study the ground and change her plan of attack after she saw that a blatant come-on hadn't worked with Auerbach, she had more brains than he'd figured. 'My hat's off to you,' he said, and fit action to word. 'It took a little more than that, though, didn't it?'

'I showed him I could ride, I showed him I could shoot, I showed him I could shut up and take orders,' she answered. 'He was looking for people who could do those things, and we're so short of the ones who can that he didn't much care if I had to go at my uniform with scissors and needle and thread before it'd fit right.'

He looked her up and down. 'If you don't mind my saying so – if it won't make you kick like a bronc – it fits you just fine.'

'Captain, you can say whatever you please,' she answered. 'You got me out of Lakin, out from under the Lizards' thumbs. I owe you more than I can figure out how to pay you back for that.'

Back when she'd offered him a roll in the hay to get what she wanted, he hadn't been interested. Now he was – now she sounded interested in him as a person, not a stepping stone. But if she was bound and determined to be a soldier, she'd be a hell of a lot better off not going to bed with an officer. If women were going to fight, the fewer the rules that got bent out of shape, the better for everybody, women and men.

Instead of making any suggestions, then, Auerbach asked, 'How's Penny getting along these days? I hadn't seen you since I came back here, and I haven't seen her, either.'

Rachel Hines's sunny face clouded. 'She's not so good, Captain. She's got a room in the rooming house off the street here, and she mostly just stays in it. Even when she does come out, it's almost like you're watching a ghost, not a real person, if you know what I mean. Like she's here but not quite really all here.'

'That's what I saw before,' Auerbach said glumly. 'I was hoping she'd started to snap out of it by now.'

'Me, too,' Rachel said. 'She was so much fun to be with when we were in high school together.' She came to an abrupt halt. Nothing much was left of the Kearny County Consolidated High School, not after the Lizards set up their local base there, the Americans drove them out of it, and then they came back and pushed the Americans back toward the Kansas-Colorado line.

As he had before, Rance wondered what would happen to the generation of kids whose schooling the Lizards had interrupted. Even if mankind won, making up for lost time wouldn't be easy. If the Lizards won, odds were that nobody would have an education ever again.

He didn't care to think about that. He didn't care to think about a lot of the ways the war was going. 'Maybe I ought to go over there and see her,' he said after a moment. 'It's my fault she's here, after all – my fault you're here, too, come to that.'

'I wouldn't call it a fault, Captain,' Rachel Hines said. 'If we hadn't come with you, we'd still be back in Lakin, doing what the Lizards told us. Anything is better than that.'

'Tell it to – what was his name? – Wendell Summers,' Auerbach answered harshly. 'He hadn't tried to get out of Lakin, he'd be alive back there today.'

'We all knew there was a chance of that when we went with you people – it was a chance we all wanted to take.' Auerbach didn't know whether Rachel had seen action, but she talked and shrugged like a veteran. She continued, 'Penny has taken that hard, I will say.'

'I know.' Auerbach kicked at the sidewalk. 'Maybe she won't want to see me at all. God knows I couldn't blame her for that.'

'The worst thing she can tell you is no,' Rachel said. 'If she does, how are you worse off? But if she doesn't, you may do her some good.' She saluted again and headed up the street. Auerbach turned to watch her go, then laughed at himself. He didn't remember admiring a cavalry trooper's backside before.

'And a good thing, too,' he said with a snort. He walked over to the rooming house where Penny Summers was staying. The place was always packed, but with a shifting population: refugees who had been there for a while headed farther west into more securely held territory, while a continuous stream of newcomers from Kansas took their place. Penny had kept her room ever since she came from Lakin, which made her well-nigh unique.

Auerbach's nose twitched as he walked upstairs. The rooming house smelled of unwashed bodies, garbage, and stale piss. If you bottled the odor, you'd call it something like Essence of Despair. No sergeant worth his stripes would have tolerated a tenth of it for a second. But the Army had all it could handle fighting the Lizards and trying to keep itself on its feet. The civilian part of Lamar had been left to sink or swim on its own. He didn't think that was good management, but he didn't feel like belling the cat, either.

He knocked on Penny Summers's door. He didn't know whether she'd be there or not. A lot of civilians in Lamar spent their days working for the Army, one way or another. He hadn't seen Penny busy with any of that, though, and Lamar was small enough that he thought he would have if she'd been doing it.

Somewhere down the hall, a baby started to scream. The sound ground at Auerbach's nerves like a dentist's drill digging into a molar. You had to be crazy to want to bring up a kid in times like these. Of course, just because you were bringing up a kid didn't necessarily mean you wanted one, only that you had one.

He knocked on the door again. He was about to turn and go (a prospect not altogether unwelcome, because the baby was doing a pretty good impression of the noise that came from a Lizard jet fighter engine) when Penny Summers opened it. She looked surprised to see him. He got the idea she would have looked surprised to see anyone.

'Captain Auerbach,' she said, and gestured vaguely. 'Come in.'

The room was cramped and, even with the window open, stifingly hot. Dust lay think on every surface. Auerbach thought about shouting at her like a tough sergeant, but decided it would do more harm than good. Shouting wouldn't snap her out of the state she was in. He didn't know what would, but he was sure of that.

He said, 'I'm worried about you. You should be out and doing things, not sitting here cooped up like a canary in a cage. What do you do all day, anyhow?' That vague gesture again. 'I sit, I sew sometimes. I read my Bible.' She pointed to the book with the limp leatherette covers and gold leaf that sat on the little table next to the bed.

'It's not enough,' he said. 'There's a whole big world out there.'

'I don't want any part of it,' she answered, laughing. 'There are all sorts of worlds out there. The Lizards showed us that, didn't they?' He'd never heard her laugh, not since her father was blown to bits before her eyes, but this was so bitter he'd sooner never have heard of it, either. 'I don't want any part of them. I just want to be left alone.'

Two things ran through Auerbach's mind. First was Greta Garbo. Second, Texan that he was, was the defiant rallying cry of the Confederacy against the damnyankees: *All we want is to be left alone*. But neither one fit Penny Summers, not really. What she'd wanted was to grow up in Lakin, marry a farmer who lived nearby, raise a flock of kids, and get as old as she was going to get, all without going fifty miles from where she was born.

It might not have happened even if the Lizards hadn't come. The war could have put her in a factory somewhere in the city, and who would guess what she might have done after that? Once you saw a city, going back to a small town or a farm often didn't look the same. But he couldn't tell her that her life might not have gone as she'd planned it, because here and now her life sure as hell hadn't gone as she'd planned it.

He said, 'Miss Penny, sitting here like a broody hen on a nest doesn't do you any good. Things won't get better on account of it. The more you go out and do things, the sooner you'll be able to put what's past behind you and go on with the rest of your life.'

'What difference does it make?' she answered dully. 'The world can go on without me just fine, it looks like. And I don't like what the world's turned into. I'd sooner stay here and let things happen. If a bomb lands on this place this minute or tomorrow or a week from now, I'll be sorry for the other people who live here, but not for me.'

He'd had troopers who talked like that after they'd been through more battle than a man could stand. Shell shock, they'd called it back in the First World War; combat fatigue was the name it went by these days. Penny had been in only that one fight, but how many troopers got to watch their fathers turned to cat meat right before their eyes? You couldn't guess beforehand what would send any one person over the edge.

You couldn't tell what would snap anybody out of it, either. Sometimes nothing would. Some of his men weren't fit for anything better than taking care of horses here in Lamar. A couple had seemed well enough to ride, but didn't bother taking any precautions when they went up against the Lizrds. They weren't around any more. And a couple of others had been through the worst of it and got better again. No way to know who would do what.

He took her by the shoulders and hugged her, hard. She was an attractive girl, but it wasn't like holding a woman in his arms. It reminded him more of the embraces he'd given his grandfather after the old man's wits started to wander: the body was there, but the will that directed it wasn't minding the store.

He let her go. 'You've got to do this for yourself, Miss Penny. Nobody on God's green earth can do it for you.'

'I think you'd best go now,' she said. Her face hadn't changed, not even a little bit.

Defeated, he opened the door to her room and started for the stairs. In the room down the hall, the baby was still screaming bloody murder. A couple of doors farther down, a man and a woman shouted angrily at each other.

Almost too soft for Auerbach to hear, Penny Summers called after him, 'Be careful, Captain.'

He spun around. Her door was already closed. He wondered if he should go back. After a moment's hesitation, he headed down the stairs instead. Maybe he hadn't lost, or not completely, after all.

Since the British army was swinging southward anyhow, the better to fight the remaining Lizard forces on English soil, Moishe Russie got to go into London for a day to see if he could find his family.

The instant he reached the outskirts of the great city, he realized he could throw off his Red Cross armband and desert, and no one would ever be the wiser. London had been battered before; now it seemed nothing but ruins. A man might hide in there for years, coming out only to forage for food. By the filthy, furtive look of a good many people on the street, that was just what they did. A lot of them in better condition carried guns. Russie got the idea those weren't only for defense against possible Lizard paratroopers.

Making his way through the rubble towards his family's Soho flat was anything but easy. Street signs had been missing since the Nazi threat in 1940; now whole streets had disappeared, so choked with rubble and cratered by bombs as to be impassable. Worse, a lot of the landmarks he'd used to orient himself as he went about the city were no longer standing: the tower of Big Ben, Marble Arch in Hyde Park, the Queen Victoria Memorial near Buckingham Palace. On a cloudy day like this one, even knowing which way was south was a tricky business.

He'd walked along Oxford Street for a couple of blocks before he realized where he was: no more than a block from the BBC Overseas Service studio. The brick building that housed it had not been wrecked by bomb or shell. A man with a rifle stood outside. At first Russie thought he was one of the soldiers who had guarded the studio. He needed a moment to realize Eric Blair wore a tin hat and bandolier of cartridges.

Blair took even longer to recognize Russie. As Moishe approached, the Englishman brought the rifle up in unmistakable warning. He handled the Lee-Enfield with assurance; Moishe remembered he'd fought in the Spanish Civil War. Then Blair let the stock of the rifle fall to the grimy sidewalk. 'Russie, isn't it? he said, still not quite sure.

'Yes, that's right,' Moishe answered in his uncertain English. 'And you are Blair.' If he could put a name to the other, Blair might be less inclined to shoot him. He pointed to the doorway. 'Do we still work here?'

'Not bloody likely,' the Englishman said with a shake of the head that threatened to throw off his helmet. 'London's had no power for a fortnight now, maybe longer. I'm here to ensure that no one steals the equipment, nothing more. If we were doing anything, they'd set out fitter guards than I.' He scowled. 'If any fitter are left alive, that is.'

Off to the south, artillery spoke, a distant mutter in the air. The Lizards in the northern pocket were dead, fled, or surrendered, but in the south they fought on. Moishe said, 'My family – have you heard anything?'

'I'm sorry.' Blair shook his head again. 'I wish I could tell you something, but I can't. For that matter, I can't say with certainty whether my own kinsfolk are alive or dead. Bloody war.' He started to cough, held his breath till he swayed, and managed to calm the spasm. 'Whew!' he said. 'Those tear me to pieces when they get going – I might as well be breathing mustard gas.'

Russie started to say something to that, but at the last minute held his peace. No one who hadn't seen the effect of the gas at close range had any business talking about it. But, by the same token, no one who hadn't seen it would believe it.

To his surprise, Blair went on, 'I know I shouldn't be speaking of it so. Gas is a filthy business; the things we do to survive would gag Attila the Hun. But Attila, to be fair, never had to contend with invaders from another world.'

'This is so,' Russie said. 'Good luck to you. I go now, see if I can find my family.'

'Good luck to you, too,' Blair said. 'You should carry a weapon of some sort. The war has made beasts of us all, and some of the beasts are more dangerous to a good and decent man than the Lizards ever dreamt of being.'

'It may be so,' Moishe answered, not meaning a word of it. Blair was a good and decent man himself, but he'd never been in the clutches of the Lizards – or the Germans, either, come to that.

Russie walked south down Regent Street toward Soho. A Lizard plane darted overhead. Along with everyone else close by, he threw himself flat and rolled toward the nearest hole in the ground he could find. When the plane had passed over, he picked himself up and went on. He hardly thought about it. He'd been doing the same sort of thing since 1939.

The only difference he could find between Soho and the rest of London was that misery was expressed in more languages in the cosmopolitan district. The Barcelona, a restaurant Eric Blair favored, was still open for business on Beak Street. Boards covered what had been a glass front; from the smoke that rose from the rear of the place, the proprietor used more boards with which to cook. If London's electricity was gone, surely no gas flowed through its mains, either.

When Moishe trudged past the Barcelona, he knew his own block of flats was not far away. He picked up the pace, desperate to find out what had become of his wife and son and at the same time dreading what he might learn.

He turned off Beak Street into Lexington Street and then into Broadwick Street, in which his block of flats lay. No sooner had he done so than he let out a long sigh of relief: the building still stood. That did not necessarily prove anything. The neighborhood, like all London neighbourhoods he'd seen, had taken heavy damage. If Rivka and Reuven had been outside at the wrong moment ... He did his best not to think about that.

In the street, strewn though it was with bricks, broken chunks of concrete, and jagged shards of glass, life went on. Boys shouted as they kicked around a football. The goal posts on the improvised pitch were upright boards undoubtedly scavenged from some wrecked house of shop. The boys played with the same combination of abandon and grim intensity their Polish counterparts would have shown, shouting and laughing as they ran. Not until later would they turn into the calm, undemonstrative Englishmen Moishe found so strange.

A crowd of children, a few adults scattered through it, stood watching the football match and cheering on one team or the other. Moishe took no special notice of the adults. Seeing so many children idling on the sidewalks, though, left him sad. Even when things were worst in Warsaw, hundreds of schools had gone on under the Nazis' noses. Children might die, but they would not die ignorant. He noted much less of that spirit here than he had in the ghetto.

One of the football teams scored a goal. One of the watching men reached into a pocket and passed a coin to the fellow behind him. The English did like to gamble. Boys swarmed onto the pitch to pummel the lad who'd sent the ball past the opponents' goalkeeper.

Moishe ran onto the pitch, too. The boy he swept up into the air was too small to have been a player. The boy squeaked in surprise. Then he shouted, 'Papa!' The word was English, not Yiddish or Polish, but Moishe didn't care. Reuven stared at him and said, 'What happened to your beard, Papa?'

'The gas mask won't fit over it tight enough, so I shaved it off,' Russie answered. Naked cheeks, however strange they felt, were better than a lungful of mustard gas. He'd seen that. Heart pounding in his chest, he asked the next question: 'Where is your mother?'

'In the flat,' Reuven said indifferently, as if to ask, *Where would she be?* 'Could you put me down, please? They're starting to play again, and I want to watch.'

'I'm sorry,' Moishe said, his voice full of mock humility. However important his homecoming was to him, his son seemed well able to take it in his stride. Moishe got out of the street just in time to evade a football flying past his ear. Reuven squirmed and again demanded to be released. Moishe set him on the scarred sidewalk and climbed the stairs to his flat as fast as he could.

From behind the door across the hall came the sounds of a hideous row: Mr and Mrs Stephanopoulos were going at it hammer and tongs. Russie couldn't understand a word of the Greek they were using to slang each other, but it made him feel at home anyway. The Stephanopouloi cared about each other, cared enough to yell. Englishmen and women seemed much more given to cold, deadly silences.

He tried the knob to the door of his own flat. It turned in his hand. He opened the door. Rivka was bustling across the front room toward the kitchen. Her gray eyes widened in astonishment; maybe the racket the Stephanopouloi were making had kept her from hearing him in the hall. Maybe, too, she needed a moment to recognize him, clean-shaven as he was and in the khaki battledress of a British solider.

Astonishment of one sort turned to astonishment of another. 'Moishe!' she whispered, still sounding disbelieving, and ran to him. They held each other. She squeezed him so tight, he could hardly breathe. Against his shoulder, she said, 'I can't believe you're really here.'

'I can't believe *you're* here, you and Reuven,' he answered. 'I've prayed you would be, but we know what prayers are worth these days. And with everything the Lizards have done to London . . .' He shook his head. 'In this war, civilians behind the line are liable to catch it worse than soldiers at the front. We've seen that ever since the Nazis started bombing Warsaw. I was so afraid for you.'

'We're all right.' Rivka's hands flew to her hair in an automatic, altogether unconscious effort to spruce up. 'The kitchen is full of soot because I've had to cook with wood since the gas went out, but that's all. I was going *meshuggeh* worrying over you, there without even a gun in the middle of all the bullets and bombs and the terrible gas. The bombs here—' She shrugged. 'It was terrible, yes, but nothing we haven't known before. If they don't land right on top of you, you're all right. And if they do, you probably won't know about it anyhow. That's not so bad.'

'No,' Moishe agreed. After almost three years of slow starvation and disease in the Warsaw ghetto, such fatalism came easy. Next to them, sudden, probably painless death could look downright attractive.

Rivka said, 'There's still some – veal left from last night, if you're hungry.'

The slight hesitation told Moishe the 'veal' was probably pork, and that his wife was trying to shield him from knowingly eating forbidden food. He'd done the same for her in Warsaw. Accepting the pretense at face value, he said, 'I can always eat. Field rations are thin.'

Civilian rations were even thinner, and he knew it. He left a good deal on the plate. Rivka hadn't expected him to show up. She and Reuven would need to make a meal, or more than one, out of what she'd fixed. When he said he couldn't possibly hold another bite, she looked knowingly at him, but did not protest as she would have before the war.

She dipped water out of a bucket to accompany the meal. It was lukewarm, and had the flat, airless taste that said it had been boiled. He smiled. 'I'm glad you're being careful with what you drink.'

'I've seen what happens when people aren't careful,' she answered seriously. 'Being married to a medical student taught me that much, anyhow.'

'I'm glad,' he said again. He carried plate and fork to the sink. It was fully of soapy water: even now, it made a good washbasin. He washed his dishes and set them by the sink. Rivka watched him, somewhere between amusement and bemusement. Defensively, he said, 'Being apart from you, I've learned to do these things, you see.'

'Yes, I do see,' she said. From her tone, he couldn't tell whether she approved or was scandalized. She went on, 'What else have you learned, being apart from me?'

'That I don't like being apart from you,' he answered. Through the window came fresh cheers from the street below; one of the boys' football teams had just scored. In a speculative voice, Moishe remarked, 'Reuven really seems to enjoy watching the match down there.'

'Enough for us to hope he won't come upstairs for the next little while, do you mean?' Rivka asked. Moishe nodded, his head jerking up and down in hopeful eagerness. From the way his wife giggled, he suspected he looked like a perfect *shlemiel*. He didn't care, especially not after she said, 'I suppose we can do that. Privacy is where you find it, or make it.'

He tried to remember the last time he'd lain on a bed. It hadn't happened more than once of twice since he'd been shoe-horned into the forces fighting desperately to keep Britain free of the invading aliens. They'd given him a bag of medical supplies, a uniform, an armband, and a gas mask, and they'd sent him out to do his best. Comfort hadn't been part of the bargain.

As if by way of experiment, Rivka kissed his bare cheek. 'Bristly,' she said. 'I think I like your beard better, unless you can shave your face very smooth.'

'Getting my hands on a razor hasn't always been easy,' he answered. 'I never would have done it at all, but it makes a mask fit properly.'

He didn't want to think about gas masks and the things that could go wrong if they failed to fit properly, not when he lay beside his wife in an oasis of peace and calm in the midst of chaos and war. For the next little while, he didn't think about anything but Rivka.

But try as you would to stretch such moments, they had to end. Rivka sat up and began to dress as fast as she could. Partly that was ingrained modesty, and partly a well-justified fear that Reuven would choose the most inconvenient time possible to walk into the flat. Both those concerns also drove Moishe back into his clothes. The shoddy serge of his battledress scraped his skin as he pulled it on.

Rivka reached behind her neck to fasten the last catch. As if that were a signal that the everyday, dangerous world had returned, she asked, 'How long will you be able to stay here?'

'Just tonight,' he answered. 'I have to go south tomorrow, to help the wounded in the fighting against the Lizards there.'

'How is the fight really going?' Rivka asked. 'When there's power for the wireless and when they can print newspapers, they say they're smashing the Lizards the way Samson smote the Philistines. But Lizard planes keep on pounding London, the boom of artillery never goes away, and shells keep falling on us. Can I believe what they claim?'

'The northern pocket is gone – *kaputt*,' Moishe said, borrowing a word he'd heard German soldiers use. 'As for the southern one, your guess is as good as mine. All I know about the fighting is what I've seen for myself, and that's like asking a fish in a pool to tell you everything about the Vistula. If England were losing the fight badly, though, you'd be talking with a Lizard right now, not with me.'

'That is so,' she said thoughtfully. 'But after people – human beings – have lost so many fights, it's hard to believe that just holding the Lizards back should count as a victory.'

'When you think of how many people couldn't slow the Lizards down, let alone stop them, then holding them back *is* a victory, and a big one. I don't ever remember them pulling back from a fight the way they did from the northern pocket. The English have hurt them.' Moishe shook his head in wonder. 'For so long, we didn't think anything or anyone could hurt them.'

The front door to the flat opened, then closed with a slam. Reuven shouted, 'Is there anything to eat? I'm hungry!' Moishe and Rivka looked at each other and started to laugh. The noise let Reuven find them. 'What's so funny?' he demanded with the indignation of a child who knows a joke is going over his head.

'Nothing,' his father answered gravely. 'We slipped one by you, that's all.'

'One what?' Reuven said. Rivka sent Moishe a warning glance: the boy was really too young. Moishe just laughed harder. Even with the rumble of artillery always in the background, for this little while he could savor being with his wife and son. Tomorrow the war would fold him in its bony arms once more. Today he was free, and reveled in his freedom.

The silvery metal did not look like much. It was so dense that what the Metallurgical Laboratory had managed to produce seemed an even smaller amount than it really was. Appearances mattered not at all to Leslie Groves. He knew what he had here: enough plutonium, when added together with what the Germans and Russians had stolen from the Lizards and the British brought over to the USA, to make an atomic bomb that would go boom and not fizzle.

He turned to Enrico Fermi. 'There's the first long, hard step, by God! After this, we have a downhill track.'

'An easier track, General, yes, but not an easy one,' the Italian physicist answered. 'We still have to purify the plutonium, to shape it into a bomb, and to find a way to explode the bomb where we want it.' 'Those are all engineering concerns,' Groves said. 'I'm an engineer; I know we can meet them. The physics was what worried me – I wasn't sure we'd ever see enough plutonium metal.' He waved toward the small silver lump.

Fermi laughed. 'For me, it is just the opposite. The physics, we have found, is straightforward enough. Advancing from it to the finished bomb, though, is a challenge of a different sort.'

'Whatever sort of challenge it is, we'll meet it,' Groves declared. 'We can't afford to be like the Russians – one shot and out. We'll hit the Lizards again and again, until we make 'em say uncle.'

'From what I understand of the Russians' design, they are lucky to have achieved any explosion at all,' Fermi said. 'A gun-type device with plutonium—' He shook his head. 'It must have been a very large gun, with a very high velocity to the slab of plutonium it accelerated into the larger plug. Otherwise, fission would have begun prematurely, disrupting the mass before the full power of the nuclear reaction built up.'

'They could build it any size they wanted, I suppose,' Groves said. 'They weren't going to load it in a bomber, after all.' He laughed at that, a laugh edged with bitterness. 'For one thing, they don't have a bomber big enough to carry even a small nuclear bomb. For another, if they did the Lizards would shoot it down before it got where it was supposed to go. So why not build big?'

'No reason I can see,' Fermi answered. 'The same applies to us, in large degree: we will not be able to deliver the bomb from the air once we have it. Putting it in the proper place at the proper time will not be easy.'

'I know.' Groves rubbed his chin. He didn't like thinking about that. 'The way the Russians did it, from what they say, was to leave the bomb hidden in a position they knew the Lizards were going to overrun in a few hours. They set their timer and waited for the big boom. We'd have a harder time finding a position of that sort.'

'Chicago,' Fermi said quietly.

'Mm, yeah, maybe,' Groves admitted. 'That's a meat grinder, no mistake about it. I see two problems with it, though. Getting the bomb from here to Chicago once it's done is one. Hell, getting a bomb from here to anywhere is going to be a problem. So that's number one. And number two is pulling our boys back so we don't take out one of our own divisions along with the Lizards.'

'Why should that be a problem?' the physicist asked. 'They simply retreat, allowing the Lizards to move forward, and that is that.'

Leslie Groves smiled down at him. Groves had been an engineer throughout his years in the military; he'd never led troops in combat, nor wanted to. But he'd forgotten more about strategy than Fermi had ever learned – nice to be reminded there were still some things he knew more about than the eggheads he was supposed to be bossing. As patiently as he could, he answered, 'Professor, we've been fighting the Lizards tooth and toenail outside of Chicago, and now in it, ever since they came down from space. If we all of a sudden start pulling back without an obvious good reason, don't you think they're going to get suspicious about why we're changing our ways? I know I would, if I were their CO.'

'Ah,' Fermi said. He might have been naive, but he wasn't dumb, not even a little bit. 'I see what you mean, General. the Russians were already in full-scale retreat, so the Lizards noticed nothing out of the ordinary when they passed the point where the bomb was hidden. But if we go from stout resistance to quick withdrawal, they will observe something is amiss.'

'That's it,' Groves agreed. 'That's it exactly. We'd have to either convince 'em that they'd licked us and we were getting out of Dodge—'

'I beg your pardon?' Fermi interrupted.

'Sorry. I mean, retreating as fast as we can go,' Groves said. Fermi spoke with a thick accent, but he usually understood what you said to him. Groves reminded himself to be less colloquial. 'Either we do that or else we pull back secretly – under cover of night, maybe. That's how I see it, anyhow.'

'To me, this is a sensible plan,' Fermi said. 'If the time comes, will they think of it in Chicago?'

'They should. They're solid professional soldiers.' But Groves wondered. Fermi was naive about the way soldiers handled their job. Every reason he should have been, too. But why should anyone assume the generals out there actually fighting the Lizards would be anything but naive about what an atomic bomb could do? Calculations from a bunch of scholarly people who went around carrying slide rules instead of carbines wouldn't mean much to them.

Groves decided he'd better sit his fanny down and bang out a memo. He couldn't be sure anyone would pay any attention to that, either, but at least it would have *Brigadier General, U.S. Army* under his name, which might make soldiers sit up and take notice. The only real thing he was sure of was that they certainly wouldn't know what to expect if he *didn't* sit down and write. That was all a man of caution needed to know.

'Excuse me, Professor Fermi,' he said, and hurried away. The typewriter was waiting.

Atvar studied the computer display of the slow track of Tosev 3 around its parent sun. 'Equinox,' he said, as if it were blasphemy against the revered name of the Emperor.

'Truth, Exalted Fleetlord.' Kirel didn't sound any happier at the self-evident astronomical fact than had his superior. He put the reason for his distaste into words: 'Winter will now approach in the northern hemisphere, where so many Tosevite not-empires remain unsubdued.'

Both high-ranking males contemplated that for a while in unhappy silence. The probe the Race had sent to Tosev 3 centuries before had warned that the planet's weather grew extremely intemperate in winter. Still, the Race's equipment was imperfectly adapted for such climates: the ruling assumption had been that the conquest would be over and done long before such things mattered. And no one back on Home had imagined that the Tosevites could have industrialized in the space of a few short centuries, let alone developed equipment better designed than anything the Race had for dealing with all the appalling varieties of muck and frozen water indigenous to Tosev 3 in winter.

Still gloomily, Kirel resumed, 'During the last winter, we lost the strategic advantage over broad areas of the planet. When bad weather begins, the Big Uglies will assail us with more sophisticated weapons than they employed two of our years ago. This does not cause me to look on the likely results of the upcoming combat with optimism unrestrained.'

'I assure you, Shiplord, I have not looked on this conquest with optimism unrestrained since we discovered the Big Uglies knew enough to employ radio,' Atvar answered. 'But we are not in an entirely disadvantageous position in regard to the Tosevites, either. We have made serious inroads on their industrial capacity; they produce far less than they did when we first arrived.'

'Our own industrial capacity on Tosev 3, however, remains effectively nil,' Kirel said. 'We can produce more ammunition: all well and good, though even there we rely to some degree on captured Tosevite factories. But who in his wildest nightmares would have thought of the need to manufacture landcruisers and killercraft in large numbers to replace combat losses?'

'No one, but it remains a reality whether we thought of it or not,' Atvar said. 'We have serious weaknesses in both areas, as well as in antimissile missiles. We were lucky to have brought any of those at all, but now our stocks are nearly exhausted, and demand remains unrelenting.'

'The Deutsche, may their eggshells be thinned by pest-control poisons, not only throw missiles at us but load them with their poisonous gases rather than with ordinary explosives. These missiles must be shot down before they reach their targets, or they can do dreadful damage. Our ability to accomplish this is degraded with every antimissile missile we expend.'

'We have knocked the island of Britain out of the fight against us for some indefinite time,' Atvar said. That was true, but it was also putting the best possible face on things, and he knew it. The campaign on Britain had been intended to annex the island. Like a lot of intentions on Tosev 3, that one had not survived contact with the Big Uglies. The losses in males and matériel were appalling, and certainly had cost the Race far more than the temporary neutralization of Britain could repay.

After what looked like a careful mental search, Kirel did find an authentic bright spot to mention: 'It does appear virtually certain, Exalted Fleetlord, that the SSSR possessed but the single atomic weapon it used against us. Operations there can resume their previous tempo, at least until winter comes.'

'No, not until winter, not in the SSSR,' Atvar said sharply. 'Long before that, the rains begin there and turn the local road network into an endless sea of gluey muck. We bogged down there badly two years ago, during the last local autumn, and then again in the spring, when all the frozen water that had accumulated there through winter proceeded to melt.'

'Truth, Exalted Fleetlord. I had forgotten.' Kirel seemed to fold in on himself for a moment, acknowledging his error. Almost angrily, he continued, 'The Big Uglies of the SSSR are a pack of lazy, incompetent fools, to build a road system unusable one part of the year in three.'

'I wish they were a pack of lazy, incompetent fools,' Atvar answered. 'Lazy, incompetent fools, though, could not have built and detonated an atomic device, even if the plutonium was stolen from our stockpile. As a matter of fact, prisoner interrogations imply that the roads are so shoddy for a strategic reason: to hinder invasion from Deutschland to the west. They certainly had reason to fear such invasion, at any rate, and the measure taken against the Deutsche have also served to hinder us.'

'So they have,' Kirel hissed in anger. 'Of all the Tosevite not-empires, I most want to see the SSSR overthrown. I realize that their emperor was but a Big Ugly, but to take him from his throne and murder him—' He shuddered. 'Such thoughts would never have crossed our minds before we came to Tosev 3. If males ever had them, they are vanished in the prehistory of the Race. Or they were, until the Big Uglies recalled them to unwholesome life.'

'I know,' Atvar said sadly. 'Even after we do conquer this world, after the colonization fleet sets down here, I fear Tosevite ideas may yet corrupt us. The Rabotevs and Hallessi differ from us in body, but in spirit the Empire's three races might have hatched from the same egg. The Big Uglies are alien, alien.'

'Which makes them all the more dangerous,' Kirel said. 'If the colonization fleet were not following us, I might think sterilizing Tosev 3 the wisest course.'

'So Straha proposed early on,' Atvar replied. 'Have you come round to the traitor's view?' His voice grew soft and dangerous as he asked that question. Straha's broadcasts from the USA had hurt morale more than he liked to admit.

'No, Exalted Fleetlord. I said, "If the colonization fleet were not following us." But it is, which limits our options.' Kirel hesitated, then continued, 'As we have noted before, the Tosevites, unfortunately, operate under no such restraints. If they construct more nuclear weapons, they will use them.'

'The other thing I doubt is the effectiveness of nuclear weapons as intimidators against them,' Atvar said. 'We have destroyed Berlin, Washington, and now Tokyo. The Deutsche and Americans keep right on fighting us, and the Nipponese also seem to be carrying on. But when the Soviet Big Uglies detonated their device, they intimidated us for a long period of time. That is not how warfare against a primitive species should progress.'

'One thing the Tosevites have taught us: technology and political sophistication do not necessarily travel together,' Kirel said. 'For us, dealings between empires are principles to be absorbed out of old texts from previous conquests; for the Big Uglies, they are the everyday stuff of life. No wonder, then, that they find it easier to manipulate us than we them. By the Emperor' – he cast down his eyes – 'that might have been true even if they were as technologically backwards as our probes led us to believe.'

'So it might, but then they would not have had the strength to back up their deviousness,' Atvar said. 'Now they do. And sooner or later, the Soviets will manage to build another nuclear weapon, or the Deutsche, or the Americans – and then more difficult choices will present themselves to us.'

'Difficult, yes,' Kirel said. 'We suspect the Americans and the Deutsche and the British as well of having nuclear programs, as the Soviets surely do. But what if we cannot find the source of their production, as we were lucky enough to manage with the Nipponese? Shall we destroy one of their cities instead, taking vengeance for their nuclear attacks in that way?'

'It is to be considered,' Atvar answered. 'Many things are to be considered which we had not contemplated before we came here.' That made him nervous in and of itself. Maneuvering through uncharted territory was not what the Race did best. It was seldom something the Race had to do at all, for those who led knew their kind's weaknesses full well. But on Tosev 3, Atvar found himself with only the choice of too many choices.

The ruined gray stone castle before which Ussmak had halted his landcruiser seemed to him immeasurably old. Intellectually, he knew the frowning pile of some could hardly have stood there for more than a couple of thousand years (half that, if you counted by Tosev 3's slow revolutions around its primary – hardly a flick of the nictitating membrane in the history of the Race.

But his own people had not built such structures since days now more nearly legendary than historical. None survived; a hundred thousand years and more of earthquakes, erosion, and constant construction had seen to that. Chugging up the hill to the castle at Farnham, Ussmak had felt transported in time back to primitive days.

Unfortunately, the British were not so primitive now as they had been when they ran up the castle, either. Otherwise, Ussmak's landcruiser would not have had to retreat from its attempted river crossing to aid the males in the northern pocket. The northern pocket had no males left in it now. Some had been evacuated. More were dead or captured.

Back in the turret, Nejas called out, 'Front!'

Ussmak peered through his own vision slits, trying to find the target the landcruiser commander had spotted. He waited for Skoob to answer, 'Identified!' Instead, the gunner said doubtfully, 'What have you found, superior sir?'

'That group of Tosevite males advancing along the highway, bearing as near zero as makes no difference,' Nejas answered. 'Give them a round of high explosive. It will teach them not to show themselves so openly.'

'It shall be done, superior sir,' Skoob said. The autoloader clanged as it slammed a shell into the breech of the landcruiser's main armament. 'On the way,' Skoob said, an instant before the big gun roared and the landcruiser rocked back on its tracks, absorbing the recoil.

The Big Uglies knew enough to move forward in open order, which left them less vulnerable to artillery fire. Even so, several males went down when the shell burst among them. Those who had not been hit quickly joined their comrades on the ground. 'Well aimed, Skoob!' Ussmak exclaimed. 'One round and you stopped the advance cold.'

'Thank you, driver,' Skoob answered. 'I'm not used to retreating. Of course I obey for the good of the Race, but I don't much fancy it.'

'Nor I,' Ussmak said. Every time he sneaked a taste of ginger, he was filled with the urge to charge forward into the ranks of the Big Uglies, smashing them with the landcruiser's tracks while the gunner and commander used the weapons in the turret to work a great slaughter.

He knew that was the herb doing his thinking for him, but knowing it made the urge no less urgent.

'No one fancies retreating,' Nejas said. 'Landcruiser males are trained to be first into battle, to tear holes in the enemy's force through which others may pass. Now our task is to keep the British from tearing holes in our force and to be the last ones out of battle. Difficult, I grant you, but less far removed from our basic role than you might think.'

'Truth,' Ussmak said, 'but not satisfying truth. Forgive me for speaking so boldly, superior sir.'

'I do forgive you, driver, but I also remind you of our task here,' Nejas said. 'The Race has but one airstrip on this island out of range of British artillery: that at the place called Tangmere south of here, not far from the sea. As long as we can hold the British away from it, we can freely bring in supplies and evacuate wounded males as well as those being withdrawn.'

'Truth,' Ussmak repeated. He followed the strategy, but giving up ground to the Tosevites still seemed strange to him. The Deutsche were probably better warriors in a technical sense than the British, but here every Tosevite, whether formally a warrior or not, was an enemy. He hadn't felt that in the SSSR or France; some there had seemed willing to serve the Race on its terms. Not in Britain. Here they fought with everything they had.

As if thinking along with him, Nejas said, 'We can't let them get within artillery range of Tangmere. If they do, they'll plaster the airstrip with that hideous poison gas of theirs.' He paused for a moment, then went on, 'And from what I've heard, we have it lucky. The Deutsche are using a gas that makes this one seem tame: one good whiff and you fall over dead.'

Ussmak said, 'Superior sir, if what we have here is good luck, I don't ever want to see the bad.'

'Nor I,' Skoob agreed. To Nejas, he added, 'I see more Big Uglies in the fields and along the road to the north. Shall I give them another couple of rounds of high explosive?'

'Pick your own targets, Skoob,' the landcruiser commander answered. 'Remember what ammunition resupply has been like lately, though. We have to hold this position and keep on holding it till we're ordered to fall back again. That probably won't be until our time for evacuation comes up: they're using armor for a shell, and pulling back all the soft meat behind it.'

'Back when we first started the campaign on Tosev 3,' Ussmak said, his words punctuated by the deep rumble of the landcruiser's main armament, 'one of our landcruisers could sit out in the middle of open country and dominate as far as its cannon could reach.' He let out a long, hissing sigh. 'It's not like that any more.'

'Not there, that's certain,' Nejas said. 'Britain hardly has open spaces worthy of the name. There are always trees or hedgerows or stone fences or buildings to give cover to the Big Uglies. When we first landed, too, they didn't have any antilandcruiser weapons worthy of the name: nothing this side of big guns, anyway, and big guns are easy to spot and neutralize. But now any sneaking infantrymale can carry a rocket or one of those spring-launched egg-addlers the British use. They still can't hurt us from the front, but from the sides or rear ... we've lost too many landcruisers that way.'

Skoob traversed the turret a couple of hundredths, fired again. Two other landcruisers held positions slightly lower on the hill that led up to Farnham Castle. They also sent high-explosive rounds into the loose ranks of the oncoming British males. Again and again, the British went to ground. Again and again, the survivors got up and kept moving forward.

'I wish we had more infantrymales in the ruins of the town down there,' Ussmak said. 'Some of those Big Uglies will get in among them – as you said, superior sir – and work their way toward us.'

Neither of his crewmales argued with him. He wondered if this was what the Tosevites had felt at the outset of the campaign, when for a while the Race swept all before it: the numbing sense that, try as you would to stop it, something would go wrong and you'd end up dead or maimed on account of it.

A flight of killercraft roared low overhead from out of the south, dropping bombs on the Big Uglies and strafing them with their cannon. A series of runs like that, by multiple flights, would have ruined the British, but the Race had neither the aircraft nor the munitions to expend in such lavish quantities.

That meant the British would not be ruined. It also probably meant the Race's forces in Britain would. Ussmak desperately wanted a taste of ginger. Without the herb, the world was a depressing, gloomy, cold place – not that he'd ever found Tosev 3 anything but cold, even with a taste or two inside him. But the cloud that settled over his spirit when he'd gone too long without ginger made the world feel even worse than it was and defeat seem a certainty.

No sooner had that thought crossed his mind than something exploded against the side armor of one of the landcruisers farther down the hill. One of the revolting things about the British spring-launched antilandcruiser bombs was that they gave no clue about their launch site, as, say, a missile did.

This bomb, by good fortune, did not penetrate the landcruiser's armor, perhaps because it hadn't landed squarely. After the initial blast, no smoke mounted skyward. No escape hatches popped open. No males bailed out of the landcruiser. Instead the turret slewed rapidly through a quarter of a circle. The machine gun coaxial with the main armament chattered angrily. But if anything in the ruins of Farnham stirred, Ussmak didn't see it.

'The Big Uglies' weapons get better all the time,' he said. 'We have the same ones we started out with, and we don't have as many of them. The

Tosevite substitutes we're getting are shoddy, and we don't have enough of those, either. Why can't we be the ones who invent something new for a change?'

Neither Nejas nor Skoob answered him. They did not need to answer him; he had already answered himself. The Race looked warily on invention. When it did happen, the results were fed into the culture of the Empire a tiny bit at a time, so as not to create instability. Steadiness counted for more than quickness. The past hundred thousand years, that had worked well. It did not work well on Tosev 3.

His crewmales also had another, less abstract reason for not answering him: they were trying to spot the Big Ugly who'd launched the bomb at the nearby landcruiser. Ussmak peered through his own vision slits, but his field of view was too narrow to offer him much hope of getting a glimpse of the dangerous Tosevite.

He heard a metallic rasp from the turret: Nejas was sticking his head out for a direct look around. That was what a good landcruiser commander was supposed to do. Looking out at the world through the periscopes that ringed the cupola didn't let you see enough to be sure you were safe.

But if you did stand up in the cupola, by definition you were no longer safe. The moment Nejas emerged, British males started shooting at him. Two bullets ricocheted off the turret and another cracked past before he ducked back down and slammed the cupola lid with a clang.

'I didn't see any Big Uglies,' he said, the words punctuated by swift, harsh breathing. 'That doesn't mean they didn't see me. By the Emperor, I hope that other landcruiser took out the male with the bomb launcher. If he didn't—'

'If he didn't, we'll find out quite soon,' Skoob said. The silence that rollowed probably meant his mouth had fallen open in a laugh. He went on, 'I haven't come close to spotting him. He's good at what he does. By now, on this planet, the males who aren't good warriors are mostly dead, on their side and ours both.'

Ussmak was still alive, so he supposed he was good at what he did, by Skoob's standard, at any rate. He wished he could taste some ginger. Then he'd feel alive, too. He hissed bemusedly. Even when he tasted, he imagined himself triumphantly wielding weapons, never inventing them. Somehow fantasy and hard work in a laboratory failed to come together.

Was that movement in the rubble, right at the edge of his field of vision? He moved his head to one side, trying to look farther in that direction. If it had been movement, it was stopped now.

He opened his mouth to speak up about it anyhow. *Better safe* was a motto drilled into the Race from hatchlinghood. Back on Home, it usually meant avoiding annoyance or discomfort. Here, it had more to do with preventing agony and gruesome death.

Before he could say anything, Skoob's machine gun started rattling away. Hot brass cartridge cases clattered down onto the floor. '*Got* him!'

Skoob shouted, almost as excitedly as if he'd tasted ginger himself. 'Tosevite male with a rifle – probably one of the ones who was shooting at you, superior sir.'

'Good riddance to him,' Nejas said.

The turret of the landcruiser that had taken the bomb hit swung back toward the north. The landcruiser started shelling the advancing British males once more. The flames that spurted from the muzzle, the smoke and dirt that flew with each shellburst, impressed Ussmak less than they had before. Armed Tosevites were already inside Farnham, sneaking toward the landcruisers like biters looking to slide needle-nosed mouths between a male's scales. Swat as you would, you never could quite get rid of all of them. For that, you needed a spray – but here on Tosev 3, the biters were the ones with the poisonous gas.

Clang-pow! For a moment, Ussmak thought the main armament had fired. But this jolt slewed the landcruiser sideways. Warning lights blazed all over the instrument panel. A klaxon started to hoot, loud enough to make his hearing diaphragms feel like vibrating drumheads. That meant fire loose in the engine compartment in spite of everything the extinguishers could do, which in turn meant the landcruiser could brew up at any moment. Hydrogen wasn't so enthusiastically explosive as the hydrocarbon fuels the Big Uglies used, but it burned. Oh, it burned …

All of that went through Ussmak's mind far faster than conscious thought. Even before Nejas screamed 'Bail out!' Ussmak had the hatch over his head open. He paused only to grab his little jars of ginger, stuff them into a belt pouch, and, almost as an afterthought, pick up his personal weapon. Then he was scrambling up and out, fast as legs and arms would propel him.

A rifle bullet whined past his head, close enough for him to feel, or imagine he felt, the wind of its passage. He skittered across the smooth, sloping surface of the glacis plate, jumped down, and landed heavily on torn-up asphalt, the bulk of the landcruiser between him and the Tosevite guns.

Skoob already sprawled there. 'We can't stay here,' he said, his eyes swiveling wildly as he looked for danger every which way at once. 'This thing is liable to go up whenever the fire gets to the ammunition, or to the fuel, or if that cursed Big Ugly sends another bomb into the fighting compartment.'

'Tell me something I didn't know,' Ussmak answered. 'Where's the commander?'

Just then, Nejas jumped down on both them. Blood dripped from a surprisingly neat hole in his forearm. 'They hit me when I started to climb out,' he said, barely opening his mouth so as to show as little pain as he could. Skoob reached for a bandage, but Nejas waved him off. 'We have to get clear first.'

The commander scurried away from the hull of the stricken landcruiser, keeping it between himself and the Tosevites. Ussmak and Skoob followed. Ussmak wanted to spray bullets back at the Big Uglies, but that would have reminded them he was there. He would sooner have had them forget all about him.

Clang-pow! The sound was quite different from outside the landcruiser, but unmistakable all the same. Another of those spring-launched bombs – Ussmak and his crewmates had got away just in time. Turning one eye backwards, he saw flame race over the whole vehicle. Then ammunition started cooking off inside. A perfect black smoke ring shot out through the opening atop the cupola.

The pyrotechnics finally alerted the crews of the other two landcruisers that something had gone wrong behind them. They both broke off shelling the advancing British Big Uglies and lashed the ruins of Farnham with fire, trying to rout out the fighting males already sneaking through those ruins.

Ussmak doubted they would succeed in exterminating the Tosevites. He was past the point of caring. As long as they made the Big Uglies lay low long enough to let him find shelter, that would do. He'd given up hoping for anything better than temporary respite.

Nejas dived behind a couple of gray stone blocks that had been blasted off the wall of Farnham's castle. Ussmak and Skoob followed him to earth as if they were hunted beasts. *We might as well be hunted beasts,* Ussmak thought. In combat and out of his landcruiser, he felt naked and soft and hideously vulnerable, like some crawler cruelly torn from its shell.

'Let's see that now, superior sir,' Skoob said, pointing to Nejas's wound.

Nejas held out the arm. His eyes wandered vaguely. When he opened his mouth to speak, only a wordless hiss came out. The interior of his mouthparts was a pale, pale pink. He hadn't lost that much blood, but he did not look good. 'Shock,' Ussmak said, his voice worried.

'Truth,' Skoob said. He wrapped a wound bandage around the landcruiser commander's arm. 'I hope one of those other crews will radio for an evacuation helicopter; our own set just went up in flames.' He turned both eyes toward Nejas. 'If we have to walk out – and I'm afraid we will – he'll be a burden unless he comes out of it.'

No rescue helicopter appeared. Nejas sank further into sludgy semiconsciousness. Ussmak grew more and more sure they would have to retreat on foot. If they were going to do that, they needed Nejas on his legs and moving. Trying to carry him, they'd be desperately slowed, and easy meat for any armed Big Uglies whose path they chanced to cross. Abandoning the landcruiser commander never crossed Ussmak's mind; for all he'd been through, he was still in some ways a well-drilled male of the Race.

But how to get Nejas up on his legs? Skoob was looking around helplessly, perhaps for some males to lend them a hand. Ussmak did not think anyone would magically materialize, not unless another landcruiser got killed, in which case the crewmales would likely have wounded of their own.

He got an idea of a different sort. He reached into the pouch in which he'd stored his ginger, took out a vial, and poured some of the powdered herb into the palm of his hand. Skoob stared at him in astonishment. He ignored the gunner. Holding his hand just in front of the tip of Nejas's muzzle, he said, 'Superior sir? Taste this.'

His greatest fear was that Nejas was far too gone to hear him, or to respond if he did. But the commander's bifurcated tongue flicked out, almost of itself, and brought into his mouth a fair-sized taste of ginger. Ussmak waited tensely to see if it would do any good.

The membranes that had fallen halfway across Nejas's pupils suddenly peeled back, leaving the landcruiser commander's eyes bright and alert. His tongue shot forth again, and cleared the last of the ginger from Ussmak's palm. 'By the Emperor, what is that stuff?' he demanded. 'Whatever it is, it's marvelous.'

Skoob spoke before Ussmak could: 'That's the Tosevite herb, isn't it? The one we've had so much trouble with, I mean.' He turned one eye from Nejas toward Ussmak. 'What are you doing with it? Possession of ginger is against regulations and subject to punishment.'

'What do you think I'm doing with it?' Ussmak snapped, irritated by the manifest stupidity of the question. 'I'm a ginger taster, that's what. And it was the only thing I could think of to get the commander moving again.' He shifted his eyes to Nejas. 'I'm sorry, superior sir. This way, we can sort things out later. If I hadn't given it to you, I didn't think there'd be a later.'

'You were right,' Nejas declared, which silenced Skoob. The landcruiser commander's voice was vibrant, full of life. Moments before, his wound left him all but unconscious. Now he seemed to have forgotten he'd been hurt. 'Where's my personal weapon?' he asked, looking around for it. 'If I can get my hands on it, the three of us should be plenty to drive all the Big Ugly fighting males out of this damp, grimy little town.'

Now Skoob stared at him, as if certain the ginger had robbed him of his wits. And so, in a way, it had. Ussmak recognized the symptoms from his own first tastes of ginger: the certainty that you could do anything, regardless of the odds. He still felt that when he tasted, but now he knew it was the herb's illusion. Nejas didn't have the experience to recognize it for what it was.

Gently, Ussmak said, 'Superior sir, you remain yourself, nothing more, however powerful the herb may make you feel. Use logic, if you can: if we could not drive the Big Uglies from Farnham from inside our landcruiser, we won't do it now that the machine is wrecked. We need to get out of here and get you and your wounded arm seen to.'

Ginger made you think faster than you did without it. It also made you think you were thinking better than you did without it, though that wasn't always so. After only the briefest pause, Nejas said, 'Truth. We must leave. Logic.' Ussmak wasn't sure how clear his commander's wits really were, but he wanted to get Nejas moving and get all three of them out of Farnham before the ginger's exhilaration wore off and the first dreadful depression crashed down to take its place.

Without warning, Nejas broke cover, skittering southward toward another pile of rubble. A bullet kicked up earth between his feet; another struck sparks from the stonework behind him. With a headlong leap, he reached the new shelter. 'Come on!' he called to his crewmates. 'Nothing to it!'

Ussmak wished he'd also tasted; it would have helped nerve him for the dash across open, empty space. 'Go on,' Skoob said. 'I'll cover you.' He fired a few shots as Ussmak poised, sprinted, dived. Ussmak returned the favor when Skoob made the dangerous crossing.

From rubble to wreckage, from wreckage to house, they made their way south out of Farnham. The houses, those few of them that hadn't been ruined in the fighting, looked tidy and comfortable, at least by Tosevite standards. As he scurried from one of them to the next, always wondering when a bullet he never heard would hit him, Ussmak began to see how a Big Ugly who was faced with the loss of such comfort might fight hard to keep it.

Houses thinned out and gave way to open country. That worried Ussmak. It gave him and his crewmales fewer hiding places than they'd had in town. And untold enemies could lurk behind the hedgerows that separated one miniature field from the next. Ussmak eyed those hedgerows with mingled fear and respect. Some of them had been growing for the Emperor only knew how long; even a landcruiser had trouble crashing through them.

Hedgerows, however, were not his only concern. As he'd known it would Nejas's ginger charge wore off, leaving the landcruiser commander very much a drained battery. Nejas slumped bonelessly to the rough asphalt of the road. 'I can't go on,' he moaned, after-tasting depression holding him in its teeth. 'And even if I could, what good would it do?'

'Here, superior sir, taste this.' Ussmak got out more ginger. He didn't know if a brand-new user could stand having so much course through him, but he did know the alternative was abandoning Nejas. He'd had commanders he would have happily abandoned, but Nejas wasn't one of them.

'I don't want it,' Nejas said; now he knew what Ussmak was giving him. But Ussmak had never heard a more obvious lie. Nejas's eyes never moved from the palm that held the ginger. When Ussmak brought his hand close to the other male's muzzle, Nejas's tongue flicked out and licked it clean.

Quietly, Skoob said to Ussmak, 'We ought to report you for punishment when we get to an area where such things are possible.'

'Do whatever you're going to do,' Ussmark answered, as weary as he ever remembered being. 'The point is that we got to one of those places, not what we do afterwards.' 'Let's go.' Nejas surged to his feet again. His eyes had a hectic glow to them, as if fires burned uncontrolled in his brain. Ussmak knew about those fires, and the herbal wind that fanned them. He hoped he hadn't given the commander too much ginger. Voice crackling with unassailable certainty, Nejas pointed south. 'That way. Before long we shall surely encounter one of our bases intended to hold down this land.'

Unless we encounter Big Ugly infiltrators first, Ussmak thought. *If they were in Farnham, no reason they can't have slipped south of it. They're good at such things. After all, this is their planet.* Over the days since the Race came to Tosev 3, he'd got a thorough education as to what that meant.

Something moved at the bottom of the hedgerow. He didn't pause to wonder about what it might be; males who hesitated once seldom got the chance to hesitate twice. He fired a short burst, his first bullet an instant ahead of Skoob's.

Only after his finger came off the trigger did he see what he and the landcruiser gunner had been shooting at: a round little spiny animal with a pointed snout. It was dead now, dead and torn and bleeding, its tiny black eyes staring up in blind reproach. For the first time since he woke up from cold sleep on Tosev 3, Ussmak felt guilty about killing something.

13

Mutt Daniels crouched in a broken house, peering out through the glassless window and down the wreckage-filled street. The Lizards were still moving forward; between their onslaughts and the stubborn American defense, Chicago was being ground to meal, and fine meal at that.

The wind that whistled through the window and through the gaping holes in the roof had a chilly edge to it. The sun was going down early these days, too, when you could see it through the clouds, both natural and of smoke.

'Never thought I'd be one rootin' for an early winter an' snow on the ground, but I sure as hell am,' Mutt muttered to himself. The winter before, the Americans had kicked the stuffing out of the Lizards, who didn't seem to have a clue about fighting in the cold. In the summertime, though – Mutt marveled that he was still alive.

A noise from behind him made him whirl around. His first sergeant, a burly Irishman named Herman Muldoon, nodded to him and said, 'We got some new fish comin' in out of the north, Lieutenant; replacements, by Jesus! They're all going to be green as paint, poor lads.'

'Yeah, well, that's one thing ain't nobody can say about the likes of us,' Mutt answered. Muldoon's answering chuckle showed crooked teeth, a couple of them broken. He was a few years younger than Daniels; like Mutt, he'd been Over There in what had been optimistically called the War to End War. As best they could figure it, they'd been only a few miles apart in the Argonne, though they had't met.

Muldoon took of his old British-styled tin hat and ran a hand through matted hair that had been red but now was going gray. He said, 'I seen a few of 'em when they was back a ways. Christ on His cross, they've got guns, they've got helmets, some of 'em even got uniforms. They look like soldiers on the outside, but inside a couple weeks – hell, maybe, inside a couple days – half of 'em's gonna end up dead.'

'I know,' Mutt answered gloomily. 'That the way it works. The ones who live, we'll make soldiers out of some of 'em.'

''S true,' Muldoon said. ''S a fuckin' waste, but it's true. The real bitch of it is, some o' the ones who stop a bullet early would

make pretty decent men if they had any luck. Just how you roll
the dice.'

'Yeah,' Mutt said again. He fell silent. He didn't like thinking about
that, though he'd seen it in France and here in Illinois. If chance ruled,
if skill played no part on the battlefield, you could die any old time,
no matter how good a soldier you'd got to be. Of course you could. He
knew that. Knowing it and contemplating it were two different things,
though.

A couple of hundred yards off to the left, back toward Lake Michigan,
shooting stared up. It was just a spattering of rounds, but Daniels hunkered
down without conscious thought. Muldoon said, 'Probably some of the
rookies coming into the line. They get up here, they think they gotta start
shootin'.'

Mutt nodded. It had been like that in France. His granddad – hell,
both his granddads – had said it was like that in the States War. It had
probably been like that since the day Alley Oop, Jr., joined up with his
dad and chucked a rock at the first dinosaur he saw.

More noises from the rear. The firing wasn't spreading, not yet. Daniels
risked a peek back over his shoulder. Crawling through the wreckage of
what had been a quiet North Side residential neighbourhood came six or
eight – they weren't dogfaces, not yet. Puppyfaces, maybe.

Those faces were all dirty, but only a couple of the rookies had struck
up any serious acquaintance with a razor. To Mutt's jaundiced eye, they
all looked too pale and too skinny. Down in Mississippi, his guess would
have been hookworm. Here, he knew better. He thumped his belly, what
was left of it. Nobody'd been eating good, not this whole past year – one
more reason to hate the Lizards' scaly hides.

Muldoon slid back and took charge of the kids, moving them into the
houses to either side of the one Mutt was in. Daniels had the heady feeling
of actually being part of a real fighting line again, not just a picket of
a band of skirmishers. That quickly went away. The new fish not only
wouldn't know when to shoot and when not to, they wouldn't shoot worth
a damn when they did open up.

Sure as hell, one of them let lose with a long burst from a tommy gun.
Through the racket – and after it abruptly fell silent – Daniels listened
to Muldoon raking the kid over the coals: 'You go blowin' it off like that
again, you worthless no-brain turd, and the lieutenant'll chew on your
ass, not just me. You don't ever want that to happen, buddy, believe me
you don't.'

Mutt snorted rueful laughter as Muldoon came back to him by way of
a battered trench (in France in 1918 it hardly would have deserved the
name; they'd known how to build trenches then) that ran across what had
been a neat urban lawn. When Daniels had been a noncom, he, too, had
warned privates about the fearsome wrath of their officers. Now he was
one of those officers, awesome and distant as some minor league god. He

hadn't changed, but when he'd got his gold bar the way people looked at him had, sure as the dickens.

The Lizards, worse luck, weren't asleep at the switch. When somebody shot at them, they shot back. Mutt didn't know if they really had all the ammo in the world, but they sure as hell acted that way. He threw himself flat; he'd return fire after the storm calmed down. A thump told him Muldoon had gone down on his belly, too. Muldoon knew how things worked.

A couple of houses away, somebody started screaming for his mother in a high, broken voice. Mutt bit on his lip. One of the rookies had just found misfortune, or rather, it had found him. He hoped the kid wasn't wounded too badly. Any kind of gunshot wound hurt enough and was bloody enough to scare the piss out of you, even if it didn't set you pushing up the daisies.

He looked out through a hole in the wall, saw a couple of Lizards skittering forward under cover of all the lead they were laying down. He fired in their direction. They dived for cover. He nodded to himself. Some ways, he had more in common with the Lizards these days than he did with raw recruits on his own side.

A buzzing in the air made him scoot back from that hole. Anything in the air nowadays most likely belonged to the Lizards. When machine guns began to yammer, he congratulated himself on his good sense and hoped none of the new fish would get killed.

But the machine-gun bullets, by the sound of them, were slamming into the Lizard position, not his own. He grinned wickedly – the scaly bastards didn't often screw up like that. The aircraft, whatever it was, passed right overhead. A bomb landed on the Lizards, close enough to batter his ears and make the ground shake under him.

Even the most cautious man will take a chance every once in a while. Daniels wriggled forward, ever so warily peeked out through the hole in the wall. He burst out laughing, a loud, raucous noise altogether at variance with the racket of combat.

'What the hell?' Muldoon grunted.

'You know what just strafed the Lizards, Muldoon?' Daniels held up a solemn hand to show he was telling the truth: 'A so-help-me-God Piper Cub with a couple machine guns, one slung under each wing. Got away, too. Flew in maybe ten feet off the rooftops here, or what's left of 'em, shot up the Lizards, dropped that light bomb, and got the hell out of there.'

'A Piper Cub, Lieutenant?' Muldoon didn't sound as if he believed his ears. 'Jesus God, we really must be scraping the bottom of the barrel.'

'I dunno about that,' Mutt answered. 'I heard somewheres the Russians been giving the Lizards fits with these little no-account biplanes, fly so low and slow they're damn near impossible to stop until they're right on top of you – they can do stuff a regular fighter plane can't.'

'Maybe,' Muldoon said doubtfully. 'I tell you one thing, though, sir: you wouldn't get me up on one of those little crates, not for all the tea in China. Hell, the Lizards can pick out which eye they're gonna shoot you through. No, thanks. Not for me, no way, nohow.'

'Not for me, either,' Daniels admitted. 'I ain't never been on an airplane, an' it's too late for me to start now. But this here ain't exactly a safe line o'work we done picked ourselves, neither.'

'Boy, don't I wish you was wrong.' Muldoon slithered up beside Mutt. 'But them Lizards, half the time they ain't aiming at me in particular. They're just throwin' bullets around, and if I happen to stop one, I do. But if you're up there in an airplane and they're shooting at you, that's *personal*, you know what I mean?'

'I guess maybe I do,' Mutt said, 'but a dogface who stops one of those bullets with his head, he's just as dead as the Red Baron who got shot down all personal-like.'

Muldoon didn't answer. He was looking out through the hole in the wall. Mutt got up on one knew and peered through the window. The strafing run from the Piper Cub had taken the wind right out of the sales of the Lizards' pounding of his position. That made him think he could maybe do a little pounding of his own.

'Stay here and give us some coverin' fire,' he told Muldoon. 'I'm gonna see if we can head south for a change, 'stead o' north.'

At Muldoon's acknowledging nod, Daniels crawled through the trench to the ruins of the house next door. The men who had dug it had broken both gas and water mains, but, since neither had worked for months, that didn't matter. A soldier he didn't recognize gave him a hand up out of the trench.

He pointed southward. 'They're hurting there. Let's go take us back some houses before they remember which end is up.'

The young soldiers cheered with an intensity that made him proud and frightened at the same time. They'd do whatever they thought it took, the same way a young outfielder would chase a fly ball right into a fence. Sometimes the fence would be wood, and give a little. Sometimes it would be concrete. Then they'd cart the kid off on a stretcher.

They'd cart a lot of these kids off on stretchers before the fight was through. Mutt tried not to think about that. They'd carted him off on a stretcher once already. Now he was back. He hoped he'd stay in there this time.

'Come on, we can't waste time here,' he said. He told some men to move forward with him, others to say back and give covering fire. The ones he told to stay back squawked and pouted like spoiled children deprived of a lollipop. He held up a hand: 'Don't get in a swivet, boys. This here'll be fire and move. Soon as we find cover up ahead, we'll hunker down and start shootin' so you-all can move on up ahead of us. You'll get your share, I promise.' *Your share of shattered skulls and splintered bones and belly wounds.*

Exploiting such eagerness filled Mutt with guilt. He'd never again feel it himself.

Yelling like fiends, his men moved forward, some shooting from the hip to add to the Americans' firepower and make the Lizards keep their heads down. Mutt dived behind the burnt-out hulk of somebody's old Packard. Sheet metal wouldn't keep bullets from biting him, not the way a good pile of concrete or dirt would. But if the Lizards couldn't see him, they wouldn't send as many bullets toward him.

A couple of men were down, one twisting, one ominously limp and still. The Lizards weren't sending out the wall of lead they had before, though. Daniels waved for the troops who had been covering to move forward, past and through the detachment that had accompanied him. Those men, in turn, laid down covering fire for their buddies. They did a better job than Mutt had thought they had in them. Maybe he would be able to push the Lizards out of their forward positions.

One Lizard had other ideas. He'd pop up in a window like a jack-in-the-box, squeeze off a few rounds, and duck back down before anybody could nail him. He was a good shot, too. Somebody brave and stubborn and lucky like that, whether human or twisty-eyed alien critter, could derail an advance.

Mutt gauged the distance from himself to the house in which the Lizard sheltered: maybe fort yards. The window the Lizard was using wasn't a very big one, which wasn't surprising – being a twisty-eyed alien critter didn't make you stupid. The Lizard let loose with another burst. Off to Mutt's right, a human voice started screaming.

He grimaced, shook his head, and took a grenade from his belt. His arm had got him to the majors, even if that was a long time ago – and even if his lousy bat hadn't let him stay there. Almost without conscious thought, he went into a catcher's crouch in back of, not the plate, but the trunk of the Packard.

He yanked the pin out of the grenade, popped up (knocking off his helmet with the back of one wrist, as if it had been a catcher's mask), and let fly. He went down behind the car before the grenade sailed through the window. It went off with a *bang!* different from those of the rifles and submachine guns and Lizard automatic weapons all around.

A GI dashed for that window. The Lizard didn't pop up to shoot him. The young dogface leaned in (suicidally stupid, had the Lizard been playing possum), and fired a long burst from his tommy gun. 'Hell of a peg, Lieutenant!' he yelled. 'Little bastard's raw meat now.' Cheers rang amid the shooting.

Move and fire, more and fire ... and then the Lizards were moving and firing, too, in retreat. Mutt ran to a corner of the house where the tough Lizard had holed up, fired at its buddies as they pulled back. For the time being, a block of ruined North Side Chicago was back in American hands.

By the hideous standards of fighting in the city, that counted for a victory. He owed the kids a mental apology. They'd done great.

Ttomalss wondered again how any Tosevite ever lived to grow up. The hatchling he was hand-rearing was more than half a year old; it had also had a year and a half of growth inside the female who bore it. It was still helpless. It still had no control over its messy bodily functions; the chamber in which it lived – in which Ttomalss perforce did most of his living, too – smelled unpleasantly of stale Tosevite waste.

Several times a day, Ttomalss wished he had left the Big Ugly hatchling with the female from whose body it had so disgustingly emerged. She'd fought like a wild thing to keep the little squalling creature. If she had had it all this time, Ttomalss was confident she would have been willing to hand it over to him decorated with whatever the Big Uglies used to signify a gift.

It was lying on the soft mat where it slept – when it slept. Lately, Ttomalss had had to install wire mesh around the mat, because the hatchling had – finally – developed enough neuromuscular control to roll over. At this stage of their lives, hatchlings of the Race were aggressive little predators: keeping them from hurting themselves and others counted for more than anything else in raising them. The only way the Tosevite could hurt itself would be to roll off a high place and fall down. No hatchling of the Race would have been so foolish.

The little Big Ugly looked up at Ttomalss out of its dark, narrow eyes. Its elastic face twisted into the grimace Tosevites used to show amiability. It kicked its arms and legs, as if that added to the effect of the facial grimace. Most of the time, it seemed sublimely unaware of its limbs, though it was beginning to suspect it had hands.

It let out a long sequence of meaningless noises. That still unnerved Ttomalss every time he hard it. Hatchlings of the Race were silent little things, which made sense in evolutionary terms: if you were small and quiet, you were less likely to get eaten than if you were small and raucous.

Ttomalss said to it, 'You are the most preposterous specimen of a preposterous planet.'

The hatchling made more burbling noises. It liked him to talk to it. Its arms and legs kicked more. Then it started to whimper. He knew what that meant: it wanted to be picked up.

'Come here,' he said, bending over and lifting it off the mat. Its head didn't flop around so loosely that it had to be supported, as had been true at the onset. Now it could hold that big, ungainly head up and look around. It liked being held against his warm skin. When its mouth fell onto his shoulder, it started sucking, as if he secreted nutrient fluid. He found the wet, slimy touch most unpleasant. It would suck on anything its mouth could reach; it would even suck when it was asleep.

'What am I going to do with you?' he asked it, as if it could understand. Males of the Race often embarked on lifetime research projects, but raising a Tosevite up to what passed for adulthood in the species? He'd had something like that in mind when he took the work the job involved. But it kept on being so much work for years to come ...

'I'll fall over dead,' he told the hatchling. It wiggled at the sound of his voice. It was a social little thing. 'I'll fall over dead,' he repeated. It seemed to recognise the repetition, and to like it. It made a noise which, after a moment, he recognized as a hatchling-sized version of the vocalization Big Uglies used for laughter.

'I'll fall over dead,' he said, again and again. The hatchling found that funnier and funnier for several repetitions, laughing and squealing and kicking its feet against his chest. Then, for whatever reason, the joke wore thin. The hatchling started to fuss.

He gave it a bottle of nutrient fluid, and it gulped avidly. He knew what that meant: it was sucking in air along with liquid. When it did that, the air had to be got out of the hatchling's stomach; it commonly returned along with slightly digested fluid, which stank even worse than the stuff that came out the other end.

He was glad the hatchling seemed healthy, such revolting characteristics aside. The Race's knowledge of Tosevite biochemistry and pathogens still left a great deal to be desired, while the Big Uglies were as ignorant about that as they were about everything else save military hardware. Some of their not-empires knew how to immunize against some of their common diseases, and had begun to get the idea that there might be such things as antibiotics. Past that, their knowledge stopped.

Ttomalss wondered if he should give the hatchling such immunizations as the Big Uglies had developed. The little Tosevite would eventually encounter others of its own kind. The Big Uglies had a concept called 'childhood diseases': illnesses that were mild if a hatchling contracted them but could be serious if caught in adulthood. The notion made Ttomalss, who had never suffered from any such misfortunes, queasy, but research showed the Race had shared it in the earliest days of recorded history.

The hatchling started to wail. Ttomalss had heard that particular cry many times before, and knew it meant genuine distress. He knew what kind of distress, too: the air it had sucked in was distending its stomach. He resignedly picked up one of the cloths used for containing bodily wastes and draped it over his shoulder.

'Come on, get the air out,' he told the hatchling as he patted its back. It twisted and writhed, desperately unhappy at what it had done to itself. Not for the first time, the Big Uglies' feeding arrangements for their young struck him as being inefficient as well as revolting.

The hatchling made a noise astonishingly loud and deep for something its size. It stopped thrashing, a sign its distress was eased. The sour odor that reached Ttomalss' chemoreceptors said it had indeed spit up some of the nutrient fluid he'd given it. He was glad he'd draped himself with the cloth; not only did the fluid smell bad, it also dissolved his body paint.

He was about to lay the hatchling back on the mat when it made another noise with which he was intimately familiar: a throaty grunt. He felt sudden warmth against the arm under the hatchling's hindquarters. With a weary, hissing sigh, he carried it over to the cabinet, undid the fastenings that held the cloth round the hatchling's middle closed, and tossed that cloth into a sealed bin along with several others he'd put there that day.

Before he could put another cloth under the hatchling, it dribbled out a fair quantity of liquid waste to accompany the solid (or at least semisolid) waste it had just passed. He mopped that off the hatchling and off the cabinet top, reminding himself to disinfect the latter. While he was cleaning up, the hatchling almost rolled off the cabinet.

He caught it with a desperate lunge. 'You are the most troublesome thing!' he exclaimed. The hatchling squealed and made Tosevite laughing noises. It thought his displays of temper were very funny.

He noticed the skin around its anus and genitals looked red and slightly inflamed. That had happened before; luckily, one of the Race's topical medications eased the problem. He marveled at an organism whose wastes were toxic to its own integument. His scaly hide certainly never had any such difficulties.

'But then,' he told the hatchling. 'I don't make a habit of smearing waste all over my skin.' The hatchling laughed its loud Tosevite laugh. Fed, deflated, and cleaned, it was happy as could be. Tired, bedraggled Ttomalss wished he could say the same.

Clouds rolled across the sky, more and more of them in bigger and bigger masses as the day wore on. The sun peeked through in ever-shorter blinks. Ludmila Gorbunova cast a wary eye upwards. At any moment the autumn rain would start falling, not only on Pskov but all over the western Soviet Union. With the rains would come mud – the fall *rasputitsa*. When the mud came, fighting would bog down for a while.

And Pskov still remained in human hands. She knew a certain amount of pride in that, even if some of those hands were German. She'd done her part in the battle to hold the Lizards, and the alien imperialist aggressors were not pushing attacks with the élan they'd shown the year before. Maybe, when snow replaced rain and mud, the human forces in Pskov (yes, even the fascist beasts) would show them the proper meaning of the word.

The Lizards didn't like winter. The whole world had seen that the year before. She hoped this winter would bring a repetition of the pattern. She'd already proved a *Kukuruznik* would fly through almost anything. Its radial engine was air-cooled; she didn't have to fret about coolant turning to ice, as happened in liquid-cooled engines forced to endure Russian winter. As long as she had fuel and oil, she could fly.

With Georg Schultz as her mechanic, she sometimes wondered, not quite jokingly, whether she might not be able to fly even without fuel and oil. The more he worked his magic on the little U-2, the more she wondered how the planes she'd flown had kept from falling apart before they enjoyed his ministrations.

She opened and closed her hands. She had black dirt and grease under her nails and ground into the folds of skin on her knuckles; not even a steam bath could sweat the dirt out of her. She did a lot of work on her own aircraft, too, and knew she made a better mechanic than most Russian groundcrew men. But Schultz had an artist's touch with spanner and pliers, to say nothing of an instinct for where trouble lay, that made Ludmila wonder if he was part biplane on his mother's side.

Houses thinned as she walked toward the airstrip just east of Pskov. It lay between the city and the great forest where partisans had sheltered until they and the Germans made uneasy common cause against the Lizards.

If you didn't know where the airstrip was, you'd walk right past it. The Russian passion for *maskirovka* made sure of that. The Lizards had repeatedly bombed a dummy strip a couple of kilometers away, but they'd left the real one alone. The *Kukuruzniks* all rested in shelters covered by netting with real sod laid over them. More sod replaced ruts in the grass the aircraft made on takeoff and landing. No sentries paced nearby, though several marched at the dummy airstrip.

Ludmila reached into her pocket and pulled out a compass. She didn't trust the one on her instrument panel, and wondered if some idiot groundcrew man had somehow got near it with a magnet. Whether or not that was so, now she'd have one against which to check it.

She had to look sharp to find the first mat that concealed a U-2. When she did, she started counting; her aircraft was fifth in line. She paused outside the trench in which it rested, bent down, leaned her head toward the mat. Yes, someone was down in there; she could hear soft, muffled noises.

'*Bozhe moi*,' she whispered silently. The better to preserve the *maskirovka*, no one, not even groundcrew, hung around the airplanes when they weren't heading out to a mission or coming back from one. Had the Lizards managed to find a human being who would do sabotage for them here? Ludmila hadn't imagined such a thing was possible, but then, she hadn't imagined how many Soviet citizens would go over to the Germans, either.

As quietly as she could, she drew her pistol out of its holster. Then she tiptoed around to the deep end of the trench, where her arrival would be least expected. Before she lifted up a corner of the mat, she paused to listen again. The noises seemed fainter here. She nodded in grim satisfaction. She'd give the wrecker in there something to remember as long as he lived, which wouldn't be long.

She slid under the mat and dropped down to the dirt beneath. The bottom of the trench was almost three meters below ground level. She landed hard, but didn't try to stay on her feet. If by some mischance the wrecker had a gun, too, a prone figure made a smaller target than an upright one.

It was dim and dark under the matting. Even so, she had no trouble picking out the pale body – no, bodies: there were two of them, something she hadn't thought of – under one wing of the *Kukuruznik*. They both lay on the ground, too. Had she alerted them when she jumped down into the trench?

'Stop what you're doing!' she yelled at the top of her lungs, swinging the muzzle of the Tokarev automatic toward them.

Only then did she realize the two bodies seemed so pale and white because she was seeing skin, not clothes. '*Gott in Himmel*, is that you, Ludmila Vadimovna?' Georg Schultz demanded. 'You don't want me, and now you want to kill me for finding somebody else? Are you crazy?'

'*Bozhe moi*,' Ludmila repeated, this time quite loudly. She started to giggle. The giggles turned to guffaws. 'I thought you were sabotaging the *Kukuruznik*, not, – not—' Laughter swallowed speech.

'Not funny,' Schultz muttered. He was on his feet now, getting into his clothes as fast as he could. So was his partner. Ludmila's eyes were more used to the gloom now. They widened as she recognized Tatiana Pirogova.

'I *am* sorry,' Ludmila said, speaking very quietly and taking only tiny breaths to hold mirth in check. 'The only reason I came here was to mount a spare compass on the aircraft, and—' She thought too much about the use of the word *mount* in another context, and couldn't go on. Tears filled her eyes as she sputtered and coughed.

Tatiana Pirogova strode up to her. The blonde sniper was several centimeters taller than Ludmila, and glared down at her. 'If ever you speak a word of this to anyone – to *anyone*, do you understand me? – I will kill you,' she hissed. Even in the dimness under the matting, her blue eyes glittered dangerously.

'Your top tunic is still undone, dear,' Ludmila answered. Tatiana's fingers flew to it of themselves. Ludmila went on, 'I'm not in the habit of gossiping, but if you threaten me, you are making a big mistake.' Tatiana turned her back. Ludmila looked over to George Schultz, switching to German as she did so: 'Will you please make her believe I'm just as glad to have you with someone else so you're not pestering me any more? Just thinking of that is more likely to keep me quiet than her bluster.'

'It's not bluster,' he answered, also in German.

That was probably – no, certainly – true. Tatiana with a scope-mounted rifle in her hand was as deadly a soldier as any. And Ludmila had also seen that Schultz was a viciously effective combat soldier even without his panzer wrapped around him. She wondered if that shared delight in war was what had drawn him and Tatiana together. But she'd been in enough combat herself to keep Tatiana or Georg Schultz from intimidating her.

Schultz spoke to Tatiana in the same sort of mixture of German and Russian he used to talk with Ludmila. Tatiana angrily brushed aside his reassurances. 'Oh, go away,' she snapped. Instead, she went away herself, slithering out from under the netting at the shallow end of the trench that hid the *Kukuruznik*. Even in her fury, she carefully smoothed out the net after she got free of it, so as not to damage the *maskirovka*.

'You might have waited another minute or two before you jumped down in here,' Schultz said petulantly. He hadn't finished, then. That set Ludmila laughing yet again. 'It isn't funny,' he growled. It occurred to her then that the two of them were alone under the netting. Had she not had the Tokarev, she would have worried. As things were, she knew she could take care of herself.

'Yes, it is,' she said, the weight of the pistol reassuring in her hand. 'Look, if you want to come down here again, move one of the rocks that holds down the netting so it's just off the edge instead of just on. I had no idea anyone was down with the aircraft, and when I did hear noise, I thought it was wreckers, not – not lovers.'

Somewhat mollified, Schultz nodded. 'I'll do that,' he said, adding gloomily, 'If there is a next time.'

'There probably will be.' Ludmila surprised herself at how cynical she sounded. She asked, 'Why was Tatiana so upset at the idea of anyone finding out she's with you? She didn't care who knew she was sleeping with the Englishman – Jones, his name is.'

'*Ja*,' Schultz said. 'But he's an Englishman. That's all right. Me, I'm a German. You may have noticed.'

'Ah,' Ludmila said. It did make sense. The fair Tatiana used her sniping talents against the Lizards these days, but she'd honed them against the Nazis. She made no secret of her continued loathing for Germans in general – but not, evidently, for one German in particular. If word got out, she would be compromised in a whole unpleasant variety of ways. 'If she hates Germans so much, what does she see in you?'

'She says we're both killers.' Georg Schultz shuffled his feet, as if unsure whether he liked the sound of that or not.

As far as Ludmila was concerned, it not only had a lot of truth in it, it also confirmed her earlier guess, which made her feel clever. She said, 'Well, *Gospodin* Killer – you, a German, would be angry if I called you *Tovarishch* Killer, Comrade instead of Mister – I think we had both better go now.'

She was nervous as she got out from under the netting. If Schultz wanted to try anything, that was the moment he'd do it. But he just emerged, too, and looked back toward the place where the U-2 was hidden. 'Damnation,' he said. 'I thought sure nobody would ever bother us there.'

'You never can tell,' Ludmila said, which would do as a maxim for life in general, not just trying to fornicate with an attractive woman.

'*Ja*.' George Schultz grunted laughter. After the fact, he'd evidently decided what had happened was funny, too. He hadn't thought so at the time. Nor had Tatiana. Ludmila didn't think she would find it funny, not if she lived another seventy-five years.

Ludmila glanced over at Schultz out of the corner of her eye. She chuckled softly to herself. Though she'd never say it out loud, her opinion was that he and Tatiana deserved each other.

David Goldfarb sat up in the hay wagon that was taking him north through the English Midlands toward Nottingham. To either side, a couple of other men in tattered, dirty uniforms of RAF blue sprawled in the hay. They were all blissfully asleep, some of them snoring enough to give a creditable impression of a Merlin fighter engine.

Goldfarb wished he could lie back and start sawing wood, too. He'd tried, but sleep eluded him. Besides, looking at countryside that hadn't been pounded to bits was a pleasant novelty. He hadn't seen much of that sort, not lately.

The only thing he had in common with his companions was the grubby uniforms they all wore. When the Lizards invaded England, nobody had thought past fighting them by whatever means came to hand. After Bruntingthorpe got smashed up, he'd been made into a foot soldier, and he'd done his best without a word of complaint.

Now that the northern pocket was empty of aliens and the southern one shrinking, though, the Powers That Be were once more beginning to think in terms longer than those of the moment. Whenever officers spied an RAF man who'd been dragooned into the army, they pulled him out and sent him off for reassignment. Thus Goldfarb's present situation.

Night was coming. As summer passed into autumn, the hours of daylight shrank with dizzying speed. Even Double Summer Time couldn't disguise that. In the fields, women and old men labored with horses, donkeys, and oxen to bring in the harvest, as they might have during the wars against Napoleon, or against William the Conqueror, or against the Emperor Claudius. People would be hungry now, too, as they had been then.

The wagon rattled past a burnt-out farmhouse, the ground around it cratered by bombs. The war had not ignored the lands north of Leicester, it merely had not been all-consuming here. For a moment, a pile of wreckage made the landscape seem familiar to Goldfarb. He angrily shook his head when he realized that. Finding a landscape familiar because the Lizards had bombed it was like finding a husband familiar because he beat you. Some women were supposed to be downtrodden enough to do just that. He thought it madness himself.

'How long till we get to Watnall?' he called to the driver, softly, so he wouldn't wake his comrades.

'Sometime tonight, Ah reckon,' the fellow answered. He was a little old wizened chap who worked his jaws even when he wasn't talking. Goldfarb had seen that before. Usually it meant the chap who did it was used to chewing tobacco and couldn't stop chewing even when tobacco was no longer to be had.

Goldfarb's stomach rumbled. 'Will you stop off to feed us any time before then?' he asked.

'Nay, no more'n Ah will to feed mahself,' the driver said. When he put it that way, Goldfarb didn't have the crust to argue further.

He rummaged in his pockets and came up with half a scone he'd forgotten he had. It was so stale, he worried about breaking teeth on it; he devoured it more by abrasion than mastication. It was just enough to make his stomach growl all the more fiercely but not nearly enough to satisfy him, not even after he licked the crumbs from his fingers.

He pointed to a cow grazing in a field. 'Why don't you stop for a bit so we can shoot that one and worry off some steaks?'

'Think you're a funny bloke, do you?' the driver said. 'You try lookin' at that cow too long and some old man like me back there in the bushes, he'll blow your head off for you, mark ma words. He hasn't kept his cow so long bein' sweet and dainty, Ah tell you that.'

Since the driver was very likely right, Goldfarb shut up.

Night fell with an almost audible thud. It got cold fast. He started to bury himself in the hay with his mates, then had a second thought and asked the driver, 'Besides the Fighter Command Group HQ, wot'n 'ell's in Watnall?' By sounding like a Cockney for three words, he made a fair pun of it.

If the driver noticed, he wasn't impressed. 'There's nobbut the group headquarters there,' he answered, and spat into the roadway. ''Twasn't even a village before the war.'

'How extremely depressing,' Goldfarb said, going from one accent to another: for a moment there, he sounded like a Cambridge undergraduate. He wondered how his fellow radarman was faring these days, and then whether Jones was still alive.

'Watnall's not far from Nottingham,' the driver said, the first time since he'd stepped up onto his raised seat that he'd actually volunteered anything. 'Nobbut a few miles.'

The consolation Goldfarb had felt at the first sentence – Nottingham was a good-sized city, with the promise of pubs, cinemas when the power was on, and people of the female persuasion – was tempered by the second. If he couldn't lay hands on a bicycle, a few miles in wartime with winter approaching might as well have been the far side of the moon.

He vanished into the hay like a dormouse curling up in its nest to hibernate. One of his traveling companions, still sleeping, promptly stuck an elbow in his ribs. He didn't care. He huddled closer to the other RAF man, who, however fractious he might have been in his sleep, was also warm. He fell asleep himself a few minutes later, even as he was telling himself he wouldn't.

When he woke again, something had changed. In his muzziness, he needed a moment to figure out what: they weren't moving. He sat up, brushing straw from his hair. 'What's happened?' he asked.

One of the other RAF men, a Liverpudlian whom Goldfarb knew only as Henry, answered before the driver could: 'We're in Nottingham, we are. They're going t'give us some grub after all.' His clotted accent said he was a factory worker from a long line of factory workers.

'Jolly good!' Goldfarb brushed at himself again, trying to get as close to presentable as he could. It was wasted effort, because of his own disheveled state and because the night was too dark to let anyone see anything much. Stars glittered in a black, black sky, but shed little light, and the moon, some days past full, hadn't yet risen.

'We've soup for you, lads,' a woman's voice said out of the gloom; Goldfarb could make out her silhouette, but no more. 'Here, come take your panikins. Have a care – they're hot.'

Hot the soup was, and full of cabbage, potatoes, and carrots. Goldfarb didn't find any meat in his tin bowl, but the broth tasted as if it had been somewhere within shouting distance of a chicken in the not too distant past.

'Sticks to your ribs, that does,' Henry said happily. The other RAF men made wordless noises of agreement. So did the driver, who was also getting outside a bowl of soup.

'Pass me back your bowls when you're done, lads, and we'll serve 'em out again to the next lot who come through hungry, or maybe to some of our own,' the woman said. Goldfarb couldn't see her, couldn't tell if she was young or old, ugly or beautiful. Food – and even more, kindness – made him feel halfway in love with her just the same.

When all the bowls and spoons had been returned, the driver said, '*Get* along there,' and the horses ambled on. Goldfarb called thanks back to the woman who'd given them the soup.

As the driver had said, they got into Watnall in the middle of the night. The transition was abrupt: one minute they were rolling through open country, the next in among Nissen huts and Maycrete buildings that seemed to have sprung from the middle of nowhere – which made a pretty fair description of Watnall, now that Goldfarb thought on it. They rattled by a couple of ack-ack guns, whose crews jeered at them: 'Coming back to work, are you, at last, dearies? Did you have a pleasant holiday?'

'Bugger off,' Goldfarb said, which summed up his comrades' responses pretty well, too. The ack-ack gunners laughed.

Henry said, 'What they were shootin' at, it were up in the sky, and they weren't in range of the bleedin' Lizards every minute of every bleedin' day. 'Ad it right soft, they did, you ask me.'

'Amen to that,' Goldfarb said, and the other RAF men on the wagon added not only agreement but profane embellishment. If you weren't a pilot, you were probably safer in the RAF than as an infantryman. You certainly lived softer in the RAF than in the poor bloody infantry, as you learned if you found yourself at the thin end of the wedge on the ground, the way Goldfarb had.

The driver pulled back on the reins. His two-horse team stopped. One of the animals bent its head and began pulling up grass. 'Taxi ride's done, lads,' the driver said. He pointed, 'You go over there now.'

'Over there' was a Nissen hut, its semicylindrical bulk black against the slightly lighter sky. Goldfarb scrambled down from the wagon. He led the way toward the hut. Several of the other RAF men hung back, grumbling. He was glad he'd be returning to a job that could use his special skills. Any bloke could make an infantryman.

He opened the door and pushed his way through two blackout curtains. The light inside came from candles and lanterns, not electric fixtures, but still seemed bright to his night-accustomed eyes. A tired-looking flight sergeant waved him over to a desk piled high with forms. 'All right, let's see what we can do with you,' he said. He examined Goldfarb's draggled uniform. 'You've not had the easiest time of it, seems like.'

Goldfarb shrugged. 'You do what you have to do.'

'That's the way of it,' the flight sergeant said, nodding. He pulled out a form and a short nub of pencil. 'Very good – stand and deliver.' Goldfarb rattled off his name – surname first, Christian name (an irony in his case), middle initial – rank, and service number. The flight sergeant wrote them down, then asked, 'And your speciality, uh, Goldfarb?'

'I'm a radarman, sir.'

The flight sergeant started to write that down, too, then looked up sharply at Goldfarb. 'Radarman? Somebody should have his bloody head examined, turning you into a ground-pounding Tommy. How the devil did that happen?'

'Sir, I was on duty south of Leicester when the Lizards hit my establishment. We beat them back, but they wrecked the place and scattered us to the four winds. I fell in with some soldiers, and—' He spread his hands. 'You know how it is, sir. I was separated from my unit, but I still wanted to fight, and so I did.'

The flight sergeant sighed. 'If I had a farthing for every time I've heard that story this past fortnight, I'd be the richest man in England, sure as hell. But a radarman—' His grin suddenly made him look younger than he had. 'I'll get a "well done" for coming up with you, I will. What was your establishment, and what were you doing there?'

'I don't like to say, sir,' Goldfarb answered. Radar had been a secret vital to conceal from the Germans when the war was young. The Lizards knew more about radar than any Englishman was likely to learn for the next generation, but old habits died hard.

'What was your establishment, and what did you do there?' the flight sergeant repeated with the air of a man used to cutting through multiple layers of nonsense. 'Don't waste my time.'

The rest of the RAF men stood before other desks, giving out their service records. Goldfarb surrendered: 'Sir, I was at Bruntingthorpe, working under Group Captain Hipple to fit radar into Meteor jets and to see what we could learn from captured Lizard radars.'

'Then you bloody well ought to be court-martialed for letting anybody – and I mean up to the field-marshal's rank – take you away from what you were doing,' the flight sergeant said. At Goldfarb's alarmed expression, he went on, 'Don't worry. That's not going to happen. But getting yourself shot up would have been a bloody waste.'

'Sir, Bruntingthorpe had taken a hiding,' Goldfarb said defensively. 'I don't even know if Group Captain Hipple is alive or dead.'

'If he's dead, someone else will be minding that store.' The flight sergeant spoke with conviction. 'And if everyone above you has bought his plot, why then, the store is yours.'

'Mine?' Goldfarb was mortified when his voice rose to a startled squeak, but couldn't help it. He stammered on: 'I'm – I don't know enough on my own. I—'

'If you know more about it than anyone else who might do it, it'll be yours,' the flight sergeant said. He turned to the flying officer at the desk next to his. 'Pardon me, sir, but I've a chap here who's not only a radarman but has also been working on a couple of what sound like Most Secret projects.'

'Just you wait one moment,' the flying officer said to the aircraftman standing in front of him. He grilled Goldfarb for a minute or two, then raised his eyes to the heavens in an expression of theatrical despair. 'You were at Bruntingthorpe, you say, and they drafted you into the infantry? Dear God in heaven, I sometimes think we deserve to lose this war as punishment for our own stupidity.'

'Sir, after the base took a pounding, I wanted to hit back at the Lizards any way I could,' Goldfarb said. 'I wasn't drafted into the infantry – I wanted to fight.'

'Young man, that only makes you a fool, too.' The flying officer might possibly have been two years older than Goldfarb. 'You can do them much more damage fighting with your head than with a rifle. Flight Sergeant, get on the telephone to London. Ask them where the most fitting possible billet for your man is, then see that he gets to it.' He gave his attention back to the patiently waiting aircraftman. 'Do carry on. You were saying landing gear was your maintenance speciality?'

'You come with me,' the flight sergeant told Goldfarb, rising from his desk.

Goldfarb came. 'You can ring up London?' he asked, following the other RAF man out into the night. 'I thought all telephone lines were long since wrecked.'

'All the civilian ones are, and likely to stay so,' the flight sergeant answered. 'You want to be careful here; if you step off the path, you'll be ankle-deep in muck. Can't very well run a military outfit, though, without being able to talk back and forth, eh?'

'I suppose not.' Goldfarb couldn't see the path he wasn't supposed to step off of, which gave each step a certain feeling of adventure. He went on, 'It must have been a bit dicey while the Lizards stood between here and London.'

'Oh, it was,' the flight sergeant agreed cheerily. 'We were cut off a couple of times, as a matter of fact. But ground-laid cable is not what you'd call conspicuous, and we managed to infiltrate men to make repairs the couple of times it did get broken. Ah, here we are.'

He opened the door to a Maycrete building whose walls were already beginning to crumble even though they'd been up for only a couple of years. After the usual pair of blackout curtains, he and Goldfarb went into a stuffy little room where a corporal sat relaxing by what looked like a fancied-up version of an ordinary field telephone.

The corporal nodded to the flight sergeant. ''Ello, Fred,' he said, dropping his aitches like the lower-class Londoner he undoubtedly was. ''Oo's this bloke wiv yer?'

'Flying officer says we've got to ring up London, figure out what the devil to do with him,' the flight sergeant – Fred – answered. 'Get them on the horn for me, would you?'

'Right y'are.' The corporal vigorously turned the crank on the side of the telephone, then picked up the handset. Goldfarb watched the process with interest. Any new gadget fascinated him, and he hadn't seen this model of telephone before. He wished he could ask questions, but the corporal was intent on his task. Suddenly the fellow grinned and began to talk: ''Ello, darlin', I was 'opin' you'd be on tonight. 'Ow's tricks?'

'Chat her up another time, Nigel,' Fred said dryly. 'This is business.'

The corporal nodded, saying, 'Listen, love, put me frew' – it came out *frew* – 'to the blokes in Personnel, would you? That's a lamb – we got us a square peg wot wants a round 'ole.' He waited, then passed the handset to the flight sergeant.

Fred told Goldfarb's story to whoever was on the other end in London. The longer he talked, the more excited he sounded and the more details he asked of Goldfarb. 'Very good, sir. Thank you, sir,' he said at last. 'I'll see that he's sent on there straight away.' He hung up.

'Sent on where?' Goldfarb asked.

'Dover,' the flight sergeant answered. 'The Lizards never got that far, and I gather something which may interest you is going on there, though they wouldn't tell me – What's so funny?' 'Nothing, sir, not really,' Goldfarb said. He'd been thinking of a song from an American film he'd seen back before the war began, a catchy number called 'California, Here I Come.' After all this time, he'd be right back where he started from.

* * *

Barbara Yeager folded her hands over her belly. More forcefully than a shout, the wordless gesture reminded Sam she was pregnant. After not showing for what seemed a very long time, these past couple of months she'd ballooned. A couple of months more and he'd be a father.

'I wish you weren't going away,' Barbara said. She was a trouper; that was as close as she would come to reminding him things didn't always work out exactly as planned. Just because the baby was due around Christmastime didn't mean it had to wait that long.

He shrugged. 'They gave me my orders, hon. It's not like I have a whole lot of choice.' He patted the stripes on his shirtsleeve.

'You don't fool me one bit, Sam Yeager,' Barbara said, laughing at him. Maybe they'd been married only seven months or so, but she read him like a book. 'You're champing at the bit, and you know it. You and your pulp fiction.'

She said it affectionately, so it didn't sting, or not much. But he'd heard similar noises from so many people that his response sounded more nettled than it was: 'It's science fiction, not just any pulp fiction. And with the Lizards here, it's not fiction any more, it's the straight goods, same as ... what the Met Lab was working on.' They were alone in their room, but he didn't mention atomic bombs by name.

Barbara spread her hands. 'That's all true, and I admit every word of it. But you're as excited about working with a real live spaceship as a little kid would be with an all-day sucker.'

'Well, what if I am?' he said, yielding the point. 'I earned this chance, and I want to make the most of it. If I do a good job here, the way I did with the work on that light-amplifier gadget, maybe – just maybe – they'll turn me into an officer. And that's not minor league at all. I spent too much time in the bushes, babe – I want to hit the bigs.'

'I know,' Barbara answered. 'I think that's good – I think it's better than good, as a matter of fact. But as I said, you can't fool me. If we start building spaceships of our own, you want to ride one, don't you?'

Sam hugged her. The way her belly pressed against his reminded him again of the child growing within her. He said, 'Having a wife who understands me is a darn good thing. Sure, I'd love that, if it ever happens. And the only way it will is if I get real good at talking with the Lizards about how rockets work and what you're supposed to do with 'em. I don't have the education to know how to make 'em myself, or the training – and the reflexes – to be a pilot.'

'I understand all that,' she said, and kissed him fiercely. 'And I'm proud of you for it, and I love you for working hard to make something of yourself – and I wish you weren't going.'

'But I've got to.' He started to show her his wristwatch. Before he could, somebody knocked on the door. He quickly kissed her. 'I've got to go now, hon.' She nodded. He opened the door.

Standing in the hall were an Army major and a Lizard who wrote pretty fancy body paint. 'Morning, Yeager,' the major said. He wore horn-rimmed glasses and a thin, sandy mustache. The name tag above his right breast pocket said TOMPKINS.

'Morning, sir.'

The major glanced toward to the Lizard. 'And you'll know Vesstil, I expect – Straha's pilot for his flight down here.'

'Oh, sure.' Sam shifted into the Lizards' language: 'In the name of the Emperor, I greet you and wish you health.' Every time he talked with a male of the Race, he was reminded of just how informal a language English was. He'd never thought about that till he started picking up Lizard talk.

'I return your wishes in the Emperor's name,' Vesstil said in fair English. Even using English, he lowered his eyes at the mention of his sovereign.

'Okay, let's go.' Tompkins sounded like a man in a hurry. Yeager waved to Barbara one last time and set off behind him. To Vesstil, Tompkins said, 'We have clothes downstairs for you, to make you look like a human being if your friends upstairs are watching.'

'They are not my friends, not now,' the Lizard pilot said. 'If they were my friends, I should not be here assisting you.' The remark held an unmistakable note of reproof. Sam wondered if Tompkins heard it.

A Lizard in trousers and shirt and wide-brimmed hat could not help looking anything but ridiculous, not at close range. From the air, though, he'd seemed just another Big Ugly, which was the point of the exercise. He and his human companions got into a buckboard. A driver dressed like a hayseed clucked to the horses and flicked the reins. The wagon rattled off.

'We'd go faster if we were riding horses,' Sam said. 'We would if Vesstil here could ride one, anyway.' He translated the remark for the Lizard's benefit.

'I am willing to teach you how to fly the shuttlecraft the Race has made,' Vesstil said with dignity. 'I am not willing to learn to barbarously balance myself on the back of a beast. These creatures strike me as being more dangerous than flying between the stars, which is but a matter of routine. Beasts are unpredictable.' By the way he said it, that was an inexpiable sin.

They were on the road north for several days. The highways held little traffic, and all of it drawn by horses or mules. Yeager felt transported back into the days of his father's youth. Once they passed out of the pine woods and into those where broad-leafed trees predominated, the fiery colors of autumn replaced green. They interested Vesstil. None of the humans in the wagon could explain why the leaves changed color every year.

A sign on US 63 said they'd just passed from Arkansas up into Misorri. They'd also passed into what looked as if it had been one hell of a forest fire not so long ago. Yeager wondered if it had started when the rocket ship – the shuttlecraft, Vesstil called it – landed. He turned to Tompkins and said, 'Sir, how do you go about hiding a shuttlecraft?'

'You'll see when we get there,' the major answered, and set a finger alongside his nose. Sam didn't know what to make of that, but he kept quiet.

Before long, the wagon was jolting down winding country roads and then along unpaved tracks that would turn into hub-deep glue at the first good rain. Off in the distance, Yeager saw what looked like the wreckage of the biggest tent in the world. About half a mile farther on, he spotted another enormous canvas Big Top, this one with a couple of bomb craters close by.

The proverbial cartoon lightbulb went on above his head. 'We built so many tents, the Lizards never figured out which one had the pea under it.'

'Well, actually, they did,' Tompkins said. 'But by the time they did, we'd managed to strip it pretty completely. They manufacture these critters the same way we do Chevvies, except maybe even better – everything comes apart real easy so you can work on it if you have to.'

'How else would you build something?' Vesstil asked.

'You'd be amazed,' Major Tompkins answered, rolling his eyes behind the horn-rims. 'Your people have had a long, long time to learn to do everything the smooth way, the easy way, the efficient way. It's not like that with us. A lot of the stuff we're doing now, we're doing for the very first time. We aren't always as good at it as we might be, and we make a lot of dumb mistakes. But one way or another, we get it done.'

'This the Race has learned, often to its sorrow.' Vesstil made one of the leaky-kettle noises Lizards used when they were thinking hard. 'The shiplord Straha, my commander that was, has this trait also, in larger measure, at least, than is usual for a male of the Race. Because the fleetlord would not heed him, he decided to join his fate to you.'

And yet Straha had had kittens about unauthorized body-paint designs. Even a radical Lizard, Sam thought, was a reactionary by human standards. He said, 'I don't really get to go aboard a real live spaceship, then? Too bad. Even working with the parts will be pretty good, though.'

'A question, if I may,' Vesstil said: 'How does your English have a word for spaceship and the idea of a spaceship without having the spaceship itself? Does not the word follow the thing it describes?'

'Not always, not with us,' Yeager answered with a certain amount of pride. 'We have something called science fiction. That means stories that imagine what we'll be able to build when we know more than we do now. People who write those stories sometimes have to invent new words or use old ones in new ways to get across the new things or ideas they're talking about.'

'You Tosevites, you imagine too much and you move too fast to make what you imagine real – so the Race would say,' Vesstil answered with a sniffy hiss. 'Change needs study, not – stories.' He hissed again. Sam felt like laughing, or possibly pounding his head against the side of the buckboard. Of all the things *he'd* never imagined, a Lizard sneering at the concept of science fiction stood high on the list.

They came to a little hamlet called Couch. Yeager had been in a lot of little backwoods towns before. He'd waited for the locals to give them the suspicious once-over he'd got more times than he could count. Having Vesstil along should have made things worse. But the Couchians or Couchites or whatever they were went about their business. Sam wondered how many visiting firemen had come to look over the spaceship. Enough to get them used to the idea of strangers, anyway.

The driver pulled up at a general store across the street from a big shed, much the largest building in town. Yeager wondered what it had been for: curing tobacco, maybe. It had that look. But, to his surprise, Tompkins didn't take them over to the shed. Instead, they walked into the general store.

The fellow behind the counter was on the scrawny side and had a scraggly gray beard. Those details and some bare shelves aside, he and his store might have been pulled out of a Norman Rockwell painting and set in motion. 'Mornin',' he said with the hillbilly twang Yeager had heard from players in ballparks scattered all across the country.

'Morning, Terence,' Major Tompkins answered. 'Mind if we use your back room?' Terence (*hell of a name*, Sam thought) shook his head. Before the major could lead Yeager and Vesstil through the door to the back room, it opened, and three men came out into the store.

Sam stared. He knew he was staring, but he couldn't help it. Of all the people he never would have expected to see in a small-town general store, Albert Einstein ranked high on the list – so high, in fact, that he needed a moment to realize one of the physicist's companions was Benito Mussolini, complete with the enormous concrete jaw that showed up in all the newsreels.

Einstein eyed Vesstil with the same fascination Yeager felt toward *him*. Then the third man spoke to Tompkins: 'Bob's still back there. He's the one you'll want to see, isn't he, Major?'

'Yes, General Eisenhower,' the major answered. By then, Yeager had given up staring. When you got to the point where a mere general's company made him not worth noticing till he opened his mouth, you'd come a hell of a long way from the Three-I League.

Eisenhower shepherded his VIPs out of the general store. Tompkins shepherded his not-so-VIPs into the back room. Terence the storekeeper took everything in his stride.

The back room had a trapdoor set into the floor. As soon as he saw it, Yeager figured out what was going on. Sure enough, it led not to a basement but to a tunnel, formidably shored up with timber. Tompkins carried an old-fashioned lantern to light the way. The lantern might once have burned kerosene, but now the smell of hot fat came from it.

The tunnel came out inside the shed, as Sam had expected it would. The interior of the building did smell powerfully of tobacco, though none was curing there now. Sam sighed. He still missed cigarettes, even if his wind was better these days than it had been for the past ten years.

But he forgot all about his longing when he looked around. These tanks and lines and valves and unnameable gadgets had come out of a veritable spaceship Vesstil had flown down from outer space to the surface of the earth. If people could figure out how to duplicate them – and the frame in which they'd flown – space travel would turn real for mankind, too.

Prowling among the disassembled pieces of the Lizard shuttlecraft was a tall, gray-haired man with slightly stooped shoulders and a long, thoughtful face. 'Come on over with me – I'll introduce you,' Tompkins said to Sam. Nodding to the tall man, he said, 'Sir, this is Sergeant Sam Yeager, one of our best interpreters. Yeager, I'd like you to meet Robert Goddard. We filched him from the Navy when Vesstil brought Straha down in the shuttlecraft. He knows more about rockets than anyone around.'

'I'm very pleased to meet you, sir,' Yeager said, sticking out his hand. 'I've read about your work in *Astounding*.'

'Good – we won't be starting from scratch with you, then,' Goddard said with an encouraging smile. He was somewhere in his fifties, Yeager thought, but not very healthy ... or maybe, like so many people, just working himself to death. He went on, 'Hank – your Major Tompkins – is too kind. A good many Germans know more about this business than I do. They've made big ones; I've just made small ones. But the principles stay the same.'

'Yes, sir,' Yeager said. 'Can we build – one of these?' He waved at the collection of hardware.

'The mechanical parts we can match – or at least we can make equivalents for them,' Goddard said confidently. Then he frowned. 'The electric lines we can also match. The electronic controls are another matter altogether. There our friends here' – he nodded to Vesstil – 'are years, maybe centuries, ahead of us. Working around that will be the tricky part.'

'Yes, sir,' Sam repeated. 'What will you want me to do, sir?'

'You're supposed to be a hot translator, aren't you? You'll run questions and answers back and forth between me and Vesstil. Between what we already know and what he can tell us – it'll be a while before we get spaceships of our own, I expect, but even big rockets like the ones the Germans have would help us a lot. Hitting the Lizards from a couple of hundred miles away is a lot better than going at 'em face-to-face.'

'That's true, sir.' Sam wondered how big a rocket would have to be to carry an atomic bomb. He didn't ask. Vesstil had no business hearing of such things, and he didn't know whether Goddard was cleared from them, either.

He laughed a little. The United States didn't have a big rocket, and it didn't have atomic bombs, either – and here he was, putting the two together. From everything he'd seen of the Lizards, they didn't make leaps of imagination like that – which was why human beings still had a chance to win this war.

14

Nieh Ho-T'ing glowered at Liu Han. 'You are the most exasperating woman in the history of the world,' he snarled.

Liu Han smiled back across the table at the dingy Peking rooming house. She sipped tea, nibbled at a rice cake, and said nothing. She'd been saying nothing every since he'd let him know she had a good idea weeks before. He still had no notion what her idea was. She'd wanted to keep more control over it than he was willing to give: basically, she wanted to become one of the leaders in the Communists' Peking underground. Nieh hadn't been willing to pay that kind of price.

Beside him, Hsia Sho-Tao laughed raucously. 'You sound like you're in love with her, for heaven's sake,' he said. Nieh glowered at him, too. Hsia thought of everything in terms of his crotch, not economics. But he also thought he knew how to get what he wanted. 'If she won't open up, we can always liquidate her. No one would miss her, that's certain.'

Nieh glanced over to Liu Han to see if the threat had put her in fear. He didn't think it had, and he was expert in gauging such things. She said, 'If you kill me, you will never find out what I have in mind.'

'We don't have to kill you,' Hsia said, his voice all the more frightening because he sounded so genial. 'All we have to do is hurt you for a while.'

'Do what you want with me,' Liu Han said. 'But who will trust you with his ideas if you torture me?'

That made Nieh wince. Mao had written that guerrillas should be like a fish concealed within the school of the people. If they scared the people away from them, they would stand alone and exposed to the wrath of the little scaly devils. Sighing, he made his first retreat: 'I will give you what you ask, but only if I think your idea is good enough.'

'Then you will tell me you think it is bad, ignore me, and use it anyhow,' Liu Han said.

'I could do that now: make all the promises in the world and then break them,' Nieh Ho-T'ing reminded her. 'If you want your idea used against the little devils, sooner or later you will have to tell me what it is. And if you want your reward, you will have to trust a promise that you will get it.'

Liu Han looked thoughtful when he was through. But then he said, 'Any time anyone has promised me anything – men and little scaly devils both – it's turned out to be a lie. Why should you be any different?'

'Because we are comrades in a fight against the same enemy,' Nieh answered. 'If you show me a way to hurt the scaly devils, you *will* be rewarded. The People's Liberation Army does not exploit the women who fight side by side with their sons, fathers, husbands and brothers.' He kicked Hsia Shou-Tao under the table. He had spoken sound doctrine, and wished Hsia were better at living up to it.

Hsia, for a wonder, kept his mouth shut. And, after keeping silent so long, Liu Han at last wavered. 'I wish I could do this on my own,' she muttered. 'Then I wouldn't have to believe another pack of lies. But if I want to hurt the little devils – and I do – I need help. So—'

She talked for some time. The longer Nieh Ho-Ting listened to her low-voiced description of what she had in mind, the more impressed he got. Hsia Shou-Tao said 'A beast show!' in disparaging tones, but Nieh kicked him again. He wanted to hear every word of this.

When Liu Han finished, he dipped his head to her and said, 'I think you may deserve everything you have been saying you wanted for so long. If it works as it should, this will let us get in among the scaly devils: to spy certainly, and maybe, as you say, to kill.'

'That is what I want,' Liu Han said. 'I want the little devils to know I did it to them, too. They will know my name. It is in their records, and the machines that think for them will find it. They stole my child, my tiny daughter. Maybe I can force them to give her back.'

Nieh Ho-Ting sent her a severe look. 'And if they returned the child to you, you would abandon the campaign against the scaly imperialist aggressors?' he demanded. If she said yes to that, he would throw her out of the rooming house and think hard about having her liquidated. The dialectic of the class struggle was more important than merely personal concerns.

But Liu Han shook her head. 'Nothing would make me stop fighting the little scaly devils. I owe them too much for that. You Communists seem to be doing more to fight them than anyone except maybe the Japanese, and I hate the eastern devils, too. So I will work with you whether or not I have my child – but I want her back.'

'Good enough,' Nieh said, relaxing. Injuries suffered at the hand of oppressors often led folk to the People's Liberation Army. Once they learned the true doctrines the Communist Party espoused, they were likely to remain loyal members all their lives, and to be eager to help others escape from similar maltreatment.

Liu Han said, 'Our best chance to smuggle weapons and explosives in amongst the little scaly devils, I think, is to use the men who display dung beetles and mice. The scaly devils, I have seen, are squeamish about these little creatures. They will not search the containers that carry them as thoroughly as they would if something else were inside.'

'That is a very good thought,' Nieh said.

'That is a *very* good thought,' Hsia Shou-Tao echoed. He looked at Liu Han as if he'd never seen her before. Perhaps he hadn't, in any real sense of the word. He certainly hadn't taken her seriously until this moment.

'The idea has one weakness,' Nieh Ho-T'ing said. 'If the scaly devils search only by hand, we shall defeat them, and yours is a good way to do it. But if they use the machines that see into things, we shall be discovered.'

'That is true of any scheme for bringing weapons in among the little devils,' Liu Han said. Nieh Ho-T'ing nodded; she was right.

'Two weaknesses,' Hsia said. 'The other is that those who will use the guns and grenades probably will not come out alive. It is hard to find men willing to die like that. Every time you use them up, too, finding more like them gets harder.'

'Do not tell the men giving the shows what we're loading in among their creatures,' Liu Han said.

Nieh and Hsia both laughed. 'You're ruthless enough, that's plain,' Nieh said. 'But bombs and grenades aren't light and are bulky. They would know the containers for their beetles or mice had been altered.'

'They would not know why, though,' Liu Han answered. 'If the explosives were in a metal case painted black, we could say it was one of the scaly devils' machines for making the films that they show on their little cinema screens. The animal show men will be honored to believe that, and they probably will not ask the little devils about it.'

Nieh and Hsia Shou-Tao looked at each other. 'This woman has the spirit of a people's commissar in her,' Nieh Ho-T'ing said admiringly.

'Maybe she does, maybe she does,' Hsia said. He leered at Liu Han across the table. 'She has other assets, too.'

Nieh wished Hsia would stop evaluating women principally on how beddable they were. He, too, had noticed that Liu Han was far from bad-looking, but that did not mean he thought she was beddable. He had the idea that any man who tried to force his way through her Jade Gate was likely to end up a eunuch like one of those who had served at the court of the old, corrupt Ch'ing emperors. If Hsia wasn't smart enough to realize as much, he might have to find out the hard way.

'You have the idea now – I've given it to you,' Liu Han said, sounding unsure whether or not that had been wise. 'Now to use it.'

'Now to use it,' Nieh Ho T'ing agreed. 'First we need to find the animal-show men we will need, and to get them to co-operate with us. Then we have to spread this idea far and wide throughout China. We need to learn of some great holiday the little scaly devils will be celebrating, and to attack them in many places at the same time. Each time we come up with a way to get inside their quarters, we can only use it once. We want to wring the most advantage we can from this.'

'Yes,' Liu Han said. 'That would be a good beginning to my revenge.'

Nieh sipped tea as he studied her. A good beginning to her revenge? Most people would have been satisfied with that as the whole of it. He nodded thoughtfully. The demands she'd made of him before she would reveal her idea seemed more and more reasonable. Even if she was a woman, she had a soldier's ruthless spirit.

He lifted the handleless cup in salute to her. 'To the people's revolution and to liberation from all oppression!' he said loudly. She smiled at him and drank to the toast.

A new idea slid through his mind: if a woman was already a revolutionary, did that not give wanting her a sound ideological basis? It was, he told himself, purely a theoretical question. Had he not already told himself Liu Han was not beddable? He glanced her way again. It was a pity ...

The freighter drew close to New York City. Vyacheslav Molotov stared at the great towers with loathing and envy he concealed behind his usual expressionless façade. As he had when he visited Hitler in Berlin, he felt he was entering a citadel of the enemy of everything he and the Soviet Union stood for. Molotov on Wall Street! If that wasn't an acting-out of the struggle inherent in the historical dialectic, he didn't know what was.

And yet, just as fascist Germany and the Soviet Union had found common cause a few years before, so now the Soviet Union and the United States, already allies against Hitlerism, joined forces against a worse invader. When you looked at life without the dialectic to give it perspective, it could be very strange.

Pointing ahead to the arrogant, decadent skyline, Molotov's interpreter said, 'The Americans have taken their share of damage in this war, Comrade Foreign Commissar.'

'So they have,' Molotov said. Most of the glass in the windows of the tall, thrusting skyscrapers had been shattered. Black scorchmarks running up the sides of the buildings showed where fires had blazed out of control. A couple leaned drunkenly to one side, as if unlikely to stand much longer. Molotov surveyed the scene with a cold eye, then added, 'Only fit that they be reminded they are in a war. Against the Germans, they did the building and we did the dying.'

A tugboat came puffing out to greet the freighter. A man with a megaphone stood at the bow and bellowed something in English. The interpreter translated: 'He says, "Ahoy, Lithuanian ship! You're a long way from home." This, I believe, is intended as a joke.'

'Hey, hey,' Molotov said, just like that. He'd forgotten his vessel still flew the extinct gold, green, and red banner of what was now, and rightfully, the Lithuanian Soviet Socialist Republic (he also managed to forget that the

Lithuanian Soviet Socialist Republic had been under Nazi occupation till the Lizards came, and still showed no delight at the prospect of bowing to the authority of Moscow).

'How shall I reply?' the interpreter asked.

Molotov was tempted to send the American greetings in the name of the Lithuanian Congress of People's Deputies, but refrained. 'Tell him I greet him in the name of the Soviet people and of General Secretary Stalin.'

More shouts in English. The interpreter said, 'This time he replies correctly. He says we are to let him assist us in berthing.'

'Then we shall do so,' Molotov answered. 'Take this up with the ship's officers, not with me. I had thought they might bring proper diplomatic personnel to meet with us here, but if this is not the case, we shall proceed into New York.' He spoke as if he were about to enter some jungle filled with wild and savage tribesmen. That was how he felt: to him, capitalists were no more than predatory wild beasts, and New York their principal lair.

Following the lead of the tug, the freighter sailed into the East River. The battered ship left behind the Statue of Liberty, standing tall and proud on Bedloes Island. Molotov had nothing in principle against the ideals the statue epitomized, but thought the United States, with its exploitation of Negroes by whites, of poor by rich, of proletarians by capitalists (which was not quite the same thing), did a poor job of living up to them.

The freighter tied up at Pier 11, quite near the shore. The interpreter pointed to a sign in English. 'Comrade Foreign Commissar, do you know what there is between this and Pier 12, the next one over?' he said, his voice quivering with indignation. 'There is what is called the Municipal Skyport, where the rich capitalists can land their private seaplanes conveniently close to their Wall Street offices.'

'That any man should be rich enough to own his own seaplane—' Molotov shook his head. How many men went hungry so a handful could afford these useless luxuries?

But he had not come here to mock the capitalists, he had come to deal with them. He'd dealt with the Nazis; he could stand this. He looked around at the bustling activity on the docks. Even invaded, America remained formidably productive and economically strong. He even saw some petrol-powered lorries hauling goods away once they'd been taken off their ships. Back in the USSR, every drop of petrol and diesel fuel went directly to the war effort, to tanks and airplanes. Donkeys and horses and strong backs hauled goods from one place to another.

Waiting on the pier was, not a taxicab as he'd half expected, but a horse-drawn buggy of American design. Molotov was not insulted at failing to rate a motorcar of his own. The Lizards had a habit of strafing automobiles, on the assumption that whoever was in them was liable to be important. As a result, people who were genuinely important traveled for the most part in horse-drawn conveyances, like everyone else.

When Molotov and his interpreter climbed aboard the carriage, the driver surprised him by greeting him in good Russian: '*Dobry dyen, Gospodin Molotov.*'

'Good day to you as well, but I am *Tovarishch* Molotov, if you please,' the foreign commissar answered. *Gospodin* was what you would have called an aristocrat before the Revolution. The simple *comrade* showed proper egalitarianism.

'However you like,' the driver said, equably enough. Molotov did not think him a native Russian-speaker; he had a trace of the sibilant accent English gave to Russian. Perhaps his parents had come to the United States and he'd learned his ancestral language from them – or could have been an American who'd studied Russian thoroughly, as Molotov's interpreter had studied English.

The interpreter leaned forward in his seat as the carriage began rolling. He looked petulant. Molotov understood that: if the interpreter was not useful, he would soon be performing a function where he was, most likely a function that involved carrying a rifle, living on whatever he could scrounge, and trying to survive against superior Lizard firepower.

'You are going to the Subtreasury Building, Comrade Foreign Commissar,' the driver said. 'Our first President, George Washington, took his oath of office in front of the old city hall that used to stand there. Inside, in a glass case, is the very stone he stood on.'

'How interesting,' Molotov lied.

'Comrade Foreign Commissar,' the interpreter said hoarsely, pointing to a sign on a corner, 'we are traveling down Wall Street at this very moment.' He looked around in alarm, as if he expected an assault from a regiment of swag-bellied plutocrats in toppers, cutaways, and spats, each one sporting a diamond ring bigger than the last and puffing a fat cigar.

Molotov looked around, too. Some of the people on the fabled street did wear business suits, but more were in workmen's clothes or uniforms. They didn't look quite so shabby as men on the street in war-ravaged Moscow, but they didn't seem wildly wealthy, or even prosperous, either.

In a helpful tone of voice, the driver said, 'The Subtreasury Building is right across the street from the New York Stock Exchange.' Had Molotov's interpreter had an apotropaic amulet, he would have taken it out and brandished it at the mention of that tool of the Soviets' ideological devil.

The Subtreasury Building was a dignified structure in the Greek Revival style of the previous century. To Molotov, for whom socialist realism was as much an article of faith as the doctrine of the Incarnation was to Pope Pius XII, having a building pretend to be something it wasn't summed up the dishonesty of the capitalist system. That the skyscrapers along Wall Street dwarfed the Subtreasury Building told him everything he needed to know about where economic power in the United States really lay.

A bronze statue of a man in outmoded clothing stood on the steps. As Molotov went past it, his interpreter said, 'There is George Washington, the first President of the United States.'

Molotov dismissed the first President in half a dozen words: 'He is dressed like an aristocrat.' The offhand condemnation made the man who had driven him to the Subtreasury Building mutter something under his breath. Behind the impassive mask Molotov always wore, he chuckled to himself.

Inside, a smiling flunky led him and the interpreter to a large, airy, well-lit chamber. The men waiting behind the tables there rose politely as he came in. 'Good morning, Comrade Foreign Commissar,' Cordell Hull said. 'Excellent to see you again.'

'I am pleased to have this opportunity to consult with my allies in the joint struggle against the imperialist aggressors from the stars,' Molotov answered, keeping any dealing on a personal level to a minimum. 'It is also good to have representatives of Great Britain here, after the heroic resistance her people have shown against the aliens' invading forces.'

'Do you know Lord Beaverbrook and Lord Halifax?' the American Secretary of State asked. 'I had the honor of meeting Lord Beaverbrook in Moscow two years ago, when he headed the Anglo-American mission on sending aid to the Soviet Union after the unprovoked and perfidious fascist attack,' Molotov said, nodding to the present British Minister of Supply.

'Good to see you again, Molotov,' Lord Beaverbrook said, sticking out his hand. He was a tall, ruddy, balding man in his mid-sixties, with a shrewd, blunt-featured face and an air of energy that would have done credit to someone half his age.

'You will introduce me to Lord Halifax?' Molotov said. 'We have never met in the flesh.'

What he did know about Halifax, he did not fancy. The British ambassador to the United States had been Foreign Secretary under Neville Chamberlain before war broke out and during most of its first year, till the Chamberlain government fell in the aftermath of disasters in Scandinavia, the Low Countries, and France. All through his time in office, he'd advocated appeasing the Hiterlerite beast by tossing one country after another into its ravening maw.

Now, though, he nodded civilly to Molotov and extended his right hand. The left sleeve of his coat hung limp; his left arm had been withered from birth, and lacked a hand. 'A pleasure to meet you at last,' he murmured.

'Indeed,' Molotov said, looking up at him. He was taller and balder than Beaverbrook – he had to be within a few centimeters of two meters tall. Most men, though, were taller than Molotov; he refused to let that, or anything else, intimidate him. 'Now that we have dealt with the formalities, shall we move on to the business at hand?'

'Yes, yes, by all means.' With his own hands, Cordell Hull pulled out a chair for Molotov, and then another for his interpreter. Molotov felt faintly scandalized; that was not proper work for a man whose rank matched his own. The American passion for showing equality of upper and lower classes even – sometimes especially – where that equality did not in truth exist always struck him as hypocritical.

But diplomacy without hypocrisy was almost a contradiction in terms. Molotov said, 'Let us review the present state of our alliance and plan our future moves against the common foe.'

'Not all such planning is practicable,' Lord Beaverbrook put in. 'The damned Lizards have plans of their own, as we found out to our sorrow this past summer.'

'We were invaded first by the Nazis, then by the Lizards,' Molotov said. 'We know in great detail what you have experienced.'

'Russia being a large state—' Lord Halifax began.

Molotov corrected him with icy precision: 'The Soviet Union being a large state—'

'Yes. Quite. Er, the Soviet Union being a large state,' Lord Halifax resumed, 'you enjoyed the luxury of trading space for time, which allowed you more strategic options than were available to us.'

'Thus your immediate use of poison gas,' Molotov said. 'Yes. That, like our bomb from explosive metal, does seem to have been something which found the Lizards ill-prepared.'

He watched Halifax and Beaverbrook preen, as if they'd been personally responsible for throwing mustard gas at the Lizards. Maybe Beaverbrook actually had had something to do with the decision; he'd been active in weapons development. Molotov reckoned poison gas an altogether mixed blessing. Not long after the English started using it, the Germans also did – a more lethal species, too. And the Germans had rockets to throw their gas farther than they could directly reach. Not for the first time, Molotov was glad the Lizards had landed in Poland. He would have liked their landing in Germany even better.

The Nazis' poison gas also seemed to be on Beaverbrook's mind, for he said, 'Technical co-operation among the allies is still not all it might be. We have yet to receive from Berlin—'

'You won't get anything from Berlin, any more than you would from Washington,' Cordell Hull said. 'Or Tokyo, either, come to that.'

'From the Germans, I should say,' Lord Beaverbrook replied. 'Ahem. We've not received from the Germans the specifics of their new suffocating gas, nor indeed any word from them on their progress toward nuclear weapons for some time.'

'We and they were enemies before; our present alliance with them is nothing more than a convenience,' Molotov said. 'We should not be surprised when it creaks.' The Anglo-American-Soviet alliance against the Hitlerites had also been one of convenience, as had the Nazi-Soviet pact before that. You didn't stay wedded to an alliance because it was there; you stayed because it was useful for you. What had Austria said, refusing to help Russia during the Crimean War after the Romanovs rescued the Hapsburg throne? "We shall astonish the world by our ingratitude" –

something like that. If you were in the game, you knew it had slippery rules. The British had some clues along those lines. Molotov wondered about the Americans, though.

Because he still worried about the Germans almost as much as he did about the Lizards, Molotov said, 'We have reports that the Nazis will be ready to begin using those bombs next spring.' He didn't say he'd heard that himself, straight from Ribbentrop's mouth. The United States and Britain endangered the future of the Soviet Union hardly less than the Nazis.

'We can match that,' Cordell Hull said placidly. 'We may even beat it.'

That was more than Molotov had heard from Ribbentrop. He wondered if it was more than Ribbentrop knew. For that matter, he was always amazed when Ribbentrop knew anything. 'If that is so, the war against the Lizards will take on an entirely different tone,' he observed.

'So it will,' Hull said. 'You Russians should have more of these weapons coming up soon, too, shouldn't you?'

'So we should.' Molotov let it go at that. Unfortunately, just because the Soviet Union should have had more explosive-metal bombs coming into production didn't mean it *would* have them. He wondered how long the physicists would have before Stalin started liquidating them out of frustration. The Great Stalin's virtues were multifarious – he would tell you as much himself. Patience, however, was not among them.

Lord Halifax said, 'If we show the Lizards we are their match in destructive power, my hope is that we shall be able to negotiate a just and equitable peace with them.'

Once an appeaser, always an appeaser, Molotov thought. '*My* hope is that we shall drive them off our world altogether,' he said. 'Then the historical dialectic can resume from the point where it was interrupted.' *And its processes can finish throwing Britain onto the rubbish heap.*

'That would not be easy under the best of circumstances,' Lord Beaverbrook said. 'And circumstances are not of the best. The Lizards, as you will probably recall, have a colonization fleet traveling toward Earth, much as the *Mayflower* brought Englishmen and women to what we then called the New World. Will their military forces flee, leaving the colonists nowhere to land? I think not.'

Molotov hadn't considered it from that perspective. He was certain Stalin hadn't, either. And yet it made sense, even in dialectical terms. The Lizards were imperialists. So much was obvious. But what did the imperialists do? They didn't just conquer locals. They also established colonies – and would fight to protect what they saw as their right to do so.

Slowly, he said, 'I do not wish to accept the permanent presence of these aliens on our world.'

'I daresay the Red Indians weren't overjoyed at the prospect of Pilgrim neighbors either,' Beaverbrook answered. 'We must first make certain we aren't simply overwhelmed, as they were.'

'That's an important point,' Cordell Hull said. 'And one of the reasons the Indians got overwhelmed as that they never – or not often enough, anyway – put up a common fight against the white men. If a tribe had another tribe next door for an enemy, they wouldn't think twice about joining with the new settlers to clear 'em out. And then, a few years later, it would be their turn, and they probably wondered what the devil happened to them. We can't afford that, and we have to remember it. No matter how bad we think our neighbors are, living under the Lizards would be a damn sight worse.'

Molotov thought not of Red Indians but of the tsars expanding Russian might at the expense of the nomads of the steppe and the principalities in the Caucasus. The principle, though, remained the same. And Hull was right: all the world's leaders, even the Great Stalin, needed to remember it.

'I shall convey your thoughts, and my agreement with them, to the General Secretary,' Molotov said.

Cordell Hull beamed. 'Thank you, Comrade Foreign Commissar. I hope you won't mind my saying that this is, I believe, the first time you've expressed a personal opinion in all our talks.'

Molotov considered. Slowly, he nodded. 'You are correct, Mr Secretary,' he said. 'I apologize for the error. It was inadvertent, I assure you.'

Heinrich Jäger accepted three francs in change from a shopkeeper after he bought a couple of meters of twine. Two were solid prewar coins. The third, instead of Marianne on the obverse, had a double-headed axe, two stalks of wheat, and the legend ETAT FRAN•AIS. It was made of aluminium, and felt weightless in his hand.

The shopkeeper must have noticed the sour stare he sent the franc. 'Vichy says we have to use them,' the fellow said with a shrug. 'So do the Lizards.'

Jäger just shrugged and stuck the coin in his pocket. The less he had to put his halting French on display in Albi, the happier he was. He and Otto Skorzeny had already been here longer than they wanted. Other raids Skorzeny planned had run like clockwork. Here, the clock was slow.

He rolled up his twine and walked out of the shop onto the Avenue du Maréchal Foch. As always when he looked about in Albi, a line from some English poet sprang to mind.' A rose-red city half as old as time.' Pink and red brickwork predominated hereabouts, though brown and muddy yellow added to the blend. If one – or, here, two – had to resticate, there were worse places than Albi in which to do it.

The aluminium coin from Marshal Pétain's mint went when he bought a kilo of *haricots verts*. He carried the beans back to the flat he and Skorzeny were sharing.

He hoped his comrade in arms hadn't brought home another tart. When

Skorzeny had a mission directly before him, he was all business. When he didn't, his attention wandered and he needed something else to keep him interested in the world. He'd also been drinking an ungodly lot lately.

But when Jäger got back to the flat, he found Skorzeny alone, sober, and beaming from ear to ear. 'Guess what?' the big SS man boomed. 'Good old Uncle Henri finally shipped us the last piece we need to put our toy together.'

'Did he? That's first-rate,' Jäger said. A mortar was not an impressive-looking piece of lethal hardware, especially disassembled; a sheet-metal tube, an iron base plate, three legs for the tripod, and some straps and screws and a sight. Any individual component could go through the still-functional mails of Vichy France without raising a Gallic eyebrow. But now that the base plate had finally come, they could turn everything back into a mortar in a matter of minutes.

'Let's go do it now,' Skorzeny said excitedly.

'In daylight?' Jäger shook his head. That idea still appalled him. 'The plant runs three shifts. We'll do just as much damage if we hit it at night, and we'll have a better chance of getting away clean.'

'Sometimes, Jäger, you're a bore,' Skorzeny said.

'Sometimes, Skorzeny, you're a crazy man,' Jäger retorted. He'd long since learned that you couldn't let Skorzeny grab any advantage, no matter how tiny. If you did, he'd ride roughshod over you. The only thing he took seriously was a will whose strength matched that of his own, and God hadn't turned out a whole lot of those.

Now Skorzeny laughed, a raucous note that filled the little furnished flat. 'A crazy man? Maybe I am, but I have fun and the Lizards don't.'

'They'll have even less fun once we're through with them,' Jäger said. 'Shall we walk by the factory one last time, make sure we're not overlooking anything?'

'Now you're talking!' The prospect of action, of facing danger, always got Skorzeny's juices flowing. 'Let's go.'

'First smear that glop over your scar,' Jäger said, as he did whenever Skorzeny was about to go out in public in Albi. The Lizards were terrible at telling people apart, but that scar and the SS man's size made him stand out. They made him stand out for human collaborators, too.

'Bore,' Skorzeny repeated, but he rubbed the brown makeup paste over his cheek. It left him looking as if his face had been burned, but the Lizards weren't looking for a man with a burn. They were after a man with a scar – *and they won't be shy about snapping up any friends he has along, either,* Jäger thought.

Baggy trousers, a tweed jacket, a cloth cap ... to Jäger, they make Skorzeny look like a German in down-at-the-heels French clothes rather than a down-at-the-heels Frenchman, but he did know the Lizards were a less demanding audience. He thought the beret he wore made him look dashing. Skorzeny insisted it looked like a cowflop on his head. He took the chaffing in good part; wearing a beret in France these days meant you supported Vichy, which was exactly the impression he was trying to create.

The factory was on the Rue de la Croix-Verte, in the northeastern part of the city. Jäger and Skorzeny walked past the theater and the Jardin National on their way to it. They ambled along, hands in their pockets, as if they had all the time in the world. Skorzeny gave a pretty girl the eye. She stuck her nose in the air, ignoring him with Gallic panache. He laughed as raucously as he had back in the apartment.

A stream of lorries rolled out of the gas-mask plant as the two Germans came up to it. The lorries headed off to the east, to help save Lizards from German gas. The factory itself was a large, nondescript building of orange brick, utterly unremarkable from the outside. Only the Lizard guards who paced its perimeter with automatic rifles made it seem at all important.

Jäger didn't even turn his head toward it. He just glanced at it out of the corner of his eyes as he mooched on past. As for Skorzeny, he might not even have suspected the place existed, let alone that it manufactured goods which hurt the *Reich*. He was pompous and arrogant, no doubt about that, but a mission made him all business.

He and Jäger bought lunch at a little café a couple of blocks from the gas-mask factory. The chicken – actually, almost chickenless – stew was pretty bad, even by wartime standards, but the house wine that went with it was noticeably better than *ordinaire*. After a couple of glasses, you stopped noticing the stringy carrots and sad potatoes that accompanied the little diced-up bits of chicken – or rabbit, or maybe cat.

Lunch finished, Jäger and Skorzeny walked back the way they had come. The Lizards took no notice of them. Skorzeny started whistling something. After the first few bars, Jäger gave him a shot in the ribs with an elbow. A good thing, too; it was the 'Horst Wessel Song.'

When they got back to the flat, Skorzeny hopped up and down like a kid with a new toy. 'I want to do it now,' he said, over and over.

'Better we wait till tonight,' Jäger kept answering. 'Less chance of someone noticing us setting up a mortar in the middle of the Parc Rochegude.'

'But they're more likely to notice us carrying the stuff at night,' Skorzeny argued. 'You carry boxes during the day, you're a workman. You carry boxes at night, if you're lucky people think you're a burglar on your way to do a job. You aren't so lucky, they think you've already done it and they try to rob you.'

'No,' Jäger said yet again. 'The park is just a short distance away – that's why we took this flat, remember? We can carry all our gear in one trip, set up in the middle of that nice stand of elms we found, and start firing. We can get off eight or ten bombs in a minute or so and then get the hell out of there. What could be better than that?'

'Watching the fur fly,' Skorzeny answered without hesitation. Then he sighed. 'I don't suppose we could do that anyway. Wouldn't be a good idea to walk past the factory on our way out of town.'

'Why?' Jäger said in mock astonishment. 'Just because we'll have lobbed eight or ten bombs full of Tabun into it and around the neighborhood? All we'd have to do is hold our breath as we went by.'

'You're right – maybe we could get away with it.' Before Jäger could explode, Skorzeny laughed at him. 'I'm joking, son, I'm joking.'

'Tabun isn't anything to joke about.' Jäger cast a respectful eye on the mortar bombs he and Skorzeny had carried down through the Lizard lines from Germany. Had one of those bombs developed the tiniest leak, the sun would have gone dark in the sky, his lungs would have stopped working, and he wouldn't have made it to Albi.

'Well, I don't say you're wrong about that,' Skorzeny answered. 'It's some very nasty stuff, for a fact. 'The *Führer* wasn't going to use it, even against the Lizards, till the British hauled out their mustard gas. Then I suppose he decided he might as well be hanged for a sheep as a lamb.'

'The *Führer* knows about gas,' Jäger said. 'He was in the trenches in France himself.' He remembered his own days there, the frantic cries of alarm when the gas shells started landing, the struggle to get your mask on and tight before the tendrils of poison reached you and started eating your lungs, the anguished cries of comrades who hadn't grabbed their masks fast enough, the stifling feel of very breath, the way you started wanting to tear off the mask after you'd worn it for hours on end, no matter what happened to you once you did ... Across a quarter of a century, those memories remained vivid enough to make the fear sweat prickle up under his arms.

Grumpily, Otto Skorzeny said, 'All right, Jäger, we'll do it your way, tonight when it's nice and dark. Should be clear, too, which won't be bad if we can spy the North Star through the trees. Give us a better gauge of true north than our compasses would if somebody's tampered with our marks.'

'That's true,' Jäger said. They'd picked the spot from which they would fire a good while before. Thanks to some excellent maps of Albi their French friends (no, not friends, partners: the Frenchmen had been enemies of Vichy when Pétain collaborated with the Germans, and remained enemies now that he was collaborating with the Lizards), they knew the range and bearing from their chosen copse in the Parc Rochegude to the gas-mask factory, to within a few meters and minutes of the arc. It was just a matter of getting the mortar pointing in the right direction, fiddling with the elevation screw, and firing away.

To kill time till darkness fell, they played skat. As he usually did, Skorzeny won money from Jäger. They were playing for Vichy francs, though, so the losses hardly felt real. Jäger though of himself as a pretty fair cardplayer, and wondered if Skorzeny cheated. He'd never caught him at it, and if he did, Skorzeny would make jokes about it and turn it into a lark. What could you do?

When twilight came and the sky turned purple-gray, Skorzeny stuck the cards in his pocket and said, 'Shall I make us some supper?'

'I thought you wanted us to live till tonight,' Jäger said, which earned him a glare from the bigger man. As anyone does who spends time in the field, Skorzeny had learned to cook after a fashion: roasted meats, stews made from whatever was handy thrown into a pot and stuck over the fire for a while. Since Jäger cooked the same way, he waved a hand to tell Skorzeny to go ahead.

You couldn't do a lot to mess up cabbage and onions and carrots and potatoes. The stew was bland and boring, but it filled the belly. At the moment, Jäger didn't care about anything else. The flat had good blackout curtains. That let him turn on the electric lights after supper and let Skorzeny win more funny money from him with those possibly trained pasteboards.

Seven, eight, nine, ten, eleven . . . the hours crawled slowly past. When midnight struck, Skorzeny loaded the thirty kilos of mortar onto his back, slung into a big cloth bag. Jäger carried the bombs in the packs he and the SS man had used to bring them down from German-held territory.

They closed the door behind them and went downstairs and then outside as quietly as they could. Jäger wondered how many people were peering at them as they trudged east down the Avenue du Maréchal Foch toward the park.

He also wondered if he would make it to the park. Added together, the mortar bombs and powder charges were at least as heavy as the weapon that fired them, while he was not nearly so big and burly as Otto Skorzeny.

He was staggering but still moving along when they got to the Parc Rochegude. A rustle in the bushes made him snatch for the pistol he wore in the waistband of his trousers. 'Just a couple playing games,' Skorzeny said with a coarse laugh. 'Might have been a couple of men, but it's too dark for me to be sure.'

The tree-surrounded open space they'd picked to set up the mortar had no couples using it, for which Jäger was heartily glad: he had found a discarded French letter in it one morning. 'We won't need the compass or the North Star,' he said with relief. A few days before, Skorzeny had splashed whitewash on a branch of one of the elms in the grove. Set the base plate of the mortar on the gray stone Jäger had placed in the grass, aim the barrel over the white splash, and the Lizards – and the humans who worked for them – would learn collaboration had its price.

Skorzeny assembled the mortar, swearing softly when he barked his knuckles in the darkness. He'd practiced so often in the flat that the lethal little device quickly grew from a collection of innocent-looking hardware to an artillery piece. He lined it up roughly on the marked branch, then turned the traversing screw to bring it to exactly the bearing he wanted. At last he grunted in satisfaction and began adjusting the elevation screw so the mortar would fling its bombs just the right distance.

Jäger, meanwhile, had been taking the bombs out of the packs and standing them on their tailfins by the mortar. Even without knowing the particularly lethal freight they carried, anyone would have recognized them as intended for no good purpose: nothing painted flat black and full of sharp curves and angles was apt to be a kiddie toy.

'Flick on your lighter,' Skorzeny said. 'I want to make sure I have the elevation right. Wouldn't do to shoot over or under.'

'No, it wouldn't.' Jäger dug the lighter out of his pocket, flicked the wheel with his thumb. His breath came short and quick, as if he'd spied a Lizard panzer's turret traversing to bring its main armament to bear on him. A cry of *Qu'est-ce que c'est?* and feet pounding toward the corpse would be just as disastrous now.

After what seemed like an eternity but couldn't have been more than half a minute, Skorzeny said, 'Everything's fine. Douse it.' Jäger flicked the cover over the flame. Even that little noise made his heart pound. Well, the Parc Rochegude would know bigger noises any minute now.

Skorzeny softly slapped him on the back. He took that as his signal to begin. Snatching up a bomb, he dropped it down the barrel of the mortar.

Wham! The noise hit harder than that of a panzer's cannon; he didn't have several centimeters of steel shielding him from most of it now. He grabbed another bomb, sent it after the first one. *Wham!*

Between shots, he tried to use his stunned ears to listen for any outcry, and for whistle blasts from the French gendarmerie. He didn't hear anything, and prayed that meant there wasn't anything to hear. He'd brought a dozen bombs in all. He'd hoped to be able to fire most of them before the uproar started. In just over a minute, he sent every one of them on its way.

Skorzeny slapped him on the back again, this time hard enough to stagger him. 'You can be on my mortar team any day!' the burly SS man bawled, his mouth as close to Jäger's ear as if he'd been a lover.

'That's wonderful,' Jäger said dryly. 'Now let's get back to the flat before somebody spots us out here and puts two and two together.'

'Just a minute.' Skorzeny grabbed the mortar by the tripod, heaved it up off the ground. Jäger started in alarm; the plan had called for leaving it behind. But Skorzeny didn't carry it far. Close by the copse was a little pond. He heaved the mortar in with a splash. 'They won't find it till sunup this way, and maybe not for a while afterwards. By then, *Gott mit uns*, we'll be on our way.'

'*Gott mit uns*,' Jäger echoed. 'Now come on, damn it.'

They'd just shut the front door to their building when several men came round the corner and dashed toward the park. Jäger and Skorzeny hurried upstairs. The biggest worry in the plan had been that people would come out of their block of flats when the mortar started banging. That would make them notice the two men in Number 14 had been outside – and wonder why. They probably wouldn't have wondered long.

But the hallway was empty when Jäger closed the door behind him. He let out a long sigh of relief. Off in the distance, sirens wailed and bells clanged: ambulances and fire engines. Solemnly, he stuck out his hand. As solemnly, Skorzeny shook it.

The SS man pulled the cork from a bottle of wine, took a swig, and passed it to Jäger. Jäger wiped it on his sleeve and then drank, too. 'Success,' he said. Skorzeny's big head bobbed up and down. After a moment, Jäger thought about what his toast had meant: some unknown number of Frenchmen – Frenchwomen, too, very likely – asphyxiating, not because they'd harmed him in particular but because, to support themselves and their families, they were turning out goods the Lizards could use.

The wine turned to vinegar in his mouth. 'This is a filthy business we're in,' he said.

'You just figured that out?' Skorzeny said. 'Come on, Jäger, you're not a virgin, except maybe in your left ear. If we don't hurt the Lizards, we lose. If hurting the Lizards means hurting civilians, too, well, too bad. These things happen. We did what we were supposed to do, what our superiors ordered us to do.'

'*Ja*,' Jäger said in a hollow voice. What Skorzeny didn't get and wouldn't get if he lived to be a hundred – not likely, considering how the SS man lived – was that *what we were supposed to do* and *what our superiors ordered us to do* weren't necessarily one and the same thing.

Soldiers didn't commonly have to draw that distinction. Jäger hadn't worried about it, not until he found out how the Germans dealt with Jews in the east. Since then, he hadn't been able to look away. He knew what sort of disaster awaited the world if the Lizards won the war. Like Skorzeny, he was willing to do just about anything to keep that from happening. Unlike the SS man, he wasn't willing to believe everything he did was fine and virtuous.

That made for another subtle distinction, but he clung to it.

Panting, Jens Larssen stopped at the top of Berthoud Pass. His breath smoked in the thin, cold air. Snow dappled the ground and turned the pines and firs into a picture right off a Christmas card. Snow and ice also turned US 40 into a slippery slalom course that had to be treated with the utmost respect.

'Downhill from here,' Jens said. That was literally true; he'd lose more than a mile of altitude before he made it back to Denver, a bit more than fifty miles away. It also normally implied everything would be easy the rest of the way. Heading back to Denver wasn't going to be easy. If your bike hit an icy patch and skidded while you were slogging uphill to the

Continental Divide, you'd fall and scrape your shin. If you lost it while you were speeding down some of these steep grades, you'd break a leg - or your neck.

'Slow and easy,' he said out loud, reminding himself. 'Slow and easy.' He'd spent some of his time getting up to the pass walking the bicycle; he'd spend even more coming down. All the same, with luck he'd be in Denver in a couple of days, and then, before long, the Metallurgical Laboratory could pack up and head for Hanford and the Columbia.

Up in Tabernash, a ways to the north, he'd bought a knitted wool sailor's cap. God only knew what it was doing there; Tabernash was about as far from the sea as you could get in North America. He kept it pulled down over his ears, even though that made them itch. He also hadn't bothered shaving since the leaves started turning colors. His beard had come in thick and strawberry blond; it did a surprisingly good job of keeping his cheeks and chin warm.

'I wonder if Mary Cooley would know me,' he muttered; Idaho Springs law only twenty miles or so to the east. His hand went over his shoulder and briefly caressed the barrel of the Springfield he wore slung on his back.

But, now that he found himself close to Idaho Springs, he also found he wasn't killing angry at the waitress who'd given him the clap, not anymore. The sulfa tablets Dr Henry had given him in Hanford had done the job. The disease wasn't bothering him at all now. He didn't even have the morning drop of pus he had to piss away with the day's first whizz, so he supposed he was cured. *I'll let the bitch live*, he thought, and felt magnanimous.

The sky was the grayish-yellow color that warned of more snow coming. He made the best speed he could down US 40; the lower he was when it started to fall, the happier he'd be. One thing growing up in Minnesota did: it taught you what to do in a blizzard. And if he hadn't learned then, traveling cross-country the winter before would have imparted a lesson or three.

He rolled past an abandoned Studebaker. Dead cars and trucks lined the highway, here one, there a clump, here another. They'd make decent shelters if it really started coming down hard.

Somewhere up off the road, a cougar yowled. The wildlife was probably having a high old time these days. Not a lot of people were able to get up here and go hunting, as they had once. Thinking of the Lizards' being good for something on Earth felt odd.

Jens' hands tightened on the black rubber grips of the handlebars. The Lizards hadn't been good for him, not even slightly. If they'd just stayed on the pages of the pulp magazines where they belonged, he and Barbara would still be married and happy. He meant to say a thing or two to her when he got back to Denver - and to Sam Yeager, too. He'd been thinking about that, on and off, ever since he headed west.

He reached back and patted the gun barrel again. That might end up doing some of his talking for him.

He didn't quite make it into Idaho Springs before darkness descended like a cloak. A few minutes later, the snow started falling. Larssen kept rolling along until he came to a dead car in the middle of the road. 'A Cadillac, no less,' he said as he came up to it. It would be roomier than a lot of the autos in which he'd taken refuge during his travels.

The Cadillac's windows were rolled up and the doors locked, as if the fellow who'd been driving it had been sure he'd be back to get it pretty soon. Jens took savage pleasure in smashing the driver's-side window with the butt of his rifle. He unlocked the door, opened it with a squeak of rusty hinges, and reached inside to unlock the back door. Then he shut the front door again. He wondered if he should have shot out the front-door lock instead, to keep cold air from blowing in, and thought about going on and finding another car.

'Hell with it,' he said. The window still had some glass in it, and he would have rolled it down a couple of inches for the fresh air anyhow. Even if the Cadillac was full of the musty smell of mildew, he wouldn't find any better place to spread out his sleeping bag. The backseat was plenty long and plenty wide. It would have made a wonderful backseat for making out, though he doubted whether people who owned Cadillacs needed to use backseats for such purposes.

He unrolled the sleeping bag, and also took a couple of thick wool blankets from the pack he'd tied to the bicycle's carrying rack. He still had bread and homemade butter he'd got in Tabernash. He ate some of that. He'd eaten like a pig all through this jaunt, and was skinnier now than he had been at the start of it.

With the sleeping bag around him and the blankets on top, he was plenty warm enough. He slid the rifle down into the space between the backseat and the front; the transmission hump made it stick up a little. 'Anybody who tries messing with me for any reason at all will regret it,' he said.

He woke up, unmessed with, the next morning, to some of the most supernal quiet he'd ever known. It was as if the snow of the night before had coated the whole world with a thick blanket of muffling feathers. The shift of the car springs under him as he sat up was the only sound in the land.

Keeping on the road would be more interesting than it had been. No snow plows, not now, nor salt that let tires grip even as it rotted fenders. 'Slow and easy,' he told himself again.

As it had when he came through westbound, Idaho Springs had sentries out to check on who entered their little town. When Jens started to produce his letter signed by General Groves, the men stood aside. 'You go right on ahead, buddy,' one of them said. 'I 'member you and that there letter from back a few months, don't I?'

Larssen pedaled through Idaho Springs and then struggled up to the top of Floyd Hill, which wasn't that much lower than Berthoud Pass. After that, the road got better. Even if it wasn't plowed, what looked from the marks like a wagon train had been through ahead of him, defining the roadway and shoving aside the worst of the snow. He made good time coming down into Denver.

Before the Lizards came, the town had held better than a quarter of a million people. What with evacuations, simple flight, and bombings, not nearly so many lived there nowadays. All the same, the sight of so many men and women on the streets felt strange and untoward, and made Larssen nervous. He'd got very used to his own company and nobody else's on his travels. He wondered how he'd fit on the Met Lab team once he got back to the University of Denver.

'Hell with 'em,' he muttered. 'If they can't make room for me, that's their problem.'

A man riding east alongside him on US 40 – no, they called it Colfax Avenue here in town – overheard that and gave him a curious look. He stared back, so fiercely that the Nosy Parker found some business elsewhere in a hurry.

Jens swung south onto University Boulevard just as the sun, which had come out in the afternoon, sank behind the Rockies. That didn't bother him. He knew just where he was going now, and he didn't figure the Met Lab crew were working eight-hour days and then knocking off.

The buildings on the university campus were dark, but that didn't mean anything. Except on the East Coast, blackouts had been kind of a joke in the United States after the first few panicky days that followed Pearl Harbor, but the coming of the Lizards turned them into deadly serious business once more. A lot of work got done behind blackout curtains.

He stopped the bike outside the Science Building, then opened the door and went in, pushing his way through the curtains that shielded the electric lights from view. The shining bulbs made his eyes water, not just for their brilliance but also as a sign the twentieth century still lived.

A sentry stood a few paces inside the doorway. By the time Jens got through the yards of black cloth pinned to the ceiling, the fellow had a rifle aimed at his brisket. 'Who goes there?' he demanded, and then, after a moment, with visible reluctance, moved the rifle aside. 'Oh, it's you, Dr Larssen. Welcome back.' His tone gave the lie to the words.

'Hello, Oscar.' Jens tried to keep what he was feeling out of his voice. Oscar had been his bodyguard – his keeper, if you wanted a less polite word for it – when he got into Denver. Oscar had also slugged him when he had tried to talk sense into Barbara. All right, he'd grabbed her, but still, the bitch hadn't had any business squawking like that. He fought down the red rage that made him want to throw himself at the soldier. 'Is General Groves still working?'

'Yes, sir, he is.' Oscar sounded relieved to be sticking to business. 'He works late 'most every night. You want to see him now, sir?'

'Yeah, I do,' Larssen answered. 'I've been on the road a long time. The sooner he hears what I have to say, the sooner he can start doing something about it.'

'Okay, Dr Larssen, you can go upstairs.' Oscar hesitated. 'Uh, sir, you want to leave that Springfield down here with me?' It was phrased as a request, but it didn't sound like one.

Jens unslung the rifle and leaned it against the wall, not without an inward pang. He did his best to sound light as he said, 'Don't suppose I'll need to shoot anybody before I come back down.' The one he really wanted to shoot was Oscar. By the way the soldier's eyes clung to him as he walked over to the stairwell, Oscar knew it, too.

The door to Leslie Groves's office was ajar. Jens rapped on the frosted glass panel set into the top part of it. 'Who's there?' Groves demanded gruffly. Taking that as all the invitation he was likely to get, Jens went in. Surprise spread over Groves's heavy features. He got up from behind his desk, stuck out a big, thick hand. 'Dr Larssen! We were beginning to be afraid you wouldn't make it back. Come in, sit down.'

Mechanically, Jens shook hands. 'Thanks,' he said, and sank into one of the wooden chairs in front of the desk. With a sigh, he shrugged off his pack.

'You look like something the cat dragged in,' Groves said, surveying him. He picked up the phone, dialed for numbers. 'That you, Fred? Listen, send me up some fried chicken, maybe half a dozen of those nice rolls, and some honey to go with 'em. I've got a prodigal to feed here, so don't waste time.' He slammed the receiver down on its cradle. Even in ordering up some supper, he was a man who brooked no nonsense.

Jens fell on the food like a starving wolf, even if all the choices had been Groves's rather than his own. When he'd reduced it to gnawed bones and crumbs, Groves pulled a bottle of bourbon out of his desk drawer, took a snort, and passed it to him. He had a hefty swig himself, then gave it back.

'Okay, now that you're not going to fall to pieces right before my eyes, tell me about your trip,' Groves said. 'Tell me about this town in Washington you were supposed to be scouting. Did you actually manage to get there?'

'Yes, sir, I sure did.' Larssen looked at him with irritation the whiskey only fueled. He did his best to sound enthusiastic as he went on, 'Hanford's the perfect place to move the Met Lab, sir. The Columbia's got all the water in the world in it, there aren't any Lizards for hundreds of miles, and there's a railhead into town. What more do we need?'

He waited for Groves to leap in the air, shout *Whoopee!* and start moving people around with the same verve and aggressiveness he'd used in getting the fried chicken brought up. But instead, the Met Lab's chief administrator said, 'I appreciate all you did, and I sure as the devil congratulate you for getting there and coming back again. But things have changed since you left—'

'Changed how?' Jens demanded suspiciously. 'What have you done, started turning out dental floss instead of atomic bombs?'

He wanted to make Groves made, but the engineer just laughed. 'Not quite,' he said, and explained. The more Jens heard, the less he liked. It wasn't so much everything the Met Lab crew had accomplished while he was gone – good God, Groves was talking glibly about kilogram quantities of plutonium! What really grated was that the team had done all these important things, had come to the very edge of being able to fabricate a bomb, *without Jens Larssen*.

He wished Oscar hadn't made him leave his rifle downstairs. He wanted to do some shooting now, starting with Groves and maybe ending with himself. If the Met Lab was going to stay here in Denver, everything he'd done since he rolled out of town was wasted effort – spinning his wheels in the most literal sense of the word. And they hadn't missed him one single, solitary bit while he was gone, either.

'But, General,' he said, hearing the desperation in his own voice, 'you don't understand what a swell place Hanford really is, how perfect it would be for us to work there—' He hadn't thought it was perfect when he rode into town. He'd thought it was a wide spot in the road, nothing better. But in retrospect, it was starting to take on aspects of the earthy paradise. He didn't want to think he'd spent so much time in vain.

Gently, Groves said, 'I'm sorry, Dr Larssen, I truly am. But while you were away, we've put down deep roots here. We'd need months to make the move and get set up and producing again, and we don't have months to spare. We don't have days to spare; hell, Larssen, I grudge every inessential minute. We're making the best of things here, and the best has turned out to be pretty good.'

'But—' Jens stared at the jumble of chicken bones on his plate. He'd have just as easy a time putting the meat back on them as he would of persuading Groves. He offered a new gambit: 'I'll take this up with Fermi and Szilard.'

'Go right ahead,' Groves said, accepting the move without a qualm. 'If you can convince them, I'll listen to you. But you won't convince them, and I'll bet money on that. They've got our second pile up and running under the stadium here, and the third won't be far behind. And our reprocessing plant is doing just fine, separating plutonium from the uranium slugs where it's made. We'd have to uproot that, too, if we headed for Washington State.'

Jens bit his lip. If things were as Groves said, the physicists wouldn't want to move. Logically, rationally, he didn't suppose he could blame them. They'd lost months once already, coming from Chicago to Denver.

They wouldn't want to lose more time, not when they were so close to the success the United States needed so badly.

Sometimes, though, you couldn't go by logic and reason and nothing else. Clutching at straws, Larssen said, 'What if the Lizards start a big overland push to toward Denver? There's nothing much to stand in their way – you couldn't ask for better tank country than eastern Colorado.'

'I won't say you're wrong about that, but it hasn't happened yet and I don't think it will happen soon,' Groves answered. 'It's long since started snowing – you'd know more about that than I do, wouldn't you? Last year, the Lizards didn't do much once the snow started falling. They seem to be pretty predictable, so it's a good bet they won't get aggressive till spring. And by spring, we'll give them enough other things to worry about that they won't even be thinking of Denver.'

'You've got it all figured out, don't you?' Jens said bitterly.

'Oh, Lord, how I wish I did!' Groves rolled his eyes. 'In case I haven't said so, though, I'm damned glad to have you back. You'll be able to ease the strain on a lot of people who've been stretched real thin for a long time.'

Jens heard that as, *You'll be a spare tire. We'll put you on whenever we need to patch a blowout, and then we'll have you back in the trunk again.* He almost told Groves just what he thought of him, just what he thought of the whole Met Lab: crew, project and all. But Groves held the whip hand here. Telling him off wouldn't do anything but ruin the chance for revenge.

Voice tightly controlled, Jens asked, 'How's Barbara doing these days? Do you think there's any chance she'd want to see me?'

'I really couldn't tell you about that one way or the other, Dr Larssen.' Groves sounded wary, which wasn't like him. 'The thing is, she and – and her husband left the Met Lab staff not long after you headed west. Yeager got a new assignment, and it was one where she could be useful, too, so she went along.'

'I – see,' Jens said. The first time he'd gone away, Barbara hadn't waited for him to come home; she'd slid out of her skirt for that damn dumb ball-player. Now when he went off to do something else for his country, she hadn't wanted so much as to set eyes on him when he got back. Wasn't the world a hell of a place? He asked, 'Where did she – where did they – go?

'Afraid I can't tell you that,' Groves answered. 'I couldn't tell you even if you didn't know either one of them. We do try to keep up security, no matter how irregular things get sometimes. And what with the troubles you've had, it'd be better for you and for them if you didn't know where they were.'

'Yeah, maybe.' Jens didn't believe it for a minute. It might be better for the whore who had been his wife and the bastard she was shacked up with, but for him? He shook his head. Getting his own back would be better for him. Changing the subject again, he asked, 'Where are you going to put me up for the night?'

'Let's see. If I remember right, you were BOQ over at Lowry, weren't you?' Groves did have an impressive ability to remember detail. 'Why don't we send you back there for the time being, anyhow? Things are pretty cramped right around the campus here.'

'Okay,' Jens said. *Spare tire, sure as hell.* 'You have to remember, though, that I am going to keep trying to convince you and everybody else that Hanford is a better place than Denver for making bombs.'

'Oh, I believe you,' Groves said. 'What I don't believe is that it's enough better to justify shutting down here and making tracks to start up again over there. You get yourself a good night's sleep, look around and see what we've done while you were away, and see if you don't change your mind yourself.'

'I'll do that,' Larssen said, but he was damned if anything would change his mind, not now, not after all he'd been through. He got up and started for the door.

'Wait,' Groves said. He scrawled rapidly on a sheet of paper. 'Show this to the sentries at Lowry Field. Show it to Colonel Hexham, too, if he doesn't want to give you a room at the inn.'

'Right.' Larssen took the paper, left Groves's office, and went downstairs. He reclaimed his rifle from Oscar and walked out into the night. 'Good old Colonel Hexham,' he muttered as he climbed onto his bicycle. If Hexham had just let him send a letter to Barbara before it was too late, he'd probably still be married to her today. A fling with that son of a bitch Yeager wouldn't have mattered so much; after all, she had thought Jens was dead. But when she got herself knocked up, that ruined everything.

And now Groves wanted him to deal with Hexham. He rode slowly up University to Alameda, then turned right to go on to Lowry Field. As he pedaled east toward the air base, the temptation rose in him to keep on going past it, to keep heading east till he got to somewhere not far from the Colorado-Kansas border. Nobody was going to listen him here, no matter how right he was. He could see that, plain as the nose on his face. But if he headed out and talked to the Lizards, they'd be very interested in finding out what was going on in Denver.

He'd had that thought before. He'd almost ridden east instead of west when they sent him out to look Hanford over. He'd fought it down then; he'd still figured his first obligation was to mankind.

'But what if the only thing every goddamn human being in the world wants is to give me a hard time?' he asked the silent, chilly darkness.

He got no answer. When he came to the Lowry Field turnoff, he stopped his bicycle and stood unmoving for two or three minutes. At last, he rode on toward the airfield. He didn't want to admit, even to himself, how close he'd come to choosing the other path.

15

Rain drummed down out of a leaden sky. Most of the leaves were off the trees in Pskova Park; they lay, brown and forlorn, on the yellow dying grass below. As George Bagnall walked toward the Pskov *Krom*, he thought the bare-branched beeches and birches looked sad and miserable, like skeletons with their arms held high in surrender to approaching winter.

Sheets of water ran over the concrete slabs of the pavement. Rain collected in bomb craters, turning them to muddy little ponds. If you stepped into one, not watching where you were going, you could sink deeper than your waist – or deeper than your head. Two or three people had already drowned that way, or so rumor said.

The sentries at the *Krom* stood inside the entrance, both to keep dry and to keep the Lizards from spotting them from the air. Pskov's ancient fortress had taken a couple of bombs in the early days of the Lizard invasion, but the aliens had pretty much left it alone since. Everyone in town hoped they would go right on doing that.

'Who comes?' the German sentry demanded, while his Soviet opposite number raised the barrel of his submachine gun. Bagnall swept back the hood on the rain cape he was wearing. 'Ah, the Englishman,' the German said, first in his own language and then in Russian. The Soviet sentry nodded and gestured with his weapon: go ahead.

'*Spasebo*,' Bagnall said. His German, after months of intensive practice, was pretty fluent. His Russian wasn't so he used it whenever he could.

He went upstairs to the office of the local German commandant, *Generalleutnant* Kurt Chill. 'Good day, Mr Bagnall,' Chill said in excellent English. 'Brigadiers German and Vasiliev, I fear, have not yet arrived. I thank you, at least, for being punctual.'

Bagnall shrugged. If you let Russian habits of punctuality get you down, you would go mad. 'They'll be here, General,' he said. And so they would, in five minutes or half an hour or a couple of hours. The concept of having *0900* mean anything more than a way of saying *sometime this morning* was beyond the Russian mental horizon.

The two partisan leaders showed up at twenty of ten. If they knew why Kurt Chill was gently steaming, they didn't show it. 'So,' Nikolai

Vasiliev said, 'let us discuss our moves against the imperialists from another world. We should be able to drive them back from Pskov while winter conditions prevail.' His comrade, Aleksandr German, translated Russian into Yiddish, which was close enough to German for Chill – and Bagnall – to understand.

On his own, Aleksandr German added, 'They are weak in winter, weaker even than you Germans were that first year.'

Chill was used to such sniping, and gave as good as he got. 'We were strong enough then to hold you out of Pskov,' he said with a chilly smile, 'and we have got better since. My hope is that the Lizards will not do the same.'

'I think they probably won't,' Bagnall said in German; Aleksandr German translated for Vasiliev. 'They seem to do the same old things over and over.'

'Their old ones are quite bad enough,' Vasiliev said through Aleksandr German. 'They are not imaginative fighters' – which was a hell of a thing for a Russian, the product of the world's most rigid military system, to say – 'but with their weapons and machines, they do not always need to be. We are lucky to have withstood them so long.'

'For them, this is a subsidiary front,' General Chill said. 'Had they put full effort into it, they might well have overrun us.'

Nikolai Vasiliev puffed out his broad chest. With his dark, curly beard, he looked like a proud bandit chieftain – which in many ways he was. The flickering lamplight only added to the impression. But he was also a Soviet citizen and proud of it, for he said, 'The marvelous bomb the Great Stalin touched off south of Moscow taught the Lizards better than to risk too much against us in any one place.'

Bagnall glanced over at Lieutenant General Chill. The *Wehrmacht* officer looked as if he'd bitten into something sour. The Germans set great store on their scientific ingenuity. To have to listen to someone he probably thought of as a Slavic *Untermensch* going on about the achievements of Soviet science had to be galling – and all the more so because the Nazis hadn't matched that bomb.

Aleksandr German said, 'We cannot count on the Lizards' holding back forever. We need to force them to retreat wherever we can, to regain the soil of the *rodina*, the motherland. General Chill, will our men fight side by side in this, as they have the past year and more?' *Except when they were shooting at one another*, Bagnall glossed silently to himself.

Despite that reservation, he looked for Chill to give hearty assent. Chill better give his assent, if any planned winter offensive was to get anywhere. The Russians had more soldiers in Pskov than the Nazis did, but their men were armed with rifles and submachine guns and a few machine guns. The Germans were the ones who had the artillery, the lorries, the carefully husbanded panzers, the even more carefully husbanded petrol.

'I shall have to examine the overall strategic situation,' was what Chill did say. 'Standing on the defensive until spring may prove a wiser, mo economical choice.'

Vasiliev and Aleksandr German both shouted at him. *Coward* was on of the kinder words they used. Bagnall found himself speechless. Up t now, Chill had always been an aggressive commander, willing, even eage to spend lives to gain territory. Of course, a lot of the lives he'd spe around Pskov were Russian ...

Not only were a lot of the lives Chill had spent Russian, so was a l of the matériel. The German garrison at Pskov had done plenty of har fighting, and the Lizards in Poland cut them off from the *Vaterland* (one these days, he'd have to think about what the differences between *rodin* and *Vaterland* implied, but not now, not now).

As innocently as he could, Bagnall asked, 'How is your supply situatio General Chill?'

'Given all we have done, it is not bad,' Chill answered. Bagnall ha heard a great many more responsive replies. The German officer's fac said more; it reminded Bagnall of the look a poker player wore whe he'd got himself into a big hand and had to own up to holding nothin more ferocious than a pair of nines.

From strident, Aleksandr German's voice went soft, persuasive *'Generalleutnant*, supplies from the Soviet Union would probably b available. The routes and the amounts are not always what they migh be, but they do exist. Surely your well-trained men would not have muc trouble getting used to Soviet weapons.'

'Hardly – we captured enough of them on the way here,' Chill said wit as much aplomb as he could muster: more than Bagnall had guessed h had in him. He was indeed a formidable man. When he continued, he cu straight to the heart of the problem: 'If I take Soviet supplies and grov to depend on them to keep my force in being, then before long I have t take Soviet orders, too.'

'If you don't, then before long you have no supplies and it no longe matters whose orders you take, because you won't be able to carry the out in any case,' Aleksandr German said.

Nikolai Vasiliev's eyes lit up with a fierce light. 'And when you have n supplies left, no point to our truce any more, either. We will restore Pskov to the *rodina* then, and we will remember what you have done here.'

'You're welcome to try, at any time you choose,' Chill answered calmly 'This I tell you, I do not lie: we have plenty to knock any number of partisan back into the woods, or into graves in them. By all means feel free to tes what I say.' The German soldier glared fiercely back at Vasiliev. By th look in *his* eye, he would sooner have killed Russians than Lizards any day of the week.

'Enough, both of you!' Bagnall exclaimed. 'The only ones who gai when we bicker are the Lizards. We would do well to remember that We can hate one another later, after the main war is won.'

Kurt Chill and Aleksandr German both stared at him as if he'd suddenly started spouting Swahili. After Aleksandr German translated, Nikolai Vasiliev gave Bagnall that same dubious look. But slowly, one by one, the three leaders nodded. 'This is truth,' Chill said. 'We *would* do well to remember it.'

'*Da*,' Aleksandr German said. But he could not resist twisting the knife: 'Also truth, *Herr Generalleutnant*, is that sooner or later, hoard them or use them, your German munitions will be exhausted. Then you will use those of the Soviet Union or you will cease being soldiers.'

Lieutenant General Chill looked as if he'd found a worm – worse, found half a worm – in his apple. The prospect of becoming not just allies but dependents on the Soviet Union, after being first overlords and then at least superior partners because of superior firepower, had to be anything but appetizing for him.

'It can work,' Bagnall insisted, not just to the *Wehrmacht* officer but also to the partisan brigadiers. And yet it wasn't their shaky truce that made him speak with such conviction; it was the passionate affair that German mechanic who'd come into Pskov with Ludmila Gorbunova was having with the fair Tatiana (much to Bagnall's relief, and even more to Jerome Jones's). The pair still didn't like each other much, but that didn't stop them from coming together every chance they got. *They should be a lesson for all of us*, Bagnall thought.

'This should be a lesson for all of us,' Atvar said, looking with one eye at the video of the damage to the gas-mask factory in Albi and with the other at Kirel. 'Whatever we thought of our security procedures, they have been starkly revealed as inadequate.'

'Truth, Exalted Fleetlord,' Kirel said. 'And yet, the destruction was not as bad as it would have been had these mortar rounds contained explosives rather than poison gas. Now that the plant has been decontaminated, it is ready to resume full operation.'

'Ready physically, yes.' Atvar felt ready himself, ready to bite something. In lieu of an actual enemy, poor Kirel would have to do. 'Of course, the decontamination cost us four irreplaceable males of the Race. Of course, the gas attack itself killed most of one entire shift of highly trained Big Uglies. Of course, the Big Uglies who work the other two shifts are afraid to go back into the plant even if it is decontaminated, for one thing because they don't believe it truly is and for another because they fear the Deutsche will attack once more – and how can we blame them for that when we fear it ourselves? Other than these minor details, the plant is, as you said, ready to start up again.'

Kirel crouched down, as if he expected to be bitten. 'Exalted Fleetlord, it is merely a matter of bringing in other Tosevites who have this skill: either that or making it plain to the locals that if they do not do this work, they will not eat.'

'Bringing Tosevites into one area from another is far more difficult than it would be on a properly civilized world,' Atvar said, 'for they are not simply Tosevites, essentially the same regardless of from which part of the planet they spring. Some are Français Tosevites, some are English Tosevites, some are Italiano Tosevites, some are Mexicano Tosevites, and so on. They all have their own foods, they all have their own languages, they all have their own customs, and they all think their ways are superior to everyone else's, which touches off fights whenever groups from two regions come together. We've tried; the Emperor knows we've tried it.' He cast down his eyes not so much in reverence as in worn resignation. 'It does not work.'

'The other approach will, then,' Kirel said. 'No matter what foods they eat, all the Big Uglies must eat some foods. If they fail to produce what we require of them, they will also fail to be fed.'

'This has some merit, but again, not as much as I would wish,' Atvar said. 'The sabotage level in Tosevite factories producing goods for us is already unacceptably high. Wherever we try to coerce the workers to produce more or produce under harsher conditions, it goes higher. This is intolerable when the product under discussion is as important as a gas mask.'

'Truth,' Kirel said again, this time wearily. 'The Big Uglies' poison gas has already lowered the morale of fighting males to the point where they have shown reluctance to go into combat in areas bordering the Deutsche. And now the Americans are also beginning to deploy it in large quantities. If males cannot have confidence in their protection, their fighting spirits will plummet further, with unfortunate consequences for our efforts here.'

'Unfortunate consequences indeed,' Atvar said. What if his males simply upped and quit fighting? He'd never imagined such a thing. No commander in the history of the Race (and perhaps not in its prehistory, either) had ever had to imagine such a thing. The Race's discipline had always proved reliable – but nothing had ever tested it as it was being tested now.

'If the males waver, Exalted Fleetlord,' Kirel said, 'perhaps we can bolster their spirits with the Tosevite herb known as ginger.'

Atvar stared at him.

Kirel crouched again, lower than he had before. 'It was intended as a joke, Exalted Fleetlord, nothing more.'

'It is *not* funny,' Atvar said. It also wasn't the worst idea he'd ever heard, not in the present circumstances. That frightened him more than anything.

The Lizards' air-raid alarms went off in Lodz. They weren't sirens, as they would have been had human beings made them. Instead, they reminded Mordechai Anielewicz of nothing so much as the sound of a cauldron full of sizzling fat – except the cauldron had to be half the size of Poland. They were, he gathered, an enormously amplified version of the noise a Lizard made when something frightened it.

All that ran through his mind in less time than he needed to snatch up a gas mask and stick it on his head. Then, along with the rest of the Jews in the offices above the fire station, he dashed for the sealed room. People got in one another's way, cursing and stumbling and falling down.

He made it to the sealed room just as a Nazi rocket came down with a crash. He tried to gauge how far away it had landed by the sound of the explosion, but that was tricky these days. The rockets that carried gas didn't make a bang nearly so big as that from the ones carrying explosives – but they were much more to be feared, even so.

'Shut the door!' four people bawled at once.

With a slam, somebody obeyed. Packed into the middle of the sardinelike crush and turned the wrong way anyhow, Mordechai couldn't see who. He looked up at the ceiling. Fresh plaster gleamed all around its periphery, covering over the cracks between it and the walls. Similar plaster marred the paint on those walls where they joined one another and also covered the molding that had marked their separation from the floor. Even if a gas-carrying rocket hit close by, the sealed room would – everyone inside hoped – let the people it sheltered survive till the deadly stuff dissipated.

Splashes said people nearest the doorway were soaking cloths in a bucket of water and stuffing them into the cracks between the door and the wall. The German poison gas was insidious stuff. If you left a chink in your armor, the gas would find it.

The Lizards' alarm kept hissing. Before long, the merely human air-raid siren added its wail to the cacophony. 'Does that mean we're not done, or just that people are too addled to turn those noisy things off?' one of the secretaries asked, her voice muffled by the mask she wore.

'We'll find out,' Anielewicz said, along with three other men and a woman. Lately, the Nazis had found a new way to keep the Lizards and humans in Lodz from getting anything done: lobbing rockets at the city every so often, making people take shelter and stay there for fear of gas. Not everyone had a sealed room to which to go, and not all sealed rooms were as cramped as this one, but the ploy was good enough to tie Lodz in knots.

'I wish the Lizards would shoot down the rockets, the way they did when the Nazis first started firing them at us,' a woman said.

'The Lizards are almost out of their own rockets,' Mordechai answered. 'These days, they only use them when one of the Germans' happens to head straight for an installation of theirs.' That wasn't an everyday occurrence; while the Lizards could make rockets that went exactly where they wanted, those of the Nazis were wildly inaccurate. Anielewicz went on, 'If a rocket lands in the middle of Lodz, that's just too bad for the people under it.'

'The Race is doing what it can for us,' David Nussboym declared.

Several people nodded emphatically. Mordechai Anielewicz rolled his eyes. He suspected he wasn't the only one, but with everybody in concealing gas masks, he couldn't be sure. The Jewish administration and fighters in Lodz were in a delicate condition. They had to co-operate with the Lizards, and some – Nussboym among them – still did so sincerely. Others, though, hurt the aliens every chance they got, so long as they could do it without getting discovered. Keeping track of who was in which camp made life more interesting than Anielewicz liked.

Another blast, this one close enough to shake the fire station. Even without a large charge of explosive, several tons of metal falling out of the sky made for a big impact. Anielewicz shivered. Working against the Lizards often meant covertly working with the Nazis, even when their poison gas was killing Jews inside Lodz. Some Jews supported the Lizards simply because they could not stomach working with the Nazis no matter what.

Anielewicz understood that. He sympathized with it, but not enough to feel the same way himself. The Nazis had been gassing Polish Jews before the Lizards arrived, and they'd kept right on doing it even after the Lizards took Poland away from them. They were without a doubt bastards; the only good thing Mordechai could think to say about them was that they were human bastards.

Minutes crawled slowly past. Mordechai kept hoping, praying for the all-clear signal. Instead, another rocket landed. The siren and the alarm hiss went on and on. He drew in breath after breath of stagnant air. His feet began to hurt. The only place to sit – or rather, squat – in the sealed room was over a latrine bucket in a tiny curtained corner. Just getting there wasn't easy.

At last the amplified hiss faded and the sirens changed to a warbling note before ceasing altogether. '*Gevalt!*' somebody said. 'Let's get out of here.'

'Is it safe?' somebody else asked. 'Just because the rockets aren't coming, does that mean the gas has gone away?'

'We can't stay here forever,' Mordechai said. 'I'll go out and look around, see if anyone close by is down from the gas. If I don't come back in five minutes . . . you'll know I shouldn't have gone.' With such gallows humor, he elbowed his way toward the door.

When he got outside, he was relieved not to find people lying dead on Lutomierska Street in front of the fire station. He hadn't expected he would find that; none of the explosions had sounded close enough to produce such a result. But the Germans' gas was insidious stuff, and sometimes spread more in one direction than another. The minute you stopped assuming it could kill you, it probably would.

He looked around. One column of smoke was rising from the north, from the Polish part of Lodz, the area where Germans who'd called the place Litzmannstadt had settled before the Lizards came. Not many of them were left; the Poles and the Jews had had their revenge. Too bad, n a way. There would have been delicious irony in the Nazis' gassing he Germans they'd sent out to dwell in a land that wasn't theirs.

More smoke, though, rose from closer to home. One of the rockets had it in the Jewish district. That must have been the second one, Mordechai thought, the one that shook the station. He snarled. Even now, fighting the Lizards, the Nazis were killing Jews. He was sure they knew it, too. They robably thought it was a hell of a good joke – and that some of the Jews vere co-operating with them against the Lizards an even better one.

He went back inside before the people in the sealed room decided he'd ecome a casualty, too. He hurried upstairs. 'It's safe to come out,' he said. We had a hit in the ghetto, though.' Now that the Germans were gone, it vasn't formally a ghetto any more. It still functioned as one, though, and he name lingered.

'The fire engine will have to go to tend it,' David Nussboym said. 'I volunteer to ride along.' That took courage; the Germans' gas could kill ou not only if you breathed it but if it got on your skin. Anielewicz would ave preferred to think of anyone who collaborated with the Lizards as a spineless coward. Nussboym complicated his picture of the world.

He wanted to volunteer himself, to show Nussboym people who lisagreed with him had spirit, too. But he made himself keep quiet. With the collaborator away from the offices, people who wanted to deal vith the Lizards instead of sucking up to them could speak freely.

'Come on,' said Solomon Gruver, the big, burly man who led the ire brigade and drove the engine. His men and Nussboym ran for he stairs.

'I hope the people in the area are already hosing down the streets nd the buildings,' Anielewicz said. 'Between them and the engines, they should be able to flush most of the gas down the mains.' He laughed, a aunted, hollow sound inside his mask. 'We're so used to dealing with he unspeakable that we've got very good at developing procedures for t. Either that proves we're clever and quick or that we're utterly damned. Maybe both.'

The fire engine roared away, bell clanging. 'Do you think we can take ur masks off?' a woman named Bertha Fleishman asked. She was drab nd mousy; no one human or Lizard, took any special notice of her. That nade her one of the most valuable spies the Jews in Lodz had: she could o anywhere, hear anything, and report back.

'Let's find out.' Anielewicz pulled the mask off his head. He took a couple of deep breaths, then gasped and crumpled to the floor. Instead of crying out n alarm and dismay, people swore at him and looked around for things to hrow. The first time he'd played that joke, they'd been properly horrified. Now they halfway looked for it, though he didn't do it all the time.

The rest of the people in the sealed room took off their masks, too. Whew! someone said. 'It's just about as stuffy in here with them off as t is with them on.'

'What are we going to do?' Bertha Fleishman said. 'If we get rid of the Lizards, we get the Germans back. For us in particular, that would be worse, even if having the Germans win and the Lizards lose would be better for people as a whole. After we've suffered so much, shouldn't we be able to live a little?' She sounded wistful, plaintive.

'Why should this time be different from all other times!' Anielewicz said. The reply, so close to the first of the Four Questions from the Passover Seder but expecting a different response, brought a sigh from everyone in the room. He went on, 'The real question should be, what do we do if the Lizards get sick of the Germans harassing them and decide to put everything they have into smashing the *Reich*?'

They tried that against the English,' a man said. 'It didn't work.'

'And thank God it didn't,' Mordechai said, wondering if he'd sent Moishe Russie into worse danger than that from which he'd escaped. 'But it's not the same. The Lizards' logistics in England were very bad. They had to fly all their soldiers and all their supplies up from southern France, so it was almost as if they were trying to invade by remote control. It wouldn't be like that if they attacked the Nazis. They're right next door to them here and in France both.'

'Whatever they do, they probably won't do it right away, not with snow on the ground,' Bertha Fleishman said. 'They hate the cold. Come next spring, it may be something to worry about. Until then, I think they'll hold back and try to ride out whatever the Nazis throw at them.'

Thinking about the way the Lizards did things, Anielewicz slowly nodded. 'You may be right,' he said. 'But that only gives us more time to answer the question. It doesn't make it go away.'

Teerts did not like flying over Deutschland. He hadn't liked flying over Britain, either, and for much that same reason: more and more Tosevite jets in the air, along with antiaircraft fire that seemed thick enough to let him get out of his killercraft and walk from one shell burst to the next.

His mouth dropped open in ironic laughter. Fire from the Big Uglies' antiaircraft guns had done more than put a couple of holes in the skin of his killercraft. As best he could figure, the one time he'd been shot down was when he'd had the colossal bad luck to suck infantrymales' bullets into both engine turbines in the space of a couple of moments ... and his luck had only got worse once he descended inside the Nipponese lines.

He never, ever wanted to be captured again. 'I'd sooner die,' he said.

'Superior sir?' That was Sserep, one of his wingmales.

'Nothing,' Teerts said, embarrassed at letting his thoughts go out over an open microphone.

He checked his radar. The Deutsche had some killercraft in the air, but none close enough to his flight to be worth attacking. He also watched the Tosevites' aircraft to make sure they weren't pilotless machines like the ones he'd encountered over Britain. Orders on conserving antiaircraft missiles got more emphatic with every passing day. Before long, he expected the fleetlord to issue one that said something like, *If you have already been shot down and killed, it is permissible to expend one missile against the enemy aircraft responsible, expenditure of two will result in severe punishment.*

He spotted a dark gray plume of smoke rising from the ground and hissed with glee. That was a railroad engine, burning one of the incredibly noxious fuels the Tosevites' machines employed. Whatever a railroad engine was hauling – Big Uglies, weapons, supplies – it was a prime target. He spoke to Sserp and Nivvek, his other wingmale, to make sure they saw it, too, then said, 'Let's go shoot it up.'

He dropped down to lose altitude and reduced his airspeed to make sure he could do a proper job of raking the target. His fingerclaw stabbed at the firing button of the cannon. Flames stabbed out from the nose of his killercraft; the recoil of the cannon and the turbulence form the fired shells made it shudder slightly in the air.

He yelled with savage glee as puffs of smoke spurted from the railroad cars. As he shot over the locomotive that pulled the train, he yanked the stick back hard to gain some altitude and come around for another pass. Acceleration tugged at him; the world went gray for a moment. He swung the killercraft through a ninety-degree roll so he could look back at the train. He yelled again; either Sserep or Nivvek had hit the engine hard, and it was slowing to a stop. Now he and the other two males could finish destroying it at their leisure.

Off in the middle distance on his radar set, something – half a dozen somethings – rose almost vertically into the air. 'What are those?' Nivvek exclaimed.

'Nothing to worry about, I don't think,' Teerts answered. 'If the Deutsche are experimenting with antiaircraft missiles of their own, they have some more experimenting to do, I'd say.'

'Truth, superior sir,' Nivvek said, amusement in his voice. 'None of our aircraft is even in the neighborhood of those – whatever-they-ares.'

'So I see,' Teerts said. If they were missiles, they were pretty feeble. Like other Tosevite flying machines, they seemed unable to exceed the speed of sound in the local atmosphere. They climbed toward the peak of their arc in what looked to be a ballistic trajectory ... whereupon Teerts forgot about them and gave his attention over to smashing up the train.

It had been carrying infantrymales, perhaps among other things. The first pass hadn't got all of them, either; some had bailed out of the damaged coaches. The gray-green clothes they wore were hard to see against the ground, but muzzle flashes told Teerts some of them were shooting at him. Memories of the Nipponese made fear blow through him in a choking cloud – what if the Big Uglies got lucky twice with him?

They didn't. His killercraft performed flawlessly as he flailed them with canon fire. Shells smashed at them' they boiled like the waves of Tosev

3's oversized oceans. He hoped he'd slaughtered hundreds of them. They weren't Nipponese, but they were Big Uglies, and in arms against the Race. No qualms about killing civilians diluted his revenge, not here, not now.

He pulled back on his stick again. The train was afire at several places up and down its length; one more run would finish the job of destroying it. Now that the nose of his killercraft was pointing upward again, he checked the radar screen to make sure no Deutsche aircraft were approaching.

Sserep must have done the same thing at the same time, for he shouted, 'Superior sir!'

'I see them,' Teerts answered grimly. The Deutsche machines he'd dismissed as experimental – and inept – antiaircraft missiles were diving on his flight of killercraft, and plainly under intelligent control. For the Tosevites, that meant they had to be piloted, the Big Uglies didn't have automatic systems good enough for the job.

With a small shock, he saw that the Tosevite aircraft were flying faster than his own machine. At least momentarily, that let them choose terms of engagement, something rare in their air-to-air engagements with the Race. He gave his killercraft maximum power; acceleration shoved him back against the seat. The Big Uglies wouldn't keep the advantage long.

'I am firing missiles, superior sir,' Sserep said. 'After we get back to base, I'll argue about it with the males in Supply who seem to spend all their time counting pieces of eggshell. The point is to be able to get back *to* base.'

Teerts didn't argue. The missiles streaked past his killercraft, trailing thin plumes of smoke. The Tosevites' aircraft had smoky exhaust, too, far more smoky than that of the missiles. With hideous speed, they swelled from specks to swept-wing killercraft of peculiar design – just before he stabbed his firing button with a fingerclaw, he had a fractional instant to wonder how they maintained stability without tailfins.

Whatever the details of the aerodynamics, maintain stability they did. One of them managed to sideslip a missile. Electronics would have been hard-pressed to do that; for mere flesh and blood to accomplish it was little short of a miracle. Sserep's other missile exploded its targets in a spectacular midair fireball that made Teerts' nictitating membranes flick out to protect his eyes from the flash. What in the name of the Emperor were the Big Uglies using for fuel?

That thought, too, quickly faded. He blazed away at the strange machine heading straight for his killercraft. Winking flashes of light at its wing roots said it was shooting at him, too. Deutsche killercraft carried cannon; they could do real damage if they scored hits.

Without warning, the Big Ugly aircraft blew up as violently as the one Sserep's missile had hit. 'Yes!' Teerts shouted. The only feeling that matched midair triumph was a good taste of ginger.

'Superior sir, I regret to report that my aircraft is damaged,' Nivvek said. 'I waited too long before firing missiles, and they shot past the Tosevites: they were still too close to me to arm their warheads. I am losing speed and altitude, and fear I shall have to eject. Wish me luck.'

'Spirits of Emperors past go with you, Nivvek,' Teerts said, gnashing his teeth in anguish. Urgently, he added, 'Try to stay away from the Big Uglies on the ground. As long as you can keep clear of them, your radio beacon gives you some chance of being rescued.' How good a chance, here in the middle of Deutschland, he tried not to think about. His own memories of captivity were too sharp and dreadful.

Nivvek did not answer. Sserep said, 'He has ejected, superior sir; I saw the capsule blast free of his killercraft and the parachute deploy.' He paused, then went on, 'I don't have the fuel to loiter till rescue aircraft come.'

After a quick glance at his own gauges, Teerts said, 'Neither have I,' hating every word. He checked his radar. Only one of the Deutsch killercraft was still in the air, streaking away at low altitude. Sserep and Nivvek hadn't been ideal – nor had he. He turned and expended one of his missiles. It streaked after the strange little tailless aircraft and blew it out of the sky.

'That's the last of those,' Sserep said. 'The Emperor grant that we don't see their like again soon.'

'Truth,' Teerts said feelingly. 'The Big Uglies keep coming up with new things.' He said that as if he'd been accusing them of devouring their own hatchlings. Against what they'd had when the Race landed on Tosev 3, combat had been a walkover. Only males who were unlucky – as Teerts had been – got shot down. Now, at least above the western end of the main continental mass, you had to earn your living every moment in the air.

'We won't even be able to cannibalize spares from Nivvek's aircraft,' Sserep said, his voice sad.

Somewhere down there in a Deutsch factory, Big Ugly technicians were welding and riveting the airframes for more of their nasty little killercraft. Somewhere down there, Big Ugly pilots were learning to fly them. The Race made do with what it had brought along. Day by day, less and less of that remained. What would happen when it was all gone? One more thing to think about.

Teerts used satellite relay to call both his base in southern France and the nearest air base the Race held east of Deutschland, in the territory called Poland. Nivvek's rescue alarm should have been received at both of them, but Teerts was taking no chances. He got the feeling the base in Poland had more things to worry about than Nivvek; the male to whom he spoke spent half his time babbling about a Deutsch rocket attack.

Teerts wondered why antimissile missiles didn't protect the base. The most obvious – and the most depressing – answer was that no missiles were left. If that was so . . . how soon would he be flying without antiaircraft missiles? What would happen when his radar broke down and no spare parts were left?

'We'll be even with the Big Uglies,' he said, and shuddered at the thought of it.

Liu Han stared at the row of characters on a sheet of paper in front of her. Her face was a mask of concentration; the tip of her tongue slipped out between her lips without her noticing. She gripped a pencil as if it were a dagger, then remembered she wasn't supposed to hold it that way and shifted it back between her index and middle fingers.

Slowly, painstakingly, she copied the characters written on the sheet of paper. She knew what they said: *Scaly devils, give back the baby you stole from Liu Han at your camp near Shanghai.* She wanted to make sure the little devils could read what she wrote.

When she'd finished the sentence, she took a pair of shears and clipped off the strip of paper on which she'd written. Then she picked up the pencil and wrote the sentence again. She had a great bundle of strips, all saying the same thing. She was also getting a new callus, just behind the nail on her right middle finger. A lifetime of farming, cooking, and sewing had left her skin still soft and smooth there. Now that she was doing something less physically demanding than any of those, it marked her. She shook her head. Nothing was as simple as it first seemed.

She started writing the sentence yet again. Now she knew the sound and meaning of each character in it. She could write her own name, which brought her its own kind of excitement. And, when she was out on the streets and *hutungs* of Peking, she sometimes recognized characters she'd written over and over, and could occasionally even use them to figure out the meanings of other characters close by them. Little by little, she was learning to read.

Someone knocked on the door to the cramped little chamber she used at the rooming house. She picked up her one set of spare clothes and used them to hide what she was doing before she went to open the door. The rooming house was a hotbed of revolutionary sentiment, but not everyone was to be trusted. Even people who did support the revolution might not need to know what she was doing. Living in a village and especially in a camp had taught her the importance of keeping secrets.

But waiting outside in the hall stood Nieh Ho-T'ing. She didn't know whether he knew the secrets of everyone in the rooming house, but he did know all of hers – all, at least, that had anything to do with the struggle against the little scaly devils. She stood aside. 'Come in, superior sir,' she said, the last two words in the scaly devils' language. No harm in reminding him of many ways she could be useful to the people's cause.

Nieh knew next to nothing of the little devils' tongue, but he did recognize that phrase. It made him smile. 'Thank you,' he said, walking past her into the little room. His own was no finer; anyone who could believe he had become a revolutionary for personal gain was a fool. He nodded approvingly when he noticed trousers and tunic covering up her writing. 'You do well to keep that hidden from prying eyes.'

'I do not want to let people know what I am doing,' she answered. As she shut the door behind him, she laughed a little before going on. 'I think I would leave it open if you were Hsia Shou-Tao.'

'Oh? Why is that?' Nieh Ho-T'ing asked, a little more sharply than her comment deserved.

'You know why perfectly well, or you should,' Liu Han said, irritated at his obtuseness. *Men!* she thought. 'All he wants to do is see my body' – a euphemism for doing other things with it than merely seeing it.

Nieh said, 'That is not all Hsia Shou-Tao wants. He is a committed people's revolutionary, and has risked much to free the workers and peasants from the oppression first of the upper classes and then of the scaly devils.' He coughed. 'He is also fond of women, perhaps too fond. I have spoken to him about this.'

'Have you?' Liu Han said, pleased. That was more action than she'd expected. 'Men usually look the other way when their comrades take advantage of women.'

'Er – yes.' Nieh paced around the chamber, which did not have a lot of room for pacing. Liu Han took her spare clothes off the table. Nieh not only knew what she was doing, he had started her on the project. He came over and examined what she'd done. 'You form your characters more fluidly than you did when you began,' he said. 'You may not have the smooth strokes of a calligrapher, but anyone who read this would think you had been writing for years.'

'I have worked hard,' Liu Han said, a truth that applied to her entire life.

'Your labor is rewarded,' he told her.

She didn't think he had come to her room for no other reason than to compliment her on her handwriting. Usually, though, when he had something to say, he came out and said it. He would have called anything else bourgeois shilly-shallying ... most of the time. What, then, was he keeping to himself?

Liu Han started to laugh. The sound made Nieh jump. She laughed harder. 'What do you find funny?' he asked, his voice brittle.

'You,' she said, for a moment seeing only the man and not the officer of the People's Liberation Army. 'When I complained about Hsia Shou-Tao, that left you in a complicated place, didn't it.'

'What are you talking about?' he demanded. But he knew, he knew. She could tell by the way he paced again, harder than ever, and by the way he would not look at her.

She almost did not answer him, not directly. A proper Chinese woman was quiet, submissive, and, if ever she thought about desire between woman and man, did not openly say so. But Liu Han had been through too much to care about propriety – and, in any case, the Communists talked a great deal about equality of all sorts, including that between the sexes. *Let's see if they mean what they say*, she thought.

'I'm talking about you – and about me,' she answered. 'Or didn't you come up here now to see if you could get down on the mattress with me?'

Nieh Ho-T'ing stared at her. She laughed again. For all he preached, for all the Communists preached, down deep he was still a man and a Chinese. She'd expected nothing different, and so was not disappointed.

But, unlike most Chinese men, he did have some idea that his prejudices were just prejudices, not laws of nature. The struggle on his face was a visible working out of – what did he call it? – the dialectic, that's what the word was. The thesis was his old, traditional, not truly questioned belief, the antithesis his Communist ideology, and the synthesis – she watched to see what the synthesis would be.

'What if I did,' he said at last, sounding much less stern than he had moments before.

What if he did? Now she had to think about that. She hadn't lain with anyone since Bobby Fiore – and Nieh, in a way, had been responsible for Bobby Fiore's death. But it wasn't as if he'd murdered him, only that he'd put him in harm's way, as an officer had a right to do with a soldier he commanded. On the scales, that balanced.

What about the rest? If she let him bed her, she might gain influence over him in that way. But if they quarreled afterwards, she would lose not only that influence but also what she'd gained through her own good sense. She'd won solid respect for that; the project for which she was writing her endless slips had been her own idea, after all. There, too, the scales balanced.

Which left her one very basic question: did she want him? He was not a bad-looking man; he had strength and self-confidence aplenty. What did that add up to? *Not enough*, she decided with more than a twinge of regret.

'If I let a man take me to the mattress now,' she said, 'it will be because I want him, not because he wants me. That is not enough. Never again will that be enough for me to lie with anyone.' She shuddered, remembering time with Yi Min the village apothecary after the little scaly devils captured them both – and even worse times with men whose names she never knew, up in the little devils' airplane that never came down. Bobby Fiore had won her heart there simply by being something less than brutal. She never wanted to sink so low again.

She hadn't directly refused Nieh, not quite. She waited, more than a little anxious, to see if he'd understood what she'd told him. He smiled crookedly. 'I will not trouble you any more about this, then,' he said.

'Having a man interested in me is not a trouble,' Liu Han said. She recalled how worried she'd been when her husband – before the Japanese came, before the scaly devils came and turned the world upside down – had wanted nothing to do with her while she was carrying their child.

That had been a bleak and lonely time. Even so— 'When a man does not listen when you say you do not want him, that is trouble.'

'What you say makes good sense,' Nieh answered. 'We can still further the revolution together, even if not in congress.'

She liked him very much then, almost enough to change her mind. She'd never known – truth to tell, she'd never imagined – a man who could joke after she'd turned him down. 'Yes, we are still comrades,' she said earnestly. 'I want that'. *I need that*, she did not add, not for him to hear. Aloud she went on, 'Now you know the difference between yourself and Hsia Shou-Tao.'

'I knew that difference a long time ago,' he said. 'Hsia, too, is still a revolutionary, though. Do not think otherwise. No one is perfect, or even good, in all ways.'

'That is so,' Liu Han clapped her hands. 'I have an idea. Listen to me: we should arrange to have our beast-show men give a couple of exhibitions for the little scaly devils where nothing goes wrong – they simply give their shows and leave. That will tell us how the little devils search their cages and equipment and will also make the scaly devils feel safer about letting beast shows into the buildings they use.'

'I have had pieces of this thought myself,' Nieh Ho-T'ing said slowly, 'but you give reasons for doing it more clearly than I had thought of them. I will discuss it with Hsia. You may talk with him about it, too, of course. It may even interest him enough to keep his mind off wanting to see your body.'

His smile said he was joking again, but not altogether. Liu Han nodded; as he'd said, Hsia *was* a dedicated revolutionary, and a good enough idea for hurting the scaly devils would draw his attention away from fleshly matters ... for a while.

Liu Han said, 'If he likes the notion well enough, it will only make him want me more, because he will think someone who comes up with a good idea is desirable just on account of that.'

She laughed. After a moment, so did Nieh Ho-T'ing. He found an excuse to leave very soon after that. Liu Han wondered if he was angry at her in spite of what he'd said. Had he done what she'd said Hsia would do: decided he wanted her not so much because of the woman she was as in admiration of her ideas for the struggle against the little scaly devils?

Once the idea occurred to her, it would not go away. It fit in too well with what she'd seen of how Nieh Ho-T'ing's mind worked. She went back to writing her demand on strip after strip of paper. All the while, she wondered whether she should consider Nieh's ideologically oriented advances a compliment or an insult.

Even after she set aside pen and paper and scissors, she couldn't make up her mind.

*   *   *

Behind the glass partition, the engineer pointed to Moishe Russie: *You're on!* Russie looked down at his script and began to read: 'Good day, ladies and gentlemen, this is Moishe Russie speaking to you from London, still the capital of the British Empire and still free of Lizards. Some of you have no idea how glad I am to be able to say that. Others have the misfortune of suffering under the Lizards' tyranny and know for themselves whereof I speak.'

He glanced over at Nathan Jacobi, who nodded encouragement for him to go on. It was good to be working with Jacobi again; it felt like better days, the days before the invasion. Moishe took a deep breath and continued: 'The Lizards sought to bring Great Britain under their direct control. I can tell you now that they have failed, and failed decisively. No Lizards in arms remain on British soil; all are either fled, captured, or dead. The last Lizard airstrip on the island, that at Tangmere in the south, has fallen.'

He hadn't seen that with his own eyes. When it became clear the Lizards were abandoning their British toehold, he'd been recalled to London to resume broadcasting. He checked his script to see where he'd resume. It was Yiddish, of course, for broadcast to Jews and others in eastern Europe. All the same, it sounded very much like what a BBC newsreader would have used for an English version. That pleased him; he was getting a handle on the BBC style.

'We have now proved decisively what others began to demonstrate last year: the Lizards are not invulnerable. They can be defeated and driven back. Moreover, just as their weapons have on occasion discomfited us, we too have devised means of fighting for which they have as yet developed no countermeasures. This bodes well for future campaigns against them.'

How it boded for the soul of mankind was another question, one he felt less confident about answering. Everyone was using gas against the Lizards now, and praising it to the skies because it killed them in carload lots. But if they vanished off the face of the earth tomorrow, how long till earthly nations remembered their old quarrels and started using gas on one another? How long till the Germans started using it on the Jews they still ruled? For that matter, how did he know they weren't using it on the Jews they still ruled? Nothing came out of Germany but what little Hitler and Goebbels wanted known.

Even as he thought about what mankind would do after the Lizards were vanquished, he realized beating them came first. And so he read on: 'Wherever you who hear my voice may be, you, too, can join the fight against the alien invaders. You need not even take up a gun. You can also contribute to the war against them by sabotaging goods you produce if you work in a factory, by not paying, paying late, or underpaying the exactions they seek to impose on you, by obstructing them in any way possible, and by informing their foes of what they are about to do. With your help, we can make Earth so unpleasant for them that they will be glad to pack up and leave.'

He finished the last line of the script just as the engineer drew a finger across his throat to show time was up. In the soundproof control room, the engineer clapped his hands, then pointed to Nathan Jacobi, who began reading the English version of Russie's talk.

Jacobi was a consummate professional; the engineer took for granted his finishing spot on. What struck Moishe about his colleague's reading was how much of it he understood. When he'd first begun broadcasting for the BBC, he'd had next to no English. Now he could follow it pretty well, and speak enough to get by. He felt less alien in London than he sometimes had in purely Polish sections of Warsaw.

'There, that's done it,' Jacobi said when they were off the air. He clapped Moishe on the back. 'Jolly good to be working with you again. For a while there, I doubted we should ever have the chance.'

'So did I,' Moishe said. 'I have to remind myself that this is warfare, too. I've seen altogether too much of the real thing lately.'

'Oh, Yes.' Jacobi got up and stretched. 'The real thing is a great deal worse to go through, but you and I may be able to do more damage to the Lizards here than we could on campaign. I tell myself as much, at any rate.'

'So do I,' Moishe said as he too rose. 'Is Eric Blair broadcasting after us, as he often does?'

'I believe so,' Jacobi answered. 'You've taken a liking to him, haven't you?'

'He's an honest man,' Russie said simply.

Sure enough, Blair stood outside the studio door, talking animatedly with a handsome, dark-skinned woman who wore a plum-colored robe of filmy cotton – from India, Moishe guessed, though his knowledge of people and places Oriental had almost all been acquired since he came to England. Blair broke off to nod to the two Jewish broadcasters. 'Hope you chaps have been giving the Lizards a proper hiding over the air,' he said. 'I hope we did, too,' Jacob answered, his voice grave.

'The princess and I shall endeavour to do the same,' Blair said, dipping his head to the woman from India. His chuckle had a wheeze in it that Russie did not like. 'I think that's what they call an alliance of convenience: a princess and a socialist joining together to defeat the common foe.'

'You wanted dominion status for India no less than I did,' the woman said. Her accent, so different from Moishe's, made her hard for him to understand. He reminded himself to tell Rivka and Reuven he'd met a princess: not something a Jew was likely to do in Warsaw – or, from what he'd seen, in London, either.

'India has more than dominion status these days, *de facto* if not *de jure*,' Eric Blair said. 'It's the rare and lucky ship that goes from London to Bombay, and even luckier the one that comes home again.'

'How are things here?' Moishe asked. One thing he'd learned since coming to England was how narrow his perspective on the world had been. He wanted to learn as much as he could about places that had been just names, if that, to him.

Blair said, 'You will not be surprised to learn that Mr Gandhi has made himself as unpleasant to the Lizards as he ever was to the British *raj*.'

'The aliens do not know how to deal with masses of people who will not fight them but also refuse to labor for them,' the princess said. 'Massacre has only made the Mahatma's followers more eager to continue their nonviolent campaign against oppression and unjust rule – from anyone.'

'That last bit would have brought out the censor's razor blades and red ink had you tried to say it before the Lizards came,' Blair said. He looked at his watch. 'We'd best get in there, or we shall be late. Good to see you, Russie, Jacobi.' He and the Indian woman hurried into the studio, closing the door behind them.

The sun of early November was a cool, pale, fickle thing, scurrying through the sky low in the south and scuttling behind every cloud and bit of mist that passed. Even so, Moishe faced the weather with equanimity. In Warsaw, snow would have started falling a month earlier.

He said his good-byes to Nathan Jacobi and hurried home to his Soho flat. Having been separated from his family when the Lizards invaded England made him appreciate them all the more. But when he got up to the flat, before he could even tell his wife he'd met a princess, she said, 'Moishe, someone came round here looking for you today – a man with a uniform.' She sounded worried.

Moishe didn't blame her. That news was enough to worry anyone. When he first heard it, ice prickled up his spine. He needed a moment to remember where he was. 'This is England,' he reminded Rivka – and himself. 'No *Gestapo* here, no *Juden Heraus?* Did he say what he wanted of me?'

She shook her head. 'He did not say, and I did not ask. Hearing the knock on the door, opening it to find the man with those clothes there ...' She shivered. 'And then he spoke to me in German when he saw I did not understand enough English to know what he needed.'

'That would frighten anyone,' Moishe said sympathetically, and took her in his arms. He wished he could forget about the Nazis and Lizards both. He wished the whole world could forget about them both. The next wish that produced the desired effect would be the first.

Someone knocked on the door. Moishe and Rivka flew apart. It was a brisk, authoritative knock, as if the fellow who made it had a better right to make it, had a better right to come into the flat, than the people who lived there. 'It's him again,' Rivka whispered.

We'd better find out what he's after,' Moishe said, and opened the door. He had all he could do not to recoil in alarm after that: except for the different uniform, the man who stood there might have come straight off an SS recruiting poster. He was tall and slim and muscular and blond and had the dangerous look in his eye that was calculated to turn your blood to water if you ended up on the receiving end of it.

But instead of shouting something like, *You stinking sack of shit of a Jew*, he politely nodded and in soft tones asked, 'You are Mr Moishe Russie?'

'Yes,' Moishe said cautiously. 'Who are you?'

'Flight Lieutenant Donald Mather, sir, of the Special Air Service,' the blond young soldier answered. To Russie's surprise, he saluted.

'C-come in,' Moishe said, his voice a little shaky. No SS man would ever have saluted a Jew, not under any circumstances. 'You have met my wife, I think.'

'Yes, sir,' Mather said, stepping past him. He nodded to Rivka. 'Ma'am.' Social amenities apparently complete, he turned back to Moishe. 'Sir, His Majesty's Government needs your help.'

Alarm sirens began going off in Moishe's mind. He slipped from English back into Yiddish: 'What does His Majesty's Government think I can do for it? And why me in particular and not somebody else?'

Flight Lieutenant Mather answered the second question first: 'You in particular, sir, because of your experience in Poland.' He left English, too, for German. Moishe's hackles did not rise so much as they might have: Mather made an effort, and not a bad one, to pronounce it with a Yiddish intonation. He was plainly a capable man, and in some not-so-obvious ways.

'I had lots of experience in Poland,' Moishe said. 'Most of it I didn't like at all, not even a little bit. Why does anyone think I would want to do something that draws on it?'

'You're already doing something that draws on it, sir, in your BBC broadcasts,' Mather replied. Moishe grimaced; that was true. The Englishman continued, making his German sound more Yiddish with every sentence: 'I will admit, though, we have rather more in mind for you than sitting in front of a microphone and reading from a prepared script.'

'What do you have in mind?' Moishe said. 'You still haven't answered what I asked you.'

'I was coming round to it, sir, by easy stages,' Donald Mather said. 'One thing you learned in Poland was that co-operating with the Lizards isn't always the best of notions, if you'll forgive the understatement.'

'No, not always, but if I hadn't co-operated with them at first, I wouldn't be here arguing with you now,' Moishe said.

'Saving yourself and your family—' Mather began.

'—And my people,' Russie put in. 'Without the Lizards, the Nazis would have slaughtered us all.'

'And your people,' Flight Lieutenant Mather conceded. 'No one will say you didn't do what you had to do when you joined the Lizards against the Nazis. But afterwards, you saw that mankind as a whole was your people, too, and you turned against the Lizards.'

'Yes to all of this,' Moishe said, beginning to grow impatient. 'But what does it have to do with whatever you want from me?'

'I am coming to that,' Mather answered calmly. No matter how well he spoke, that external calm would have marked him as an Englishman; in his place, a Jew or a Pole would have been shouting and gesticulating. He went on, 'Would you agree that in His Majesty's mandate of Palestine, no effort to exterminate the Jews is now under way, but rather the reverse?'

'In Palestine?' Moishe echoed. The mention of the name was enough to make Rivka sharply catch her breath. Moishe shook his head. 'No, you aren't doing anything like that. *Nu?*' Here, the multifarious Yiddish word meant *Come to the point.*

He would have explained that to Mather, but the flight lieutenant understood it on his own. Mather said, 'The nub of it is, Mr Russie, that there are Jews in Palestine who are not content with British administration there and have been intriguing with the Lizards in Egypt to aid any advance they might make into the Holy Land. His Majesty's Government would like to send you to Palestine to talk to the Jewish fighting leaders and convince them to stay loyal to the crown, to show them that, unlike yours, their situation is not so bad as to require intervention by the aliens to liberate them from it.'

'You want to send me to Palestine?' Moishe asked. He knew he sounded incredulous, but couldn't help it. Beside him, Rivka made an indignant noise. He corrected himself at once: 'You want to send us – me and my family – to Palestine?' He couldn't believe what he was saying. Occasionally, in Poland, he'd thought of emigrating, of making *aliyah*, to the Holy Land. But he'd never taken the notion seriously, no matter how hard the Poles made life for a Jew. And once the Nazis came, it was too late.

Now this Englishman he'd known for five minutes was nodding, telling him the long-hopeless dream of his exiled people could come true for him. 'That's just what we want to do. We can't think of a better man for the job.'

With a woman's practicality, Rivka asked the next question: 'How do we get there?'

'By ship,' Donald Mather answered. 'We can get you down to Lisbon without any trouble. Outbound from Lisbon, your freighter will meet a submarine to take you through the Straits of Gibraltar. From the submarine, you'll board another freighter for the journey to Haifa. How soon can you be ready to leave?'

'It wouldn't be long,' Moishe said. 'It's not as if we have a lot to pack.' That was, if anything, an understatement. They'd come to England with only the clothes on their backs. They had more than that now, thanks to the kindness of the British and of their relatives here. But a lot of what they had wouldn't come with them – why bring pots and pans to the Holy Land?

'If I came for you the day after tomorrow this same time, you'd be ready, then?' Flight Lieutenant Mather asked.

Moishe almost laughed at him. If they had to leave, he and Rivka could have been ready in half an hour – assuming they found Reuven and dragged him away from whatever game he was playing or watching. A couple of days' notice struck him as riches like those the Rothschilds were said to enjoy. 'We'll be ready,' he said firmly.

'Good. Until then—' Mather turned to go.

'Wait,' Rivka said, and the Englishman stopped. She went on, 'For how long would we be going to – to Palestine?' She had to fight to say the incredible word. 'How would you bring us back, and when?'

'As for how long you'd stay, *Frau* Russie, it would be at least until your husband completed his mission, however long that might take,' Mather answered. 'Once that's done, if you want to return to England, we'll arrange that, and if you want to stay in Palestine, we can arrange that, too. We do remember those who help us, I promise you that. Have you any other questions? No?' He saluted, did a smart about-turn, and headed for the stairwell.

Moishe and Rivka stared at each other. 'Next year in Jerusalem,' Moishe whispered. Jews had been making that prayer since the Romans sacked the Second Temple almost nineteen hundred years before. For almost all of them, it expressed nothing more than a wish that would never be fulfilled. Now—

Now Moishe seized Rivka. Together, they danced around the inside of the flat. It was more than exuberance; he felt as if he could dance on the walls and ceiling as well as the floor. Rivka slowed sooner than he did. She kept a firm grasp on the essentials of the situation, saying, 'They are not doing this for you, Moishe – they're doing it for themselves. Who are these Jews conniving with the Lizards, anyhow?'

'I don't know,' Moishe admitted. 'What could I know of what goes on in Palestine? But I know this much: if they want to play games with the Lizards, they're making a mistake. The British aren't starving them and killing them for sport, and that would be the only possible excuse for choosing the Lizards.'

'You've seen that for yourself,' Rivka agreed, and then turned practical once more: 'We'll have to leave a lot of these clothes behind. The Holy Land is a warmer country than England.'

'So it is.' Moishe hadn't been thinking about such mundane things. 'To pray at the Wailing Wall—' He shook his head in wonder. The idea was just starting to sink down from the front of his mind to the place where his feelings lived: he'd gone from stunned to joyful, and the joy kept growing. It was the first thing he'd ever imagined that might improve on being in love.

It had seized Rivka, too. 'To live the rest of our lives in Palestine,' she murmured. 'England here, this is not bad – next to Poland even before the Nazis came, it's a paradise. But to live in a land with plenty of Jews and no one to hate us – that would really be paradise.'

'Who else lives in Palestine?' Moishe said, once again realizing his ignorance of the wider world was both broad and deep. 'Arabs, I suppose. After Poles and Germans, they can't be anything but good neighbors. If Reuven grows up in a country where no one hates him—' He paused. To a Polish Jew, that was like wishing for the moon. But here, even though he hadn't wished for the moon, Flight Lieutenant Mather had just handed it to him.

'They speak Hebrew in Palestine along with Yiddish, don't they?' Rivka said. 'I'll have to learn.'

'I'll have a lot of learning to do myself,' Moishe said. Men read the Torah and the Talmud, so he'd learned Hebrew where Rivka hadn't. But there was a difference between using language to talk to God and using it to talk with your fellow men. *When I get to Jerusalem, I'll find out what the difference is,* he thought, and shivered with excitement.

It occurred to him then that he owed his chance of going to the Holy Land to the Lizards. Before them came, he'd been one more Jew among tens of thousands, hundreds of thousands, of others starving in the Warsaw ghetto. He'd been out on the streets in dead of night, trying to cadge some food to stay alive and praying to God to grant him a sign that He had not forsaken His people. He'd taken the sunlike glow of the explosive-metal bomb the Lizards had set off high above the city as an answer to that prayer.

A lot of other people had taken it the same way. Almost willy-nilly, they'd made him into their leader, though becoming one had been the last thing in his mind. Because he'd looked like a leader to his people, he'd looked like one to the Lizards, too, when they drove. Hitler's thugs out of Warsaw. Had it not been for them, he would have stayed ordinary till the day he died – and he'd probably be dead by now.

Haltingly, he spoke that thought aloud. Rivka heard him out, then shook her head. 'Whatever you think you owe them, you paid it off long ago,' she said. 'Yes, they saved us from the Nazis, but they did it for themselves, not for us. They just used us for their own purposes – and if it suits them to start killing us the way the Nazis did, they will.'

'You're right, I think,' Moishe said.

'Of course I am,' she answered.

He smiled, but soon sobered. Rivka had repeatedly shown she was better at dealing with the real world than he was. If she made a pronouncement like that, he would be wise to take it seriously. Then, all at once, he started to laugh: who would have thought that going to the Holy Land was part of the real world?

16

Inside the landcruiser which was inside the heavy transporter, Ussmak was thoroughly shielded from the outside world. What he was not shielded from was fear. After all he and his crewmales had endured in Britain, he knew he would never again be shielded from fear.

He spoke into the intercom microphone: 'How does your wound feel today, superior sir?'

'Getting better all the time,' Nejas answered. 'High time I was back on duty.' He hesitated, perhaps making sure the crew of the transporter could not hear the next thing he had to say. Once he was sure they were out of the circuit, he went on, his words all at once quick and breathy: 'Do you by any chance happen to have another – taste of ginger, landcruiser driver?'

'I'm sorry, superior sir, but I don't have any even for myself,' Ussmak answered. He wished he hadn't had to start his commander tasting. If he hadn't, though, he and Skoob would have had to leave Nejas behind. The landcruiser commander would never have made it to Tangmere and evacuation. Maybe none of them would have made it out of Britain alive.

'Too bad,' Nejas said. 'Oh, too bad. How I crave the herb!'

'As well you can't get it, then, superior sir,' Skoob told him. The gunner and commander had been crewmales since long before Ussmak joined them; Skoob had earned the right to speak bluntly to his chief. 'That filthy stuff's no good for any male, believe you me it's not.'

He'd said as much back in Britain, but he hadn't turned Ussmak in to the disciplinarians once they'd escaped the chaos of evacuation and reached the relative safety of southern France – relative safety, because even there the Big Uglies proved themselves able to lob poison gas at males and females of their own kind who labored on behalf of the Race. And Skoob had turned both eye turrets away from Nejas when his commander kept tasting while recovering. Skoob disapproved, but was too loyal to do anything about it.

Shame licked at Ussmak like the flames from a burning landcruiser. Hidden away in the driver's compartment, he had several – maybe more than several – tastes of ginger. He told himself he'd liked to Nejas because he didn't want to see the landcruiser commander plunge into degradation as he had done. It was even true – to a degree. But the main reason he'd said he had no more ginger was simple and selfish in the extreme – he didn't want to share it.

'Attention, landcruiser crews.' The voice of the transporter pilot filled the audio button taped to Ussmak's hearing diaphragm. 'Attention, landcruiser crews. We are beginning our descent to the landing. Please be alert for possible abrupt motions of the aircraft. Thank you.'

'Thank *you* – very much,' Ussmak muttered, having first made sure he was not transmitting even to his crewmates. *Please be alert for possible abrupt motions of the aircraft*, indeed! He'd flown into Britain in a landcruiser aboard a heavy transporter. He knew too well what that innocent-sounding euphemism meant. Had the pilot wanted to be honest, he would have said something like, *We may have to dodge like maniacs because the stinking Big Uglies are doing everything they can to shoot us down.*

What Ussmak didn't know was how much the local Big Uglies *could* do to shoot him down. Britain had been a dreadful place to fly into or out of. Not only was it a cramped little island, but the locals had a great many killercraft, some of them jet-powered, and radar to help guide those killercraft to their targets. No wonder, then, the transporters had taken such a beating over British skies.

Here in the eastern portion of the SSSR, that part of the mission was supposed to be easier, although Ussmak had grown heartily tired of experts telling him things about the Tosevites that soon turned out not to be so. But he'd fought in the SSSR before, if farther west, and knew that the Soviets, while they made good landcruisers by Big Ugly standards, lagged behind in other areas of the military art and lacked the doctrine to get the best results from the equipment they did have.

Or rather, he knew the Soviets *had* lagged behind in other areas of the military art and *had* lacked proper doctrine. He hadn't fought them in two of his years, one of Tosev 3's. Against his own people, or the Rabotevs, or the Hallessi, that wouldn't have mattered. For the mutable Big Uglies, it was as good as an age. Fearfully, he wondered what new destructive skills the Soviets had learned while he was busy elsewhere on this planet. Suddenly he shuddered. They were the ones who had used atomic weapons.

Nejas said, 'Pilot, how bad is the weather in the area to which we're flying?'

'It's cold, landcruiser commander,' the pilot answered. 'There's frozen water on the ground already, for instance.'

'That seems to happen a great deal on this planet,' Nejas said, his tone halfway between weary resignation and making the best of things. 'I don't suppose this Siberia place can be too much worse than the rest.'

'Last Tosevite winter, we were on duty in the southwestern part of the great land mass, what the Big Uglies call Africa,' Skoob said. 'That would have been downright pleasant if it hadn't been so damp. It was warm enough, anyhow, which is more than you can say for a lot of Tosev 3.'

Ussmak had spent most of the previous winter in a hospital ship, recovering from radiation poisoning after he'd had to bail out of his landcruiser into plutonium-contaminated muck when the Big Uglies raided the area for metal for their nuclear devices. The climate inside the ship had been salubrious enough. Getting there by way of radioactive mud was not a route he recommended, though.

Even through the steel and ceramic armor of the landcruiser in which he rode now, Ussmak could hear the roaring whine of the transporter's turbofans. He listened closely for any abrupt change in their tone, and braced himself in his seat. Especially on its landing descent, the huge, clumsy aircraft wasn't much faster than a Tosevite killercraft. Instead of feeling safe within the twin eggshells of transporter and landcruiser, he felt doubly trapped.

A swing to the side set his heart pounding. A moment later, the pilot came on to say, 'We are experiencing some violent crosswinds, you males in there who can't see out. Nothing to worry about; radar reports no Tosevite killercraft airborne in our vicinity. We'll be on the ground shortly.'

'What do you know?' Skoob said. 'Good news for a change.'

'The Emperor knows we could use some, after the fiasco in Britain,' Nejas said. He sounded like a male who needed a taste of ginger. When you hadn't had any for a while, the world seemed a grim place indeed. Ussmak had slowly learned that it was the herb – or rather, the lack of it – talking, not the world itself. Some tasters took a long time to figure that out. Some never did.

The transporter jet jerked in the air. Ussmak jerked in his seat. You didn't want to try to sit bolt upright; you'd smash your head against the roof of the driver's compartment. He remembered just in time. The pilot said, 'Flaps are down. We'll be landing momentarily. Landcruiser crews prepare to roll out the cargo bay.'

Another jolt announced the landing gear coming down. Then the transporter hit the runway. Despite its bulk, it jounced back into the air for an instant, then rolled to a stop. the turbofans screamed as they reversed thrust to help slow the enormous aircraft.

Ussmak was eager to escape from the transporter. Tosev 3 had too much water and not enough land, but they'd just flown one of the longest all-overland routes possible on the planet. He wanted to get out, look around at his new duty area (or as much of it as he could see through the vision slits of a landcruiser), and, more important still, meet some of the males here and find out where he could get some more ginger after his present supply ran out.

The nose of the transporter swung up, filling the cargo bay with light other than that of its own fluorescents. The light was white and very cold. 'Driver, start your engine,' Nejas said.

'It shall be done, superior sir,' Ussmak said, and obeyed.

No sooner had he obeyed than Nejas slammed the lid of the cupola down with a clang. 'It's a freezer out there,' he exclaimed. 'Worse than a freezer! You'd go into a freezer to warm up.' As if to support him, the landcruiser's heating elements came on, hissing gently as they blew warm air through the interior of the machine.

When Ussmak saw the male with a light wand who came up to direct the landcruiser out of the aircraft, he believed every word Nejas had said. The poor guide had an electrically heated suit of the sorts pilots used in the chilly air of high altitudes, and over it a hooded coat and boats made from the furry hides of Tosevite animals. In spite of all that, he looked desperately cold as he waved the landcruiser ahead. Ussmak put the machine in gear and rumbled down the ramp. Snow blowing almost horizontally greeted him. The landcruiser's heater hummed as it worked harder. He hoped it was made to withstand a challenge like this. Snow also started clogging his vision slits. He flicked the button that sent a stream of cleaning liquid onto them. It got rid of the snow, but froze in place, so it was as if he was trying to see out through a pane of ice.

'Careful!' Nejas shouted. 'You almost ran down the guide.'

'Sorry, superior sir,' Ussmak answered. 'If you have vision out your cupola, command me.' He explained what had gone wrong with his own optics.

Between them, the male with the light wand and Nejas directed Ussmak to a point in front of a building he saw only as a large, solid lump of snow in the midst of all the swirling stuff. A door opened in the side of the solid lump. The guide gestured. 'We're supposed to bail out and go in there, I think,' Nejas said. 'I just hope we don't freeze to death before we make it.'

With a single convulsive motion, Ussmak threw open the hatch above his head and scrambled out. The cold was stunning. His nictitating membranes drew over the surface of his eyes to protect them from the icy blast of the wind, but he had to blink hard to make them return to where they belonged; they had started to freeze in place. His lungs felt as if he was breathing fire. His skin burned for a moment, too, but then went cold and numb.

'This way! This way!' the guide shouted. Stumbling, Ussmak and his crewmales threw themselves at the entrance to the building. It was only a couple of his own bodylengths away, but he wondered if he would freeze into a solid block of ice before he got to it.

As soon as the landcruiser crew was inside, the male who had guided them off the transporter slammed the door and dogged it shut. Then he opened the inner door to the chamber. Delicious warmth flowed out. The chamber between the blizzard outside and the oasis of comfort within might almost have been a spaceship airlock. As far as Ussmak was concerned, the environment from which he'd just escaped was far more hostile than the unchanging vacuum of space.

'New hatchlings!' the guide called as he went into the barracks room that seemed a tiny piece of Home magically transported to Tosev 3. 'I've got some new hatchlings here – poor fools don't know they've just been stuck up the cloaca of this miserable world.'

Males in the body paint of landcruiser and fighting vehicle crews crowded round Ussmak and his companions. 'Welcome to Siberia,' one of them called. 'This place is so bad, they say even Big Uglies got exiled here.'

'The ground is frozen half the year,' another male added.

'The atmosphere doesn't freeze – it just seems that way,' said a third.

Ussmak had never run into such a cynical band of males. They had to be ginger tasters, he decided, and felt better for a moment.

Nejas waved his hands, trying to get a word in edgewise. 'Where is this railroad we're supposed to be interdicting? How can we even move about in this hideous weather, let alone fight?'

'The railroad's south of here, but not far enough to do us any good,' their guide answered. 'We've broken it; the trick is to keep the Russkis from hauling anything across the break and shipping it one way or the other. They have all sorts of animals, and sometimes they even use motor transport. When we come on one of their convoys, it's usually a massacre.'

'Coming on them is the problem, though,' another male said. 'Even radar has trouble seeing through these storms – when it's not frozen up, that is.'

Yet another male said, 'And we don't even have it too bad – when we're out there, we're in our vehicles. It's the poor infantrymales I really pity. They have to head out without a nice, warm eggshell around them.'

'Infantrymales!' Skoob exclaimed. 'How could you possibly go out there and fight on foot in – that? And even if you could, why would you?'

'Because the Russkis can,' said the male who'd guided them. 'If we didn't have infantry patrols out there, the cursed Big Uglies would sneak within mortar range and start dropping their stinking bombs right down on top of our heads. Either that or they'd get into our vehicle parks and work the Emperor knows how much havoc there. They've done both, and they probably will again.'

Ginger or no ginger, Ussmak wanted to hide. 'I thought nothing could be worse than Britain and all that poison gas. Maybe I was wrong.'

In a ragged chorus, the guide and the other males in the barracks sang out: 'Welcome to Siberia!'

Rance Auerbach looked to the cloudy skies, hoping for snow. Thus far his prayers had gone unanswered. Low, dirty-gray clouds hung over the prairie of eastern Colorado, but whatever snow or even rain – he would gladly have taken rain – they held refused to fall.

He waved to the troopers of his company, urging them to spread out farther. If a Lizard helicopter spotted them, they were on the way to becoming raw meat. The winter before, from all he'd heard, the Lizards hadn't got so frisky so late in the year. This time, they'd sent a force west by helicopter to occupy Cheyenne Wells, and were pushing infantry west along US 40 to try to consolidate their position. If they did, that would put Lamar, due south of Cheyenne Wells down US 385, in a hell of a bind.

Worse still, the next town west of Cheyenne Wells on US 40 was called First View: it was the place where the Rockies first poked up over the horizon of the Great Plains. In the Rockies lay Denver. Because he'd traveled with Leslie Groves, Auerbach got the idea something important was going on in Denver, even if he didn't know – and had no business knowing – what. Lizard thrusts that headed toward Denver needed stopping, no matter what.

The prairie seemed utterly empty but for his men and their horses. Turn those into buffalo and you'd have things back the way they were before the white man came – before the red man, too, come to that.

He turned in his saddle and called to Bill Magruder: 'Now I know what the Indians must have felt like, going up against the US Cavalry back in my grandpa's day.'

His second-in-command nodded. 'Sitting Bull licked General Custer, but look at all the good it did him in the end. We can't just win fights now and again. We have to win the whole shootin' match.'

Auerbach nodded. He'd been trained to think in terms of campaigns, which Sitting Bull certainly hadn't. He wondered what sort of global strategy the Lizards were trying to maintain. They'd plainly had one at the start of their invasion, but it seemed to have broken down in the face of unexpected human resistance.

As soon as his company passed Sheridan Lake, Auerbach waved them off US 385. No tracked vehicle could match a horse for cross-country performance. So he told himself, anyhow, although the rule applied more in mountains and marshes than on the rolling plains near the Kansas border. But his troopers and their mounts would be harder to spot in the mix of stubble and unharvested crops than on the asphalt of the highway.

'Sir, will you want to strike US 40 east or west of Arapahoe?' Magruder asked.

Auerbach's orders gave him discretion. Arapahoe lay about ten miles east of Cheyenne Wells, close to the Kansas line. If he came to the highway west of the little town, he risked drawing notice from the Lizards who'd been helicoptered into Cheyenne Wells. If he reached the highway on the Kansas side of Arapahoe, though, he was closer to what had been the Lizards' main forward bases.

'We'll go in to the east of Arapahoe,' he decided after a few seconds' thought. 'The farther east we can damage them, the more we draw their attention away from moving west, which is what we want to try to do.' That operating as far east as possible made it easier for the Lizards to damage him was something he tried not to think about.

He and his men camped for the night on an abandoned farm not far south of US 40. When they set out the next morning, they left their horses behind, toting on their backs the supplies they needed, as if they were infantrymen.

Auerbach had scouts out. He and most of his men sprawled in tall, yellow grass while the scouts advanced to make sure no Lizard patrols were on the highway. He watched through field glasses as the scouts crept forward, their khaki uniforms almost invisible against the brown earth and dying plants.

Only when they waved did he go forward with the demolition team. Two men laid charges on the surface of the road, connecting each one with the electrical detonator. They ran wire back to a little gully a couple of hundred feet away and then, crouching in it, blew the charges.

The earth shook under Auerbach. Chunks of asphalt rained down on the improvised trench. Somebody swore: 'Goddamn thing hit me right in the ass, Howard. Whose side you on, anyway?'

Howard was the trooper who'd pushed down the detonator plunger. He said, 'I'm on the good guys' side. Reckon that leaves you out, Maxwell.'

'Let's see what we've done,' Auerbach got up and trotted over to US 40. He nodded in solemn approval. Through swirling dust, he saw they'd blown a crater across both lanes of blacktop. Anybody who sent a tracked vehicle down into it would get his teeth rattled. Nobody would try to send a wheeled vehicle into it – you'd have to go around.

The demolition team finished their job in the area, then became ordinary cavalrymen-turned-foot soldiers like the rest of the company. Auerbach positioned his men on the north side of US 40, although that put the highway between them and their horses. The ground rose toward the low ridge of the Smoky Hills there, and offered better firing positions.

Once the men had dug in, there was nothing to do but wait. He gnawed jerked beef and fidgeted. He hadn't wanted to blow the road too close to Cheyenne Wells, not least for fear the Lizards there would respond before all his preparations were ready. Now he began to worry that they hadn't noticed the explosion at all.

Bill Magruder let out a hiss, then said, 'Sir, something coming down the road from the east.'

Auerbach peered in that direction. 'Something' was a motor vehicle – no, a couple of motor vehicles. That meant they were Lizards, all right. He raised the field glasses to his eyes. The vehicles leaped closer: a couple of armored personnel carriers. He grimaced. He'd hoped for one of those and a truck. Well, you didn't always get everything you hoped for.

The carriers – he would have thought of them as half-tracks, but the Lizards fully tracked their machines – slowed when they saw the crater ahead. Auerbach kept a wary eye on their turrets. They mounted light cannon, not machine guns like American half-tracks.

A Lizard crawled out of a hatch and went up to the edge of the broken asphalt. No one fired at him. He got back into the machine. Auerbach waited to see what would happen next. If the Lizards decided to wait and send for a road repair crew, a mighty good plan would have gone up in smoke.

After a moment, several Lizards emerged from the lead armored personnel carrier. A couple of them scrambled up onto the deck behind the turret and unshipped a dozer blade, which the others helped them fit to the front of the personnel carrier's hull. They were going to do a hasty job of road repair themselves. The waiting cavalrymen did not interfere.

The Lizards got back into the carrier. It rolled off onto the soft shoulder of the road. The dozer blade dug in to pick up dirt to fill in the hole in the road. The engine's note, though quiet to anyone used to American armor, got louder.

Hunkered down behind a tumbleweed, Auerbach bit his lip and waited, fingers crossed. When the explosion came, it wasn't as loud as the one that had blasted the crater in US 40, but far more satisfying. Antitank mines carried a charge big enough to wreck a Sherman. That didn't always suffice to take out the tougher Lizard tanks, but it was plenty to ruin an armored personnel carrier. Smoke and flame spurted up from the vehicle, which slewed sideways and stopped, the right track blown off the road wheels.

Hatches flew open. Like popcorn jumping up in a popper, Lizards started bailing out of the stricken machine. Now Auerbach's cavalry company opened up with almost everything they had. The Lizard infantry men fell, one after another, although a couple made it to the ground unhurt and started shooting back.

The turret of the unhurt Lizard personnel carrier swung north with frightening speed. Both the cannon and machine gun coaxial with it opened up on the machine-gun position the Americans had dug for themselves. No, the Lizards weren't fools, Auerbach thought as he fired at one of the males who'd succeeded in escaping from his vehicle: they went after the most dangerous enemy weapon first.

Or rather, they went after what they *thought* was the most dangerous enemy weapon. Auerbach had posted a two-man bazooka crew as close to the road as he dared: about seventy-five yards away. Like antitank mines, bazookas were iffy against Lizard tanks; frontal armor defeated the rockets with ease, while even side or rear hits weren't guaranteed kills. But the ugly little rocket bombs were more than enough to crack open lesser vehicles.

An American half-track would have become an instant fireball after a bazooka hit. The hydrogen fuel the Lizards used was less explosive than gasoline, and they had better firefighting gear than the handheld extinguishers half-tracks and American tanks carried. That helped, but not enough. After a couple of heartbeats, the Lizards the bazooka round hadn't killed or maimed began to try to escape their burning machine.

As with the males who'd left the first personnel carrier, most of them didn't get away from the vehicle, but some skittered off behind bushes and returned fir. At Auerbach's urgently shouted orders, flanking parties moved out on both wings to envelop the Lizards. They had to be wiped out quickly, or—

Auerbach didn't want to believe he heard the rotor blades of a helicopter chewing their way through the air, not so soon. It was coming from out of the west, from Cheyenne Wells. His mouth went dry. Killing two infantry fighting vehicles was splendid, but a bad bargain if it cost him his whole company – and himself.

Fire rippled from the weapons pod under the belly of the flying beast. The Lizards didn't know exactly where his men were positioned, but a rocket salvo made precision anything but mandatory. Auerbach dug his face into the musty ground as the rockets flailed the prairie. Blast picked him up, flipped him onto his back, and slammed him down, hard. Through stunned ears, he heard screams amidst the explosions.

Nose-mounted Gatling twinkling like some malign star, the helicopter bored in to finish exterminating the humans who had presumed to challenge the might of the Lizards. Auerbach and his comrades – those still alive and unwounded – returned fire. He imagined the helicopter crew laughing in the cockpit; their machine was armored against rifle-caliber rounds.

Perhaps because they were so close to US 40, the bazooka team had not drawn the helicopter's notice. As it hovered not far from the burning armored personnel carrier, an antitank rocket drew a trail of flame in the air toward it.

A bazooka was not supposed to be an antiaircraft weapon. If it hit, though, it was going to do damage. It hit. The helicopter staggered, as if it had run into an invisible wall up there in the air. Then it heeled over onto its side and crashed down on US 40. For good measure, the bazooka team put another round into its belly as it lay there. Ammunition started cooking off, tracer rounds going up like the Fourth of July fireworks.

'Let's get the hell out of here!' Auerbach yelled, his voice blurry even to himself. A few Lizards were still shouting, but the Americans made short work of them. Collecting the human wounded took longer and hurt more, spiritually as well as physically. Auerbach's driving urge was speed. He wanted to be away and under cover before the Lizards sent any more aircraft after his men.

'Even if they nail the whole lot of us, they won't have bought anything cheap today,' he muttered. While that was undeniably true, he still wanted to escape. Victory was a lot sweeter if you lived to enjoy it. And once he got back to Lamar, he'd have some fine stories to tell Rachel Hines ... and Penny Summers, too.

Returning to Dover made David Goldfarb feel he'd stepped back to an earlier time in the war. Things had been simpler then, with only the Jerries to worry about. And Hitler's finest, after all, hadn't managed to invade England in spite of all the *Führer's* threats and promises: 'Don't worry ... he's coming.' But he and the *Wehrmacht* hadn't come. The Lizards had.

Basil Roundbush came into the little room in the natural sciences building at Dover College where the radarman was working. The mustachioed pilot was whistling something whose words Goldfarb didn't recognize; whatever it was, it sounded as if it ought to be bawdy.

Working again with Roundbush brought the months at Bruntingthorpe back to the top of Goldfarb's mind. He looked up from his oscilloscope and said in mock disgust, 'All the time I was playing at infantryman, I felt sure you'd be dead and out of my hair for good.' After a moment too long, he added, 'Sir.'

Roundbush took the chaffing in good part. With a grin that made him look like a lion that had just brought down its zebra, he said, 'Dead? Something even worse than that happened: I got promoted.'

'Yes, sir, most illustrious Flight Lieutenant Roundbush, sir!' Goldfarb cried, springing to his feet to deliver a salute so vehement it threatened to snap off his arm. 'Oh, put a sock in it,' Roundbush said genially. 'Let's get down to work, shall we?'

'Right,' Goldfarb said. His sportiveness covered an admiration for the flier that fell only a little short of awe. He'd been through danger enough and to spare in his stint at ground combat. His own fighting skill had had little to do with coming out the other side intact, though. Bullets and shell fragments flew through the air almost at random. If you were lucky, they missed you. If you weren't you ended up dead or crippled.

But Basil Roundbush had survived flying mission after mission against the Lizards while in an aircraft and with weapons far inferior to theirs. Luck undoubtedly had something to do with that. But a fighter pilot, unlike a ground-pounder, needed more than luck. You had to be good at what you did, or you wouldn't keep doing it long.

And Roundbush had not merely survived. The Distinguished Flying Cross he wore on the front of his tunic testified to that. He wasn't commonly given to boasting – most often when chatting up a barmaid – but Goldfarb had heard he'd brought down one of the Lizards' immense transport aircraft, the ones that, when roaring overhead, looked as if they could carry a regiment. They made the Dakotas the RAF had started getting from the Americans not long before the Lizards came seem like children's models of wood and paper by comparison – and the Dakotas had far outclassed anything the British had before them.

That kill had earned Roundbush his DFC. What he'd said about it was to the point: 'Pack of ruddy fools back in London. The lasses must hate them, one and all – they think size is more important than technique. Even if it was the size of a whale, the transport couldn't shoot back. Their fighter planes are another piece of business altogether.'

Goldfarb looked out at the rain splashing down from a leaden sky and said, 'If the Lizards had been smart, they would have come now. We'd have been all but blind to them in the air, what with the autumn clouds and mist and rain, but their radars are good enough to let them carry on as if this were high summer.'

'They don't fancy cold weather,' Roundbush said, 'and I've heard it said they invaded us to get some of their own back after the Reds lit off that explosive-metal bomb under their scaly snouts.' He snorted. 'Letting the politicians set strategy for their own reasons will make you sorry, no matter whether you're a human being or a Lizard.'

'Now that we've won, I'm glad they did it.' Goldfarb waved to the electronic apparatus filling the shelves and tables of the room in which he and Roundbush labored. Some of it, like the gear they'd been analyzing at Bruntingthorpe, was wreckage, but some was intact, taken from aircraft and vehicles either captured after minimal damage or else abandoned in the retreat.

Basil Roundbush's wave was similar but more extravagant, seeming to take in not just what was the room but all the Lizard equipment the British had captured. He said, 'As I see it, we have two jobs of work ahead of us. The first is putting to use the devices we've captured that are still in working order. After that comes cannibalizing the damaged ones for parts so that, say, we can build two working ones from the hulks of four.'

'Understanding how the bleeding things work as well as what they do might also be a good notion,' Goldfarb observed.

To his surprise, Roundbush shook his head. 'Not necessary, not insofar as what we're about now. The Red Indians hadn't the faintest notion how to smelt iron to make gunpowder, but when they got muskets in their hands, they had no trouble shooting at the colonials in America. That's where we are right now: we need to use the Lizards' devices against them. Understanding can come at its own pace.'

'The Red Indians never did understand how firearms work,' Goldfarb said, 'and look what became of them.'

'The Red Indians didn't have the concept of research and development, and we do,' Roundbush said. 'For that matter, we were on the edge of our own discoveries in these areas before the Lizards came. We had radar: not so good as what the Lizards use, I grant you, but we had it – you'd know more of that than I. And both we and the Jerries seem to have been playing about with the notion of jet propulsion. I'd love to fly one of their Messerschmitts, see how it stands against a Meteor.'

'I wonder where Fred Hipple is these days,' Goldfarb said, and then, more somberly, 'I wonder if he's alive.'

'I fear not,' Roundbush said. He too sounded more serious than was his wont. 'I've not seen the little fellow, nor heard word of him, since the Lizards raided Bruntingthrope. My guess is that he was one of the officers killed in the barracks. He wasn't among those who reassembled afterwards: that much I know.'

'Well, neither was I,' Goldfarb answered. 'I got separated in the fighting and ended up in the army.'

'They'd not have commandeered a group captain in quite so cavalier a fashion, nor would Fred Hipple have been shy about pointing out the error of their ways had they made the attempt,' Roundbush said. Then he sighed. 'On the other hand, they might not have listened to him. No one paid the jet engine much heed before the war, and that's a melancholy fact.'

'Why not?' Goldfarb asked. 'Do you know, sir? It seems so obviously a better way of doing things. Try as you will, you'll never tweak a Spitfire to the point where it can match a Meteor's performance.'

'All true. I've flown both; I should know.' Roundbush thought for a moment. When he put his mind to it, he was quite a clever chap. He was also handsome and brave. When Goldfarb was in an intolerant mood, he found the combination depressing. Roundbush went on, 'A couple of things went into it, I think. We had a large investment in piston engines, an investment not just in the factories that made them but also in close to forty years' thinking they were the right and proper way to go about powering aircraft. The other factor is, piston engines were *proved* by those forty years. It takes a bold man, or a desperate one, to make the leap into the unknown and abandon the tried and true.'

'Something to that, I expect,' Goldfarb said. 'Against the Germans, we could make gains by squeezing out an extra fifty horsepower here or a hundred there. They were doing the same against us, I expect, or those jet Messerschmitts of theirs would have started showing up over England a year ago and more. But against the Lizards, it's pretty clear we had to try something new or go under.'

'There you have it in a nutshell,' Basil Roundbush agreed. 'Now, to business: are we going to be able to mount these Lizard radars in any of our aircraft? They're small and light enough, that's certain, and we'll finally be able to see as far as the Lizards can.'

'I think it should be possible, if we have enough sets,' Goldfarb answered. 'They don't draw a lot of power, and we've figured out the voltage and cycles per second they use – about two-thirds of the way from our standard down towards what the Americans prefer. We are still working to calibrate their ranges, though, and we still have to decide how many we want to mount on the ground to add to our air defense. Seeing the Lizards counts there, too.'

'That's so,' Roundbush admitted reluctantly. 'The other side of the coin is, the Lizards' radar should be less susceptible to being tracked by their missiles and confused by their interference. That matters a great deal when you're up past Angels twenty.'

'It matters when you're on the ground, too.' Goldfarb remembered the opening days of the Lizards' invasion of Earth, when their missiles had homed unerringly on radar transmitters throughout the British Isles, knocking them out again and again. 'Try tracking their fighter-bombers with binoculars, if you want a treat for yourself.'

'Binoculars? Old chap, try tracking them with the Mark One eyeball.' Roundbush could also deliver a convincing impersonation of an overbred, underbrained aristocratic twit, of the sort who made Bertie Wooster seem a philosopher-king by comparison. Now he leered horribly, aiming a pair of Mark One eyeballs (rather bloodshot) at Goldfarb. 'Bit of a bore in the cockpit, don't you know?'

'I know you're quite mad,' Goldfarb retorted. 'Sir.'

Roundbush stopped twisting his features into that bucktoothed grimace and let his voice lose the nasal whine he'd affected. 'What I know is that I need a pint or three after we knock off today. What's the name of that pub you dragged me to, the one with the blonde and the redhead?'

'That's the White Horse Inn, sir. I don't think Daphne, the blonde one, works there any more; she was just visiting old friends.' From what he'd heard, Daphne was in the family way, but he kept that to himself. He hadn't done it, and in any case he'd been sweet on Sylvia when last he was in Dover.

'The White Horse Inn, that's it. Couldn't recall the name for love nor money.' Roundbush coughed significantly. 'Only thing about the place I'm likely to forget, though. The beer's not bad – made locally, I'd say – and that little redhead ... Ah!' He kissed his fingertips, like an actor playing a comic Italian. 'She's quite a piece of work, she is.'

'Can't argue with you there, sir.' Goldfarb had been trying to get back into Sylvia's good graces – to say nothing of her bed – ever since he returned to Dover. He'd been making progress with the one, if not the other. Now he waved a fond farewell to any hope of seeing the inside of Sylvia's flat again. Women had a way of throwing themselves at Basil Roundbush – his problem wasn't catching them but in throwing back the ones he didn't want. If he did want Sylvia, odds for anyone else drawing her notice were abysmally poor.

Sighing, Goldfarb bent low over the radar he'd been working on when Roundbush came in. Work couldn't make you forget your sorrows but if you kept at it, you found yourself too busy to do much fussing over them. In a world that showed itself more imperfect with every passing day, that was about as much as any man had a right to expect.

Because it was large and round, the Met Lab crew had dubbed their first completed bomb the Fat Lady. Leslie Groves eyed the metal casing's curves with as much admiration as if they belonged to Rita Hayworth. 'Gentlemen, I'm prouder than I can say of every one of you,' he declared. 'Now we have only one thing left to do – build another one.'

The physicists and technicians stared at him for a moment, then burst into laughter and applause. 'You had us worried there for a moment, General,' Enrico Fermi said. 'We are not used to unadulterated praise from you.'

Another man might have taken that for an insult. Groves took it in his stride. 'Dr Fermi, when the war is over and the United States has won, I will praise all of you to the skies and ten miles further. Till that day comes, we have too much work to do to waste time saying nice things.'

'No one ever accused you of wasting time in this fashion,' Leo Szilard said, drawing a fresh round of laughter from the Met Lab crew. Groves even saw a smile flicker on the face of Jens Larssen, who had been more gloomy and taciturn than ever since he got back from Hanford, Washington, and found the whole program not only wasn't moving there but had moved on without him. Groves understood how all that could grate on a man, but didn't know what to do about it.

It was, in any case, far down on his list of worries. He knew what was at the top of the list: 'I wasn't joking there, my friends. We had help with this bomb: the plutonium we got from the British, who got it from the Polish Jews, who got it from the Germans, who got it from the Lizards with help from the Russians. Next time, we make it all ourselves, all *by* ourselves. How long till the next bomb?'

'Now that we have made the actual product once, doing it again will be easier; we will make fewer mistakes,' Szilard said. That drew nods from almost everyone, Groves included. Any engineer knew half the trouble in making something for the first time lay in figuring out what you were doing wrong and figuring out how to do it right. 'We have almost enough plutonium for the second weapon now,' Fermi said. 'Once we use it in the bomb, though, we will for a time be low. But production is steady, even improving. With what we have now, with the third atomic pile coming into full production, from now on we will be manufacturing several bombs a year.'

'That's what I want to hear,' Groves said. The production numbers had told him the same thing, but hearing it from the man in charge of the piles was better than inferring it from figures.

'The next question is, now that we have these bombs, how do we place them where we want to use them?' Szilard said. He waved a stubby hand toward the Fat Lady. 'This one would have to go on a diet before it could fit in an airplane, and the Lizards would shoot down any airplane before it got where it was going, anyhow.'

Both those points were true. The Fat Lady weighed nearly ten tons, which was more than any bomber could carry. And anything bigger than a Piper Cub drew the Lizards' immediate and hostile attention. Groves didn't know how to make a nuclear weapon small enough to fit into a Piper Cub, but he did know that, no matter what the *Luftwaffe* thought, you didn't have to deliver a bomb by air.

'I promise you, Dr Szilard: we will manage when the time comes,' he said, and let it go at that. He didn't want everybody to hear what the delivery plans were. Security wasn't as tight as it had been with the Japs and Nazis to worry about; he had trouble imagining anybody vile enough to want to betray American atomic secrets to the Lizards. But he was just an engineer, and knew his imagination had limits. What was unthinkable for him might not be for someone else.

'How do we even get the thing out of the reprocessing plant?' a technician asked. He worked at one of the piles, not here where the plutonium was extracted and the bomb made. Groves just pointed to the wooden cart on which the Fat Lady sat. It had wheels. The technician looked foolish.

He needn't have. Moving ten tons was no laughing matter, especially when those ten tons included complicated gadgetry and had to be moved in utmost secrecy. Groves had most of the answers now. Inside a week, he needed all of them. He was confident he'd get them. Moving heavy things from one place to another was a technology mankind had had under control since the days of the Pharaohs.

Somebody said, 'We got our bombs now. How soon will the Germans have theirs? When will the Russians set off another one? What about the Japs?'

'If there are no other questions, class is dismissed,' Groves said solemnly. That got the laugh he'd hoped for. When it was over, he went on, 'The Germans aren't very far behind us. If they hadn't had their, ah, accident, they might be ahead of us.'

The intelligence information on which he based that wasn't firsthand. Much of it came from things Molotov had said when he was in New York. Where Molotov had got it, Groves didn't know. The Russians had been wrong about the Germans before, generally to their sorrow.

Groves also took special care in describing what had gone wrong with the Germans' first effort to set up a pile that went critical. Though the Germans seemed to have been spectacularly careless about safety precautions, it wasn't as if running a pile was an exact science. Things could go wrong here, too.

'What of the Russians?' Enrico Fermi echoed. 'They were first with their bomb, but only silence from them since – a long silence now.'

'They say they'll be ready with another bomb come spring,' Groves answered. 'If I had to make a guess, I'd say you shouldn't hold your breath waiting for them. They got a jump start with the plutonium they and the Germans stole from the Lizards. That was enough to give them the one bomb. Past that ...' He shook his head. 'Russia simply does not have the precision industry, technical skill, or scientific numerical strength to come even close to manufacturing their own. Not yet.'

'How long do you think they'll need?' In almost identical words, three people asked the same question.

'Oh, I don't know – 1955, maybe,' Groves answered, deadpan. That got another laugh. He didn't really think the Reds would take that long, but he didn't look for a new bomb from them next Tuesday, either.

'And the Japanese?' Leo Szilard asked, as if he expected Groves to forget. 'What of them?'

Groves spread his hands. 'Dr Szilard, there I just don't know what to tell you. They were on the track of something, or the Lizards wouldn't have blown Tokyo off the map. How much they knew, how many of their top people got killed when the bomb hit, how far they've come toward rebuilding their program – I don't know, and I'd be lying if I said I did.'

Szilard nodded. 'That is fair, General. So often, people are in the habit of saying they know more than they do. Seeing a case where this is not so makes a pleasant change.'

That was the first compliment Groves had got from Szilard in as long as he could remember. He cherished it for that very reason. For the sake of his own peace of mind, though, he wished he could give the Hungarian physicist a more authoritative answer. The Japanese worried him. Before Pearl Harbor, the United States hadn't taken Japan seriously: not a white man over there, for one thing, he thought. But whether the Japs were white, yellow, or bright blue, their warships had proved as good as those Americans made, and their airplanes probably better. Buck-toothed, slant-eyed little bastards they might be, but if you thought they couldn't fight – if you thought they couldn't engineer – you had another think coming.

'Anything else?' he asked.

'Yeah,' said the technician who'd asked him about getting the bomb out of the reprocessing plant. 'How come that arrow that says 'this end up' is pointing down at the floor?'

'What arrow?' Groves blurted, a split second before he realized the technician was pulling his leg. 'Wise guy,' he said, through the laughter sent at him. He didn't mind it. He knew hostility aimed at him was sometimes what kept the crew working together and working hard. That was fine. As long as they *were* working together and working hard, he couldn't kick.

He walked out of the reprocessing plant to let the gang cuss at him when he wasn't there to hear it. His breath smoked. To the west, the Rockies were white. It had snowed in Denver more than once, but not for the past week. He hoped it would hold off a bit longer. Moving the Fat Lady with ice on the ground wasn't something he wanted to think about, though he would if he had to. Actually, getting the bomb moving wouldn't be such a problem. Stopping it, though ...

Ice wasn't something Pharaoh's engineers had had to worry about. *Lucky dogs*, he thought.

His office back in the Science Building wasn't what you'd call warm, either. He refused to let it get him down. Like a bear before hibernation, he had enough adipose tissue to shield him from the chill. So he told himself, at any rate.

He pulled an atlas off the shelf and opened it to a map of the United States. The one thing you couldn't do without aircraft, at least not easily, was deliver a bomb to the heart of the enemy's territory. You had to place the weapon somewhere along the frontier between what you held and what he did. Given the state of the war between humanity and the Lizards, that didn't strike Groves as an insurmountable obstacle to using it effectively.

Once the Fat Lady got aboard a freight car and headed out of Denver, where would they use it? That wasn't his responsibility, which would end when the bomb went onto the train. Even so, he couldn't help thinking about it.

His eyes kept coming back to one place. Nowhere else in the whole country had a rail network that even approached the one going into and out of Chicago. The Lizards had cut a lot of those routes, of course, but you could still reach the outskirts of town from the north or from the east. And with all the fighting going on there, you couldn't help but knock out a lot of Lizards if the bomb went off there.

He nodded to himself. Chicago was a good bet, probably *the* good bet. And where would they use the second bomb? That was harder to figure. Where it would do the most good, he hoped.

Mutt Daniels had known snow in Chicago before. He'd been snowed out of an opening-day series here in 1910 – or was it 1911? He couldn't recall. A hell of a long time ago, whichever it was. The Cubs hadn't even been playing in Wrigley Field yet, he knew that; they were still over at West Side Grounds.

When it snowed in April, though, you knew things were winding down: pretty soon it would be hot and muggy enough to suit you even if you were from Mississippi. Now, though, winter looked to be settling in for a nice long stay.

'No gas heat, no steam heat, not even a decent fireplace,' Mutt grumbled. 'I went through all o' this last winter, and I don't like it worth a damn. Too stinkin' cold, and that there's a fact.'

'I'm not saying you're wrong, Lieutenant,' Sergeant Muldoon said, 'so don't make it out like I am, but the Lizards, they like it even less than we do.'

'There is that. It's almost reason enough to get fond of snow, but not quite, if you know what I mean.' Mutt sighed. 'This here overcoat ain't real bad, neither, but I wish I didn't have to wear it.'

'Yeah.' Muldoon's overcoat was a lot more battered than the one Daniels was wearing, and smelled overpoweringly of mothballs; Mutt wondered if it had been in storage somewhere since the end of the Great War. The sergeant, though, was good at making the best of things. He said, 'We may not have a decent fireplace like you was talkin' about, Lieutenant, but Lord knows we got plenty of firewood.'

'Ain't that the truth,' Daniels said. Every other house in Chicago – some parts of town, every single house – was wrecked. Places where fire hadn't done the job for you, you could burn a lot of wood staying warm.

The neighbourhood in which the platoon was presently encamped was one of those areas where next to nothing was left upright. Since winter arrived, the Americans had pushed their front south a couple of miles. The Lizards weren't grinding forward any more; they were letting humanity come to them. The price was ghastly. One thing the cold weather did do: it kept the stink of rotting flesh from becoming intolerable instead of just bad.

Fighting back and forth across the same stretch of ground also produced a landscape whose like Mutt – and Muldoon, too – had seen over in France in 1918. Not even an earthquake shattered a town the way endless artillery barrages did. In France, though, once you got out of town, you were back in the country again. Chewed-up countryside was pretty bad, too, but it didn't have quite the haunted feel of stretches where people used to be crowded together. And Chicago wasn't anything but stretches where people had been packed close together.

'One thing,' Mutt said: 'I don't believe in ghosts no more.' He waited for a couple of people to wonder why out loud, then said, 'If there was such a thing as ghosts, they'd be screamin' to beat the band at what we done to Chicago and done to their graveyards in partic'lar. I ain't seen none o' that, so I reckon ghosts ain't real.'

Off to the rear, American artillery opened up. Mutt listened to the shells whistling by overhead. That was a reassuring noise, nothing like the roaring screech they made when they were coming straight at you. They landed a couple of miles south of the house in whose wreckage he was squatting. The explosions sounded flat and harsh, not as big as they might have been. Mutt grimaced. He knew the why of that.

So did Muldoon. 'Gas,' he said, as if tasting something sour.

'Yeah.' It was one of the big reasons the Lizards had stopped advancing in Chicago, but that didn't mean Daniels liked it. Nobody who'd ever been on the receiving end of a gas bombardment liked the idea of gas. 'All the hell we let loose on this city our own selves, us and the Lizards, I mean, maybe it's no wonder we ain't seen any ghosts. By now, I reckon they're liable to be more scared of us than we are of them.' He scratched his head. 'What the dickens was the Irving Berlin song from the last war? "Stay Down Here Where You Belong," that's it – the one where the devil tells his son not to go up to earth on account of it was worse than it was down in hell. Maybe the devil knew what he was talkin' about.'

'Maybe he did.' Muldoon nodded. 'Thing of it is, though, it's either do what we gotta do or else have the Lizards do somethin' worse.'

'Yeah,' Daniels said again. 'An' that reminds me – I'm gonna go up and heck on the sentries, just to make sure the Lizards ain't doin' somethin' vorse right here.'

'Sounds good to me,' Muldoon said. 'I sorta got fond of living, all that ime between the wars – I'd like to keep on doin' it a while longer now. 3ut you wanna watch yourself, Lieutenant. The Lizards, they can see like ats in the dark.'

'I seen that already,' Mutt agreed. 'Dunno whether it's their eyes or the gadgets they got. Don't reckon that matters anyway. They sure can do it, and that's what counts.'

Most officers just used .45s. Mutt had been a noncom and a dogface oo long to trust his neck to anything less than the best weapon he could carry. It that meant he had to lug around the extra weight of a tommy un, he was willing to put up with it.

He paused a while outside the ruined house where his men were sheltering, so his eyes could adapt to the dark all around. He didn't see like a cat, and he didn't have any gadgets to help him do it, either. No moon in the sky, and even had there been, the cloud cover would have kept him from seeing it. The only light came from the fires that turned parts of the skyline orange. Chicago was so big, it never seemed to run out of things that would burn.

The Lizards' lines lay about half a mile to the south of the positions the Americans were holding. Between them were both sides' sentry posts, along with American barbed wire and Lizard razor wire coiling through the ruins of what had been middle-class homes not long before. Those ruins made the no-man's-land an even more dangerous place than it had been in France back in 1918. They gave snipers wonderful cover.

As if the blamed war isn't bad enough, what with the gas and the tanks and the shells and the planes and the machine guns and all that other shit, Mutt thought. *But no, you gotta worry about some damn sniper puttin' a bullet through your head while your damn underpants are down around your ankles so you can take a dump.* Some things didn't change. One of his grandfathers had fought in the Army of Northern Virginia during the States War, and he'd complained about snipers, too.

Going out to the sentry positions, Mutt used a route he'd worked out that kept him behind walls most of the way: he didn't believe in making a sniper's job any easier. He had three or four different ways to get from the main line to the pickets in front of it, and he didn't use any one of them more than twice running. He made sure the sentries took the same precautions. His platoon hadn't had a man shot going up to sentry duty in weeks. A low but threatening whisper: 'Who's that?'

Daniels answered with the password: 'Cap Anson. How they hangin', Jacobs?'

'That you, Lieutenant?' The sentry let out a low-voiced chuckle. 'You give us those baseball names for recognition signals, why don't you make 'em people like DiMaggio or Foxx or Mel Ott that we've heard of, not some old guy who played way back when?'

Mutt remembered hearing about Cap Anson when he was a kid. Was that way back when? Well, now that you mentioned it, yes. He said, 'The Lizards'll know about today's players. They might fool you.'

'Sure, okay, yeah, but we can forget the old guys,' Jacobs said. 'Then we're liable to end up shooting at each other.'

Did I talk back to my officers in France like that? Mutt wondered. Thinking back on it, he probably had talked like that. American soldiers were a mouthy lot, no two ways about it. That had been true for a long time too, and even more so a long time ago. Some of the things his granddads said they'd called the officers back then would curl your hair.

He signed and said, 'Sonny, if you don't want your buddies shootin' at you, you better remember, that's all.'

'Yeah, okay, sure, Lieutenant, but—' Jacobs quit bitching and stared out into the darkness. 'What was that?'

'I didn't hear nothin',' Daniels said. But his voice came out as the barest thread of whisper. His ears were old-timers, and knew it. Jacobs couldn't be a day over nineteen. He had more balls than brains, but he could hear. Mutt made sure he was under cover. Jacobs pointed at the direction from which the sound had come. Mutt didn't see anything, but that didn't signify.

He picked up a fist-sized lump of plaster, hefted it in his hand. 'Be ready, kid,' he breathed. Jacobs, for a wonder, didn't say *For what?* He just took a firmer grip on his rifle and nodded.

Mutt tossed the plaster underhand through the air. It came down maybe thirty feet to one side, clattering off what sounded like a brick chimney. Out in no-man's-land, a Lizard cut loose with his automatic rifle, squeezing off a burst whose bullets whined through the area where the plaster had landed.

Jacobs and Daniels both fired at the muzzle flashes from the Lizard's weapon. 'Did we get him?' Jacobs demanded, shoving a fresh clip into his Springfield.

'Damnfino,' Mutt answered. His ears were still ringing from the racket the tommy gun made. 'It ain't always – how do you say it? – cut and dried like that. Next thing we gotta do is, we gotta find you a new position. We just told 'em where this one's at.'

'Okay, Lieutenant,' Jacobs said. 'I hadn't thought of that myself, but it makes sense now that you've said it.'

Daniels sighed, a long, silent exhalation. But he was used to thinking strategically, and a lot of people weren't. 'We gotta be careful,' he whispered. 'If we didn't get that son of a bitch of a Lizard, he'll be out there waitin' to nail us. Now if I remember straight, there was a house over that way' – he pointed west with his right hand – 'maybe a hundred yards that'd fill the bill. Lemme go check it out. That Lizard starts shootin' at me, keep him busy.'

'Sure, okay, yeah, Lieutenant,' Jacobs said. Throwing those words into varying combinations seemed to be his sport for the evening.

Down on his belly like a reptile, Mutt slithered through rubble toward the house he had in mind. Part of its second storey was still standing, which made it damn near unique around these parts – and made it a good observation point, too, at least till the Lizards figured out somebody was up in it. Then they were liable to expend a rocket or a bomb just to knock down the place.

Something skittered by, a few feet in front of Mutt. He froze. It wasn't Lizard; it was rat. That much he saw. His imagination filled in the rest: a fat, happy rat like the ones he'd seen in the trenches of France, with a diet it was better not to think about.

He made it to the house he had in mind without getting shot at, which he took a sign, if not a sure one, that he and Jacobs had hit the Lizard would-be infiltrator. The house seemed all right. The stairway wobbled a little when you went up it, but considering that half the second floor wasn't there, he didn't suppose you could expect miracles. And you could see a long way from the second storey window.

He returned to the current sentry post and told Jacobs, 'Everything's okay. Come on with me and I'll show you where I'm moving you.' Once he'd installed the sentry in his new position, he said, 'I'll go back and give your replacement word about where you'll be.'

'Yeah, okay, Lieutenant,' Jacobs said.

When Mutt had almost made it back for the second time to the ruins where Jacobs had been stationed, the Lizard out there in no-man's-land fired at him. He dug his face into the dirt as bullets cracked all around him and ricocheted with malignant whines from stones and chunks of concrete.

'Sneaky little bastard, ain't you?' he muttered, and squeezing off a burst of his own, just to let the Lizard know he was still among those present. The Lizard shot back. They traded fire for a few minutes in a surprisingly sporting way, then gave up. Mutt went back to his lines; he wouldn't have been a bit surprised if the Lizard did the same thing.

Go on ahead, Lizard, he thought. *You had your at-bats this summer. Now that cold weather's here, we'll throw your scaly ass right out of Chicago. Just wait and see if we don't.*

The Tosevite hatchling rolled over on the floor of the laboratory chamber that had been its home since Ttomalss had taken charge of it. After a little while, it rolled over again, and then again. All three rolls were in the same direction. Ttomalss thought the hatchling was beginning to get the idea of going some particular way.

Any sign of neuromuscular progress in the little creature interested him, since all such signs were few and far between. By the standards of the Race, hatchling Tosevites had no business surviving to grow up to become the Big Uglies who had proved such complete nuisances ever since the conquest fleet arrived. Were they to be separated from those who cared for them for the first years of their lives, they could not survive. The Race had many stories of feral hatchlings who came from untended clutches of eggs and survived to adulthood, most of them well-authenticated. Among the Tosevites, such tales were vanishingly rare, and even when told often had more of the feel of legend than fact.

Something crinkled – the little female had got its hands on a crumpled-up piece of cellophane that had fallen unnoticed off some work surface. Ttomalss bent quickly and took the cellophane out of the Tosevite's mouth.

'That is not edible,' he said in what he hoped was a severe voice.

The hatchling laughed at him. Anything it could reach went into its mouth. You had to watch it every walking moment. *A miracle all the Big Uglies didn't poison themselves or choke on things they swallow*, Ttomalss thought. He picked up the hatchling. It had soiled itself again.

With a hissing sigh, he carried it over to the table where he kept the waste-absorbing (or at least partially absorbing) cloths. It babbled cheerfully all the while. Some of the babbles were beginning to sound as if they were emulating the hisses and clicks that made up a good part of the Race's language. Those were nothing like the sounds it would have been hearing had it stayed among the Big Uglies. Its linguistic talents, he suspected, would prove very adaptable.

After he had cleaned it, it gave the whining cry that meant it was hungry. He felt it suck from the bottle, then walked back and forth with it as it fought a losing battle against sleep. At last, with a sigh of relief, he set it down on the pad where it rested.

'The Emperor be praised,' he said softly when the hatchling did not wake up. Since he'd taken it up here, he measured the time that was his own by the spaces during which it slept. Even when he left the laboratory, he always wore a monitor attached to his belt. If the Big Ugly started to squawk, he had to hurry back and calm it. He hadn't been able to trust any other males to do the job properly; no one else had his unique and hard-won expertise.

No sooner had he taken a couple of steps away from the pad on which the hatchling lay than another psychologist, a male named Tessrek, tapped with his fingerclaws on the doorjamb to the chamber to show he wanted to come in. When Ttomalss waved that he could enter, he said, 'How is the little Tosevite treating you, today, Mother?' His mouth dropped open in amusement at the joke.

Ttomalss did not think it was funny. By now, he'd heard it from a lot of his colleagues. Most, like Tessrek, borrowed the word *mother* from the Tosevite language with which they were most familiar. That seemed to make it doubly amusing for them: they could imply not just that Ttomalss was an egg-laying male, but one who'd hatched out a Big Ugly.

He said, 'The creature is doing very well, thank you. It's definitely been displaying increased mobility and a greater sense of purpose lately.' It still couldn't come close to matching what a hatchling of the Race was able to do the moment the eggshell cracked, and he'd been thinking disparaging thought about it only moments before. But mocking the Big Ugly hatchling was mocking his chosen research topic, and that he would defend as fiercely as he had to.

Tessrek's mouth opened in a different way: to show distaste. 'It certainly is an odoriferous little thing, isn't it?' he said.

'Have you any other pleasantries to add?' Ttomalss asked, his tone frigid. He and Tessrek were of identical rank, which complicated matters: as neither owed the other formal deference, they had no social lubricant to camouflage their mutual dislike. Ttomalss went on, 'My scent receptors do not record the odor to any great degree. Perhaps I have grown used to it.' That was at best a quarter-truth, but he would not let Tessrek know it.

'That must be because you have spent so much time with the creature,' Tessrek said. 'Continual exposure had dulled your chemoreceptors – or perhaps burned them out altogether.'

'Possibly so,' Ttomalss said. 'I have been thinking I spend an inordinate amount of time here with the hatchling. I really do need someone to relieve me of creature-tending duties every so often, not least so I can pass on some of the data I have gathered.' He swung both eye turrets towards Tessrek. 'As a matter of fact, you might make an excellent choice for the role.'

'Me?' Tessrek recoiled in alarm. 'What makes you say that? You must be daft to think so.'

'By no means, colleague of mine. After all, did you not study the Tosevite male Bobby Fiore, whose matings with the Tosevite female brought into our spacecraft for research purposes led to her producing the hatchling here? You have a – what is the term the Big Uglies use? – a family attachment, that's it.'

'I have no attachment at all to that ugly little thing,' Tessrek said angrily. 'It is your problem and your responsibility. At need, I shall state as much to superior authority. Farewell.' He hurried out of the laboratory chamber.

Behind him, Ttomalss's mouth opened wide. Sometimes jokes had teeth, as he'd show Tessrek. He'd put forward a suggestion in an effort to make the other psychologist's skin itch right down under the scales where you couldn't scratch. But, now that he thought about it, it struck him as a pretty good idea. He could use help with the Tosevite hatchling, and Tessrek was the logical male to give it to him.

Still laughing, he picked up the telephone and called the office of the seniormost psychologist.

17

Sam Yeager paced back and forth in the Army and Navy General Hospital waiting room. He wondered how much experience the doctors had with delivering babies. Soldiers and sailors being of the male persuasion, they weren't likely to end up in a family way themselves. How often had the medical staff here helped their wives. Lots and lots, he devoutly hoped.

From the delivery room beyond the swinging doors came a muffled shriek. It made him clench his fists till nails bit into flesh, bite his lip till he tasted blood. That was Barbara in there, straining with all her might to bring their child into the world. Part of him wished he could be in there with her, holding her hand and reassuring her everything was all right. (*Please, God, let everything be all right!*) Another part of him was grimly certain he'd either lose his lunch or pass out if he watched what she was going through.

He paced harder, wishing he had a cigarette to calm him and to give him something to do with his hands. He'd actually smoked a couple of pipefuls up in southern Missouri; they grew tobacco around there. But when word came that Barbara was going to pop any day now, he'd hurried back to Hot Springs fast as horseflesh would carry him. Robert Goddard had been good about letting him go; he owed his boss one for that.

Barbara shrieked again, louder. Sam's guts churned. For a man to have to listen to his wife in agony just wasn't right. But the only other things that came to mind were charging into the delivery room, which he couldn't do, and sneaking off somewhere like a yellow dog and holing up with a bottle of booze, which he could do, either. He just had to stay here and take it. Some ways, going into combat had been harder. Then, at least, the danger had been his personally, and he'd had some small control over it. Now he couldn't do anything but pace.

Maybe the worst was that he couldn't hear anything the doctors or nurses were saying in there, only Barbara's cries. He didn't know whether she was supposed to be making noises like that. Were things going okay, or was she in trouble? He'd never felt so helpless in his life.

He sat down in a hard chair and made a conscious effort to relax, as if he were stepping into the batter's box against some kid pitcher who could fire a fastball through the side of a barn – if he could hit the side of a barn. He blanked everything but the moment from his mind, took a couple of deep breaths. His heart stopped pounding so hard. *That's better*, he thought.

Barbara chose that moment to make a new noise, not a scream exactly, but cry and grunt and moan all mixed together. It was a sound of supreme effort, as if she were trying to lift the front axle of a car off somebody pinned underneath it. Sam bounced out of his seat, all efforts at relaxation out of the park like a line drive off the bat of Hank Greenberg.

Barbara made that appalling noise again, and then once more. After that, for maybe a minute, Sam didn't hear anything. 'Please, God, let her be all right,' he mumbled. He wasn't usually much of a praying man; when he asked God for something, it was something he really wanted.

Then another cry came through the swinging doors: a thin, furious wail that said only one thing: *what is this place, and what the devil am I doing here?* Sam's knees sagged. It was a good thing he was standing next to that chair, because he would have sat down whether or no.

The swinging doors opened outward. A doctor came through them, gauze mask fallen down under his chin, a few splashes of blood on his white robe. In one hand he held a crudely rolled cigar, in the crook of his other elbow the littlest person Sam had ever seen.

He handed Yeager the cigar. 'Congratulations, Sergeant,' he said. 'You've got yourself a fine baby boy here. Haven't put him on the scales yet, but he'll be around seven and a half pounds. He's got all his fingers, all his toes, and a hell of a good set of lungs.' As if to prove that, the baby started crying again.

'B-B-B-B—' Sam took one more deep breath, made himself talk straight: 'Barbara? Is she all right?'

'She's doing just fine,' the doctor said, smiling. 'Do you want to see her?' When Yeager nodded, the doctor held out the baby to him. 'Here. Why don't you take your son in, too?'

Your son. The words almost made Sam's legs buckle again. He stuffed the cigar into a trouser pocket and wearily reached out for the baby. Seeing his inexperience, the doctor showed him how to hold it so its head wouldn't flop around like a fish out of water.

Now he could pass through the doors that had held him back before. The delivery room smelled of sweat and of the outhouse; a nurse was taking a bucket away from the table with the stirrups. Sam gulped. Birth was a process with no dignity to it.

His son wiggled in his hands. He almost dropped the baby. 'Bring him here,' Barbara said from the table. 'They only showed him to me for a couple of seconds. Let me see him.'

She sounded beat up. She looked it, too. Her face was pale and puffy, with big purple circles under her eyes. Her skin glistened with sweat, even though the delivery room wasn't what you'd call warm. If a guy caught two doubleheaders back to back on the same day in ninety-degree heat and ninety-percent humidity, he'd look a little like that when it was finally over.

Sam showed her the baby. The smile that spread over her face cut through her exhaustion like a sharp knife through tender steak. 'Give him to me,' she said, and held out her hands.

'You can nurse him now, if you like,' the doctor said from behind Sam. 'In fact, it would be good if you did. There aren't going to be many bottle babies, not any more.'

'I suppose that's true,' Barbara said. 'Before the war, of the people I knew who had babies, hardly any nursed theirs. Bottles seemed so much more modern and sanitary. But if there aren't any bottles—' She drew aside the sheet that was draped over the top part of her body. For a moment, Sam was startled that she'd bare her breasts to the doctor. Then he told himself not to be an idiot. After all, the fellow had just helped guide the baby out from between her legs.

Barbara set the baby on her breast. He knew what he was supposed to do. If he hadn't known, people would long since have been as extinct as dinosaurs. He made little slurping noises, just like the calves and lambs and piglets on the farm where Sam had grown up.

'What are you going to name him?' the doctor asked.

'Jonathan Philip,' Barbara answered. Sam nodded. It wasn't the most imaginative way to name a kid – after his father and hers – but it would do the job. Had it been a girl, they would have called it Carol Paulette, for her mother and his.

He said, 'I wish we had some kind of way to let our folks know we had a baby.' After a moment, he added, 'Heck, I wish we had some kind of way to let our families know we're married, or even that we're alive. I wish I knew whether my folks were alive or dead, too; from what I hear, the Lizards have been in Nebraska just about since they landed.'

'What I wish,' Barbara said, sitting up and draping the sheet over her like a toga,' 'is that I could have something to eat. I feel as if I'd spent the last two weeks digging ditches.'

'We can take care of that,' the doctor said. 'In fact, we should be taking care of that right about now.' As if his words were a cue, a nurse came in carrying a tray that bore a huge steak, a couple of baked potatoes, a pumpkin pie, and two large mugs. Pointing at those, the doctor said, 'I know they should be full of champagne, but that is the best homebrew we've made yet. Call it a wartime sacrifice.' He pushed a little wheeled table next to the one on which Barbara was sitting.

Since she was still nursing Jonathan, Sam did the honors with knife and fork, cutting alternate bites for her and himself. As far as he could remember, he'd never fed anybody like that before. He liked it. By the way Barbara smiled as she ate, so did she. She hadn't been kidding about being hungry, either; food disappeared off the plate at an astonishing rate. The homebrew was as good, and as potent, as promised.

Barbara said, 'If the beer goes to my milk, will it make Jonathan drunk?'

'Maybe,' the doctor answered. 'If it does, it'll probably make him sleep better, and I don't think you'll complain about that.'

Sam wondered how they'd do: a man, a woman, and a baby, all in one room. People did manage, so he supposed they would. Then he remembered he'd be going back up to Missouri any day now. That didn't seem fair, either to him or to Barbara, but he didn't know what he could do about it. No, that wasn't true. He did know what he could do about it: nothing.

When they were done eating, the nurse took away the tray. Sam waited for her to come back with a wheelchair for Barbara, then realized that wouldn't do any good, not without the elevators running. 'She can't walk upstairs to our room,' he protested.

'Oh, she probably could,' the doctor said. 'One thing you find out pretty fast is that people are tougher than you'd imagine. But we're not going to let her. You and I, Sergeant, we'll get her up there.'

They did, too, in a sort of modified fireman's carry that had them both pausing by the time they made it to the fourth floor. The nurse followed with Jonathan. When they finally came out into the hallway, Barbara said, 'If it weren't for the honor of the thing, I'd rather walk.'

Walk she did, toward their room. It was more shamble than stride; her feet were as wide apart as if she'd spent the last twenty years in a saddle. While that wasn't true, she had spent a good long while in the stirrups.

Straha came out of his room to see what was going on in the hall. He kept his body paint unsmeared and in the magnificent shiplord's pattern he'd worn when defecting: no Official American Prisoner markings for him. He came skittering up to the nurse. She drew back a pace, as if to protect the baby from him. 'It's okay,' Sam said quickly. 'We're friends. Let him see Jonathan.'

The nurse looked doubtful, but held out the baby boy. As Straha examined it, he looked doubtful, too. 'This is a Tosevite hatchling?' he said in his own hissing language. 'It is a Little Ugly, not a Big Ugly.' His mouth fell open in appreciation of his own wit.

Barbara answered in the same tongue: 'Shiplord, that is *my* hatchling, and it is not ugly.' For good measure, she tacked on an emphatic cough. Yeager added one of his own, to show he agreed. Among the Lizards, that was grammatically uncouth, but it got the message across.

'Familial attachments,' Straha said, as if reminding himself. 'No insult was intended, I assure you. For a Tosevite hatchling, this is undoubtedly a paragon.'

'What's he talking about?' the doctor asked.

'He says we've got a cute kid,' Sam answered. He was skeptical about Straha's sincerity, but the Lizard was too big a cheese for him to make a fuss over it. Besides. except for an exaggerated sense of his own brilliance an worth – hardly a trait unique to Lizards – he was a pretty good fellow.

Barbara returned to English: 'I may be able to walk, but I can't stan in one place very long. I'm going inside and lying down.' She waddle the last few steps toward their door and started to go into the room. Th nurse followed with the baby.

Before she got there, Ristin and Ullhass came out to look over the new arrival. They were politer than Straha, but still curious. When Jonathan opened his mouth to squawk, Ristin exclaimed, 'The hatchling has n teeth! How can it eat if it has no teeth?'

Barbara rolled her eyes. 'If the baby did have teeth, it wouldn't ea from me,' she said feelingly.

'That's right – you Tosevites nourish your hatchlings yourself.' Ullhass was more thoughtful, less high-spirited than Ristin. 'I am sure you will do everything you can to make this little – is it a male or a female? – this little male an upstanding member of your race.'

'Thank you, Ullhass,' Barbara said, 'but if I'm on my feet another minute I'm going to be a downfalling member of my race.' She went into the room she and Sam would now share with their son.

The nurse brought in the baby. 'Y'all holler if there's anything we can do,' she said as she gave it to Barbara. 'Good luck to you, honey.' Then she left, and closed the door behind her. All at once, in spite of what the nurse had said, it seemed to Sam that he, his wife, and their child were the only people left in the world. He gulped. Could he handle responsibility like that? After a moment, he realized the question hardly mattered. He wouldn't ge that much chance to handle the responsibility of being a father, not when Jonathan was here and he'd be heading back up to Missouri.

Barbara set Jonathan in the crib he'd bought at a secondhand store in Hot Springs. The crib wasn't very large – even if it did crowd the already-crowded room – but the baby all but disappeared in it. With a long, shuddering sigh, Barbara lay down. 'You all right, hon?' Sam asked anxiously.

'I think so,' she said. 'I don't know for sure, though. I've never done this before. Am I supposed to feel as if a steamroller just mashed me?'

'I can't tell you from what I know myself, but by everything my mother used to say, that is how you're supposed to feel.'

'That's good. I'm going to sleep for a while, I think, while the baby's resting, and then, if he's still asleep, I'll stagger down the hall and take a shower. Thank heavens the hot springs give us all the hot water we need, because I don't think I've ever felt so … greasy in my whole life. That was hard work.'

'I love you, honey.' He bent down and kissed her on the cheek, then turned and shook a severe finger at Jonathan. 'And you, buster, keep it quiet for a while.' He laughed. 'There, I'm already showing our kid who's boss.'

'That's easy – he is.' Barbara closed her eyes.

Sam sat down in the one chair the room boasted. Barbara dropped off almost at once. Her slow, deep breaths mixed oddly with Jonathan's quick, uncertain ones. The baby was a restless sleeper, wiggling and thrashing and sometimes trying to suck at the sheets or the blanket that covered him. Every so often, Yeager got up to peer at him. He tried to figure out whom the baby looked like. He couldn't tell. What Jonathan mostly looked was squashed. Even his head almost came to a point at the top. None of the doctors or nurses had got upset about that, so Sam supposed it was normal.

After an hour or so, Barbara woke up, stretched, and said. 'Isn't he a little angel, sleeping like that? I am going to get clean. I won't be long. Pick him up and hold him if he fusses while I'm gone.'

Sam hadn't thought about that. He was going off and leaving Barbara on the spot for God only knew how long. But she was a woman – she was supposed to be able to take care of babies. What would he do if Jonathan started crying?

Jonathan started crying. One minute he was quiet except for snorts and grunts, the next he sounded like an air-raid siren in the little room. Gulping, Sam picked him up, careful to support his head as the doctor had shown him. One thing immediately became obvious: the kid was wet.

Next to the crib stood a pile of diapers; safety pins lay on top of the chest of drawers. Sam undid the diaper Jonathan had on, and discovered he was more than wet; he had a mess in there, too. Sam stared at it: was it supposed to be greenish black? He didn't know, but figured he'd assume everything was normal there, too, till he heard otherwise.

Growing up on a farm had inured him to dealing with messes of most sorts. He wiped his son's bottom, which made Jonathan fuss more, then folded a diaper into a triangle and got it onto the kid. He stuck himself with a pin only once, which he reckoned a victory of sorts. The doctors hadn't circumcised the baby. He wasn't circumcised himself, so that didn't bother him. *One less thing to have to worry about*, he thought.

Jonathan kept fussing. 'It's okay, kid, it really is,' Sam said, rocking the baby in his arms. After a while, the cries subsided to whimpers. Jonathan drifted off to sleep. Ever so carefully, Sam put him back in the crib. He didn't wake up. Sam felt as if he'd caught a fly ball that clinched a pennant.

Barbara came back a couple of minutes later. 'Is he *still* asleep?' he exclaimed, looking at the baby.

Sam pointed to the galvanized bucket where he'd tossed the dirty diaper. 'I managed,' he said, which, with his ballpark thought of a little while before, made him wonder how Mutt Daniels was doing these days. The news coming out of embattled Chicago lately was better than it had been earlier in the year, but still not good.

'I wish you didn't have to go back tomorrow,' Barbara said that evening as they got ready for bed.

'So do I.' Sam passed her the cigar the doctor had given him: they were sharing it for a treat. 'But I can't do anything about that. I'm just lucky Dr Goddard was a good enough guy to let me get down here at all.'

By the time he crawled out of bed the next morning, Sam wasn't so sure he was sorry to go. He wondered if it might not be more like an escape. He'd expected Jonathan to wake several times in the night, and the baby did. Whenever he roused, Barbara nursed him. What he hadn't expected – nor Barbara, either, by her increasingly haggard look – was that the baby could wake them without waking up himself. Every little snort or grunt or slurping noise Jonathan made would bring his parents alert their eyes wide, wondering what they needed to do next. Often the answer was *nothing*, but they couldn't know that in advance.

As he put on his khakis, shirt, and jacket, Sam felt himself moving as if underwater. Barbara looked to be in worse shape than he was. 'Jesus,' he said, his voice a rusty croak, 'I wish there was coffee.'

'Oh, so do I,' Barbara said fervently. She managed a wan smile. 'One thing about the shortages, though: I don't have to worry about your falling asleep at the reins of your horse and driving him into a tree or a ditch.'

'Something to that,' Sam said. 'Not much, but something.' He hugged her, then smiled himself. 'I don't have to lean over your belly any more. That's pretty good.'

'I'm still all—' Barbara gestured. 'I hope I'll have my figure back when I see you again.' She shook her head. 'No, I don't, because that would mean I won't see you for a while, and I want you back here as soon as you can come. I love you, Sam, and besides, Jonathan needs to know who his daddy is.'

'Yeah.' The baby was asleep for the moment. Yeager kissed the tip of his own finger, brushed it against Jonathan's cheek. 'So long, kiddo.' He hugged Barbara again. 'So long, hon. Love you, too.' Sighing, he lurched out the door and headed down the hall to the stairs.

From behind him, Straha called in peremptory tones: 'I must tell you that your hatchling's howls last night disturbed me and, I have no doubt, other males of the Race on this floor. How long can we expect this unseemly cacophony to continue?'

'Oh, about six months, more or less,' Sam answered cheerfully. 'That's one of your years, isn't it? So long. I'm going back to Missouri, away from the noise.' He ducked down the stairway, leaving the shiplord staring after him.

George Schultz spun the U-2's prop. The five-cylinder Shvetsov radial engine caught at once. Being air-cooled, it was less susceptible to cold weather than a lot of aircraft powerplants. When the weather got cold enough, oil didn't want to flow, but it wasn't quite that bad today. It had been, on and off, and Ludmila Gorbunova had no doubt it would be again before long.

Schultz got out of the way in a hurry. Ludmila released the brake and let the *Kukuruznik* bounce down the rutted dirt of the airstrip. When she'd built up enough speed, she pulled back on the stick and clawed her way into the air. Getting the little biplane off the ground always made her feel that, if you wanted to badly enough, you could run along with your arms spread and take off and fly all by yourself.

The slipstream that came over the windscreen threatened to freeze her cheeks and mouth, the only flesh she bared to it. She went into a wide turn and flew over the airstrip on her way south. George Schultz was already out of sight. *Probably on his way to Tatiana's bed*, Ludmila thought scornfully. But he was right: she really had no business complaining. She didn't want him, and was just as glad to have him out of her hair once for all.

She buzzed over the defense lines south of Pskov, built with such unflagging and dreadful civilian effort the summer before. Soldiers in the trenches waved at her. And, as happened fairly often, a couple of fools shot at her, not believing anything built by human beings could be in the air. She saw muzzle flashes, heard a couple of bullets crack past.

'Who do you think I am, the devil's grandmother?' she shouted. That helped relieve her own feelings, but the men on the ground couldn't hear her. Sometimes, when bullets came closer than they had today, she thought longingly about machine-gunning the trenches of her own side.

Then she was over the Lizards' lines. She gunned the U-2 for all it was worth, but that, as she knew only too well, was a matter of kopecks, not rubles. A couple of Lizards shot at her, too. They didn't come any closer than the Russians had. That wasn't what worried her. They'd use their radios to let their side know she was out and flying, and the Lizards had antiaircraft weapons far more deadly than automatic rifles.

Once she was past the Lizards' main line, she swung the *Kukuruznik's* nose west, then south, then west again, then north for a little ways, and then east for an even shorter time. The less predictable she made her path, the less likely they were to blow her out of the sky.

Some kilometers south of the Lizards' forward positions, she spotted a convoy of tanks and soft-skinned vehicles slogging around a dirt road. Now that snow had replaced the fall rains, roads were passable again: what had been mud was frozen solid.

That wasn't what drew her notice to the convoy, though. The tanks and lorries weren't moving up to help the Lizards advance on Pskov. Instead, they were heading south themselves, away from the city. They had artillery with them, too, some self-propelled and some towed weapons captured from the Red Army and the Germans.

She didn't get too close to the convoy. A lot of those vehicles mounted machine guns for defense against low-flying aircraft, and her best hope for surviving such a barrage was not drawing it in the first place. As soon as she was sure they really were southbound, she flew away as fast as the U-2 would take her.

'What *are* they doing?' she wondered aloud. Had she not been wearing thick gloves and a leather flying helmet, she would have scratched her head. She'd never seen such a large-scale withdrawal by the Lizards before.

She skimmed along a few meters above the treetops, drawing occasional potshots from the woods below, but was gone before the Lizards could do her any damage. She was thinking hard. The evasive maneuvers she'd performed south of the Lizards' lines had left her a trifle disoriented, but if she was where she thought she was, she ought to strike another road if she flew southeast for a couple of minutes.

And there it was! Like most roads between Soviet cities, it was dirt-surfaced. But it also had Lizard armor on it, and lorries with the tanks and fighting vehicles. This was a bigger column than the one she'd seen before, and also heading south – southwest, actually, given the direction of the highway, which ran toward Daugavpils in what had been Latvia till the Soviet Union reclaimed it a couple of years before.

'What *are* they doing? she repeated, but that seemed pretty obvious. They were pulling back from Pskov, or at least pulling back the forces with which they could advance farther rather than merely holding in place.

She found another question: 'Why are they doing it?' She didn't think it was because they'd despaired of conquering Pskov. They had to want the armor somewhere else. Where, she had no idea, and it wasn't her job to worry about such things anyhow. But she needed to get the information to someone whose job *was* worrying about them.

Not for the first time, she wished the *Kukuruznik* had a radio. She sighed; a lot of Soviet aircraft and tanks went without radios. That saved the expense of building and installing them, and the trouble of training personnel who were liable to be illiterate peasants just off the farm. Whether such economies were worth the disadvantage of being without good communications was another question entirely.

When she bounced in for a landing outside Pskov, no Soviet groundcrew men waited for her. The possibility that she might come back early had never entered their minds. She taxied as far from the concealed airplanes as she could, leaving her own at the very edge of the trees. With luck, the Lizards would be so intent on their retreat that they wouldn't notice the *Kukuruznik*.

Without luck ... '*Nichevo*,' Ludmila said: 'It can't be helped.'

She hurried into Pskov. By the time she got to the *Krom*, she was sweating; if anything would keep you warm, flight gear would. She almost ran into George Bagnall as he was coming out. 'What's going on?' he asked in his bad Russian.

She poured out the story, in Russian and then, when she realized she was going too fast for him to follow, in German instead. 'And so I must see *Generalleutnant* Chill and the Soviet brigadiers *sofort* – immediately,' she finished. German was a good language in which to sound urgent. If you didn't get your way, it seemed to warn, something terrible would happen.

But Bagnall only nodded. '*Da*, they all need to know that,' he said, and, etting a hand on her shoulder to show she was with him, he marched er through layers of sentries and subordinates to the commandants f Pskov.

She told them the story in the same mix of languages she'd used with Bagnall. Aleksandr German translated from the Russian for Kurt Chill nd form the German for Nikolai Vasiliev. The leaders were as excited s Ludmila had been. Vasiliev slammed a fist down on the tabletop. 'We an drive them far from our city?' he shouted.

'They're already going,' Chill said. '*Where* are they going – and why? We nust have more intelligence reports. I shall order up additional flights.' He eached for a field telephone.

Until they got more data, the commandants weren't about to order nything irrevocable, which struck Ludmila as sensible. She and Bagnall oth withdrew. He said, 'You did well to come back so soon. You showed lot of—' He had trouble with the word, both in Russian and in German. 'inally, after some fumbling, Ludmila decided he was trying to say *nitiative*.

She shrugged. 'It needed doing, so I did it.' Only after the words were ut of her mouth did she realize that was unusual, at least among the oviets. You did what you were told, and nothing else. That way you ever got in trouble. From what she'd seen, the Germans were looser, nore demanding of imagination from their lower ranks. She didn't know ow the English did things.

'*Das ist gut*,' he said, and then repeated himself, this time in Russian: Khorosho.' Ludmila supposed that meant he thought initiative was a good hing, too. Like a lot of Soviet citizens, she mistrusted the concept. How ould social equality survive if some people shoved themselves ahead of he rest?

Coming out of the gloomy confines of the *Krom* took such ideological oncerns from her mind. The sun had escaped the clouds while she was assing her news on to the local commandants. It glittered off the snow n the ground and made the whole world dazzlingly white. The day vasn't warm – they wouldn't see a warm day for months – but it was eautiful.

Bagnall must have felt it, too. He said, 'Shall we walk along he river?'

Ludmila looked at him out of the corner of her eye. Yes, he definitely elieved in initiative. After a moment, she smiled. 'Well, why not?' she aid. Maybe she had a weakness for foreign men, something that struck er as vaguely – well, not so vaguely – subversive. Then she shook her ead. Georg Schultz was foreign, but she'd never had the slightest yen for im. Maybe she had a weakness for *kulturny* men. In the Soviet Union, she ometimes thought, they were almost as hard to come by as foreigners.

The Pskova River was frozen over, ice stretching from bank to bank.

Here and there, men had cut holes in it and were fishing. A couple ha plump pike and bream out on the ice to show their time wasn't goin to waste.

'Fish here keep fresh all winter long,' Bagnall said.

'Well, of course,' Ludmila answered. Then she paused. England wa supposed to have warmer winters than the Soviet Union. Maybe it wasn an *of course* for him.

After a while, he stopped and looked across the river. 'Which churc is that?' he asked, pointing.

'I think that is the one they call the church of Sts Cosmas and Damia on Gremyachaya Hill,' Ludmila answered. 'But I ought to be asked yo these things, not the other way round. You have been in Pskov muc longer than I have.'

'That's true, he said, and laughed in some embarrassment. 'But it' your country, after all, so I think you should know these things. Eas to forget you could drop England anywhere in the Soviet Union and i would disappear.'

Ludmila nodded. 'After the Lizards came, I flew once into Swede and Denmark and Germany.' She did *not* say she'd taken Molotov t Berchtesgaden. 'Everything seemed so small and so . . . so – used. Her we have more land than we know what to do with. I have seen it is no like that all over the world.'

'No, hardly,' Bagnall said. 'With us, the trouble is finding the land to d all the things we want to do with it.' He hesitated, then laughed. He had good laugh; even when he was laughing at himself, he sounded genuinel amused. He went on, 'Here I am with a pretty girl, and I'm talking abou churches and land. I must be getting old.' Ludmila looked up at him. H was a few years older than she, but – 'I do not think you are ready fo the dustbin yet,' she said. She didn't know how to say *dustbin* in German and getting it across in Russian took almost as much work as he'd ha to make *initiative* comprehensible.

When he finally understood, he laughed again and said, 'Then it mus be my young, fiery blood that makes me do this.' He slipped an arm around her shoulder.

When George Schultz tried putting his hands on her, she'd always go the feeling she had to shake him off right away, that if she didn't, he woul tear off whatever she happened to be wearing and drag her to the ground Bagnall didn't give the same impression. If she said no, she thought he'd listen. *Yes, I do like* kulturny *men.*

Because she thought she could say no any time she wanted to, she didn't say it right away. That emboldened Bagnall to bend down and try to kiss her. She let his lips meet hers but, after a moment's hesitation, she didn't kiss back.

Schultz wouldn't have noticed, or cared if by some chance he had noticed. Bagnall did. He said, 'What's wrong?' When Ludmila didn't answer right away, his brow furrowed in thought. Then he smote his forehead with the heel of his hand, a gesture she'd seen him use before. 'I'm an idiot!' he exclaimed. 'You have someone else.'

'*Da*,' she said, and in an odd sort of way it was true, though all she and Heinrich Jäger had together was time best measured in hours and a couple of letters. Then, to her amazement and dismay, she burst into tears.

When Bagnall patted her shoulder this time, it was in pure animal comfort. No, perhaps not quite pure; anyone who finds someone else attractive will always have mixed motives in touching that person. But he was doing the best he could. 'What's wrong?' he asked again. 'You don't know if he's all right?'

'No, I don't know that,' she said. 'I don't know very much at all.' She looked up at his long face, set now in lines of concern. She would never have told her story to a countryman. Speaking to a foreigner somehow felt safer. And so, in a torrent where Russian soon swamped her German, she poured out what she'd hidden from everyone for so long. By the time she was done, she felt as if she'd been flattened by a bulldozer.

Bagnall rubbed his chin. Bristles rasped under his fingers; both razors and hot water for shaving were in short supply in Pskov. The RAF man uttered something in English. That meant nothing to Ludmila. Seeing as much, Bagnall dropped back into his mix of German and Russian: 'You don't do anything the easy way, do you?'

'*Nyet*.' She scanned his face, trying to figure out what he was thinking. It wasn't easy. What they said about Englishmen was true: whatever went on inside their head, they kept it to themselves. At least he hadn't called her a traitor and a whore for ending up in the German's bed when they found each other in Berchtesgaden. That was something.

Slowly, Bagnall said, 'You must know something of what the fair Tatiana' – *die schöne Tatiana*, he called her; which made Ludmila smile in spite of herself – 'feels because she is carrying on with George Schultz.'

'Yes, perhaps so, though I don't think she'd give me much sympathy.' Ludmila didn't think Tatiana gave anyone much sympathy. She looked Bagnall in the eye. 'Now you know why I cannot, do not want to – how did you say it? – carry on with you. And so?' *What are you thinking? Your face is as quiet as Molotov's.*

'Yes, I see that,' Bagnall answered. He didn't sound happy about it, either. Ludmila felt obscurely good about that, even though she'd just told him she didn't want to have an affair with him. Picking his words with care, he went on, 'Your German had best be a good man, if he is to be good enough to deserve you.'

Your German. Ludmila's guilt came flooding back. Even after a year and a half of uneasy alliance with the Nazis against the Lizards, the memory of the war against Hitler's invading minions would not go away. But the rest of it – Ludmila stood on tiptoe and kissed Bagnall's whiskery cheek. 'Thank you,' she whispered.

He chuckled, a little uncomfortably. 'If you do that sort of thing, you will make me forget my good intentions.'

'With you, I will take the chance.' There was a notion believers had, one Ludmila, a thoroughgoing athiest, had always scorned. Now, though, for the first time in her life, she understood the idea of absolution. No matter that an Englishman rather than a priest had given it to her. Given her own secular beliefs, that only made it better.

The fellow who made his living exhibiting dung beetles was talking so fast and so excitedly, Nieh Ho-T'ing could hardly follow him. 'They loved it, loved it, I tell you,' he exclaimed, gulping down one glass after another of *samshu*, the potent, triple-distilled brew made from *kaoliang* – millet beer. 'They paid me three times as much as I expected, and they want me to come back again as soon as I can.' He stared at Nieh in sodden gratitude. 'Thank you so much for arranging my performance before them.'

'Hou Yi, it was my pleasure,' Nieh Ho-T'ing said expansively. 'Anything I can do to make the lives of the little scaly devils more pleasant, that I shall do.' He smiled. 'Then they pay me, which makes *my* life more pleasant.'

Hou Yi laughed a loud, sozzled laugh. He poured the last few drops from the jar of *samshu* into his cup, then lifted a finger to show he wanted another. After a while, a girl brought it to him. He was drunk enough to pat her on the backside by way of showing thanks. She made a face as she hurried away. She might well have been available, but making a show of that demeaned her.

Nieh let Hou freshen his cup of *samshu*. The tavern – it was called the *Ta Chiu Kang*: the Big Wine Vat – was only a couple of blocks from his rooming house, but he assumed an altogether different persona here. Instead of being the scaly devils' staunchest foe, he acted the part of a medium-important tout for them, someone who was always looking for new ways to keep them entertained. Thanks to the connections the People's Liberation Army had with men and women in the little devils' employ, he had no trouble living up to the role.

The *Ta Chiu Kang* was different from his usual haunts in other ways besides the part he played here. *Mo T'an Kuo Shih*, a sign announced: do not talk politics. Every time he looked at it, Nieh snickered. In a revolutionary situation, all speech was political speech. As if to underline that, a smaller banner below the sign read, PLEASE KEEP YOUR HONORABLE MOUTH SHUT. In less inherently futile fashion, other signs declared *cash only* and *no credit*.

Hou Yi said, 'The little devils want me back. Oh, I told you that, didn't I? Well, they do. One of them told me as much, as I was capturing my bugs and getting ready to go. Can you arrange it for me?'

'Arrange it for you? My friend, I can do better than that,' Nieh answered. 'Do you know what I've learned? The little scaly devils want to make films of some animal-show performances – *of your* beetle show – so they can show them far away from here, in countries where the foreign devils have no such shows. Before you go to them next time, you will visit me, and I will fix a special camera from the scaly devils inside your case. It will take just the pictures they need, by some magic I am too ignorant to understand.'

Hou Yi goggled at him, then bowed his head – and almost banged it on the top of the table. 'You are much too generous to me. I am unworthy of such an honor.'

Nieh knew that was politely insincere. 'Nonsense,' he said. 'The little scaly devils demanded it of me – they insisted, I tell you. Could I say "no" to my masters, especially when I know what enjoyment you give them?'

'This is wonderful, wonderful,' Hou Yi babbled. 'I am your slave for life.' He looked close to the maudlin tears of drunkenness.

'Just remember,' Nieh said, no idle warning in view of the showman's condition, 'before your next performance in front of the little scaly devils, you come to me with your case of insects, and I will mount the camera inside. Do not act as if you know it is there; the little devils want you to put on your show exactly as you would otherwise.'

'I shall obey you as a dutiful son obeys his father,' Hou Yi giggled, belched, set his head down on the table where he and Nieh Ho-T'ing were drinking, and went to sleep.

Nieh looked down on him, then shrugged and left coins on the table to pay for the *samshu* they had been drinking. He walked out of the Big Wine Vat and into the maze of Peking's *hutungs*. Torches and candles and lanterns and the occasional electric light made the alleys almost as bright as day. Nieh used every trick he knew to make sure no one was following him before he made his way back to the rooming house where the Communist cause flourished.

Sitting in the dining room there was Hsia Shou-Tao. To Nieh's relief, his aide was alone; he never stopped worrying that one of the tarts Hsai brought back here would prove to be an agent of the scaly devils or the Kuomintang or even the Japanese. Hsai simply was not careful enough about such things.

In front of him stood a jar of *samshu* identical to the one from which Hou Yi had been drinking. He also had plates with crackers and meat dumplings and pickled baby crabs and a salad of jellyfish and gelatin. When he saw Nieh, he called, 'Come join my feast. There's enough here for two to celebrate.'

I'll gladly do that,' Nieh said, waving to the serving girl for a cup and a pair of chopsticks. 'What are we celebrating?'

'You know Yang Chüeh-ai, the mouse man? The little scaly devils liked his act, and they want him back. He says they didn't do a careful search of the cages he carries his mice in, either. We shouldn't have any trouble planting our bomb inside there.' Hsia slurped at his *samshu*. 'Ahh, that's good.'

Nieh poured himself a cup of the potent millet liquor. Before he drank, he ate a couple of crackers and pickled crab. 'That is good news,' he said as he finally lifted his cup. 'Hou Yi, one of the fellows who shows dung beetles, told me the same thing. We can get bombs in amongst the little scaly devils; that much seems clear. The real trick will be to have them invite all the beast-show men at the same time, so we can do them as much damage as possible.'

'You're not wrong there,' Hsia said with a hoarse, raucous chuckle. 'Can't use the beast-show men more than once, either, poor foolish fellows. Once should do the job, though.' He made a motion of brushing something disgusting from the front of his tunic.

To Hsia, the beast-show men were to be used and expended like any other ammunition. Nieh was just as willing to expend them, but regretted the necessity. The cause was important enough to use innocent dupes to further it, but he would not forget the blood on his hands. Hsia didn't worry about it.

'The other thing we need to make sure of is that we have good timers on all our explosives,' Nieh said. 'We want them to go off as close to the same time as we can arrange.'

'Yes, yes, Grandmother,' Hsia said impatiently. He'd had a good deal to drink already, unless Nieh was much mistaken. 'I have a friend who is dickering with the Japanese outside of town. From what he says, they have more timers than they know what to do with.'

'I believe that,' Nieh said. With the coming of the little scaly devils to China, Japanese forces south of their puppet state in Manchukuo were reduced to little more than guerilla bands, and, unlike the Communist guerrillas, did not enjoy the protection of the populace in which they moved. Too many atrocities had taught the Chinese what sort of soldiers the Japanese were.

But Japan was an industrial power. It had been able to manufacture for its troops all sorts of devices the Chinese, unable to produce the like locally, had to beg, borrow, or steal. They had got matériel from the British, the Americans, and the Russians, but now both capitalist imperialists and fraternal socialist comrades were locked in their own struggle for survival. That left the Japanese remnants as the best source for advanced munitions.

Nieh said, 'A pity the little scaly devils did not wait another generation before beginning their imperialist onslaught. The spread of industry over the world and the advance of revolutionary progressive forces would have made their speedy defeat a certainty.'

Hsia Shou-Tao reached for a dumpling with his chopsticks. They crossed in his fingers, leaving him with a confused expression on his face. If he was too drunk to handle them properly, he had indeed had quite a lot of *samshu*. He said, 'We'll beat them anyway, and the damned eastern dwarfs from Japan, and the Kuomintang, and anybody else who gets in our way.' He tried for the dumpling again, and succeeded in capturing it. He popped it into his mouth, chewed, swallowed. 'Jus' like *that.*'

Nieh thought about lecturing him on the difference between something being historically inevitable and it being easy to accomplish, but concluded he'd be wasting his breath. Hsia didn't need a lecture. What he needed was a bucket of cold water poured over his head.

Hsia belched heroically. From confused, his face took on a look of drunken foxiness. 'You think Liu Han is going to get her brat back?' he asked, breathing *samshu* fumes across the table into Nieh Ho-T'ing's face.

'That I don't know,' Nieh said. Like any scientific doctrine, the historical dialectic considered the motion through time of mankind as a mass; the vagaries of individuals were beneath its notice.

Leering, Hsia found another question: 'You get inside her Jade Gate yet?'

'None of your business,' Nieh snapped. How did Hsia know he wanted her? He was sure he'd been discreet – but evidently not discreet enough.

His aide laughed at him. 'That means no.'

Looking at Hsia Shou-Tao's red, mirth-filled countenance, Nieh decided Hsia didn't need just a bucket of water poured over him. Clobbering him with the bucket afterwards seemed a good idea, too.

Kirel stood beside Atvar and studied the evolving dispositions of the Race's infantrymales and armor. For a moment, one of his eye turrets slid away from the map and toward his superior. 'Exalted Fleetlord, this had better work,' he said.

'I am aware of that, yes,' Atvar answered. He was painfully aware of it, and having Kirel remind him of it so bluntly didn't make him feel any easier about what he'd set in motion. 'If spirits of Emperors past look down on us in approval, we shall smash Deutschland once for all.'

Kirel did not say anything, but his tailstump twitched a little. So did Atvar's, in irritation. He could read his subordinate's thoughts: not so very long ago – though it seemed an age – he'd promised to smash Britain once for all. That hadn't worked out. In spite of hurting the British, the Race had hurt itself worse, and Britain remained in the war.

'This time, it will be different,' the fleetlord insisted. 'This time, our logistics are far better than they were for the invasion of that pestiferous island.' He brought up highlights on the map. 'Instead of having to fly males and matériel long distances to bring them into the battle, we shall be operating from our own long-established strongholds on either side of the Deutsche, from France and Poland. We shall move forward with both forces and crush the Big Uglies between us.'

'So the operational planners have maintained,' Kirel said. 'So they would maintain, the better to underline their usefulness to our efforts. If reality matches the computer simulations, this operation will succeed. But how often, Exalted Fleetlord, does reality match simulations on Tosev 3?'

'We know what the Deutsche have,' Atvar said. 'We have even extrapolated that they will have some new weapons, with performance improved over those with which we are familiar: when dealing with the Big Uglies, as you say, an upward slope on the projection line seems as reasonable as one that is flat for us. Even given that, though, the projections show us beating them.'

'Do the projections take into account the wretched weather on that part of the planet at this time of its year?' Kirel stroked computer keys. A corner of the screen that displayed the simulations map went first to a satellite image of endless storm systems rolling east from Deutschland toward Poland, and then to a video of wind whipping crystallized frozen water across a desolate landscape that resembled nothing so much as the inside of some tremendous refrigeration plant. 'Our males and our equipment do not perform at optimum levels in such conditions.'

'Truth. But we have improved over our levels during the previous local winter,' Atvar said stoutly. 'And the cold, ironically, also hinders the activities of the Deutsche. Their poisonous gases are far less effective now than when the weather is warmer. We've also succeeded in developing filters to keep most gases out of the interior compartments of our fighting vehicles. This will boost both performances and morale.'

'Except, perhaps, among the infantrymales still compelled to leave their fighting vehicles from time to time and perform their duties in the open,' Kirel said.

Atvar sent him a suspicious look. Ever since Straha's attempted coup, Kirel had been scrupulously, almost ostentatiously, loyal. Unlike Straha, he did not believe in adventure for its own sake. Indeed, he hardly believed in adventure at all, as witness his protests against the upcoming campaign. But his very conservatism, a quality that endeared him to most males of the Race, might yet make him the focus for disaffected shiplords and officers. Atvar had enough troubles worrying about the political effects on his campaign on the Big Uglies. When he also had to worry about its political effects on his own males, he sometimes thought he was having to bear too heavy a burden.

'Let us look at the benefits of success,' he said. 'With Deutschland defeated, the whole northwest of the main continental mass comes under our control. We gain improved positions for any future assaults, whether by air alone or with ground forces, against Britain. We go from active combat to pacification over that whole area, freeing up troops for operations elsewhere. And the psychological impact on the remaining Tosevite not-empires will be profound.'

'Truth, all of it, Exalted Fleetlord,' Kirel said. 'But, as the saying goes, to get the hatchling, you first must have the egg.'

Atvar's tailstump lashed harder now. 'Let us not mince words, Shiplord,' he said coldly. 'Do you advise me to abandon this planned effort, or shall we go forward with it? Proceeding in the face of your obstructionism is difficult.'

'I obstruct nothing, Exalted Fleetlord,' Kirel said. Almost involuntarily, he hunched down into the posture of obedience. 'I merely question methods and timing to obtain the best possible results for the Race. Have I not labored long and hard to support the implementation of this plan?'

'Truth.' Atvar knew he sounded reluctant to admit as much, but he couldn't help it. Externally, Kirel had done as he'd said. The fleetlord had been inferring the thoughts behind his actions. Maybe he was wrong. He hoped he was. Sighing, he said, 'Blame it on Tosev 3, Shiplord. Anything that has anything to do with this cursed planet goes wrong one way or another.'

'Exalted Fleetlord, there we agree completely,' Kirel said. 'As soon as we detected radio signals from it, we should have realized all our previous calculations needed revising.'

'We did realize that,' Atvar said. 'What we didn't have, what we should have had, was a feel for *how much* revising they needed.'

'And yet,' Kirel said in tones of wonder, 'we may yet succeed, in spite of having to abandon plans already made.' For a Big Ugly, as Atvar had seen him after time – generally to his consternation – abandoning plans and making new ones on the spur of the moment (or even going ahead and acting without making new plans) was so common as hardly to be worth noting. For the Race, that attitude started at traumatic and got worse from there. Routine, organization, forethought – thanks to them, the Empire had endured for a hundred millennia, had made two other species reverence the Emperor in the same way the Race did. Adhering to routine on Tosev 3 as often as not led straight to disaster, for the Big Uglies anticipated and exploited routine behavior.

But deviating from routine had dangers of its own. The routine pattern was often the best one; deviations just made things worse. And the Race wasn't good at thinking under such stress: the snap decisions males came up with were usually bad decisions. The Big Uglies exploited those, too.

Atvar removed from the screen the map of the planned campaign against Deutschland. In its place he substituted a detailed chart of an urban area on the lesser continental mass. 'As you say, we may yet succeed,' he told Kirel. 'Here in Chicago, we have reversed the setbacks the American Tosevites inflicted upon us when the weather first turned, and are now moving forward once more. If the trend continues, the entire city may be in our hands by the end of local winter.'

'May it prove so,' Kirel said. 'Even if we do achieve victory there, the cost has proved very high. We threw many males, many fighting vehicles, many landcruisers into that grinding machine.'

'Truth,' Atvar said sadly. 'But once having begun the campaign to wrest control of the city from the Big Uglies, we had to go forward with it. If we abandoned it, the Tosevites would conclude we dared not press our attacks in the face of stiff opposition. We invested more than our males in the fight for Chicago, we invested our prestige as well. And that prestige will rise with a victory.'

'This is also truth,' Kirel agreed. 'Once joined, the battle could not be abandoned. Had we been able to anticipate the full cost, however, we might not have initiated the battle in the first place.' He let out a hissing sigh. 'This has proved true in all too many instances on Tosev 3.'

'Not always, though,' Atvar said. 'And I have a special reason for hoping the conquest of Chicago will be successfully completed. Somewhere in the not-empire called the United States skulks the oh-so-redoubtable shiplord Straha.' He laced his voice with all the scorn he could muster. 'Let the traitor see the might of the Race he abandoned. Let him have some time to contemplate the wisdom first of revolt against me and then of treachery. And, when our triumph is at last complete, let us bring him to justice. On Tosev 3, his name shall live forever among the colonists as a symbol of betrayal.'

The Race's memory was long. When Atvar said forever, he intended to be taken literally. He thought of Vorgnil, who had tried to murder an Emperor sixty-five thousand years before. His name survived, as an example of infamy. Straha's would stand alongside it after the conquest of Tosev 3 was complete.

Mordechai Anielewicz strode down the sidewalk, as if enjoying every moment of his morning outing. That the temperature was far below freezing, that he wore a fur cap with ear flaps down, two pairs of wool trousers one inside the other, a Red Army greatcoat and felt boots, and heavy mittens, that his breath smoked like a chimney and crystals froze in his beard and mustache – by the way he strolled along, it might have been spring in Paris, not winter in Lodz.

He was far from the only person on the street, either. Work had to get done, whether it was freezing or not. People either ignored the weather or made jokes about it. 'Colder than my wife after she's talked with her mother,' one man said to a friend. They both laughed, building a young fogbank around themselves.

The Lizards were busy on the streets of Lodz, too. Alien police, looking far colder and more miserable than most humans Mordechai saw, labored to get traffic off the main east-west streets. They had their work cut out for them, too, for as fast as they shooed people away, more spilled onto the boulevards they were fighting to clear. Not all of that was absentminded cussedness; quite a few men and women were being deliberately obstructive. Anielewicz hoped the Lizards didn't figure that out. Things might get ugly if they did.

Finally, the Lizards cleared away enough people and wagons to get their armored column through. The males peering out of the cupolas of tanks and armored personnel carriers looked even more miserable than the ones on the street. They also looked absurd: a Lizard wearing a shaggy wolfskin cap tied on under his jaws resembled nothing so much as a dandelion gone to seed.

Four tanks, three carriers ... seven tanks, nine carriers ... fifteen tanks, twenty-one carriers. He lost track of the lorries, but they were in proportion to the armored vehicles they accompanied. When the parade was done, he whistled softly between his teeth. West of Lodz, the Lizards had something bit laid on. You didn't have to be Napoleon to figure out what, either. West of Lodz lay ... Germany.

Still whistling, he walked down to the Balut Market square and bought a cabbage, some turnips, some parsnips, and a couple of chicken feet. They'd make a soup that tasted meaty, even if it didn't have much real meat in it. Next to what he'd got by on in Warsaw, the prospect of a soup with any meat in it – the prospect of a soup with plenty of vegetables in it – seemed ambrosial by comparison.

He wrapped his purchases in an old ragged cloth and carried them back to the fire station on Lutomierska Street. His office was upstairs, not far from the sealed room where people took refuge when the Nazis threw gas at Lodz. If they'd known what he knew, their rockets would have been flying an hour earlier.

He fiddled around with the draft of a letter for Mordechai Chaim Rumkowski to present to the Lizard authorities, asking them to release more coal for heating. Having to rely on the Lizard's dubious mercy grated on him, but every so often Rumkowski did win concessions, so the game was worth playing. Rumkowski had begged Himmler for concessions, too, and won a few. As long as he could be a big fish in the little pool of Jewish Lodz, he'd debase himself for the bigger fish in the bigger pools.

People wandered in and out. Bertha Fleishman's sister had had a baby girl the night before; along with everyone else, Anielewicz said *mazeltov*. Even as people kept blowing one another to bits, they were having babies, too. He'd seen that in the ghetto. In the midst of horror worse than any he'd imagined, people kept falling in love and getting married and having children. He wondered if that as absolutely *meshuggeh* or the sanest thing they could possibly do.

Finally, three o'clock rolled around. That hour corresponded to a change of shift at the telephone exchange. Anielewicz picked up the phone, waited for an operator to come to the other end of the line. When one did, he called his landlady, Mrs Lipshitz, and told her he'd be working late. She bore up under the news with equanimity. He tried again. When he heard the operator's voice, he asked her to put him through to Rumkowski's office. He asked a meaningless question about the upcoming request for more coal, then hung up. Muttering under his breath, he picked up the telephone once more. When the operator answered, he brightened. 'Is that you, Yetta?' he said. 'How are you this afternoon, darling?'

'Saul?' she asked, as she'd been trained to do. Yetta wasn't her real name. Mordechai didn't know what it was, or what she looked like. The less he knew, the less he could give away if he fell into the Lizards' hands.

'The same. Listen, sweetheart, I need to talk to Meyer the baker. You know the one – his shop is right next to the Balut.'

'I'll try to put you through,' Yetta said. 'We've been having some trouble with the wires down there, so it may take a while. Please be patient.'

'For you darling, anything,' Anielewicz said. The Balut was code for Breslau, the nearest major city in German hands; had he wanted Poznan, he'd have asked for an establishment on Przelotna Street. Telephone lines between Lodz and Breslau were supposed to be down. In fact, they *were* down, but here and there illicit ground lines ran between Lizard-held territory and that which the Germans still controlled. Getting through on those lines wasn't easy, but people like Yetta were supposed to know the tricks.

Mordechai hoped she knew the tricks. He didn't want to call Breslau, not so you'd notice, but he didn't see that he had any choice, either. The Nazis, curse them, needed to know something large and ugly was heading their way. One reason the Lizards were relatively mild in Poland was that they had the Germans right next door, and needed to keep the locals contented. If Hitler and his crew folded up, the Lizards would lose their incentive to behave better.

Gevalt, *what a calculation to have to make*, Anielewicz thought.

Sooner than he'd expected, the phone on the other end of the line started ringing. Somebody picked it up. *'Bitte?'* came the greeting in crisp German. The connection was poor, but good enough.

'Is this the shop of Meyer the baker?' Mordechai asked in Yiddish, and hoped the Nazi on the other end was on the ball.

He was. Without missing a beat, he answered, *'Ja. Was willst du?* – What do you want?'

Anielewicz knew that was the *du* of insult, not intimacy, but held on to his temper. 'I want to give an order I'll pick up a little while from now. I want you to bake me fifteen currant buns, twenty-one onion bagels, and enough bread to go with them. No, I don't know how much yet, not exactly; I'll try to call you back on that. Do you have it? Yes, fifteen currant buns. How much will that come to? ... Meyer, you're a *gonif*, and you know it.' He hung up in a good display of high dudgeon.

A voice came from the doorway: 'Laying in supplies?'

'As a matter of fact, yes, Nussboym,' Mordechai answered, hoping he sounded calmer than he felt. 'I was going to bring it all in so we could celebrate Bertha's niece. Children deserve celebrating, don't you think?' Now he'd have to go over to Meyer's and buy all that stuff.

David Nussboym walked into Mordechai's room. He was several years older than Anielewicz, and a lot of the time acted as if he thought Mordechai had no business doing anything more than wiping his snotty nose. Now, scowling, he spoke in the manner of professor to inept student: 'I'll tell you what I think. I think you're lying to me, and that you were passing on code of some kind. There's only one kind of code you're likely to be passing, and only one set of people you're likely to be passing it to. I think you've turned into Hitler's *tukhus-lekher.*'

Slowly, deliberately, Anielewicz got to his feet. He was three or four centimeters taller than Nussboym, and used that height advantage to look down his nose at the older man. 'I'll tell you what I think,' he said, his voice silky with menace. 'You gabble on about *tukhus-lekhers* – I think you can lick *my* arse.'

Nussboym stared. Nobody had talked to him like that since the Lizards ran the Germans out of Lodz. He'd had a year and a half to get used to being *somebody*. But he also had considerable native spirit, and the awareness that those in authority backed him. After drawing back a pace in surprise, he thrust his chin forward and snapped, 'I wouldn't talk so fine if I were you. I've been doing some quiet checking, Mr Mordechai Anielewicz – oh, yes, I know who you are. Some males of the Race back in Warsaw would be very interested in having a word or two with you. I haven't said anything to my friends there because I know these things can be misunderstandings, and you've done good work since you got here. But if you're going to bring the Nazis back into Poland—'

'God forbid!' Mordechai broke in, with complete sincerity. 'But I don't want the Lizards in Germany, either, and you can't understand that side of the coin.'

'I want Hitler dead. I want Himmler dead. I want Hans Frank dead. I want every Nazi bastard with SS on his collar tabs dead,' Nyssboym said, his face working. 'That wouldn't begin to be payment enough for what they did to us. I'd sooner kill them all myself, but if I have to let the Race do it for me, I'll settle for that.'

'And then what happens?' Anielewicz demanded.

'I don't care what happens then,' David Nyssboym answered. 'That's plenty, all by itself.'

'But it's not, don't you see?' Mordechai said, something like desperation in his voice. 'After that, who stops the Lizards from doing exactly as they please? If you know who I am, you know I've worked with them, too. They don't make any bones about it: they intend to rule mankind forever. When they say forever, they don't mean a thousand years like that madman, Hitler. They mean forever, and they aren't madmen. If they win now, we won't get a second chance.'

'Better them than the Germans,' Nussboym said stubbornly.

'But you see, David, the choice isn't that simple. We have to—' Without changing expression, without breaking off his flow of words, Anielewicz hit Nussboym in the belly, as hard as he could. He'd intended to hit him in the pit of the stomach and win the fight at the first blow, *blitzkrieg*-fashion, but his fist landed a few centimeters to one side of where he wanted to put it. Nussboym grunted in pain but instead of folding up like a concertina, he grappled with Mordechai. They fell together, knocking over with a crash the chair on which Anielewicz had been sitting.

Mordechai had done a lot of fighting with a rifle in his hand. It was a different business altogether when the fellow you were trying to beat wasn't a tiny spot seen through your sights, but was at the same time doing his best to choke the life out of you. Nussboym was stronger and tougher than he'd figured, too. Again, he realized being on the opposite side didn't turn you into a sniveling coward.

Nyssboym tried to knee him in the groin. He twisted aside and took the knee on the hip. He would have thought it even less sporting had he not tried to do the same thing to Nussboym a moment earlier.

They rolled up against Mordechai's desk. It was a cheap, light, flimsy thing, made of pine and plywood. Mordechai tried to bang Nussboym's head against the side of it. Nussboym threw up an arm just in time.

A heavy glass ashtray fell off the desk. Anielewicz was damned if he knew why he'd kept the thing around. He didn't smoke. Even if he had smoked, nobody in Poland had any tobacco these days, anyhow. But the ashtray had been on his desk when he got the office, and he hadn't bothered getting rid of it.

It came in handy now. He and David Nussboym both grabbed for it at the same time, but Nussboym didn't reach it. Mordechai's arm was longer. He seized it and hit Nussboym in the head. Nussboym groaned but kept fighting, so Mordechai hit him again. After the third blow, Nussboym's eyes rolled up and he went limp.

Anielewicz struggled to his feet. His clothes were torn, he had a bloody nose, and he felt as if he'd just crawled out of a cement mixer. People crowded in the doorway, staring. 'He was going to tell the Lizards who I am,' Mordechai said. His voice came out raw and rasping; Nussboym had come closer to strangling him than he'd thought.

Bertha Fleishman nodded briskly. 'I was afraid that would happen. Do you think we have to shut him up for good?'

'I don't want to,' Mordechai answered. 'I don't want any more Jews dead. He's not a bad man, he's just wrong here. Can we get him out of the way for good?'

She nodded again. 'He'll have to go east, but we'll manage. I have enough Communist friends to be sure he'll get into Russia without ever having the chance to speak his piece to the Lizards.'

'What'll happen to him there?' Anielewicz asked. 'They're liable to ship him to Siberia.' He'd meant it for a joke, but Bertha's sober nod said it was indeed a possibility. Mordechai shrugged. 'If that's how it is, then that's how it is. He'll have a chance to stay alive there, and we'd have to kill him here.'

'Let's get him out of here for now,' Bertha said. More quietly, she added, 'You ought to think about disappearing, too, Mordechai. Not everyone who favors the Lizards is as open as Nussboym. You could be betrayed any time.'

He bit his lip. She was right. He knew she was right. But the idea of going on the road again, finding another alias and joining a partisan band, pierced him with a chill worse than any winter's gale. 'Good-bye, Lodz. Good-bye, flat,' he muttered as he took hold of David Nussboym's feet.

18

Heinrich Jäger felt like a table-tennis ball. Whenever he returned from a mission, he never knew where he would bounce up next: to Schloss Hohentübingen to help the men with the thick glasses and the high foreheads drive the explosive-metal bomb project forward, off on another run with Otto Skorzeny to tweak the Lizards' snouts, or to lead panzers into battle, something he actually knew how to do.

After he got back from Albi, they'd stuck him in a panzer again. That was where the powers that be stuck him when the war was going badly. If the Lizards overran the *Vaterland*, everything else became irrelevant.

He stood up in the cupola of his Panther. The wind tore at him, even through his reversible parka. He wore it white side out now, to go with the panzer's whitewashed turret and hull. The machine, large and white and deadly, reminded him of a polar bear as it rumbled east from Breslau. As for the parka, it kept him from freezing. Next to the makeshifts the *Wehrmacht* had used two winters before in Russia, it was a miracle. With it on, he was just cold. That seemed pretty good; he knew all about freezing.

His gunner, a moon-faced corporal named Gunther Grillparzer, said, 'Any sign of the Lizards yet, sir?'

'No,' Jäger answered, ducking back down inside the turret to talk. 'I tell you the truth: I'm just as glad not seeing them.'

'*Ach, ja*,' Grillparzer said. 'I just hope that call from the damned Jews wasn't a pack of damned moonshine. For all we know, the bastards want to make us motor around and burn up petrol for no reason.'

'They wouldn't do that.' *I hope they wouldn't do that*, Jäger added to himself. After what the *Reich* had done to the Jews in Poland, how could he blame them if they wanted revenge? Aloud, he went on, 'The commandant seems convinced the call was legitimate.'

'*Ja, Herr Oberest*,' Grillparzer said, 'but those aren't angels that come out the commandant's arse when he squats on the WC, are they?'

Jäger stood up again without answering. Russians and Lizards – and SS *Einsatzgruppe* men – followed orders without thinking about them. The *Wehrmacht* trained its soldiers to show initiative in everything they did

– and if that made them less respectful of their superiors than they would have been otherwise, well, you had to take the bad with the good.

They reached the crest of a low rise. 'Halt,' Jäger told the driver, and then relayed the command to the rest of the panzers in the battle group: an *ad hoc* formation that essentially meant, *all the armored vehicles we can scrape together for the moment*. 'We'll deploy along this line. Hull down, everyone.'

When a polar bear prowled through ice and snow, it was the most deadly predator in its domain. Foxes and badgers and wolverines stepped aside; seals and reindeer fled for their lives. Jäger wished – oh, how he wished! – the same held true for his Panther, and for the Panthers and Panzer IVs and Tigers with it.

Unfortunately, however, in straight-up combat it took anywhere from five to a couple of dozen German panzers to knock out one Lizard machine. That was why he had no intention of meeting the Lizards in straight-up combat if he could possible help it. Strike from ambush, fall back, hit the Lizards gain when they stormed forward to overwhelm the position you'd just evacuated, fall back again – that was how you hurt them.

He wished for a cigarette, or a cigar, or a pipe, or a dip of snuff. He'd never tasted snuff in his life. He just wanted tobacco. There were stories that people had killed themselves when they couldn't get anything to smoke. He didn't know if he believed those or not, but he felt the lack.

He had a little flask of schnapps. He took a nip now. It snarled its way down his gullet. It might have been aged half an hour before somebody poured it into a bottle. Then again, it might not have. After he drank, he felt warmer. The doctors said that was nonsense. *To hell with the doctors*, he thought.

What was that off in the distance? He squinted through swirling snow. No, it wasn't a horse-drawn wagon: too big and too quick. And there came another behind it, and another. His stomach knotted around the schnapps. Lizard panzers, heading this way. Down into the turret again. He spoke two brief sentences, one to the gunner – 'The Jews weren't lying' – and one to the loader – 'Armor-piercing'. he added one more sentence over the wireless for the benefit of the battle group: 'Hold fire to within five hundred meters.'

He stuck head and shoulders out into the cold again, raised binoculars to his eyes for a better look. Not just Lizard panzers coming this way, but their personnel carriers, too. That was good news and bad news. The panzers could smash them, but if they disgorged their infantry before they were hit, they were very bad news. Lizard foot soldiers carried antipanzer rockets that made *Panzerschrecks* look like cheap toys by comparison.

The panzer troops he commanded had plenty of fire discipline, *danken Gott dafür*. They'd wait as he had ordered, let the Lizards get close and then hit them hard before dropping back to the next ridge line. They'd—

Maybe the crew of the Tiger a few hundred meters away hadn't been paying attention to the wireless. Maybe their set was broken. Or maybe they just didn't give a damn about fire discipline. The long-barreled 88 roared with the leaders of the Lizard force still a kilometer and a half away.

'Dumbheaded pigdog!' Jäger screamed. The Tiger scored a clean hit. One of the personnel carriers stopped dead, smoke spurting from it. Through the dying reverberations of the cannon shot, Jäger heard the crew of the Tiger yelling like drunken idiots. The resemblance didn't end there, either, he thought bitterly.

He ducked into the turret once more. Before he could speak, Gunther Grillparzer said it for him: 'The Lizards know we're here.'

'*Ja*.' Jäger slapped the gunner on the shoulder. 'Good luck. We'll need it.' He spoke to the driver over the intercom. 'Listen for my orders, Johannes. We may have to get out of here in a hurry.'

'*Jawohl, Herr Oberst!*'

They were a good crew, probably not quite so fine as the one he'd had in France – Klaus Meinecke had been a genius with a cannon – but damn good. He wondered how much that was going to help them. Exactly what he'd feared was happening. Instead of motoring blithely down the highway toward Breslau and presenting their flanks for close-range killing shots, the Lizard panzers were turning to face his position straight on. Neither a Tiger's main armament nor a Panther's could penetrate their glacis plates and turrets at point-blank range, let alone at fifteen hundred meters.

And the personnel carriers were pulling back even farther. He got on the all-panzers circuit: 'They know we're here now. Panzer IVs, concentrate on the carriers. *Gott mit uns*, we'll come out of this all right.' *Or some of us will, anyhow*, he glossed mentally. Some of them wouldn't.

The Panzer IVs along the line of the ridge opened up, not only with armor-piercing shells to wreck the personnel carriers but also with high-explosive rounds to deal with the Lizards who'd left before being hit. The order was cold-blooded calculation on Jäger's part. The IVs had the weakest cannons and the weakest armor of the machines in the battle group. Not only were they best suited for handling the carriers, they were also the panzers Jäger could best afford to lose when the Lizards started shooting back.

He'd hoped the Lizard panzers would come charging up the slope toward his position, cannon blazing. The Russians had made that mistake time and again, and the Lizards more than once. That kind of rush would give his Panther and Tiger crews close-range shots and shots at the Lizards' side armor, which their cannon could penetrate.

The Lizards were learning, though. Their panzer crews had been through combat, too, and had a notion of what worked. They didn't need to charge; they could engage at long range. Even at fifteen hundred meters, a hit from one of their monster shells would blow – did blow – the turret right off a Panzer IV and send it blazing into the snow. Jäger clenched is fists. With luck, the commander, gunner, and loader there never knew what hit them.

Nor were the armored personnel carriers helpless against panzers. Their light cannon wouldn't penetrate turret armor, but some of them carried rockets on launch rails on the sides of their turrets. Like the ones the Lizard infantry used, those had no trouble cracking a panzer.

'Retreat!' Jäger bawled on the all-hands frequency. 'Make them come to us.' The Maybach in the Panther he personally commanded bellowed louder as it stopped idling and went into reverse. 'This'll be interesting,' Grillparzer shouted up at Jäger. 'Will we be in our new position before they get up here where we are now and start blasting away at us?'

Interesting wasn't the word Jäger would have used, but it would do. The trouble was, the Lizard panzers were not only better armed and armored than the ones the *Wehrmacht* had, they were faster, too. General Guderian hadn't been joking when he said a panzer's engine was as important a weapon as its gun.

A Tiger maybe half a kilometer off to the north of Jäger took as it was about to reach the cover of pine woods. It brewed up spectacularly, with a smoke ring going out through the cupola as if the devil were enjoying a cigar, and then with the ammunition cooking off in a display of orange and red fireworks. Some of the smoke that boiled out of it came from the burning flesh of its five crewmen.

Grillparzer got a decent shot at one of the Lizard panzers, but its armor held the round out of the fighting compartment. A trail of fire appeared from out of a snowdrift, with no Lizard panzers nearby: the Lizard infantry had come up. The rocket hit a Panzer IV in the engine compartment, which burst into flames. Hatches popped open. Men ran for the trees. A couple of them made it. Machine-gun fire cut down the rest.

Voices were screaming in Jäger's earphones: 'They're flanking us, *Herr Oberst!*' 'Two enemy panzers have broken through. If they get in our rear, we're done for.' 'Can you call for reinforcements, sir?'

If you were commanding a battle group, you didn't have much hope of calling for reinforcements: battle groups got formed from the scrapings at the bottom of the barrel. Jäger's men were right – if the Lizards got behind them, they were in big trouble. That made the requisite order easy, no matter how distasteful it was.

'Retreat,' Jäger said on the all-panzers circuit. 'We'll fall back to the first line of defenses around Breslau.'

Three belts of fortifications ringed the city on the Oder. If they were penetrated, Breslau itself could hold for a long time, perhaps even in the way Chicago was holding in the United States. Though Jäger had distant relatives on the other side of the Atlantic, nothing he'd seen in the First World War or heard in this one till the Lizards came left him thinking much of Americans as soldiers. Chicago made him wonder if he'd been wrong.

But Chicago was far away. Breslau was close, and getting closer all the time as the driver retreated westward. The town had lots of bridges. If you managed to blow them all, Jäger thought, the Lizards would have a rough time crossing the Oder. When that occurred to him, he realized he didn't really believe the *Wehrmacht* could make a stand at Breslau. But if they couldn't hold the Lizards there, where could they?

'So you see, General Groves—' Jens Larssen began.

Before he could go on, Groves was glaring at him again, like a fat old bulldog getting ready to growl at a stranger across the street, 'What I see, Professor, is somebody who won't listen when I tell him to,' he said. 'We aren't packing up and moving to Hanford, and that's all there is to it. I'm sick of your whining. Soldier, shut up and soldier. Do you understand me?'

'Oh, I understand you, all right—' Larssen clamped his jaw down hard on the scarlet rage that welled up in his mind. *You goddamn pigheaded son of a bitch.* He got more creative from there. He'd never seen an atomic bomb go off, but the explosion inside his head felt like one.

'They aren't paying you to love me,' Groves said. 'They're paying you to do what I tell you. Get on back to work.' The boss of the Metallurgical Laboratory crew held up a hand. 'No, take the rest of the day off. Go back to your quarters and think it over. Come tomorrow morning, I expect you to throw everything you have into this project. You got it?'

'I've got it,' Jens said through clenched teeth.

He left the office and went downstairs. He'd leaned the Springfield he always carried against the wall down there. Now he slung it back over his shoulder. Oscar the guard said, 'You don't really need to tote that thing, sir. Not like you're in the Army.' His companion, a jug-eared yahoo named Pete, laughed. His big, pointy Adam's apple bobbed up and down.

Jens didn't answer. He went out to the row of parked bicycles, lifted the kickstand to his with the side of his shoe, and started to head off north on the road back to Lowry Field, as Groves had ordered.

Oscar's voice pursued him: 'Where are you going, Sir? The piles are that way.' He pointed down toward the athletic field.

The piles are on your miserable, snooping ass. With no tone at all in his voice, Larssen said, 'General Groves wants me to take the day off and think about things in my quarters, so I'm not going back to the piles.'

'Oh. Okay.' But instead of letting it go at that, Oscar spoke quietly to Pete for a moment, then said. 'I guess I'll come with you then, sir, make sure you get there all right.'

Make sure you do what you're told. Oscar didn't trust him. Nobody here trusted him. Between the Met Lab and Colonel Hexham, they'd all got together to screw up his life eight ways from Sunday, and now they didn't trust him. Wasn't that a hell of a thing? 'Do whatever you damn well please,' Larssen said, and started pedaling.

Sure as shit, Oscar climbed aboard his own bicycle and rolled after him. Up University Boulevard to Alameda, then east on Alameda to the air base and the delightful confines of BOQ. Jens didn't think much of the place as somewhere to do any serious contemplating, but he'd take the day off and see what sprang from it. Maybe he'd be able to look at things differently afterwards.

The day was cold but clear. Jens's long winter shadow raced along beside him, undulating over snowdrifts by the side of the road. Oscar's lumpier shadow stayed right with it, just as Oscar clung to Jens like a leech.

For a long while, they had the road to themselves. Oscar knew better than to try any casual conversation. Larssen despised him quite enough when he was keeping his mouth shut.

About halfway between the turn onto Alameda and the entrance to Lowry Field, they met another bicycle rider coming west. The fellow wasn't making any great speed, just tooling along as if out for a constitutional. Jens's jaw tightened when he recognized Colonel Hexham.

Hexham, unfortunately, recognized him, too. 'You – Larssen – halt!' he called, stopping himself. 'What are you doing away from your assigned post?'

Jens thought about ignoring the officious bastard, but figured Oscar wouldn't let him get away with it. He stopped maybe ten feet in front of Hexham. Oscar positioned himself between the two of them. Oscar was a bastard, but not a dumb bastard. He knew how Jens felt about Colonel Hexham.

'What are you doing away from your post?' Hexham repeated. His voice had a yapping quality, as if he were part lapdog. His face, as always, was set in disapproving lines. He had pouchy, suspicious eyes and a shriveled prune of a mouth with a thin smudge of black mustache above it. His hair was shiny and slick with Wildroot or some other kind of grease; he must have had his own private hoard of the stuff.

Jens said, 'General Groves ordered me to take a day off, go back to my quarters and just relax for a bit, then get back to it with a new attitude.' *Fat chance, if I have to deal with a slug like you.*

'Is that so?' By the mockery Hexham packed into the question, he didn't believe a word of it. He wasn't any fonder of Jens than Jens was of him. Turning to Oscar, he said, 'Sergeant, is what this man tells me true?'

'Sir, it's exactly the same thing he told me,' Oscar replied.

Hexham clapped a dramatic hand to his forehead, a gesture he must have stolen from a bad movie. 'My God! And you didn't check it with General Groves yourself?'

'Uh, no, sir.' Oscar's voice suddenly went toneless. He might have been trying to deny he was there while standing in plain sight, a trick Larssen had seen enlisted men use before.

'We'll get to the bottom of this,' Colonel Hexham snapped. 'We'll all go back to the University of Denver and find out just precisely what – if anything – General Groves told Professor Larssen to do. Come on!' He made as if to start riding again.

'Uh, sir—' Oscar began, and then shut up. A sergeant had no way to tell a colonel he was being a damn fool.

'Come on!' Hexham growled again, this time staring straight at Jens. 'We'll get to the bottom of this malingering, damn me to hell if we don't. Get moving!'

Jens got moving. At first he seemed to be watching himself from outside. He slung the Springfield, flipping off the safety as he did so. He always carried a round in the chamber. But as the rifle came up to his shoulder, he was back inside his own head, calculating as abstractly as if he were working on a problem of atomic decay.

Tactics ... Oscar was the more dangerous foe – not only was he closer to Jens, he was a real fighting man, not a pouter pigeon in a uniform. Jens shot him in the face. Oscar never knew what hit him. He flew off the bike saddle, the back of his head exploding in red ruin.

Jens worked the bolt. The expended cartridge jingled cheerily when it hit the asphalt. Colonel Hexham's eyes and mouth were open as wide as they could be. 'Good-bye, Colonel,' Jens said sweetly, and shot him in the head, too.

The clank of the second cartridge on the roadway brought Jens back to himself. He felt exalted, as if he'd just got laid. He even had a hard-on. But two bodies sprawled in spreading pools of blood would take some explaining he couldn't give, no matter how much both the stinking bastards had it coming.

'Can't go back to BOQ, not now, nosiree,' Jens said. He often talked to himself when he was alone on the road, and he sure as hell was alone now. He'd made certain – dead certain – of that.

Couldn't go to BOQ. Couldn't go back to the pile, either. Okay, what did that leave? For a second, he didn't think it left anything. But that was just a last bit of reluctance to face what had been in the back of his mind for a long time. Humanity didn't have any use for him any more. People had been rubbing his nose in that ever since Barbara let him know she'd been spreading her legs for the lousy ballplayer she'd found. They didn't need him in Denver. They wouldn't listen to his plans, they'd gone ahead and built a bomb – built a couple of bombs – without him.

Well, to hell with humanity, then. The Lizards would care to hear what he had to tell them. Yes, sir, they sure would (dim memories of Thornton Burgess stories floated up in his mind from childhood). They'd know how to reward him properly for telling them, too. But he wouldn't be doing it for the reward. Oh, no. Getting his own back was a lot more important.

He carefully put the safety back on, slung the Springfield over his shoulder, and headed east. The sentries at the entrance of Lowry Field just nodded to him as he rolled past. They hadn't heard the rifle shots. He'd worried a little about that.

A map unrolled in his mind. They'd find the bodies. They'd chase him. If they understood he was heading east toward the LIzards, they'd probably figure he'd go east on US 36. That was the straight route, the route a crazy man who wasn't hitting on all cylinders would take.

But he wasn't crazy, not even slightly. Not him. He had US 6 and US 34 north of US 36, and US 24 and US 40 south of it, plus all the little back roads between the highways. Before long, he'd pick one. Somewhere not far from the Colorado-Kansas border, he'd find the Lizards. He bent his back and pedaled harder. It was all downhill from here.

'Yes, sir,' Mutt Daniels said. The way he said it told what he thought of the order. Cautiously, he added, 'We been doin' a lot of retreating lately, ain't we, sir?'

'So we have,' Captain Szymanski also looked sour about it. Seeing that, Mutt pushed a little harder: 'Seems like we ain't needed to do most of it, neither, not from the way the fightin' went beforehand. And this latest, this here, is just a skedaddle, nothin' else but. Sir.'

His company commander shrugged, as if to say he couldn't do anything about it no matter what he thought. 'Major Renfree and I have been screaming to the colonel, and he's been screaming to the high command. There's nothing he can do to get the orders changed. From what he says, they came right from the top, from General Marshall himself. You want to call up FDR, Lieutenant?'

'It would take somethin' like that, wouldn't it.' Daniels sighed. 'Okay, sir, I don't know what the hell's going on. I'll just shut my damnfool mouth and do like I'm told. Anybody'd think I was in the Army or some damn thing like that.'

Szymanski laughed. 'I'm glad you are in the Army, Mutt. You keep everybody around you all nice and loosey-goosey.'

'*I'm* not glad I'm in the Army, meanin' no offense to you, sir,' Mutt said. 'I done my bit in the last war. Only reason they need old farts like me is on account of the Lizards. Wasn't for them bastards, I'd be lookin' ahead to spring training, not tryin' to figure out how to pull my men back without lookin' too much like I'm doin' it.'

'We've got to do it,' Captain Szymanski answered. 'I don't know why, but we do. And if that's not the Army for you, what the devil is?'

'Yes, sir.' If Mutt laid down the bunt sign, the fellow at the plate had to try and bunt, whether he liked Mutt's strategy or not. Now it was his turn to do something he really hated because the higher-ups thought it was a smart move. *They better be right*, he thought as he climbed to his feet.

Sergeant Muldoon looked anything but happy when he brought the news from on high. 'Jeez, Lieutenant, they're sandbaggin' so hard, they could build a wall around these damn Lizards with all the sand,' he said. 'We should be kickin' their ass instead o' letting them push us around.'

'You know, I know it, the captain knows it, the colonel knows it, but General Marshall, he don't know it, and he counts for more'n the rest of us put together,' Daniels answered. 'I just wish I was sure he had some kind of notion of what he was up to, that's all. What's that they say about "Ours is not to wonder why?"'

'The other part of it goes something like, "Ours is to let the bastards kill us even when they don't have a clue,"' Herman Muldoon said. He was cynical enough to make a sergeant, all right. And, like any decent sergeant, he knew fighting city hall didn't pay. 'Okay, Lieutenant, how we gonna make this work?'

Mutt let stories from his grandfathers give him the clues he needed to do the job right. He thinned his main line down to what either granddad would have called a line of skirmishers, then to nothing but pickets. To disguise that as best he could, he made sure the pickets had automatic weapons and both the bazooka launchers in the platoon.

To try to hold back Lizard armor, the brass also had a lot of tanks and antitank guns well forward. Mutt didn't quite follow that: it was as if they wanted the Lizards to go forward, all right, but not too far or too fast. He hoped the big picture made sense, because the little one sure as hell didn't.

His men had the same feeling. Retreat was hard on an army; you felt as if you were beaten, regardless of whether you really were. The troops didn't look ready to bug out, but they didn't act like men with their peckers up, either. If they had to fight and hold ground, he wasn't sure they could do it.

Not that much of Chicago looked like ground worth holding, anyhow. As far as that went, one stretch of rubble was pretty much like another. Even tanks had a rough time making their way through piles of brick and stone and craters big enough to swallow them whole.

He was taken by surprise when he came upon one stretch of halfway decent road as his unit trudged north. 'You can go that way if you want to,' an MP doing traffic control said, 'but it makes you easier for the Lizards to spot from the air.'

'Then what the hell did anybody build it for?' Mutt asked. The MP didn't answer. Odds were, the MP couldn't answer because he didn't know. Maybe nobody knew. Maybe the Army had cleared the road just so people walking along it could get killed in carload lots. Mutt was past the stage where anything had to make sense.

Not far from the southern end of the road, he watched a team of soldiers busily repairing a house. They weren't repairing it to look like new, they were repairing it to look like the wreckage all around it. It looked as if they'd knocked down the whole side nearest the road. Inside was a wooden crate big enough to make a pretty good Hooverville shack. In a little while, though, you wouldn't be able to see it because the soldiers would have restored the wall they'd knocked down. By the time they were done, the place would look as ugly as it had before they started.

'Ain't that a hell of a thing?' Muldoon jerked his thumb at the soldiers. 'Are we fighting the Lizards or are we building houses for 'em?'

'Don't ask me,' Daniels answered. 'I gave up a long time ago, tryin' to figure out what's goin' on.'

'They ain't gonna stay there and try and hold on to that box, are they?' Muldoon asked. The question wasn't aimed particularly at Mutt, who didn't have any answers, but at whoever in the world might know. Muldoon spat in the mud. 'Sometimes I think everybody's gone crazy but me, you know?' He gave Daniels a sidelong look. 'Me and maybe you, too, Lieutenant. It ain't like it's your fault.' From Muldoon, that was a compliment, and Mutt knew it.

He thought about what the sergeant had said. He also thought about the way the brass was running the fight here in Chicago. If they'd just kept at what they were doing, they could have pushed the Lizards back to the South Side, maybe even out of Chicago altogether. Oh, yeah, it would have cost, but Mutt had been through the trenches in the First World War. He knew you had to pay the price if you wanted to gain ground.

But instead, they were pulling back. Mutt turned to Muldoon. 'You're right. They must be crazy. It's the only thing that makes any sense a-tall.' Solemnly, Muldoon nodded.

Heinrich Jäger slammed his fist down on the cupola as his Panther rumbled out of Öels, heading west toward Breslau. He was wearing gloves. Otherwise his skin would have peeled off when it hit the frozen metal of the panzer. He wasn't crazy – no, not he. About his superiors, he had considerable doubts.

So did Gunther Grillparzer. The gunner said, 'Sir, what the devil's the point of pulling out of Öels now, after we've spent the last three days fighting over it as if it were Breslau itself?'

'If I knew, I would tell you, either.' Jäger answered. 'It doesn't make any sense to me, either.' Not only had the *Wehrmacht* done a good job for fortifying Öels as part of the outer ring of Breslau's defensive system, the fourteenth-century castle up on the hill made a first-class artillery observation post. And now they were abandoning the town, the castle (or what was left of it), and the works the engineers had made, just letting the Lizards take them while the panzers pulled back closer to Breslau.

Artillery shells whistled overhead, plowing up the frozen ground between the retreating panzers and Öels, as if to tell the Lizards, *Thus far and no farther.* Jäger wondered if the Lizards would listen. They were hitting hard in this latest onslaught, probably fighting better than they had since the days when they first came to Earth and swept everything before them.

His Panther had two narrow rings and one wide one painted on the cannon, just behind the muzzle brake: two armored personnel carriers and one panzer. The Lizards were still tactically sloppy; they didn't watch their flanks as well as they should, and they walked into ambushes even Russians would have seen. Half the time, though, they fought their way out of the ambushes, too, not because they were great soldiers but because their panzers and rockets broke the trap from the inside out. As always, they'd inflicted far more damage than they suffered.

Even now, Lizard artillery shells fell around the panzers as they withdrew. Jäger feared them almost as much as he feared the Lizards' panzers. They spat little mines all over the bloody place; if your panzer ran over one of those, it would blow a track right off, and maybe send you up in flames. Sure enough, his Panther passed two disabled Panzer IVs, their crews glumly trudging west on foot.

He gnawed on his lower lip. Öels was only about fifteen kilometers east of Breslau. The Lizards were already shelling the city that sprawled across the Oder. If they established artillery in Öels, they could pound Breslau to pieces, scattering about so many of their little mines that no one would dare walk the streets, let alone drive armored vehicles through them.

And yet, he'd been ordered to give up a position he could have held for a long time – ordered in terms so peremptory that he knew protest would have been useless. Stand-fast orders were what he'd come to expect, even when standing fast cost more lives than retreating would have. Now, when standing fast made sense, he had to give ground. If that wasn't insanity, what was it?

His discontent deepened when his panzer finally reached its new assigned position. The village just outside of Breslau that was the linchpin of the new German line might have held fifty people before the war. It was on flat ground and, as far as he could see, had no special reason for existing. Some rolls of barbed wire strung across the landscape and a few trenches for infantrymen didn't constitute a line of defense as far as he was concerned, no matter how imposing the wire and trenches might seem on a map in a warm room out of the range of the guns.

His driver thought the same thing. 'Sir, they made us pull back to *this?*' he said in incredulous dismay.

'Johannes, believe you be, I wouldn't have given you the order on my own,' Jäger answered.

Somebody had at least some small sense of how to defend a position. A soldier in white parka over black panzer coveralls directed the Panther to a barn with a doorway that pointed east: a good firing position if the Lizards broke out of Öels and stormed toward Breslau. A couple of hundred meters farther west lay a stone farmhouse behind which he could retreat after firing, and which would do for a second position. But if the Lizards broke out of Öels, nothing here, at least, was going to stop them from breaking into Breslau.

To give the artillery its due, it was trying to make sure the Lizards didn't break out of Öels. Just west of the town, the ground jerked and quivered and shook like a live thing. Every gun the Germans had around Breslau must have been pounding that stretch of terrain. Jäger hadn't seen such a bombardment since his days in the trenches in World War I.

He didn't see any shells falling *in* Öels, though. The *Wehrmacht* had conceded the town to the Lizards, and for the life of him he didn't understand why. They could consolidate there at their leisure for the next big push. They were taking advantage of everything the Germans gave them, too. Through field glasses, he watched panzers and lorries coming into Öels and gathering east of the town.

'What the hell's going on?' Gunther Grillparzer demanded, out and out anger in his voice. 'Why aren't we throwing gas into Öels? The wind's blowing in the right direction – straight out of the west. We've got a wonderful target there, and we're ignoring it. I've seen the high mucky-mucks do some really stupid things, but this takes the cake.'

Jäger should have pounded on that open profession of heresy, but he didn't. He couldn't. He felt the same way himself. He peered through the field glasses for another thirty seconds or so, then lowered them with a grunt of disgust. He'd risked his neck to throw nerve gas at the gas-mask factory in Albi. Why the devil wasn't the artillery heaving it toward the Lizards now?

'Tear me off a chunk of that bread, will you, Gunther?' he said. When the gunner handed him a piece of the brown loaf, he dug out a tinfoil tube of meat paste and squeezed a blob onto the bread. Just because your commanders belonged in an institution for the feebleminded was no reason to starve. Die, yes; starve, no.

He was looking down at the bread and meat when the gloomy interior of the barn suddenly filled with light as bright as – brighter than – day.

Johannes, the driver, let out a cry in his earphones: 'My eyes!'

Jäger looked up, just for an instant, then lowered his gaze once more. Like the sun, the fireball in what had been Öels was too brilliant to look at. The light that filled the barn went from white to yellow to orange to red, slowly fading as it did so. When Jäger looked up again, he saw a great fiery pillar ascending toward the heavens, coloring the clouds red as blood.

The ground shook under the treads of the Panther. A wind tore briefly at the barn doors, then subsided. Stuck inside the turret, Grillparzer demanded, 'What the fuck was that?'

'I don't know,' Jäger said, and then, a moment later, 'My God!' He knew what an explosive-metal bomb had done to Britain; he'd heard about what had happened to Washington and Tokyo and south of Moscow. But knowing what such a bomb could do and seeing the bomb do it – the difference between those two was like the difference between reading a love poem and losing your virginity.

'They really did it,' he breathed in amazement.

'Who really did what, sir?' the panzer gunner asked indignantly.

'The physicists at – oh, never mind where, Gunther,' Jäger answered; even in the midst of such awe as he'd not felt in church for years, he did not forget his worship of the great god security. 'The point is, we've just given the Lizards what they gave Berlin.'

The panzer crew shouted like men possessed. Jäger joined the exultation, but more quietly. That sense of awe still filled him. Some of the explosive metal was what he'd snatched, Prometheus-like, from the Lizards. It was seldom given to a colonel of panzers to feel he'd personally turned the course of history. Jäger had that feeling now. In an odd way, it seemed larger than he was.

He shook himself, bringing the real world back into focus. 'Johannes, how are your eyes?' he asked over the intercom.

'I'll be all right, sir, I think,' the driver answered. 'It was like the world's biggest flashbulb went off a centimeter in front of my nose. I still see a big ring of smeary color; but it's getting smaller and dimmer.'

'That's good,' Jäger said. 'Think of it like this: for the Lizards over there in Öels, it's as if the sun went off a centimeter in front of their snouts – and they'll never see anything again.'

More cheers rang out. Gunther Grillparzer said, 'You know what, sir? I have to apologize to the mucky-mucks. Never thought I'd live to see the day.'

'I tell you what, Corporal,' Jäger said: 'I won't tell them. That way they won't die of shock.' The gunner laughed loud and long. Jäger added, 'I thought they'd gone round the bend myself, and I'm not ashamed to say so. But it makes sense now: they let the Lizards concentrate on Öels, didn't shell the town itself, both to hold the Lizards there and to make sure the bomb didn't get hit by accident, and then—'

'Yes, sir,' Grillparzer agreed enthusiastically. 'And then!'

In color and shape, the cloud rising from the explosive-metal bomb put Jäger in mind of Caesar's amanita. It was more nearly the hue of apricot flesh than the rich, bright orange of the mushroom prized for its flavor since Roman days, but that was a detail. He wondered how many kilometers into the sky the cap of the mushroom rose.

'Well,' he said, half to himself, 'I think Breslau has held.'

Gunther Grillparzer heard him. *'Jawohl!'* the gunner said.

An alarm hissed insistently. Atvar thrashed and twisted in free fall, fighting to stay asleep. Before long, he knew the fight was lost. As consciousness returned, fear came with it. You didn't wake the fleetlord to report good news.

One of his eye turrets swiveled toward the communications screen. Sure enough, Pshing's faced stared out of it. The adjutant's mouth worked, but

o sound emerged. He looked extraordinarily ugly that way, or perhaps
Atvar was grumpy at being roused so suddenly.

'Activate two-way voice,' he told the computer in his rest chamber, and
hen addressed Pshing: 'Here I am. What's the commotion?'

'Exalted Fleetlord!' Pshing cried. 'The Big Uglies – the Deutsch Big
Uglies – set off a fission bomb as we were about to overrun their fortified
position at the town called Breslau. We had been concentrating males and
equipment in the forward area for the assault on their works immediately
outside the city, and suffered large losses in the blast.'

Atvar bared his teeth in a grimace of anguish a Tosevite who knew a
little about the Race might have taken for laughter. His plan for the attack
on Deutschland had allowed for the Deutsch Big Uglies' having better
weapons than the Race knew them to possess, but had not anticipated
their having atomic bombs.

Tensely, he asked, 'Is this a case like that of the SSSR, where they've
shaped a device from plutonium they stole from us?'

'Exalted Fleetlord, results of analysis are at present both preliminary
and ambiguous,' Pshing answered. 'First approximation is that some of
the fissile material was indeed taken from us, but that some may well
have been independently produced.'

Atvar grimaced again. If that report was accurate, it was what he'd
dreaded most. The SSSR had used the one bomb, apparently of plutonium
stolen from the Race, but had shown no signs of being able to produce its
own. That was bad, but could be lived with. If the Deutsche knew not
only how to exploit radioactives that fell into their hands but also how to
produce those radioactives, the war against the Big Uglies had just taken
a new and altogether revolting turn.

'What are your orders, Exalted Fleetlord?' Pshing asked. 'Shall we bomb
the Deutsch positions in Breslau, and avenge ourselves in that fashion?'

'Do you mean with your own nuclear weapons?' Atvar said. When
his adjutant made the affirmative gesture, he went on, 'No. What would
be the point of that? It would only create more nuclear zones for our
males to cross, and the fallout, given Tosev 3 weather patterns, would
adversely affect forces farther east. Unfortunately, we have not succeeded
in tracking down the area where the Deutsche are conducting their nuclear
experiments.'

'That is not surprising,' Pshing answered. 'They so contaminated a
stretch of their own territory when a pile went out of control that
the radioactivity in the area could mask a successful experiment on
their part.'

'Truth,' Atvar said bitterly. 'Even their incompetence may work in
their favor. And, after the lesson we taught the Nipponese, they
must know we respond severely to nuclear development efforts on
the part of Big Uglies. They will be shielding their program as well
as they can.'

'Surely you will not leave them unpunished merely because we canno locate their nuclear reactors,' Pshing exclaimed.

'Oh, by no means,' Atvar said. If he did nothing, the revolt Straha ha led against him would be merely a small annoyance, when compared t what the shiplords and officers would do to him now. Unless he wante Kirel holding his position, he had to respond. 'Have the targeting specialis select a Deutsch city within the zone of radioactive contamination. We sha remind the Big Uglies we are not to be trifled with. Report the targeting choice to me as soon as it is made – and it had best be made soon.'

'It shall be done.' Pshing's face vanished from the screen.

Atvar tried to go back to sleep. That would have been the perfect way to show his latest setback did not unduly concern him. The setback *did* concern him, though, and sleep proved as elusive as victory over the Big Uglies. *So much for enhancing my reputation among the males*, he thought He laughed in self-mockery. By the time this war was done, if it ever was he'd be lucky to have any reputation left.

The communicator screen lit up again. 'The largest Deutsch city within the contaminated zone is the one they call München, Exalted Fleetlord,' Pshing reported. A map showed Atvar where in Deutschland München lay. 'It is also a major manufacturing center and transport hub.'

Atvar studied the railroad and highway networks surrounding the city. 'Very well,' he said, 'let München be destroyed, and let it be a lesson to the Deutsche and to all the Big Uglies of Tosev 3.'

'It shall be done,' Pshing said.

The *goyim* had a legend of the Wandering Jew. With a knapsack on his back and a German rifle slung over his shoulder, Mordechai Anielewicz felt he'd done enough wandering to live up to the legend.

There weren't as many woods and forests around Lodz as there were farther east: fewer places for partisan bands to take refuge against the wrath of the Lizards. He hadn't been able to find a band to join, not yet. Lizards had rolled past him a few times in their armored vehicles. They'd paid him no special heed. Armed men were common on Polish roads, and some of them fought for, not against, the aliens. Besides, the Lizards were heading west, toward the battle with the Nazis.

Even from many kilometers away, Anielewicz had listened to the sullen mutter of artillery. The sound hung in the air, like distant thunder on a summer's day. He tried to gauge the progress of the battle by whether the rumble grew louder or softer, but knew he was just guessing. Atmospherics had as much to do with how the artillery duel sounded as did advances and retreats.

He was walking toward a farmhouse in the hope of working for his supper when the western horizon lit up. Had the sun poked through the clouds that blanketed the sky? No – the glow seemed to be coming from *in front* of the clouds.

He stared in awe at the great, glowing mushroom cloud that rose into the sky. Like Heinrich Jäger, he quickly realized what it had to be. Unlike Jäger, he did not know which side had touched it off. If it was Germans, he, too, knew he played a role, and no small one in their getting at least some of the explosive metal they'd needed.

'If it *is* the Nazis, do I get credit for that, or blame?' he asked aloud. Again unlike Jäger, he found no sure answer.

Teerts checked the radar in his head-up display. No sign of Deutsch aircraft anywhere nearby. The thought had hardly crossed his mind before Sserep, one of his wingmales, said, 'It's going to be easy today, superior sir.'

'That's what Nivvek thought, and look what happened to him,' Teerts answered. The Race hadn't been able to rescue the other male before the Deutsche captured him. From some reports, the Deutsche treated prisoners better than the Nipponese did. For Nivvek's sake, Teerts hoped those reports were true. He still had nightmares about his own captivity.

He suspected more nightmares were heading his way. He wished – how he wished! – Elifrim had chosen a different male to lead the protection for the punishment killercraft now flying toward München. Had the Deutsche known the load that killercraft carried, they would have sent up everything that would fly in an effort to knock it down. They'd used an atomic bomb against the Race, and they were going to be reminded they could not do that without paying the price.

Tokyo had already paid that price, thanks to Teerts, and the Nipponese hadn't even had nuclear weapons – they were just trying to acquire them. They were only Big Uglies, but Teerts felt guilty anyhow. And now he was going to have to watch a Tosevite city go up in atomic flame.

The pilot of the punishment killercraft, a male named Jisrin, had no such qualms. Mechanical as if he were a computer himself, he said, 'Target is visually obscured. I shall carry out the bombing run by radar.'

'Acknowledged,' Teerts said. He spoke to Sserep and his other wingmale, a relatively inexperienced flier named Hossad: 'We'll want to swing wide of the punishment killercraft after it releases its bomb. From everything I've heard and reviewed in the training scenarios, blast effects and winds can do dreadful things to aircraft handling if we're too close to the site of the explosion. You'll follow my lead.'

'It shall be done,' Sserep and Hossad said together.

In his flight-leader's circuit, Teerts listened to his opposite number on the other side of the punishment killercraft, giving his wingmales almost identical instructions. Then Jisrin said, 'I am releasing the weapon on the mark ... Mark. Ignition will delay until proper altimeter reading. Meanwhile, I suggest we depart.' He hit his afterburner and streaked away from the doomed city.

Teerts swung his killercraft through a wide turn that would bring him back on course for the air base in southern France. His wingmales followed.

Up till now, everything had run as smoothly as if it were a training mission. That relieved him – such things didn't happen very often on Tosev 3 – and alarmed him, too: what would go wrong now?

Nothing. Not this time. A great ball of fire burned through the clouds below and behind him, flinging them aside, scattering them, vaporizing them. The glare was terrifying, overwhelming; Teerts's nictitating membranes flicked across his eyes to protect them, as if the piercing light were a grain of sand or grit that could be physically pushed aside.

Moments later, the blast wave caught up with the fleeing killercraft and flicked it through the air. It was stronger and sharper than Teerts had expected. The airframe groaned under the sudden strain, but held. Together, Teerts and the killercraft's computer rewon control.

'By the Emperor,' Hossad said softly as he, too, mastered his killercraft. 'We take for granted what the atom can do. It gives us electric power, it electrolyzes hydrogen and oxygen for our vehicles, it powers our ships between the stars. But when you let it loose—' He didn't go on. He didn't need to go on. Teerts wished he had a taste of ginger.

Jisrin, still matter-of-fact, put the capper on the mission: 'The target is destroyed. Returning to base.'

Atvar listened to the bestial howls of rage that came over the crackling shortwave frequencies from Deutschland. One thing the atomic bomb that had smote München had not done: it had not got rid of Hitler, the non-emperor of Deutsche. Even without understanding a single word of the Deutsch language, Atvar also gathered that it had not persuaded Hitler to yield.

He turned away form the incomprehensible rantings of the Deutsch not-emperor to a translation: 'We shall have vengeance!' Hitler was saying; the translator added an emphatic cough to show the stress the Big Ugly put on the words. 'Our strength lies not in defense but in attack. Mankind has grown strong in eternal struggles. We shall once more make the heroic decision to resist. Our idea – our people – is right, and so is invincible; every persecution will lead to our inner strengthening. This war is one of the elemental conflicts which will usher in a new world era. At its end, Deutschland will either be a world power or will not be at all! If the Deutsch people despair now, they will deserve no better than they get. If they despair, I will not be sorry for them if God lets them down.'

The translator added, 'Speaking in my own voice for a moment, I should note that all of these not particularly rational utterances are accompanied by vehement and prolonged applause from the Big Uglies in the audience. Rational or not, Hitler has a strong hold on the Tosevites of his not-empire.'

When he resumed, the febrile tone he assumed showed he was once more passing on Hitler's words: 'We shall have vengeance, I say again! For every bomb the Lizards use against us, we shall use six, eight, ten, a hundred bombs against them. We shall destroy them so completely, it shall be as if they never were. They have dared test themselves against the master race, and they shall fail!' The translator added another emphatic cough, then said, 'This preposterous and vain pronouncement was greeted with more applause.'

Atvar turned off the Tosevite's speech. 'Well, what do you think of that?' he asked Kirel.

'Destroying München has failed to intimidate the Deutsche, ' Kirel answered. 'I find this most unfortunate.'

'Unfortunate, yes,' Atvar said, with an emphatic cough of his own. Kirel's restrained pattern of speech could sometimes be most effective. Atvar went on, 'What do you make of this Hitler's threat, to respond bomb against bomb?'

'My opinion, Exalted Fleetlord, is that he will do so if he has the ability,' Kirel said. 'And, since analysis confirms that this latest bomb was made partly from nuclear material not stolen from us ...' His voice trailed away.

'—He either does have the ability or will have it soon,' Atvar finished unhappily. 'That is my conclusion also. My other conclusion is that this war has just grown a great deal worse. Spirits of departed Emperors willing, I shall not have to say that so often in future.'

Mutt Daniels opened his canteen, poured from it into his cup. The liquid that went from one to the other was a deep amber color. He lifted the cup in salute before he drank. 'Mud in your eye, Miss Willard,' he said, and gulped the whiskey down.

'Ain't this a hell of a thing, Lieutenant,' said Sergeant Muldoon, who had his own canteen full of whiskey. 'Havin' a drink in the Frances E. Willard Home, I mean.' He drank, too. 'All the little old ladies from the WCTU must be spinning in their graves, I figure.'

'I seen plenty o' the Women's Christian Temperance Union down home in Mississippi when I was growing up,' Mutt answered. 'I figured anything those sour old prunes were against had to be good enough for me to want to be for it. And you know what? Put it all together, I reckon I was right.'

'Damn straight you were,' Muldoon said, taking another drink.

'But that ain't why I chose this here house for us,' Daniels said.

Herman Muldoon laughed. 'I know why you chose it: it's standing up.'

'You ain't just joking.' Even here in Evanston, north of the Chicago city line, devastation was heavy. The Northwestern University campus had been pounded hard. The water filtration plant close by was just a ruin. Maybe it was the whiskey – though he'd had only the one swig – and maybe just frustration boiling up in him, but he burst out, 'God damn it to hell, we don't need to be in Evanston. We should be takin' the fight to the Lizards down in Chicago.'

'Tell me somethin' I don't know, Lieutenant,' Muldoon said. 'But as long as we're here, we got ourselves a nice fire goin', an' we can get snug as a couple of bugs in a rug.'

The fireplace in the sitting room of the Willard House still worked fine, and there was anything but a shortage of wood to feed it. A plaque on the wall of the room said it was dedicated to Miss Anna Gordon, Frances Willard's lifelong companion and a world president of the WCTU in her own right. Mutt wondered exactly what *lifelong companion* meant. Lucille Potter, who was dead now, had shown him that even if it meant what he suspected it did, it wasn't necessarily as shocking and sinful as he'd been brought up to believe.

'You know what?' he said, almost plaintively, to Muldoon. 'You get stuck in a war, you don't just set your body on the line. Everything you knew or thought you knew goes up into the front lines with you, and some of it ends up dead even if you don't.'

'That's over my head, Lieutenant,' Muldoon said. 'I'm a dumb noncom, nothin' else but. I leave the thinking to officers like you.' He laughed to show Mutt wasn't supposed to take him all that seriously. 'What I think is, sounds like you could use another drink.'

'I'd like to, don't you doubt it for a minute,' Daniels answered. 'But if I'm gonna keep track of this platoon full of wild men, I can't afford to get me lit up.'

Later, he wondered if God had been listening to him. A brilliant yellow-white light blazed through the south-facing window of the sitting room, printing his shadow against the far wall, the one with the plaque on it. It reminded him of the way a flashbulb could do the same thing. But a flashbulb was there and then it was gone, while this light was not only brighter than any flashbulb but went on for several seconds, though it got fainter and redder as time went on.

The ground jerked under Daniels's feet. As he exclaimed in surprise and alarm, he heard a report that reminded him of a big artillery piece being fired maybe a hundred yards away. The few shards of glass that remained in the sitting-room window blew out. By luck, none of them pierced him or Muldoon. 'What the *hell* was that?' the sergeant burst out. 'Biggest darn boom I've ever been through, and I've been through some doozies. Somebody's ammunition dump going up, maybe. Hope to Jesus it was theirs and not ours.'

'Yeah.' Mutt went to the window to see what he could see. Muldoon joined him a moment later. For perhaps half a minute, they stared south together. Then, very softly and not in the least irreverently, Mutt whispered, 'Goddamn.' Muldoon's head bobbed up and down. He seemed to have lost the power of speech.

Mutt had seen plenty of explosions and their aftermaths. He'd seen an ammunition dump go up, too, maybe from a lucky hit, maybe because

omebody got careless – not enough was left afterwards for anyone to
e sure. But he'd never seen anything like this.

He had no idea how high into the night the glowing cloud mounted.
Miles, that was all he could be sure of. Other thing was, the base of that
loud looked a lot farther away than he'd figured it would – which meant
he explosion was even bigger than he'd guessed.

'Goodgodalmightydamnwillyoulookitthat!' Muldoon said, as if words
ad just been invented and nobody quite knew yet where they stopped
nd started. Mutt had the feeling that words to describe what he was
eeing hadn't been invented yet, and maybe never would be.

What *was* he seeing, anyhow? Pursuing his earlier thought, he said,
That ain't no ammo dump. You could blow up all the ammo in the world,
nd it wouldn't make a cloud like that there one.'

'Yeah,' Muldoon agreed, almost with a sigh. 'Whatever it is, it came
own on the Lizards' heads, not ours. Look where it's at, Lieutenant –
hat's the part of Shytown we retreated out of.'

'Yeah, you're right,' Mutt said. 'Maybe we was lucky to get out of there
vhen we did. Or maybe—' He stopped, his eyes going wide. 'Or maybe,
n' I hate like hell to say it, the brass ain't so dumb after all.'

'What the hell you talkin' about, uh, sir?' Muldoon said. Then he got a
araway look on his face, too. 'Jesus, Mary, and Joseph, Lieutenant, you
hink we pulled back on purpose so those scaly bastards could walk right
nto that big boom like they was moths divin' into a fire?'

'Don't know if it's so, but it stands to reason,' Daniels answered. 'The
Russians, they figured out last year how to make one of them big bombs
he Lizards use, and the Nazis, they fired one off last week, I hear, less'n
he radio's tellin' more lies'n usual.'

'Fat lot of good it did 'em, too,' Muldoon retorted. 'The Lizards went
nd blew one of their cities to hell and gone right afterwards.'

Mutt refused to let that distract him. 'If the Reds can do it and the
goddamn Nazis can do it, though, why the hell can't we? You think we
lon't got a bunch o' guys with thick glasses and what d'you call 'ems
– slide rules, that's it – tryin' to figure out how to make our own bombs?
You're crazy if you do. And you ain't never seen an explosion like that,
nd neither have I, so what do you think it's liable to be?'

'That makes sense, sounds like,' Muldoon said reluctantly. Then he
rightened. 'Jeez, if that's what it was, Lieutenant, a whole bunch o'
izards and all their gear just went up in smoke.'

'Reckon that was the idea.' Daniels thought back to the crew who'd
een hiding the big crate in what looked like more rubble. Had they been
etting the bomb there so it would be waiting for the Lizards when they
dvanced in pursuit of the withdrawing Americans? He didn't know for
ure; no way he ever would, but he couldn't think of any better reason
or wanting to conceal a crate. He laughed. You'd have a devil of a time
roving him wrong, that was for sure.

'Let's say it was one o' those bombs, Lieutenant, Muldoon persisted 'When the Germans used one, next thing you know the Lizards knocked on of their towns flat, like I said. They gonna do the same thing to us?'

Mutt hadn't thought about that. Now that he did, he found he didn' fancy any of the answers that popped into his head. 'Damnfino,' he sai at last. 'We'll just have to wait and find out, seems like to me. That'd b a damned ugly way to fight a war, wouldn't it? You blew up all o' m guys in this city over here, so I'll go and blow up all o' yours in that on over yonder.'

'Shit, that's what the krauts and the limeys were doin' to each othe when the Lizards got here,' Muldoon said. 'But doin' it with one boml to a city makes you start runnin' out o' cities pretty damn quick.'

'Lordy, don't it just,' Mutt said. 'Like two guys playin' Russian roulette 'cept they're pointin' the guns at each other an' five o' the chambers ar loaded. Maybe all six of 'em, you come to that.'

The cloud to the south of them was fading now, dispersing, the win sweeping it away toward Lake Michigan. Pretty soon it would be gone But the horrible dilemmas it raised would not disappear so soon.

Uneasily, Mutt looked north, east, west, and then last of all south onc more, toward and past the dissipating cloud. 'What you tryin' to d Lieutenant?' Muldoon asked. 'You tryin' to figure out where the Lizard are gonna drop the one they use to answer ours?'

Daniels scowled. He didn't like being that obvious. But he didn't wan to be a liar, either, not when he was talking about something as importan as this. He sighed. 'Yeah,' he said.

The alarm hissed hideously. When Atvar woke, for a moment he though he was dreaming about the last time the alarm had gone off. Then incontestably, his senses came to full alertness, and the alarm was stil yammering away. And there was Pshing's face in the communicato screen, just as it had been that dreadful, all-too-recent night.

'Activate two-way voice,' Atvar said to the computer, as he had then Whatever disaster his adjutant had to report, it couldn't be as hideous a news of the Deutsche with nuclear weapons. So the fleetlord told himself even as he was asking Pshing, 'What now?'

'Exalted Fleetlord—' Pshing began, and then had trouble going on Gathering himself, he finally managed to continue: 'Exalted Fleetlord, regret to have to inform you that the Tosevites of the not-empire of th United States detonated a fission bomb in the northern sector of the city known as Chicago. As our males had only just succeeded in occupying this sector, and as the front lay not far north, our concentrations in th area of the explosion, and thus our losses, appear to have been heavy.'

A predator in the warm, friendly deserts of Home dug a pit in the sand and hid at the bottom. When an animal stumbled into the pit, it woul scrabble at the loose sand, but generally slide down deeper and deeper ntil the trapmaker came out and devoured it with a minimum expenditure f effort. Atvar felt now like a creature trapped in one of those sand pits. o matter what he did on Tosev 3, things kept getting worse.

He gathered himself. 'Tell me the rest,' he said, as if knowing the rest uld somehow restore what the Race had lost.

Pshing clung to what had been normality with some of the same esperation Atvar felt. 'Exalted Fleetlord, the bomb appears to have een of the same type as that which the Deutsche employed against us: at is to say, some of the plutonium in it was stolen from us, while the ig Uglies produced the rest for themselves.'

'But the American Big Uglies are on the other side of an immense ocean om the Deutsche and the Russkis,' Atvar said, 'and we have made air assage between the continental masses rare, difficult, and dangerous for e Tosevites to attempt. To think they could have smuggled the explosive etal across in one of the few successful flights—' He checked himself. Wait. I am overlooking something.'

'Exalted Fleetlord?' By the tone of his interrogative cough, Pshing didn't ee what Atvar was missing.

'Water. It is the curse of this world whether liquid or frozen,' Atvar said. The Big Uglies have so much of it to deal with, they transport goods on it uch more readily than ever became the norm back on Home. We've not roperly dealt with their ships and boats because we've assumed them be of relatively small importance – and because we've had so many ther commitments on this miserable iceball of a world that seemed more rgent. We may now be paying the price for our inability to think as the ig Uglies do.'

Pshing made an eloquent gesture of distaste. 'If becoming like the ig Uglies is a condition for victory over them, I for one would almost ather lose.'

'A distinct point,' Atvar admitted. 'Were it only my own personal choice, should agree with you. But we have committed ourselves to bringing this orld and its noxious inhabitants under the rule of the Emperor.' He cast own his eyes. What would his sacred sovereign think when he learned f the difficulties the Race was having in annexing Tosev 3? First reports f combat were already on the way Home, but at laggard lightspeed would ave completed only about a sixth part of their journey.

'For the Emperor, I would brave anything,' Pshing said, seeming to ake fresh spirit. Sometimes Atvar thought loyalty and reverence to the mperor were all that kept his males performing as they should on a orld where the weather and the natives both seemed calculated to drive hem mad.

Atvar forced himself to think clearly, even if not like a Tosevite. 'The omposition of the bomb, like the one the Deutsche used, means the mericans will soon have more such weapons, of production entirely ative. For that matter,' he added, as if reminding himself, 'they may already have more such weapons, and be saving them for future strike against us.'

'Underestimating the capacity of the Big Uglies has caused us grie and misfortune ever since we arrived here,' Pshing said.

'Truth,' Atvar answered wearily. 'Even when we build their advance in technology into our planning, as we did with the campaign against th Deutsche, we still underestimate them – and pay the price for it.' He le out a long, hissing sigh. 'Rouse the targeting specialists. Also rouse th shiplord Kirel and summon him to the operations chamber. We must pla our response to the American bomb.'

'It shall be done, Exalted Fleetlord,'

When Kirel reached the operations chamber, Atvar couldn't decide if h looked sleepy or stunned. A bit of both, perhaps. 'Another nuclear weapon your adjutant tells me,' the shiplord said. 'From the Americans this time Did I hear that correctly?'

'You did,' Atvar said. 'As at Breslau, our progress at Chicago has bee halted, and the spearhead of our forces destroyed.' He hissed again, thi time thoughtfully. 'In both instances, we were led to impale ourselves o the bomb by unforced or lightly forced retreats on the part of the Bi Uglies. In future, we shall be more wary.'

'A worthy plan, Exalted Fleetlord,' Kirel said, 'but the very recen past has been extremely damaging to us. Have we any notion wher the Americans prepared their fission bomb?'

'I wish we did,' Atvar said. 'That site would no longer exist. Th Americans cannot hide their program in an already radioactive area, a the Deutsche seem to be doing. They are simply careful about allowin leaks to pinpoint their atomic piles and reprocessing plants.'

'That is a problem,' Kirel said – a good-sized understatement. 'If the destroy fighting males with their bombs and we only civilians with ours do they not gain advantage from that?'

'Some, certainly, but we also destroy industrial sites, and were thi planet not industrialized, it would long since have been incorporate into the Empire,' Atvar answered. Kirel could not disagree with that Atvar went on, 'We also put pressure on the Tosevites' not-empires t accommodate themselves to us while they still have a significant civilia population.'

'None of the Tosevite empires and not-empires we have bombed ha yet chosen to accommodate itself to us,' Kirel remarked, but he let i go at that. He knew better, these days, than to criticize Atvar. After a moment, he called up the map of the United States and highlighted two cities the targeting specialists had chosen. Pointing to one, he said, 'Here is a centrally located target, Exalted Fleetlord, if you want one.'

Atvar read the name of the place. 'Denver? No, I don't want that one See how relatively close our males to the east of it are. The prevailing wind will sweep radioactive waste in among them.'

'Truth,' Kirel said. Very well, then. Your adjutant gave me to understand that you are concerned about the Big Uglies' traffic on the water. He brightened the light that showed the other town. 'This one is a waterside city, and we have no great numbers of males nearby.'

· 'Seattle?' Atvar considered. 'Yes, that is a good choice, for exactly the reasons you name. We shall bomb it. The Tosevites have begun this game – let us see if they have the liver to play it out to the end.'

19

Leslie Groves stared down at his hands. They were big and blunt and battered, the hands of a working engineer. He didn't bite his nails, though. He was proud of that. If he hadn't been so proud of it, he probably would have started.

He'd led the team that made the Fat Lady. The bomb had worked exactly as advertised, maybe better than advertised. A big chunk of the North Side of Chicago would never be the same – but a whole bunch of Lizards would never be the same, either, and that was the point of the exercise.

'So I should be on Easy Street, right?' he asked the walls. In the privacy of his office, he sometimes talked to himself. One of these days, he'd do it in public. 'So what?' he said, out loud again. People who didn't like him already thought he was crazy. He didn't care if he gave them more ammunition. He'd got the job done, crazy or not.

But he wasn't on Easy Street. All he knew about Jens Larssen was that he'd shot two people and then headed east. The sentries at Lowry had seen him ride by, but they hadn't stopped him. They hadn't known he'd shot anybody. They also hadn't known Groves had ordered hi back to his quarters in the BOQ to calm down.

Groves slammed a fist onto the desk, making papers and the In and Out trays jump. 'If I hadn't sent him back to Lowry, would he still be all right now?' he asked. 'The walls didn't give him any answers.

He wished Larssen hadn't gone east. East was where the Lizards lived. You wouldn't think anybody would go running off to the Lizards, but you wouldn't think anybody would gun down a colonel and a noncom in cold blood, either. Once you'd done the shooting, taking refuge with the Lizards looked a lot more likely than it had before.

They hadn't managed to catch the son of a bitch, either. One thing Larssen had proved, traveling cross-country from White Sulphur Springs to Chicago and then from Denver to Hanford and back again: he knew how to live off the land. You couldn't count on him freezing to death in a Colorado winter or doing something dumb to give himself away. If he was heading toward the Lizards, he might well get to them.

'Next question,' Groves said in his orderly fashion: 'What will he do if he does get to them? Will he spill his guts?'

By all the signs, Larssen hated the Met Lab and anybody who had anything to do with it. Sure, he'd blamed Hexham for the breakup with his wife, but that had sprung from the secrecy surrounding the project, too. So, the sixty-four dollar question was, if he got to the Lizards, would he blab about what was going on in Denver? If he did, the town would become radioactive gas and dust in short order. No less than the Americans, the Lizards were playing for keeps.

As if he needed more proof of that, he turned on the battery-powered radio he'd ordered into the office when news of the destruction of Seattle came over the wires. When the set warmed up, he caught an announcer in the middle of a word: '—several hundred thousand believed dead, as we've told you before. Newly released information from the Secret White House indicates that one of them was Vice President Henry Wallace, who was visiting war workers in the stricken city to improve their morale.'

Groves whistled softly and turned off the radio. That *was* news. The last time he'd seen FDR, a few months before, the President had looked like death warmed over. If he did drop dead, who was next in line now? The Speaker of the House, assuming he was still alive – Groves didn't know for sure. President Sam Rayburn? He thought about that. He'd always figured Wallace for a custardhead, so Rayburn might be an improvement. All the same, he hoped Roosevelt would die of old age at about a hundred and thirty-one.

He turned the radio back on. The newsman was still talking about the hideous things that had happened to Seattle. The same kind of things had happened to Berlin and Washington and Tokyo and Munich, and to the Lizards outside Moscow and Breslau and inside Chicago. After a while, hearing them repeated numbed the brain, not so they seemed unreal but so their horrors no longer struck the mind as quite so horrific. As with anything else, acquaintance made what had once been unimaginable take on the comforting cloak of familiarity.

Men had gone through four years of trench warfare in World War 1, and thought man's inhumanity to man could sink no lower. Then, just to prove they were wrong, they'd found ways to bomb noncombatants from the air. And now more than half a dozen atomic bombs had been used, with more liable to come. How soon would those dreadful clouds come to be taken for granted – by those who survived them?

'But if it's that or letting the Lizards conquer us?' Groves asked. Again, the walls were silent. He didn't need their answer, not to that question. The second bomb had already gone out of Denver. When the time came, people would use it, and a Lizard force would go up in fiery ruin. And then, very likely, an American city would join that force on the pyre. Would anything be left of the country when it was over?

What was that line doctors used? *The operation was a success, but the patient died.* If the Lizards finally gave up, but you presided over nothing but devastation afterwards, had you won? That had a flip side, though. If you didn't do everything you could to stop the Lizards and they ended up conquering you, what then? You couldn't plan revenge against them down the line, the way you could against an Earthly neighbor. If you lost now, it was forever.

'Maybe there'll be some pieces left to pick up after all this is done,' Groves said: 'Have to hope so, anyhow.'

Vyacheslav Molotov did not care for meetings that convened at two in the morning. Stalin was notorious for calling meetings at hours like that. Molotov concealed his distaste. The stony countenance he raised as a shield against rapacious capitalists and alien imperialist aggressors also helped protect him from his own superior.

Stalin seemed amiable enough at the moment, offering him vodka, a glass of tea (it was made from leaves flavored with blackberry extract, and pretty vile), cakes sweetened with honey, and cigarettes of course Russian tobacco. *The condemned man ate a hearty meal,* ran through Molotov's mind. Stalin could be most appalling just after he'd been most polite.

Now he drank and ate and blew smoke up toward the ceiling of the little Kremlin room he used as his own. At last, quite casually, he remarked, 'I have learned something interesting about the explosive-metal bombs the Germans and Americans used against the Lizards.'

'And what is that, Iosef Vissarionovich?' Molotov asked. 'That they were made with metal that damned German managed to smuggle back through Poland? A pity, I know, but we couldn't reasonably have expected him to survive.'

'Reasonably.' Stalin said it as if it were a swear word; his throaty Georgian accent the term sound even more menacing. But then he went on, 'No, we've known he got through for some time; nothing we can do about that now but make sure no similar mistakes happen in future.' Molotov wondered how many men had died or gone to the *gulag* expiating such mistakes. Stalin continued, 'No, this thing I have learned has nothing to do with that. It was obtained by our diligent wireless operators monitoring Lizard frequencies.'

'This is good,' Molotov said, nodding. 'We cannot place inconspicuous intelligence operatives among them, so we had better learn something by monitoring their communications.' He waited. Stalin did not go on. At last, he had to ask, 'What did the diligent wireless operators learn from the Lizards?'

In the space of a heartbeat, Stalin's face went from mild and serene to coldly furious. A film seemed to draw itself over his eyes, giving his gaze the menacing steadiness of a serpent's. Molotov had seen the transition many times; it never failed to alarm him. When the unwinking stare appeared on the General Secretary's countenance, dreadful things followed.

Hissing out the words, Stalin said, 'Vyacheslav Mikhailovich, they learned the bombs the Hitlerites and capitalists used were made partly from the explosive metal stolen from the Lizards and partly from that which they manufactured themselves.'

'This is not surprising,' Molotov said. 'Our physicists told us neither of the other parties with the explosive metal had enough for a bomb of his own - that is how we exploded ours first last summer.' He stopped in chagrin; for once, his mouth had outrun his brains. In an entirely different tone of voice, he said, 'Oh. I see the difficulty, Comrade General Secretary.'

'Do you?' Stalin's gaze was even more hooded than before. '*Khorosho. Ochen Khorosho.* I thought I should have to draw you an illustration. The Nazis have made this explosive metal for themselves. The Americans had made this explosive metal for themselves.' His voice grew soft and deadly. Why have we not made this explosive metal for ourselves?'

Molotov gulped. 'Iosef Vissarionovich, our physicists warned from the outset that this would be a slow project, requiring well over a year, not merely a time measured in months.' They'd spoken of two or three years or even more, but he hadn't dare tell Stalin that. 'We had so much to do to bring the Soviet Union to a point where it could hope to resist the onslaughts of the fascists and capitalists that in such matters as abstract research we lagged behind them. We have made great strides in catching up, but we cannot have everything at once.'

'But this is something the Soviet Union requires,' Stalin said, as if demanding explosive metal could make it spring into being on the table next to the cakes. 'If the incompetents now laboring to accomplish the task cannot succeed, we should uproot them and bring in others with great understanding of the subject.'

Molotov had been dreading that pronouncement since Igor Kurchatov told him they would for the time being have no more than one bomb. He saw nothing but disaster in dismantling the team Kurchatov had assembled: for all practical purposes, everyone in the Soviet Union who knew anything about nuclear physics was gathered at the carefully disguised farm outside Moscow. If that set of physicists was liquidated, only charlatans would be left to try to build an explosive-metal bomb. The Soviet Union could not afford that.

Cautiously, as if he were walking through a minefield, he said, 'They need more time to do what they said they would. Displacing them, I think, might have a disruptive effect on our progress.' Displacing them would wreck the project as effectively as if an explosive-metal bomb had gone off on that disguised farm, but he couldn't tell Stalin that. Disagreeing with the Soviet ruler, even indirectly, made his heart thud and sweat spring out on his high forehead.

Stalin looked petulant. 'They have shown themselves to be bunglers, and you want to give them more time to prove it?'

'They are not altogether bunglers, Comrade General Secretary,' Molotov answered, sweating harder. 'Had it not been for the bomb they did succeed in detonating, Moscow would now be overrun.' He wondered if they could have carried on the fight against the Lizards from Kuibishev. He might yet be faced with the prospect of finding out.

'That was one bomb,' Stalin said. 'We need more. The Hitlerites will have more, which means the *rodina* will be endangered even leaving the Lizards out of the account.'

'Hitler will not use the bombs against us while the Lizards lie between Germany and the Soviet Union,' Molotov said. 'We shall have our own by the time they are cleared from Poland.' He briefly contemplated the irony of a Georgian talking about the Russian motherland, but did not come close to having the nerve to remark on it.

Stalin said, 'The devil's uncle take Poland.' He used Russian expressions all right, sometimes with a sardonic twist that showed he knew how strange they could sound in his mouth, others, as now, as if he really felt himself to be a Russian. 'How, without more bombs, are we going to clear the Lizards from our own land?'

'Winter is our ally,' Molotov insisted. 'We have gained a good many kilometers south of Moscow, and our forces are also advancing in the Ukraine. And in the west and north, the Lizards have reduced the forces opposing us to concentrate on the Germans.'

'Which means only that they hold us in contempt,' Stalin snapped. 'The Nazis, they think, are more dangerous to them. But us? They can deal with us at any time. And why do they think this? Because the Nazis can make these bombs on their own and we, it seems, cannot. It all comes down to these bombs.'

Molotov thought about pointing out that the Lizards had reduced their forces in the north and west of Russia to attack Germany before they knew the Nazis had explosive-metal bombs, and that the one the Germans set off came as a complete and most unpleasant surprise to them.

He kept quiet, though. This once, it wasn't because he feared what would happen if he contradicted Stalin – although that would be bad. In the end, though, the General Secretary was right. It did all come down to those bombs. If the Soviet Union could make more, it might survive. If it couldn't, it would go under, if not to the Lizards, then to the Germans and Americans.

Kurchatov and his crew *could* make more bombs; Molotov was certain of that. He was just as certain nobody else in the Soviet Union could in any conceivably useful amount of time.

Stalin glared at Molotov, in lieu of glaring at the entire world. 'These bunglers you have gathered together, Vyacheslav Mikhailovich, have six months. If they have not made an explosive-metal bomb by then, they shall suffer the consequences – and so shall you.'

Molotov licked his lips. Stalin did not forget threats like that. Molotov took a deep breath. 'Comrade General Secretary, if that is how you feel, call the People's Commissariat of Internal Affairs and have them deal with me now. The Kurchatov group cannot make us a bomb within six months. No one else you can find will do better.'

He hated taking such a risk. Stalin might very well ring up the NKVD, in which case the Soviet Union would have a new foreign commissar in short order. But defusing Stalin now would also defuse the threat half a year away.

Stalin kept staring at him, now musingly. Molotov did not talk back to him; that was like a law of nature. Molotov went hot and cold at the same time; his legs felt like jelly. Facing Churchill, even facing Hitler, was one thing, facing Stalin quite another. He was in Stalin's power, and he knew it.

At last, the General Secretary said, 'Well, we shall see.' Molotov almost spilled out of his chair and onto the floor in relief – he'd won. He'd managed to talk the leader of his country into not destroying it – and, incidentally, into not destroying him. It shouldn't have been as hard as it was. Hard or easy, though, he'd survived. So had Kurchatov's team. The war would go on, and the Soviet Union, too.

Liu Han hated Peking winter. She was from hundreds and hundreds of *li* farther south; the cold months were bad enough there. Here, every time she went outdoors she was acutely reminded the Mongolian steppe lay just to the west. She piled on quilted garments till she looked like a perambulating pile of bedding, and she was still cold.

Nevertheless, tonight she was out on the streets, making her way on *hutungs* and broader avenues toward the Forbidden City, where the little scaly devils, like the Chinese Emperors before them, made their headquarters. Let the icy wind do with her as it would. Tonight, she wanted to be close to the little devils' center.

She turned to Nieh Ho-T'ing. 'I hope their Emperor has a happy birthday,' she said savagely.

'Yes.' His smile was more a predator's grimace than one of genuine mirth. 'They are the strangest creatures in all the world – the little devils, I mean. They celebrated their Emperor's birthday – they call it hatching day – six months ago, too, in summertime. How can a man, or even a scaly devil, have two birthdays each year?'

'They tried to explain this to me when I was on their plane that never came down,' Liu Han said. 'They were talking about different worlds and different years. I didn't understand much of it, I'm afraid.' She hung her head. Time in the plane that never came down, in the scaly devils' camp, and in the city had shown her how ignorant she was. If she'd stayed in her village the rest of her life, as most Chinese peasant women did, she never would have known.

Nieh said, 'Yes, they are from a different world. That is so. I had not thought on what it might mean for birthdays and such, to have a world with a different year from ours.'

Even knowing things, sometimes, was not enough. She'd seen that, too. You also had to know how the things you knew fit together. Knowing one thing here and one there wasn't worth much. If you could put them together, you had something.

'How much longer?' she asked him.

He took a watch from his pocket, looked at it, quickly replaced it. 'Fifteen minutes,' he said. If you openly showed you had a watch these days, you ran the risk of being mistaken for one of the little devil's rich running dogs, or, conversely, having the lackeys think you were a resistance leader who needed to know exactly what time it was so your raid would go as you'd planned. If you were, in fact, such a leader, you didn't want people to know it.

Fifteen minutes. Save for when she was in labor, Liu Han had never known time to pass so slowly. 'Will we be able to hear the songs we're listening for?' she asked, guarding her meaning in case any of the people milling around was a spy.

'Oh, yes,' Nieh assured her. 'I'm sure my friend from the Big Wine Vat will sing very loud and clear, and he is far from the only man in the chorus.' He lowered his voice, careful even though he was speaking in code. 'This song will be heard all over China tonight.'

Liu Han hugged herself, partly against the numbing cold and partly from excitement. If all went as she hoped, she would soon have the beginning of her revenge on the little scaly devils who had brought her to much grief. A boy ran past her with a bundle of strips of paper in one hand and a paste pot in the other. He found a blank stretch of wall, slapped paste onto it, and put up a couple of the strips. Then he ran to look for a spot where more might go.

'You had a clever idea there,' Liu Han said, nodding toward the ragamuffin. 'Picking boys who can't read makes it harder for the little scaly devils to trace those messages. All the boys know is that someone gave them money to put them up.

'Doctrine,' Nieh said. 'If you use someone for a purpose like that, the less he knows, the better.' He chuckled. 'Our singers are the same way. If they knew just what sort of songs we were asking them to perform, some of them might want to do something else instead.'

'Yes.' Liu Han thought about doctrine. Nieh often seemed to know what to do without having to consider first. The thing he called doctrine told him what he needed, almost as if it let him toss the coins for the *I Ching* inside his own head. That made it a valuable tool. But he also sometimes seemed unable to think outside the framework his doctrine gave him, as if it were not tool but master. The Communists in the scaly devils' prison camp had acted the same way. She'd heard Christian missionaries gabble about a Truth they claimed to have. The Communists thought they owned truth, too. It sometimes made them uncomfortable allies, even if she could never have struck the little devils such a blow without them.

Nieh Ho-T'ing was casually tapping the palm of his hand against a trouser leg. His mouth shaped silent words: *eight, seven, six* ...

As he said the word *five*, a sharp, deep *bang!* came from inside the walls of the Forbidden City. 'Early,' Nieh said, 'but not so bad.' The grin he was wearing belied even the partial criticism.

He'd hardly finished the sentence when another *bang!* went off, and then another. Liu Han felt as if she were drunk on *samshu*, though she'd had nothing stronger than tea. 'We give the Emperor a happy birthday,' she said, and added the emphatic cough for good measure.

Two more bombs went off among the scaly devils, then one, then silence. Nieh Ho-T'ing frowned. 'We had eight arranged for in all here in Peking,' he said. 'Perhaps two timers failed, or perhaps they ran late and the little devils found them before they could blow up.

That made Liu Han remember the bombs had not got in among the little scaly devils by themselves. The Communists had promised her they'd care for the families of the beast-show men killed in the explosions, and she believed them; they had a good reputation in such things. But money did not pay for the anguish the wives and children of those men would know. She knew how hard losing a family was. It had happened to her twice now.

Had she not had her idea, those beast-show men would still be living, working at their trade. She hung her head. Hurting the little scaly devils might justify what she'd done, but could not make her proud of it.

The little devils' hissing alarms started going off. Gunfire came from inside the Forbidden City. That wasn't the raiders. That was the little scaly devils, shooting either at innocent people (there were waiters and other servants who'd also still be alive and well if she hadn't had her idea; she remembered them, too, or at one another.

Suddenly Liu Han and Nieh Ho-T'ing stood almost alone, not far from the walls of the Forbidden City. People in Peking had seen a lot of war. They knew that, when explosions went off anyplace nearby, going elsewhere was one of the best ideas you could have. She started drifting away with the crowd, and tugged at Nieh's sleeve when he didn't move fast enough to suit her.

'You're right,' he said sheepishly, once she'd finally got his attention. They'd just ducked back into a *hutung* out of sight of the wall when a little scaly devil up there started shooting with his automatic rifle. A moment later, others up and down the wall poured fire at the humans out and about in the night. What had been a withdrawal became a stampede, some people screaming in panic, others because they were hit.

'Hurry!' Liu Han cried. 'We have to get away. If they send their males out of the Forbidden City, they'll slaughter everyone they can find.'

Nieh hurried but, to her surprise, wore a big, fierce grin on his usually solemn face. 'What's funny?' Liu Han demanded indignantly. 'They're killing us.'

'That is what's funny,' he answered, which made no sense to her till he explained: 'They play into our hands. If they kill people who had nothing to do with setting off the bombs among them, they do nothing to help themselves and only make people hate them. Even some of their lackeys will think twice about backing them now, and may come over to us or give us useful information. The scaly devils would have been wiser to do nothing till they found out who had bombed them, then to strike hard at us. That way, they could have claimed they were punishing the guilty. Do you understand.'

He'd taken that tone — almost as if he were a village schoolmaster — with her before when he was instructing her in matters of doctrine. She thought as she fled. Nieh looked at the world cold-bloodedly, more so than anyone else she'd ever known. But he was a war leader. Such men could not afford to be anything but cold-blooded.

She said, 'We'll have to stay in the shadows for a while, till the little devils stop hounding us.'

Nieh Ho-T'ing shook his head. 'No. Now we hit them harder than ever, harass them in every way we can, so we keep them too busy to launch a proper campaign against us. If we can keep them off balance, they will be foolish.'

Liu Han thought about that as they trotted along through the *hutungs*. They went arm in arm to keep from being swept apart by the crowds surging away from the Forbidden City. She decided it made sense. If you were in a fight with someone, you didn't hit him once and then stand back to see what he'd do next. You hit him again and again, as often as you could, to make sure he gave up or at least didn't have the chance to hit you back.

The landlord of their rooming house screamed at them to close the door and stop letting out the heat. 'What's all the commotion outside?' he added.

'I don't know,' Nieh and Liu Han said together, and then laughed. She'd picked up a good deal of doctrine listening to him. If she showed undue knowledge, the landlord might wonder how she came by it.

Hsia Shou-Tao sat at a table in the eating room. With him was a pretty young woman in a brocaded silk dress with so many slits in it that Liu Han wondered how she kept from freezing to death. A jar of *samshu* sat between them. By the foolish expression on Hsia's face, it was not the first one that had been there.

'Is all well?' he called to Nieh Ho-T'ing.

'I think so,' Nieh answered, with a pointed glance toward Hsia's companion. She glared at him like a cat with ruffled fur. If she wasn't a security risk, Liu Han had never seen one. Could Hsia keep his mouth hut after he took her upstairs to see her body? Liu Han hoped so, but hope wasn't enough in a game of this importance.

'Join us?' Hsia Shou-Tao asked.

'No, thank you,' Nieh Ho-T'ing answered, rather coldly. The pretty girl muttered something through her painted lips; Liu Han had no doubt it wasn't a compliment. She was pleased at Nieh's answer. She didn't want to sit at the same table with Hsia, even if he had another woman to distract him from her.

She and Nieh Ho-T'ing went to the stairway together. She saw Hsia smirking at the two of them, which only made her more angry with him. The stairwell was cold and dark. She stumbled. Nieh caught her elbow before she could fall. 'Thank you,' she said.

'My pleasure,' he answered, and then laughed at himself. 'I sound like a perfect member of the bourgeoisie, don't I? But it *is* my pleasure. This was your idea, Comrade. I wouldn't want you to hurt yourself just as it begins to unfold. You deserve the credit.'

'Thank you,' she said again. Her room was a couple of floors higher than Nieh's, but she didn't mind when he walked up past his floor with her. She wondered why she didn't. Maybe she'd decided to pay Hsia Shou-Tao back for that smirk, maybe she felt filled with the triumph of finally paying back the scaly devils for all they'd done to her. Her mouth twisted. Maybe, after so long, she just wanted a man. Her hand was all right in its way – it knew exactly what she liked – but it couldn't hold her and hug her afterwards. Of course, not all men did that, either, but the hope was always there.

She'd told Nieh she didn't want to lie with him. That hadn't been long ago, either. Neither of them mentioned it now. Liu Han opened to her room. A lamp still flickered in there. She used the flame to light the little brazier that gave the place such heat as it had – not much.

Even after she'd shut the door behind them, Nieh Ho-T'ing still hesitated. 'It's all right,' she said. 'It's better than all right, in fact.'

That made him smile. He didn't smile often. When he did, his whole face changed. It wasn't hard and watchful – committed – any more. Not only did he seem happy, he seemed surprised at being happy, as if he wasn't sure how he was supposed to react.

'No *k'ang* to lie on up here,' Liu Han said sadly. 'Even with blankets' – she pointed to the mount under which she burrowed – 'it won't be warm.'

'We'll have to make it warm, then,' he said, and smiled that uncertain smile once more. It grew broader when she smiled back at him. He glanced toward the little brass lamp. 'Shall I blow that out?'

'I don't think it matters,' she answered. 'We're going to be covered up anyhow.'

'True.' But Nieh did blow out the lamp, plunging the room into blackness. Liu Han got out of her layers of clothes as fast as she could and dived beneath the covers. Nieh almost stepped on the bedding – and her – when he walked over in the dark after undressing himself.

She shivered when he ran his hands up and down her body, partly from excitement and partly because they were cold. But he was warm elsewhere; his erection rubbed against her thigh. When she took him in her hand for a moment, he shivered, too, probably for both the reasons she had.

He kissed her. She stroked his cheek. It was almost as smooth as her own, not furry with beard or rough with the nubs of scraped-off whiskers as Bobby Fiore's had been. Nieh's chest was smooth and hairless, too, with nothing like the black jungle the American had had growing there. When she'd first been forced to couple with Bobby Fiore, she'd thought that mat of hair disgusting. Then she'd got used to it. Now smoothness felt strange.

His mouth was warm, too. It came down on her left breast. His tongue teased her nipple. She sighed and rested a hand on the back of his head. But although the caresses felt good, they also reminded her of the baby – even if it was only a daughter – who should have been nursing there.

His mouth moved to her other breast. His hand took its place, squeezing her hard enough to be pleasurable and not quite enough to hurt. She sighed again. His other hand was busy between her legs, not yet stroking her most secret places but teasing all around them till she – almost – forgot how cold the room was. He understood patience in a way she'd had to teach to Bobby Fiore.

After a while, he grew too patient to suit her. She closed her fingers around him, gently tugging back his foreskin. He gasped and scrambled onto her. She spread her legs and arched her back to make his entry easy. The darkness was so complete, she could not see his face above hers. It didn't matter. She knew that, when their lips weren't joined, it had to bear the same intent, inward, searching expression as her own. His hips bucked steadily, driving him in and out of her.

Her breath came in short gasps, as if she'd run a long way. Nieh grunted and shuddered, but kept moving inside her until, a moment later, she also quivered in release. Then, still thoughtful, he rolled off beside her so his weight, which suddenly seemed much heavier, wouldn't flatten her.

He touched her cheek. 'You are everything I thought you'd be, and more besides,' he said.

The words warmed her and left her wary at the same time. 'I am not going to be your toy or your – what do you say? – your lackey, that's it, because of what we just did,' she said. Her voice came out sharper than she'd intended, but that was all right, too. He needed to know he couldn't take advantage of her, in bed or out, because she'd laid with him once. The Communists preached of better days for women. As she'd seen from Hsia Shou-Tao, not all of them meant what they said. She thought Nieh was different. Now she'd find out.

'Fair enough,' he said. He sounded wintry, too, as he went on, 'And just because you've lain down with me, don't think I will press for your schemes unless they have merit.' Then he softened that by leaning up on an elbow and kissing her. 'The one tonight certainly did.'

'I am glad you think so,' she said. Had she been wondering if she could use her body to influence Nieh and advance her own position among the revolutionaries who fought the scaly devils? She had to admit to herself that it had crossed her mind. In a man's world, a woman's body was sometimes the only weapon she had – and she did want to rise to where all her ideas were taken seriously, the better to avenge herself against the little devils. What Nieh said marked a better way, though. 'Comrade, we have a bargain.'

As if by accident, his hands strayed along her body toward the joining of her legs. 'How shall we seal it?' he asked slyly.

She hesitated, feeling him stir against her side and start to rise. She wouldn't have minded another round, but – '*Not* like that,' she said, and took his hand away. 'Didn't you listen to what I told you.'

To her relief, he didn't sound angry when he answered, 'I listened, but sometimes – often – people do nothing but mouth empty phrases. The Kuomintang, for instance, calls itself a revolutionary party.' His contemptuous snort showed what he thought of that. 'But you, Liu Han, you mean what you say. This is something I need to know.'

'Good enough,' Liu Han said after a moment. 'We seal it like this, then.' Now she kissed him. 'It is enough for now.'

The Emperor's holographic image beamed down on the shiplords' celebration aboard the *127th Emperor Hetto*. On three worlds of the Empire, billions from the Race, the Rabotevs, and the Hallessi were celebrating their sovereign's hatching day at just this moment. Knowing that made Atvar feel part of the great community the Race had built, not the embattled outsider into which he sometimes seemed transformed by the pestilential war on Tosev 3.

Some of the shiplords were behaving so boisterously, he wondered whether they'd illicitly tasted ginger before their shuttlecraft brought them here to the bannership. He didn't like to think high-ranking commanders could fall victim to the insidious Tosevite herb, but on Tosev 3 what he liked and the truth were often – too often – far apart.

There over to one side floated Kirel, his usual standoffishness forgotten, talking animatedly with a couple of males who had been of Straha's faction back in the days when Straha was around to have a faction. Atvar was glad to see his chief subordinate happier than usual, less glad to see the company with which he chose to enjoy himself. On the other fork of the tongue, a considerable majority of males had voted for Atvar's ouster after the SSSR set off its nuclear bomb, so for Kirel to ignore all of them would have left him on good terms with only a few shiplords.

And there was poor hardworking Pshing. He had in his hand a squeezebulb filled with the fermented juices of certain Tosevite fruits. The Big Uglies, being unable to enjoy the intoxicating effects of ginger, made do with ethanol and various flavourings. Males of the Race found some of those vile – why anyone, even a Big Ugly, would drink whiskey, was beyond Atvar – but others might be worth exporting to Home after the conquest was complete.

Atvar drifted over to Pshing, checked himself by snagging a grab ring with the claws of one toe. 'How does it feel not to be waking me up to report some disaster?' he asked.

Pshing's eyes didn't quite track. He'd probably had several bulbs full of red wine already. 'Exalted Fleetlord, it feels *wonderful!*' he exclaimed, tacking on an emphatic cough that threatened to become a coughing fit. 'Stinking Big Uglies are quiet for a change.'

'Indeed,' Atvar said. 'Now if only they remain so.' He floated toward the console that dispensed bulbs of potations brought from Home, and toward the local drinks kept in bins with lids alongside it. He didn't want to celebrate the Emperor's hatching day with a product of Tosev 3. The Emperor represented Home and all it stood for. Far better to drink hudipar-berry brandy, then, than wine.

The male who came into the chamber was conspicuous not only for his subdued body paint but also for the purposeful way he went about looking for Atvar. The fleetlord's momentary good spirits flickered and blew out. Rokois was Pshing's subordinate, taking the duty for the adjutant so he could enjoy himself. If Rokois was here, instead of waiting in front of a communicator, something had gone wrong – again.

Atvar had a strong impulse to hide himself inside a floating cluster of males so Rokois could not spot his body paint. Just for once, he, like Pshing, deserved a respite from bad news. But even if he escaped that, he would not be able to evade the Emperor's eyes. Some trick of the hologram made them follow you wherever you were in the chamber. And had that trick not been there, he knew his duty too well to flee from it.

But oh, the temptation!

Instead of fleeing the adjutant's assistant, Atvar pushed off the console toward him (he did carry along the bulb of hudipar-berry brandy). Rokois folded into the posture of respectful obedience and began, 'Exalted Fleetlord, I regret to report that—'

Although he had not spoken loudly, those words were plenty to bring near-silence to the festival chamber. Atvar was far from the only male to have noted his arrival and to wonder what news was urgent enough to disturb the fleetlord at the celebration. Had Britain or Nippon or some other, previously discounted, Tosevite empire or not-empire touched off an atomic bomb? Had Duetschland or the United States or even the SSSR touched off another one?

'Tell me, Rokois,' Atvar interrupted. 'What do you regret to report ow?'

'Exalted Fleetlord, the Big Uglies appear to have discovered our custom honoring the Emperor's hatching day,' the adjutant's assistant answered. ertain of them were invited to perform with their trained Tosevite beasts observances of the day in cities on the eastern part of the main continental ass: this is in the large, populous not-empire known as China. Due to adequate security, they were able to smuggle explosives in amongst ir officers and administrators along with their beasts.'

'They died themselves, then?' Atvar said. Defending against males illing to do that was next to impossible. Fortunately, such fanatics ere rare even among the fanatical Big Uglies.

'Exalted Fleetlord, in many instances they did,' Rokois answered. 'We aptured a couple of these males and disarmed their explosives before etonation. They insist they were duped, that they thought the bombs ere, in fact, video equipment to allow us to record their performances.'

A rising mutter of anger and outrage came from the shiplords. Atvar nderstood that; he felt it himself. If you told lies, you didn't need to cruit fanatics without fear of death. Any race, the Race included, had s share of dupes.

As he usually did in the face of misfortune, he tried to look on the bright de of things. 'If we have some of these beast exhibitors in custody, they ay be able to lead us to the males who induced them to undertake their issions.'

'May events prove you correct, Exalted Fleetlord,' Rokois said. 'The ming devices on the captured explosives are of Nipponese manufacture, though the males unanimously insist Chinese were the intermediaries ho paid them and arranged for their performances.'

'More than one level of dupery may have been involved,' Atvar said.)r, conversely, the timers may have been used merely to deceive us. urther investigation should shed more light on that. What else have you arned?'

'There is one other thing to support the view that this was a Chinese ow against us,' Rokois answered. 'In the areas surrounding several of our dministrative centers, we have found small handbills that, if translated rrectly – the Chinese write with a peculiarly abominable script – demand e return of the hatchling taken from the Big Ugly female Liu Han for irposes of research.'

'The Big Uglies may not make demands of us,' Atvar said indignantly. hen he wondered why not. In matters military, they had earned wary tention if not full equality. 'We shall have to evaluate this further.'

'Truth, Exalted Fleetlord.' Rokois held no responsibility there, and was lithely aware of it. He disseminated policy; he did not shape it. After moment's hesitation, he went on, 'Exalted Fleetlord, reports indicate at casualties among senior administrators and officers in China may be especially heavy. They naturally had seats closest to the Big Uglie presenting the beast shows, and so took the full brunt of the blasts.'

'Yes, that does make sense.' Atvar sighed again. 'No help for it. Som junior males will get new marks and colors for their body paint. Some them won't have the experience or the sense to do their jobs as well they should. As they show that, we'll cull them and put others in the place. We shall rule China. We shall rule Tosev 3.' *And I shall dri enough hudipar-berry brandy to forget I'm orbiting above this miserabl hateful world.*

Despite that gloomy thought, his outward demeanor inspired Roko who exclaimed, 'It *shall* be done, Exalted Fleetlord!'

'Yes, spirits of past Emperors aiding us, it shall.' Now Atvar pause before resuming, 'When you came in here, I feared you were bringing n word the Big uglies had touched off another nuclear device. The Emper be praised, I was wrong.' Instead of lowering his eye turrets, he turne them toward the hologram of his ruler.

'May it not come to pass,' Rokois burst out, also gathering strengt from the image of the Emperor.

'Indeed. May it not.' The fleetlord squirted a long pull of brandy dow his throat.

Teerts's radar gave him a new target. He didn't have it visually, not yet. A he saw through his windscreen were clouds and, through occasional rent in them, the wave-chopped surface of the ocean that stretched between th main and lesser continental masses.

He was just as glad not to be flying over Deutschland any more. Mayb München had deserved what the Race gave it; he was no targeting specialis or shiplord, to be able to judge such things from full knowledge. Flying ove the glassy ruins of what had been a large city, though, left him glum. Th sight made him think of Tokyo, which, but for him, might still be standing To hate the Nipponese was one thing, to visit on them nuclear fire quit another.

They would have visited the same fire on the Race, had they possesse it. Teerts knew that full well. It salved his conscience, but not enough.

He thought about tasting ginger, but decided to wait until his body' need could no longer be denied. 'I think faster with ginger,' he said, firs making sure his radio was off. 'I don't think better. Or I think I don think better, anyhow.' He puzzled through that, finally deciding it wa what he meant.

He dived down beneath the clouds. This would be the third ship he' attacked on his flight to the lesser continental mass. They seemed almos as thick as parasites on the water. The males with the fancy body paint wer right to start paying more attention to them, as far as he was concerned The Race had automatically discounted water and travel on it.

'Trust the Big Uglies to do things we'd never think of,' he muttered. Yo ould use up a lot of aircraft and a lot of munitions trying to suppress the osevites' nautical commerce. If you tried shutting down all of it, would ou have any aircraft left to commit to other tasks?

That wasn't his judgment to make. But attacking ships wasn't like lowing cities off the face of Tosev 3. It was a real part of war, easily omprehensible to any male at all. For once, Elifrim had assigned him omething he didn't loathe.

There! Sheet metal and wood, crude and homely, slow and wallowing, elching a trail of smoke into the cloudy sky. You didn't need missiles or this. He'd used up his laser-guided bombs on the two previous targets, ut he still had cannon and plain bombs taken from a Tosevite arsenal. hey should do the job.

The ship swelled monstrously fast. His killercraft screamed toward it a shallow dive. The targeting computer told him to release the bombs. he aircraft's nose tried to come up as they dropped away. He and the utopilot kept it on its proper course.

He spotted Tosevites scrambling about on the deck of the ship. The illercraft bucked in the air as he thumbed the firing button of the cannon. e poured shells into the ship before the blasts from the bombs, and the ater they kicked up, obscured it from sight. 'Good-bye, Big Uglies,' he aid, pulling out of the dive so he could make another pass and inspect e damage.

He hadn't sunk this one. Radar told him as much, before he got a good ok at it. But smoke spurted from places it hadn't before. Some of the ig Uglies were down and motionless now, others struggling to repair e damage he'd done.

And others – Fire spurted from the front end of the ship, again and gain and again. They had an antiaircraft gun aboard, and were using with great vim even if the shells they threw up weren't coming very ose to him.

'Praise the Emperor's name for that,' he said. If he was unlucky enough get shot down twice, he wouldn't be taken prisoner, not here. He'd go into e water and see whether he froze before he drowned or vice versa.

This time, he fired a long burst at the Tosevite's popgun. He knew e'd damaged their vessel some more, and had no intention of coming und again to find out how much. That antiaircraft cannon might not ave been wrecked.

Up above the clouds once more, to broaden the radar's range. He looked rward to landing in what the locals called Florida. The air base in southern rance from which he'd been flying had turned unpleasantly cold, by his tandards if not by those of Tosev 3. But Florida stayed close to temperate roughout its winter season, even if the air was moist enough to make im inspect his scales for mold whenever he got up in the morning.

He checked his fuel supply. The attack runs he'd made had left him ather low on hydrogen to make it all the way across this ridiculously wide stretch of water. The Race kept a couple of refueling aircraft flying above the ocean for such contingencies. Satellite relay quickly put him in touch with one of them. He swung north for a rendezvous.

Guiding the prong from the refueling aircraft into his own took delicacy and concentration. He was glad he hadn't tasted beforehand; he knew how jumpy and impatient he got with ginger in him. Unfortunately, he also knew how sad and morose he got with no ginger in him.

He attacked one more ship on his way to Florida. The fog was so thick over the water that he carried out the run almost entirely by radar. He saw the wallowing Tosevite craft only at the last instant, just in time to add a few rounds from his cannon to the bombs he'd dropped.

Before long, he left behind the clouds and fog. The sky above him was a deep blue, the water below an even deeper shade of the same color. For once, Tosev 3 seemed almost beautiful – if you liked blue. It was a color far less common on Home than here. A proper world, to his way of thinking, was supposed to have an abundance of yellows and reds and oranges. Blue should have been an appetizer, not a main course.

Radar spotted the land ahead before he did – but radar was not concerned with aesthetics. Teerts didn't think much of the low, damp terrain toward which he was flying. Its hideous humidity meant that everything not recently cleared was covered by a rank, noxious coat of vegetation. He wasn't any too fond of green, either, though he did prefer it to blue.

Only the sandy beaches reminded him of Home, and they should have been broad expanses, not narrow strips hemmed in by more of Tosev 3's omnipresent water. He sighed. He wasn't going to have to do anything complicated from here on out, so he let himself have some ginger.

'I might as well be happy when I land,' he told the cockpit canopy as he followed the seacoast south toward his destination. Every so often, he'd fly over a little Tosevite town. Some of them had ships in their harbors. The aggressiveness the herb put in him made him want to blast those ships, as he had the ones out on the ocean. But the Race had held this territory for a long time, and any traffic was likely to be in authorized goods.

Staying rational through that first jolt of pleasure and excitement was never easy – the ships were just sitting there, as if begging to be destroyed. But Teerts knew how to separate the urgings of the ginger from those he would have had without it. He didn't let the herb make him as stupid as he once had.

The radar was linked to a map that listed the names of the cities over which he flew. Coming up was Miami, and past that the landing strip the Race had taken for its own. Miami was easy to recognize, being much the largest center the Big Uglies had built hereabouts. He could see it coming up in the distance. It had a large harbor, with tens upon tens of ships. Teerts's mouth fell open in a ginger-induced amusement as he imagined the havoc he could wreak upon them with a good strafing run.

It was almost – but not quite – worth braving the wrath of his superiors once he'd landed.

Then, right before his eyes, the whole harbor – for all he could tell, the whole city – went up in a fireball.

Ginger made you think faster. That much he knew. He swung the killercraft away from that fireball in as tight a turn as it would take. He knew what the fireball was. He'd seen one of the same sort over the Deutsch city Jisrin had incinerated. This one, in fact, wasn't quite so large as the other, and looked to be a ground burst rather than one in the air. But nothing could be mistaken for the explosion of a nuclear bomb.

The blast slapped the killercraft like a blow across the muzzle. For a dreadful moment, he thought he had no control. The ocean here was supposed to be warmer than it was farther east and north, but that didn't mean he wanted to go into it. And if Miami had just exploded in radioactive fire, who would rescue him, anyhow?

He was starting to review ejection procedures in his mind when the aircraft decided to answer the controls. He wondered how much radiation he'd picked up from being all too close to two nuclear blasts in a matter of days. Nothing he could do about that, not now.

His next query was much more urgently relevant: was his landing site still on the map? He got on the radio: 'Flight Leader Teerts to south Florida air base. Are you there?' He'd never before meant that question literally.

To his relief, the answer came back in moments, though it was hashed with static. 'Reading you clearly, Flight Leader Teerts. Were you damaged in the explosion? Was that . . .? Could that have been . . .?'

Teerts didn't blame the male for not wanting to say it out loud. But the ginger in him made him impatient with subterfuge and euphemism. 'That was a nuclear bomb in Miami, air base. Whatever we had in the city, it's gone now.'

'How could they have done that?' The male on the other end of the radio connection sounded stunned, disbelieving. 'Our radar spotted no aircraft to deliver the weapon, nor missiles, either. And we've chased the Big Uglies out of this peninsula. They couldn't have smuggled the weapon in by land. What does that leave?'

Maybe ginger really did make Teerts think better, not just faster. Or maybe his mission had freed his mind from the Race's usual patterns of thought. Without a moment's hesitation, he replied, 'Maybe they brought it in by water.'

'By water?' The fillip the male added to his interrogative cough made him sound incredulous, not just curious. 'How could they do that?'

'I don't know exactly how.' Teerts' right eye turret swung back toward the capped cloud still rising above Miami. 'But I'd say they seem to have managed.'

*　　*　　*

Atvar was growing to hate the reports he got from the targeting specialists, and to hate the sessions he spent with Kirel translating the recommendations from those reports into an order that would throw another city into the fire. Kirel called up a map of the United States. 'Once again, Exalted Fleetlord, Denver is a recommended target, along with this other, more peripheral one.'

'There is enough radiation loose on this continental mass, thanks to the Big Uglies,' Atvar answered. Somehow, catastrophe endlessly repeated didn't seem so catastrophic as it had the first time. One Tosevite atomic bomb had had the shiplords hissing for his skin. Now that the Big Uglies had touched off a whole string of them, the males stopped worrying about Atvar. They had a new kind of war on their hands.

Kirel said, 'The Emperor be praised we didn't delay another generation in attacking this planet, as some of the budget-cutters proposed. Even if we'd kept our nuclear armory intact, we'd have faced more nuclear weapons than we brought along. We might not even have effected a planetfall, let along conquest.'

'Truth,' Atvar said. 'This device, you will note from the analysis, was prepared entirely from the Big Uglies' own plutonium. They would have had nuclear arms all too soon in any case, even if we had not come to this miserable world. Of course, if we had come a generation later, they might also have succeeded in fighting their own full-scale atomic war, which would have solved most of our problems for us.'

'Ours, yes, but not those of the colonization fleet,' Kirel said.

'If the Big Uglies slagged Tosev 3 themselves, the colonization fleet could stop here just long enough to pick up reaction mass for the motors, and then honorably return Home,' Atvar answered. 'But since the Big Uglies have not quite wrecked the planet, we cannot do so, either. We know limits; they seem unaware of the concept.'

'We have spoken before of how the restraint we feel compelled to observe has been the Tosevites' biggest single safety factor,' Kirel agreed. He illuminated the other possible bomb site the targeting specialists had chosen. 'I don't know why they reckon this place a candidate for annihilation, Exalted Fleetlord. By planetary standards, it's far away from everything.'

'Only if you look at matters from the perspective of a male of the Race,' Atvar said. 'To the Tosevites, in its own way it is as important a nexus as Chicago.' *Which they went and destroyed themselves,* he added mentally. 'You are going to choose the out-of-the-way site, then,' Kirel said, not quite in resignation, but with the clear intention of conveying that, had he been fleetlord, he would have come to a different conclusion.

Well, he wasn't fleetlord, and Atvar now had reason to hope he never would be. A small or medium-sized crisis agitated males; in a large one, they got behind the leaders they had. The fleetlord said, 'That is my choice, yes.'

'Very well,' Kirel said. 'Per your orders, it shall be done. We shall bomb this Pearl Harbor place.'

Ttomalss did not read Chinese well. He was one of the few males of the Race who read Chinese at all. Learning a separate character for each word struck him as far more trouble than it was worth, and he had a computer to help him recognize the angular squiggles and remind him of what they meant. How a Big Ugly ever learned to cope with this cumbersome system was beyond him.

He did not need to know a great many characters to decipher those on the strips of paper that had been brought up to him from cities throughout the eastern stretch of China the Race occupied. Those strips had been found pasted up around sites the Chinese Tosevites had bombed; some of them had been captured in the cases of beast-show males before the bombs in those cases exploded.

The Tosevite female called Liu Han not only wanted her hatchling back, she was in a position with the Chinese who still resisted the Race's rule to make her demands widely known and to exert force to persuade the Race to yield to them.

Ttomalss turned an eye turret toward the hatchling in question. That was partly in reaction to the demands for its return and partly a simple caution to make sure it wasn't getting into anything it shouldn't. It could move around on all fours now, and could reach for things with at least some chance of having a hand actually land on them. And, as always, whatever it touched went straight into its mouth.

None of the beast-show males who hadn't blown themselves to small, gory fragments admitted to having heard of Liu Han. Ttomalss wished he'd never heard of her, either. Give the amount of trouble her hatchling had caused him, he might well have been delighted to give it back to her, would that not have disrupted his research program. As things were, though, he hated to abandon the experiment just when its results were beginning to seem interesting.

'What have you to say for yourself?' he asked the hatchling, and tacked on the usual interrogative cough at the end.

The hatchling turned its head to look at him. He'd been around Big Uglies enough that he no longer found that unnerving. The creatures were just too poorly made to move their eyes as the Race did. The hatchling's face twisted into a Tosevite gesture of amiability: the rest of its features were far more mobile than Ttomalss's. He didn't think that made it superior; he thought it made the hatchling and its race even uglier than they would have been otherwise.

It screwed up its face and let out a noise that sounded amazingly like an interrogative cough. It had done that two or three times already. As best he could tell, it began by making all sorts of sounds, and then gradually started picking out those the beings around it used in their language.

He wondered if its vocal apparatus would be able to handle the language of the Race. By two or three thousand years after the conquest, all the Big Uglies would be speaking that tongue; they would, unlikely as the notion now seemed, be normal subjects like the Rabotevs and Hallessi. A lot of them were good at languages. With so many different ones on Tosev 3, that was hardly surprising. But one of the things Ttomalss needed to learn was how they would handle the Race's tongue when learning it from hatchlinghood. If this hatchling was returned to Liu Han, he would have to start that process over again.

Tessrek struck his head into the laboratory. 'Enjoy your Little Ugly while you have it,' he said.

What Ttomalss would have enjoyed was sending Tessrek out the airlock with no space suit. 'The creature is not here to enjoy,' he said stiffly. 'Animals are to exploit, not to befriend as the Big Uglies do.' Remembering his earlier thought, he added, 'Not that the Tosevites are animals. Once the conquest is complete, they will be our subjects.'

'It would be much more convenient if they *were* animals,' Tessrek said. 'Then this world would be ours. Even if they were barbarians – remember the image of the Tosevite warrior the probe sent Home?'

'The sword-swinging savage in rusty iron, mounted on a beast? I'm not likely to forget.' Ttomalss hissed out a sigh. Would that the image were still truth on Tosev 3. It would have made his life – the Race's life – ever so much simpler. But he wasted only a moment on the barbarous past of the Tosevites. 'What do you mean, enjoy the hatchling while I have it? No decision to abandon it to the Big Uglies has reached me.'

'As far as I know, the decision hasn't been made,' Tessrek admitted. 'But when it is made, what do you think it will be? Everybody's eye turrets are swiveling every which way because of the atomic bombs the Tosevites have started using against us, but the Chinese raids cost us a lot of capable males, too. If giving back one hatchling can get us a respite from more of those, don't you think we ought to take it?'

'That depends,' Ttomalss said judiciously. 'If we do return the hatchling, we encourage the Big Uglies to make other demands of us, and then to harm us if we don't obey. They're supposed to be afraid of us, not the other way round.'

'If they are, they hide it very well,' Tessrek said, 'and who can blame them? Now that they have atomic weapons, they can do us severe damage. We may have to treat with them as equals.'

'Nonsense,' Ttomalss said automatically. The Race recognized no equals. The Rabotevs and Hallessi had legal equality in most areas of life, and had their own social hierarchies, but their worlds were in the Race's hands even so. Yet, on reflection, maybe it wasn't nonsense. Tosev 3 wasn't in the Race's hands, not yet. Ttomalss still assumed it eventually would be, but the assumption looked less and less assumable all the time.

Tessrek said, 'Besides, as I and other males have noted, the presence of the small Tosevite aboard this vessel has had noxious consequences for the local environment. In short, the creature still stinks. Many males would be glad to see it gone for that reason alone, and have stated as much.'

'My personal attitude is that that viewpoint has a far more noxious odor than the Tosevite,' Ttomalss answered. He did his best to disguise the stab of fear that ran through him. If all the other researchers and psychologists banded together against his experiment, it might be terminated regardless of its virtues. That wasn't fair, but sometimes it was the way the egg hatched.

He wondered if the Big Uglies let personalities get in the way of scientific research. He doubted it. Otherwise, how could they have so quickly moved forward from barbarism to rivaling a Race unified perhaps before their species had evolved its present form? It was itchy to think of the Tosevites as more advanced, in a way, than his own people, but the logic seemed inescapable.

He said, 'Until I am told otherwise, the experiment will continue in its present form. Even if I am told otherwise, I shall not surrender the hatchling to the inept mercies of the Big Uglies without an appeal to highest authority. And I, too, have backers for my cause. This work is an important part of understanding not only our future relations with the Tosevites but also that of their sexuality and its consequences for their species. Terminating it would disrupt several research tracks.'

'And probably send you back down to the surface of Tosev 3,' Tessrek said maliciously.

'At least I've *been* down to the surface of Tosev 3,' Ttomalss retorted. Though he regarded that surface and the Big Uglies who dwelt on it as rivaling each other for unpleasantness, he added, 'Some males seem to be of the opinion that research can be conducted only in sterile laboratory settings; they do not understand that interactions with the environment are significant, and that results obtained in the laboratory are liable to be skewed precisely because the setting is unnatural.'

'Some males, on the other fork of the tongue, simply enjoy stepping into lumps of excrement and stooping to wash it out from between their toes,' Tessrek turned his eye turrets toward the Tosevite hatchling. 'And some males, I might add, are in a poor position to sneer at the practices of others when they themselves are comfortably ensconced in a laboratory aboard ship.'

'Being here is a necessary component of my research,' Ttomalss answered angrily. 'I am trying to determine how well the Big Uglies can be made to conform to our practices if those are inculcated into them from hatchlinghood. Just as one intending fraud goes to a computer for access to resources, I have brought the hatchling here for access to the Race undiluted by contact with the Tosevites. Such would be most difficult to arrange down on the surface of Tosev 3.'

'You've certainly given the rest of us undiluted olfactory contact with the wretched little creature,' Tessrek said. 'The scrubbers up here are designed to eliminate *our* wastes from the air, not its, and some of those odors have proved most persistent and most disgusting.' He added an emphatic cough.

The hatchling made a noise that, if you were in a charitable mood, you might have recognized as an emphatic cough. Perhaps you didn't need to be in a charitable mood; Tessrek's eyes swung sharply toward the little Tosevite, then moved away as if to say he refused to acknowledge what he'd just heard.

Triumphantly, Ttomalss said, 'There, you see? The hatchling, despite its deficiencies, is being socialized toward our usages even at this early stage in its development.'

'It was just another in the series of loud, unpleasant sounds the creature emits,' Tessrek insisted. 'It held no intelligible meaning whatsoever.' To show he meant what he said, he let out a second emphatic cough.

Now Ttomalss looked anxiously toward the hatchling. Even he would have been willing to concede it did not know the meaning of the noises it made in imitation of his. It seemed likely to learn meanings by observing what the beings around it did in response to the stimuli varying sounds evoked. But despite his knowledge, he would have yielded a pay period's wages to have it come out with another emphatic cough.

He didn't think it was going to happen. But then, just when he'd given up hope, the little Tosevite did make a noise that sounded like an emphatic cough – sounded more like one, in fact, than its first effort had.

'Coincidence,' Tessrek declared, before Ttomalss could say a thing. Yet no matter how dogmatically certain he sounded, he did not presume to tack yet a third emphatic cough on behind his assertion.

'I think not,' Ttomalss said. 'This is how the Big Uglies go about acquiring language. Since we are the language possessors with whom the hatchling is in constant contact, it is imitating our repertoire of sounds. Eventually, I believe, it will attach mental signification to the sounds it uses: in other words, it will begin to speak intelligibly.'

'The Big Uglies have enough trouble doing that no matter what language they use,' Tessrek said. But he did not try directly refuting Ttomalss, from which Ttomalss inferred he conceded the point.

Ttomalss said, 'Since video and audio monitors constantly record the activities in this chamber, I want to thank you for adding to our store of data concerning Tosevite language acquisition.'

Tessrek hissed something unpleasant and departed more quickly than he'd come in. Ttomalss let his mouth fall open in a long laugh, which he thought well-earned. The Tosevite hatchling emitted one of the squeals it used in place of a sensibly quiet gesture. Sometimes those squeals, so unlike any sound the Race made, annoyed Ttomalss no end. Now he laughed even harder. The hatchling had understood his mirth and responded with its own.

For the benefit of the recorders, he emphasized that point aloud, adding, 'This growing level of successful interspecies communication appears to me to warrant further serious investigation.' He looked at the little Tosevite with something more nearly approaching warmth than he ever remembered showing it. 'Let's see them try to take you away from me now. Even if you are a nuisance, you're too valuable to give back to the Big Uglies.

20

Jens Larssen peered out of the window of the farmhouse where he'd taken shelter for the past several days. That was what he'd been doing lately: peering out the window and waiting for the searchers to give up and go away. 'They aren't going to catch me,' he muttered. 'I'm too smart for them. I won't let them catch me.'

He was pretty sure he could have outrun pursuit from Denver and made it to Lizard-held territory. Pursuit wasn't the only problem, though. People would have been waiting for him out east. He hadn't forgotten telegraph and telephone lines (even if those were likely to be down, could you take the chance?) and radio and even carrier pigeons. They'd know he was coming, oh yes they would.

So he'd been waiting for them to give up and quit looking for him. Sooner or later, they'd figure he'd got caught in a snowstorm and frozen to death, or that he'd managed a clean getaway, or else the war would heat up and they'd forget all about him and go off to fight. Then he'd start moving again. The time, he judged, was nearly ripe.

He laughed. 'They aren't going to catch me,' he repeated. 'Hell, they were right in this house and they didn't have a clue.'

He'd been smart. He was a physicist – he was supposed to be smart. He'd picked a house with a storm cellar in it. Whenever prying eyes came around, he'd ducked down into the cellar. He'd even tied a throw rug to a chair near the cellar door so it kept that door covered up after he went down below. He'd heard combat boots thumping up above his head, but none of the soldiers had had a hint that he was sitting in the darkness with his finger on the tripper of his Springfield in case anything had gone wrong.

He laughed again. The soldiers hadn't had the brains to look beyond the ends of their noses. He'd expected nothing different, and he'd been right. 'I usually am,' he said. 'If those fools would have listened to me—' He shook his head. They hadn't listened. The Lizards would.

Even though they hadn't been physicists, the people who'd built this farm had been pretty smart, too. They weren't around, though, so they hadn't been smart enough to escape the Lizards. Or maybe they hadn't been lucky enough. You never could tell. Whichever way it was, they were gone.

But they'd left behind that storm cellar, stocked with enough home-canned goodies to feed a platoon for a month. That's how it seemed to Jens, anyhow. Beef, pork, chicken, vegetables – they didn't seem to have had any fruit trees, and he missed sweets till he came upon a gallon jar of tapioca pudding. The wife of the house must have made a lot more than she could use right away, and put up the rest. He ate tapioca till it started coming out of his arse.

He'd found cigarettes down there, too, but he hadn't smoked any. The odor would linger in the house. When he got on the road again – ah, that was another matter. He looked forward to it, although the first couple of times he'd lit up after going without for a long time, he'd been like Tom Sawyer after Huck Finn gave him his first pipe.

He walked over to the window that looked across the fields toward US 40. It was snowing again, not as hard as it had back when he was a kid in Minnesota but plenty hard enough to cut way back on visibility. In a way, that was bad, because he couldn't tell who, if anybody, was out there. He didn't think anybody was. The highway had been quiet since that search party stomped through the house, and that was days ago now. And the snow could work for him, too. It would make him harder to spot, and harder to recognize if somebody did spot him.

'Well, then, time to get moving,' he said. He was just the Denver side of Limon. Once he made it past there, he'd be getting close to frontier country. He'd have to be careful again: the frontier meant soldiers. But unless he had it all wrong, they'd be worrying about Lizards, not about him.

And he didn't have it all wrong. He couldn't have it all wrong. The only mistake he'd made was not doing something like this a hell of a lot sooner. He went down into the storm cellar and hauled out his bicycle. As soon as he was on the road, he lit up a King Sano. Yeah, it made him halfway want to puke, but goddamn did it taste good.

The Russies had been buried alive before, first in the bunker under a Warsaw block of flats and then in the submarine that brought them from Poland to England. That didn't mean Moishe enjoyed repeating the process. There were, however, worse choices these days.

A sandy-haired naval officer named Stansfield commanded the HMS *Seanymph*. 'Welcome aboard,' he'd said as, somewhere off the coast of Portugal, or perhaps Spain, Moishe, Rivka, and Reuven transferred to his boat from the freighter that had brought them down from England. 'I'd wager you'll be glad to submerge for a spell.'

Like a lot of military types Moishe had met – Poles, Nazis, Englishmen, Lizards – he seemed almost indecently offhanded about the implications of combat. Maybe the only way he could deal with them was not to think about them. Moishe had answered, 'Yes,' and let it go at that.

When the British decided to send him to Palestine, getting him and his family there hadn't looked like a problem. The Lizards hadn't acted very interested in attacking ships. But then the Americans had touched off atomic bombs, first in Chicago and then in Miami. When Moishe thought of Chicago, he thought of gangsters. He'd never heard of Miami before it abruptly ceased to be.

What he thought of those places didn't much matter, though. The Lizards must have thought ships had something to do with their destruction, because from then on they'd started hitting them a lot harder than they ever had before. Moishe didn't know how many times his eyes had flicked to the air on the long, rough haul down from England. It was, he realized, a pointless exercise. Even if he spotted a Lizard fighter-bomber, what could he do about it? That didn't keep him from looking anyhow.

Diving with the *Seanymph* had seemed reassuring at first. Not only was he ought of sight of the Lizards, he was also out of the waves that had made the passage something less than a traveler's delight. No rolling and pitching, down however many meters they went.

That was just as well, too, for the submarine was not only cramped but also full of pipes and projecting pieces of metal and the ruins of watertight doors, all of which could bang heads or shins or shoulders. In a proper design, Moishe thought, most of those projections would have been covered over by metal sheeting or hidden away behind walls. He wondered why they hadn't been. In his halting English, he asked Commander Stansfield.

The naval officer blinked at the question, then answered, 'Damned if I know. Best guess I can give you is that S-class boats are built in such a tearing hurry, no one cares about anything past getting them out there to sink ships. Give us another couple of generations of engineering and the submarines will be much more comfortable to live in. Compared to what we had in the last war, I'm told, this is paradise.'

To Russie's way of thinking, paradise was not to be found in a narrow, smelly, noisy metal tube lit by dim orange lights to that it resembled nothing so much as a view of the Christian hell. If this was an improvement, he pitied the men who had put to sea in submarines about the time he was born.

He, Rivka, and Reuven shared what normally would have been the executive officer's cabin. Even by the dreadful standards of the Warsaw ghetto, it would have been cramped for one and was hideously crowded for three. When set against the sailors' triple-decker bunks, though, it seemed a luxury flat. A blanket attached with wires to one of the overhead pipes gave some small semblance of privacy.

In Yiddish, Rivka said, 'When we went from Poland to England, I was afraid to be the only woman on a ship full of sailors. Now, though, I don't worry. They aren't like the Nazis. They don't take advantage.'

Moishe thought about that. After a little while, he said, 'We're on the same side as the English. That makes a difference. To the Nazis, we were fair game.'

'What's "fair game" mean?' Reuven asked. He remembered the ghetto as a time of hunger and fear, but he'd been away from it most of a year now. In the life of a little boy, that was a long time. His scars had healed. Moishe wished his own dreadful memories would go away as readily.

After being submerged for what he thought was most of a day – though time in tight, dark places had a way of slipping away from you if you didn't hold it down – the *Seanymph* surfaced. Hatches let in fresh air to replace the stale stuff everyone had been breathing over and over again. They also let in shafts of sunlight that clove straight through the gloom inside the submarine. No winter sun in London or Warsaw could have shone so bright.

'We'll lay over in Gibraltar to recharge our batteries and pick up whatever fresh produce they have for us here,' Commander Stansfield told Moishe. 'Then we'll submerge again and go on into the Mediterranean to rendezvous with the vessel that will take you on to Palestine.' He frowned. 'That's what the plan is, at any rate. The Lizards are strong around much of the Mediterranean. If they've been as vigorous attacking ships there as elsewhere—'

'What do we do then?' Moishe asked.

Stansfield grimaced. 'I don't precisely know. I gather your mission is of considerable importance: it must be, or it wouldn't have been laid on. But I've neither fuel nor supplies to take you there, I'm afraid, and I don't really know where I should acquire more. Here, possibly, though I should have to get authority from London first. Let us hope it does not come to that.'

'Yes,' Moishe said. 'Let us.'

He and his family stretched their legs on the deck of the *Seanymph* a few times while she resupplied. The sun beat down on them with a vigor it seldom found in summer in more northerly climes. Like those of the sailors, their skins were fish-belly pale. Before long, they began to turn pink.

The Germans and Italians had bombed Gibraltar, back when the war was merely a human affair. The Lizards had bombed it since, more persistently and more precisely. Nonetheless, it remained in British hands. No great warships used the harbor, as they had in earlier days, but Moishe spotted a couple of other submarines. One looked considerably different in lines from the *Seanymph*. He wondered if it was even a British boat. Could the Axis powers be using a harbour they'd tried to destroy?

When the crew dogged the hatches, Moishe felt a pang, as if he were being dragged unwilling into a cave. After the spirited Mediterranean sun, the dim interior lamps seemed particularly distressing. A couple of hours later, though, he'd got used to the orange twilight once more.

Time crawled on. The sailors were all either asleep or busy keeping the submarine running. Moishe had slept as much as he could, and he was useless on the boat. That left him as bored as he'd ever been in his life. In the bunker under the Warsaw ghetto flats, he'd passed a lot of time making love with Rivka. He couldn't do that here.

Keeping Reuven out of mischief helped occupy him. His son was every bit as bored as he was, and couldn't understand why he wasn't allowed to go out and get under people's feet. 'It's not fair!' he said, again and again. He was probably right, but not right enough to be turned loose.

The *Seanymph* sailed east, altogether cut off from the outside world. Moishe wondered if traveling between worlds in a Lizard spaceship was anything like this. If it was, he pitied the Lizards. They had to endure it for a lot longer than mere hours.

When the submarine surfaced, it was black night outside. That made transferring Moishe and his family safer, but also harder. 'Like trying to find a black cat in a coal cellar at midnight,' Commander Stansfield grumbled. 'And we're not even certain the cat is here.'

'How well can you find where you are going when this ship is underwater?' Russie asked.

'Boat,' Stansfield corrected absently. 'That is the rub, of course. If we're a couple – or more than a couple – of miles from where we ought to be, we might as well have sailed to Colorado.' He smiled, as if at some remembered joke. Whatever it was, it made no sense to Moishe. Stansfield went on, 'It's a clear night. We can read our positions from the stars and move at need. But dawn will be coming before too long – now that we're further south, night ends earlier than it would in British waters – and I'm not keen on being spotted around here.'

'No, I understand this,' Moishe said. 'Can you sail back to Gibraltar all under the sea?'

'We'll use the diesels to charge the batteries,' the Royal Navy man answered. After a moment, Russie realized that wasn't a fully responsive reply. The *Seanymph* had sailed into danger to take him and his family where they were supposed to go.

Stansfield was getting out the sextant when a sailor came down from the conning tower and said, 'Sir, we've spotted a ship maybe half a mile to port. No sign she knows we're anywhere about. Is that the one we want?'

'It's not likely to be anybody else,' Stansfield said. 'And if it happens to be, he won't go telling tales out of school. We'll make certain of that.' Moishe hadn't heard the idiom before, and needed a moment to figure out what it meant. Yes, Stansfield was a military man – he talked with complete equanimity of killing people.

The *Seanymph* glided quietly toward the waiting ship. Moishe wished he could go up on deck to help, but realized he would be as much underfoot there as Reuven was down below. He hated waiting for others to decide his fate. That had happened too often in his life, and here it was again.

Shoes clattered on the rungs of the iron ladder that led up to the conning tower. 'Captain's compliments, sir, ma'am,' a sailor said, 'and please to get your things and come along with me.' He actually said *fings* and *wiv*, but that didn't bother Moishe, who had trouble with the *th* sound himself. He and Rivka grabbed their meager bundles of belongings and, shooing Reuven ahead of them, climbed up to the top of the conning tower.

Moishe peered out into the darkness. A tramp steamer bobbed alongside the *Seanymph*. Even in the darkness, even to Moishe's inexperienced eye, it looked old and dingy and battered. Commander Stansfield came over and pointed. 'There she is,' he said. 'That's the *Naxos*. She'll take you the rest of the way to the Holy Land. Good luck to you.' He held out a hand. Moishe shook it.

With a rattling of chains, the *Naxos* lowered a boat. Moishe helped his wife and son into it, then put in what they'd brought with them, and last of all climbed in himself. One of the sailors at the oars said something in a language he didn't understand. To his amazement, Reuven answered in what sounded like the same language. The sailor leaned forward in surprise, then threw back his head and shouted loud laughter.

'What language are you speaking? Where did you learn it?' Moishe asked his son in Yiddish.

'What do you mean, what language?' Reuven answered, also in Yiddish. 'He uses the same words the Stephanopoulos twins did, so I used some of those words, too. I liked playing with them, even if they were *goyim*.'

To Rivka, Moishe said, 'He learned Greek.' He sounded almost accusing. Then he started to laugh. 'I wonder if the Stephanopoulos boys speak Yiddish and surprise their mother.'

'They were using some of my words, too, Papa,' Reuven said. 'It's all right, isn't it?' He seemed anxious, perhaps afraid he'd revealed too much to his friends. In the ghetto, you quickly learned giving yourself away was dangerous.

'It's all right,' Moishe assured him. 'It's better than all right, in fact. I'm proud of you for learning.' He scratched his head. 'I just hope you won't be the only one who can talk with these sailors.'

When they got up onto the *Naxos's* deck, the captain tried several languages with Moishe before discovering they had German in common. 'Panagiotis Mavrogordato, that's me,' he said, thumping his chest with a theatrical gesture. 'They're your enemies, they're my enemies, and we have to use their tongue to talk with each other.' He spat on the deck to show what he thought of that.

'Now the Lizards are everyone's enemies,' Moishe said. The Greek rubbed his chin, dipped his head in agreement, and spat again.

The *Seanymph* slid beneath the surface of the Mediterranean. That made the *Naxos* rock slightly in the water. Otherwise, there was no trace the submarine had ever been there. Moishe felt alone and very helpless. He'd trusted the British sailors. Who could say anything about the crew of a rusty Greek freighter? If they wanted to throw him over the side, they could. If they wanted to hand him to the first Lizards they saw, they could do that, too.

As casually as he could, he asked, 'Where do we go from here?'

Mavrogordato started kicking off destinations on his fingers: 'Rome, Athens, Tarsus, Haifa. At Haifa, you get off.'

'But . . .?' Was Mavrogordato trying to bluff him? Rome is in the Lizards' hands. Most of Italy is.'

'That's why we go there.' Mavrogordato mimed licking something from the palm of his hand. 'The Lizards there will be mighty *gamemeno* glad to see us, too.'

Moishe didn't know what *gamemeno* meant. Reuven let out a shocked gasp and then a giggle, which told him what sort of word it was likely to be – not that he hadn't figured that out for himself. Even without the word, he understood what the Greek was talking about. So he was running ginger, was he? In that case, the aliens *would* be glad to see him – and he was less likely to turn over a family of Jews to Lizard officialdom. Mavrogordato went on, 'They give us all kinds of interesting things in exchange for the' – he made that tasting gesture again – 'we bring them, yes they do. We would have had a profitable trip already. And when the British paid us to carry you, too—' He bunched his fingertips together and kissed them. Russie had never seen anybody do that before, but he didn't need a dictionary for it, either.

The captain of the *Naxos* led them to their cabin. It had one narrow bed for him and Rivka, with a pallet on the floor for Reuven. It was cramped and untidy. Next to the accommodations aboard the *Seanymph* they'd just left, it seemed like a country estate.

'Don't turn on the light at night unless you shut the door and pull the blackout curtain over the porthole first,' Mavrogordato said. 'If you make a mistake about that, we will be very unhappy with you, no matter how much the British paid us for you. Do you understand?' Without waiting for an answer, he squatted and spoke in slow, careful Greek to Reuven.

'*Nee, nee,*' Reuven said – that's what it sounded like to Moishe, anyhow. His son was obviously impatient at being talked down to, and added, '*Malakas,*' under his breath.

Mavrogordato's eyes went wide. He started to laugh. Getting to his feet in a hurry, he said, 'This is a fine boy you have here. He will make a fine man if you can keep from strangling him first. We'll have rolls and bad tea for breakfast in a couple of hours, when the sun rises. Come join us then.' With a last dip of his head, he went out of the cabin.

Rivka shut the door and used the blackout curtain.

Then she clicked on the light switch. A ceiling bulb in a cage of iron bars lit up the metal cubicle. The cage was much like the ones aboard the *Seanymph.* The bulb, though, made Moishe squint and his eyes water. It wasn't – it couldn't have been – as bright as Gibraltar sunshine, but it seemed that way.

Moishe looked around the cabin. It didn't take long. But for rivets and peeling paint and a couple of streaks of rust, there wasn't much to see. In his mind's eye, though, he looked farther ahead. 'Halfway there,' he said.

'Halfway there,' Rivka echoed.

'Mama, Papa, I have to make a *pish*,' Reuven said.

Moishe took his hand. 'Come on,' he said. 'We'll find out where you do that here.'

Ussmak was dressed in more clothes than he'd ever worn in his life. Back on Home, he hadn't worn anything beyond body paint and belts hung with pouches. That was the way you were supposed to go through life. But if he went out that door as if he were on Home, he'd freeze to death before he ever got to his landcruiser.

He turned an eye turret down toward the large, heavy gloves on his hands. 'How are we supposed to do any sort of work on the machine in clumsy things like these?' he complained, not for the first time. 'My grip has about as much precision as if I were using my tailstump.'

'We have to maintain the landcruiser, no matter how hard it is,' Nejas answered. The landcruiser commander was bundled up as thoroughly as Ussmak. 'It has to be perfect in every way – no speck of dirt, no slightest roughness in the engine. If the least little thing goes wrong, the Big Uglies will swoop down and kill us before we even know they're around.' He paused, then added, 'I want a taste of ginger.'

'So do I, superior sir,' Ussmak said. He knew he'd probably saved Nejas's life by giving him ginger when he was wounded in the invasion of Britain. But ginger fit Nejas's personality only too well. He'd been a perfectionist before; now the least little flaw sent him into a rage. The herb also exaggerated his tendency to worry about everything and anything, especially after he'd been without it for a while.

A lot of males in this Emperor-forsaken frozen Soviet wasteland were like that. But for goin. on patrol and servicing their landcruisers, they had nothing to do but sit around in the barracks and watch video reports on how the conquest of Tosev 3 was going. Even when couched in broadcaster's cheerily optimistic phrases, those reports were plenty of incitement for any male in his right mind to worry about anything and everything.

'Superior sir, will this planet be worth having, once the war of conquest is over?' Ussmak asked. 'The way things are going now, there won't be much left to conquer.'

'Ours is not to question those who set strategy. Ours is to obey and carry out the strategy they set,' Nejas answered; like any proper male of the Race, he was as good a subordinate as a commander.

Maybe it was all the ginger Ussmak had tasted, maybe all the crewmales he'd seen killed, maybe just his sense that the Race's broadcasters hadn't the slightest clue about what the war they were describing was really like. Whatever it was, he didn't feel like a proper male any more. He said, 'Meaning no disrespect to the fleetlord and those who advise him, superior sir, but too much of what they've tried just hasn't worked. Look what happened to us in Britain. Look at the poisonous gas and the atomic bombs the Big Uglies are using against us.'

Skoob was also climbing into the gear a male needed to survive in Siberia, the gear that turned quick death into prolonged discomfort. The gunner spoke in reproving tones: 'The leaders know better than we what needs doing to finish the conquest of Tosev 3. Isn't that right, superior sir?' He turned confidently to Nejas.

Skoob had come through the British campaign unwounded; he'd also managed to keep from sticking his tongue in the powdered ginger, though he turned his eye turrets the other way when his crewmates tasted. But for that toleration, though, he still seemed as innocent of the wiles of the Tosevites as all the males of the Race had been when the ships of the conquest fleet first came to Tosev 3. In a way, Ussmak envied him that. He himself had changed, and change for the Race was always unsettling, disorienting.

Nejas has changed, too – not as much as Ussmak, but he'd changed. With a hissing sigh, he said, 'Gunner, sometimes I wonder what is in the fleetlord's mind. I obey – but I wonder.'

Skoob looked at him as if he'd betrayed their base to the Russkis. He sought solace in work: 'Well, superior sir, let's make sure the landcruiser is in proper running order. If it lets us down, we won't be able to obey our superiors ever again.'

'Truth,' Nejas said. 'I don't want to quarrel with you or upset you, Skoob, but I don't want to lie to you, either. You'd think I was talking out of a video screen if I tried it.' He didn't think much of the relentless good news that kept coming from the fighting fronts either, then.

Trying to keep the landcruiser operational was a never-ending nightmare. It would have been a nightmare even had Ussmak himself been warm. Frozen water in all varieties got in between road wheels and tracks and chassis and cemented them to one another. The intense cold made some metals brittle. It also made lubricants less than enthusiastic about doing their proper job. Engine wear had been heavy since the landcruiser was airlifted here, and spare parts were in constantly short supply.

As he thawed out the cupola lid so it would open and close, Ussmak said, 'Good thing we have those captured machine tools to make some of our own spares. If it weren't for that and for cannibalizing our wrecks, we'd never keep enough machines in action.'

'Truth,' Skoob said from back at the engine compartment. So Ussmak thought, at any rate The howling wind blew the gunner's words away.

Ussmak took tiny, cautious sips of air. Even breathed through several thicknesses of cloth, it still burned his lungs. Little crystals of ice formed on the mask. His eyes, almost the only exposed part of him, kept trying to freeze open. He blinked and blinked and blinked, fighting to keep them working.

'Good enough,' Nejas said some endless time later. 'What we really need is a flamethrower under the chassis of the landcruiser. Then we could melt the ice that freezes us to the ground in a hurry.'

The crew started back toward the barracks. Ussmak said, 'I've been talking with some of the males who've been here a long time. They say this is bad, but local spring is a hundred times worse. All the frozen water melts – by the way they make that sound, it happens in the course of a day or two, but I don't think that can be right – and whatever was on top of the ground sinks down into the mud. Sometimes, if you're lucky, you can get it out again.'

'You served in the SSSR before, didn't you?' Nejas said. 'Did you see any of that for yourself?'

'I saw the mud in local fall, before I was wounded,' Ussmak answered. 'That was bad. It just comes from rain falling on the ground, though. From all I've heard, the mud that comes in spring, when a winter's worth of frozen water melts, is a lot worse.'

He looked around at the white expanse through which they slogged. A lot of the drifts were higher than a male was tall. Winter had a long way to go, too; all of Tosev 3's seasons were twice as long as those of Home in any case, and here in Siberia winter seemed to rule most of the local year.

His sigh turned the air around him smoky. Softly, he said, 'I hope we last long enough to see how bad the local mud is.'

Rance Auerbach stared out across the snowy east Colorado prairie. He didn't see anything much, which suited him fine. He wanted to be off fighting the Lizards, not making like an MP. What he wanted and the orders he got weren't the same beast.

He wasn't the only one on whom those orders grated, either. Lieutenant Magruder rode up to him and asked, 'Who is this guy we're supposed to be looking for again? Waste of time, if you ask me – not that anybody did.'

'Fellow's name is Larssen, says Colonel Nordenskold.' Auerbach laughed. 'One squarehead telling us to go find another one. The colonel got word from General Groves that this Larssen plugged two guys and then headed east. They don't want him to make it into Lizard country.'

'Why do they give a damn? That's what I want to know, and nobody's told me yet,' Magruder said. 'If he's a bastard and he's heading toward the Lizards, why shouldn't we let him be their headache?'

'Colonel Nordenskold told you just as much as he told me,' Auerbach answered, 'so I don't know, either.' He could make some guesses, though. He'd led the cavalry detachment that had escorted Groves – who'd been a colonel then – all the way from the East Coast to Denver. He didn't know for certain what Groves had carried in that heavy, heavy pack of his, but he suspected. The explosions in Chicago and Miami hadn't done anything to make him think he was wrong, either.

If Groves wanted this Larssen stopped, it was probably because Larssen had something to do with those explosions. If he made it through to the Lizards, who could say what would happen next? The likeliest thing Auerbach could think of was Denver going up in a flash of light. If that happened, the USA's chance to beat the Lizards would probably go up with it.

If, if, if ... All of it was guesswork, and he knew as much. All the same, that wasn't why he kept quiet about it. The fewer people who knew about heavy-duty bombs, the less the chance word about them had of reaching the Lizards. Other speculations he would have shared with Magruder, but not these. He wished he hadn't been in the position to make these particular guesses himself.

Magruder changed the subject: 'He's going to get past us on a *bicycle*?' He patted his horse's neck. The animal whickered softly.

'He's supposed to be good at roughing it,' Auerbach answered. 'Maybe he'll ditch the bike and try it on foot. This is a big country, and we're spread thin. He might slip through. Hell, Bill, he might already have slipped through. And the other thing of it is, he might not be within a hundred miles of here. No way to know.'

'No way to know,' Magruder echoed. 'So here we are, out beating the bushes for this one guy instead of doing something to twist the Lizards' little scaly tails. That's a hell of a thing. He must be one really important so-and-so if they want him caught so bad.'

'Does sound that way,' Auerbach agreed. He felt Magruder's eyes on him, but pretended he didn't. His lieutenant might not know as much as he did, but wasn't bad at piecing things together.

Auerbach peered south from US 40. Somewhere a couple of miles down there was the little town of Boyero. A squad was going through there now. The rest of his men were strung out along the dirt road that led from Boyero to the highway, and north of US 40 toward Arriba on US 24. Farther north, troopers from Burlington took over for his company. One lone man shouldn't have been able to slip through that net, but, as he'd told Magruder, it was a big country, and they were spread thin.

'One thing,' Magruder said, perhaps trying to look on the bright side: 'It's not like he's going to be able to fool us by making like he's somebody else. There's nobody else on the road to pretend to be.'

'You're right about that,' Auerbach said. 'Country like this, there wouldn't have been a lot going on even before the Lizards came. Now there's nothing.'

Behind heavy clouds, the sun slid toward the distant – and now obscured – Rockies. Auerbach wondered if Larssen had the guts to move at night. He wouldn't have wanted to try it, not on a bicycle. Maybe on foot ... but while that upped your chances of slipping through, it also slowed your travel and left you running the risk of being far from cover when day found you.

A rider came pounding down the dirt road toward US 40. Auerbach spotted blonde hair around the edges of the helmet and nodded to himself – Rachel Hines was the most recognizable trooper in his command.

She reined in, saluted, and said, 'Sir, Smitty and me, we think we seen somebody heading our way across the fields, but as soon as whoever it was spotted us, he went to ground. He couldn't hardly think we were Lizards, so—'

'So he must have thought we were looking for him,' Auerbach finished. Excitement tingled through him. He hadn't expected to run across Larssen, but now that he had, he was ready to run him down. 'I'm with you,' he said. 'We'll pick up every other soldier on the way to where you and Smitty were at – that way, in case this turns out not to be Larssen, we won't give him a free road east.' He turned to Magruder. 'Bill, you stay here and ride herd on things. If we run into trouble, send more men after us.'

'Yes, sir,' Magruder said resignedly. 'Why did I know you were going to tell me that?'

'Because you're smart. Come on, Rachel.' With knees and reins, he urged his horse up into a fast trot. Rachel Hines had galloped to give him the news, but stayed with him now. Every few hundred yards, they'd gather up another trooper. By the time they got back to where Smitty was waiting, they headed up a squad's worth of men.

'We're gonna get the guy, eh, Captain?' Rachel said. Something of the eagerness he felt Auerbach heard in her voice as well. 'Don't quite know why we want him, but we're gonna get him.'

'Yeah, reckon we are.' Auerbach heard the question in Rachel's voice, but if he wouldn't give out his guesses for Magruder, he wouldn't do it for her, either. He turned to the troopers he'd brought in his wake. 'Isbell, you and Evers hold horses. If we get in trouble out there, one of you ride like hell back to the highway and tell Lieutenant Magruder to get reinforcements up here.' The men he'd designated both nodded. He peered out over the prairie. He saw no signs anybody was out there, but Larssen was supposed to know what he was doing. 'Okay, let's spread out and get him. Be on your toes. He's got a gun and he uses it.'

Before she separated from the rest, Rachel Hines said, 'Thanks for not making me stay back with the critters, Captain.'

Auerbach realized he hadn't even thought of that. He'd accepted her as a soldier like any other. He shook his head. Would he have imagined such a thing before the war? Never in a million years.

He strode across the chilly ground. These had probably been wheat fields before the Lizards came, but they didn't look to have been harvested the last couple of years. Even after the winter die-off, a lot of the brush was waist high. Bushes had taken root here and there among the grain, too. The country looked pretty flat, but it gave better cover than you'd think. The grain and bushes also broke up the snow on the ground, making it harder to spot somebody's tracks.

If Larssen was smart, he'd just sit tight wherever he was and hope they'd miss him – if he was really here. But being that smart wasn't easy – and if Auerbach turned the whole company loose on this stretch of ground, anybody hiding would get found.

He didn't want to do that, in case he was wrong. Pulling in a raft of men would leave a hole in the screen the Army had set up to keep the fugitive from slipping east. 'Larssen!' Auerbach shouted. 'Come out with your hands up and nobody'll get hurt. Make it easy on yourself.' *Make it easy on us, too.*

Larssen didn't come out. Auerbach hadn't expected that he would. He took another couple of steps toward where Rachel and Smitty had seen whoever it was take cover. A bullet cracked past his ear. An instant later, he heard the sound of the gunshot. He was already throwing himself flat.

'Down!' he yelled from behind a tumbleweed. He looked around, but dead plants didn't let him see far. He shouted orders: 'Spread out to right and left and take him.' Now they knew where Larssen was. Getting him out wouldn't be any fun, but it was something they knew how to do, tactics that came almost as automatically as breathing. Larssen fired again, not at Auerbach this time. 'You're all against me,' he shouted, his voice thin in the distance. 'I paid back two. I'll pay back the rest of you sons of bitches if it's the last thing I ever do.'

Out on either flank, a couple of Auerbach's troopers started shooting at Larssen, not necessarily to hit him but to make him keep his head down while their buddies slid forward. Not far from Auerbach, Rachel Hines fired a couple of shots. That was his cue to dash ahead and then flop down in back of another bush. He squeezed off three rounds from his own M-1, and heard Rachel and a couple of other troopers advancing on either side of him.

If you were being moved in on from the front and both flanks the way Larssen was, you had only two choices, both bad. You could stay where you were – and get nailed – or you could try and run – and get nailed.

Larssen sat tight. A cry from off to Auerbach's left said he'd hit somebody. Auerbach bit his lip. Casualties came with the job. He understood that. When you went up against the Lizards, you expected not to come back with a full complement, and hoped you'd do them enough damage to make up for your own losses. But having somebody wounded – Auerbach hoped the trooper was just wounded – hunting down one guy who'd gone off the deep end ... that was a waste, nothing else but.

He was within a hundred yards of Larssen now, and could hear him even when he was talking to himself. Something about his wife and a ballplayer – Auerbach couldn't quite make out what. He fired again. Rachel Hines curried past him. Larssen rose up, shot, flopped back down. Rachel let out a short, sharp shriek.

Larssen bounced to his feet. 'Barbara? he shouted. 'Honey?'

Auerbach fired at him. Several other shots rang out at the same instant.

Larssen reeled backwards, collapsed bonelessly. His rifle fell to the ground. He wasn't going anywhere, not any time soon. Auerbach ran up to Rachel Hines. She already had a wound dressing out, and was wrapping it around her hand.

She looked up at Auerbach. 'Clipped the last two joints right off my right finger,' She said matter-of-factly. 'Don't know what I'll do about a wedding band if I ever get married.'

'You'll figure out something.' Auerbach bent down and kissed her on the cheek. He'd never done that for a wounded noncom before. Seeing that she wasn't seriously injured, he said, 'I'm going to make sure of the son of a gun now. I think maybe hearing you yell like that startled him into breaking cover.'

'It's not like I done it on purpose,' she answered, but she was talking to his back.

Jens Larssen was still twitching when Auerbach got up to him, but he didn't see any point in calling for a corpsman. Larssen had taken one in the chest, one in the belly, and one in the side of the face. He wasn't pretty and he was dead, only his body didn't quite know it yet. As Auerbach stood over him, he let out a bubbling sigh and quit breathing.

'Well, that's that,' Auerbach said, bending to pick up Larssen's Springfield – no point in leaving a good weapon out to rust. 'Now we can get on with the important stuff, like fighting the war.'

The *Naxos* chugged on toward Rome. It flew a large red-white-and-blue tricolor Captain Mavrogordato had hauled out the flag locker. 'I want the Lizards' airplanes to think we are French,' he explained to Moishe. 'We have friends on the ground in Rome who know we are bringing them good things, but the pilots – who can say what they know? Since the Lizards hold southern France, this will help them believe we are perfectly safe.'

'What happens when we leave Rome and head for Athens and Tarsus and Haifa?' Moishe asked. 'Those places, they won't be so happy to see a ship that might have come out of Lizard-held country.'

Mavrogordato shrugged. 'We have plenty of flags in the locker. When the time comes, we will pick another one that better suits our business there.'

'All right,' Russie said. 'Why not?' He'd never known such a blithe swashbuckler before. Mavrogordato was smuggling things to the Lizards, undoubtedly smuggling things away from them, and was smuggling him and his family right past their scaly snouts. For all the Greek captain worried about it – airplanes aside – he might have had the whole Mediterranean to himself.

'But what if something goes wrong?' Moishe had asked him, some hundreds of kilometers back toward the west. He himself was a chronic worrier, and was also of the opinion that, considering everything that had happened to him over the past few years, he'd earned the right.

But Mavrogordato had shrugged then, too. 'If something goes wrong I'll deal with it,' he'd answered, and that was all he would say. Moishe reluctantly concluded he didn't say any more because he didn't know any more. Moishe would have had plans upon plans upon plans, each one ready in case the trouble that matched it arrived.

Whether the plans would have worked was another question. Given his track record, it wasn't obvious. But he would have had them.

'How far from Rome are we now?' he asked as the Italian countryside crawled past beyond the starboard rail.

'Thirty-five kilometers, maybe a bit less,' Mavrogordato answered. 'We'll be there in a couple of hours – in time for lunch.' He laughed.

Moishe's stomach rumbled in anticipation. Neither the British freighter that had brought him down near Spain nor the *Seanymph* had had a galley that could compare to the *Naxos's*. Mavrogordato's crew might be short on shaves and clean clothes and other evidence of spit and polish, but they lived better than British seamen imagined. Russie wondered if the English had some sort of requirement denying them as much pleasure as possible. Or maybe they were just a nation of bad cooks.

'I hate to say it, but I wish the Germans were in Italy instead of the Lizards,' Moishe said. 'It gives them too good a base for pushing north or east.'

'They tried pushing east into Croatia last year, and got their snouts bloodied for them,' Mavrogordato said. 'But you're right. Anybody who looks at a map can tell you as much. Hold Italy down and you're halfway toward holding down the whole Mediterranean.'

'Mussolini didn't have much luck with the whole Mediterranean,' Moishe said, 'but we can't count on the Lizards' being as incompetent as he was.'

Captain Mavrogordato slapped him on the back, hard enough to stagger him. He spoke a couple of sentences in Greek before he remembered Russie didn't know what he was talking about and shifted back to German: 'We kicked the Italians right out of our country when they invaded us. The Nazis beat us, yes, but not those clowns.'

The difference between the Italians and the Germans was that between inept tyrants and effective ones. Inept tyrants roused only contempt. No one was contemptuous of the Germans, the Russians, or the Lizards. You could hate them, but you had to fear them, too.

Moishe said, 'Ginger is the worst weakness the Lizards have, I think. A Lizard who gets a taste for ginger will—'

He broke off, a flash of light from the north distracting him. He wondered what it could be – it was as bright as the sun. And no, it wasn't just a flash – it went from white to orange to red, a fireball swelling fantastically with each moment he stood there watching.

'*Meter theou!*' Panagiotis Mavrogordato exclaimed, and crossed himself. The gesture didn't bother Russie; he wished he had one to match it. The aptain of the *Naxos* went on, 'Did they hit an oil tanker between us and Rome? You'd think we would have heard the airplanes, or something.'

They did hear something just then, a roar that rocked Moishe harder than Mavrogordato's slap on the back had a few minutes earlier. A great column of smoke, shot through with crimson flames, rose into the air. Moishe craned his neck to watch it climb.

Slowly, softly, he said, 'I don't think that was anything between us and Rome, Captain. I think that *was* Rome.'

For a moment, the Greek stared at him, blank incomprehension on his face. Then Mavrogordato crossed himself again, more violently than he had before. 'Is it one of those terrible bombs?' he demanded in a hoarse whisper.

'I don't know,' Moishe said. 'I've never seen one before. but I don't know what else it could be, either. Only the one blast and – that.' He nodded toward the glowing, growing cloud of dust and fire. 'If God is kind, I'll never see such a thing again.'

Captain Mavrogordato pointed over the water. A large wave was approaching the *Naxos* at unnatural speed, as if flying through the air rather than being part of the sea. The freighter's bow rose sharply, then plunged into the trough behind. The wave sped past them, out toward Corsica and Sardinia and Sicily. Moishe wondered if it would wash up against distant Gibraltar. Mavrogordato shouted orders in Greek. The *Naxos's* engine began to work harder; the deck thrummed under Moishe's feet and thick clouds of black smoke rose from the stack. Those clouds, though, were misshapen dwarfs when set alongside the one still swelling above Rome. Moishe could not tear his eyes away from that terrible beauty. He wondered how many people – and how many Lizards – had perished in the blast.

'There goes the Pope,' Mavrogordato said, one step ahead of him. 'I'm no Catholic, but that's a hell of a thing to do to him.'

How the Poles would wail when the news reached them! And, if they could find a way, they'd blame it on the Jews. This time, though, the Lizards and the Nazis looked to be much more likely candidates. Now, too, the Jews had guns (Moishe wondered briefly how Mordechai Anielewicz fared these days). If the Poles started trouble, they'd get trouble back.

The bow of the *Naxos* began swinging away from what had been its destination. Russie glanced toward Mavrogordato, a question in his eyes. The merchant captain said, 'Nobody's going to take delivery of what we were bringing, not here, not now. I want to get as far away as I can, as fast as I can. If the Lizards were hunting ships before, what will they do after this?'

'*Gevalt!*' Moishe said; he hadn't thought of that.

Maybe the Greek had heard that bit of Yiddish before, or maybe tone and context let him figure out what it meant. He said, 'It'll be better once we get away from Italy; Lizard planes don't range quite so widely in the eastern half of the Mediterranean as they do here. Only trouble is, I'm going to have to coal once before we make Athens. I would have done it at Rome, but now—'

'Will they let you go into an Italian port after this?' Moishe asked.

'Only one way to find out,' Mavrogordato answered, 'and that's to try it. I know some people – and some Lizards – in Naples. I could unload the ginger there, *theou thelontos*, and take on the fuel I need to get you to where you're going. All we have to worry about is getting sunk before we make it that far. Well, friend, did you want life to be dull?'

'What difference does it make?' Moishe said. 'Life hasn't cared what I want ever since the war started.' After a moment's thought, the Greek solemnly nodded.

Like all the other landcruiser drivers at the Siberian base, Ussmak had installed grids of electricity-heated wire over his vision slits. They melted the frozen water that accumulated on the slits and let him see what he was doing. Nejas had mounted similar grids over the panoramic periscopes in the cupola. The local mechanics had slapped white paint on the landcruiser too, to make it less visible as it ranged across the icy landscape.

Ussmak let his mouth fall slightly open in a bitter laugh. Making the landcruiser less visible was a long way from making it invisible. The Big Uglies might not realize it was there quite as soon as they would have otherwise, but they'd get the idea too quick to suit him any which way.

'Steer a couple of hundredths closer to due south, driver,' Nejas said.

'It shall be done.' Ussmak adjusted his course. Along with two others, his landcruiser was rumbling down to smash a Soviet convoy trying to cross from one end of the break in their railroad to the other. The Russkis had probably hoped to get away with it while camouflaged by the usual Siberian blizzards, but a spell of good weather had betrayed them. Now they would pay.

Clear weather. Ussmak corrected himself. *Not good weather*. From what the males unlucky enough to be long-timers at the base said, good weather in Siberia was measured in moments each long Tosevite year.

'Let's slaughter them and get back to the barracks,' Ussmak said. 'The faster we do that, the happier I'll be.' He was warm enough inside the landcruiser, but the machine was buttoned up at the moment, too. If the action got heavy, Nejas, good landcruiser commander that he was, would open up the cupola and look around – and all that lovely heat would get sucked right out. All the crewmales had on their cold-weather gear in case of that dreadful eventuality.

Wham! Ussmak felt as if he'd been kicked in the side of the head. The round from the Soviet landcruiser hadn't penetrated the side armor of his own machine, but it did make the inside of the landcruiser ring like a bell.

'Turn toward it!' Nejas shouted, flipping up the cupola lid. Ussmak was already steering his landcruiser to the left – you wanted to meet enemy fire head on, to present your thickest armor to the gun. He knew they'd been lucky. Soviet landcruiser cannon could pierce some spots in the side armor.

He peered through his defrosted vision slits. It was already getting cold inside the landcruiser. Where among the dark, snow-draped trees and drifts of frozen water was the enemy lurking? He couldn't spot the Big Uglies, not till they fired again. This time the round hit one of the other landcruisers, but did no damage Ussmak saw.

'Front!' Nejas sang out.

'Identified,' Skoob answered.

But instead of smoothly going on with the target-identifying routine, Nejas made a strange, wet noise. 'Superior sir!' Skoob cried, and then, in anguish, 'Sniper! A sniper killed the commander!'

'No,' Ussmak whispered. Votal, his first landcruiser commander, had died that way. A good commander kept standing up in the cupola, which let him see much more than he could through periscopes and made his landcruiser a far more effective fighting machine – but which also left him vulnerable to small-arms fire he could have ignored if he'd stayed snug inside the turret.

As if the snow and ice themselves had come to malignant life, a figure all clad in white stood up not far from the landcruiser and ran toward it. 'Bandit!' Ussmak shouted to Skoob, and snatched for his personal weapon.

Skoob fired, but by then the camouflaged Big Ugly was too close to the landcruiser for its turret-mounted machine gun to bear on him. He tossed a grenade up and through the open cupola. It exploded inside the turret.

Ussmak thought he was dead. Fragments of the grenade ricocheted off the inside of the fighting compartment. One scraped his side; another tore a long, shallow cut across his right forearm. Only as he felt those small wounds did he realize the grenade somehow hadn't touched off the ammunition inside the turret. If it had, he never would have had the chance to worry about cuts and scrapes.

He shoved the muzzle of his personal weapon out through a firing spot, sprayed the Big Ugly with bullets before he could check another grenade into the landcruiser. Skoob was screaming: terrible cries that grated on Ussmak's hearing diaphragms. He couldn't help the gunner, not yet. First he had to get away from the fighting.

With one male in the turret dead and the other disabled, the landcruiser was no longer a fighting machine. Ussmak could operate the gun or he could drive the vehicle. He couldn't do both at once. He put it into reverse, moving away from the Soviet landcruisers in the forest.

The audio button taped to a hearing diaphragm yelled at him: 'What are you doing?' The cry came from the male who commanded one of the other landcruisers, 'Have your brains addled?'

'No, superior sir,' Ussmak said, though he wished for ginger to make the answer yes. In three or four short sentences, he explained what had happened to his landcruiser and its crew.

'Oh,' the other commander said when he was through. 'Yes, you have permission to withdraw. Good luck. Return to base; get your gunner to treatment as soon as possible.'

'It shall be done,' Ussmak said, above Skoob's wails and hisses. He would have withdrawn with or without orders. Had the other commander tried ordering him to stay, he might have gone up into the turret and put a round through his landcruiser. Keeping a crewmale alive counted for more than killing Big Uglies. You could do that any time. If your crewmale died, you'd never get him back.

When he'd withdrawn far enough from the fighting (or so he hoped with all his spirit), he stopped the landcruiser and scrambled back to do what he could for Skoob. By then, the gunner had fallen silent. His blood and Nejas's had puddled on the floor of the fighting compartment. With the cupola still open – no one had been left to close it – the puddles were starting to freeze.

As soon as he saw the wounds Skoob bore, Ussmak despaired of saving him. He bandaged the gunner all the same, and dragged him down beside the driver's seat. Then he scrambled past Nejas's corpse and slammed the lid of the cupola. That gave the landcruiser's heater some chance against the stunning Siberian winter. Skoob would need every bit of help he could get.

Ussmak radioed back to the base to alert them that he was coming. The male who took the call sounded abstracted, as if he had other things on his mind, things he reckoned more important. Ussmak switched off the radio and called him every vile name he could think of.

He took a large taste of ginger. He wasn't in combat now, and decided he could use the quickened reflexes the herb gave him without endangering himself or the landcruiser. He tried to get Skoob to taste ginger, but the gunner was too far gone to extend his tongue. When Ussmak opened Skoob's jaw to pour in the stimulant powder, he realized the gunner wasn't breathing any more. Ussmak laid a hearing diaphragm over the gunner's chest cavity. He heard nothing. Some time in the last little while, Skoob had quietly died.

The ginger kept Ussmak from feeling the grief that would otherwise have crushed him. What filled him instead was rage – rage at the Big Uglies, rage at the cold, rage at the base commandant for sending males out to fight in these impossible conditions, rage at the Race for establishing a base in Siberia and for coming to Tosev 3 in the first place. As the base drew near, he tasted again. His rage got hotter.

He halted the landcruiser close by the anticold airlock. The crew of mics started to protest. 'What if everybody wanted to park his here?' one of them said.

'What if every landcruiser came back with two crewmales dead?' ssmak snarled. Most of the mechanics fell back from his fury. When ne started to argue further, Ussmak pointed his personal weapon at him. he male fled, hissing in fright.

Still carrying the weapon, Ussmak went into the barracks. He looked own at himself as he waited for the inner door to open. The blood f Nejas and Skoob still covered the front of his protective garments. everal males inside exclaimed in startled dismay when he came into ne communal chamber. More, though, were watching a televisor screen. ne of them turned an eye turret toward Ussmak. 'The Big Uglies just atched another atomic egg,' he said.

Fueled by his rage and loss – and by the ginger – Ussmak shouted, Ve never should have come to this stinking world in the first place. Now aat we're here, we ought to quit wasting lives fighting the Big Uglies nd figure out how to go Home!'

Some of the males stared at him. Others turned their eye turrets away, s if to say he didn't even deserve to be stared at. Somebody said, 'We ave been ordered to bring Tosev 3 under the rule of the Emperor, and shall be done.'

'Truth,' a couple of males said, agreeing with the fellow.

But others shouted, 'Truth!' in a different tone of voice. 'Ussmak is ight,' one of them added. 'What have we got from Tosev 3 but death nd misery?'

That brought another, louder, chorus of 'Truth!' from the males who'd upported Ussmak in the first place, and from a few who hadn't. A lot f his backers, he saw, were males who had their tongues deep in the inger vial. Not all, though, not by any means. That made him feel good. ven full of ginger, he knew males full of ginger were not similarly full f good sense.

'We want to go Home!' he yelled, as loud as he could, and then again: Ve want to go *Home!*' More and more males added their voices to the ry. It filled the communal chamber and echoed through the base. Having he other males follow his head lifted Ussmak's spirits almost the way inger did. This had to be what the fleetlord knew, or even the Emperor imself.

A few males who refused to join the outpouring of anger fled the chamber. ut more came rushing in, first to see what the commotion was about and hen, more often than not, to join it. 'We want to go *Home!*' Ussmak's earing diaphragms throbbed with the rhythmically repeated roar.

'Attention all males! Attention all males!' A countering shout rose from he intercom speaker on the wall: 'End this unseemly display at once nd return to your duties. I, Hisslef, base commandant, so order. Return o your duties at once, I say!;

One or two males meekly squeaked, 'It shall be done,' and skittered way.

With ginger still in him, though, Ussmak wasn't as inclined to pay th
strict attention to subordination he would have when he first came t
Tosev 3. 'No!' he shouted. A lot of males in the command chamber wer
tasting ginger. 'No!' they yelled with him. Somebody added, 'Fancy body
paint's not enough!' In a moment, that became a new war cry.

Had Hisslef let the males shout and carry on till ginger exhilaratio
gave way to after-ginger gloom, the uprising probably would have die
a natural death. Instead, he chose to stalk into the communal chambe
and shout, 'Who has perpetrated this outrageous conduct?'

'I have sup—' Ussmak said. He'd automatically started to add Hisslef'
honorific, but choked it down. What honor did Hisslef deserve? Fanc
body paint *wasn't* enough.

'You will place yourself under arrest,' Hisslef said coldly. 'You are
disgrace to the Race, and shall be punished as you deserve.'

'No,' Ussmak answered. Half the males in the communal chamber stare
at him in astonishment. Disobeying an intercom speaker was one thing
disobeying a direct personal order quite another. But the repeated loss o
cherished crewmales – and the ginger in him – took Ussmak to a place
far outside the Race's normal patterns. And when he went to that place
he was able to take the rest of the males in the chamber with him. Afte
their moment of surprise, they screamed abuse at Hisslef.

The base commandant spread his hands so all the claws showed,
gesture showing he was ready to fight. 'You will come with me *now*, yo
egg-addled wretch,' he ground out, and took two steps toward Ussmak.

Ussmak raised the personal weapon he'd been holding ever since h
frightened the mechanics with it. A ginger-quickened impulse made hin
squeeze the trigger. The burst crumpled Hisslef and flung him backwards
like a sheet of wastepaper. Ussmak was amazed at how little he cared
With Nejas's blood, and Skoob's, on his coat, what did having Hisslef's
on his hands matter?'

'We'll clean them all out!' he shouted. 'The base is ours!'

Again, he'd stunned the males in the communal chamber. Again, he
was able to take them with him to a place where they might never have
gone otherwise. 'Clean them out!' they bayed. 'The base is ours!'

Atvar wished with all his spirit that the Race had never come to Tosev
3. He wished that, if the Race had to have come to Tosev 3, it would have
done so under a different fleetlord. 'By the Emperor, maybe Straha *should*
have overthrown me after the first atomic bomb the Big Uglies touched
off,' he said savagely. 'I'd like to see how he'd enjoy coping with these
latest ones.'

'The loss of Rome was a heavy one for us in many ways, Exalted
Fleetlord,' Kirel agreed. 'Not only were military and administrative
casualties heavy, the bomb also destroyed the Big Ugly who called himself
'12th Pope Pius, and that male had been a leading factor in accommodating

e large number of Tosevites of his theological persuasion to our rule. His aditional authority reached back almost two thousand Tosevite years, hich for this planet gives most antique status.'

'Unlike a good many others on this world, he was able to recognize e advantages of co-operating with authority,' Atvar answered, 'and he ould not have lost all his power after the conquest, as the emperors and ot-emperors here so bitterly fear. As you say, Shiplord, an unfortunate ig Ugly to lose.'

'Targeting the Deutsch city called Hamburg for retaliation seems tting, Exalted Fleetlord,' Kirel said, 'it being a center for waterborne ommerce.'

'Yes, we shall destroy it. In fact' – Atvar flicked one eye toward a ronometer – 'it is already destroyed. Thus we avenge ourselves for ome; thus we visit horror on Deutschland in exchange for the horror e Deutsche visited upon us.' He signed wearily. 'And for what? The eutsche continue to resist us. This latest bomb had nuclear materials tirely of their own making. And much of the radiation from our nuclear xplosions on Deutsch territory – and from that of their first weapon, the e east of Breslau – is blown east and contaminates our holdings and r males in Poland.'

'It contaminates the Deustsche first and worse, Exalted Fleetlord,' irel said.

Atvar hissed out a sad sigh. 'Truth, and I thank you for trying to cheer e with it. But another truth is that the Deutsche, whether out of sheer norance or simply their own savagery – given some of their practices efore we arrived, the latter strikes me as not at all unlikely – well, as I ay, whatever the reason may be, the Deutsche do not seem to care what appens to their own males and females.'

'What happens in the generations to come will make them care,' irel said.

'Truth again,' Atvar answered, 'and if you put this truth to the Deutsch ot-emperor – the *Führer*, he calls himself – I know precisely what he would ay: "So what?" If something suffices for the moment, the Big Uglies care othing for long-term consequences.'

'This irony bites us again and again,' Kirel said. 'We must have a care r the future management of Tosev 3 in order to preserve it more or less tact for the settlers aboard the colonization fleet, while those native to e planet would cheerfully fling it into the cremator for the sake of a mporary advantage.'

Pshing's face appeared on the communicator screen. 'Exalted Fleetlord, xcuse the interruption,' Atvar's adjutant said, 'but, per your orders, I eport the successful destruction by atomic weapon of the Deutsch city f Hamburg. All aircraft involved in the mission have returned safely base.'

'Thank you,' the fleetlord said, and Pshing's image vanished. Atvar

turned his eye turrets back toward Kirel. 'The war has grown unpr
dictable.' No stronger curse could have come from a male of the Rac
'Deutschland and the United States both continue to produce atom
weapons; the SSSR may yet succeed in building one of its own. All th
Tosevite powers now use poisonous gases of various sorts against us. Th
Deutsche have joined them to missiles. How long will it be before the
or some other empires or not-empires develop missiles whose guidan
systems are more accurate than the crude ones they now use, or unt
they make missiles large enough, or nuclear weapons small enough,
use together?'

'Those are major technological steps, Exalted Fleetlord,' Kirel sai
'They would require many decades, perhaps many centuries—'

'—For us,' Atvar broke in. 'For the Big Uglies, who can say? Who ca
say, Shiplord? The more contact we have with the Tosevites, the mo
demoralized our males become. Where will it end? What is happening t
us here?'

'Exalted Fleetlord, I thin—'

Before Kirel could say what he thought, he was interrupted again, no
by Atvar this time but by Pshing, whose features came back on th
communicator screen. Like Kirel, he began, 'Exalted Fleetlord—'

Atvar knew a sinking feeling. This was not an ordered call, whic
meant it had to be an emergency. 'Speak,' he said, dreading what h
adjutant would say.

'Exalted Fleetlord—' Now Pshing hesitated on his own, searching, n
doubt, for the least appalling way to frame whatever the latest disaste
was. At last, he went on, 'Exalted Fleetlord, we have reports a landcruise
and infantry base in the region of the SSSR known as Siberia no longe
ah, responds to orders.'

'It has fallen to the Big Uglies?' Atvar asked.

Pshing hesitated again, longer this time. 'Exalted Fleetlord, it wou
appear not. The fragmentary communications we had before it stoppe
responding or transmitting suggest internal disorders instead. The bas
commandant, Hisslef, is believed slain.' The adjutant hissed in anguishe
dismay. 'Exalted Fleetlord, it appears to be a – a mutiny.' He hissed agai
once the awful word was out.

'A mutiny?' Atvar stared at the communicator screen. He was to
shocked even to be angry. That might come later, but not yet. Males o
the Race – loyal, obedient, cohesive – rising up against their commanders
Killing their commanders, if the report Pshing had was correct? It coul
never have happened, not on any world under the Emperor's dominior
On Tosev 3 – As he had to Kirel, Atvar cried, 'What is happening to u
here?' His voice came out a frightened moan.